STORM AND SILENCE

Storm and Silence

Robert Thier

2016

First Printing: 2016

ISBN: 978-3-00-051351-0

This book is also available in eBook format. More information on this and any other subject connected with Robert Thier's books on: www.robthier.com

Dedication

This story is dedicated to all my awesome fans and fiery little Ifrits without whom the book would never have been possible. All of you have been an inspiration!

Firstly, I would like to thank the contributors to the publishing campaign who have opened their hearts (and their wallets!) to get this book into print. The most generous contributions came from (**taking a deep breath**): Alexis Rose Stinson, Ammarah Maryam Abbasi, Bianca van den Berg, Cailin Ingram, Cindy Susana Orozco-Cazapa, compulsiveeater, Daisy Orozco, Dakota Trauth, Deb Caputo, Dominique C. Mohler, Elisabeth Nettesheim, Eve McManus, Faryal Motiwala, Filipa Silva, Gabriela Grant, Jodie Perry, Julia Davis, Julia Hazima, Katrin Störmer, Kuini Erika, Laura F. Carlson, Laurianne Wohlscheid, Leisa Zaharis, Madeline Bunde, Marcia Robichaud, Marnurwani Bte Mohd Noordin, Michele Marquez, Mohsanh Omar, Natalie Y. Young, Nicole Strong, Nina Lawrence Akpovi, Noelia Wehrhahn, Reman Jawar, Romina Avaness, Shelby Nunn, Sonali Chander, Tahani H. and Tasneem Hiba. Thank you! Without your generosity, this book would never have made it into print.

Additional thanks is due to Deb Caputo, who indicated a number of points that helped me significantly in fine-tuning historical accuracy. And a big cartload of thanks goes to Iris Chacon, the wonderful editor who volunteered her time to edit this opus from front to back.

Last, but certainly not least, I want to thank all those fiery fans and Ifrits who might not have had the means to contribute funds to the publication campaign, but who inspired me with their encouragements, during a mighty Twitter battle helped this book win the People's Choice Award in the Wattys, drew wonderful portraits of Lilly and Mr Ambrose or scattered glowing reviews of this book all over the web. I truly have the most amazing fandom south of the North Pole! Three cheers for you all! Lilly would be proud of you, and even Mr Ambrose would be mildly impressed. I look forward to scribbling many more stories for your enjoyment, knowing that you shall be with me every step of the way.

CONTENTS

ARRESTED FOR GOOD MANNERS

The young man's reflection glared back at me out of the shop window, suspicion etched into his roundish face. He probably thought I was doubting whether he looked manly enough, and, to be honest, I was.

'Come on,' I muttered, morosely. 'Manliness, manliness... give me some manliness!'

I turned sideways, and he turned with me, thrusting his chest out at the exact same moment I did. It looked flat as a board, betraying not a hint of femininity, so that, at least, was going to be no problem.

Farther down though... My eyes wandered to the young man's behind, where my Uncle Bufford's old trousers bulged in a distinctly un-manly way. Yes. The young man's behind was definitely a bit too fa–

No.

Not the f-word. Generous. That was the word. It was just a bit too generous.

'Hell's whiskers!'

I made an impolite gesture at the young man in the window, which he duly reciprocated. Who was he trying to fool? He was no man. He was a girl. Which meant that, as much as I would have liked to pretend otherwise, so was I.

'I don't like you,' I informed my reflection in no uncertain terms. It scowled at me, not at all pleased about being spoken to so disrespectfully.

'It's your own fault.' I scowled right back. 'If you were skinnier, and didn't have so much of this–' I pointed to my derrière, 'then you'd look a bit more convincing in this getup.'

Distastefully, I tugged at the tailcoat and trousers, which felt odd over the tight corset.

'If we get caught, it's your fault for looking so... so chubby! We're trying to look *manly* here. Couldn't you at least get hold of a false beard or a prominent, masculine jaw?'

A pedestrian walking by gave me an odd look.

I decided that if I wanted to appear more masculine, it was probably time to stop talking to my reflection in a shop window and be about my business.

Throwing a last, discontented look at the well upholstered, tanned young man in the shop window, I hurriedly stuffed my hair under the huge, heavy top hat that was part of my disguise from my uncle's wardrobe. My hair wasn't too long to be a man's, really, it only reached down to my shoulders. But not many young men had shoulder-length brown locks. Silently thanking my uncle for unknowingly providing such a monster of a hat, I turned to face my destination.

It was still some way away and concealed by the thick layer of mist that obscured most of London's streets at this time of day, but I knew exactly where I was going. I had spied out the place days ago, in preparation for my secret mission.

Secret, solitary, and illegal.

I started down the street again and felt my throat go dry. The stop in front of the shop window had been a temporary one, a last chance to confirm that I looked the part I was trying to play. It had granted me a short reprieve, but now the time had come.

Blast! What if they recognize me? If they realize I'm a girl? Panicked thoughts shot through my head like bees in a beehive rattled by a hungry bear. *What if they grab me and... God only knows what they might do!*

Calm down, Lilly, I told myself. *You are on a mission for all womankind. If you should fall, hundreds will follow in your footsteps.*

Which didn't exactly make me feel better, since that meant they would trample over my remains.

Suddenly, the mist before me parted, and there it was: the place I had come to infiltrate. The place I was forbidden, by law, to enter. White columns supported a wide, classical portico that overshadowed the steps leading up to the entrance. The door had two massive wings of oak, and a guard beside it. Over the door hung a dark red banner, proclaiming, in black letters the words 'POLLING STATION'.

And I suppose that says it all. That explains why I was here, why I was wearing ridiculously baggy men's clothes which I had pinched from my uncle and why I was so mad at my own reflection. That explains why I was afraid. That explains what was illegal about my plans. That explains everything.

No? It doesn't? Not to you, anyway?

Count yourself fortunate, then. You apparently live in a country which actually allows its female inhabitants the right to vote.

Not so the United Kingdom of Great Britain and Ireland, I thought, gritting my teeth in anger. Its politicians had thoroughly deliberated on the subject of women's suffrage and come to the conclusion that women should never be allowed to vote, for the following reasons:

1. Women's tiny brains had no capacity for logical thought. Their emotional nature made them incapable of understanding politics.
2. If women were to get involved in politics, they would be too busy to marry and have children, and the entire human race would die out, which would be very bad indeed.
3. If women got involved in politics, they would be on an equal footing with men, thus creating the appalling condition of equality of the sexes and putting an end to all need for male chivalry and gentlemanly behaviour, which would be even worse.
4. All government ultimately rested on brute force. Since the gentle nature of women made them incapable of that, they were simply not suited for politics.[1]

---

[1] This list is not a work of fiction. It is taken, virtually word for word, from articles arguing against women's suffrage which were published in renowned newspapers such as the London Times.

Would it surprise you to hear that all the politicians who put forward the reasons on that little list were men? I had taken the time to think very long and sincerely about their arguments, finally coming to the conclusion that said arguments were complete and utter poop. I really wished I could have a private meeting with the fellow who suggested that women were incapable of brute force. Just five minutes alone with him in a sound-proof room would do.

Not looking right or left, I marched down the street towards the polling station, trying to keep my heart from jumping out of my chest. Every minute, I expected someone to raise an accusing finger and start shouting, 'A female! A female in men's clothes! Grab the vile abomination!'

Nothing happened. Nobody even gave me a second glance.

That might, however, have had something to do with the thick fog that let one see clearly for only a few yards. Everything beyond that was just a hazy outline. As I walked on, the fog thickened even more, and for a moment, even the polling station at the other end of the street was consumed by it.

Yet even without the fog, there didn't seem to be a great chance of my being recognized by passers-by. Only a few people were out on the streets, and they rushed past quickly. I hoped it would be the same inside the station. The only exception to the rule here, outside, was a large group standing half-way down the street. Although they were visible to me only as hazy silhouettes, I could tell that two of the men were in intense conversation.

'... tell you, it is in perfect condition,' the older of the two said. His double chin wobbled as he spoke and he made energetic gestures with his pudgy hands to underline his speech. 'The best of all the houses I have.'

'Indeed?' The other man sounded curt and cool. I didn't see his face since he stood with his back to me. All I could see was his lean black figure, erect as a rod of iron. 'Interesting that you are willing to part with such a treasure.'

'It is out of the goodness of my heart, Sir, out of the goodness of my heart!' the fat man assured him. 'Wilding Park is a treasure, and I hate to part with it, but I know that with you it will be in good hands.'

I hadn't really paid attention to their conversation before, but the name caught my ear. Wilding Park? Surely not *the* Wilding Park?

'Bah.' The young man waved his hand depreciatively. 'I have no time for this. Karim, pay the man and let's be done with it.' He raised a hand, pointing at the fat man. 'However, you should remember: If you haven't told the truth, I shall be very... displeased.'

Even through the fog I could see the double-chin of the fat fellow tremble.

'Karim? The money.' The young man snapped his fingers.

A gigantic fellow, one of the people surrounding the two, started forward but stopped and turned his head abruptly when I took a few steps in the direction of the group and cleared my throat.

Stupid, stupid, stupid! What was I doing? What was it to me if some rich chauvinist fellow got swindled and lost a few thousand quid? Nothing. But then, this might be a brilliant opportunity to test my disguise.

It was also a brilliant opportunity to procrastinate and put off my attack on the fortress of male political power for just a few moments more.

'Excuse me, Sir?' I wanted to tap the lean man on the shoulder, but the giant called Karim grabbed my arm before it even got near him and pulled me back, towering over me.

'On your way, you lout!' he growled in some thick, uneven accent I couldn't identify. I looked up at him, eyes wide. Now that he was so close, with no mist obscuring his form, I could see he was a mountain of a man, with a face as dark as his long black beard, and a turban, yes, an actual turban on his head. What freak show had I wandered into? A turban? In the middle of London?

'On your way, I said!' he growled, twisting my arm painfully. 'The *Sahib* has no time for beggars!'

Beggars? I was more than a little peeved, I had to say. I was dressed in my uncle's Sunday best, after all. And all right, the clothes were three sizes too big for me and hadn't been used or washed in years, but still.

At least he hadn't said 'The *Sahib* has no time for girls who dress up as men.'

'I don't want any money from him,' I retorted. 'In fact, I want to help him save some!'

'Save Money? Karim – let him go, now!' the young man commanded, turning to look at me.

The big fellow did what he said so quickly that it was obvious he was a very obedient servant. His master was staring at me intently, but because of the fog I still couldn't see much of him – except his eyes.

'You,' the man said, fixing me with his dark gaze, dark as the sea, somewhere between blue, green and grey. 'What do you speak of? How exactly can you help me save money?'

I swallowed, wishing I hadn't said or done anything at all. I could be safe in the polling station by now. Instead I was stuck here, because once again I couldn't keep my nose out of things that didn't concern me.

When I tried to step towards the man, thinking I should bow or shake his hand, the big dark-skinned servant blocked my way and put his hand to his belt. For the first time, I noticed the giant sabre that hung there. Obviously he didn't think much of handshakes, bows and formal introductions. So I simply spoke from where I stood.

'I couldn't help overhearing part of your conversation with...' my gaze strayed to the fat man.

'Mr Elseworth,' the man with the sea-coloured eyes supplied, curtly.

'...with Mr Elseworth. Am I right in thinking that you intend to purchase Wilding Park, Sir?'

'You are.'

'If you don't mind my saying so, Sir, I would advise against it.'

'Why?'

'My... my grandmother lives in the vicinity of Wilding Park, Sir. I visit her now and again and have caught glimpses of the house. It is not pretty.'

'I am not concerned with whether it is pretty or not. Is it sound?'

'That it is, Sir, that it is,' the fat man cut in, throwing me an evil glare. 'Don't listen to this foolish youth!'

'It is not sound,' I snapped.

4

'And you know that how?' the man with the dark eyes asked.

'Half the roof tiles are missing, and I have seen unhealthy-looking stains on the walls. Once, in passing, I heard the steward complain about the wilderness in the grounds and an infestation of rats. The road up to the house, from what I could see from my coach as I drove by, also looked in bad disrepair.'

'And you remember all that just from passing?'

'Yes?' I responded nervously.

He gave a curt nod. 'I see. Exactly what I have been looking for.'

That statement slightly confused me. 'But I just told you the house is dilapidated and...'

The shadowy stranger cut me short with an impatient gesture. 'Not the house, young man. You.'

I blinked, totally taken off guard. '*Me?*'

'Yes, you.' Carelessly, the lean figure in the fog waved a hand towards the fat man. 'Karim, get rid of that individual. Our business relationship is terminated. I have no further use for him.'

'Yes, *Sahib*.'

Seizing the stunned Mr Elseworth by the scruff of the neck, this fellow Karim hauled him off into the mist without so much as a second to consider. The protesting shrieks of the man could be heard for about two or three seconds, then abruptly ceased.

'Now to you,' said the dark-eyed man as if nothing particularly strange had happened. 'I know a good man when I see one, and I need a bright young man with a good memory and quick mind as my secretary. The last one I had has just left my employment for some unfathomable reason. I think you would be exactly the man for the job.'

I managed to turn my involuntary laugh into a cough. 'Err... the *man* for the job? Sorry, but I don't quite think that I'm the one you want, Sir.'

'Can you read and write?'

'Yes, but...'

'Do you have employment?'

Again, I had to work hard to stifle a giggle.

'No, Sir, but...'

'Well then it's settled. Be at my office, nine sharp Monday morning.'

He walked forward and held something out to me.

'Here.'

As he approached, the tendrils of fog uncurled around him, and for the first time I could see him clearly. My mouth experienced a sudden, inexplicable lack of saliva.

For a man he looked... quite acceptable.

Hard. That was what he looked like. That was what you first noticed about him: a hard, chiselled face, like that of some ancient Greek statue. Except of course that all the stone statues I had met at the museum looked a lot more likely to suddenly smile than he did. They, after all, were made of marble, which was really a quite soft kind of stone, maybe capable of a changeable facial expression. He, on the other hand, wasn't soft. He looked as though he were hewn from granite. Like most of his fellow statues in the museum, he wore no beard. Against the current fashion, his face was meticulously clean-shaven, making it appear even more angular and stark. And then, finally, there were his eyes... His dark blue-green eyes that I had already seen through the mist. They were dark pools of immeasurable depth, pools you could drown yourself in and never again come up for air.

All right, all things considered he probably looked slightly better than just 'acceptable'.

I instantly and absolutely mistrusted him. I disliked all men as a matter of principle, but handsome men, especially ones with a strong chin and overbearing manner, were at the top of my 'things to exterminate to make this world a better place'-list. This particular specimen of manhood in front of me looked like just the kind of fellow who might have come up with the brute force argument.

'Hello, young man? Are you listening to me?'

I shook my head, trying to chase away my wandering thoughts and concentrate. I was in disguise! This was a test, and I had to act accordingly.

'Err... yes. Yes, I am,' I stuttered. 'You just surprised me, Sir. I must admit,' I added truthfully, 'that it's not every day I get an offer like that.'

'See that you're not "surprised" too often when you are in my employ,' he said without moving a muscle of his angular, stony face. 'I have no use for baffled fools standing around gawking for no good reason.'

Fools, was it? His capacity for politeness seemed about equal to his ability to force a smile on that statue's face of his. I had a sudden, mad urge to ask him what he thought about point number four. Maybe it really had been him...

Again, he stepped closer and jerked his hand forward.

'My card,' he said, his voice curt and commanding. Only then did I notice what he was holding out to me: a small rectangular piece of cardboard. I took it and examined it. In clear, precise lettering without any embellishments were printed the words:

Rikkard Ambrose
Empire House
322 Leadenhall Street

Nothing else. No titles, no embellishments, no profession.

I looked up at him again. Ambrose, hm? Like the stuff the Greek gods used to eat for breakfast? Well, he certainly looked good enough to eat, I thought as my eyes swept up and down his lean form appreciatively.

No! What was I thinking? I didn't want or need men. I didn't need anyone who thought my brain was too small to understand politics, thank you very much! I was a proud suffragette[2] and should be thinking about promoting

---

[2] Suffragettes were women who advocated women's right to vote in political elections, which was against the law in most countries in the 19th century. The word comes from 'suffrage'. That suffragettes dressed up as men in order to gain this right secretly is no fiction:

women's rights, not the contents of men's tights! Did men even wear tights under their trousers? I would have to ask my twin sisters about that. They would probably know from personal experience.

'Don't be late,' he added, his dark eyes flaring. 'I don't tolerate tardiness.' Then, without a further word, he turned and vanished into the fog, his long black cloak flapping behind him. The others who surrounded him silently followed, as if he were the centre of their little solar system and they all revolved around him. I stared after him, flabbergasted.

The nerve of the man! He didn't even wait to hear me say yes or no? He just left, expecting I would do his bidding. Who was he? Some industrialist with too much money for his own good? No, that didn't fit the cut and colouring of his clothes, which was very simple: sleek black from head to toe. So was he just a simple tradesman? But then again... He had all those attendants with him. That suggested someone important.

Maybe he was a government official. I snorted, staring intently at the card. Yes, that would fit! One of those fellows who were to blame for me being out here in this strange getup in the first place. I should just chuck his card away and be done with it. It wasn't as if I intended to go there on Monday.

I hesitated for a moment.

Then I pocketed the card and turned to the polling station again.

Why was I feeling so annoyed? I should be happy. This had been an excellent test. I had been in the company of one of the most masculine men I had ever met, and he hadn't noticed I was in fact a girl. Great job!

Yet, deep down, I knew exactly why I was peeved. It was because I had been in the company of the most masculine man I had ever met and he had completely, I mean absolutely and completely, *not noticed that I was in fact a girl!*

Be sensible, I chided myself. *A moment ago you were worried about looking too feminine. Now you've been proven wrong. Problem solved.*

Yes.

There was definitely no reason for me to feel annoyed. No reason at all.

Banishing all thoughts of the strange Mr Rikkard Ambrose from my mind, I again started towards the building at the end of the street. The fog lifted slightly and revealed the menacing figure of a police officer posted outside the door. Sweat broke out on my forehead despite the cold, and for a moment I was convinced he was stationed there for the express purpose of catching young ladies daring to try and vote against the supreme will of the British Government.

Then I remembered he was probably not there for the women, but for the millions of men who still weren't allowed to vote either, because they didn't have a penny in their pocket. Women were probably not even important enough to be taken into consideration. Well, I would show them!

As I walked up the steps to the front door, the bobby took off his hat respectfully. 'Good day, Sir.'

---

in 1853, a woman disguised as a man attempted to vote in Cincinnati, was caught, and served a prison sentence.

7

Oh God! He'd lifted his hat in greeting. Why hadn't I thought of this? What should I do? Take off my hat in return? I couldn't do that, considering the mass of hair that was piled up underneath it like a haystack crammed into a shopping bag. So I just nodded silently. Better to be thought rude than to be polite and subsequently arrested.

Quickly I pushed past the bobby and threw open the door to the polling station. A thick stench of cigars and sweat wafted towards me out of the darkness.

My hands clenched into tight fists, and I stood there, immobile. Could I do this? Was I brave enough? Would I get caught? Would I get lynched by an outraged male mob?

Before I could think better of it, I plunged forward, into the darkness, towards my goal.

~~**~*~*

For a moment, I stood still while my eyes accustomed themselves to the gloom. Slowly, shapes appeared out of the dark, and I could distinguish a sort of counter at the other end of the room, where an official sat with several lists and thick books. Men formed a line in front of the counter. They scribbled something in the books with a fountain pen, then bowed to the official and departed.

Was I supposed to write in there, too? I had no idea how this 'voting'-thing actually worked. Oh heavens, I should never have tried this...

Come on, I chastised myself. Do it! *Do it for your friends, Patsy, Flora and all the rest! Do it for the oppressed masses of women who are too lazy to protest themselves! Do it against all those arrogant male chauvinists who think the brains of a woman wouldn't fill a tea spoon!*

Unfortunately, this last thought brought a certain image to my mind: the image of Mr Rikkard Ambrose as he disdainfully handed his card to his new 'secretary'.

Was I really so ugly that a man like him would not even recognize me as a girl? I refused to believe so! Admittedly, my skin was rather tanned, and my face was rather round with a perky chin, not at all demure and ladylike. But still, not even to recognize me as a girl...?

Forget about him. He's not important. You have a job to do! I repeated over and over in my mind. Still, the image of Rikkard Ambrose persisted in front of my inner eye as I approached the line of men at the counter.

Just before I could get into line, a thin little man in a bright yellow waistcoat stopped me. Or maybe he was a woman in disguise, too? How should I know, after all?

'Excuse me, Sir,' he said in a voice high enough to make the theory at least possible. 'You will have to show me your passport.'

Ah! I breathed a sigh of relief. At least this was one eventuality I had provided for. At a dinner party, I had heard the gentlemen once talking about the government introducing this measure: you had to show your passport when you voted, to prove who you were.

So how could I try and vote, you may ask yourself?

Well, I had pinched my uncle's passport.

Why not? I had already taken his trousers, jacket, waistcoat and top hat. And it wasn't like he was going to vote. He never left his room except to work or complain about things.

'Um... of course. Here.

With fluttering fingers I removed the rectangular piece of paper from my pocket and unfolded it. The little man took it and looked at it without really paying attention.

'In his Majesty's name... Passport for the person of the name Bufford Jefferson Brank... signed by... and so on and so on... yes, all appears to be in order.' He handed the document back to me, and I quickly tugged it back into my pocket. 'Please continue, Mr Brank,' he said, gesturing towards the line of waiting men and already looking somewhere else, having lost all interest in yours truly.

That was fine by me.

Hurriedly, I placed myself behind the last man in the line, thanking the Lord that the British government hadn't yet adopted the practice of putting pictures of people in passports. I might be able to pass for a man by putting on a pair of trousers and a top hat, but I doubted I would be able to pass for a grumpy sixty-year-old by availing myself of a false white beard and pretending to limp.

'Next, please,' the man at the counter called in a bored voice. The line moved forward, and I moved along with it, step by step, voter by voter. In that way, I slowly approached the counter, getting more nervous with every passing minute. How exactly did you 'cast a vote'? Did you actually have to throw something? I presumed it was only a figure of speech, but I wasn't entirely sure.

The men before me didn't seem to be throwing things around, though. They just bent as if to write something down, and then went away. That didn't look so bad.

Suddenly, the last man in front of me stepped aside and I was facing the official behind the counter. He held out a piece of paper, on which the names of two candidates were printed with little circles beside them.

'Cast your vote, please,' he said, his voice still dripping boredom.

'What?' I stared at the man, surprised. 'Do you mean anyone will be able to see who I voted for?'

He looked at me as if I had just asked whether the sea was really made out of water. 'Of course. If you're ashamed of your political affiliations, you shouldn't be here. Haven't you voted before?'

Trying desperately not to let my nerves show, I shook my head. 'No. First time.'

'Oh, well, that explains it.' His expression changed from bored to superior, and he pointed to a place on the paper. 'We vote publicly here, young man. That's the way it's supposed to be. You'll get none of those absurd new political ideas the Chartists are proposing in my polling station. Did you know those fools don't just want to have secret ballots, they actually demand universal suffrage?'

'Incredible.'

'Just what I said! This is a decent, British polling station, young man. Everybody who comes here to vote is a gentleman with a residence in town and a good income, and everybody sees who everybody else votes for.'

He paused, and I, as was obviously expected, nodded my agreement to his political wisdom. The official seemed pleased. He tapped on the paper in front of me.

'Just make your mark there, or there, young Sir, depending on which candidate you wish to vote for.'

'Thank you, Sir.' I grabbed the fountain pen and immediately made my mark for the Whig candidate.

'The Whigs, hmm?'

The official's face soured, and he glanced at me disapprovingly. 'Didn't you hear what I was just saying? The Whigs actually support those Chartist extremists and rebels who want votes for the common people. Do you really know what you are doing, young man? Those infernal reformers will be the death of our great country, some day!'

'Well, we'll just have to see, won't we, Sir,' I said with a smile and curtsied.

The entire room went suddenly deadly quiet as everybody turned to stare at me. The voters, the officials, even a fellow in the corner who looked like he had just come in to warm himself up a bit – they all stared at me with open mouths.

What was the matter with them?

Then I realized. Oh, blast! I curtsied! I didn't bow, I *curtsied*!

~~**~*~*

They needed to call a second police officer to 'restrain the madwoman in the polling station' as the government official put it to the messenger boy who was sent to the police. The boy was obviously impressed with my performance, because he returned not with one, but with three additional Bobbies, truncheons in hand.

Now don't get me wrong, I didn't try to strangle anybody. Far from it. I simply had decided that since I was discovered anyway, I might as well use the opportunity and set up an impromptu demonstration for women's rights in the polling station. The government officials in charge of the place didn't seem to take kindly to the idea.

Thus it was that at 9:30 am on 22 August 1839 I was dragged out of an inconsequential polling station in the middle of London, with the firm assistance of four protectors of the people. Two of the officers held my arms, while another two marched ahead to warn any passers-by of the dangerous madwoman.

'Chauvinists!' I yelled. 'Oppressors of womanhood!'

One of the Bobbies winced, covering his ears.

'Can we gag her?' he asked his sergeant.

'No, lad, that's against regulations,' the older man grunted.

'What about a straitjacket?'

'We ain't got one of those, more's the pity.'

Digging my heels into the ground, I continued to express my opinion of the oppressors of womanhood in no uncertain terms. To my considerable satisfaction they had a great deal of trouble moving me five inches, let alone down the steps from the doors of the polling station.

We had just reached the last porch step when out of the bank on the opposite side of the misty street stepped a figure I remembered all too well: Rikkard Ambrose, his classical features as hard as ever, his black cloak wrapped tightly around him. When he caught sight of me being dragged away, he stopped in his tracks.

'Officer!' In three long strides he was in front of us. His face was just as unmoving as before, but there was a steely glint in his dark eyes. 'Officer, what are you doing with this young man, may I ask?'

The sergeant turned, and paled as he saw the visage of the much younger man. He took one hand off my arm to salute. My, my. Mr Rikkard Ambrose had to be someone of importance to elicit that kind of reaction from one of London's stoic defenders of the law.

I tried to use the opportunity to wrestle free, but immediately the sergeant stopped saluting and clapped his hand around my arm again.

'Good morning, Mr Ambrose, Sir!' he said, trying to stand at attention while not loosening his grip on yours truly. 'Um... Sir, if I may ask, what young man are you speaking of?'

With a sharp jerk of his hand, Mr Ambrose pointed at me.

'That one, of course. Are you blind? What are you doing with him?'

'Not *him*, Sir.' Reaching up, the sergeant gripped my top hat and pulled it off, so my chestnut bob cut was freed and tumbled downwards. '*Her*. That's a girl, Mr Ambrose, Sir.'

The expression on the face of Mr Rikkard Ambrose at that moment was quite possibly the funniest thing I had ever seen in my life. His stone face slackened and he gaped at me like he hadn't seen a single female before in his entire life.

'Something wrong, Sir?' the sergeant inquired, dutifully. When no answer was forthcoming from the stupefied Mr Ambrose, the sergeant shrugged, and made an awkward little bow. 'Well, if you'd excuse us, Sir, we have to take this one,' he nodded at me like he would at a rabid horse, 'away to where she belongs. Maybe a night in the cells will teach her not to do what's only for men.'

'Aye,' one of the constables chuckled. 'Women voting? Who ever heard of something like that? Next thing we know they'll want decent jobs!'

His colleagues laughed at his joke and started dragging me to a police coach standing not twenty yards away.

In that moment, I made a decision.

I turned my head around to look back. Mr Rikkard Ambrose still stood there, pale and unmoving as a block of ice. Even though he was already a dozen yards away, and the Bobbies dragged me further and further, I could see his stone face very clearly. I could see his dark eyes starting to burn with cold anger. A grin spreading across my face, I yelled:

'Looking forward to seeing you at work on Monday, Sir!'

APE BOBBY

By the next morning I didn't feel quite so cocky anymore. That might have had something to do with spending the night in a prison cell, or with the fact that I had made a total mess of my plan, or with the fact that I hadn't been able to get myself calmed down enough to sleep until midnight.

And when I finally did fall asleep on the hard, uneven bunk bed in the prison cell, I dreamed of a dozen Bobbies, reinforced by a whole platoon of Ancient Greek statues, chasing me through the dark streets of London all night, shouting: 'Stop her! Stop the feminist! She has to be at work on Monday! At nine sharp! Catch her!' I'm not sure which was more disturbing, the horrifying chase or the fact that the stone statues on my tail looked suspiciously like Mr Rikkard Ambrose.

I awoke sometime around three am, my heart hammering so fast I knew I would never be able to go to sleep again.

Instead, I surveyed the luxurious hotel suite the nice policemen had put me in for the night: six square feet of the best of what London's police stations had to offer. The walls of my temporary home were decorated in an intricate pattern of mould and graffiti. The panorama window – about two square feet covered with a beautiful set of iron bars – offered a spectacular view over the gutter of one of London's finest dingy alleyways. The door, of course, was designed to fit the standards of the window and was similarly crafted from highly decorative iron bars. The bed, as my back could attest, was also made to fit the highest standards, and was able to reduce your back muscles to a tangle of aching knots within five minutes. All in all, it was a breath-taking place with a charming atmosphere. The previous tenant had even left me a little present in the form of a puddle of well-matured goo in the corner. It emitted the most delicious, stomach-turning odour and completed the whole ambience to misery in perfection. The pale light of the moon which filtered in through the small window didn't make the scene any cheerier.

At least there was no one else in the cell with me. The policemen had put me in solitary confinement. I would have liked to think that was for my protection, but truth be told, they probably thought it was safer for the other prisoners. After all, they couldn't want those poor misunderstood thieves, burglars and murderers in the same cell as a raving madwoman who had dressed up as a man and thus had given proof of the fact that she had absolutely no morals whatsoever, could they?

Groaning, I shuffled until I was sitting on the bunk, my chin resting in my open palm. A truly philosophical position, ideally suited for pondering my fate. What would be my punishment for my little subterfuge? Would I be sent to prison for daring to defy the laws of England? Or put in the stocks? Or transported to the colonies like a common thief?[3] That last thought cheered me up

---

[3] British Criminals were often not put into prison, but instead simply shipped off to one of the British colonies. Australia was a particularly popular prison-continent.

considerably. I had heard that some of the colonies were much more civilized and advanced when it came to the independence of women than our dear mother country. Plus, my aunt and uncle would then be a few thousand miles away from me.

But then I thought of my friends and of my little sister, Ella, and immediately regretted my selfish desire to be shipped off to a criminal colony. I couldn't leave. And even if I could get out of England, I knew I would rather stay and fight for my rights. Running from my problems had never been my style. Grabbing them by the throat and shaking them until they capitulated, that was more my way of dealing with things.

Not that this particular strategy had proven very helpful to me recently. After all, I had tried to grab political freedom for women by the throat, and it had just slipped through my fingers. Would it be like that with every other kind of freedom? Yes, it probably would. It wasn't just voting that ladies weren't allowed to do. I was well aware that there were other, even more essential, freedoms.

Shifting uncomfortably, I could feel Mr Ambrose's card pressing against my skin where I had stuffed it into my sleeve to conceal it from the Bobby who had taken my personal effects. Yes, a lady definitely lacked certain freedoms. Such as the right to work for a living, for instance.

You are not seriously thinking about going to his office on Monday morning, are you? I heard a nagging little voice from the back of my mind. *Forget it! Forget about him. Forget he ever existed, or that you met, or that he offered you a job. He won't give it to you now, knowing who you really are.*

He wouldn't, would he?

No, certainly not.

Almost certainly.

But...

But if there was a chance, even a tiny chance, that he might still hire me, shouldn't I take it? This wasn't just about demonstrating my will to be free to the oppressors of womanhood. This was more serious. Often enough had I wondered about what would happen with me if my uncle, the one who took me and my siblings in after our parent's death, were suddenly to die. Deep inside, I knew the answer. There was no one to take care of us. We would be out on the streets faster than you could say Jack Robinson. We would be reduced to begging or seeking charity. And there were already plenty of people in line for that.

What could a young lady like me do, really do, to earn money? Would they even let me into a factory? There were tens of thousands of working-class men, women and children available for those jobs, and I suspected they were ten times better at spinning and weaving cotton than I would be. For one thing, they'd had a few decades of practise.

Besides, these jobs were bone-breaking work for little money. I had taken the time once to calculate whether I could survive on my own out there if I were able to get such a job. A factory worker earned about 1s 3d per day. That made about 400s per year, or in other words, £20.[4] The average rent for a nice, comfortable home was about £100. So, if I took up factory work, I would be able to rent one fifth of a house, provided I managed to live without food, water or clothes for an entire year. I really wasn't that keen on intense fasting or full-time nudity.

Sometimes I wondered how those working-class people managed to live at all. But I soon stopped wondering, because I had enough problems of my own.

Once again I thought of the card in my sleeve. Yes, factory work was out of the question. *This* kind of work, however... Mr Ambrose had offered me a job as a private secretary. That was a prestigious post, and well-paid. It could be the way to my freedom, the opportunity I had hoped for all my life. What if I just tried to go there and...?

No!

I shook my head. But the card in my sleeve didn't seem to think much of my denial. It pressed into my skin in an ever nastier manner, proving itself to have quite sharp and annoying edges. Well... I looked around. There was nobody here but me. Nobody would see. It couldn't hurt to just take out the card and look at it again, could it?

Quickly, I fished it out and held it up into the moonlight filtering in through my panorama gutter-window.

Rikkard Ambrose
Empire House
322 Leadenhall Street

Hm. It still appeared strange to me that it didn't say anything about his titles or occupation – as if the man expected everybody to know who he was. And maybe, just maybe, he might be right to assume so. Leadenhall Street... the name rang a bell somewhere.

With sudden realization, my head jerked up from where it rested on my knees and I snapped my fingers. That was it! Wasn't Leadenhall Street in the very heart of the banking district? Where all the largest banks and companies, even the East India Company and the Bank of England, had their offices? What was Mr Rikkard Ambrose doing there if, as I had assumed, he was a simple government official?

Maybe I had misjudged him. There apparently were a few things hidden under that cold, flinty exterior.

What would he say if I took him at his word and on Monday actually... no! Again, I instinctively shook my head, trying to chase the mad thought away. I

---

[4] In Victorian England, there was no decimal coin system similar to the one we have today. Instead, Victorians used three kinds of coins: the pound (£), which was worth 20 shillings (s), one of which in turn was worth 12 pence or pennies (d). It may at first seem strange that 'penny' would be abbreviated with a 'd' and not a 'p', but it makes sense if one takes into consideration that the name of the ancient Roman coin equivalent of the penny is called 'denarius'. It is also worth noting that one pound back then was worth vastly more than it is today, which is not surprising, considering that the coins were made out of pure gold.

had to forget about it. It had been a preposterous idea in the first place. He would kick me out of his office as soon as he caught sight of me, or get his goons to do it. Maybe that mountainous fellow Karim. He looked like he could kick you all the way from here to Hampshire. And that wasn't considering what he could do with that pig sticker of his.

And still... still the possibility was tempting. My eyes glazed over as I considered the possibilities. My own job! My own money, earned with my own hands. Money to do with as I pleased. No longer would I be dependent on my miserly relatives, no longer would I have to dodge my aunt's not-so-subtle attempts at marrying me off.

The mental image of a vulture-like little woman violently cut short my daydream of independence. Ah yes, my beloved aunt, Mrs Hester Mahulda Brank. Like most greedy people on this wonderful earth, she was most desirous of obtaining what she could not have. First and foremost among those desires was a craving for social status, which her nieces, as daughters of a gentleman, automatically had, and she, as the daughter of a pawnbroker and a lady of questionable honour, was incredibly jealous of.

Mrs Brank was determined, as recompense for all her expense in feeding and clothing us girls for all those years, to squeeze as much social advancement out of us as humanly possible, and would have happily auctioned us off to the highest bidder if by so doing she could have gained an invitation to a duchess's tea party. The sale of relatives, however, unfortunately being illegal in England, she was confined to trying to marry each of us off to as rich and noble a bridegroom as possible, thus killing two birds with one stroke: not only would she be ridding herself of expensive mouths to feed, but she also would be gaining entrance into higher society through her nephews-in-law. In this way, the six bothersome girls who had infested Mrs Brank's home for years would finally be turned from unremunerative properties into valuable investments.

Hitherto, this brilliant scheme had met with little success. All six of us were still unmarried, and if I had my way, things were certainly going to stay that way, at least in my own case.

My dear aunt, with the natural instinct of the born financier, sensed this reluctance on the part of her property – i.e. me – to be dispensed with at a good profit, and was not very pleased about it. She had pointed out more than once that we would not always be able to count on her and her husband's generosity, and that after their death, nobody would provide for us if we were not married.

'And what if I want to provide for myself?' I had asked her once when the subject had come up.

She had stared at me as if I had been speaking a foreign language, and then given me a sour grimace which was probably supposed to have been a smile. She had thought I was joking.

Well, here and now was a chance to provide for myself. A real chance. Thoughtfully, I stared at the card again. Money. Money to earn for myself. A way to freedom.

If I didn't take it... then it would be the street for me. Or worse, the work-house.[5]

I looked around. Not that I had ever seen a workhouse, myself – but I had heard the stories whispered all around London. This charming little cell might actually give a good indication of what life in such a pigsty of humanity would be like. Criminals and poor people were about the same thing in this glorious *metropole*[6] of the British Empire, and their accommodations were probably similar. Of course, as a poor workhouse inmate, I wouldn't have the luxury of a cell to myself, and the food would probably be scarcer, because, unlike criminals, poor people don't generate paperwork when they die of hunger. But it was only to be expected that criminals would get better treatment. After all, thieves and murderers were of some interest to the general public: they were the subject of heroic ballads and gripping newspaper articles. They had to be kept alive until they could be hanged to the cheers of the crowd. Poor people, on the other hand, were just dirty and dull. Who would want to waste food and living space on them?

And that was the bright future that awaited me. Unless... Unless Mr Ambrose...

Suddenly, I heard a faint noise. Was it really what I thought? Yes! The jingle of keys. Someone was coming. Quickly, I tucked the card away and looked up. Startled by the sudden bright glow, I blinked and shielded my eyes with my hand. I had been so deep in thought that I hadn't noticed how the time had flown by. Now I saw a faint orange glow falling through the window into the cell. The sun was rising. The jingling from outside the cell grew louder and was joined by the sound of heavy footsteps.

I watched the cell door apprehensively. After a few more moments, a thick-set bobby appeared from around the corner. I could see him approach through the iron bars of the door. He unlocked it with a rusty key and pulled it open, gesturing for me to exit.

'What now?' I asked, not managing to keep apprehension from creeping into my voice.

The portly constable frowned. 'What do ye mean, "what now", Miss?'

'What will happen to me? How will I be punished?'

He blinked like a little piggy. Then, he opened his mouth and started to laugh. He continued to laugh for some time, holding his belly all the while. The keys jingled in the rhythm of his merriment.

'Oh my God, Miss,' he gasped, still holding his belly. 'We ain't gonna punish people for things like that! A woman trying to vote? We might as well punish every nutter running around in the streets, and then we'd be busy till kingdom come. Why, only the other day I met a man in a pub who told me that we're all

---

[5] The place where all the people who had no work or other means of supporting themselves ended up in Victorian London. It was an image of horror Victorian parents used to frighten their children with, a fact that reveals much about the conditions in such places.

[6] The central city of an Empire.

16

descendants of apes!'[7]Clearly off his rocker, the chap. And I didn't even reprimand him.' He chuckled once more. 'Now come on, Miss. It's time for ye to go.'

'I'm not going to be thrown into prison?' I demanded, actually sounding a little offended. I had expected some horrendous punishment. After all, I had bravely defied the chauvinist establishment. That deserved some recognition, at the very least, didn't it? A few years ago, at the Peterloo massacre, the authorities had come down hard on a crowd of working-class men demonstrating for *their* right to vote, resulting in twelve dead and three-hundred injured. And now they were simply going to let *me* go, just because I was a woman? There was no justice in this world! 'That's not fair! They're not even going to put me on trial?'

The bobby shook his head.

'Nay. We wouldn't want to bother a judge with this, he'd fine us for wasting his time. Now come on, Miss.'

For a moment, I considered whether I should insist on my right to go to prison. But at heart I was a practical person, and I really didn't want to spend another night on that bunk bed. So, grudgingly, I rose and followed the constable out of the cell to the small office of the police station, which smelled faintly of spit tobacco and bacon.

'Just wait a moment, Miss, while I get your things,' the still-smiling bobby said and waddled off to a cupboard in the corner. Opening the cupboard door, he rummaged around inside and came back with something big and black in his hand. 'There ye go, Miss,' he said in a stern and annoyingly fatherly manner, handing me all my personal belongings, contained in the top hat I had worn when I first set out on my little adventure. 'I really hope this will be a lesson to ye.'

'Yes it will,' I assured him, adding to myself, too quietly for him to hear: 'I'll make sure not to curtsy next time.'

Yes, next time I wouldn't get caught. Next time, I would succeed, because now I knew how hazardous good manners could be. I had never entirely agreed with my aunt, who had always thought them of such great importance, and now I finally knew I had been right all along. They were superfluous and dangerous – they could get you thrown into prison!

The bobby escorted me to the door of the police station, obviously wanting to make sure he would be rid of the madwoman, now that she was out of the cell and could start climbing up the walls or spouting feminist nonsense again at any moment. I was more than happy to oblige him and stepped out of the brick building into a glorious Saturday morning. The sun was shining and the fog was only slight today, the wind blowing in the opposite direction from the River Thames, making the morning air comparatively clear by London standards.

---

[7] In the early 19th century, the forerunners of Darwin's theory of evolution first appeared, such as Lamarck's 1809 'Theory of Transmutation'. For many Victorians, finding out that they were supposed to be the cousins of apes instead of creations of God's divine will was a rather big disappointment, which led to many people simply ignoring such new scientific discoveries.

I immediately set out towards home. I wasn't sure what my aunt had made of my overnight absence. She might not even have noticed it. With six of us in the house, and ninety per cent of her brain cells occupied with saving house-keeping money, she sometimes forgot one or another of her nieces. Sometimes I got lucky and it was my turn. Maybe, if I was really lucky, that had been the case last night.

At least I knew she hadn't completely run haywire and contacted the police, fearing I had been abducted or some such nonsense. If she had, the police would have informed her that her dear niece was perfectly safe, though a bit bedraggled and sitting, dressed in men's clothes, in one of their cells. If she had heard that, my aunt would have come to get me. And I don't know whether I would have survived the encounter. As it was, I had hopes of escaping relatively unscathed.

As if in answer to my hopeful attitude, the rows of dark houses parted before me and granted me a beautiful view of Green Park. In the warm glow of the sunrise, the small park looked like a fairy kingdom planted between the strict, orderly houses of middle-class London. A few birds were hopping on the grass, and the wind rippled the surface of a little pond surrounded by wildflowers. Through a clump of trees on the opposite side of the park, I could see the houses of St. James's Street.

My Uncle Bufford had lived on St. James's Street ever since I could remember, and we had lived with him and his wife ever since I could walk. We – that is my five sisters and I – had had to quit our family's country estate years ago, after our mother and father died and the estate went to the next male heir of the line. If you believed the stories of my older siblings, who could still remember the place, it had been a veritable palace with hundreds of servants and doorknobs made of gold. I didn't. Believe their stories, I mean. But I did somewhat resent the thing about this supposedly 'rightful heir' snatching away our family's estate just because he was a dratted man!

Oh well, to tell the truth, I didn't remember our childhood home in the country well, and I didn't want to. I was a city girl, and the few trees and lawns of Green Park were as much country as I could deal with at any given time.

Squaring my shoulders, I made my way through the park, enjoying the songs of the birds in the trees and the fresh morning breeze. The country was a nice thing, as long as it was in the middle of town and you could reach a civilized place with shops, libraries and newspapers within five minutes or so.

Five minutes and thirty-seven seconds later, I had reached the wall that encircled our little garden, a rare thing in the city of London. Over the wall, I could see the plain, orderly brick house with its plain, orderly windows, plain, orderly curtains and plain, orderly smoke curling out the chimney in a discreet and economical manner. The flowerbeds around the house were well-kept, but strict and simple. Everything was rectangular and neat. There wasn't a piece of decoration in sight. Sometimes, when I looked at this house I had been living in for years now, I thought it should have a sign over the door saying, 'Fortress of the Bourgeoisie, centre of the realm of hard work and stinginess. Beware of the aunt. She bites!'

There was only one bright spot among all the neat tediousness: the window of a first floor room. It afforded a wonderful view over Green Park – which was why, when we had arrived at this house years ago, the room had been dusty and unused, and my uncle had never set foot in it. He had probably been afraid the annoyingly beautiful view might distract him, or worse, tempt him to actually take a walk and thus waste valuable time he otherwise could have spent working.

But that had been just fine with me. When we had arrived at my uncle's, I had seen the dusty, deserted old room, fallen in love with it and taken possession before any of my sisters could complain. I had defended my conquest with my very life! Only Ella, my youngest sister, and of all of them the one I could stomach best, had been allowed to enter my dominion and make her abode there along with me.

Right now, the fact that my room looked out over the back garden came in handy in a way which had nothing whatsoever to do with the beautiful view. Hurrying across the street, I opened the little door in the garden wall with the key I had secretly 'borrowed' from my uncle, along with his clothes and passport. Inside, I quickly made my way to the garden shed. Taking out the rickety old ladder that had been in there since time immemorial, I carefully put it to the wall of the house and started climbing up to the window which I had taken care to leave unlatched. If I was lucky, I would get back into the house without anybody being the wiser.

Climbing up the ladder proved to be considerably more difficult than climbing down had been. My muscles were aching from the night in the cell, and there seemed to be several large lead weights tied to my behind, pulling me down. Or maybe it was just my behind that felt so heavy...

No! It was just generous, after all, not fat. Definitely not fat.

Sweat ran down my face in rivulets by the time I had reached the top of the ladder. I clung to the windowsill for a moment, making sure my aching legs would be up for the task, then I hoisted myself inside and landed rather inelegantly on the floor. Done! I was back home, and nobody had seen me sneak in. I remained kneeling on the floor for a moment longer to catch my breath, and then turned and got up – to find my sister Ella sitting just a few feet away on her bed, staring at me, her mouth agape in shock.

Oh, did I happen to mention she hadn't known anything of my leaving yesterday?

Blast, blast, blast!

WHO HE REALLY IS

'Where have you been?' Ella demanded in a breathless voice, jumping up from the bed, where, judging from the dampness of her pillows, she had spent half the night crying in despair. 'Oh Lilly, I've been so worried!'

She definitely looked worried. Her normally cream-coloured face had taken on the hue of a freshly whitewashed wall, except for her large almond eyes, which were shining with suppressed anguish. With both hands, she held a hand-kerchief to her mouth as if to stifle a scream that was on the tip of her tongue. Glittering tears decorated her face like diamonds. I had to hand it to her: she looked like a perfect damsel in distress. And it hadn't even been she who had spent the night in prison. How did she do it?

'What has happened to you, Lilly? Were you abducted? Who were you with? Where were you? And... *Why are you wearing Uncle Bufford's old striped trousers?*' At the last question, she actually stopped crying. Apparently, my wearing striped trousers had a calming effect on her. I should try to do it more often.

'Don't worry,' I told her, patting her on the head. 'I'm perfectly fine.'

'Yes, but *where were you?*' she repeated the question with more force.

I shrugged. 'Out.'

'Where?'

'Somewhere in town.'

'You've been gone the whole night!'

'Have I?' I tried to sound surprised. It didn't sound very convincing, unfor-tunately. 'My, my, how time flies.'

'Why are you wearing Uncle Bufford's trousers?' she asked again. Appar-ently, this point was of extraordinary significance to her.

'Well, I...' Desperately I wracked my brain for some legitimate reason why a girl should be wandering through London dressed in trousers.

Instinctively, my eyes slid up and down Ella's figure. She was dressed in what was considered normal and decent for a young lady to wear: a pale cotton gown with wide, puffed sleeves and lace trimmings, and, of course, the crinoline, a structure for supporting enormous hoop skirts that was made out of the bones of whales. The poor sea creatures had to suffer to give the rear end of every lady within the British Empire preposterous dimensions. This was what was consid-ered 'normal'.

Taking this into consideration, was there a legitimate reason why a woman would want to wear trousers?

Well, maybe because she actually had some brains...

'Why don't you answer, Lilly? What is the matter?'

But no, that wouldn't work as an argument with Ella. I bit my lip, trying des-perately to think of something to say.

'Please,' she pleaded, clasping her hands together like a little child. 'Please tell me where you were!'

Darn it! How could I resist her? But I simply couldn't tell her what had really happened.

Don't get me wrong, it wasn't that I didn't trust her. I loved her. I would have trusted her with my deepest, darkest secrets – if she hadn't been afraid of the dark, that is. If I told her that I went out, dressed in men's clothes, to illegally vote at a parliamentary election, was offered a job as a secretary, got caught by the police, then got thrown into jail and spent the night next door to three fa-mous murderers, she would have nightmares for the next three years.

'I... I wanted to go out last night to visit Patsy,' I fibbed. 'And you know... it was so late, and the streets were so dark... I was afraid something might happen to me, a lone girl, in the dangerous city.' I affected a quite convincing shudder. 'And I had read in some book – I don't remember the title right now – of girls dressing up as men when they did not want to be harassed, so I thought why not do the same, and so I did. But then it was so terrible out in the dark streets, and Patsy said I could stay the night if I didn't want to return in the dark. I was afraid, so I stayed. Sorry for worrying you.'

I waited for the admonishment. No doubt even my sweet, unsuspecting sister would see through this feeble lie. When in the world had I ever been afraid of anything, let alone something as ridiculous as the dark? Rather than dressing in my uncle's clothes to avoid trouble, I would have taken my uncle's cane to deal with trouble if it chose to appear. What would I say next if Ella didn't believe me?

'Oh, my *poor, poor* Lilly.' Ella rushed towards me. The next thing I knew she was hugging me tightly, though slightly awkwardly because of her enormous hoop skirt getting in the way. 'That must have been so *terrible*! You must have been *really* frightened.'

'Err... yes,' I mumbled. 'I was, I was really.' Dear Lord, she had actually swallowed it!

'*Poor* Lilly. You are so brave. Oh, I would have *died* from fear if I had to set a foot outside the house at night.'

'Well it's fortunate that I went out then, and not you,' I said, patting her head reassuringly. 'I like you alive and kicking.'

'We must go to Aunt Brank, Lilly, immediately,' Ella insisted, stood back and grasped me by the hand. 'She wanted to know where you had disappeared to. I'm sure she's frantic with worry.'

Oh blast! Ella, the sweet little angel, might be easy to fool, but my aunt was another matter. If she saw me in striped trousers it would most definitely not have a calming effect on her. Quite the opposite, I suspected.

Ella was already turning and starting towards the door when I grasped her by the arm. 'Stop! Wait.'

'Why? We shouldn't wait. She must be terribly worried!'

Worried? Not worried for me, that was for sure. Worried that I had committed some humongous, scandalous transgression, maybe. That was always her first assumption when anything out of the ordinary happened near me: blame Lilly. And in this case she would actually be right.

'Um... I can't let her see me like this.' I gestured at Uncle Bufford's old trousers. 'She would be very upset.'

To be honest, 'very upset' was putting it mildly. But I thought it better to couch it in gentler terms for the benefit of my little sister.

Ella clutched her hands in front of her chest. 'Oh, you are right! Oh, Lilly, what shall we do?'

'Err... change?' I suggested. 'At least I should. You are fine as you are.'

'Quite right!' A beaming smile spread across Ella's face. 'And then we will go down to see Aunt?'

'Yes, yes.'

Quickly I went to the big old wardrobe that took up a considerable portion of the room. Its size was hardly justified by its contents: one coat and two dresses for each of us. No ball gowns, no large collection of dresses like many of the ladies in town possessed.

Originally, there had even been only one dress for each of us, until I had pointed out to my dear aunt and uncle that if one dress got dirty, you needed a second one to change into, since it was hardly proper for a lady to run around stark-naked. Grudgingly, my uncle had conceded the point and opened his precious purse to buy each of us another dress. The plainest and cheapest that could be found in the city of London.

This was the dress I now took out of the wardrobe, not forgetting to thank the Lord for my uncle's stinginess. The very fact that it was so plain made it a marvellous camouflage for dodging the prospective suitors my aunt flung at me at regular intervals.

'Here, hold this for a moment, will, you?' I asked Ella, with one hand starting to open the belt which held Uncle Bufford's old trousers in place, and handing her my favourite armour against suitors with the other.

You aren't likely to need it to fend off many suitors, though, are you? said a nasty little voice in the back of my head. *Not as long as you look so unlike a girl that the most masculine of men doesn't even recognize you as female.*

'Help me put this on, will you?' I said to Ella, to drown out the annoying voice in my head. I would *not* think of Mr Ambrose again. I had done more than enough of that in prison.

'Of course,' she responded with a sweet smile and was just about to unbutton the dress when a knock from the door froze her in place. That knock managed to drive all thoughts of Mr Ambrose out of my head far more successfully than any attempts on my part.

'Ella? Ella, are you still in there? Who are you talking to?' The high tones of my aunt's voice penetrated the door. I would have said her voice sounded something like a piece of chalk being dragged across a blackboard, but that would be an insult to chalk all over the world.

Before I could stop her, Ella smiled and cried, elated: 'It's Lilly, Aunt! She has come back!'

There was a pause. It was filled with the threat of sudden and violent doom. 'Lillian? Is it true? Are you in there?'

For a moment I considered shouting back, 'No, not really' – but then I gave up. There was no sense in pretending anymore.

'Yes, Aunt, I am here.'

'Come out at once! I wish to speak with you. You have a lot to explain, young lady!'

On tiptoes, I went to the door and bolted it.

'What are you doing?' Ella mouthed at me, her eyes wide.

'Protecting our necks,' I mouthed back at her.

'I'm sorry, Aunt, but that will have to wait a while,' I called out. 'I'm dressing at the moment.'

'So what? I am your Aunt. I have seen you dress since you were a little girl.' She turned the doorknob and pushed – but the door wouldn't budge. 'Lillian? Lillian, don't tell me this door is bolted!'

'That's fine,' I answered in as light a tone as I could manage while frantically unbuttoning Uncle Bufford's waistcoat. 'I won't tell you, I promise.'

'Don't get smart with me, young lady! Is this door bolted?'

'You just asked me not to tell me that. So I can't, even though technically it actually might be true.'

'Lillian!'

Oh-oh... maybe I shouldn't push her too far.

'Yes, Aunt, it is bolted.'

'Then unbolt and open it at once.'

'Sorry, I can't do that.' Quickly, I ripped the waistcoat off and stuffed it under my pillow. Now I was standing half-naked in my room, dressed only in striped trousers, a corset and a top hat which for some reason hadn't fallen off my head yet. 'I, err... I am preparing a special look for myself today. You always say how I don't look ladylike enough, don't you? Well, I'm giving it a special effort today, and I want to surprise you.'

'Is that really true?'

'Yes.' I glanced down at my corset and striped trousers. 'You wouldn't believe how I look right now – it's so different from the usual. Trust me.'

'I want to know where you were last night.'

'I'll tell you as soon as I'm finished dressing.' That would give me a little more time to prepare a convincing variation of the lie I had told Ella.

'Were you with a man?'

I rolled my eyes. Of course that would be the first conclusion my aunt would come to.

'Will he make an honest woman of you?' she demanded.

'No,' I hissed. All this talk was distracting. Angrily, I fumbled at a waistcoat button which wouldn't do what I wanted. I needed to get these clothes off fast.

'What? What kind of rake have you gotten yourself mixed up with?'

'I didn't mean no as in "no he won't make an honest woman of me". I meant no as in "no, I wasn't with a man".'

'Oh.' She pondered that for a moment, and then demanded: 'Well, where were you, then?'

Quickly I looked around for a place to hide the top hat. There wasn't any place I could see, so I just chucked it out of the open window. I would get it later when all the hubbub was over.

'Like I said, Aunt, I'll tell you when I'm finished preparing my special look.'

'What kind of special look? What exactly is it that you are doing in there?'

'Um... Ella will tell you. I'm too busy with dressing.'

I climbed out of the trousers and stuffed them inside my second dress in the wardrobe. When I turned to her, Ella was gaping at me in horror.

'What am I supposed to tell her?' she mouthed.

'Think of something,' I mouthed back and then transferred my attention to the dress I would have to worm myself into.

Handing it to me, Ella hurried to the door.

'Err... Aunt, well, Lilly is... Lilly is...'

Furiously I tried to struggle into the crinoline while Ella stood at the door and with a quivering voice told my aunt some nonsense story about how I was doing my hair in a special new style. God, couldn't she think of a good lie for once? It would be a special day when I decided to style my hair at all, let alone in some special way. My brown locks always looked as if a hurricane had just gone through them in any case, so why bother?

But amazingly, my aunt seemed to swallow the story. She stopped trying to come in, and, after a time, went off grumbling.

Five minutes later I was completely dressed, styled and mentally prepared. Ella had even lavished her skills on me and provided me with a hasty yet luscious hairdo, to give at least a little bit of credence to her story. She squeezed my hand in silent encouragement. Finally, I took a deep breath, unbolted the door, plastered a bright smile on my face and stepped out into enemy territory.

My aunt was waiting for me on the landing, her thin arms folded in front of her chest, the glower of her narrow eyes directed at me like that of the ancient Roman god Jupiter at some poor wrongdoer he was just about to smite with a thunderbolt. All she was missing was the toga and the long white beard.

'Where were you?' she demanded, the beady little eyes in her vulture-like face narrowing with suspicion. 'And be warned – I will brook no evasions this time!'

'Oh, me?' I said brightly. 'I was at Patsy's and stayed the night. Just came back, in fact. Don't you remember? I told you the day before yesterday that I would stay at her place.'

Keep it simple. Don't say anything else. Just keep it simple and for God's sake, don't blink.

My aunt's glower flickered. I waited, holding my breath. I had gambled on her nature: my dear aunt was suspicious to the bone, but she also didn't actually care tuppence about how I spent my time, as long as it didn't threaten her social standing or the contents of her purse. If I had gotten myself killed last night she wouldn't have cared, if I had done it in a nice, quiet manner. I saw the suspicion gradually lift from her bony face to be replaced by her usual expression of mild distaste. 'Um... err... yes, now that you mention it I do recall something of the kind,' she said slowly. 'The day before yesterday, you say?'

'Exactly,' I confirmed, letting my smile grow even more bright and confident. 'Where did you think I was? Did you think I spent the night in prison?'

Her mouth thinned. 'Lillian! Don't even joke about such a thing! It is unbecoming of a lady!'

'Of course. I am sorry.'

Behind me, I heard Ella carefully step out of the room. She had obviously listened and knew that the danger of actual bloodshed was passed.

'Shall we go down to breakfast?' I suggested. 'I am hungry after my walk.'

Nodding, and still frowning slightly, my aunt turned and led the way down the stairs. Behind her, I let out a deep breath. Thank the Lord for uncaring relatives.

Breakfast. The most important meal of the day, it is said. And, in many families under the glorious rule of Her Majesty Queen Victoria, an occasion for the entire household to gather around the table and make polite small talk about their plans for the day, while consuming luscious delicacies. I had read once, when for some reason I had peeked into a cookbook, that in the usual upper middle-class family, the following was brought to the table, for *one* breakfast:
- fresh sausages
- boiled eggs
- a cold ham
- porridge with fresh cream & butter
- kippers
- a pheasant pie
- fresh curds and whey
- corn muffins
- fresh bread
- marmalade
- honey
- coffee
- tea

The cookbook had also suggested that a red and white chequered tablecloth should be avoided since it could have adverse effects on the digestion.

Breakfast at my uncle's house was slightly different. For one thing, my dear Uncle Brank only owned one tablecloth – a dark brown one, so stains would not be visible and it wouldn't have to be washed so often. For another, the meal was not quite so opulent. And as for the polite small talk at table, that was inhibited slightly by the fact that my uncle wasn't actually present.

Mr Brank had not come down into the dining room to take his meals for years, not since his sister and her husband had died, leaving him the task of looking after six of these strange, unpleasant little creatures commonly referred to as 'girls'. Mr Brank was not fond of female company. He'd had to acquire a wife at some point in his life, of course, in order to produce an offspring who could someday take over the business, but at least she was a sensible, economical woman. These... 'girls' were another matter entirely.

Thus it was that when we arrived in the dining room that morning, the big chair at the head of the table was empty, and my aunt bore an especially sour expression on her thin face. Leadfield, our only servant, who held the position of butler, valet, scullion and shoeblack all at the same time, was waiting for us and bowed as far as his ancient back would allow.

'Breakfast is served, Madam.'

'Thank you, Leadfield,' my aunt said in a cool voice, repeating the ritual that had taken place in our household for over a decade. With another bow and a sweep of his bony arm Leadfield directed us to the table.

'Will Mr Brank be joining us at the breakfast table today, Leadfield?' my aunt asked, continuing the ritual.

'The master is very busy and left early for work this morning,' Leadfield gave the expected answer. 'I brought him his breakfast earlier, up in his study.'

'I see.'

I saw my aunt throw a piercing glower up at the door of Uncle Brank's study, just visible upstairs. It had long been his inner sanctum and impenetrable fortress, where no female, not even my aunt, was allowed to enter.

When Mr Brank's sister and her husband, my beloved mother and father, had been so inconsiderate as to die in an accident, and this horde of chattering miniature females had invaded his home, Mr Brank had wisely decided to retreat and establish a secure base in his upstairs study, where these small creatures would not dare to venture. Instead of coming down to breakfast, lunch and dinner, he preferred to have his meals brought up to him by the aged butler, or to simply eat at work. Needless to say that this did not endear us girls to his wife, who lost many an opportunity to discuss at the table with her husband such important subjects as her latest efforts in household savings and the profligacy of the neighbours.

This time, things were no different. My aunt pursed her lips as the other doors to the dining room opened and my other sisters filed in from various parts of the house, yet my uncle remained absent.

'Are you sure he is already gone, Leadfield?'

'Yes, Madam.'

She sniffed. 'Well, hopefully he will join us tomorrow.'

'Hopefully, Madam,' Leadfield concurred.

'You may serve the first course.'

The first and only, I thought, shaking my head.

'Yes, Madam. Thank you, Madam.'

With all the dignity of a host of royal lackeys serving a voluptuous feast, Leadfield took the lid off the porcelain bowl in the middle of the table and poured each of us a healthy portion of porridge. To this he added some potatoes and salted herrings – the cheapest and most nourishing food that could be found on the London market. Say what you will, my uncle didn't starve us. Over the years, I even had gotten quite a taste for salted herrings.

My aunt obviously didn't feel like that. She eyed the fish on her plate with ambivalence. I could clearly see two of her strongest instincts warring with one another: her stinginess, which told her that this was the cheapest food you could get without poisoning yourself, and her social aspirations, which told her that a lady would under no circumstances eat something that also formed the regular diet of Irish peasants. In the end, stinginess, aided by a rumbling stomach, seemed to win out. She poked one of the potatoes with her fork as if she expected it to come alive and attack her. When it didn't, she impaled it and picked up her knife.

I had already started shovelling porridge into my mouth while my aunt was occupied, taking the opportunity to actually get some serious eating done before my lack of table manners was noticed. Beside me, Ella ate with considerably better manners but equal enjoyment. Gertrude, my eldest sister and the old maid in the family, didn't seem to mind the plain food either. The others, however, – Lisbeth and especially the twins, Anne and Maria – looked rather contemptuously at their plates and took a long time to start eating.

Even when they finally stuck their forks into the herring, they did not eat very much, and this was not just the case because they didn't like their food: unlike me, they considered themselves to be very fine ladies. Very fine ladies could under no circumstances talk with their mouths full, which meant they hardly ever could put a bite in their mouths.

'Have you heard?' Anne burst out as soon as we were all seated. 'Lord Tilsworth is engaged! And to a frightful girl, too. She is supposed to be one of the most low-minded creatures in London – and with horrible freckles all over her face. What in God's name induced him to marry her I cannot imagine! She's not even of the gentry, from what my friend Grace told me the other day.'

'No!' gasped Maria. 'Can it be true that he is throwing himself away on somebody like that? I can hardly believe it!'

'It is true, I swear it. As I said, I had it from Grace, who had it from Beatrice, who had it from Sarah, who had it from her second cousin, who heard it all from the cousin of Lord Tilsworth's second chambermaid.'

'Which of course means that it *must* be true,' I mumbled, rolling my eyes and chewing my potatoes.

'Lillian!' snapped my beloved aunt. 'Don't talk with your mouth full.'

'Yes, Aunt.'

'Such a pity,' Maria sighed. 'Tilsworth would have been such a catch. And he was quite taken with me at the last ball.'

I rolled my eyes again and hoped my aunt wouldn't see. She would probably consider that unladylike behaviour, too. Oh yes, *the last ball*. Anne and Maria had been talking about it for days and days now. They were the only ones of us who actually ever got invited to any balls, because they were the only ones pretty enough in the eyes of the gentlemen. No, that wasn't quite true. Ella could have given them a run for their money – if she hadn't been so painfully shy. But as it was, Anne and Maria, pale, tall and sickly-looking, with dark circles under their eyes and that demure look that gentlemen favoured so much, were the only ones of us ever getting into society.

Which was pretty much how I liked it. They were welcome to all the balls and all the men they could get. They could have thousands and thousands of men, and have illicit affairs with them or marry one or all of them, or cook them for dinner if they really wanted to. I would wish them the best of luck. But why oh why did they have to bore the rest of us to death by talking about it?

'...and the Earl of Farthingham is supposed to be engaged to Lady Melrose.'

'Really, Anne? I hadn't heard that.'

'Yes, Maria. You see, it's a frightful secret because...'

I ignored them to the best of my ability and concentrated on my salted herrings, while they kept gossiping about the famous Admiral this and the rich Mister that. My thoughts were neither on my food nor on society, however. They were on a certain tall, dark-eyed individual and on one question that kept coming back to the forefront of my mind ever since he had given me his card: *Should I go there?*

I didn't even know why I was still thinking about it. A normal lady wouldn't even consider trying to get a job.

Ah yes, that snarky little voice in the back of my mind said, *but then, a normal lady wouldn't try to go voting dressed up as a man, would she? Ladies simply weren't supposed to be independent. They were expected to marry, sit at home and look pretty. And that's not exactly what you have in mind for your life, is it?*

I threw a glance at Anne and Maria. They obviously were content with this lot in life. And why not? They were pretty, they could sit still very well, and to judge from the effort which they put into their social exploits, they would marry well, too. The young men of London where, from what I could gather, full of praise for their beauty and accomplishments, and were only quarrelling about which of the two to praise more. Quite a hard decision, since they were twins and identical to the last lock of their golden hair.

Indeed, Anne and Maria would make very fine ladies. I, on the other hand, had always had a rather stormy temperament that didn't lend itself well to the idea of marriage. Not as long as the vows included an oath of obedience to a man, anyway.

I definitely wanted to do more with my life than exist as an appendix to some chauvinist blockhead. So why did I hesitate, now that this golden opportunity had presented itself?

Maybe because I remembered with crystal-like clarity the darkness in Mr Ambrose's eyes. I remembered how that muscled mountain, Karim, had dragged off the fat man at his master's command. Mr Ambrose was no friendly or gentle man. There was a good chance that going there would cost me dearly. Still, his offer was a once-in-a-lifetime opportunity.

Now the question was: for this opportunity, was I prepared to enter the lion's den without knowing if an open maw awaited me?

In my mind, I again saw an image of his dark eyes – dark eyes so deep you could drown in them. They seemed to draw me towards them. Suddenly, I didn't feel as hesitant about going as I had a moment ago.

His offer, I reminded myself. *That is the only reason you're thinking about him, the only reason for going to see him again. This man is your ticket to freedom. Remember that, and while you're at it, forget about his hard, chiselled face and those deep, dark eyes...*

But somehow I couldn't seem to manage. His eyes seemed to stare at me constantly out of my memory, burning holes into my mind. In those eyes I saw ruthlessness, arrogance, anger and more icy cold than in an arctic blizzard.

Why couldn't I stop thinking about them? About him? I had never thought much about a man before. The way they behaved themselves, regardless of their looks, had always been enough to make me want to give them a good kick in the backside. But there was something about Mr Ambrose, something about those dark sea-coloured eyes, his granite face and the way he held himself, ramrod-straight and immovable, which I couldn't get out of my head. I had a feeling that if I tried to kick him, I would end up breaking every single one of my toes.

I wanted to go to him, to grab this golden opportunity, and at the same time I wanted nothing so much as to run away to hide in some corner where his dark eyes couldn't find me. If I only knew more about him, knew who or what he was and what I would be facing, maybe I could work up the courage to go to his office. But how in the world could I find out anything about him?

'...and Sir Ralley was so taken with the French Countess, I doubt he'll be able to resist another week. If he doesn't propose soon, I know nothing about London society. And I'm an expert, trust me. It's a marvel that...'

My hand froze in mid-air, half a herring hanging from my fork. Anne's words, which I had only heard by accident, had struck me like a thunderbolt.

I'm an expert. Trust me.

That was it! I just might find out more about him simply by asking! After all, I had a veritable fountain of information about London's society at my disposal. Two of them, in fact, or even three if you counted my aunt, who, although she wasn't able to go out as much as Anne and Maria, was just as addicted to the gossip of the high society. And to the high society, I was sure by now in spite of his simple attire, Mr Ambrose belonged without a doubt.

It was still unlikely that they would know of him. There were thousands of upper-class people residing in London, the capital of the world. But asking couldn't hurt.

'Err... I have a question,' I said, laying down my fork and bisected herring.

Maria waved a hand. 'Oh, leave us alone with your talks of politics and adventure stories and God knows what else, Lilly. We're too busy with serious talk to be bothered with your nonsense.'

'A question about society.'

The table went silent. All eyes were on me, even those of Gertrude, who normally was content to stay in her own little world.

I cleared my throat. 'Um... Does anybody know a Mr Rikkard Ambrose?'

Holding my breath, I waited for an answer. If he was nothing but a simple government official, they wouldn't know of him. But if not, if he was somebody more important, or rich, or powerful...

Maria laughed a high, nervous laugh, somewhere between hysteria and giggling.

'Oh Lord, Lilly, you're so funny. Do you honestly mean to tell us you don't know who Rikkard Ambrose is? I mean, *the* Rikkard Ambrose?'

SWEET AND SOLID

'No,' I said, suddenly feeling stupid in comparison to my sister Maria for the very first time in my life. I didn't like the feeling. 'Have you met him?'

'Met him?' Now Anne joined Maria's laughter. It wasn't considered polite for a lady to laugh at someone, but when they were in the family circle and I was the subject of their mirth, they frequently seemed to forget that rule. 'Silly girl! Of course we haven't met him. No one has been that lucky.'

I have. And be careful about who you call a silly girl.

'Then how do you know who he is?' I asked politely, suppressing the urge to chuck a salt shaker at my sister's head.

Maria rolled her eyes as if this should be obvious.

'We've heard the talk, of course. Half of London has been talking about nothing but him for the last three months, ever since he's returned from the colonies.'

It must have been the wrong half of London, because I hadn't heard the talk. I fixed a glare on the twins. They were annoying enough under normal circumstances, but now that they knew something I didn't, their level of annoyance had passed the point of tolerance.

'Well, what does the talk say, exactly?'

The twins exchanged a meaningful glance.

'That he's tall,' giggled Anne.

'That he has eyes as dark as night,' said Maria, fluttering her eyelashes.

'I wouldn't say like the night,' I mumbled. 'More like the sea on an overcast day.'

They ignored me.

'That he's mysterious,' continued Anne in the same annoying sing-song. 'He landed out of the blue a few months ago at the Port of Dover, returned from God only knows where in the biggest ship they've ever seen down there, with an army of servants and armed guards, and he started buying up property all over town. Nobody has been able to find out who exactly he is or what he wants, and they haven't failed for lack of trying. Half of Fleet Street[8] has been after him for weeks, but still nobody knows where he or his fortune came from.'

Fortune? So he was rich, then. Yes, I could see by the longing sparkle in my sisters' eyes that he was. Rich and powerful.

Slowly, I put down my knife. I didn't feel much like eating, all of a sudden.

'That he's secretive and secluded,' added Maria, the corners of her mouth going down. 'He's practically shut himself up in that place he's had built in Leadenhall Street – almost never comes to any balls or dinners. And if he does, he acts as if the ladies in the room don't even exist.'

The corners of her mouth went down a little farther, and her delicate white hand tightened into a fist. At any other time, I might have enjoyed speculating about the reasons behind this, but right now I was far too busy. On top of half a bowl of porridge, I now had a big lump of information to digest.

Government official my ass! Mr Rikkard Ambrose was considerably more than an official. Considerably more dangerous. An official had to answer to the government. This man... did he answer to anyone? Again, I remembered how his henchman had hauled off the fat swindler into the mist. For the first time I realized that I had no idea what happened to the fat man. I didn't even know whether he was still alive.

---

[8] A street in London where ever since the Victorian Era, a lot of newspapers are based. For this reason, 'Fleet Street' was and is a synonym for 'British Journalists', much as 'Wall Street' is a synonym for 'American Finance'.

And then there was the question of which mysterious methods Mr Rikkard Ambrose had employed to acquire the fortune he apparently possessed. Not by inheriting it from a noble ancestor, apparently, which was the approved method for good, upper-class English gentlemen.

'Um...' I had to swallow to get rid of the lump in my throat. 'You mentioned his wealth. How wealthy is he, exactly?'

'How wealthy?' Maria scoffed. 'Why, he is only rumoured to be one of the richest men in the entire British Empire. That is all.'

'Lilly?' Ella asked suddenly, her voice sounding concerned. 'Are you not all right?'

I clutched the edge of the table with both hands, not knowing how to answer. I wasn't sure myself. What had I gotten myself into? 'I... I feel a little faint,' I finally mumbled. 'That's all.'

But that wasn't all. Definitely not.

The rest of the meal passed in a blur. I couldn't force another bite down. I could hardly force myself to remain in my seat. As soon as the others put down their forks and knives, I sprang up and rushed out the door.

'Lillian,' I heard my aunt call after me. 'Lillian, stay here! You can't go! It is time for your embroidering lesson.'

I didn't listen. The only thing I ever managed to do at embroidering was perforate my fingers, anyway.

Bounding down the hall, I rushed out through the back door and into the little garden. The small green space welcomed me, its high walls shielding me from all that lay beyond – the bustle and noise of the city, the stench of smoke drifting over from distant factories, and of course... *him*.

Quickly, I crawled into a little shady space behind a few bushes and hid. It was a favourite place of mine whenever I wanted to be away from my aunt or be alone with my thoughts. With the gently swaying green brush around me, almost hugging me close, I felt safe and protected from the world for a change. A world that seemed determined to turn me into something I was not and would never be.

And when I attempt to break free, I thought, *this has to happen.*

One of the richest men in the British Empire. Yesterday, I had met, ridiculed and insulted one of the richest men in the British Empire. What was I to do?

Stay here, said a little frightened voice in the back of my mind. A voice that sounded a bit like Ella. *He doesn't know who you are yet. He's only seen your face. If you don't go to meet him, he'll never find you, and that will be the end of it.*

I bit down on my lip. Exactly. That would be the end of it. The end of my only chance for freedom ever. And I wanted freedom. I wanted the chance to go where I pleased, do what I wished, and not to have to answer to any man for my actions.

So what was I to do now?

~~**~*~*

31

A lazy morning spent lying on my back and staring at the clouds drifting by hadn't helped to find an answer to that question. After two hours or so, when my back, still not recovered from being tortured by the police station bunk, began to protest at its treatment from the hard ground, I made myself get up. This wasn't helping.

Scrambling out from behind my bushes, I slipped through the little garden gate and set out towards Green Park. I felt as tense as a taut wire, and only relaxed a little when I reached the edge of the park. What I needed now was to get a breather, to clear my head of any thoughts about heavy life-altering decisions by means of good company. Which meant, of course, female company. I could only hope they were where I thought they would be...

'Hey! Lilly!'

Quickly, I turned towards the voice I had been hoping for.

That deep bellow was unmistakable! Unlike you would suspect on first hearing it, it didn't belong to a big, beefy bulldog, but to my best friend Patsy. She and the others already awaited me on the wrought iron park bench under the big oak, the usual meeting place of our little band of wrongdoers.

'Hello! Here we are!'

Passing gentlemen looked askance at Patsy, clearly indicating by their looks that ladies weren't supposed to bellow. They forbore however from making any disapproving remarks, probably because Patsy, with a figure like that of a boxing champion and a face like a horse, cut a pretty impressive figure, even for a girl in a hoop skirt. I certainly wouldn't have liked to come to blows with her.

She picked up her parasol and waved it like a victory flag. 'Where have you been, Lilly? Get your behind over here!'

The other two turned around and spotted me, too. Flora smiled shyly, and Eve raised her tiny pink parasol, waving it so energetically one could have mistaken it for a fluttering hummingbird's wing.

'Patsy is holding a speech,' she yelled across the remaining distance. I quickened my step, already feeling better. This would take my mind off other things. 'She's telling us how she will convince all the stinking rich people of London to give up their money for her latest charity.'

'You could threaten to impale them on your parasol,' I suggested, settling down on the only free place on the bench and grinning from ear to ear. It was good to see my friends.

Patsy snorted. 'That might be the only way to actually get it done. You wouldn't believe how tightly some people hold on to their money. Oh wait, I forgot about your uncle. You *would* believe.'

'I would,' I concurred. 'So, what is this charity event you're organizing?'

Patsy rolled her eyes. 'Ask rather how many dozen I'm organizing. One in favour of the workhouses, one in favour of St. Vincent's Orphanage, one in favour of everything you can think of, and I'll be lucky if I get more than a few pennies for any of them. But it's the event in favour of women's suffrage that has me really worried.'

'Why?' I wanted to know. 'Aren't any of the guests likely to give money?'

A scowl appeared on Patsy's face, and for a moment she really did look like a Rottweiler. 'Hardly. The problem is that there likely won't be any guests. So far, nobody has accepted my invitation.'

'Nobody? Honestly?'

'Honestly. I even got a note back from Lady Metcalf, saying that... how did she put it again? Ah yes, saying "how scandalous" it is that I am "trying to erode the pillars of civilization by destroying woman's natural role in life".'

I patted her hand.

'That's horrible! And after you gave yourself so much trouble in organizing everything. I'm so sorry for you.'

'Don't be.' The scowl on Patsy's face was replaced by a look of grim satisfaction. 'Be sorry for Lady Metcalf. You don't know what I said in my answering note.'

I couldn't prevent a grin from spreading over my face. No, I didn't know. But I knew Patsy, and could imagine.

'By the way,' I asked, 'how did the election go? I didn't catch the results.'

'How could you not catch them?' Patsy gave me a strange, sideways look. 'It was in all the papers.'

Well, I was sitting in prison all day, you know. We don't get papers there.

That's what I would like to have said, just to see the look on her face. But I didn't. My friends didn't know anything about my little adventure on Friday, and if I could, I wanted to keep it that way. They didn't need to know what a fool I had made of myself. It had been a crazy idea from the beginning, this whole dressing-up-as-a-man thing, and I just wanted to forget it as quickly as possible. So instead, I said:

'I... was busy. Very busy.'

'Well, you didn't miss anything worth hearing.' Patsy stabbed at the air with her parasol, as if it were a conservative politician. 'You want the result? A landslide victory for the Tories, of course! The Whigs were flattened. So no reforms on women's suffrage, nor on any other sensible subject by the way!'

A depressive silence fell over our little group for a while, and the morning, which had seemed cheerful right up until then, suddenly wasn't quite as enjoyable any more.

Without warning, Eve clapped her hands together and woke us from mourning over our lost freedom. 'Time for a little cheering-up! Look what a treat I've brought!' She fished something out of her pocket and held it out: four brown, rectangular objects. They didn't look very appetizing.

'What are those?' I asked, suspiciously.

'It's a new invention, just come on the market,' Eve trilled excitedly. 'It's chocolate.'

'Don't be silly. Chocolate is a drink,' Patsy objected. 'It's not solid.'

'Not usually no. But,' she lowered her voice conspiratorially, 'this fellow – Fly or High, I think he's called – developed a method to *make* it solid.'[9]

---

[9] This would be Joseph Fry & Sons, a British pioneer in chocolate making. The clever inventors at Fry & Sons produced some experimental forms of solid chocolate as early as the

I carefully tapped against one of the brown objects. It was quite hard. 'And it stays that way? A bit hard to swallow, wouldn't it be?'

'No, no. It dissolves in your mouth.'

'Really?'

'Yes, yes. Well, that's what it said in the advert, anyway.'

That didn't inspire much confidence in me.

'Why would anyone *want* to make chocolate solid?' Patsy demanded. 'If it only dissolves again afterwards, what's the point?'

'Oh, don't be such a stick-in-the-mud!' Eve was almost bouncing with excitement now. 'It's something new, something exciting. People call it a chocolate bar, and they say they're fantastic! So try them out already, will you? I spent all my pocket money on them!'

That final argument persuaded me. I knew enough about what it was like not to have much money to understand the sacrifice. Slowly, I took one of the 'bars' of chocolate and carefully deposited it in my mouth. The others followed my example. A tense silence settled over our group as we waited. The bars didn't explode or attack our teeth, which was a good sign to begin with. On the other hand, they didn't taste much like anything.

At least at first.

Then, the brown stuff suddenly started growing softer and softer, and the taste began to flood my mouth. I started licking and chewing faster and faster.

'Goodness!' Flora fanned herself. 'That really isn't fair! To have something that looks so plain and unappetizing, and then have it attack you like that... Dear me. Dear, dear me.'

'Is it good?' asked Eve, who still hadn't put her piece into her mouth, but seemed to be anxiously awaiting our judgement.

I sighed contentedly. Finally something that made me forget my troubles for a minute or two. I opened my mouth long enough to say: 'More than good. It's... yummy! The best thing I've ever tasted. The fellow who invented it, has he been knighted yet?'

'I don't believe so.'

'Just one more sign that there's no justice in this country,' I groaned, and Patsy as well as Flora nodded their consent, chewing energetically.

'So we have one more thing on our to-do list,' laughed Patsy, in her deep, throaty horse-laugh. 'Achieve women's suffrage and get the inventor of solid chocolate bars knighted for his achievements.' Suddenly despondent, she shook her head. 'Sometimes I just despair and think that women will never have equal rights with men in this lousy excuse for a country,' she sighed. 'We might as well forget about campaigning for women's suffrage and just start dressing up in men's clothes for the next election.'

I coughed, and almost choked on my chocolate bar. Luckily, the others were too busy with eating to notice, and I quickly forced it down.

1830s, but the modern chocolate bar as we know it was not invented until 1847, a few years after this book takes place.

Eve cleared her throat and winked at her large friend. 'Not to put too fine a point on it, Patsy... That might work for you, but I doubt the rest of us could pull it off.'

Patsy pounded the ground with her parasol. 'And why I and not the rest of you, Eve?'

'Because, my dear Patsy, you have a nose like a lumpy potato and enough bone in your chin for three good men. If we put you in a suit, everybody would bow to you and call you Sir.'

'Do you want a parasol hammered on your head, Eve?'

'Not particularly, no.'

'Then I suggest you quickly take yourself out of my reach.'

Eve sprang up laughing, snatched up a bird and racket I hadn't seen before and gaily ran off into the Park, dancing around, hitting the bird, catching it with the racket and hitting it skywards again. She missed as often as she hit, but that didn't seem to bother her.

'I don't think I could do it,' Flora offered shyly. 'Dressing up as a man, I mean. You could, Patsy, but not I.'

'Of course you could, Flora!' Patsy gave her a hearty slap on the back that almost catapulted the little girl off the bench. 'Come, Lilly, back me up! Everybody could do it, couldn't they?'

I contemplated the question carefully for a moment. 'No,' I said, finally, shaking my head. 'I think I would end up getting thrown in prison and landing myself in all sorts of troubles I hadn't counted on.'

~~**~*~*

My friends and I continued to sit long after that on the little bench under the oak and discussed politics, fashion, and the folly of men. But I had to admit that once the soothing effects of the wondrous solid chocolate waned, Mr Ambrose intruded more and more often on my thoughts.

Patsy kept shooting suspicious glances in my direction. Of our unofficial little secret society for women's suffrage, she was certainly the most observant one, Eve being too hyper and Flora too shy to remark anything. Patsy noticed my altered behaviour: how I sometimes stared into the air without seeing anything, how I crossed my arms more often than usual as if about to confront an invisible enemy. I'm sure she would have said something if the other two hadn't been there. So I made sure I was the first to leave, excusing myself on account of having to help my aunt with supper. If she wanted to find something out, Patsy could be determined as an Ascot race horse[10], and I didn't want to get trampled underfoot.

---

[10] Ascot is a little village in Berkshire, England. For over three centuries, ever since 1711 to be exact, the British aristocracy have been flocking there to bet their money on horses at the great Ascot horse race.

I didn't go home immediately, though. My beloved aunt wouldn't appreciate any help in preparing a meal she considered far too simple for such a good family as hers. Instead, I went around the little clump of trees in Green Park to a small pond, and fed the ducks for a few minutes. They seemed to appreciate the pieces of dry bread I threw them very much, and it soothed my nerves. Although I felt miserable right now, it was good to know that at least I could make somebody else happy, even if it was only some silly, feathery little beast. The last piece of bread landed in the pond with a soft 'plop'. I turned and started towards home.

The rest of the day flew by in a whirl of disjointed images. It seemed to take no time at all until I stared at the candle on my nightstand. Around the lone candle flame there was darkness. I was lying in my bed, listening to Ella's steady breathing in the other bed across the room and staring into the flame so hard it almost hurt my eyes.

This is it, I thought. If I blow out this candle, the day will be over and there will be only one day left before Monday. One day before I have to face him or forget my dream of freedom.

What would I do?

More importantly: What would *he* do if I did the wrong thing?

He was no jolly fat bobby who would laugh the whole thing off. He might do anything, and a man with his position and power actually could do just about anything he wanted – to me and to my family. Getting me arrested for disturbing the King's Peace, ruining my uncle's business... the possibilities were chilling, and not unlikely to come to pass. I remembered every cold, hard line, of his face. Mr Ambrose definitely didn't look like the kind of man who appreciated being made to look like a fool.

But this was my only chance! The only chance I would ever get to be free.

For the first time in my life I was afraid of the dark. But I screwed up all my courage, leant forward and blew out the candle.

~~**~*~*

The next day was even worse. In church, I didn't hear above one word in ten of what the reverend was saying. I tried not to look at him too much because I knew of whom a tall black figure with a stern expression would remind me – only Reverend Dalton wasn't half as good-looking as... *he.*

What did I do once I got home?

I honestly couldn't say. Maybe I actually went through one of my aunt's embroidering lessons for once. Ella was starting to look worried whenever she glanced my way. I would have liked to reassure her, tell her that everything was all right, but it would have been a more blatant lie than even I was capable of.

Evening came, and then the night. I lay in my bed again, staring at the candle and wondering whether to blow it out or not.

If I did, that was it. No more time to think or evade. It would be Monday, my first day at 'work'. Or in prison, if *he* put his mind to it. What was he going to do to me?

36

I crossed my arms and rolled myself up into a tight, protective ball. Why oh why did things have to be so difficult? Why couldn't I have a job and my independence without having to fear retribution from one of the most powerful men in the British Empire?

Maybe, if I didn't blow out the candle, I wouldn't fall asleep and tomorrow would never come. Yes, that sounded like a good plan!

I lay there, gazing up at my protection, the candle, and wishing fervently that tomorrow would never arrive.

Suddenly, a gust of wind from the open window ruffled the curtains and blew out the candle, plunging me into darkness.

Not fair!

EMPIRE HOUSE

I awoke and thought: *Oh God, please don't let it be Monday.*

Beside me, in the other bed, Ella yawned and stretched, looking first out of the open window, through which bright, golden sunlight streamed into the room, then turning to beam at me. 'What a beautiful Monday morning!'

Thank you very much, God.

Faced by the inescapable fact that Judgement Day was upon me, I simply lay there for a while, contemplating my doom. Ella, however, didn't seem to be aware of the fact that her sister was about to face a masculine monster from the pit. She was already up and dressing herself, humming a merry tune.

'Come on, Lill,' she said, calling me by my nickname she only used when nobody else was around. 'Get out of bed. It's already eight thirty.'

So what, I wanted to answer, but the words stuck in my throat. Eight thirty? In my mind I heard Mr Ambrose's cool voice echoing: *Be at my office, nine sharp Monday morning.*

'Eight thirty?' I choked.

'Yes, why?'

Not daring to waste time with an answer, I jumped out of bed, struggled out of my nightdress, and hurriedly started throwing on the dozens of petticoats that we poor females had to stuff under our dresses.

'What's the matter?' cried Ella, alarmed.

'I have to be somewhere at nine!' My own voice was slightly muffled because I was trying to force my way through three petticoats at once.

'Where?'

'Can't tell you. But it's frightfully important. Please, Ella, help me with these infernal things? I think I'm stuck!'

'Here, let me.' Ella, ever the helpful spirit, didn't even think of questioning me. Instead she untangled the knotted mess of petticoats I had been trying to ram my head through, and then handed me my dress.

'Not that one,' I said, shaking my head at my favourite, simple, gown. 'The other one.'

Now even Ella's curiosity was roused. She handed me the fancier of my two dresses, the one with lace trimmings she knew I hated wearing. When I had slipped into it, I rushed to the mirror and started untangling my hair. 'How do I look? Well? What do you think? Am I presentable?'

Ella stood behind me, watching something that was rarer than a volcano eruption in Chiswick: me, trying to make myself look stylish. In the mirror I could see her mouth open in a silent 'Oh' and a blush suffuse her cheeks.

'Oh, Lill!' She clapped her hands together, a sudden smile spreading over her face. 'You have a rendezvous, haven't you? A rendezvous with a young man!'

My jaw dropped, and I whirled around.

'No! Of course not!'

Ella didn't seem to have heard me. Quickly, she stepped to my side, that silly, secretive, girly smile still plastered on her face. Her hands came up, starting to style my hair and smooth my dress at a pace I would never have been capable of. It was as if she had ten arms. 'It's all right,' she giggled. 'I won't tell. Is he nice? Is he handsome?'

Yes he is. Very.

I pushed the thought out of my mind as soon as it appeared. It wasn't like that! I wasn't going to meet a man. Well, in a sense I was, but not 'meeting' as in meeting to do... well, to do whatever romantic couples get up to when they're alone. Why did every female's brain on earth, including that of my little sister, turn to mushy-gushy mushrooms the moment a man was mentioned? There were many legitimate reasons for a girl to meet a man, reasons that had nothing whatsoever to do with mating behaviour, such as... such as...

Well, maybe I couldn't think of anything just now, but you see my point.

'Oh Lill, come on. Tell me at least what colour his eyes are, will you?'

I stomped my foot and crossed my arms. Ella more or less ignored my signs of protest and continued to work her magic on my hair.

'I said no, didn't I? I'm not going to a rendezvous, Ella!'

She just giggled again, and then winked. My dear, demure, innocent little sister, winking? And if my eyes didn't betray me, even conspiratorially!

'I quite understand,' she whispered. 'You have to be discreet.'

Why was I even bothering to correct her? It would be good if she came up with her own explanation and I wouldn't have to engage in inventive truth-modification again to spare her concern. But the thought simply drove me insane: I was going to meet Mr Rikkard Ambrose, and all the while my little sister would be sitting at home thinking that he and I were...

I shook my head. This was no time for mushy-gushy irrationality. My interest in Mr Ambrose was purely professional, and it didn't matter what anybody else thought. Did it?

No doubt motivated by her concern for the welfare of my pining, love-struck heart, Ella finished my hair in record time. I took about two seconds to admire myself in the mirror – really, Ella had managed to make quite a presentable lady out of her raw material – and then rushed towards the door. Over my shoulder, I threw my little sister a grateful grin. 'I'll owe you forever for this! Thanks!'

'You are most welcome,' she said, winking again. It was definitely conspiratorial this time.

Dear God, had the world gone mad?

I rushed down the stairs, past a bewildered aunt and out the door before she could shriek her protest. How much time was left until nine? Not enough, probably. I was just about to start sprinting off in the direction of Leadenhall Street when I spotted a cab, just driving by on the other side of the street. Huzzah![11] My life was saved!

'Cabbie!' I waved my parasol like a castaway signalling the rescue ship.

With a 'Ho there!' the cabbie stopped his horses and peered at me curiously. I clambered into the cab before he could even think of jumping down to help me inside, and whacked my parasol against the roof.

'Leadenhall Street, cabbie, number 322. I have to be there before nine.'

The name of the famous street, full to the brim with business and money, acted like an electrical shock on the poor man. Up until then he had been looking sleepy and not too pleased by his new passenger, but when I said that name, his eyes flew wide open and he cracked the whip.

'Gee up!'[12]

The cab lurched forward and I was thrown back into the seat. Fiercely, I clung to the upholstery as we raced over the cobblestones. The uneven paving almost knocked my teeth out at the speed we were driving. We were lucky that there wasn't much traffic on the streets, or this insane tempo would have been plain suicide.

Outside the window, the buildings rushed by in a confused blur. I couldn't see much of them, but I did notice that, after a few minutes, the reddish-brown colour of brick buildings was replaced by the fancier colours of painted walls, which in turn were replaced by the gleaming white of marble. We had left the middle-class districts of London and were fast approaching the centre of the unrivalled power and wealth of the British Empire.

Anxiously, I listened for the sound of Great Paul, the bell of St. Paul's Cathedral, announcing the full hour. I had no idea if I still had twenty or only two minutes left till my appointment. If I only had a watch, then I would know! But apart from being expensive, watches were also only intended for gentlemen. As if girls didn't need to know the time of day!

'Hold tight, Miss!' the cabbie called, and I tightened my grip on the seat just in time. We swerved around a corner and I was almost thrown sideways onto the seat, but managed to right myself in time to see the black and white painted sign rush past the open window:

Leadenhall Street

Thank the Lord. Or maybe I shouldn't be too quick to thank him. That would rather depend on what would happen to me now...

'322, you said?' the cabbie called.

'Y-yes!'

---

[11] The Victorian version of 'Hurrah'.

[12] A cry uttered to a horse to make it move faster.

Abruptly, the cabbie pulled on the breaks and I was flung forward, just managing to catch myself in time to prevent my nose from being bashed in. Panting, I sat there in the coach and tried to recover my equilibrium. Outside, the cabbie jumped down and opened the door for me. Ordinarily I would have protested at such a display of male chauvinism, but right now my legs didn't feel like protesting. With shaky steps, I climbed out and even accepted the cabbie's hand, which he offered to help me down.

'Here.'

I handed the man my pocket money of about half a year – thanks to my generous uncle just enough to pay the fare – and looked up and down the street. I didn't see number 322 anywhere. Hmm... What could the office of Mr Rikkard Ambrose look like? The likeliest candidate for the headquarters of a man of his wealth was a building right across from me, with a broad, showy façade and more pillars and scrollwork than on most royal palaces.

The cabbie had followed my gaze. 'Which one is number 322?' I asked. 'That one?'

He shook his head emphatically. 'Oh no, Miss. That's India House, the headquarters of the East India Company. Number 322, Empire House, is right opposite. Behind the cab.'

Oh. I turned and with apprehensive steps circumvented the cab.

Slowly, as the black-painted wood of the vehicle blocked less and less of my field of vision, something gigantic and steel-grey came into my sight, and I knew immediately: this was it. This was the office of Mr Rikkard Ambrose.

It was built in neo-classical style like India House. That attribute, however, was just about all the two buildings had in common.

Empire House was not broad. Not ostentatious. Not richly adorned. It was the highest building in the street, stacking levels of offices upon offices in the narrowest space possible, and by doing so towered over the flatter, broader houses. Its façade was not marble, but austere dark grey stone and cast iron. The portico, normally the pride of every building with dozens of pillars, was hardly fit to be called a portico. There were only two pillars supporting the projecting roof – but what pillars they were: grey giants that seemed to threaten everybody who approached them.

Grey giants under which I had to pass.

'Looks impressive, don't it?'

I jumped. The cabbie was standing right behind me.

'W-what does?' I asked, trying to make my voice sound steady. It didn't really work.

The cabbie took a critical look at my face, which for once I'm sure, in spite of my tan, was fashionably pale according to the beauty-standards of English society.

'Sure you want me to drop you off 'ere, Miss?'

'Yes, yes, of course. Why wouldn't I?'

'Just saying.' He shrugged and hauled himself onto the cab's box again. Once more, he looked back. 'Quite sure? The gentleman who lives 'ere is supposed to be...'

For some reason he didn't finish the sentence, but glanced up at Empire House, and suddenly cut off.

'Yes, I'm quite sure. Thank you.' I nodded to him once more, and tried to give him my best imitation of a smile.

He just shrugged.

'It ain't none of my business. Good luck.'

With that, he cracked his whip and drove off, maybe a bit faster than was strictly necessary. I stared after him for a moment – then I remembered: I was running out of time. Quickly shaking off my paralysis, I turned and strode across the street.

Halfway across, the shadows of the great pillars enveloped me like giant bat wings. I couldn't help shuddering as I climbed the steep steps to the big oak front door. There was no doorman, which was a bit unusual for a building belonging to one of the world's most wealthy men, but which strangely fit the austere nature of the building and its owner. I was actually relieved – I wasn't entirely sure a doorman would have let me in. Yet deep inside I was also disappointed. A disapproving doorman might have been an excuse to turn around and go home.

Now I had no choice. No reason to excuse cowardice. I had to try. I owed it to myself.

Cautiously, I grabbed the large brass doorknob and pushed.

The door swung open, and I waited for the smoke of cigarettes to assault me as it had in all buildings ruled by men. Yet there was nothing but a draft of cool, clean air. Taking a deep breath, I entered and let the door fall shut behind me.

˷˷**˷*˷*

Inside it was dark. The sun hadn't risen above the houses of London yet, so only a little light fell through the high, narrow windows. What light there was, though, was sufficient to illuminate the scene in front of me well enough to make my throat constrict.

I was standing at the entrance to an enormous hall, at least seventy feet across. Apart from the gigantic cast iron chandelier hanging from the ceiling and the galleries high up on the walls, there was no decoration of any kind. No portraits, no draperies, nothing. The floor was dark, polished stone; the walls were painted a dark green-blue. In any other place the lack of decoration might have made one think the owner of the building was poor, but not here. The very enormity of this stark cavern repudiated poverty. And besides, it didn't take me long to realize the true reason behind the sparse decoration. I had lived too long with my dear uncle and aunt not to recognize the signs that somebody kept his purse up his arse.

Throughout the hall, people were jogging from one of the many doors to another, carrying pieces of paper, and obviously in a very great hurry to get their business done. The only person who wasn't moving an inch was a sallow-faced old man behind a plain wood counter at the back of the giant room. He simply sat, bent over a book in which he was busy scribbling notes.

Was he the receptionist? Well, there was only one way to find out.

I approached the counter and cleared my throat timidly. The man didn't seem to notice and continued writing in his book.

I cleared my throat again, louder this time, and crossed my arms. This fellow was getting my hackles up!

He finally deigned to look up and examined me over the tops of his small, steel-rimmed spectacles. The face he pulled made me think he wasn't very pleased with what he saw.

'Yes?'

This was it. Last chance to back out. Last chance to leave this place and never come back.

With great effort, I gathered all my courage and said, loudly and clearly: 'I'm here to see Mr Ambrose.'

I couldn't have gotten a more impressive reaction if I had said 'I'm here to see Father Christmas do a naked tap dance on your desk.' Everybody within hearing range stopped to turn towards me. One young clerk fell over his own feet and only just managed not to drop the large pile of papers he was carrying.

'Mr Ambrose?' asked Sallow-face incredulously. 'Mr *Rikkard* Ambrose?'

'Is there another one here?'

'Most assuredly not, Miss...?'

'Linton. Miss Lillian Linton.'

'Well, Miss Linton,' said Sallow-face, steepling his long fingers in a manner that I'm sure he meant to be threatening, 'Mr Ambrose is a very busy man. He does not have time for everybody who wishes to waste it.' He looked down at his book again. 'If you have come collecting for charity, try Lord Arlington's place, or Lady Metcalf's. I am sure they shall be more than happy to oblige you.'

'I have not come to collect for charity,' I said. 'I have an appointment.'

This time, somebody actually did drop his documents. I heard the clatter behind, me, and the hurried noises of someone running after flying bits of paper. Sallow-face had no eyes for the miscreant, however. His full attention was on me once more, sizing me up, and down, and up again.

'*You* have an appointment, Miss...?'

'Linton. Yes.'

'With whom, if I may ask?'

'With Mr Ambrose, of course. I already told you I came here to see him. I was told to be here at nine.'

Sallow-face's eyes bored into me, as if he was trying to see a note with the words 'April fool's joke' attached to the back of my head, although it was the middle of summer. 'Told by whom?' he demanded.

'By Mr Ambrose.'

For the first time, I could see a tiny little bit of uncertainty replace some of the sallowness. Mixed into it was a spark of fear. 'By Mr Ambrose himself? Personally?'

'Yes.'

'Wait a moment, please.'

I was expecting him to jump up and run off, emulating all the other people hurrying around the entrance hall, but instead he remained sitting where he was and picked up a strange metal horn from his desk, which I hadn't noticed before. It was connected to the desk by a thick tube that vanished into the wood.

'Stone? Stone, are you there?' Sallow-face spoke into the metal horn.

I stared at him, stupefied. Had he lost his marbles? Did he think this metal thing was a stone? And if so, why was he talking to it? As far as I knew, neither stones nor metal objects were very verbose.

The man held the horn to his ear – and a faint, tinny voice came out of it! My mouth dropped open. What was this? I couldn't hear what the voice said, but it was unquestionably human. He was talking to someone through that thing!

Sallow-face returned the horn from his ear to his mouth and said: 'Listen, Stone. There is a young... *lady* here,' he threw me a look that made it clear he privately had other names for me, 'who maintains she has an appointment with Mr Ambrose. Can you check that for me please? Go to Simmons and ask, will you.'

A moment of silence. Then the faint tinny voice started talking again.

'What?' Sallow-face demanded. 'Not there? What do you mean not... Oh, quit his job? I see.'

A thrill went through me, and suddenly I forgot all about the strange listening-horn. *Quit his job?* They had to be talking about the secretary! The secretary who had left. Had they wanted to check whether I really did have an appointment? That must have been it! So they were actually considering letting me up there. For a moment, I wondered whether I should mention that I was the ex-secretary's replacement. Then I remembered that I was a lady, and ladies didn't work for a living, and if I claimed such a thing, Sallow-face would throw me out for sure.

'Yes, yes,' he snapped at that very moment. 'But what am I to do? If she really has an appointment and I don't let her through, I'll be out on the street tomorrow morning. Yes? So what? What do I care? I say she can go through, so she's your problem now.'

Sallow-face put down the horn from which protesting shrieks were echoing and turned to me with a syrupy smile on his lips.

'Very well, Miss Linton. You can go up to the top floor inquiry desk. Mr Stone is already awaiting you there and anxious to help you.'

Oh, *Mister* Stone, not *a* stone. So Sallow-face wasn't barmy. Quite a relief, considering I got my directions from him. He pointed me to an open doorway behind his desk. I thanked him more graciously than he deserved, curtsied, and went through the doorway to find myself in a large hallway. Looking up, I saw steps leading up and around the walls of several floors, and these stairs were even steeper than the ones outside the building.

Dong...

Quickly, I turned my head westwards. There, a small window stood half open, letting a bit of light fall into the stark stone hallway. And through that window there now also came the sound of a bell. A deep, reverberating sound that chilled my bones. Great Paul was striking nine!

Dong...

I jumped over the first two steps, landing on the third and started to race up the stairs taking two at a time. Even so, I had hardly put half a dozen steps behind me when the clock struck again.

Dong...

I redoubled my efforts. I would not stop. I would not give up. And I would certainly not give that man any excuse not to take me on. I would make it in time!

Dong...

On the first landing I had to stop, or my heart would have burst. My legs already burned like hellfire, and my behind seemed to have an elephant attached to it. Blast it! So much for my resilience. I really needed to get more exercise!

Dong...

I reached the second landing. The noise of feet scurrying around and paper rustling that filled the hall downstairs was receding. Even over the reverberations of the bell I could hear that up here it was much quieter. Ominously quiet. My feet resounded hollowly on the steps. Third floor. Yes!

Dong...

I had just reached the fourth landing when a burst of sunlight suddenly blinded me and made me falter. I was high up now, up over the rooftops of all the surrounding houses. The cold morning sunlight penetrated the mist that was swirling around the building and streamed in through one of the narrow windows, illuminating the entire upper hallway in bright colours of gold. Quickly, I resumed my sprint up the stairs. No distractions now! The fifth landing! Onward! Once more unto the breach!

Dong...

The fifth landing. How many floors did this darn building have? I chanced a glance upwards and nearly fell over my feet. Grabbing the railing for support, I pulled myself onto the sixth landing, wheezing with the effort. But I had seen what I needed to see. Only two more floors left!

Dong...

The sixth landing! Nearly there. How many strikes of the clock were still left to me? I quickly counted in my head. Oh no, just one!

Dong...

Clutching my aching chest I stumbled onto the top landing and grabbed wildly at the air to find anything to support me. My hand caught a brass door-knob and clasped it, involuntary pushing the door open.

I had made it!

Unable to stop, I practically fell into the room beyond. I only came to a stop several fumbling steps later, falling to my knees, gasping, in front of a dark wood desk, behind which sat a narrow-faced young man who seemed rather surprised to find a young woman on the carpet before him.

'Err... Miss?' he said, tentatively.

I tried to speak, but my vocal cords didn't work quite right yet. My lungs were still too busy utilizing my throat for air supply after my sprint up seven flights of stairs. I stared at the carpet on which I was kneeling, trying to find the energy to raise my head. It was a dark carpet, with simple and rather austere geometric patterns. Somebody really should hire an interior decorator here.

Get a grip, I told myself, and clambered to my feet.

Looking around, I saw that I was standing in a longish room, almost a corridor, with doors leading off at regular intervals to the sides. At the very end of the room was a large double door of dark wood. Between me and the door stood only the desk, and behind the desk sat the anxious, narrow-faced young man.

This had to be Mr Stone.

'I'm here to see Mr Ambrose,' I panted with as much dignity as one can muster while gasping for air. Quickly I tried to smooth out the wrinkles in my dress, but they resisted stubbornly.

'Are you...?' he left the sentence hanging in the air as if afraid to finish it.

'I'm Miss Lillian Linton.'

'Ah, yes.' Mr Stone nodded. 'I was told you would be coming.' He threw a furtive look back at the double door. 'And you really have to see Mr Ambrose, Miss?'

'Yes.'

'And you have an appointment?'

'Yes.'

'Very well.'

Swallowing, Mr Stone picked up one of those horn-speak-through thingies from his desk and placed it at his mouth.

'Um... Sir? I'm sorry to disturb you, Mr Ambrose, Sir, but there is someone to see you. A Miss Lillian Linton.'

He put the horn to his ear for a few seconds, listening, then frowned and looked up at me apologetically. 'Err... Miss? Mr Ambrose says he does not know a Miss Linton.'

I gave him my very sweetest smile – sweeter than solid chocolate. 'Tell him we met last Friday in the street. I'm sure he will remember.'

'Of course, Miss.' Mr Stone cleared his throat and nodded, dutifully. He was really a very nice, accommodating young man. 'Mr Ambrose? The young lady says...'

He repeated my message. For a second or two, everything was still and silent – then Mr Stone jerked the listening-horn away from his ear. I could faintly hear someone shouting on the other end and caught a string of expletives.

'Yes, Mr Ambrose, Sir.' Mr Stone had gone as white as a sheet and was speaking hurriedly into the horn. 'Certainly, Mr Ambrose, Sir. What should I tell the young lady, Mr Ambrose, Sir?'

The answer came over the line, and Mr Stone's eyes widened, his face turning beet red.

'But Sir! I... I cannot tell her to go and do... *that*! No, not a respectable young lady!'

45

The shouting on the other end resumed, probably on the subject of my alleged respectability. It seemed that Mr Ambrose had quite a lot to say about that, and none of it was complimentary.

'Well, what then, Mr Ambrose, Sir?' asked the young man timidly. He waited again, then nodded when the answer came. 'Yes, Sir. Immediately, Sir.'

Mr Stone looked up at me, his ears still red.

'Err... Mr Ambrose wishes to see you at once, Miss Linton.'

I bet he does, I thought, but said nothing and instead merely smiled at the young desk clerk again. He was really quite nice – for a man.

Mr Stone rose, and, leading me past his desk, guided me to the large double-door that was, as I now realized, the entrance to the private office of Mr Rikkard Ambrose.

Just before the door he stopped, leaned over and whispered. 'Err... Miss? Be careful, yes? Mr Ambrose is very... um... well, just be careful.'

With that elucidating statement, he held the door open for me, and I entered, my heart hammering, knowing that the future course of my life might well depend on the man inside. Now why didn't that make me feel very good?

His Indecent Demands

As the doors closed behind me, my eyes were drawn immediately to the dark figure standing in front of the window at the opposite end of the room. Heavy curtains half covered the large windows even this early in the morning, and the lean figure of the man was cast in shadows. I could not see his face. But I could feel his eyes on me.

Quickly, I glanced around. No landscapes on the wall. No tapestries. Not even a portrait of dear X with his wife Y their three large, hairy dogs. God, did this man have an allergy to decoration? Maybe I should have chosen the simpler of my dresses for this meeting after all. To my left, massive wooden bookshelves covered one wall, but the rest of the walls weren't panelled wood as was customary in most offices. They weren't even painted, but consisted of the same dark stone as the outside of the building.

Yes, I had diagnosed the decoration allergy correctly. And I didn't even have a medical degree.

My eyes returned to the man at the window. Suddenly, he moved and sat down at the large wooden desk that, besides the bookshelves, was pretty much the only piece of furniture in the room. Light from the window fell onto his face and illuminated the hard, chiselled features of Mr Rikkard Ambrose. Again it struck me that, for a man, he didn't look half bad – maybe not even a quarter. For some reason, my heart rate picked up as I looked at him.

'Welcome,' Mr Ambrose said in a cool voice. 'Kind of you to drop by. Take a seat.'

My mouth dropped open. I had expected him to be angry. Boiling mad, even. But there he was, as cool as a cucumber.

Hesitantly I went to the visitor's chair opposite his own. As soon as I had sat down, I regretted it. The thing was made of plain, hard wood and almost hurt to sit on. I straightened my back and it got a little better.

With agonizing slowness, Mr Rikkard Ambrose rested his elbows on the desk in front of him and steepled his fingers. Over the tops of his finely manicured hands, he regarded me with those dark, sea-coloured eyes of his. Dark eyes in which I could see something roil.

'Well?' he said, after two or three seconds of silence. 'I believe I already told you that I do not appreciate time-wasters, Miss... Linton, was it?'

I nodded.

'So what do you want?'

I swallowed, and said nothing. God, how to phrase this?

He regarded me coolly for a few more moments, then added: 'If you are concerned about me pressing charges against you, do not worry. I have no desire to ruin a lady's reputation, especially the reputation of a "lady" who is not right in the head.' He looked down at his desk and studied a few papers lying there. 'If that is all, Miss Linton...'

The dismissal was obvious in his tone of voice. But I didn't pay attention. I was still too busy processing the 'not-right-in-the-head' comment. *Not right in the head?* Why? Because I put on a pair of trousers? Because I wanted a say in the government of my country?

I'll give him not right in the head!

'Actually, no,' I blurted out, my voice coming out sharper than I had intended. 'That wasn't why I came. I came because you requested it. I came to take up the position of your private secretary.'

His eyes, having perused line after line of whatever document lay before him, froze. Then they snapped up to me. His face seemed not quite as expressionless as before. Silence hovered over the two of us, thick and heavy.

Finally he said: 'But you are a girl.'

I bowed my head in what I hoped would be a demure manner. But it probably looked more sarcastic than demure.

'How kind of you to notice, Mr Ambrose.'

His gaze travelled up and down my figure, taking in the hoop skirt, my styled hair and various parts of my anatomy pushed into the right place by my corset.

'Not so very kind. The fact is rather hard to overlook.'

'You were not so observant the last time we met!'

He narrowed his eyes about a millimetre. 'The last time we met, you had taken great pains to disguise yourself, if I remember, in a manner some might call infamous and outrageous.'

I narrowed my eyes more than just a millimetre and crossed my arms defiantly.

'I was wearing trousers! Why is that infamous? They're just a piece of cloth and don't make me any less of a girl. If you went around dressed in a ball gown, would that make you any less of a man?'

'I'm afraid I've never yet made the experiment, Miss Linton,' he replied, frostily.

A mental image popped into my head of Mr Cold Masculinity Ambrose in a frilly off-the-shoulders ball gown with a big hoop skirt and a paper fan in his hand. I had to work hard to keep from laughing. His tone told me that that wouldn't have been a good idea. He didn't seem to be a person who appreciated mirth, to put it mildly.

So instead of laughing at him, I did the next best thing. I fixed him with a determined look and said: 'We're wandering from the subject. I didn't come here to talk to you about fashion. I came to work.'

Shaking his head derisively, he asked: 'So you persist in this ludicrous claim that you want to work as my secretary?'

'I do, and it isn't ludicrous. When can I take up my new duties?'

'You can't.'

'Why not?'

'Because I will most certainly not give you the position.'

'Why not?'

'I do not have to explain myself to you, Miss Linton.'

Panic started to well up inside me, and I did my best to push it back down. This was what I had feared. He wouldn't even consider taking me on. He would throw me out. Now I had only one last chance. It all depended on one question now: was Mr Rikkard Ambrose a gentleman, or only a man?

'You offered me the position,' I said in a soft voice. 'Do you break your word so easily, Sir?'

Anger flashed in his eyes, and I could see it: the wounded honour of a gentleman. Yes! I had him!

'You dare impugn my honour, Miss?' he demanded, his voice deadly quiet. I knew that had I been a man, he would have flung his glove at me, and I would have had to meet him the next day for a bloody satisfaction. But I was not a man, and he was trapped. The only thing he could do was break his word – or honour it.

'Yes,' I answered, breathless. 'If you do not keep your word, I do.'

'My word would not be broken,' he said, in that quiet voice that sent a shiver down my back. 'You deceived me.'

'How so?' My crossed arms tightened in front of my chest. This was going to be a heavy battle.

'I hired you under the misapprehension that you were a man.'

'I never said I was. In fact, I specifically told you that I wasn't the man for the job.'

He seemed stunned for just a moment. Then, taking in a deep breath, he admitted: 'So you did. Still, you can't have the position.'

'Why? Has the position already been filled?'

He hesitated for a second, then said in a slightly grudging voice: 'No.'

'Has anyone better qualified than I applied?'

'*Anyone* would be better than you.'

My face hardened. 'How so?'

He placed his hands on the desktop, as if trying to suck up calm from the even surface.

'A girl working as a secretary?' he growled. 'It is impossible! If the city were to get wind of this it would be the biggest scandal in years! Besides, females do not have the orderly mind that is required for this kind of work.'

'Of course they do! We have been kept down for centuries, but you'll see, one day women will conquer their rightful place in the world! One day, there will be hundreds, maybe thousands of women working as secretaries. We will be so good at it that we will put the men out of their jobs, and just about every secretary will be female!'

He shook his head derisively.

'That speech only shows that you have no intellect and grasp of reality. Thousands of women working as secretaries all over the world? The thought is ridiculous.'

'All I want is the chance to prove you wrong.'

'And I said no. You are a girl. I cannot have a girl in my office. I would be the laughing stock of the city of London, of the entire country even.'

'I'm sure the city and country will find funnier things to laugh about than you,' I said, regarding his stony face, not able to entirely keep the sarcasm out of my voice.

He gave me a stare from those cold, dark eyes that could have frozen lava.

'I don't appreciate being made fun of, Miss Linton.'

'I can see that, Mr Ambrose. And I do not appreciate my questions not being given full and honest replies.'

'What do you mean?'

'Has anyone better qualified than I applied for the position of your private secretary?'

A few seconds hesitation again. Then: 'No.'

'Well then.' Taking a deep breath, I unfolded my arms and rubbed my hands. 'When may I begin with my new duties?'

His hostile stare intensified to a force that almost knocked me off my chair and made the muscles in my stomach tighten with fear.

'I-need-a-man,' he said very slowly, enunciating each word. 'A man, Miss Linton. Not a girl who will run off screaming at the things she will see where my kind of business takes me.'

'I hold you to your word,' I replied, glaring just as stubbornly, though maybe not quite so impressively, back at him. 'I ask you: Are you a gentleman or a liar? *You* told me to come and work for you. I didn't ask you. And now you want to back out?'

He stared at me. And stared. And stared.

Half a minute.

An entire minute.

After two minutes, I was getting fidgety and wanted to blink, but didn't. I was not backing down on this. He would have to keep his word or throw me out into the street himself!

Three whole minutes he looked at me like this. Then, towards the end of the third minute, something seemed to spark in his dark eyes, and though his facial expression didn't really change, he somehow suddenly seemed... satisfied. Victorious. Oh no. He had decided to forget about honour and throw me out! I knew it! I just knew it!

'Fine,' he said. 'The position is yours.'

My jaw dropped. What? Had I heard correctly?

'It... it is?' I stammered, unable to contain my surprise.

'Yes,' he said, his voice as cool and calm as ever. 'I gave my word, and my honour is at stake here. Naturally, a gentleman must keep his word. The position of private secretary belongs to you.'

My heart started hammering wildly. Was this really it? Finally? My independence? My chance to build a career as a free woman?

But there was something that wasn't quite right. Mr Ambrose didn't look resigned. In spite of the fact that this should be nettling him to no end, he looked... pleased with himself. Darn pleased with himself. Though of course he didn't go so far as to actually allow a smile to appear on his stony features, I could feel it. Self-satisfaction radiated off him. Like a sleek black cat that doesn't need to smile, only show its claws to prove to the world how superior it is.

'You will, of course, be wearing the proper uniform,' he said, looking down at the papers on his desk again.

I frowned.

'Uniform?' I hadn't seen anyone in his office so far who wore a uniform. What was he talking about?

'Certainly,' he replied, still not looking up. 'The same uniform you wore on the day I first had the pleasure to meet you, *Mister* Linton.'

It took a moment or two, then the penny dropped. I jumped up from my chair as if it had bit me in the arse.

'You expect me to come and work for you dressed up as a *man*?' I gasped.

He looked up, sharply. 'I expect you to come to work dressed exactly the same as on the day I acquired your services, Mister Linton. I want exactly what I bought, and I am going to get it. Do you understand that, Mister Linton?'

'I won't do it!'

He was out of his chair and around the desk in a heartbeat.

'It is your choice,' he said, stepping so close to me that our lips were almost touching. 'Either do what I say – or get another job.'

For a moment, my heart stood still as I gazed up into his deep, dark, dangerous eyes. Then I tore myself away from the sight, turned on my heels and angrily stomped towards the door. I threw it open and rushed past the bewildered Mr Stone.

'Good day, *Miss* Linton,' he called after me, hardly concealed triumph in his voice.

Well, I thought to myself, *We'll just see about that! He wants war? He can have it!*

'Excuse me?'

Mr Stone looked up from his desk and his eyes widened.

'I would like to see Mr Ambrose, please. I have an appointment.'

Mr Stone blinked, sat motionless for a few seconds, and blinked again. Only then did he recover from his astonishment. 'Oh, err... I'm so sorry, Sir. Of course, of course. I was only distracted for a moment because just half an hour ago there was a young lady here, also asking for Mr Ambrose, and you and she...' He trailed off, gazing in amazement at the small young man with longish brown hair standing in front of him.

I tried to force a smile on my face. 'That was my sister.'

'Oh, that explains it,' said Mr Stone, a bright smile ousting the puzzled expression from his face. 'May I say, Sir, that you and she share the most *amazing* family resemblance?'

'I've often thought so myself.'

'Even your hairstyles are rather similar. It is truly intriguing.'

'Thank you.'

'And what is your name, Sir?'

'Li–' I bit my tongue. Darn! In my haste to get home, change and return, I had completely forgotten that as a man, I could hardly go by the name of Lillian. My mind was as blank as the walls of Mr Ambrose's office as I tried to think of a name, any name that I could tell Mr Stone. Finally, my thoughts landed on the royal family.

'Victor!' I blurted out. 'Victor Linton.'

Thank God. When all else failed, one could still rely on the queen of England.[13]

'Very well, Mr Linton. Wait a moment please, while I see if Mr Ambrose is ready to receive you.'

He took up the metal horn from the desk and spoke into it.

'Mr Ambrose? A Mr Linton to see you.'

In response, there came only silence from the other end.

'Err... Mr Ambrose? Are you there?'

Now there did come a noise from the other end. It sounded like something between a moan from a medieval torture chamber and the growl of a wounded Siberian tiger.

'Mr Ambrose, Sir? Are you all right?'

Apparently Mr Ambrose was all right, because he started to speak a few seconds later. I couldn't make out what he was saying, and part of me was glad for that. Stone nodded, put down the horn and then looked up at me smiling.

'Mr Linton,' he said, 'I have been informed that you have been accepted as Mr Simmons' replacement and are now a member of the staff. May I take this

---

[13] Alexandrina Victoria, Queen of the United Kingdom of Great Britain and Ireland 24 May 1819 – 22 January 1901, commonly known as Queen Victoria.

opportunity to welcome you?' He got up, walked around the desk held out a hand for me to shake.

Hesitantly, I reached out. I had never shaken a man's hand before, only curtsied. Would he be able to tell that I was a woman by a handshake? Determined not to give him any clues, I resolved to make my grip convincingly strong and masculine.

'Ouch!' Mr Stone grimaced. All right, maybe I had overdone it with the masculinity... 'Err... yes. Welcome, as I said. Now, where was I...?' Cautiously, he removed his hand from my grip and flexed his fingers.

'Ah, yes. Mr Ambrose regrets to inform you that he does not have time to receive you right now, since urgent business detains him. He wishes you to go directly into the secretary's office and wait for instructions there.'

I frowned. Urgent business that detains him? What business could be so urgent that he couldn't receive his private secretary? It should be my job to help him with his urgent business, shouldn't it? But orders were orders. And though I usually wasn't very good at obeying orders, these were different: unlike my aunt, Mr Ambrose would have to pay me for bossing me around. So I simply asked: 'The secretary's office?'

With his thumb, Mr Stone indicated a door to the right of his desk. 'That door over there. I hope you find everything to your satisfaction, Mr Linton. If there is anything I can help you with, please don't hesitate to ask.'

Wow. If all my new colleagues were like this, working for a living would actually be a piece of cake. Maybe even a chocolate cake with extra sugar.

Then I remembered my new employer, and reconsidered.

No. Not a piece of cake. Definitely not. A piece of granite might be an appropriate description.

I walked over to the door Mr Stone had indicated. I reached for the doorknob. I grasped and turned it, holding my breath. With a low 'click', the door swung open. Nervously, I peered into my new domain.

The room was just as I might have expected: bare stone walls, heavy curtains, a large desk. It looked like a smaller version of Mr Ambrose's office except that here, the desk stood against the wall and much of the space was taken up by enormous shelves holding large, differently coloured boxes. They all had numbers and letters written on them.

Good God, what was this? Seeing these vast mountains of paper, it occurred to me for the first time to wonder what the duties of a private secretary would actually be. Ever since my discovery of his wealth, I had expected Mr Rikkard Ambrose to be a rich landowner and that, as his secretary, I would maybe have to write a few letters for him when he was too lazy to do it himself. But apparently he wrote and received a hell of a lot more than just 'a few letters'. I was in for more than I had bargained for.

Tip-toeing over to one of the boxes, I could see under the cryptic message '29V118' the explanation 'Georg. G. R.' Spiffing.[14] Who was Georg G. R.? Sounded

---

[14] An old British English term for 'Great' or 'Awesome', sadly fallen into disuse, to the disappointment of learned linguists all over the globe.

foreign. He had to be a most dedicated letter-writer, though. I reached out to open the box, then hesitated.

But why not? After all, I was his secretary now. I would have to look through most of these sooner or later. Yes, that was an excellent excuse. Much better than 'I'm just nosy'.

I opened the box and took a few papers out.

What I found made me feel even more puzzled. They weren't letters. They were maps, drawings of mountains with short annotations about such things as rockers, nuggets and a whole lot of other things I had never heard of in my life.

Mystified, I put the papers back into the box and put it back on the shelf.

Then it occurred to me: why was I still waiting? Why had Mr Rich-and-Mysterious not called me yet to assist him in his oh-so-urgent business? I wanted to step out from between the shelves, but before I could do so I noticed a door behind them. From the layout of the room I supposed it to be a connecting door to Mr Ambrose's office. I approached it and carefully tried the knob.

Locked.

Blimey, this was getting on my nerves!

But it was up to him to give me work, not the other way around. Having nothing better to do, I strolled over to the window and looked out over the city. As had been evident already from the outside, Empire House was a lot taller than any of the surrounding buildings and provided a stunning view. My office – I felt a thrill go through me at the words – *my* office faced west, and in the distance I could see the white dome of St. Paul's Cathedral rising over the houses. I waited. And waited.

Great Paul struck eleven, and still I waited.

I was just about to leave the room and ask Mr Stone if anything was wrong when I heard a strange sizzling noise from the direction of my desk. Eyebrows raised, I went over to investigate.

The noise seemed to be coming from within the wall beside my desk. Whoever had put the stones there had done a shoddy job of it, because in the wall directly over my desktop was a hole, about an inch in diameter. The sizzling noise seemed to originate from there.

Curious, I bent forward and put my eye to the hole. I couldn't see anything inside; it was pitch-black. But I could hear the sizzling noise getting louder and louder, until...

'Ouch!'

Something poked me in the eye, hard, and I staggered back. I almost fell onto my rear end but managed to grab the edge of my desk and stay upright. Bright lights flashed across my field of vision. I blinked furiously. When I could finally see again, I discovered a tiny metal cylinder lying on my desk. Apparently, it had shot out of the hole in the wall and right into my eye. The hole in the wall that was separating my office from that of Mr Rikkard Ambrose. I knew where that cylinder came from.

Furious, I grabbed the thing and marched towards the door separating my office from *his*.

'Hey!'

No answer.

'Hey, I want to know why you tried to poke my eye out!'

Still no answer. I banged on the door with the hand holding the metal cylinder, and as I did, it fell out of my hand and onto the floor, breaking apart in the process. It was hollow!

Curious, I leaned forward and saw that there was a tiny piece of paper rolled up in the cylinder. Taking it out, I unrolled it, revealing a few hand-written words in a clear, precise, no-nonsense hand.

Mr Linton,
Bring me file 227B
Rikkard Ambrose.

Bring me file 227B? Just 'Bring me file 227B'? That was all? No please, no thank you. God, why did he even feel the need to sign it? No one else I know would write a message that cold, curt and discourteous. Well, maybe my uncle. But discourtesy from family didn't count.

And... 'Mr Linton'? He couldn't even acknowledge the fact that I was a female when there was nobody else around? I had been afraid he was a chauvinist. I had been wrong. He was the king of chauvinists.

But he was also the man who wrote my pay cheques. So I swallowed the adjectives I would have liked to throw at him and instead demanded of the closed door: 'Why are we communicating via tiny paper rolls? And what is file 227B?'

No answer – though he must have heard me through the door. The man didn't say a single word. But shortly after, a *plink* noise came from behind me, and I turned around only to see another missive from my master shooting out of the hole in the wall.

Stomping over to the desk, I grabbed it and read:

Mr Linton,
We are communicating via tiny paper rolls because this is the most efficient system of communication. And you should be able to find a file on your own if you want to keep your position.
Rikkard Ambrose

Most efficient form of communication my foot! The cash-carrying bit-faker[15] just didn't want to talk to me and be reminded that he suffered from the shame of having a girl as his secretary! Well, two could play at that game.

I started to rummage through my desk, opening and shutting drawers at a prodigious rate. Finally, I found what I was looking for: in the bottom drawer was a bowl full of metal cylinders and another one full of little bits of paper. I took both out, grabbed the fountain pen that was lying on the desk and began to scribble.

Dear Mr Ambrose,
May I ask with all due politeness what kind of devilish invention this is you are forcing me to use?

---

[15] An insult for a Victorian Man. Current scholarship is debating the subject of which bits of himself the man would have to be faking.

Thoughtfully, I tapped my lower lip with the pen. Then I closed the message with:

I remain
Sincerely Yours
Miss Lilly Linton

Yes! Show him that a proper girl can be courteous even if a stinking rich man cannot!

Very pleased with myself I put the cylinder into the hole in the wall. It didn't move. Frowning, I examined the hole more closely – and then discovered a little lever right beside it. Well, it couldn't hurt to try. Probably.

Cautiously, my fingers curled around the lever. Hoping fervently it wouldn't make the building explode or something like that, I pulled. There was a sucking noise, and the little metal container vanished into the hole. Phew! I hated mechanical stuff. You never knew what would happen when you pushed a button.

For a minute or two, I sat at my desk, twiddling my thumbs. But I didn't have to wait long for a reply. With another *plink*, the metal missive-container shot out of the hole and landed on my desk. I grabbed it eagerly and unrolled the message. Ha! At least this time he would have to be more courteous. He would have to accept me as a girl. Wouldn't he?

I read:

Mr Linton,
This 'devilish invention' as you deem it is the latest technical innovation for high-speed communication, called 'pneumatic tubes'. It allows me to communicate with all my employees in the entire building without leaving my office. This system has served me admirably ever since its installation. I would be required to change my modus operandi in order to communicate with you vocally. That will not happen. I do not change a working system.
Bring me file 227B.
And incidentally, I do not want you as mine, sincerely or otherwise.
Rikkard Ambrose

My eyes went wide as I read the last line before his name. The abominable, villainous... That had just been a courteous closing line! Nothing more! I hadn't meant that... well, I hadn't meant anything like the thing he obviously meant!

Seething with rage, I grabbed another piece of paper and scribbled:

Dear Mr Ambrose
I am a female, in case you still have not noticed.
How am I to give you file whateveritscalled if you do not open your bloody door?
Yours infuriatedly
Miss Lilly Linton

The reply came soon:

Mr Linton,
You are no female while you are in my employ. As, by the way, you have amply proven by your language.
Slide the file under the door.
Rikkard Ambrose

What? Now he complained about me not expressing myself in a ladylike manner, after he had forced me to come to work dressed up in a pair of striped trousers? I itched to send back another snarky remark.

But...

But...

But this man was my master now. He was the one who would hopefully one day sign my first pay cheque. He was my ticket to freedom. My only chance. Blast him!

I hurried over to the shelves that held the boxes. Two minutes of searching were enough for me to discover that whatever system my predecessor had used to sort his files, it most certainly was not an alphabetical one. Twenty minutes of searching went by, and I still hadn't discovered what I was looking for. As I was taking an extraordinarily large and heavy box from one of the upper shelves, I heard a familiar *plink* from my desk. Balancing the monument of a file container on my shoulder I tottered over to my desk, picked up the metal cylinder with one hand, opened it with my teeth and spat the removed half into the bowl on my desk.

The message fell onto my desk. Still using only my one free hand, I picked it up and unrolled it laboriously. On the paper were written two neat, concise words.

Hurry up.

'Oh thank you!' I shouted at the closed door to Mr Ambrose's office. 'Thank you so very much!'

With a grunt I deposited the gigantic box on my desk and began to look through it.

After ten more minutes of ceaseless searching, I raised my head from the dusty intestines of box 37XV227, holding my trophy aloft.

'Yes!'

Now that I had invested so much trouble into finding it, I couldn't help wondering what file 227B actually was. I took a quick peep – only to be confronted by endless columns of meaningless numbers. This was what I had spent half an hour of my precious life on? Ah, who cared what was in it! What mattered was that I had found it, finally!

Triumphantly I marched to Mr Ambrose's door, knocked, and shoved the thin file under the door. On the other side, I could hear the scrape of a chair being moved, and then footsteps. And oh, what footsteps they were – only Mr Ambrose could manage to make his step sound cool and disinterested.

I didn't wait to listen for more, though. Right now, I was so exhausted that I didn't care what he did with the bloody file. I just went to my desk, collapsed into my chair, closed my eyes and breathed a deep sigh of relief.

A *plink* from the wall made me open my eyes again. Frowning, I picked up the metal cylinder and opened it. What now?

Be quicker next time.

Rikkard Ambrose.

For a moment, I could hardly believe the words in front of my eyes. But only for a moment. Then, I saw red. Fuming, I grabbed my fountain pen and composed the following message in my best chicken scratch:

Dear Mr Ambrose,

If you want me to be quicker at finding your files, maybe you should explain the sorting system to me.

Yours (as your secretary, whether you like it or not)

Lilly Linton

I stuffed it into the tube and pulled the lever. The reply came only a minute later:

Mr Linton,

If you are not able to comprehend a perfectly logical system of sorting files, then what makes you think you are suitable for the position of private secretary? Maybe you should resign.

Rikkard Ambrose

Ha! You would just love that, wouldn't you? And what... perfectly logical? So far nothing I had seen of the supposed 'system' was perfectly logical, rather perfectly chaotic. How could anyone figure it out by themselves?

Fear suddenly lanced through my heart. What if he sacked me? The possibility hadn't occurred to me until now, because he had promised to give me the job and could not break his word. But knowing the kind of man he was, I doubted very much he would still feel honour-bound to keep me if I didn't come up to scratch. On the contrary, he would probably be delighted to throw me out at the first opportunity.

Resolving then and there not to give him that satisfaction, I got up and plunged myself into the jungle that was Mr Simmons' filing system.

~~**~*~*

When the next message landed with a *plink* on my desk, I sat there, awaiting it with a serene smile.

With a flourish, I opened the message container and studied the message inside.

Mr Linton,

Bring me file 146K. Be quicker this time.

Rikkard Ambrose

I got up, walked over to one of the shelves, took out a box, opened it, took out file 146K, closed the box again, put it back on the shelf, walked to the door with the file in hand and slid it through the slit between door and floor. Then I knocked at the door and purred:

'Your file, Sir.'

I heard him getting up and without a word taking it from the floor. All the while I stood leaning against the door, my ear pressed to the wood, grinning like an idiot and feeling like a genius.

This time, nothing came out of the hole in the wall. No message. No complaint. No scolding note. I did a little happy dance in the middle of the room.

Yay! He had nothing to complain about. And I bet the fact was riling him up good and proper.

Not long after, both files were returned in the same manner I had forwarded them. Attached to the top was a note.

Mr Linton,

Bring me file 188Q.

Not a word about being quicker. If that was at all possible, my grin widened a little bit more. Quickly I scurried over to the shelves and, after depositing the returned files in their correct place, went to the next box and got him the wished-for documents.

The following hours passed in a whirl of fetched and returned files, and curt little notes exchanged via the pneumatic tubes. If he actually read half of the files I fetched for him, I'd eat my uncle's big top hat. He seemed determined to make me mess up, to pressure me so that he would be able to find some fault with me and have an excuse to sack me.

And in every single note he sent he kept calling me *Mister* Linton.

But I didn't let him get to me. I ran between the door and the shelves like a prize race horse, fetching each file in record time. The filing system had taken me some time to figure out, but it wasn't that difficult, really, once you had taken a moment to think about it: the first two numbers on the boxes stood for years (37, for example, stood, or so I assumed, for 1837). The letters behind that were really Roman numerals, numbering the boxes relating to that particular year. And the number behind that signified the place of the box in the overall order of boxes within the room. It was really simple to find a file once you noticed that the file numbers related to that last number. You simply had to run along the shelves until you reached the right one.

Wasn't I a smart girl?

With a self-satisfied grin on my face, I pushed the fifty-second file under the door and returned to my desk to wait for the inevitable note.

In spite of my success, I couldn't really say I was looking forward to the next note. Every time I read the greeting line 'Mr Linton,' I could almost feel the sparks flying out of my eyes. The arrogant son of a bachelor was completely trying to ignore the fact that I was a girl! The fact that he was the best-looking man I had ever seen in my life didn't do much to sweeten that fact.

Why was he so determined to ignore me? Was it that he could not stand the idea of a girl in his employ, or was it me?

So what if it is you? I asked myself. *That's no problem, is it? It's not like you want to be noticed by him.*

Right. I had to remember that. It really didn't matter as who or what he thought of me, just that he gave me my salary and independence.

But... but I wanted independence as a *female!* Not independence as some cheap imitation of a man. I crossed my arms. That was it. I didn't want to be noticed by him in the way a girl wants to be normally noticed by a man, all that romantic crap and so forth. No, definitely not that, I told myself fervently. What I wanted was far harder: I wanted recognition. I wanted respect.

And I was going to get it, even if I had to shake it out of him. He couldn't avoid me forever. At the end of the day, he would have to come out of hiding, leave his office, and then I could confront him!

Or so I thought.

~~**~*~*

About two hours later, when a long time had gone by without any missives from His Mightiness and I was just beginning to wonder whether perhaps he might have choked on one of his files, somebody knocked at my office door – the one to the hallway, not to Mr Ambrose' office.

Surprised, I looked up. I was certainly not used to people knocking at my door as if they could disturb me doing something important. As if *I were* somebody important.

'Err... come in?' I called.

Mr Stone poked his head in. 'Mr Linton? Are you busy?'

'No, no.' I quickly sat up straight and tried to look very professionally secretarial. 'Come in, please.'

'Thank you.' Smiling his cautious smile, Mr Stone entered. 'I just came to give you a message. Mr Ambrose has sent me to inform you that he has gone out on urgent business and that he will not require your services for the rest of the day.'

I sat there, dumbstruck. Could this be what I thought it was? Could he actually have cut his day short in order to avoid seeing me? Why would he go to such abnormal lengths to avoid me? Was it such a blot on his honour to have a female for a secretary?

Anger boiling up inside me, I stomped past a startled Mr Stone, went down the stairs and left the building, determining there and then not to let Mr Haughty Almighty and Annoyingly Handsome Ambrose slip through my fingers tomorrow. He would have to accept me or choke on the fact of my femininity.

Disconsolately, I wandered home through the dusky streets of London. When, every now and again, couples passed me and I saw a smile on the lady's face that showed she was infuriatingly happy with her miserable lot in life as an inferior to chauvinists, I couldn't help but glower at her. The man who accompanied the woman nearly always noticed, drawing a protective arm around his charge and glowering just as fiercely back at the stranger. Chauvinism. Pure chauvinism, wherever you looked.

Since there were a lot of people out on the street and I had a lot of glowering to do, I didn't reach home for about an hour. When I finally turned the last corner and saw my uncle's house, my eyes went wide in shock.

The door to the house was wide open. Anxious, excited voices were calling out inside, and there was a large carriage right in front of the door. My uncle didn't own a carriage. Gripped by apprehension, I started to run. What the hell was going on in there?

It was infuriating to have to go in through the garden door, climb up to my window, change, climb down again and return to the front. But I didn't want to give my aunt a coronary by appearing on her doorstep in a pair of striped trousers. When I finally arrived in front, the carriage was still waiting there, and so was my aunt, anxiously looking out into the street.

'Lillian!' She rushed out of the door as I approached, her hollow cheeks flushed, a determined smile on her face. Oh no. Anything that made my aunt this happy wouldn't be good. 'Finally, there you are! Where were you? Oh, don't bother, it doesn't matter. All that matters is that you're here. Come, come quickly you have to hurry! The ball starts in an hour!'

'Ball?' I asked, dread welling up inside me. 'What ball?'

'If you, silly girl, had just stayed at home like a proper young lady, you would know all about it. Your sisters, Anne and Maria, and I have been talking about nothing else for weeks.'

That would explain why I didn't remember. My ears were good at protecting themselves against unnecessary torture.

'Now come in and hurry, for God's sake!'

She rushed inside, skirts flying around her bony figure, and I followed with trepidation. 'Why a ball?' I wanted to know. 'What has a ball got to do to me? Anne and Maria get invited to balls, not me. I don't go to balls, never ever.'

'You will today,' my aunt trilled and made a pirouette in the middle of the room that was worthy of a prima ballerina. I could see it in her eyes: the golden glint that meant she was dreaming of finally being rid of us, and at a profit, too.

The trepidation in my chest was quickly evolving into panic. Me, at a ball? I hated balls! Balls meant society, society meant people, and people meant either women or men, or worse, both! I disliked men in general because they oppressed women, and I disliked women in general because most didn't at all seem to mind being oppressed. And now I would have to face both, mixed together?

Even worse – I had heard that at balls, people had to *dance*.

With one another. Both sexes!

'But surely,' I tried to reassure myself aloud, 'only Anne and Maria are going? I mean... they are the ones that everybody admires and wants to dance with.'

My aunt nodded, the happy glow of gold coins still gleaming in her eyes. 'I agree, no man in his right mind would want to invite you.'

'Oh... err... thanks.'

'Considering how uncouth and tanned and misbehaved you are.'

'How nice of you to be so explicit.'

'But,' she continued, turning her glittering eyes on me, 'Sir Phillip was so impressed by Maria and Anne's charms at the ball the other night that, now he is giving his own ball, he has issued an invitation for the entire family.'

Oh dear God! How could I escape this deadly trap?

'Sir Philip? Philip who?' I tried to stall her, my thoughts racing.

'Sir Philip Wilkins. Surely you must remember. I told you of his dancing with your sisters at Mr Marlow's Ball only two days ago.'

Actually I didn't remember. But I thought it best not to mention that to my dear aunt.

Concentrate, I yelled at myself. *Think of some excuse! You are not going to this infernal ball. Don't you remember what Patsy told you about what balls are like? Hours of aimless chatter, and your feet hurt from dancing for days afterwards? No, no, no!*

But my aunt seemed to read my thoughts as if they were broadcast on my face. 'Don't you dare think of not coming,' she hissed and wagged a bony finger at me. 'This might very well be our only chance at getting you introduced into society. We all have to go. Even Mr Brank is coming.'

This was such an unexpected piece of information that it shook the foundation of the world as I knew it.

'Uncle Bufford? Going out into society?' I eyed my aunt suspiciously. 'How did you manage that miracle?'

She smiled back at me in a way I think the harpies of Greek legend – you know, those monsters with women's heads and the bodies of birds of prey – would have smiled. 'I pointed out to him that it would not be a wise course to offend a nobleman of such importance as Sir Philip by refusing his invitation. I also pointed out that if Maria and Anne were to be married, he would have two less mouths to feed.'

In spite of my annoyance, I had to admire her. My aunt was not a very intellectual person – but when she wanted something she knew how to get it

'Enough of this talk!' She clapped her hands and grabbed hold of my shoulder, steering me upstairs. I tried to ram my heels into the ground, but she possessed super-aunty strength, originating from the force of her determination. 'You will get dressed now, and I do not want to hear another word of protest! You are nineteen, almost an old maid now, and it is high time you were introduced into society and found a man!'

Upstairs, she deposited me in my room and entrusted me to the capable hands of Gertrude. Not having much chance to find a husband at her age, and not at all displeased about the fact, Gertrude was more than happy to attend the ball in simple attire and instead concentrated the full force of her primping skills on yours truly.

Within 20 minutes, my hair – which had been flattened into a strange shape by a box that had fallen on my head during the battle of the files – was transformed into an elaborate updo. Then I was forcibly stripped and stuffed into my other dress. With horror I discovered that my aunt had somehow found the money and time to alter it: my favourite dress was now a ball gown, with frilly lace at the sleeves and neckline, and, believe it or not, it was off the shoulders! My horror was complete when my aunt rushed in and pressed a fan into my hand.

'It's the perfect way to attract a man's attentions,' she said, smiling brightly. 'And very easy. You see, if you wave the fan like this, it means...'

'Why do I have to wave this stupid thing around to attract somebody's attention?' I demanded, panicked. 'Why can't I just walk up to him and say "Hey, I like you", or "Piss off, dick!"?'

'Lillian Linton! Mind your language. And the reason for the secret language of the fan is that it is far more discrete than actual talk.'

'I am not discreet!'

Her eyes narrowed. 'I am fully aware of that, Lillian. You had better change that quickly or else you will never find a man to take care of you.'

She rushed out of the room and I scowled at her retreating back. How I would have liked to shout after her that I didn't need a man to look after me, that I had my own job now and would soon be bringing home my own money. But I didn't dare. I knew that if I even breathed a word of it, I would be locked in my room faster than I could say 'unfair'.

So I frantically tried to memorize what waving an open fan signified, besides the fact that it was too hot and you wanted to get some air. While I waved at myself with the fan in front of the mirror and attempted to ignore the fact that for the first time in my life I was wearing an uncomfortably revealing off-the-shoulders gown, Ella entered behind me.

'Oh Lilly!' She came rushing up to me and hugged me, careful not to ruffle my hair. 'We're going to a ball! Isn't it exciting?'

'Yes, very exciting,' I mumbled. I was still busy looking at the fan in the mirror. I noticed it was quite sharp at the end when not open. Idly I wondered what the message to a gentleman would be if he got a poke in the eye with it. I didn't think one needed extensive knowledge of the secret fan language to understand that. Maybe the fan would have its uses after all. I tucked it away in my dress and turned to Ella, who was gushing excitedly.

'...can you imagine how grand the ballroom will be? And the music, Lilly? I've never heard a quadrille[16] before, let alone danced it! I would so love to dance. If only–'

She broke off abruptly.

'Yes?' I asked distractedly, still trying to figure out the best way of using a fan as a defensive weapon. 'If only what?'

'Oh... err... nothing.'

What was this? Ella, being secretive? I would probably have paid more attention to this gross deviation from her usual character had not at that very moment my aunt stormed into the room and clapped her hands.

'Girls, girls! Why are you dawdling? Come on downstairs, the coach is waiting!'

We followed her down the stairs and joined the other four waiting in the hall: Gertrude calm and composed as ever, Lisbeth even more excited than Ella, and Anne as well as Maria with the same self-satisfied smiles on their identical breathtaking faces, in the full knowledge that the rest of us owed the invitation to the ball to their charms. They probably expected us to thank them on bended knee when it was over.

---

[16] A Victorian dance, the forerunner of the square dance.

Well, I had something very different in mind for my dear sisters.

'Shall we go?' Lisbeth asked eagerly, hardly able to stand still with excitement, and eying the door longingly.

'Soon,' my aunt snapped. 'And don't fidget, Lisbeth. It does not become a true lady.'

'Yes, Aunt.'

'And straighten your ball gown.'

'Yes, Aunt.'

I held my hand in front of my face to conceal my grin. Ball gown? Lisbeth's dress was just one of her normal dresses, altered like mine. Our aunt must have worked overtime to prepare these for the ball – but it was still obvious they were not the best of ball gowns. My aunt's pride and imagination had to do what her stinginess didn't allow: change linen into muslin and glass into diamonds.

'I,' she said triumphantly and turned to the second staircase which was almost never used, 'shall fetch your uncle now, girls. Wait here.'

We waited while she ascended the steps. We waited while she entered and we heard voices. The voices got a bit louder. And a bit louder still, especially hers. Then she came out of the room again, slamming the door behind her.

'Apparently, girls,' she said, rushing past us to the door, 'your uncle feels that since we all are going, there is no need for him to leave the house and pay his respects to Sir Philip. He feels he would just be in the way.' She huffed. 'Very well then. Come!' And like a general directing his troops, she directed us down the street towards where the coach was waiting – in my case, I felt like I had been pressed into service.

'Can you imagine?' Maria said to Lisbeth in a very audible whisper. 'This is one of Sir Philip's own carriages. He sent it along to convey us to the ball. What an honour for us to be favoured in such a manner.'

And Lisbeth, as the dutiful and thankful sister she was, gave the appropriate answer: 'It is all thanks to you, sister, and to Anne. You must have made quite an impression on his Lordship.'

'Oh?' Maria giggled, and Anne joined in. 'Do you think so? Well, I must admit he seemed quite taken with me.'

That stopped Anne's giggling abruptly. 'But not quite as much as with me,' she added, throwing her twin a death-glare.

I was tempted to point out that he probably hadn't been able to tell them apart, when their conversation and our advance towards the coach was interrupted. A young man came down the street and, seeing us, stopped and bowed. I recognized him: It was Edmund Conway, our neighbour's eldest son. He was a good-looking, polite young man, but unfortunately for him, he was also neither rich nor noble. So my aunt rushed past him without even stopping to acknowledge his bow. Knowing that my aunt couldn't see, I returned his salutation. Why not, after all? He was nice enough. But in spite of my politeness, he gave me an intensive and frankly disturbing stare – then turned and walked away towards his parents' house.

'What was that that about?' I asked, turning to Ella who was standing right behind me. 'Why do you think he was staring at me like that?'

Ella blushed. 'Err... I have no idea. Let's go, shall we? The carriage and Aunt Brank are waiting.' She hurried off and I frowned after her. What was the matter with her? Must be the excitement of her first ball.

The carriage that waited for us in front of the house was indeed an impressive sight: large, bright red and with golden ornaments everywhere. Two servants in livery were sitting on the box, one of whom had jumped down to help the ladies into the coach. When he attempted to offer me his chauvinist arm, as if I couldn't even get into a coach by myself, I gave him such a deadly stare that he quickly backed away and bowed. Good for him.

I pulled myself up into the coach. Maria and Anne were of course already sitting there, and had taken the best places beside my aunt, facing into driving direction. Ella, Lisbeth, Gertrude and I had to squeeze ourselves onto the other bench. Ah well, at least I wouldn't see my doom approach.

'Gee up!' The coachman shouted. His whip cracked, and we were off. I was off to my first ball.

'Now listen carefully, girls,' my aunt said sternly, looking at all of us in turn. 'Anne and Maria have already been to balls many times, and Gertrude a few times as well, but for the rest of you, today is your coming out.[17] This first appearance in society is crucial. Therefore it is imperative that all of you, even those of you who normally exhibit strange and unladylike behaviour,' and she fixed her gaze on me, 'behave excellently tonight and show the gentlemen only their best side, understood?'

'Yes, Aunt,' we all chorused, except Anne and Maria who just kept smiling serenely.

'I'm serious,' she said, again for some reason fixing her eyes on me alone. 'This might be your best or even only chance to find a husband.'

I scowled. I knew it! I knew that was what my aunt planned. A shiver went through me at the thought of being sold off to some stranger. That was no life for me.

'Don't squander it,' my aunt continued. 'Do your best. Give a good impression, or you might never get another invitation like this again.'

I perked up. Really? So... I would just have to mess up so badly that she never ever would take me to a ball again. So badly that all the gentlemen would take me for the worst monster in town.

A small smile spread on my face and I gripped my fan inside the folds of my dress. That shouldn't present any problem, now, should it?

~~**~*~*

The carriage pulled up in front of an impressive façade. It was impressive simply because it was large. Very large. You couldn't really see anything else of it yet because of the thick pea soup[18] that was drifting in from the River Thames.

---

[17] This does not refer to being gay or lesbian. In Victorian times, 'coming out' meant being introduced into society, which usually meant a girl's first ball or dinner party.

[18] Not actual pea soup. This is an expression for the thick fog that sometimes lies over London, which, it has been attested by credible witnesses, does not taste of peas.

The house was nothing but a massive, vaguely rectangular shadow in the mist. The greenish glow of gas street lights was shining through the fog, and laughter drifted over to us. Apparently, the guests at the ball were enjoying themselves.

I shook my head. Some people had really strange tastes.

'Look! Look!' Excited, Lisbeth pointed out of the window. Before us, gates and a low stone wall had appeared out of the mist. The gates stood wide open, with servants forming an impressive welcoming committee on either side. Hm. This Wilkins fellow had to be seriously rich. No wonder my aunt had been so desperate to get us all here.

The servants stood to attention as the carriage passed. It took us down a short gravel path to the entrance of the house, flanked by two intricately wrought iron lanterns. More servants awaited us there. Good God, how many servants did this Wilkins have? And what did he use them all for? Surely one would be enough to say hello and welcome.

Gravel crunching under its wheels, the carriage stopped in front of the large front door. It stood wide open, just as the gates, and had a red carpet, an actual red carpet in front of it. Three servants jumped forward to open the door, which impressed me very much – after all, it was only one door, with one handle.

My aunt was the first to rise and descended from the carriage as if she were the Queen of England herself. All three of the servants bowed to her, and a smile appeared on her face like that of a vulture who had just found the cadaver of a fat cow. This had to be heaven for her. She hadn't had anyone bow to her in a very long time other than old Leadfield, and he didn't do it very often because of his bad back.

'Madam?' servant one asked. He held out his hand. Graciously, my aunt took out our invitation and handed it to him.

Servant one examined it carefully, then handed it to servant two, who looked at it and nodded graciously, and then handed it to servant three, who also looked at it, and nodded even more graciously. Good gracious! I was drowning in graciousness here.

'Very good, Madam,' servant number one said, bowing so deeply this time his nose almost touched the ground. 'Welcome to Lenberry Hall, home of Sir Philip Wilkins. If you and your lovely nieces would be so good as to follow me, it shall be my pleasure to conduct you into the interior of my master's abode.'

Ella leaned over and whispered to me: 'What did he just say?'

I grinned. 'I think it's his way of saying "Come on in".'

And we both burst out in a fit of giggles. Our aunt threw us a look that could have melted lead and then said to servant number one:

'Very well, my good man. Lead on.'

With a very flourishy flourish, servant one indicated to servants two and three to join again the other servants congregated around the open front door while he entered the house at a measured, dignified pace. We followed, not quite so dignified – at least not me – entering a large hallway, and I had to vigorously employ my jaw muscles to prevent my mouth from falling open at the sight of the opulent splendour awaiting us:

The walls were a pale beige colour, softly illuminated by large, glittering chandeliers that hung from the ceiling. Around the bottom, the walls were panelled in costly, dark woods that gave off a warm glow all of their own. Paintings of stately men hung on the walls, each in a frame that looked to be pure gold. What the floor was made out of I couldn't really see, for it was covered with large and fancy oriental carpets – but it was sure to be something darn expensive.

'Your coat, Miss?' I turned my head to look at servant... three? Or was it four? Who had popped out of nowhere and was holding out his arms.

'What about my coat?' I asked.

'May I take your coat, Miss?'

'No, of course not. It's mine.'

'He means to keep it for you while we are here,' my aunt hissed at me. 'You'll get it back later! Didn't you pay attention to any of my lessons in etiquette?'

Preferring not to give the rather self-evident answer to that question, I divested myself of my coat and thrust it at servant three.

'Here. Make sure nobody nicks it; it's my only one.'

My aunt closed her eyes as if in pain. Or as if counting to ten to prevent an explosion. I wasn't quite sure which.

Servant of unidentified number cleared his throat. 'Err... most assuredly, Miss.'

He hurried into a small side-room in which a multitude of hats, coats and scarves was already stored. Servants number four, five and six, who suddenly appeared out of nowhere, began to help my sisters and aunt out of their outer garments, which apparently everybody thought they were either unable or unwilling to do themselves. Chauvinism. Pure chauvinism.

Then, servant number one bowed once more and gestured down the hall.

'This way, please, Madam. Sir Phillip is awaiting you.'

Anne and Maria exchanged significant looks, which said as clear as day *I'm sure he is. But which one, damn you?* They, along with my aunt, were the first to follow servant one down the hall. After them came Lisbeth, nearly bursting with excitement, Gertrude, quiet and demure, Ella, pale, anxious and shy, and finally me, trying my best to remain invisible to any mate-seeking men in the vicinity.

At the end of the hall waited another open door. From inside the large room beyond, I could hear laughter and chatter. Servant number one placed himself beside the door and, as we entered, called:

'Mrs Brank and nieces.'

Not far from the door stood a tall, fair-haired young man. His hair was just about everything about him that could be called fair. His lips were too thin and his ears would have fit well on an elephant's head. The nose, however, any elephant would have rejected, pointing out that his conk was already large enough and he didn't need a monster like that messing up his or her perfection of elephantine beauty. An uncertain smile that quivered as if subjected to a continuous facial earthquake didn't do anything to improve the picture.

His clothes, admittedly, were posh enough: he was impeccably dressed in a black tail coat, black trousers, white shirt and, best of all, a brilliantly colourful waistcoat showing off an elaborate pattern of red and green brocade with golden embroidery. But... you know that saying, the one about the clothes making the man? Whoever came up with that saying hadn't seen this man, or his ears or nose.

Still, in his fine clothes he looked much richer than Mr Rikkard Ambrose with his simple black attire.

And why the blazes was I suddenly thinking of *him*?

I shook my head, trying to shake off the unwanted image of a familiar cold face in my mind, as the young man came towards us and bowed.

'Mrs Brank? I am Sir Philip Wilkins. Please allow me to welcome you and your lovely nieces to my humble home.'

'You are so kind, Sir Philip,' simpered my aunt. I wouldn't have thought she had that much honey in her pantry, let alone on her tongue. 'I must say you have a truly charming house, and such attentive staff.'

'I only have the *best* of *everything*,' he replied, his gaze wandering dreamily over Anne and Maria. I had a sudden desire to find a bucket to be sick in.

'That I can believe,' my aunt told him, her normally steely voice still coated in sugar.

'But... I do not see Mr Brank here, Madam. Is something the matter?'

Over the aunt's face passed a cloud of sadness that was so convincing it almost fooled even me. 'Ah, yes. Mr Brank regrets so very much that he could not attend, but he has been taken by a sudden illness and his doctor said he was not well enough to leave the house. I am to convey his sincerest apologies to you, Sir Philip.'

Sir Philip's ears drooped. 'Oh, I am grieved to hear about his condition. Please convey my wishes for his immediate recovery.'

Dear me. If they weren't finished soon I'd be smothered by an excess of good manners.

Well, time to start ignoring them and survey the battlefield for the evening...

The large ballroom was even more extravagantly decorated than the waistcoat of its owner. The floor was polished dark wood, the walls a maze of gilded floral patterns. Large windows reflected the light of the enormous sparkly chandeliers, which hung from a ceiling painted with chubby little naked boys with wings on. I supposed they were cherubs – the boys, not the chandeliers.

And the people. Oh the people. They were everywhere. At least a three hundred of them filled the vast room, conversing, bowing and curtsying to one another. And at least a hundred and fifty of them were men. One, sweet, single little me against one hundred and fifty! Now were those supposed to be fair odds?

Suspiciously I eyed the masculine beasts and wondered which of those my aunt would try to marry me off to. None of them looked particularly nice. Especially compared to somebody very nice-looking I had met recently and was determined not to think of again tonight.

Darn! I had done it again! But how was I supposed to think about not thinking about him without thinking about him?

'...and this lovely lady?' The voice directly in front of me pulled me from my thoughts. Sir Philip was standing before me, smiling his uncertain smile.

I opened my mouth to speak. 'I am–'

'That is my niece Lillian, Sir Philip,' my aunt interrupted me hastily and gave me her best don't-you-say-another-word-if-you-want-to-live-stare. Bugger! I had forgotten again. Introduction. You couldn't just speak to someone you didn't know, you had to be introduced first.

'Delighted to make your acquaintance, Miss Linton.' Sir Philip bowed, took my fingers and before I could do anything to prevent it, planted a soft, moist kiss on the back of my hand.

Eww!

I tried to wipe my hand unobtrusively on my dress while Sir Philip went on to Ella.

'And who is this lovely lady?' he asked. It seemed to be his standard sentence when seeing any previously unknown female. But then, as he took in Ella's delicate face, demure smile and fair skin, his behaviour abruptly deviated from the norm and his face was suffused by a deep blush.

'My niece Ella, Sir Phillip,' said my aunt, while Anne and Maria were competing in an ocular archery match, shooting venomous glances at Ella.

He took her hand, too, and placed a kiss on in. '*Delighted* to make your acquaintance,' he said, and it sounded like this time he really meant it. His eyes, as he looked at Ella, appeared slightly misty as if someone had hit him on the head with a wooden club. Why was he staring at her like that?

Oh no... not that. Not *he* of all people...

Ella, much too intimidated by the fact that she was being spoken to by a member of the male population to actually say anything in reply, just curtsied in silence, looking up at the knight as if he were a lion that might eat her any minute. She didn't notice his dreamy gaze. But I had. Oh yes, I had.

Sir Philip bowed to and greeted the rest of us. As soon as he was finished with Gertrude, though, he returned to stand beside my aunt, which coincidentally was also next to where Ella was standing. Anne and Maria, who, for two pretty young ladies, remarkably resembled gorgons[19] at that moment, moved closer.

'It will still be some time till the dancing begins,' said Sir Philip, speaking to my aunt, though he was looking at Ella out of the corner of his eye. 'Would you like me to introduce you to a few people?'

He could not have pleased my aunt more if he had asked whether he should gift her with the largest diamond in his jewel collection. To be introduced into the highest of London's high society, and by a member of the nobility no less, and with all her six expensive, unwanted and unmarried nieces in tow to show off to the rich bachelors of the *metropole* – it was every one of her dreams come true at once.

She concealed her rapture well, however, and simply curtsied, saying: 'It would be my pleasure, Sir Philip.'

---

[19] Monsters from Greek mythology with snakes for hair. The horror of every hairdresser.

'Excellent! Then follow me, please.'

Accompanied by a swarm of servants, which I soon gave up trying to number, we were led across the ballroom to a large group of people talking and laughing in quiet tones. They were rich, stinking rich, every single one of them. I immediately disliked them. They apparently, on beholding the makeshift ball gowns of my sisters and me, shared that feeling. Wilkins didn't seem to notice how they looked at us with their aristocratic nostrils instead of their eyes. He rushed forward and launched into a veritable storm of introductions. It wasn't long till I had forgotten half the names he had mentioned. There were some dukes and duchesses, various lords, and finally an untold number of misters and madams. None of them particularly aroused my interest, except for an older woman whom Wilkins introduced as Lady Metcalf. I tried to remember where I had heard the name before – then I had it!

'We have a mutual acquaintance, your Ladyship,' I said, curtsying.

'Do we really?' She stared at me with her nostrils like all the other ones – only in her case the nostrils were particularly impressive: large, weathered and with little hairs sticking out at the bottom that vibrated whenever she sniffed in disdain. As she did now.

'Yes, we do,' I replied, plastering a huge smile on my face. 'Miss Patsy Cusack. She told me about your very encouraging reaction to her organization of the women's rights movement. Have you received Patsy's answer yet?'

Lady Metcalf turned puce – whether from embarrassment, or anger, or simply because she liked to do that now and again, I didn't know. I was putting my money on the second option, though. Before she could say anything, Sir Philip had whisked us off to meet the next Mr Somethingorother.

I was beginning to dread that he planned to introduce us to every last person in the ballroom, just to have the opportunity to be by Ella's side for another minute or two. The way he looked at her left no doubt as to how he was feeling. As to her feelings, I wasn't quite so sure. She said little and blushed a lot – but then, she always did that. It was impossible to determine what she thought of him and his elephant ears.

Anne and Maria's feelings, on the other hand, were quite easily discernible. They had arrived here fully expecting to bask in Sir Philip's admiration for the entire evening, only to be upstaged by their little sister. They looked ready to devour Ella alive. And she, sweet thing that she was, didn't even notice.

'... and this is Colonel Remington. Colonel Remington, may I introduce–'

Just as the Colonel bowed stiffly, his waxed upturned moustache making him look like he was trying to impale something on a fork, a gong sounded from the other side of the room and Sir Philip clapped his hands.

'Ah! The musicians have arrived. That was the signal from my master of ceremonies. The first dance will begin soon.'

Oops! Quickly I retreated a few steps, to the very back on the group. Luckily, my aunt didn't notice. I had to suppress the urge to turn and run. Dancing was most definitely not my forte. Not that the idea of rhythmically moving to music was so uncongenial to me, no, that wasn't it. It was this business about having to dance in *pairs* – with a *man*, whom you were supposed to *follow*! That was not how I envisioned spending my evenings, thank you very much.

Now if one could discuss the way to move during a dance beforehand, on an equal footing with your partner, then democratically decide on a certain pattern, and then execute it, that would be a different matter entirely. But apparently nobody had ever thought of creating a dance like that.

I positioned myself out of sight, behind the bulk of a conveniently fat duchess. From my vantage point I could just see Wilkins bowing to Ella.

'Miss Ella,' he said, his lips pulling into what he probably thought was an enchanting smile. 'Will you do me the honour of granting me your hand for the first dance?'

This was simply too much for Maria to bear.

'I am not sure whether that would be congenial to my dear sister,' she said, sourly. 'This is her first night out, you see, Sir Philip, and she might not be prepared to take such a big step as opening the ball.'

'Her first night out?' Sir Philip brightened. 'All the more reason to make it a special night for her! If you have no objections, Miss Ella?'

Ella, who would not in her wildest dreams have dared to object to anything proposed by a knight of the British Empire, gave a shaky little nod and placed her hand in Sir Philip's. They went off, leaving a fuming pair of twins behind them.

I grinned and quickly ducked down behind the fat duchess when my aunt turned her head in my direction, her eyes searching.

'Lillian? Lillian, where are you?'

Thinking it unwise to respond to her question, I made my way instead to the side of the room where, behind a few extravagant tropical plants in pots, refreshment tables had been set up and chairs placed. Flopping down on one, I sighed and congratulated myself on my lucky escape. The music for the first dance had already begun to play. For now, I was saved from the mating rituals of high society.

My eyes floated to the refreshment table next to me and saw there something very agreeable – a plate of, if I was not mistaken, the same curious solid chocolate substance that Eve had brought along with her the other day in the park. What had she called it again? Ah yes, a *chocolate bar*. I took one and bit off a piece.

Aaaaah. This stuff was bliss. It seemed to fill me with peace and shoo all my worries away for a little while. The fellow who invented this should really be included in the next year's honours list. It showed that men were good for something after all.

Chewing my chocolate bar, I watched the dances from the shadow of the potted plants. Ella seemed to be doing well, if only because, unlike me, she had no problems being steered around by a man. Anne and Maria were dancing considerably less elegantly, watching their little sister with envy instead of their own feet with care. My aunt was happy in the arms of a portly admiral. Even when the first dance ended, she didn't come to look for me, preferring rather to watch Ella and Sir Philip. It looked like for the moment I was safe. Maybe I wouldn't need to stab anyone with a fan after all.

I smiled to myself. What was I really worrying about? Even if my aunt wished me to dance, first a man would have to ask me. By all accounts, that was extremely unlikely. Both she and my beloved twin sisters, kind and caring family that they were, had assured me on numerous occasions how thoroughly unattractive I was to men, with my tanned skin, wild hair and wilder manners. Apparently, according to the fashion of the day I was more likely to be taken for a fishmonger's daughter or maybe a female gorilla in a dress, than a lady men would actually be interested in, which suited me perfectly. Closing my eyes, I leaned back and popped another piece of chocolate in my mouth.

Hmm...

Just leaning back and thinking of nothing... It was so relaxing. Maybe I could sit out the entire ball like this. I mean, why would anybody come here, into this secluded corner behind the potted plants? I could just sit and wait until we went home, eating chocolate. That wouldn't be so bad. And then the awful evening would be over, and then...

Then it would be morning again.

A familiar face appeared in front of my mind's eye. It would be morning, and I would have to go to work.

Blast! Why did I have to think about him *now*, when I had just achieved a measure of peace and managed to forget all about the existence of the overbearing, annoying and infuriating species known as 'men' for a couple of minutes?

But the more I tried to force his image from my mind, the clearer it appeared: his stark, angular features, his typical look of cool disinterest and, most of all, those dark, sea-coloured eyes that seemed like pearls from a bottomless ocean. Seeing all the opulent splendour surrounding Sir Philip Wilkins, I could not help but wonder why Mr Ambrose, who was supposedly one of the richest men in London, spent his days in an office with bare stone walls. I also couldn't help wonder where he had gotten his money from, if indeed he was as rich as Maria had claimed. He didn't seem to me like a wealthy landowner, not at all the sort of man to fit into London's high society.

For a moment, I amused myself with the thought of how he would act if he were here. I couldn't help but smile. He'd stick out like a shark in a flock of peacocks.

Then, suddenly, I was jerked out of my thoughts by the most unlikely thing imaginable. A voice beside me. A man's voice. A man's voice asking, in a calm, polite tone: 'Miss Linton? Will you do me the honour of dancing with me?'

Practicing Impertinence

My eyes flew open, and I looked up to see an upright, elderly military gentleman with an enormous moustache standing before me. Not Mr Ambrose. Definitely not. It was Colonel Remington, one of the many captains and colonels Sir Philip had introduced me to.

And why the heck had I been thinking of Mr Ambrose? He wasn't even here! The Colonel cleared his throat. Maybe he thought I hadn't heard him.

'Will you do me the honour of dancing with me, Miss Linton?' he repeated.

'Err... no,' I said.

He turned a bit red in the face, and went away, looking rather affronted.

Hm... Perhaps that had not quite been according to etiquette? I racked my brains, trying to remember my aunt's lessons. Hadn't there been something about a lady never being allowed to refuse a dance unless she had already promised it to another gentleman? Well, if there was such a rule, it was complete bollocks.[20] I should have the right to choose not to dance with whomever I bloody well pleased!

Through a gap in the potted plants I could see Colonel Remington joining a few of his military friends – mostly younger officers. He was gesticulating quite energetically. No doubt he was conveying something he considered to be of some importance.

One of the young men laughed. 'Maybe she just didn't like the looks of you,' he teased the elder gentleman.

My mouth dropped open. They were talking about me. *Me!* Well, at least that would ensure that I wouldn't be bothered with any more invitations to dance this night. My lapse in courtesy would spread across the room like wildfire, and surely all those chauvinists would be revolted and shocked to the core. None of the men would even bother to give me a second glance after that.

'I must have a look at that wench,' the young officer continued with a wink, and my mouth dropped open a little farther. 'Was she pretty?'

I couldn't hear the Colonel's more muted reply to this, but the young officer laughed again. 'Come on, old boy, she must have been! And known it, too – quite a conceited little madam, to turn down an officer like that.'

He winked at the other young men around him and strode off. I could hardly believe that he was going to do what I thought he was going to do.

Nevertheless, when the dance had ended and the next one was approaching, I saw him striding towards me with a gait so pompous you could have identified him as a young military officer even if he had been missing his uniform, medals and underpants. He was accompanied by one of his friends who had already been introduced to me.

Both of them examined me not unlike one would examine a piece of meat on a butcher's counter. I ignored them with magnificent composure and took another piece of solid chocolate from the plate beside me.

'Miss Linton?' Mr Familiar Soldier made an extravagant bow, and Mr Unfamiliar Soldier followed suit.

'I don't know whether you remember me? I'm Major Rushworth. Sir Philip introduced us.'

---

[20] A British English term for nonsense (or a man's private parts, depending on the context).

I did not deign to reply immediately – after all, it was considered impolite to talk with your mouth full, wasn't it? Instead, I finished my chocolate, and then plastered a smile on my face.

'Sir Philip introduced me to a great many people,' I replied sweetly. 'Most of whom my unreliable memory has already unintroduced again. You, I'm afraid, are among them.'

It was half true. I had actually forgotten him. Nevertheless, my memory was usually very good – yet only for things I wanted to remember.

Major Rushworth blushed slightly but didn't let that deter him.

'Well, may I be permitted to introduce you to a friend of mine? To this gentleman, here, Lieutenant Ellingham.'

My eyes narrowed. I didn't know much about etiquette, but I did know that the inferior person was always introduced to the superior. By deciding to introduce me to his friend and not the other way around, he had put me on a level below him. And that was something, considering the complacent smile on the lieutenant's face, which I did not appreciate at all.

'No, you may not,' I told him. 'But you may introduce *him* to *me*, if you like.'

'Err...'

Apparently, at first the major didn't quite know what to say to that. He gazed at me for a moment, then collected himself again, cleared his throat and went on: 'Err... very well. Miss Linton, may I be allowed to introduce my friend Lieutenant Ellingham to your notice?'

'Yes, you may.' The smile on my face was widened a bit and I nodded graciously. 'Delighted to make your acquaintance, Lieutenant Ellingham,' I lied.

'As am I,' said the young man, whose arrogant smile had not in the least been reduced in radiance by my rebuff.

'Well, I'll leave you to it then,' the Major said, throwing me another odd glance and then disappearing with an eye roll at his friend. I saw the message 'It's your funeral' clearly in those eyes.

And he was right. It was.

Lieutenant Ellingham seated himself beside me. Taking the bull by the horns, I turned to him. Best to get this over with.

'Well, what should we talk about, Lieutenant? The weather would be a good subject of discussion, if we were not inside and it was night.'

'How about the society?' he asked, gesturing towards the people dancing everywhere in the grand room.

'That would be unwise. When you make conversation, it is generally considered best to say nice and polite things. And the present society would not furnish me with a lot of opportunities for that.'

He blinked at me, no doubt wondering if he had heard right. In the end, he seemed to decide that he had not. I was a lady, after all. Ladies didn't say impolite things. It was unheard of.

Instead of trying to find another topic, he cut right to the chase.

'I must admit, Miss Linton, that I had a particular reason for wishing an introduction with you.'

'Did you, now?' I couldn't entirely keep the sarcasm out of my voice. But the young man's arrogance apparently made him immune to sarcasm from ladies as well as to impudence. He gave me a smile that he probably thought was charming.

It wasn't.

'Yes, I did. I have been admiring you from afar for some time now. You have caught my eye, Miss Linton.'

'Indeed?' I raised an eyebrow. 'I can't remember you throwing it at me, to be honest. I don't have your eye on me, I promise. I never catch eyes. They are rather slippery and slimy things, not at all the kind of objects I would like to carry around in my pocket.'

'Um...' he blinked, just as dumbfounded as his friend before, clearly lacking the brains to decipher my reply. For some unknown reason, I took pity on him.

'Were you going to ask me if I would dance with you?' I asked him.

'Yes! That is it, exactly. How did you know?'

'Let's just say I am a discerning person. Well, if it is a dance you want, that makes things very simple.'

'Excellent.' He got up, his arrogant grin back on his face, and held a hand out to me.

'No,' I said, not looking up at him.

Out of the corner of my eye, I saw a look of confusion cross his face.

'Excuse me?'

'You want to dance with me – I have just given you my answer. No.'

'Oh.'

'Yes. Why don't you try that young lady over there? She looks to be in want of a partner, and unlike me, she actually wants one. Goodbye.'

He stood rooted to the spot for a few more seconds, then let his hand drop and walked off. Picking another piece of chocolate off the plate, I glanced at him out of the corner of my eye. For some reason, he didn't appear very disheartened. If I had to choose a word to describe his facial expression, I think I would have chosen 'intrigued,' though I didn't see how the bloody hell that could be.

Through the potted plants, I saw him return to his friends, and they hooted and slapped him on the back while he grinned shame-faced. I was very pleased with myself. Now, finally, there would be an end of the matter. No more invitations to dance tonight.

A few minutes later a cough distracted me, and I looked up only to be confronted with another officer asking me to dance. I turned him down like a bedspread. And the one after that. And the one after the one after that. And the other gentlemen who followed, from captains to colonels, from misters to majors. It was amazing – the more of them I sent packing, the more seemed to pop up everywhere. You'd think that by now they would have gotten the message.

During a break in the assault of dance-addicted gentlemen, I took another peep through the foliage. Ella was again being whisked across the floor in the arms of Sir Philip Wilkins and looked about ready to faint from the attention. I grinned. It would do her good to be out in society. Maybe she would get a little more confidence and experience.

But as I let my eyes wander farther over the assembled guests, I noticed something strange: I couldn't see my aunt anywhere. That was very curious indeed. Ella, Maria and Anne were busy hunting for prospective husbands. Lisbeth was doing her best, and even Gertrude was dancing with a quiet, elderly gentleman.

My aunt would hardly leave the dance floor at such a moment, unless it would be to...

And then the voice of doom spoke behind me.

'Lilly – What *in the name of the Lord* is this I have been hearing, about you *refusing to dance?*'

Oh blast!

~~**~*~*

My aunt emerged from behind a potted plant like a vulture from behind a lone desert rock and stalked towards me. I could almost see the sword of just punishment in her right and the scales in her left hand.

'Err... hello, Aunt,' I said. 'This is a nice evening. Wonderful ball, don't you think?'

But apparently, my aunt did not want to change the subject right now. 'I heard from Colonel Remington that you refused to dance with him.'

'Um... only from him?'

'Yes, he... Wait, what do you mean, *only from him*? Do you mean to say there are *others* with whom you refused to dance?'

I could have slapped myself for not keeping my big mouth shut. I wasn't usually timid, but in the face of the huge fire breathing dragon that was my aunt, I cowered on my chair, my eyes downcast.

'Err... maybe?'

'Either you did or you didn't. Well?'

'Did.'

'How many? Two? Three?'

'Err... more something like... thirteen? Maybe fourteen?'

Watching my aunt's expression, I truly believe that had we been at home, my eardrums would have been in some danger of being shattered by her reaction. However, at this very moment a gentleman stepped up to the refreshment tables and took a piece of chocolate off the plates, reminding my aunt that we were in company and that ladies did not scream like furies when they were in company.

Slowly, she stepped towards me until only inches separated us and bent down towards my ear.

'If you should be so lucky as to have another deluded gentleman apply for your hand,' she hissed into my ear, 'you will accept it or I will lock you in your room and throw the key away, understood?'

I paled. My aunt, misinterpreting my look, nodded satisfied. 'That's it. No lounging about in the park or in the garden, no going to the library, and above all no meeting with those friends of yours.'

All I could manage in answer was a shaky nod. My aunt didn't know the real force of her threat. I had obligations now. I couldn't simply be locked in my room like a spoiled child. If I wasn't punctually at work tomorrow, Mr Ambrose would dismiss me for sure.

For a fleeting moment the idea of leaving home entered my mind – but no. I wasn't even of age yet. My aunt could bring me back and forcibly lock me in my room if she wished. Though if she heard I had left her house to work for a living, she would probably lock me in an insane asylum instead.

I swallowed hard. There was nothing for it.

I had to dance.

Dance with a man.

~~**~*~*

Six or seven minutes later, a young officer approached me and bowed. Colonel Malcolm. I remembered him from Sir Philip's flood of introductions. Somewhere behind him I could see a few others, among them Lieutenant Ellingham, laughing quietly. 'Miss Linton? May I have the honour of the next dance?'

The officer braced himself for the rebuff.

'Yes.'

He stared at me, evidently taken aback.

'Really?'

I pulled a face. 'Yes, really. I said yes, didn't I?'

'Umm... yes, you did. It's just...'

I rolled my eyes at him.

'Let's just get this over with, shall we?'

The music began to play. Getting to my feet, I grabbed the surprised officer by the hand and hauled him onto the dance floor, while his friends watched in awed amazement.

'Are you wearing good, solid boots?' I asked.

'Boots?' The young man looked at me with mounting confusion. 'Yes, Miss. Why?'

'Because I've never danced before in my life and I will probably step on your feet half the time. I don't want you permanently injured.'

He grinned a little boy grin. 'That's all right. I don't mind. I'm a cavalry officer you know? Had a horse step on my foot three times already. You don't think you're heavier than a horse, do you?'

Suddenly realizing what he had said, he blushed.

'Begging your pardon, Miss. I didn't mean to imply that... well...'

Unwillingly, I had to grin back. This might just not be such an ordeal after all.

'Hmm...' I replied, pretending to contemplate the question. 'No, I don't think I'm quite as heavy as a horse. But nearly.'

He smiled, relieved. 'Then I shall take care with every step I take.'

We danced. It didn't turn out to be that terrible. Colonel Malcolm was – for a man – relatively quiet and well-behaved. He pointed me into the right direction without forcing me and didn't complain when I trampled on his toes. When we were done with the quadrille, he bowed to me in a very gentlemanly manner and said with a light smile that this had been a very novel experience.

My next partners were not quite so agreeable. While my aunt watched from the shadows of the potted plants, I wrestled with various men who seemed to think dancing consisted of pushing around the female like a piece on a chessboard. Whenever they would get too overbearing, I would make good use of my heel and aim a solid kick at the gentleman's feet, or use my fan to prod them in the ribs. This elicited very satisfying groans from the male monsters. In that way, I got through about an hour of dancing. Sweat was beginning to trickle down my forehead. I threw a pleading glance at my aunt.

She shook her head.

So I smiled at the next gentleman and said yes, he could have the honour of this dance. The fight was beginning to go out of me. My kicks became increasingly feeble. After another half hour, I turned to my aunt again, this time clasping my hands in supplication.

She considered a moment – then nodded.

Thank the Lord! I was free. What bliss.

Staggering to a chair near the refreshment tables, I flopped down on it and leaned back, closing my eyes. Whoever knew dancing could be so exhausting? If this was what you had to do in order to catch yourself an eligible bachelor, I wondered at the fact that not more ladies had decided to try and go find a job of their own. Compared with this, even working for Mr Stoneface Ambrose looked like a piece of chocolate cake.

Could I take off my shoes? My feet ached, and I wanted so much to give them a little room and air. But although this hadn't been included in any of my aunt's lectures about etiquette, I somehow believed that taking off your shoes and putting your feet on the next table wasn't considered acceptable behaviour at a high society ball.

My only consolation, I thought with a grin, was that I knew that my partner's feet would be hurting a dang sight more than mine right now. There was nothing so useful to a girl as really solid heels.

'... and abominably rude,' a voice made its way through the haze of my exhaustion to my brain. My eyelids fluttered open. The voice was coming from behind the nearest potted plant. I wasn't someone who eavesdropped, normally. Normally people didn't have anything interesting to say. But this sounded like one of those rare occasions where it might be interesting to keep an ear open. After all, they mentioned rudeness. They might be talking about me.

'Yes, that is what I heard,' I heard another voice, which I recognized as Lady Metcalf's. 'But he has certain... redeeming features.'

Oh. Not me. They were talking about some stupid man. Losing interest in the discussion, I slowly rose and started away in the direction of another refreshment table. I almost didn't catch the next sentence.

'But can anyone of you tell me what is so fascinating about him?' Another voice demanded. 'I just got back from the country and found that all London is awash with talk of him. I mean, what is so special about this Mr Rikkard Ambrose?'

I froze in my tracks.

THE SINS OF MR RIKKARD AMBROSE

'You *haven't heard?*'

The voice was full of glee and juicy gossip. I was so quickly at the potted plant behind which the group of gossiping ladies where hiding that I saw who had spoken. It was the Duchess of Brandon. I should have been able to guess from the tone.

Lady Allen, obviously the one who had asked the question, flushed a little. 'From what I've heard since I've arrived in town, he's rumoured to be one of the richest men in London,' she said defensively.

'One of the richest?' The duchess laughed. The sound almost made me want to go away again, or at least stuff my ears while it lasted. 'My dear, from what *my* sources tell me, he is *the* richest. His wealth is unparalleled. There is only one other man who can hold a candle to him.'

Lady Allen's mouth formed a little 'O', and her eyes went wide.

And I had to admit, to my shame: for once in my life I felt the same as Lady Allen and the Duchess of Brandon. I was awed, and a cold shiver ran down my back. The more I heard about Mr Ambrose, the more rich and powerful he seemed to become. Where the hell did all this wealth come from? I couldn't believe he was simply the heir of some large estate. Why would he have that monumental building in the city if his wealth came from his inheritance? And what had all those people been doing there, hurrying about, carrying papers?

The third member of the little discussion group behind the potted plant seemed to harbour similar questions.

'Yes, yes.' I knew that voice. Peeking through the foliage, I saw Lady Metcalf wave her fan. 'But does anybody know where his wealth comes from? I must say, I have my suspicions that it's not honest money, and that he is no gentleman. I have repeatedly invited him to balls and the theatre, and never once has he accepted my invitation. He hasn't even replied! The nerve of him! I say there must be something fishy about him, there is no other way to explain such dastardly behaviour.'

For some reasons those words made a grin appear on my face. Suddenly, I liked my employer a little bit better. Just a little bit.

'Well...' the duchess said in that drawn-out tone that said 'I have a shocking piece of information and I am willing to share, but you must badger me first since I cannot very well appear to be a gossip.'

'Yes?' Lady Metcalf leaned closer, eagerly. 'You know something, Duchess?'

Carefully, I stepped even closer to the potted plant, praying they would not notice me. The duchess was a treasure trove of gossip, and for once I was actually interested in what she had to say. Very much so.

'I really can't,' she protested. 'It is only a rumour, and I would never want to slander anybody.'

Amazing how people could lie without their face twitching.

'We won't tell,' Lady Metcalf assured her.

'Yes,' Lady Allen concurred. 'You know us. We don't gossip.'

Really, really amazing.

'Well... all right, if you promise not to repeat anything I say.'

'We promise,' Lady Metcalf nodded eagerly.

'It is only a rumour, mind you, and I do not have any proof.' The duchess gloried in the eager anticipation of her friends.

'Does he have anything to do with the Ambroses in the North?' Lady Metcalf tried to guess. 'A very good family, I think.'

'Dear Lord no, my dear. The Northern Ambroses? The earl's family? They may have recovered from their financial difficulties, but I assure you, they do not have the kind of money this Mr Ambrose has.'

'But if he has not inherited his wealth from them, where did it come from?'

The Duchess smiled. Lowering her voice, she said:

'That is the shocking part. I have heard,' she continued lowering her voice even more until it was only a whisper, 'that he is involved in *commerce*!'

The two ladies gasped in shock.

'Surely not!'

'Unbelievable!'

'And *trade*. And he *invests in manufacturing and industry*. Can you imagine?'

Lady Metcalf began to fan herself. 'Stop, please, my friend. Or I am going to faint. That anybody should degrade himself so...'

'You have not heard the worse of it,' the Duchess said, ominously.

'My dear, what could be worse than *that*?'

'I have heard, from a very reliable source, that during his youth he actually *worked* for money, that he did *manual labour*.'

'Dear me!'

'Heavens!'

'Yes,' the Duchess repeated with glee. 'He *worked for a living*! Among common working-class folk! It is hardly creditable, is it not?'

'Please, have mercy on us, stop!'

'And not even here in the United Kingdom – but in some wild place in the former colonies!'

'You don't mean – oh goodness, you don't mean that awful place... what do the people call it again?'

'The "United States of America".'

'God, yes. Please, Duchess, no more. Even the mere thought of that place makes me shudder!'

'They do not even have a king over there, do they?'

'Worse, my dear! They do not even take tea in the afternoon.'

I didn't catch much of the conversation after that. I had to admit, I was too blown away. Well, well, well... a gentleman who once did work for wages and earned his way to the top. What a novel idea. I couldn't suppress a grin. How very naughty of you, Mr Ambrose, to so flout the traditions of the English upper class.

But then my good mood vanished and I was overtaken by sudden anger. How dare he? How dare he judge me and my attempt to earn a living when he himself had done the same? Yes, I was a girl and he was man, but apparently a gentleman. For a gentleman to work for a living was almost more outlandish than for a female to do it. And how, by the way, had he gotten so stinking rich at it? *He* couldn't have worked as a secretary, that much was for sure.

"I will find out the truth about you, Mr Ambrose,' I vowed to myself. 'And I will make you accept me. You are my ticket to freedom, whether you like it or not.'

~~**~*~*

The ball ended about three months later. Well, it felt like that to me, anyway, although it probably only was a few hours. We were conducted outside not only by servants number one, two, three, four, seven, eleven and twenty-five, but also by an enthusiastic Sir Philip Wilkins, who kept flashing meaningful smiles at Ella and waggling his over-large ears. Though I rather think he didn't do the latter intentionally. Outside, he personally called one of his carriages to convey us home – and not the same carriage either, but an even larger and more luxurious version.

Our sitting arrangement on the way home was rather different from before. Now, a glowering Anne and Maria had taken their seats on one side, keeping everyone at bay with the bad mood radiating off them, while the rest of us were comfortably placed opposite them. Unlike on the way over, our aunt didn't give the twins a second glance. She was too busy contemplating Ella's matrimonial prospects.

'...three times he danced with you, Ella, just think! Three times. Not to speak of the compliments he made you,' she purred. I could almost see the twinkle of gold in her eyes as she contemplated the wealth of her future nephew-in-law.

Ella nodded, slightly puzzled. 'He was indeed most attentive. It is no wonder that so many fine ladies were at his ball, considering how well he behaves to all his guests.'

My aunt laughed. It sounded a little like a choking vulture.

'Oh, my dear. I doubt he would have paid so much attention to any of the other ladies.'

'But, Aunt... what special interest could he have in me?'

This made my aunt laugh again, then wink at her niece. She was about as talented at winking as she was at laughing.

'Of course, of course, my dear. You are very wise to be discreet.'

By this Ella seemed only more puzzled. Anne and Maria were staring daggers at her, choosing rather to believe her insincere than to believe anyone could actually be so innocent. I could hardly believe it myself – but unfortunately I knew it to be true. This was Ella we were talking about. I resolved to give my little sister a lecture about men once we were safely upstairs in our room.

When we got home, though, it looked like it would take some time before we could get to bed. First my aunt had to rush up to my uncle and tell him everything that had happened at the ball. Then she had to rush down and tell us how delighted he had been about everything that had happened at the ball, most of which she had to make up because my uncle probably didn't utter more than two words in response to her jubilation.

And then...

Well, then the flowers arrived. We had just managed to calm my aunt down to a certain extent, when the doorbell rang. We were all so curious to know who could be calling at this late hour that we all gathered at the entrance to the hallway to catch a peek of the front door as Leadfield shuffled down the hall.

It took him a while to manoeuvre himself into a position in which he could open the door without losing his balance and falling over, but finally he managed. The door opened, and outside a young man in livery stood, carrying something colourful and enormous.

'For Miss Ella Linton,' he said, thrusting the big thing at Leadfield, who swayed under the weight.

'Th-thank you,' he said, managing a half-bow. 'I shall deliver it directly.'

Leadfield had hardly closed the door when we all rushed out into the hallway. My aunt was leading the charge.

'Well, Ella?' she demanded of my little sister, who was holding herself in the background. 'See if there is a card! See who it is from. Hurry, hurry!'

Cautiously, Ella stepped forward and took the enormous bouquet – for that's what it was – from the swaying Leadfield. I supposed if one liked flowers and things, it was quite impressive. Some yellow flowers, dozens of white ones, and at the very top one of those red thorny things which were supposed to be so romantic. What were they called again? Ah yes, roses! Right beside the rose, a card peeked out of the bouquet.

While just managing to hold the massive flower arrangement with one hand, Ella took the card with the other, opened it, and read:

'For the most wonderful dance ever. Sir Philip.'

'Aww!' My aunt clapped her hands, her eyes glowing with triumph and the promise of untold riches. 'I knew it! I knew they had to be from him. Such beautiful flowers! And on the same evening, Ella, only imagine! I rather expected him to send a little something tomorrow, but on the same evening... That is promising, promising indeed.'

'Promising for what, Aunt?' Ella asked.

But my aunt only winked again and hurried off, muttering to herself: 'Saint Paul's Cathedral! Yes, nothing less will do. It must and will happen at Saint Paul's Cathedral. And all my old friends will be there. Oh, I can see Mrs Gullifer's face now, green with envy she'll be...'

Anne approached her little sister with a smile that could have scared off a tiger. 'Congratulations, my sister. They are truly beautiful flowers.'

'Thank you,' said Ella earnestly, blushing.

'I truly believe,' said Anne, 'that the bouquet might be even larger than the one I have got.'

'What?'

'Didn't you know?' If possible, Anne's smile got even nastier. 'Sir Philip sent me a bouquet very much like that three days ago, and one to Maria the day before that. He seems to be fond of giving away flowers.'

'Oh,' said Ella. 'I'm sorry yours wasn't as large. Do you want mine? I wouldn't mind.'

I had to steady myself against the wall, otherwise I would have collapsed from fits of silent laughter. Anne's acid-sour face was a picture!

'Don't be too confident, little sister,' she hissed, gathered up her skirts and rushed away with Maria right behind her. Ella looked after them, a puzzled expression on her face, then turned to me.

'What was that about?' she asked.

I waved the question away, while trying to conceal my smile with the other hand. 'I'll explain it to you someday, when you're ready.'

'Um... thank you very much.'

We might have said more to each other, but at that moment my aunt rushed into the room again.

'Oh Ella, Ella my dearest! Isn't it wonderful? Such beautiful flowers! Show me again, will you? We have to find a vase for them, so when he comes to visit he will see...'

She was still rotating like an overexcited top, her voice too loud to even think of going to bed in peace. So I took a book out of my uncle's library and strolled into the garden. I hadn't indulged in my favourite hobby as much as I would have liked, lately. Too much had been going on. But at least now I had a few hours before I had to go to bed.

What do you think I picked? Some wonderfully romantic novel that dealt with falling in love with tall, dark and handsome strangers? No, thank you! One tall and dark stranger in my life was quite enough. If those books gave help on how to organize a file system, that would have been one thing. But one glance years ago had been enough to tell me that all they were concerned with was strolling around gardens and mooning after men.

I preferred another kind of bedtime story: an atlas of the world from my father's old book collection. Just my kind of book: no chauvinist heroes, no soppy heroines, and plenty of strange, foreign lands promising adventure. If only I could really go there – just like Anne Thornton, who had dressed up as a man to sneak aboard a ship bound for distant lands! I had never felt so envious in my entire life as when her story had gone through the papers a few years ago. I could hardly imagine how exciting a trip to inner Africa or the unexplored, icy regions of Canada might be. Much more exciting than dreary old London, I was sure.

Slowly, I wandered through the garden and settled in the grass behind a clump of bushes, where I often sat when I wanted to avoid my aunt. The light of the moon was just enough to see by, so I opened the Atlas and started leafing through it.

I had just managed to lose myself in China, somewhere between Peking and Quingdao, when my thoughts were pulled from their Asian idyll back to Ella. I tried concentrating on my book, but just couldn't. Poor, innocent Ella. After what I had seen at the ball, it was clear as the day that Sir Philip had his eyes on her. She was just hopelessly clueless. I sighed and turned the page. Well, I would just have to talk to her and explain a few things about what went on between men and women. Was my aunt in bed and out of the way yet?

I was just about to move on from Quingdao to Hong Kong when a voice from the garden disturbed me.

'Psht!'

Or rather, not the voice disturbed me – but the fact that it was a *man's* voice. Definitely not Leadfield the butler! And my uncle? He wouldn't be seen dead in the garden. Who in God's name...

'Psht! I'm here, my love.'

My love? Now things were getting a bit thick! I sat up straight and peered through the foliage but couldn't see anybody. And in the next moment I stopped looking, because what I heard made me forget all about the man.

'I'm here! I'm here, my love,' came the answer to the lover's call in the sweet, innocent tones of my little sister Ella.

I dropped the atlas on my foot.

UNSUITABLE SUITORS

'Ouch!'

'What was that, my love? Did you hurt yourself?'

'No, my dearest Ella. Why do you ask?'

'I could have sworn I heard somebody crying out.'

'It must have been my heart crying out in joy at the sight of you, my dearest, my loveliest Ella!'

His heart? My foot, more like! Behind the bushes I was hopping on one foot, my hand clamped over my mouth to prevent any further outcries. I nearly toppled over but was able to grasp a tree and steady myself. Not more than a few feet away, hidden by the brush, I could hear the soft 'swoosh' of a gown gliding through the wet grass and my little sister's light feet as she hurried through the garden.

'Oh Ella!'

'Oh Edmund!'

Edmund? *Edmund?*

Peering between two bushes, I could see my sister standing at the wrought iron fence that separated our garden from that of the neighbours, clutching at the intricate ironwork as though it were prison bars separating her from all she desired in the world. And indeed, beyond the fence stood Edmund Conway, our neighbour's son, staring at my little sister with an expression on his face that I could only describe as... besotted.

Eww!

'Oh Ella,' he said again.

'Oh Edmund.'

'Oh my love.'

'Oh my dearest.'

They had said that already, hadn't they? Why repeat it? What was the matter with them? Squinting through the brush, I tried to get a better look at them. Were they ill, maybe? Well, they definitely both looked slightly crazy. They had silly smiles plastered on their faces and kept staring at each other like there wasn't a beautiful garden with trees and birds and a lot of other interesting things all around them. In Edmund's case I might have understood that – my little sister was an eye-catcher. But there really was no excuse for Ella's blatant staring. Our neighbour's son was a perfectly ordinary male specimen: brown hair, brown eyes, two legs, two feet, and one head on his shoulders. There was nothing about him to justify such staring. He didn't even have an interesting hunchback or a boil on his nose.

'You are growing into a real Lady, Ella,' Edmund said, his voice thick with emotion. 'I watched you from the house when you departed in your fine coach.'

He watched her? *He watched her, the villain?*

'Oh, it was nothing,' she said, blushing, and not even because she was of-fended, no! Was this believable? She was actually pleased! 'It was not our coach you saw. It was that of Sir Philip Wilkins. He invited my whole family out to his ball tonight.'

'A ball?' Edmund sighed with the pathos of a Shakespearean actor. 'How I wish I could have gone to the ball and danced with you. How I wish I could just hold you in my arms once. But always this infernal barrier of iron keeps us sep-arated!'

My eyes strayed from the pair of them to the ladder that leaned, not ten feet away, against the wall of the Conways' garden shed. I was almost tempted to say something but wisely kept my mouth shut.

'Not only this iron wall separates us, my love, as you very well know,' said Ella. There was something glinting in her eyes. Tears? Tears! That rogue had managed to make my little sister cry! I was strongly tempted to go over there and clobber him over the head with my parasol but stayed where I was. My left foot was still damaged from the atlantean collision, and I wasn't at all sure I could make it over there without landing on my nose.

'What else can separate two loving hearts?' Edmund demanded. 'Ella... I love you. I wish nothing but to love you until my dying day.'

I heard a strange sound from a sister. Hiccups? No... It sounded more like a gasp of pain. But why the heck would she be in pain? I didn't see any blood or other signs of injury.

'Oh Edmund, do not speak thus to me, I beg you!'

'Why not? Do you not love me?'

He actually looked wounded. No, more than that... devastated. Slight doubts were beginning to gnaw at me. Either he was a darn fine actor, for which I didn't really think him smart enough, or he really... No! No, that couldn't be.

'Of course!' Ella clutched the iron poles of the fence even tighter, and her knuckles turned white. 'Of course I love you, Edmund! With all my heart!'

'Then why conceal our love in the shadows, my dearest? Just think, it could have been me who danced with you at that ball.'

'Edmund, please! Do not tempt me with these enticing visions!'

'But why not?' The desperate fervour of his voice was beginning to get to me. What if he wasn't just an obnoxious, lecherous rake like ninety-nine per cent of his fellow men? What if he actually loved my little sister? I shuddered at the possibility. And even worse... what if *she* really loved him *back?*

'Why, my dearest Ella, should I not openly proclaim my love for you? My family is not rich, but we're well-off enough, and I am, while still young, a respectable man. Why should I not gain your love?'

'You already have it.'

Edmund took a deep breath as if preparing to jump off a cliff into an unknown ocean.

'What I mean, Ella, is: why should I not gain your love... and your hand?'

Ella paled and only managed to stay upright because she was clutching the iron poles of the fence. My desire to clobber young Edmund was instantly revived. How dare he upset her!

'Edmund,' Ella said, her small voice quivering, 'you know it cannot be.'

'But you say you love me?'

'As a sister would her brother.'

This time it was Edmund who paled. Yes! Now you know what it feels like, you chauvinist son of a bachelor!

'Ella! Consider what you are saying. Do you wish to pierce my heart?'

'I wish I could love you another way, Edmund. I do, I so desperately do. But I cannot.'

'Why not?' Suddenly with colour in his cheeks again, the young blackguard stepped forward. He was now almost at the fence, only inches away from my little sister. I was vigorously massaging my injured foot, preparing to charge and save her from his evil clutches if necessary.

'There is an impenetrable barrier between us, Edmund.'

'I will tear it down, my love.'

'You cannot, my dearest.'

'I can and I will.'

Now tears were running down Ella's face.

'How would you tear down our birth, Edmund?'

'Our birth doesn't separate us. We were born as soul mates.'

'We were born worlds apart, Edmund. I am of the gentry. You, though the spirit of a king may live in your breast, are the son of a tradesman.'

'An honest and prosperous tradesman. I could support you in the style to which you are accustomed. I would not dare seek the hand of a lady such as you if that were not the case.'

'Oh Edmund!' My little sister's lower lip quivered so piteously that I almost started to cry myself. Only the knowledge that this fuzz was all about nothing but a load of romantic balderdash kept me from losing my dignity. 'I have told you this a thousand times. The wealth of your family does not matter. It is the position of your family that troubles me. I know you to be good and kind and loving, but that counts for nothing with my aunt, who holds rank and pedigree above everything else. If she were to discover my love for you, the son of a common tradesman, we would be separated and never see each other again.'

'So this is it? This is why nobody must know of our attachment?'

'Nobody. Not even my dearest sister Lilly, the one who after you, Edmund, I love most in the world, knows of this, my dark and sinful secret. I have kept it close to my heart and have been most cunning in concealing it from the world.'

Covering my eyes with my hand, I slumped back into the grass. Yes, most cunning indeed – conducting a secret romance in the back garden of your family home. I mean, my dear little sister, how would it be possible for *anyone* to discover you there, or listen in on you?

Poor Ella. She would have a few nasty surprises coming for her in the real world.

I lay on my back, continuing to listen to their conversation. Some part of me was expecting Edmund to make dark and demanding overtures to my sister. I mean, he was a man, after all. But there were only flowery professions of love on both sides.

A lot of them.

A really great lot of them.

Maybe Edmund was actually a nice fellow. I had certainly thought so before this evening – before I had discovered he had his eye on my little sister. Maybe I should not immediately start to think of him as a ruthless rake. From what I could hear, he seemed decent enough, if a little soppy. Maybe I wouldn't hit him with my parasol just yet.

'But tell me, my dearest Ella...' he began, frowning slightly. I raised my head. This didn't sound like another one of those silly love-confessions. 'Might we not confide in one person at least? Your elder sister, Lilly I think her name is, of whom you have spoken so fondly?'

'Oh Edmund! How I would love to do that, to pour out my heart to my dearest sister!'

'Which one was she, by the way? I have never yet had the pleasure of being introduced to any of your family, I just saw them the other day on the street.'

Ella smiled. 'She was the one who returned your greeting. The only one. Oh, if only I could tell her how much joy she gave me in that moment! How I would love to disclose my love to her, to share with her my happiness!'

'Then why not do it? She might be sympathetic to our plight.'

I chewed my bottom lip thoughtfully. Hmm. Maybe, fellow. If you behave.

'She might also be a valuable ally, my dearest. The word of so good a lady as you described is sure to have weight with your aunt.'

Oops. Not so much luck there, I'm afraid.

I looked at Ella through a gap in the bushes. She looked slightly apprehensive. 'Err... I don't know whether telling her about us would be the best idea. Lilly is a wonderful person, only... sometimes I think she is a tiny bit prejudiced against men.'

What? Me, prejudiced? Me?

'Prejudiced against men, my love?' Edmund frowned. 'I don't quite understand. Has a man wronged her in the past?'

'Not as such. I think it's rather that she thinks all men wrong her just by breathing.'

Edmund looked even more puzzled by this.

'Why?'

Ella leaned closer to the fence. Looking quickly around her as if she were going to say something very naughty, she whispered in a voice so low I had to strain my ears to catch the words: 'You know, I think she secretly wants to be one. A man, I mean.'

My mouth dropped open. Of all the ridiculous...

I was seriously considering marching over there and giving my little sister a piece of my mind! 'Wants to be one' indeed!

'How very strange,' Edmund commented, still puzzled. I glowered at him from behind the bushes. What did *he* know? He was allowed to vote and to work for a living, and he didn't have to conceal the fact.

'That's what I thought,' Ella said, nodding eagerly. 'However, I may be mistaken. And I really shouldn't be saying such things. It is not very kind of me, after all, to insinuate that my own sister is stark raving mad. Really, deep down, she is a very gentle soul.'

Really? I certainly didn't feel very gentle at the moment!

'Then why not reveal the truth to her? She might take some time to get used to the idea, but once she got to know me that would surely change.'

Don't be so sure.

'Maybe, but... her reservations regarding men are not the only reason for keeping my silence,' Ella confessed. Looking around, she continued in hushed whispers: 'I have a feeling that if I reveal this dark secret to another soul, somehow it will be revealed to all the world. Sometimes I feel as though there is a sinister figure in the shadows, watching us and listening to every secret word we say.'

Well, well. My little sister was more intuitive than I would have believed. I had to admit I rather liked being called a sinister figure. It had an interesting ring to it.

So what are you going to do now, sinister figure in the shadows? I asked myself. *You've just discovered that your little sister, whom you thought pure as the driven snow, is in fact head over heels in love with some man and is conducting a secret romance in your own back garden! What are you going to do about it?*

The first thing that popped into my mind was telling my aunt. That would put an end to Edmund's nefarious activities, and my little sister would be out of danger.

But then... I never told my aunt anything out of principle, and so far it had worked fine for me. Maybe I should be guided by my experience in this case.

Besides, looking at the expressions on the two lovers' faces as they stared at each other... it somehow made me feel guilty for even considering to bring an end to their nocturnal meetings. *Me*, feeling guilty! I never felt guilty! Even when I did something for which I probably *should* feel guilty. And in this case I wasn't, was I? I was only trying to protect my little sister.

'Psht.' Edmund stepped nearer to her. His hands closed around the iron poles, too. Their fingers were only inches apart now. 'Do not be haunted by such dark thoughts, my love. No one is listening. Our secret is safe.'

Hmm.... Was it?

'We should be talking of happier matters,' Edmund continued, smiling at Ella in that mushy way that made me want to find a bucket to stick my head into. 'We have so little time together – I want to know about your day. You had a big day, today, didn't you? Your first ball.'

'Oh how I wished you could have been there,' Ella sighed, her voice so revoltingly infused with soppiness that it gave me an intense wish for a bucket and a quiet corner. 'I would have loved to dance with you.'

'So would I, believe me, my love. But tell me how it was. Were you much admired? I wager all the other ladies were green with envy at your beauty.'

'No, of course not!' Ella blushed, though actually Edmund wasn't so far from the truth. 'Both the gentlemen and the ladies were very considerate, particularly our host.'

She began to tell of the ball: of how they had been welcomed, of how grand everything had been, of how Sir Philip himself had been so condescending as to dance with her. At first Edmund smiled, but every time she told of how Sir Philip had come back for another dance, his smile waned a little.

'This... this Sir Philip sounds like the most attentive host I have ever met.'

'Yes indeed.' Ella smiled sweetly. 'Only think, Edmund, his attentions still continued when I had left his house. He sent me a bouquet of flowers.'

Those words, however, did not have the positive effect on her lover my sister obviously expected them to have. He paled and took a step back.

'Flowers?' he gasped. 'To your house on the same evening?'

'Yes Edmund. But my love, my dearest love, what is the matter? You are suddenly so pale. Tell me, are you ill? What ails you, my love? What is the matter?'

Looking at Edmund's face, I knew exactly what the matter was. Maybe, just maybe, I wouldn't knock him out with my parasol after all. It looked as if he'd already been dealt a blow far deadlier than I could deliver – struck down by a bouquet of flowers.

'Oh God, no,' he whispered, and I could hear he understood what the flowers meant.

Ella was staring at the young man, deep concern and longing such as I had never seen before etched into every lovely line of my little sister's face. It occurred to me that while to me this whole matter of the back garden romance seemed the most ridiculous thing ever, Ella didn't share that opinion. This was life and death to her.

I suddenly knew what I had to do.

'What is it that is wrong?' My little sister repeated with rising desperation. 'Why are you so deathly pale, my love?'

'Because...' Edmund's voice broke, and he had to start again. 'Because I think Sir Philip Wilkins might...'

He shook his head, unable to complete the sentence.

'Oh, I may be over-interpreting things. But Ella, love, you must tell me immediately if he should send you any more flowers.'

An actress would have given her right arm for the perfect expression of puzzled innocence on Ella's face at that moment. But the problem was: this expression wasn't fake.

'Flowers? Edmund, what can be so important about a few flowers?'

'Just promise me, my love,' he said with fervour. 'If what I believe is correct – oh, I shudder to think of the possibility! If what I think is correct, then every single flower from Sir Philip Wilkins is an arrow straight to my heart.'

'Then I shall throw them away directly,' Ella exclaimed, tears in her eyes again. 'What are a few flowers to me?'

'No! You must not do so. You must not do anything that would arouse suspicion.' Bowing his head against the iron poles and closing his eyes, he murmured: 'You were right. I am beneath you. If any suspicions were to enter your aunt's mind that you had given your heart to me, all would be over between us. Do not throw the flowers away. Do not do anything unusual. Act as though I didn't exist and you were leading the easy, trouble-free life that you ought to have.'

I shook my head. Dear me, this was getting a bit thick. Did all people act like this when they were in love, or was it just Edmund?

'Act as if you didn't exist?' cried Ella. 'Edmund, without you my life would be nothing! The sun would not rise and all food would turn to ashes in my mouth!'

Yes. Apparently all people acted like this.

I didn't pay much attention to what happened afterwards. Mostly they were talking about stuff that seemed pretty silly to me, like how much they loved each other, what would happen if they didn't have each other (most of which seemed pretty unrealistic) and then some more about how much they loved each other.

Finally, when I had almost fallen asleep against the tree, the lovers' talk was abruptly interrupted by my aunt's calling from the house.

'Ella! Ella, where are you girl?'

Anxiously, my little sister looked over her shoulder.

'I must go. Farewell, my love,' she whispered.

'Farewell, oh sweet Ella, light of my life.' Edmund hesitated, then plunged on: 'May I ask, something of you, before we depart?'

Instantly I was wide awake! I knew it! I knew now he was going to.... well, he was going to do whatever rakes do when they take advantage of innocent girls! I didn't quite know what that was, though from the insinuations I had read in the papers, it couldn't be anything good.

I stood up, preparing to defend my sister from that foul fiend!

'May I...' he hesitated again. 'May I touch the tips of your sweet fingers to carry with me the feeling of your love? Please, my dearest, just extend a hand to me?'

What? That was all? I wasn't too versed in rakishness, but I had at least expected something improper. He didn't even demand a kiss? He had to be kidding! This fellow was too decent to be real.

'Oh Edmund.' Again my sister had tears in her eyes, and I was amazed to see her shake her head. 'How could I? You know what my dear aunt would say? How could I so lay myself open to her disapproval and that of all my family?'

'But she will not know.'

'But my heart and conscience will.'

I tapped my foot against the ground impatiently. Well now, I was all for morals and stuff – after all, you couldn't have people running around in the streets naked – but this was taking things a bit too far! Throw the fellow a bone, Ella!

Then I realized what I had been thinking and scowled. What was wrong with me? I didn't want them to end up together. Did I? Didn't I?

'Please, my love,' Edmund breathed, leaning closer to the poles separating him from my sister. 'Just the tips of your fingers, just once. I need to know that you are real, not some apparition from the realms of angels or fairies that has come to beguile me with its loveliness.'

'No, Edmund, I can't...'

But apparently, Ella's hand and her mouth weren't quite in agreement about the matter: for while her lips denied him, her small ivory hand reached out, nearing the space between two of the iron poles. Edmund watched it, breathless, and I must admit I was pretty engrossed, too. This was better than the opera. Who knew romance could be this interesting?

Finally Ella's fingers slipped between the iron poles, and Edmund's hands flew forward, taking hold of them.

'Ella,' he breathed.

'Just a swift touch, Edmund, you promised,' she said, still with tears in her eyes.

'And I shall keep my word. One touch.' He led her fingers to his chest, to the left side where his heart was beating, and pressed them to the cloth of his tailcoat.[21] 'Here. Feel it, Ella, for it is yours. Now and forever.'

She gave a shaky nod, not having the words to reply. He let go of her hand, and she withdrew it, turning towards the house and hurrying away like a frightened doe.

~~**~*~*

I wandered back into the house some time later, deep in thought.

Well, well, well. My innocent little sister conducting a secret romance behind everybody's back. In retrospect I felt like slapping myself for not noticing it earlier. I remembered very well that odd stare Edmund Conway had given me

---

[21] Like a suit jacket, only with two long tails of cloth hanging over the wearer's bottom.

last evening as we had met in the street: yet he hadn't really been looking at me, I realized now, but rather at Ella, who had been standing right behind me.

And I had asked Ella what that had been about, and she had lied.

Ella, lying! The little vixen! A grin spread over my face. I suppose I should have been upset about my own sister lying to me, but to be honest I was delighted to discover she had a share of deviousness. It meant we had something more in common than simply the same parents.

Now that I thought about it, I remembered, too, that morning when I had first gone to work, and Ella had immediately jumped to the conclusion that I was going off to see some young man. The joy in her face back then – it was the joy of somebody who had her own personal attachment, who knew what it was to love a man and find joy in it.

I shook my head. Some people really had strange tastes.

Luckily I wouldn't have to deal with any men seeking my hand any time soon. The only man I would have to deal with again soon enough would be Mr Rikkard Ambrose, and for that particular relationship I would rather need my own pair of trousers and nerves like steel than flowery bouquets and compliments.

That night I went to bed with my head full of expectations and designs for the future, both mine and my sister's. I knew they would be very different futures, but as I looked over at the peacefully sleeping form of my little sister, I vowed that we would both be happy and successful even if I had to twist the arm of fate to achieve it!

~~**~*~*

The next morning we were awakened by a vehement knock on the door. Before either Ella or I had the time to rub the sleep out of our eyes, much less call 'enter', the door was thrown open and a mountain of flowers stumbled in, which on closer inspection revealed itself to be our aunt, carrying a cartload of bouquets and trying to conceal a triumphant smile. She did not do a very good job of the latter.

'There! There, you see, Ella?' she exclaimed, dumping her entire load at the foot of my little sister's bed. 'I knew it! I knew your beauty could not fail to capture his attention. You are almost as beautiful as I was at your age.'

Ella blinked, sleepily – then her eyes widened as she beheld the pile of flora at the foot of her bed.

'What are these?' she asked.

'Flowers from Sir Philip, of course. Get dressed, girls. It is time for breakfast.'

She rushed out and we did as she had ordered. However, I dressed with even less care than usual. It was rather superfluous, really. It was a weekday. Soon enough I would be exchanging my dress for a pair of trousers.

I felt a slight tremor run through me at the thought of encountering *him* again. Fear? No, it couldn't be fear. I was never afraid.

We went down and sat down to breakfast. For a change, my aunt was not in a sour mood over my uncle's absence. Her mind was more pleasantly engaged.

'Only look!' she proclaimed, pointing at a particularly extravagant bouquet of large roses. She had ordered Leadfield to place them all around the room in various vases. How she owned that many vases was a mystery to me, since she never would have spared one penny to buy flowers herself. 'Such beautiful flowers. This bodes well, don't you think girls?'

If she expected a reply to that, she was disappointed. Personally I didn't think it boded well at all for Ella. Ella, for her part, didn't seem to think it boded anything at all. Gertrude never spoke unless she had something serious to say, and Anne, Maria and Lisbeth, the only ones probably disposed to agree with Aunt Brank, were too green with envy to open their mouths.

Not bothered by this lack of enthusiasm, my aunt happily prattled on about her expectations while the rest of us consumed our porridge in silence, until finally somebody felt compelled to open her mouth.

'To me,' remarked Gertrude quietly, 'the gentleman's behaviour is not so delightful, my dear aunt. There seems something too rash in his manner. A gentleman must somehow show a lady admiration, that is true, but it is not quite right to be lavishing such expensive attentions on Ella so soon after showing interest in another.' Her gaze strayed to Maria and Anne, not quite sure on which to settle. They both stared daggers at her.

'Nonsense,' replied my aunt, who did not know the meaning of the words 'too rash' and who would happily have seen three or more of her nieces married to Sir Philip Wilkins if English law had but allowed it. 'The more attentions the better. It makes it more likely that we will be able secure him.'

'Secure him?' inquired Ella. 'For what, pray?'

'Is it not time to end your play-acting?' hissed Anne. 'You've gotten what you wanted, you can boast of it now.'

Ella blinked at her, dumbfounded.

Her aunt smiled at her sweetly. 'That's right dear, you go on being modest. It very well becomes you. No need to be so indelicate as to openly discuss the state of affairs until Sir Philip has acted on his resolve.'

That, I was sure, was a clue big enough that not even Ella could overlook it – but I was mistaken. My little sister appeared just as nonplussed as before. With a shake of the head, I turned from her puzzled countenance and concentrated on my porridge. It was an interesting question how, considering she was so modest as to not be able to see why anybody would want to marry her, she had managed to acquire a lover.

I would have to ask her that sometime. Or maybe I would find out soon enough by listening. I had already chosen the book I wanted to read that evening, when I would go into the garden again. Maybe I wouldn't even need it, if the exchange at the fence turned out to be interesting enough.

The doorbell rang. Leadfield went to answer it and returned with another bouquet, for which my aunt indicated he should find a vase. More flowers arrived for Ella during the course of breakfast.

I was a liberal-minded person myself, but even I began to find this a bit excessive. Our house was in a fair way to be paved and wallpapered with flowers.

Now and again, I saw Ella glance at the flowers apprehensively. Every time a new flowery message arrived, she looked more puzzled, but I was sure she would not have been worried about them if not for the words of a certain gentleman.

Edmund Conway. Every time my thoughts turned to Ella now, my thoughts couldn't help but turn to him also. It nettled me that my little sister's happiness depended on a man. Anybody with sense would seek happiness in yourself rather than in another, because yourself you could always rely upon. But then, Ella, for all her loveliness and amiability, had never had much sense.

It was my job to make up for that. And I would see her happy, or that tradesman's brat would rue the day he ever thought to play with my little sister's feelings!

Still deep in thought, I didn't look up as Leadfield came in, wheezing under the weight of the latest flowery message that, no doubt, promised marriage bells.

'Another bouquet from Sir Philip Wilkins for Miss Ella,' he breathed, as expected, and then added: 'And one from another gentleman, for you, Miss Lillian.'

I nearly bit my spoon in half.

RETURN TO THE GAME

'W-what?' I gasped.

'And one from another gentleman, for you, Miss Lillian,' Leadfield repeated stoically.

'I heard you the first time! But when? Why? And in God's name, *from whom?*'

'Err... they arrived just now, Miss. As to why...' the old butler blushed a little. 'Well, I couldn't say. And from whom... I think I saw a card with the bouquet, but I did not read it.'

Frantically I sprang up and rushed to Leadfield, desperate to know the name of my hidden enemy. I ripped the card out of the bouquet, unfolded it and read:

'In memory of the first ball where we did NOT dance together. I am looking forward to changing that soon.

Lieutenant Ellingham.'

Only when silence spread over the room did I realize that I had read aloud. The gazes of my entire family turned to me, and I wished heartily that I could sink into the floor and disappear.

'Who is Lieutenant Ellingham?' asked Gertrude.

'He wanted to dance with you?' asked Maria.

'Is he a madman?' asked Anne.

'What does he mean, "the first ball where you did NOT dance together"?' asked Lisbeth.

'He's an officer,' my aunt interrupted the barrage of questions, twirling her spoon thoughtfully. 'You could do a lot worse, Lillian. Better secure him before he changes his mind. Oh yes, you'd better hurry, before he actually gets to know you.'

I didn't really hear any of them. I was still in shock. Lieutenant Ellingham? *Lieutenant Ellingham?* He wished to make an offer to me? To seek my hand? It seemed hardly creditable.

Not that I did not believe him capable of flattering himself into the belief I might be attracted to him. From what I had seen so far, he could flatter himself into believing that the sky was brown and the earth blue. But what in the name of Jesus and all his Apostles could make *him* attracted to *me*? I had done my very best to be as ghastly to him as humanly possible!

I looked down at the card again, hoping that maybe it might have disappeared or changed its message. But there it was still, like a massive viper just waiting to bite me. Maybe it was merely a joke. Maybe he wouldn't show up here after all. Yes, that had to be it. He probably was having fun with his drinking buddies from the regiment, imagining my face at this very moment.

Resolutely, I crumpled the card and dumped it into my empty porridge bowl.

'You shouldn't have done that,' remarked Maria sweetly. 'In your place, I would have framed it and hung it on the wall – because of the scarcity value, you know.'

Not deigning to give her a reply, I rushed out of the room and into the garden. I did not have the time for either her or the oh-so-funny Lieutenant Ellingham at the moment. It was only an hour till nine o'clock and I needed to get changed.

If I remembered correctly, Mr Ambrose didn't tolerate tardiness.

~~**~*~*

Wisely I had stashed the clothes I had borrowed from my uncle in the garden shed. Nobody ever came in there, so I changed in the dusty little wooden shack without fear of discovery. I was quite glad, in fact, that I wasn't putting on the baggy, striped trousers and oversized jacket in my room: there, I couldn't have helped looking in the mirror. Oh, how I was looking forward to receiving my first pay cheque and buying clothes in which I could pass for an actual gentleman, not just a scarecrow wearing rags three sizes too big for her. Or him. Depending on your point of view.

Completely attired, I left the garden through the little back door in the wall. This time I had ample time to walk, which was fortunate since I most certainly did not have ample money to pay for another cab ride. I reached Empire House by about a quarter before nine. In the entrance hall, which was as busy as ever, Sallow-face at the front desk let me pass without comment. He had accepted me, apparently. Why couldn't his master do the same?

Maybe because he's an arrogant bastard. Or maybe because he knows you're a girl. Most probably both.

But I would be damned if I put up with this any longer! Oh no. I'd force him to look at me, to accept me, to work with me as he would with any man!

94

Smiling to myself, I began to ascend the stairs. I knew exactly what I had to do. Since he always locked the door connecting our offices, I would take another route and march in through the main door. Simple. Mr Stone wouldn't dare stop me, I'm sure. He wasn't as tough as Sallow-face. And then I would give Mr Rikkard Ambrose a piece of my mind!

My brilliant plan was smashed into ruins, however, as soon as I stepped into the long hallway at the top of the stairs. Everything was exactly as it should be – Mr Stone was behind his desk, all the doors were closed, the stone walls were still made of bare stone, and the floors were still horizontal. Yes, everything was as it was supposed to be – except for the massive figure towering behind Mr Stone, right in front of Mr Ambrose's office door.

The mountainous dark-skinned man wouldn't have needed to wear his turban or sabre for me to recognize him on the spot; I remembered him all too well. Nevertheless, Karim's accessories looked impressive. Considerably more impressive than the top hat I had with me.

Swallowing my apprehension, I walked down the hall.

'Good Morning, Mr Stone,' I said.

'Good Morning, Mr Linton.'

I stepped past his desk and tried to move towards the office door. Karim did not budge an inch.

'Excuse me, you're standing in my way,' I said.

'Yes,' he growled. He wasn't looking at me, but staring straight ahead, which meant he was focusing on a point some five inches above my top hat. He really was big. Too big.

'Well, would you mind getting out of the way?' I persisted, trying to shove past him towards the door.

'Yes.'

'But I have to speak to Mr Ambrose.'

'Yes?'

'Yes, I do. So will you let me into the office?'

'No.'

'Why not?'

At last he seemed to feel that my question merited more than a single syllable. Still staring straight ahead, he proclaimed: 'Mr Ambrose is busy.'

'With what?'

'With business.'

'Well, thank you very much for that informative answer! When will he be finished, do you think?'

'Mr Ambrose is busy for a long time.'

'He has been like this all day,' Mr Stone whispered when I turned away angrily. 'I must say I am quite perturbed. Karim is Mr Ambrose's man for... special tasks. You know, um... dangerous matters?"

He looked around anxiously as if waiting for an assassin to spring from the shadows.

'He has never been posted here yet, Mr Linton. I am afraid that Mr Ambrose perceives some terrible threat to his person.'

Oh yes, a very terrible threat, I thought, staring venomously at the bearded figure in front of the door. *A girl who doesn't want to be called 'Mister' all day! Mr Ambrose's man for special tasks indeed!*

'Well, I'll just have to talk to him later then,' I said to Mr Stone, trying to rein in my stormy temper. 'I'd better get into my office and start working.'

'Oh yes, your work!' Mr Stone slapped his forehead. 'I almost forgot. These arrived for Mr Ambrose early this morning.'

And he held out a bunch of letters. My brow furrowed in thought. Somewhere I had heard of this. Secretaries took care of their employer's correspondence, didn't they? But what exactly did they do with the letters? Read them? Answer them? Eat them for breakfast?

'Um... what am I supposed do with them?' I asked.

If Mr Stone found the question strange, he didn't let on.

'You are to separate the important from the unimportant, and only the former is to be given to Mr Ambrose.'

Taking the letters, I inquired: 'And how am I to know what Mr Ambrose considers important?'

He gave me a little smile. 'The answer to that question will determine how long you keep your job here. Good luck.'

With that he sat down and returned to his own work. I strode over to the door that lead to the room I still had difficulty thinking of as 'my office'. But it was. I had an office! Me! Sweet little me! Now all I had to do was keep it...

I laid the ominous pile of letters on my yes – yes, *my* desk! – and started looking through them.

There was a stack of invitations to various social events. Hmm. I looked at the firmly closed and bolted door connecting my office with that of my employer. Something told me that Mr Ambrose wasn't a very social person. Plus, the invitations seemed to be issued by Lady Metcalf and her circle of friends. Apparently, the fine lady was not so disgusted by Mr Ambrose's working for a living that she didn't want him at her parties and dancing with her daughters.

I smiled and, with a great deal of relish, crumpled up those letters and chucked them into the bin.

Next there were charity requests. I wasn't sure about those, but put them on the pile to go to his office, just in case. It couldn't hurt to be charitable, right?

Then there were a few letters which, on being opened, revealed themselves to be about business. I didn't understand above one word in ten they said, but it sounded important so I put them on the pile, too.

Last but not least came a letter like no other: It was no invitation. It wasn't advertising. And it sure as hell wasn't business. That was pretty obvious from the fact that it came in a pink, strongly scented envelope.

'What the...'

I almost broke out laughing when I smelled the perfume! Mr Ambrose had a lady friend? A secret love, maybe? But then I saw the address of the sender and her name. In curly, old-fashioned writing was written:

Samantha Genevieve Ambrose

Ambrose? A relative? A sister, maybe? I couldn't suppress a snort of laughter at that. To be honest, it was even harder to imagine Mr Ambrose as a family man than as a lover.

Then I noticed something printed next to the address of the sender and frowned.

'Now what is *this* doing here...?' I muttered leaning closer.

If the letter came from Mr Ambrose's family, the family of a simple, if rich, citizen, how did there come to be a coat of arms stamped on the envelope?

Quite an elaborate coat of arms, too. I didn't know much about the nobility, but I knew enough to realize that a crest like this didn't come from a simple knighthood. The coat of arms had the look of centuries on it: the rose in the upper right and the lion in the lower left corner reminded me of the little I had remembered of my lessons in English history.

In a flash, I suddenly remembered what one of the ladies at the ball had said... something about a noble family Ambrose in the North. An Earl's family.

'I'll be damned!'

But no... that couldn't be. It just couldn't be Mr Ambrose's family, could it? If he were an earl's son, he wouldn't be calling himself 'Mister' Ambrose. He would have the right to call himself Baron or Lord Somethingorother.

Curious. Very curious indeed.

And who was this lady? *Samantha?*

With a slight feeling of regret at letting go of the mystery, I placed the pink letter back on the table. For just a moment I considered throwing it away. It was obviously full of soppy romantic nonsense – nothing important, in my opinion. Yet Mr Ambrose might feel differently about the matter.

When I rose with all the letters in my hand, I realized for the first time that now was my chance to finally see him again! The thick pile of letters couldn't fit under the door, so he had to open it. Triumphantly I marched over to the door and raised my hand to knock – only to discover that in my absence, a letter slot had been installed in the middle of the thick wooden door.

Angrily, I pushed the letters through and heard them land on some kind of table. 'Here,' I called. 'I hope you choke on them!'

Shortly afterwards, the slot opened again and several of the letters fell onto the floor with a resounding 'thwack!' When I went over and picked them up, I saw that it was the charity requests and the letter from Samantha Genevieve – the latter hadn't even been opened.

A note was fastened to the top letter:

Mr Linton,

Did Mr Stone not express himself clearly? Only send those letters to me which are of interest to me.

I stared blankly at the note. Was he serious? He hadn't even bothered to open the pink letter, so clearly personal. Neither had he bothered to sign his message to me, this time – but really there was no need. There was only one person in the entire British Empire who could write like this.

Angrily I stomped over to my desk, grabbed one of the message papers and a pen and began scribbling.

Charity is important! Is the improvement of the lives of the poor of no interest to you?
The reply came almost instantly.
Not if by so doing they become richer and I poorer.
'Gah!'
Grinding my teeth, I took a look around the office: bare stone walls, no ornaments, no carpets, no nothing. Of course! He was mean with money. I should have guessed from the way he dressed – all in simple black without one piece of colourful brocade or silk on his waistcoat. He practically had the word 'SKINFLINT' printed on his forehead. In capitals.

Too bad he didn't look like a skinflint. He should be old and ugly and skinny, like my aunt, not some reincarnation of Adonis in granite. That would make working for him so much easier!

But what about the personal letter? Taking that out of the pile, I examined it closely. It really hadn't been opened. Who was it from? What was it about? Why hadn't it been opened? My fingers hesitated over the next piece of message paper. I would have loved to ask but didn't dare. I didn't want to get fired on my second day at work.

So instead I wrote:
Dear Mr Ambrose,
Be assured that you shall receive no further requests to do good deeds from me.
Yours Sincerely
MISS Lilly Linton
The reply wasn't long in coming.
Mr Linton,
It is not doing good deeds that I object to, it is the principle of charity. I do not give something for nothing. Remember that, Mr Linton.
Rikkard Ambrose
Dear God, was he threatening me?
Yes, probably.
A tingle went down my spine. It felt dangerous, dark and... exciting?
Then another message popped out of the hole in the wall.
Mr Linton,
Bring me file 38XI199.
Rikkard Ambrose
Spiffing. Here we go again.

~~**~*~*

Back and forth, back and forth I went the whole day, like a busy little ant carrying bits of leaves to the hill – only that I carried darn heavy files instead of leaves. Oh, and there also was the fact that ants could lift five times their body weight and that they couldn't get chucked out of the anthill for not working fast enough.

Lucky ants.

I, for my part, heard a fresh *plink* that announced another demand for a file every five minutes. Apparently Mr Ambrose was still determined to break my resolution and make me give him some excuse for firing me. Ha! That fellow didn't know me from Adam!

Or rather Eve, since I was a girl.

Some part of me wondered what he did with all those files. Surely, a secretary's duties consisted of more than carrying files? Having letters dictated, for example.

'Oh, but for that he'd have to actually speak to me,' I muttered, grabbing another box of files from the shelves. 'And he couldn't do that, now could he! Blast him!'

While I slaved away, my determination grew. I would keep this job. Moreover, I would make him accept me as a girl, and then I could come to work in my own clothes and stop wearing this stupid top hat! But how to make him accept me?

'I have to catch him,' I growled, grabbing the next box and imagining that it was Mr Ambrose's stiff neck. 'I have to grab him and simply make him see!'

Yesterday, I hadn't been able to get to him in time, and he had escaped. Today, he had placed his watchdog in front of the door – but he would have to come out eventually. To prevent him slipping away like last time, I cracked my office door open and kept an ear out for any steps moving out there.

As the day progressed, I got more and more excited. The thought of seeing him again – and of giving him a whopping big piece of my mind – was thrilling. I hadn't set eyes on him since the day he not-so-graciously accepted me into his service, and I was looking forward to the encounter very much. Hm... Did punching your employer count as grounds for dismissal?

Too bad I didn't have my parasol with me.

Some time around twelve o'clock, the requests for files suddenly stopped.

Ah! He was preparing to leave. Now he had to be coming soon. I sidled up to the door in anticipation.

Steps approached my door. What? Was he coming to see me? No, the steps didn't sound like him. Too slow, too timid. There was a knock on my door and Mr Stone's voice called: 'Mr Linton? May I come in?'

'Please do,' I said, stepping back, frowning.

Mr Stone entered with a slightly puzzled expression on his face. 'I am to inform you,' he said, 'that Mr Ambrose has left again and that you can finish your day early, too, if you want to.'

'What?!'

'Yes, the strangest matter indeed. He never leaves early normally, and now twice in a row? And this time he even went down the back staircase that is normally never used. I am beginning to fear for our master's safety.'

'You are, are you?' I grabbed my top hat off the desk and slammed it on my head with probably a bit too much force. 'Well, you're right to be!'

Mr Stone paled. 'So you think, too, that his life is in danger? That there is someone after him?'

'You bet there is,' I growled and marched out of the room, slamming the door behind me.

Oh that... I couldn't even think of a bad enough word for him! The next time I would get my hands on him, I would take one of those little message containers with the words 'I AM FEMALE' in it and stuff it down his throat!

~~**~*~*

I went home to lunch, but since I didn't have the wherewithal to cope with my aunt's incessant questions about Lieutenant Ellingham, I made my disappearance as soon as possible. I decided to go the King's Library to look a few things up. Maybe I'd find an interesting book on China, or a Colonial adventure story, or...

All right, I admit it. I was going to look up Rikkard Ambrose. So what? Was it a crime that I wanted to find out a bit more about the man I worked for? It was only natural that I would like to discover a few more things about him. It might help me avoid such blunders as the one with the charity requests. Maybe I'd discover that he kept a poodle, or was allergic to strawberries, or some other interesting fact.

Maybe I'd even find out whether he was, as I was beginning to suspect, more than a simple citizen. Books and newspapers could hold all sorts of interesting information.

Fortunately, unlike riding, shooting and pretty much anything else that I thought might be interesting to do in life, reading was not solely the domain of men. Nobody gave me a second glance as I walked along the gallery of the King's Library, between the mile-high shelves and imposing busts of historical personalities.

In passing, I sent up a glare at the busts. 'Of course you're all men,' I muttered, gesturing up at them threateningly. 'It didn't occur to anyone to put a bust of Queen Elisabeth or Mary Astell up there, did it? Darn chauvinist sculptors!'

An elderly gentleman passing in the opposite direction stopped when he saw me shaking my fist at the statues, and blinked as if he wasn't sure he was seeing right. I quickly hurried on to the newspaper section.

Shortly afterwards I stood in front of a row of shelves, examining the enormous books which contained the *Times* of the last few decades. Where to start? From the dates on the file boxes I knew his history went back quite some time. So I pretty randomly picked one of the massive volumes. With effort, I managed to get it down from the shelf and transported it to a table next to a bust of Julius Caesar.

'Hello there, fellow,' I said, petting Caesar on his head. 'Let's see what we have on Mr Ambrose, shall we?'

~~**~*~*

Three hours and seven volumes later, I gave up.

He was everywhere: always on the edge of things, never quite part of society yet always in the middle because all of society seemed to orientate itself around him. Mr Ambrose had been spotted near the races – but did he bet on a horse? No! Mr Ambrose had been seen talking with business partners outside the theatre. But did he go in? Of course not! Once he had been spotted at the opera but had left before the performance ended.

What did he do in his free time?

Where was his family?

What nefarious activities had he engaged in to amass his enormous fortune?

There were no articles about his past, not even the indication that at some point he might have given an interview. Nowhere in the dozens of papers I leafed through did I find a single answer to my questions. But then again – why was I so anxious to find out? What business of mine was it how he had gotten his money? Why did I so desperately want to know?

Deep down I knew why. With a shiver I remembered his words, almost a threat, on that day he had sat opposite me in his office, his dark eyes burning holes into my head:

I need a man. A man, Miss Linton. Not a girl who will run off screaming at the things she will see where my business takes me.

By that, I was sure, he had meant more than seeing the inside of file boxes.

I wanted him to accept me as his secretary. As his *female* secretary, however scandalous other people would consider that. Yet I was also slightly afraid of what would happen if he did. What would he do if I really managed to convince him to let me work for him for real? Or more importantly, what would I have to do?

~~**~*~*

When I got home, my aunt was waiting and ready for battle, glaring at me like an emaciated Valkyrie. I was half expecting her to be holding a sharp spear and riding an eight-legged horse.

'Where were you?' she demanded.

'I was in the park walking, showing off my charms to the young men there,' I lied brightly. 'Just in case I might happen to come across Lieutenant Ellingham.'

'Oh.' My aunt's thin lips relaxed a tiny little bit. 'Really? Well... good. That's very good.'

'I shall do that often now, if it is all right with you, Aunt,' I continued quickly, determined to exploit this sudden inspiration to the limits. Darn it! Why hadn't I thought of this before? 'After all, now that I have been introduced into society, there are hundreds of men I could meet. Thousands, in fact. And the more I meet....'

'You're quite right.' My aunt came up to me. For a moment I was worried that she might want to hug me, which would have been slightly awkward because (a) we were both wearing hoop skirts and (b) I hated her guts, skeleton and strict, black boots. But instead, she merely laid a hand on my arm. It was enough for me to want to run screaming and take a bath in the Thames. 'I'm very happy you've finally started behaving like a lady, Lilly. I knew you would see sense some day.'

I thanked her like a proper little lady and then hurried off. Not towards the Thames for a bath, because I knew perfectly well that it was full of dirty toilet paper. Instead, I directed my steps towards the garden.

Why the garden, you may ask?

Simple. Over all the questions about Mr Ambrose that were plaguing my poor, chocolate-deprived brain, I had not forgotten my sister and her problems. When I had entered the house, the sun had just been about to set. I knew perfectly well what that meant.

Ella and Edmund would soon have their nocturnal rendezvous in the garden. So I went out there and this time didn't even stop to take a book with me. Tonight, I was quite sure, I wouldn't need literature to take my mind off things. Judging from the number of flowers that had arrived in my absence, the evening's conversation would provide more than enough distraction.

As soon as the moon rose over the streets of London, I heard a rustle from the door and, through the bushes behind which I had concealed myself again, saw Ella hurrying past. Only a moment later, Edmund appeared on the other side of the fence.

'Ella, my love,' he called in a damnably audible whisper. 'Oh, how it fills my heart to see you!'

'And mine,' sighed Ella. Then she hesitated. 'I mean my heart is filled with joy from seeing you, not from seeing myself. That would be silly. I see myself every morning in the mirror.' She brightened. 'But now you are here!' She exclaimed. 'I have been waiting all day to see you!'

'Your words make my soul sing, Ella. Please, step closer, into the moonlight, so I may behold your lovely face.'

'I will. But first... first I have to tell you something, Edmund.'

'What?' he asked, his breath catching.

'It is the strangest thing,' Ella muttered. 'I would not even mention such a strange, trivial occurrence if not for your words yesterday, but...'

'But what? My words yesterday? What words?' Now I could hear a distinct note of anxiety in Edmund's voice.

It must have shown on his face, too, because Ella smiled at him hesitantly, caught off guard by his expression. 'Well... what you said about the flowers. You remember? You told me to tell you if Sir Philip sent me any more flowers.'

I glanced at the young man. Now the expression on his face wasn't simply anxious anymore. It was panicked.

'Yes, and? Has he sent you another bouquet?'

'One?' Ella giggled. 'No, not one. I tell you, the man must be very eccentric, I cannot otherwise account for his behaviour. He sent me *dozens* of bouquets. I had no idea there were that many flowers to buy in the whole city of London. I...' She broke off when she saw Edmund's face.

'Edmund? Edmund, what is wrong? What ails you?'

'My heart is breaking,' he answered tonelessly, staring into the distance with empty eyes. 'That is what ails me. It is as I thought. I am doomed.'

I leaned forward, resting my head on my knees. This was good. Better than the theatre, except that I couldn't throw peanuts at the actors. I doubt Ella would have appreciated that.

'What is the matter?' My little sister wrung her hands in sudden desperation. 'Oh Edmund, reveal to me this terrible secret you are carrying! What is it about those flowers that makes you fear them like death itself?'

'Worse than death,' he mutters. 'A thousand deaths and the tortures of hell.'

Dear me! That fellow had definitely read too many romantic novels. I considered interrupting and telling him he was overdoing it.

But then, on second thoughts, maybe I'd rather not.

'Tell me, Edmund! Tell me, what are they?'

'The flowers are a sign of affection,' said Edmund, his voice as hollow as a drainpipe through which all his hopes were flooding away. 'Sir Philip wishes to seek your hand in marriage.'

Ella stiffened. All colour drained from her face. I covered my eyes with my hand and let it slip down my face. Good God in heaven, she was actually surprised.

'No!'

'Yes, he does.'

'No, Edmund...'

'And who can blame him?' he continued. 'You are indeed a fair maiden, Miss Linton. Every gentleman in England should be seeking your hand. You...' his voice broke, and after a moment he continued: 'You are far too good and beautiful for common folk.'

'Edmund! What are you saying?' She cried out.

'I am saying goodbye, Miss Linton.'

'Goodbye? Edmund, why do you torture me so? And why so distant? Why call me *Miss Linton*?'

'You are right,' he said in the same hollow voice. 'I should call you Lady Wilkins. For that is who you soon shall be.'

Apparently, I had been wrong before: Ella had still some colour left to drain from her face. It vanished at Edmund's words, plummeting towards the earth's core.

Suddenly not at all amused by the scene, I sat up straight, staring whole arsenals of daggers at Edmund.

What was that bastard doing? Was he so heartless that he could just stand there and hurt my little sister? He should be pulling her into his arms and telling her all would be all right! After climbing over the fence, that is.

'I will never marry Sir Philip,' Ella proclaimed. 'Never!'

'But why not?' Edmund asked, his voice still as hollow and dead as an entire graveyard. 'Is he not a most eligible match?'

'I do not care how eligible he is,' sniffled Ella, taking two rapid steps towards the fence. Edmund stepped back hastily as she stuck her hand through the poles, trying to reach him. 'I... I...'

'Yes? You?' he inquired and his voice wasn't quite as dead as before.

'I love you, Edmund.'

'Ah. A platonic love, surely, since you are soon to be married?'

'No! A lover's love, Edmund. If I could, I would be thine, to have and to hold.'

'Oh Ella! Come into my arms!'

What the heck? Just ten seconds ago he was egging her on to marry somebody else, and now he wanted them to snuggle? If all lovers behaved like this, they should be summarily committed to lunatic asylums!

Surely, Ella would be too proud and self-respecting to throw herself at a man who had just scorned her?

'Oh, Edmund, my love!'

No, apparently she wasn't.

I watched in mingled horror and fascination as she indeed threw herself into his arms, or at least as well as she could with the fence in the way. I wondered how long it was going to take one of them to think of the ladder leaning against the garden shed. Probably a good long time still.

Anyway, both of them seemed to be much too honourable to just throw themselves at each other. I had expected at least some action and was a tiny bit disappointed when they only took hold of each other's hands and stared into each other's eyes. I had seen both of their pairs of eyes before. They weren't *that* interesting.

'So you do not simply feel friendship for me?' Edmund demanded, his voice deep with emotion. 'There is more?'

A little colour returned to Ella's cheeks. 'You know there is.'

'Yes, but the delight of hearing you say it...' He closed his eyes for a moment, sighing blissfully. 'There is no song of angels that is sweeter to my ears.'

Yes. He *really* read too many romance novels.

My little sister, not in the least repelled by his sappiness, took one of his hands and lightly pressed it to her cheek. Now we were getting somewhere!

'I love you, Edmund.'

When Edmund opened his eyes again, they looked a little more interesting than before. Certainly more intense.

'As I love you, Ella, my heart's delight.'

'Oh Edmund. You do not know how long I have been waiting for you to say these words to me.'

'They have lain ready on my tongue forever.'

He pressed her hands again.

'So you will be mine?'

Suddenly, the colour left Ella's cheeks again. The radiant smile that had lit up her features until a moment ago became laced with sadness.

'Edmund, I...'

'What? What is this? You said you loved me!'

'I do! I do! But...'

Now there again were tears in Ella's eyes. She didn't seem to be able to continue. So Edmund spoke for her, slowly and gravely:

'But the objections to our love which you so conscientiously explained to me before, still stand. Nothing has changed. The fact that we love each other does not mean that we can be together.'

Ella gave a shaky little nod.

'What if you told your aunt that you did not love Sir Philip?'

'I? Defy my dear, dear aunt? Oh please!' She clasped her hands in supplication. 'Please don't even make me think of such a thing!'

'Then what do we do?' he asked, sounding lost.

'I don't know!'

Behind the bushes, I bit my lower lip, deep in thought. Well, I didn't know either. But I'd be damned if that was going to stop me from doing something! At least I had plenty of time on my hands. My new job with Mr Ambrose was not very demanding. He didn't seem to want anything from me at all.

Had I only known then how wrong I was about that.

THE DISCOVERY

The next day I noticed that I was quite distracted by Ella's troubles. Do you want to know how I noticed? It wasn't that I forgot to go to work, oh no. I forgot to change before going to work and almost walked up to Mr Stone's desk in a long dress and hoop skirt, announcing myself as 'Mr Linton'.

That would have been a real scandal for Mr Ambrose to worry about!

I noticed my wrong attire just in time and had to hurry back and change in a wild frenzy. By the time I had run back to Empire House it was already nine o'clock. I hurried up the stairs and into my office, only giving Mr Stone a brief nod in passing. My desperate lungs lacked the air for a proper greeting. Wheezing, I collapsed onto my chair and let my head fall onto the table.

Just then, a message container flew out of the tube with a quiet *plink*. With the one hand I felt capable of moving I picked it up, opened it and unrolled the message. My eyes focused on the words:

Mr Linton

You are 1 minute and 37 seconds late. If that occurs again, you can consider yourself dismissed.

Rikkard Ambrose

This chap really knew how to give you a warm welcome. For a moment I considered telling him about my sister's romantic troubles, to make an excuse. But then I decided against it. It would be like trying to explain dancing the polka to a rock in the desert. He just wouldn't get it.

Next I considered going over there and skinning him alive. But that might not be so great an idea either. First of all, it might get me sacked. Secondly, I couldn't muster the energy to get up. And thirdly, the blasted door was still locked anyway!

A *plink* announced the arrival of the next message.

It appeared that I had to get up, whether I had the energy or not! The message read:

Mr Linton,

Fetch file S39XX300

Rikkard Ambrose.

Spiffing! Simply Spiffing! Here we go again. Rising, I started towards the rows of shelves. But then I hesitated.

Wait just a moment... file S39XX300?

I frowned. The numbering systems for the files didn't start with letters, did it? It always started with numbers proclaiming the years of the file's origin. The 39 in the name probably stood for 1839, this very year, but 'S'? What did that stand for? Snoop? Saucy? Silly?

I went looking under 39 because I didn't know what else to do. Ten minutes later, I had three open boxes standing before me and a volcano rumbling somewhere inside me.

Dear Mr Ambrose
There is no file S39XX300. I cannot find it.
Yours sincerely
Miss Lilly Linton

The reply came immediately.

Mr Linton,
There IS a file S39XX300 Have you looked in the safe?
Rikkard Ambrose.

What the heck?

Dearest Mr Ambrose,
I did not know there was a safe here. Might I inquire why you neglected to tell me this?
Yours always
Miss Lilly Linton

Angrily I shoved the message into the tube and waited. Only half a minute later, a *plink* announced the answer.

Mr Linton,
You might indeed enquire. It is because I expect my employees be capable of independent thought. The 'S' stands for safe. If that is too difficult for you to comprehend, then maybe you should look for another post. One more fitted to your limited intellectual capabilities.
Rikkard Ambrose

The arrogant.... 'limited intellectual capabilities'? Gah! I didn't even know what names to call him! The newspaper articles about women's insufficient brain size and all the other arguments against our working and voting came to mind. Oh how I would have loved to skin that man alive. And then maybe roast him slowly over an open fire...

Dear Mr Ambrose,
I will go looking for the safe directly. Do not fear – even my limited mental capacity should be sufficient to find a big metal box.
Yours always (Which means you're not getting rid of me!)
Miss Lilly Linton

I stood up. I went looking. I found the safe. It took me only five minutes and then I was back at my desk – still without file S39XX300, for a very simple reason. Fuming, I grabbed a message slip from the bowl and scrawled four simple words on it.

The safe is locked!

Had he been waiting for me to write that? Because the reply came almost instantly.

Mr Linton,

It is locked to keep things safe. That is why it is called a safe.

Rikkard Ambrose

Gah! Was this man *trying* to drive me crazy? Well... probably. To hell with him!

Dear Mr Ambrose,

I know it what a safe is, thank you very much. And I know it is locked, because I have tried to open it and not succeeded, as mentioned before. WHERE IS THE KEY?

Yours Sincerely

Miss Lilly Linton

I pushed the message into the tube with maybe a bit more force than necessary and pulled the lever. His answer came as quick as ever.

Mr Linton,

Writing in capitals is not as quick or efficient as writing in normal letters. Please refrain from such time-wasting habits while in my employ. The key I have already pushed under the door, as any observant employee would have noticed.

Rikkard Ambrose

Muttering some not very polite things about Mr Ambrose, I went over to the door and fetched the key. Then I returned to the back of the room where, in a small niche I hadn't noticed before today, a big, black metal door had been inserted into the wall, with the word 'Ambrose' written in simple steel letters at the top. I wondered for a moment why he would feel the need to write his name on his own safe. Did he have that bad a memory? Then I realized that it was probably the name of the manufacturer. So he made safes, did he? What else did he do?

Pushing the thought aside and the key into the lock, I turned it and opened the door. It went smoothly and without even squeaking. Sleek and impenetrable, just like its maker.

I had expected a metal container of maybe about three square feet to lie beyond. Instead I found myself facing the gloom of an enormous steel room, larger than my office, with scores of objects on the shelves that lined the walls.

There was everything from the mundane file box to strange rocks, painted wooden idols and large scrolls of parchment that looked as though they had already lived through several centuries. What the hell were these? If Mr Ambrose was an industrialist as the duchess had suggested, where had he gotten these from? They didn't look like anything coming out of a factory.

On the contrary – they spoke of distance, danger, mystery.

Resisting my mighty urge to go and investigate, I turned towards the file boxes and examined their numbers, one by one. There was an S39XX299 and an

S39XX301 – but no S39XX300. What was he playing at? Did he do that on purpose?

I marched back to my desk and composed a fitting message. I even managed not to put any swear words in.

Dear Mr Ambrose,
There is no box S39XX300.
Yours Sincerely
Miss Lilly Linton

The message container returned. Pulling it open, I read:

Mr Linton,
I told you to look in the safe.
Rikkard Ambrose

This was getting to be a bit too much!

Dear Mr Ambrose,
I did look in the safe. It is not there. If you cannot understand my written messages, I would offer you to read my lips. But unfortunately that is not possible since the door to your office is still locked. So let me say it in plain English once again: There is no box S39XX300 in the safe.
Yours Sincerely
Lilly Linton

When his reply came, the letters were a bit different. Not a hasty scrawl, no – they were as clear and legible as always. But one could be led to think that he had pressed the pen slightly harder on the paper as he scratched those words. Wait... He had the gall to be getting angry? *He?*

Mr Linton,
If by this subterfuge you think you can make me open my door so you can air your grievances, you are very much mistaken. Bring me file box S39XX300 or you can consider yourself dismissed.
Rikkard Ambrose

The thunderclouds of my temper began to gather, reading those words. But simultaneously I felt a tingling sensation run down my spine. This box seemed to be pretty important – and it wasn't where it was supposed to be. What was going on?

Led by this strange feeling, my reply to Mr Ambrose was considerably more conciliatory than it ordinarily would have been.

Dear Mr Ambrose,
Whatever you may think of my intelligence, it is not so slight as to risk my future merely to get a look at your profile. You are not that nice-looking. The box in question is really not here.
Miss Lilly Linton

My heart rate picked up as I pushed the message container into the tube. Would he believe me or just fire me? Did the box he wanted even exist, or was it just an excuse to get rid of me?

I looked around the bare room and felt a lump rising in my throat. Although I didn't want to admit it, I had already become accustomed to the stark surroundings, accustomed to the idea that this place was mine, my own way to freedom. What would I do if I lost it?

Slowly I pulled the lever, and my message disappeared into the tube.

The answer came not long after. I opened and unrolled it – and my eyes widened. If the situation hadn't been so serious, the reply would have made me laugh!

Mr Linton,

Do you give me your word of honour as a gentlema- as a lad- as an honourable person that you are speaking the truth?

Rikkard Ambrose.

Somehow I couldn't keep a slight grin from my face as I wrote the reply.

Dear Mr Ambrose,

I give you my word of honour as a lady who wears trousers that there is indeed no box of the aforementioned number/name in your safe.

Miss Lilly Linton

There was no reply. Nothing. For two entire minutes I sat there and waited, but nothing came. I had almost given up waiting and was chastising myself for my silly fancies. The box probably wasn't important at all. It was probably some old box he had mistakenly thrown away. That had to be all.

I had almost convinced myself of that explanation.

Then I heard the rustle of keys from the other side of the room. My head snapped up just in time to see the connecting door to Mr Ambrose's office swing open.

~~*~**~*~*

The moment I saw him I knew I had been wrong. Wrong about two things, to be exact:

Firstly, the missing file box *was* important.

And secondly, seeing his profile *might* actually be worth losing your job over.

There he stood: a lean figure, his arms crossed tightly in front of his chest, revealing taut muscles in his upper arms. In his black tailcoat, trousers and shirt he looked like some menacing manifestation of the night, come to banish the day before it was time. The fact that he had a face that seemed to have been cut from a mountain by some ancient master didn't hurt either. I was paralysed in my chair – not with fear exactly. No, certainly not! I would never be afraid! Rather with... oh, I didn't know! Whatever it was, I had to get a grip, and fast!

'Mr Linton.' His voice was just as I remembered it. Cold and clipped. He nodded at me, but before I could even open my mouth or think of a reply, he had marched past me. I stared after him until he vanished between the shelves at the other end of my office.

Mister Linton? *Mister* Linton? So he was still going to keep that up, even now that he was forced to talk to me again?

109

My paralysis suddenly lifted, and I jumped to my feet. I'd show him! I'd show that son of a bachelor!

With three quick steps I was between the shelves. There was no sign of him there, but the door to the safe still stood open. He was in there.

For one moment I was tempted to shove the door closed and lock it – but no. If I ever did choke him, I wanted my hands around his throat. Letting him suffocate in an airtight safe was much too impersonal.

Taking a deep, relaxing breath, I stepped in after him – and stopped in my tracks.

The inside of the safe room was a mess. Files were scattered everywhere on the floor. Standing before the shelves containing the boxes, Mr Ambrose was thoroughly busy dismantling and examining every part of every file box he could find, and once he was done with them, throwing them over his shoulder onto the floor. He was like a ravenous animal burrowing through the carcass of a deer. The only difference was: while a ravenous animal might have found what it needed to still its hunger in a carcass, he appeared to come up blank.

'It must be here,' he muttered. 'It must be!'

'What must be here?' I asked. He completely ignored me. By Jove,[22] what a surprise!

Why did I even bother to ask? I knew what he was looking for, didn't I? File S39XX300. But what was so bloody important about that file?

'It must be here. It must be.' He didn't say it angrily as such – but the determination in his words was like iron. Hundreds of files, which before had been in impeccable order, now lay scattered all over the metal floor of the safe, and still he continued his wild hunt.

I stood mute at the door and watched him. Even had I known how to help, I wouldn't have dared get in his way. It took him about half an hour to turn the orderly file boxes into a monumental mess. Finally, the very last file was in his hand. He looked at the number and let it drop to the floor with a clatter.

He stood like that for a moment, rock-still.

Then he whirled around. The look in his dark eyes made me retreat a step.

'You!' he hissed, coldly. He didn't say anything more. He didn't need to. I knew it was an accusation. My breathing sped up.

Dear God! He suspected me of stealing the file! *Me! Sweet little me!*

What was he going to do? Call the police? Looking into his eyes, somehow I doubted that. I remembered Karim and the huge sabre, and my heart sped up some more.

'Where is it?' he asked.

'Th-the file? I d-don't know.'

In two steps, he was in front of me. Hell's whiskers! I hadn't noticed how tall he was before. He was towering over me.

Why the hell was I so nervous? What could he do to me, anyway?

---

[22] 'By Jove' is a British English expression of surprise. Jove was an alternative name for the ancient Greek god Jupiter. Why exactly the British Victorians, all good Christians, used the name of an ancient god who hadn't been worshipped for thousands of years to express their surprise is one of the mysteries of history.

Well... looked pretty sharp the last time you saw it, don't you think?

He wouldn't harm me, would he?

'Tell me what you have done with the file,' he said in his usual cold, hard voice, 'or you will learn how to swim face down in the Thames tonight.'

All right... that answered my question pretty succinctly. My whole body felt cold all of a sudden. Darn! Was he being serious?

I looked into his eyes.

Yes, he was. Absolutely serious.

'You... you wouldn't dare!' I managed to whisper.

'Really?' Raising his hand, he counted dispassionately: 'Firstly, nobody knows you are really here. You do not exist, *Mr Victor Linton*.'

His lips didn't curve into a derisive smile, but even without that I could hear the cold venom he put into my invented name.

'Nobody will care if you vanish, and nobody will connect your disappearance to the death of some young poor lady found drowned in the Thames,' he continued.

He extended a second finger. 'Secondly, I have very discreet associates. It would be a marvel if your body was even found.'

Another finger. He caught my gaze with his, and held it. 'Thirdly, look at me. Look into my eyes and then tell me again I would not dare to get rid of you.'

Well, at least I now knew one thing. He was no industrialist who had made his fortune by producing tin cans or porcelain figurines. He was something else entirely.

'Where,' he asked in a voice so low I almost didn't catch it, 'is the file. Last chance, Mr Linton.'

'I... I...' Dammit, what was happening to me? I could feel my whole body beginning to shake, and my eyes felt strange. They felt as if they were... wet.

Oh no! No, no, no and no again! I was not going to cry like some little girl! Not in front of him. Not now. I was going to be brave and prove to him that I was just as good as any man and... and...

I started to cry.

I admit it, all right? I started to cry.

'I... I don't know,' I sniffled, lowering my head and searching desperately for a handkerchief. But these were my uncle's trousers, and he never went out, so there were no handkerchiefs in his pockets. Hurriedly, I tried to wipe away the tears with my sleeve before he could see them. 'I didn't take your file! I didn't! I...'

I blinked up at him, breathing heavily. What was he going to do now? Call his henchmen and have me killed?

To my surprise I saw him not where he had been a moment ago. He had retreated a few steps. The ice had gone out of his eyes, and he was standing in a slightly awkward position, his hands tugged into the pockets of his waistcoat as if he didn't know what to do with them.

'Um... here,' he muttered. Pulling one of his hands out of the pocket, he handed me a clean white linen handkerchief.

'You just threatened to kill me and now you're offering me a handkerchief?' I asked, tearfully.

He shrugged, and the awkwardness vanished as he fixed me with his eyes again. 'I can hardly question you further while you are... *leaking* like this. It is noisy and messy. Put an end to it. Now!'

Taking the handkerchief, I blew my nose in a noisy and not very ladylike manner. Then I held it out to him.

'Here.'

He shook his head.

'You don't want it back?'

'Are you mad?' he demanded. 'Of course I do! That thing cost three shillings and tuppence! I would simply be very obliged if you washed it before giving it back, though.'

'Oh... err... of course I will.' I paused. 'If you don't kill me, that is,' I added, as an afterthought.

'Oh, that.' He shifted uncomfortably for a moment. Mr Ambrose, uncomfortable? What was this?

Finally he waved deprecatingly. 'I have thought of a better way. A way I can determine whether you are guilty or innocent.'

'Well, I'm very glad to hear it.'

'I imagine so.' Straightening into his usual erect pose again, Mr Ambrose clapped his hand. 'Karim!'

He hadn't even called very loudly, and there was a locked door in the way. There was no way the big bearded fellow could have heard him.

'You called, *Sahib*?'

With a yelp, I sprang back and whirled to see the Mohammedan standing right behind me, towering in the safe's doorway.

With a curt wave, Mr Ambrose directed him back into my office.

'Search the room. File S39XX300.'

Apparently, Mr Ambrose was as economical with his words as with his money and facial expressions. Karim didn't need any more explanation. He went back into my office. Soon after, I heard the noise of drawers being opened.

'So what is it?' I asked. 'This better method that does not require me to learn to swim with my lungs full of water?'

Was my voice steady? I thought it was. I probably should have been more scared, but somehow this felt unreal. I was discussing with a practical stranger his reasons for not wanting to kill me. Was this really happening?

'Well, you did not have the keys for the safe until today,' Mr Ambrose reasoned, his gaze wandering up and down my body in a strange manner. 'I do not believe you are capable of cracking a safe. Ergo, if you took the file, you must have done it today. And if it is not in your office, you must still have it on you.'

'And?' I asked. 'What do you intend to do now?'

His gaze went up and down my body again. 'As I said,' he repeated, his dark, sea-coloured eyes intent. 'You must have it on you.' He took a step towards me.

And suddenly I understood.

My hands shot up to shield me. 'Oh no. No, nononono, Mister! Don't even think about it!'

I Defend my Honour, More's the Pity

He cocked his head.

'No?'

'No! Definitely no! Despite what you have been trying to tell yourself, I am still a girl and I am most definitely not going to let you rummage around in my knickers!'

'You would rather end up face-down in the Thames?'

'I would rather that you trusted me!'

'Trust...' The word came slowly over his sculpted lips as if he hadn't used them in a very long time. 'Mister Linton... in Russia they have a saying about that. Do you know it, Mr Linton?'

He took a step closer.

'How the heck should I? I'm not Russian!'

'The saying is: "trust, but verify".' He took a step closer again. 'I do not subscribe to that saying. I *never* trust. But I *always* verify.'

'You are not getting me out of my dress so you can rummage around in my underwear!' I declared, maybe a bit too forcefully. That was largely due to the fact that a part of my mind was occupied with how it would feel to have him rummage around in my underwear. And another part of my mind was busy being furious at the aforementioned part of my mind for having such thoughts.

'You are not wearing a dress, but trousers,' he pointed out in his usual cold, curt manner.

'Whatever! Are you a gentleman, Sir, or a cur?'

'That depends on the necessities of the situation.'

'And in this situation?'

'Give me back the file, Mr Linton, and I will not have to search you.'

'For the hundredth time, I do not have it!'

'For the fourth time, actually,' he corrected. 'Do not exaggerate.'

Heavy footsteps approached. They needed a few seconds to break through my concentration, and it was the same with Mr Ambrose. We were glaring at each other with such intensity that at first we didn't notice the giant bearded figure who had appeared in the doorway.

Finally, Mr Ambrose wrenched his gaze away from me.

'Yes?' he asked.

Karim shook his weighty turban and beard, as well as the head that was squeezed in between. 'Nothing, *Sahib*.'

At which Mr Ambrose's gaze returned to me with double intensity.

'You know what that means, Mister Linton?'

'What?' I snapped. 'And don't call me Mister!'

'It means that I have no choice but to search you.'

'No!' I crossed my arms. He wasn't going to touch me! Not ever!

Well, not that I really would have minded so much. But if I would ever let him take a closer look at my underwear, it would not be to search it for some stupid paper, thank you very much! I mean, every girl has to have some self-respect.

Self-respect? my inner feminist screamed at me. *Under what circumstances do you think him taking a look at your underwear would be all right with your self-respect? Have you forgotten that you despise men in whatever form they come?*

'Karim?' Mr Ambrose said, darkly. 'I'm going to take care of this. Close the safe door and lock us in. Open it only when I call again.'

My eyes widened. I rushed towards the door, but before I could reach it the huge Mohammedan had slammed it shut and plunged us into utter darkness.

~~**~*~*

'Ouch!'

'Ng!'

'Let go!'

'Stop wriggling you...'

Slap!

The noise echoed quite loudly in the dark, hollow room. There were a few seconds of silence, then I heard Mr Ambrose's calm voice – calm in the way a volcano was calm before the explosion.

'Karim? Karim, open the door again.'

Slowly, the door slid open, admitting a brilliant ray of sunlight that cut through the darkness like a red hot knife through butter. It fell on Mr Ambrose's face, which also was pretty much red hot, at least in the places where my hand had made contact with his cheek.

'You,' he said decidedly, his jaw taut, 'are either as guilty as the devil himself or have more morals than apparent at first sight.'

I narrowed my eyes. 'What is that supposed to mean, "more than apparent at first sight"?'

'It is supposed to mean more morals than one would expect from a girl who runs around dressed in men's clothes!'

'Hey, this was your idea, remember?'

'An idea I thought no sane individual would take seriously.'

'Well, I have, and now I'm here. So what are you going to do with me?'

His threatening sea-coloured eyes fixed on my face again.

'I *must* search you, Mr Linton. It is useless to resist.'

The fellow had just intended to undress me and he was still calling me 'Mister'? This was unbelievable!

'Why should I steal your stupid file?' I shouted. 'I don't even know what's in it!'

'You could have been put up to it.'

114

'By whom?'

'By one of the men who want me ruined and dead.'

He said that so coldly, so calmly, that it cut right through my anger. I looked closer and saw that behind his granite façade, emotions were boiling inside him. He was just too stubborn to admit it.

'What's so important about that file?' I asked, softly. Well, relatively softly, anyway.

'If you took it, you already know,' was his response. 'And if you didn't, I will not tell you.'

'Why not?'

'I do not have to explain myself to you!'

'So what now?' I asked again.

'I could tie you down to search you,' he threatened.

'You could try.' My hands came up defensively again. Unconsciously, Mr Ambrose's hand went to his cheek, and I had to grin. Was I crazy? It was still a very real possibility that I would end up face-down in the Thames today, and here I was, grinning like a Cheshire cat.

But I just couldn't help being excited! This was the first half-way thrilling thing to have happened in my massively mundane life.

Mr Ambrose noticed my grin. Just before he turned to his turban-wearing henchman, I thought I could see a faint scowl on his face. What? I had elicited a facial expression from Mr Granite Face? Surely not!

'Karim? Would you be so good as to search her?' Mr Ambrose inquired.

The Mohammedan's eyes flickered to me for a moment. He stood straighter and gripped the hilt of his sabre.

'I would fight an *Ifrit*[23] for you, *Sahib*... but *this* creature?' He gave me a look that reminded me of the way my aunt always looked at me. 'I must respectfully decline.'

'I thought so,' nodded Mr Ambrose.

'What in God's name is an *Ifrit*?' I demanded.

'A powerful half-demon from Arabian mythology,' Mr Ambrose informed me. 'They are over twelve feet tall, armed with huge swords and have fists and wings that burn with hellfire.'

Dear me. I had no idea Karim thought so highly of me.

Mr Ambrose started pacing up and down with long, measured strides. I watched him carefully, my heartbeat still not returned to its normal rhythm. With his impassive face, fathomless eyes and long black tailcoats fluttering behind him like bat wings, he really looked more than a little intimidating. For a moment, I considered running. Maybe I could make it to the hallway and scream for help. Mr Stone would hear me. Maybe he would run for the police.

Karim met my eyes. His small, beady specimens weren't quite as impressive as those of his master, but his were full of suspicion and animosity.

'I sent Stone away,' he stated. 'The door to the hallway is locked.'

---

[23] *Ifrit* is the most common spelling in western cultures, but the proper English pronunciation would suggest rather a spelling like *ifreet*.

Mr Ambrose didn't cease his pacing. I knew it wasn't him the comment had been meant for, anyway. I gave Karim a curt nod, which he returned. If I had the slightest doubt before that Mr Ambrose could and would kill to protect his interests, it was now gone. With such servants at his command, the deed would be easy to accomplish.

I wondered why I didn't feel more afraid.

Suddenly, Mr Ambrose stopped in his tracks and whirled around to face me.

'You,' he said curtly, 'have placed me in a difficult position, Mr Linton.'

'Because you have to kill me now?' I inquired.

'No.' Maybe I was mistaken, but I could have sworn his jaw tightened a little bit. 'Because I *cannot* kill you, Mr Linton. Any man under the same suspicion you are under now I would simply challenge to a duel and shoot like the dog he is. However,' he paused for a moment to take a breath, 'that will not be possible in your case, since you are... not quite as male as I could wish.'

There! *That* was why I was not afraid.

'You mean because I'm a *girl*,' I pointed out. 'Which means I am *female*, not male. You can say the word, you know. It's not poisonous.'

'Oh, but it is,' he responded, coolly. 'Poisonous to my reputation, and now to my interests. I must have that file, Mr Linton. However, you were right: I *am* a gentleman. And because of that unfortunate condition you conceal under your trousers, I, as a gentleman, can neither search you nor kill you to gain what I must have.'

Unfortunate condition? God, this fellow really needed his head examined!

'Why are you so bloody convinced that it was me who stole your precious papers, anyway?' I lashed out. 'Why so determined to think that I am the guilty one? Why not some other member of your staff? The file could have been gone for days.'

'No, it couldn't,' he replied curtly. 'Because nobody had access to the files in the safe.'

'Nobody else had another key? And what about the one you gave me?'

'Why these pointless questions?' he asked, shaking his head. 'We both know that you are guilty! There is no duplicate key, and the one I gave you was in my own possession the entire time since last Wednesday when–'

Abruptly, his head-shaking ceased. His whole body froze.

'Yes?' I demanded. 'When what?'

Slowly he came out of his paralysis and turned his head to face me directly. His dark eyes flashed as though a storm was raging in them. For one moment he looked so dangerous I actually took a step back.

But then I realized that for once, his anger was not directed at me. A word passed his lips like the hiss of a snake preparing to strike:

'Simmons!'

Karim let out a low oath in a language I didn't understand. But the way he said it, I didn't have to know the words to know that it was a curse. He had obviously understood. I, on the contrary, was still completely in the dark.

'Simmons?' I echoed, making it a question.

He met my eyes with his deep, dark, blue-grey ones.

116

'Yes. Simmons, Mr Linton. Simmons, my previous private secretary. Simmons, who disappeared a few days ago without any explanation. Simmons, the treacherous snake.'

With a few long strides Mr Ambrose was over at my desk and started rifling through my drawers. The wooden ones in the desk, I mean.

'What are you doing?' I demanded. 'I thought your big bull already checked those.'

Karim threw me a look that signified about a ton of displeasure. Apparently he didn't appreciate his new nickname. I made a mental note to use it again at the earliest opportunity.

'Karim did search the drawers,' Mr Ambrose agreed. 'But he searched them for the missing file, not for a sign of where the traitor who has taken the file might have gone. This was his desk once.'

'So you think that this Simmons did it now? You no longer think it was me?'

'No! I was a fool to ever have thought it. After all, you're only...' He waved his hand non-committally.

'A girl?' I piped up. 'Is that what you were going to say? We females can steal things just as well as any man, thank you very much!'

'A moment ago you were afraid of me thinking you're guilty, and now you praise your skills as a thief?'

'Not my skills, but the skills of womanhood in general! And I was certainly not afraid.'

'You were not?'

'Do I look afraid to you?'

'No,' he admitted. 'You look superfluous. Leave the room. I and my men have a thief to catch.' He nodded to the door and returned to his work of rifling through the desk, as if I had already left, or as if I had ceased to exist entirely. That, I was sure, was how he would have preferred things.

Crossing my arms, I planted myself in front of him.

'I'm not going anywhere.'

'I give you the rest of the day off,' he said, not looking at me. 'Go and enjoy your holiday. Trust me when I say I do not give holidays often.'

'With me it seems that is almost the only thing you do! I did not come here to juggle meaningless pieces of paper like a monkey trained for some circus and then be chucked out after half a day. I came here to work! And if you have a thief to catch, I will come with you!'

'Just for your information,' he said, 'the pieces of paper that you have "juggled" as you put it have most certainly not been meaningless.'

He still didn't bother to turn around and look at me. All I could do was send my furious glares at his broad, hard back, and that did nothing to calm me down.

'They all pertain to my business in a very real way,' he continued. 'And you are nothing whatsoever like a circus monkey. A monkey wouldn't talk back at me.'

'But it might bite!'

'I'm not sure I wouldn't prefer that.'

'Is that so?' I took an involuntary step towards him. 'Well, I could try if you wished.'

His neck muscles tensed. 'No need to put yourself to trouble. Go home. That is an order.'

'No!' I stamped my foot. I didn't care if I made a spectacle of myself. He was going to accept me whether he wanted to or not.

'You cannot refuse to go home if I send you away.' I wouldn't have believed his voice could grow colder than it already was. But he was reaching new heights of vocal deep-freezing. 'You work for me.'

'Exactly.' I nodded. 'I *work* for you. And just as I could protest if you were to keep me at work longer than the normal hours, I have the right to protest if you send me away early. You accepted my work in exchange for a salary, Mr Ambrose, and I intend to earn that salary. I will not accept charity from anyone, and most certainly not from you.'

He looked up then and met my gaze again. Had something in my little speech actually managed to capture his attention?

There was something in his eyes as he looked at me... Something different from before. It was intense – but I had no idea what it was.

'You are wasting my time,' he said. But his voice wasn't quite as hard and immovable as just a second ago. 'I need to catch Simmons.'

'Then let me help,' I pleaded.

Instead of answering, he returned to rummaging through the last drawer. Slamming it shut, he turned to Karim, who stood waiting at the entrance to the safe.

'Nothing here. Get the men here. The entire team. Tell Warren to go over this place with a fine-tooth comb. Anything he finds, and I mean *anything,* is to be brought to me immediately, understood?'

'Yes, *Sahib.*'

'Why not just tell the police about this?' I dared to interject.

'Because I do not want this business in tomorrow's newspapers,' was the curt reply. 'And because if we find the thief, they will get in my way.'

I had to swallow. Taking into account his recent threats towards yours truly, I could only imagine too well what he meant by that.

'So what now?' I asked.

'Now you will go home.'

'No. I will not!'

Karim, who had been striding towards the door to embark on his errand, hesitated there. 'Do you truly wish me to leave you alone with her, *Sahib?*'

I rolled my eyes. Oh, please.

Mr Ambrose nodded. 'Yes, go, Karim. I need Warren here as soon as possible.'

'As you wish, *Sahib.*' But Karim still looked doubtful under his beard as he unlocked the door and left the room.

When the door closed behind him, I stepped up to Mr Ambrose until only a few inches separated us. There was no point in beating about the bush further.

'Why won't you let me do my job? What exactly is your problem?'

His eyes, seeming darker than usual, almost black, bored into me like a steam-engine-driven drill. 'You know.'

Angrily, I put my fists on my hips. 'You mean the fact that I'm a girl?'

He didn't say anything, but from his look I knew that was it. What was the matter? This was going beyond chauvinism. Wasn't he even able to say the word 'girl' aloud? Did he have such a strong distaste for it? For me?

'Do you behave like this to all females?' I demanded.

A faint noise escaped him. It might have been a snort.

'Hardly. All females don't put on trousers and trick me into giving them jobs!'

'I did not trick you!'

'Maybe. Get to the point.'

'I already have. Why won't you let me help you, let me work for you properly?'

He shook his head in exasperation. 'You don't understand. Where I am going, what I will be doing... It will be dangerous. Very dangerous. I cannot let you accompany me.'

'Why not?' I asked, heatedly. 'Simply because I am a girl?'

He stared at me for a second, seemingly lost for words. For this one moment I saw something flicker in his eyes, something different from the iron determination that was usually there. He looked almost... frightened? Longing?

Then the shutters came done again, and he nodded. 'Yes, that's exactly the reason. I am a gentleman. As such I cannot allow any lad– person of female gender to be in danger.'

It did not pass my notice how he had avoided using the term 'lady'.

'Oh really?' Sarcasm was dripping from my voice. 'If I may remind you, you were threatening to do away with me yourself not ten minutes ago.'

'That,' he answered in a chilling voice, 'was when I thought you had betrayed me. I do not take kindly to traitors, Mr Linton.'

The sarcasm drained from my voice and face.

'I am not a traitor,' I said, my voice full of hurt.

For one instant, I thought his granite face softened a bit. 'I know. You have done an acceptable job so far – for an *Ifrit*.'

My eyes flew wide open. Had my ears betrayed me, or had Mr Ambrose, Mr Silent and Sullen Granite Face Ambrose, just made a joke?

'But your capabilities as an office worker don't have anything to do with this. You simply can't get involved in this matter! You see that, don't you?' he continued so quickly that I immediately forgot about the maybe-joke and my hackles rose.

'No! I most certainly do not see. You have taken me on to work for you!' I folded my arms in front of my chest. 'I demand work! I demand to work bloody hard for every penny you will pay me, just like Karim and this Warren fellow and every other man you employ, do you understand? I want to earn my own money, and I will, whether you want me to or not.'

119

Once again, he studied me with his dark, sea-coloured eyes. There was something growing there – slowly, very slowly. Acceptance? More likely it was resignation.

He took a step towards me. Whereas before our faces had been inches apart, now it was only a fraction of an inch.

'I will not be able to change your mind, will I?' he asked. His voice was arctic. But for some reason I didn't feel cold. Instead I felt heat rush over my body. Where his face and mine almost touched, my skin began to tingle. The tension between us was burning.

'No.' I grinned. 'And you don't have the time anyway. You have to catch a thief.'

'Good point.' Again, he studied me. 'You really wish to help?'

'Yes!'

'Very well then. Follow me.'

He whirled, and before I knew what was happening he was striding away. I followed instinctively, only now realizing how my breath had sped up during our little standoff.

Strange. Why had I reacted like this? It must have been the exhilaration of finally triumphing over him. Yes, that had to be it.

He led me back towards the entrance of the safe. There, he stopped and turned to me. I had to work hard to keep a triumphant smile off my face. This was it. He was finally going to accept me and give me responsibility.

'I have a very important assignment for you,' he said, looking me directly in the eyes. 'One of vital significance, which I expect to be finished by the time I return.'

'What is it?' I asked, breathless.

He pushed open the door to the safe, which had fallen closed behind us. Then he pointed to the chaos of files on the floor. 'Clean up that mess.'

LITTLE IFRIT

All right, so I did it. So what? He was my employer, after all, and he could order me to do anything he wanted. The fact that I was fuming and fantasizing about choking him didn't really count as an excuse to shirk my duties.

By the light of the small gas lamp Mr Ambrose had given me, I started to sort files.

Soon I found that, while the work itself was deathly boring, being positioned in the safe room had unexpected advantages. Once I had pushed open the door, which Mr Ambrose had shut, I could hear everything that was going on in my office – which was quite a lot, let me tell you.

There was a knock on the door.

'Enter,' Mr Ambrose's curt voice called.

'Mr Ambrose? Good morning, Sir,' a quiet, respectful voice said in answer. Several pairs of feet shuffled into my office. Apparently it had been selected as official HQ for the thief hunt. 'I came as soon as you called. What is the matter? Karim didn't say.'

'Warren.' No 'good morning' from Mr Stoneface Ambrose of course, and certainly no 'How nice to see you.' He got right to the point. 'Have you seen Simmons?'

'Simmons, Sir? I thought you gave me to understand that he suddenly gave up his post.'

'He did. And he took something of mine along with him, it appears.'

There was a short, heavy silence. It wasn't hard for me to imagine the merciless ice in Mr Ambrose's eyes right then. Just from the feel of the air I got the impression that the people in my office experienced a twinge of pity for Simmons.

'I see. What can we do, Sir?'

'First answer my question, Warren. Have you seen him since he left?'

'No, Sir.'

'Has he come back to pick up his belongings?'

'I can send someone and check, Sir.'

'Do that. Now.'

Footsteps hurried off. There were a few more minutes of silence, which nobody made even the slightest attempt to fill. Apparently Mr Ambrose didn't think much of small talk. What a surprise.

The moment the footsteps returned he asked: 'And?'

'His things are gone,' said a third voice. 'I asked Mr Garfield down at the lockers, and he said that Simmons took them with him on the same day he disappeared.'

'That settles it,' declared Mr Ambrose. 'He's the thief. He has been planning this.'

'It appears so, Sir,' agreed the man called Warren. 'May I ask what was stolen?'

'No.'

What was this? *No*? Just like that? No? Mr Ambrose didn't even trust his own people? Well, I shouldn't be surprised that I was stuck in here sorting files then, instead of being out there where the real work was being done.

'You are looking for a folder with the inscription "S39XX300",' Mr Ambrose told them, icily. 'That is all you need to know.'

'Yes, Mr Ambrose, Sir.'

'First you will search this office. I have some urgent business and will leave you to it. If you have any questions, ask Karim.'

'Yes, Sir.'

His footsteps receded, and the noises from the other room indicated that Mr Warren and his cronies had begun their search. I returned my attention to my work.

Quite a good idea, it appeared: I had been so distracted that I hadn't noticed I had tried to stuff a bunch of files into the open mouth of some wooden African totem. Hurriedly I removed them and started looking for their proper container.

For the next few minutes I busied with the files. Then I suddenly heard foot-steps approaching the door of the safe. Yet before I could panic and begin to wonder what they wanted with me, I heard Karim's voice.

'Not in there, Warren.'

'But Mr Ambrose said to search everywhere.'

'Everywhere in this office. Not in the safe. There is...' Karim's voice dropped to a whisper as he explained something to Warren. I didn't exactly hear every-thing, but I thought I caught the word '*Ifrit*'.

'Really?' Warren whispered. 'Are you sure?'

'I saw it with my own eyes,' Karim assured him.

'Right in there? In the safe room?'

'Indeed. So you see you had better not...'

'Of course! I'll steer clear of it, don't you worry.'

For the following few minutes my fantasies changed from strangling Mr Am-brose to braining Karim with a wooden African totem. In the end I suppose the difference didn't much matter. Men! They were all the same.

During the following hours I worked ceaselessly, clearing up the mess my dear master had left behind. He wouldn't have an excuse to accuse me of slack-ing, oh no! The task actually wasn't as hard as I had feared. All the folders strewn over the floor were numbered. Since I had already fully grasped the sorting sys-tem, and the one here in the safe was simply an extension of that in my office, I got on quickly, and orderly rows of boxes grew on the shelves.

Finally, the door to my office opened and I heard his unmistakable voice.

'Are you done, Warren?'

'Nearly, Mr Ambrose.'

'As soon as you're done here, prepare your men for a little trip, by which I do not mean a stroll in the park. Do we understand each other?'

'Yes, Mr Ambrose.'

'Very well. I shall join you in a minute, as soon as I've seen how my little *Ifrit* is doing.'

'Your what, Sir?'

'Forget what I said, Warren.'

'Yessir!'

His little Ifrit? I supposed I should have been outraged, him calling me names and all, but for some strange reason I felt warm inside. Maybe because of my flaming wings, who knew?

Mr Ambrose had obviously not intended for me to hear his words. Quickly and quietly I closed the door to the safe room, just as he had left it, and retreated to a corner, a demure little smile on my face as I looked around the room. All right, maybe the smile wasn't totally demure. Maybe it was even a little bit self-satisfied. So what?

The door was pushed open and Mr Ambrose entered. 'I will be leaving on the search soon,' he began. 'So sorry that you are occupied and can't come with us. How many hours do you think you will still need to finish your...'

As his eyes adjusted to the gloom of the safe-room, his voice trailed off.

'You were saying?' I inquired sweetly.

Slowly, Mr Ambrose's gaze wandered over the long rows of impeccably ordered boxes on the shelves of the safe room. He bent to examine the floor, maybe in the hope that he could find a stray piece of paper still lying somewhere, or at least a few flecks of dust.

When he finally straightened again, his eyes fixed on me.

'You are finished?'

'Yes. Why?' I fluttered my eyelashes at him. 'Were you by any chance expecting me to take longer?'

'No,' he lied smoothly. 'In fact I was expecting you to be finished long ago. Don't be so lazy again, or I will have to reduce your wages.'

'Well, well.' I glared at him, even though for some strange reason, inside I wasn't feeling angry. Somehow I knew he was only putting on a show, and I was dancing in triumph. 'You had better stop or you'll drown me in compliments for my work.'

'Don't be afraid,' he assured me. 'That will never, ever happen.'

I could readily believe it.

'Mr Ambrose?' The man called Warren appeared at the door to the safe room. He was an average-looking fellow with a thin moustache and a high forehead. Spotting me, he looked at me curiously for a second. Then his gaze returned to our master. 'We're ready to go, Sir.'

'I see.' Mr Ambrose's voice was as cool as could be. 'Warren, I think you haven't met before?' He indicated me. 'This...' he swallowed as if he had to get something unpleasant down his throat. 'This is *Mr Linton*. My new... *private secretary*.'

'I see. A pleasure to meet you, Mr Linton.' Warren extended his hand to me. As if in a dream, I took it and shook it.

'Likewise,' I heard myself say.

He has admitted it! He has admitted to another person that I work for him!

'Enough pleasantries,' Mr Ambrose cut short our pleasantries. Abruptly he whirled to the door. 'We have a thief to catch.' With two long strides he was outside and out of sight. 'Come!' We heard his commanding voice from outside. 'Both of you!'

I was still so thrilled by his admission that it took me a few seconds to register his words.

'W-what?' I managed. 'Me, too?'

'Are you deaf? Get a move on, Mr Linton!'

I jumped up so fast you might have thought a scorpion had stung me. Following Mr Ambrose out of the safe, I saw that he had crossed my office and was standing at the connecting door to his own. He thrust it open and we followed him inside the large, bare and empty room.

A room which was no longer bare and empty. I had been mistaken, thinking that my office was the thief hunter HQ. It had just been a temporary space until things were set up in here.

People were standing all around: men with nondescript faces, in nondescript clothes. On the desk lay a gigantic map, larger than any I had seen before, even in the British Museum. It detailed not the world, but, to judge from the web of jagged lines, some vast city in fine detail.

Immediately I knew what it had to be. A map of London. A map for the hunters.

What in heaven's name could have been stolen that Mr Ambrose was so desperate to discover? And why wouldn't he tell anyone what it was? Why wouldn't he tell *me*?

'Gather round.' Mr Ambrose took up his position at the desk and gestured for Karim, Warren and me to do likewise. The two dozen or so men whom Warren had brought with him posted themselves at either entrance to the room.

Some of the men, including Warren but excluding Mr Ambrose, took out cigars and lit them. Not used to the smell, I wrinkled my nose – but I would have to get used to this if I really intended to work among men.

'We have to come up with a strategy to track Simmons,' Mr Ambrose said. 'Suggestions, gentlemen.'

And ladies, I thought, but didn't say it. Instead I said: 'Well... maybe we should start by thinking about motive. Why did he steal the file?'

'Because he wanted it, obviously,' said Mr Ambrose. 'I should perhaps have clarified: *Intelligent* suggestions.'

'That is not what I meant,' I snapped. 'I meant... what does the file contain? Why exactly did he want it for himself?'

'None of you are to know what the file contains, Mr Linton. Nor do I see that it is in any way necessary.'

'It is necessary if we want to know where he will go next and what he will do,' I persisted. God, he really had trust issues. 'For example – if it simply is a folder containing banknotes, he'll just flee the city. If it is some important document, he might try to sell it. If it is a letter from one of your secret lady friends, he will try to blackmail you.'

Mr Warren almost swallowed his cigar. Slowly, Mr Ambrose, who had been staring down at the table, looked up at me and fixed me with his cold gaze. I tried my best to meet his eyes without flinching.

'Well, I can guarantee you, Mr Linton, that it is *not* a letter from one of my secret lady friends. They would not waste their time writing letters to me they know I would not read.'

Now it was my turn to stare. Was he being serious? Did he really have a secret lady friend or, God forbid, several? For heaven's sake, I had been trying to make a joke!

Perhaps not the best of ideas where he was concerned.

'Well,' I said as steadily as possible, 'that leaves two of the possibilities I have outlined. Which is it?'

He remained silent.

'Just a general indication,' I coaxed. 'Come on. You have got to give us something.'

Warren cleared his throat, taking this opportunity to rid himself of the bitten off pieces of his cigar that were still stuck there.

'I think I must agree with Mr Linton, Sir. Without any idea of what the document in question is, we have little hope of catching the thief.'

Mr Ambrose stayed silent for one moment longer – then he nodded curtly.

'Number two,' he stated.

I frowned. What was he talking about? 'Excuse me?'

'Number two,' he repeated. 'The second possibility you outlined. There are no banknotes in the file. It is an important document.' Taking a deep breath, he added: 'More important than you can imagine.'

'Now we're getting somewhere,' I sighed.

'Can he sell it to anyone, Sir?' Warren inquired.

'Only to the right people. And by right I do not mean "right" as in "right and honourable". I mean people with limitless cash and little conscience.'

I almost said, 'Oh, you mean people like yourself?' But I held my tongue. My natural tendency to bad manners was not well placed here if I wanted to keep my job.

'These people,' I asked, 'are they here in London, or could they be anywhere in the country?'

'Theoretically, they could be anywhere. But it is most likely that they would be here. This is the centre of the British Empire, the power-hub for a fifth of the earth's surface – the best place to transact any kind of business, whether legitimate or otherwise.'

'But we had better make sure, hadn't we?' I said with a sweet smile. 'Somebody told me once it's better to always verify.'

Mr Ambrose gave me another one of his cold stares. 'That must have been a very wise person.' Turning, he nodded to Karim. 'Go, take a few of the men and check Euston station. I want a description of all the passengers who left in the last few days and don't care how you get it. If there's anyone there who fits Simmons' description – find him, grab him, hold him. I do not care if it should happen to be the Prime Minister.'

'Is Simmons easy to recognize?' I asked as Karim marched out of the room with seven henchmen at his heels.

Mr Ambrose nodded grimly. 'Oh yes. That is the one piece of good luck in this mess. He's tall and gangly, with a long nose, long blonde hair and a thin moustache, and a scar over his right eyebrow. If anyone saw him, they'll remember him.'

'He might have altered his appearance,' I pointed out doubtfully.

Beside me, Warren nodded. 'That's very likely, Sir.'

'No, it isn't. He's always been a vain fellow. Clever, but with a too good an opinion of himself and his looks. No doubt he thinks we have no hope of catching up to him.'

'And do we, Sir?' Warren wanted to know. 'Assuming he has not left the city – and I for my part think it likely that he is still here – how are we going to find one man hidden in a labyrinth of a city among three million people?'

'The task is not as impossible as you might think, Warren.' Mr Ambrose tapped the map on the table. 'Most of those three million people are working-class folk. I doubt very much Simmons would hide out in one of their miserable little sheds. Oh no. He did this for money, and he would want to live in style.'

In quick succession he pointed out various buildings on the map, marking them with pushpins.

'These are the best hotels in town. I do not approve of such frivolous behaviour as betting, but if I did, I would bet my top hat that he is staying in one of them under some alias.'

'Just... staying in a hotel?' I asked, incredulously. 'Isn't he afraid of the police?'

'He knows my affairs,' was the curt reply. 'He knows I cannot involve the police in this. The results would be...'

His voice trailed off into nothingness. We all waited with bated breath, but not a word came. So the results would be too terrible to speak aloud, would they? What in heaven's name could be in this infernal file?

'The police are not an option,' Mr Ambrose eventually continued, 'so Simmons feels confident and secure.' For a moment, lightning flashed in his dark eyes. 'Very soon he will learn of his mistake.'

'This is all very well, but these are over a hundred hotels,' I pointed out. 'How are we to find out in which one he is staying?'

'I can take care of half,' said Mr Ambrose. Without further explanation, he strode to the pneumatic tube at the wall, wrote a message in his meticulous handwriting, and pulled the lever. Shortly after, the answer came. He checked it and returned to the desk.

'You can cross these–' pointing to about half of the hotels on the map, '–off the list.'

'How on earth can you check the guest lists of more than *fifty hotels* with just *one* message?' I demanded.

He fixed me with his dark glare.

'Because I own them.'

'You own *fifty per cent* of all the hotels in London?'

'No. I own seventy per cent of all the hotels in London. But the remaining twenty per cent are too expensive even for an escaped criminal with a bag full of ready cash to afford.'

Of course. I should have guessed.

'Well,' I asked sweetly, gesturing to the remaining hotels on the map, 'do you plan on buying the rest of them to make things easier for us?'

'That would not be making things easier, Mr Linton. Unfortunately, such things take time – time which we do not have.'

'You could always bribe someone in the hotels,' I suggested, raising an eyebrow. 'You have enough cash, don't you? And you don't seem to be above bending the law a little.'

The room went deadly quiet.

Before I knew it, Mr Ambrose was at my side, and his hard hand was gripping my arm. Slowly, he leaned down towards my ear until I could feel his breath there, tickling me in a delicious threat.

'I am perfectly well aware that you are no real lady, Mr Linton. There is no need to prove the fact further by impugning my honour in front of my associates. I will let you be a part of this only if you can behave yourself properly. For a start, when you speak to me, you will show me proper respect. You are to address me as 'Mister Ambrose' or 'Sir'. Is that clear?'

I smiled at him as sweetly as I could manage.

'Sir! Yes, Sir, Mister Ambrose, Sir!'

His eyes narrowed infinitesimally, but he didn't say anything. He just stepped back and looked down at the map again.

'So how do we deal with the remaining hotels and determine whether or not he is there?'

'We could simply ask,' suggested one of Warren's men. But Warren shook his head.

'No, Jim. We could if we knew the alias Simmons is using; that wouldn't appear too suspicious. But we can't if we only know his description.'

I nodded. 'That's right. I mean... How do you think a receptionist is going to react if you come marching into his hotel demanding to know if a man with long blonde hair is staying there, without offering any explanation as to why you're looking for him. He would throw you out.'

'He would not throw *me* out,' stated Mr Ambrose darkly.

'Err... probably, *Sir*. But he wouldn't answer the question either, would he?'

He shot me a look that was a shade darker than the one before.

'Do you have a better idea?'

Suddenly I smiled. Inspiration had struck. Yes!

'Actually,' I told him, 'I do. I know exactly how we can find him. Or more precisely, how *I* can. It'll be easy. I just need a beautiful dress and a sack full of onions.'

I Go Dress-Shopping

'A what and a what?' Mr Ambrose stared at me as if I had lost my mind, and my job was soon to follow.

I smiled at him innocently. 'Is your hearing not as good as it used to be, *Sir*?'

'How,' he asked very slowly and deliberately, 'are you going to track a thief with... with a dress and a sack full of vegetables?'

'Onions. They have to be onions. And the how,' I said, tapping my nose knowingly, 'you'll just have to leave that to me. Secrets of the trade.'

'How do I know this is going to work?'

I gave him my most sweetest smile.

'Easy. You'll have to trust me.'

~~**~*~*

127

For nearly half an hour he tried to worm my plan out of me, but I wouldn't budge. At one point he declared that, fine, we were going to try something else. When I asked him what exactly, he didn't look very pleased. Finally, Warren and a few of the others joined my side, arguing for him to let me have a go.

'We don't even know whether Simmons is still in town,' Mr Ambrose pointed out, stubbornly shaking his head.

The door to my office chose this moment to open and admit the monumental form of Karim, who bowed and with what I thought was perfect timing said: 'Nobody has seen Simmons at the train station, *Sahib*. It is safe to assume that he is still within the city.'

There was one moment more of hesitation – then Mr Ambrose grabbed his top hat from the coat stand and slammed it down on his hard head.

'Fine. We're going. Karim, come along. We're going to buy onions.'

With a slightly puzzled expression on his face, the bearded man followed his master out. I, unable to conceal a grin, was right at his heels.

'What are you planning, Mr Linton?' Warren whispered behind me, but I just shook my head.

We had to run to keep up with Mr Ambrose. Out in the street he didn't hail a cab, but began to march down the street.

'Err... Sir?' Warren cleared his throat. 'If the situation is as grave as you have indicated, the expense of a cab would surely be justifiable. It is a much quicker means of transport, very convenient in such an urgent situation.'

'Fine.'

Irritably, Mr Ambrose waved a hand and, when a cab stopped, ordered us inside with a jerk of his head. All of us, about a dozen men plus one disguised woman, into one cab! The driver looked at us as if we were completely insane, and I couldn't blame him.

The good news was I didn't end up with Karim sitting on top of me. The bad news was I ended up with Mr Ambrose sitting next to me. *Very close* next to me. I didn't want to think about how close. His lean body was nearly squashing me against the wall, and there was something hard pressing into my leg which I very much hoped was the end of his walking stick.

Through the window that connected the inside of the coach with the driver's box, Mr Ambrose threw the cabbie a look. 'Drive fast.'

The man's eyes widened. Apparently, he knew who was talking to him. The whip cracked, and we started to move with astonishing speed for a vehicle carrying three times the intended load.

'Take us to Flemming's,' Mr Ambrose shouted over the whirl and clatter of the wheels. I had no idea who or what Flemming's was – hopefully a place where one could get either dresses or onions. I didn't know if this crazy plan of mine was going to work, but if it was to succeed, I definitely needed all the right equipment.

After a ten-minute drive, the cab stopped in front of a large building with grimy windows and a lot of merchandise crammed together, displayed there. Over the door, large, ornamental letters proudly spelled out 'Flemming's'.

I took a close look at the department store. I didn't know much about fashion, but I knew enough. The frilly, cheap things displayed in the shop window were not exactly what I was after. I looked at Mr Ambrose.

'I said I needed a *beautiful* dress.'

'What's wrong with those? They're cheap.'

'That's exactly what's wrong with them.'

I knocked against the roof of the cab. 'Take us to the best dressmaker in town.'

~~**~*~*

The little dressmaker was a hunched figure with a long, hooked nose, remnants of grey hair over both ears and a resplendent waistcoat in blue and gold. He was intent on examining a few rolls of brocade and didn't look up when he heard the doorbell ring. Only when footsteps approached and the annoying presence of a customer drew him from the contemplation of the masterpiece he was no doubt thinking about creating, did he look up. A frown spread over his wrinkled face and he eyed the slight man in baggy trousers who was standing in front of him – yours truly – with obvious doubt in his eyes.

'Is there something I can do for you, Sir?' he asked. 'Or did you perhaps want to come in through the servant's entrance?'

'No.' I, shook my head. 'I'm here to pick out a dress for my sister. It's going to be a birthday present.'

Methodically, the dressmaker took a pair of pince-nez out of his waistcoat pocket, polished them on his sleeve, and clamped them on his nose. Then he studied me like he would a piece of his cloth. Apparently, he found that I was second-hand, with quite a lot of moth-holes, too.

'And you're going to pay for it?' he asked, disbelief dripping from his voice.

'Oh no. He is.' Stepping aside, I pointed behind me. A lean black figure appeared from between the shelves and mannequins and strode towards the two of us. In theory Mr Ambrose was dressed quite as simply as I. Nothing about his black tailcoat, black waistcoat or black trousers indicated wealth.

But the arrogance of his dark eyes did.

'Oh. I see.' The dressmaker swallowed. 'And the gentlemen's names are...?'

'I'm Mister Linton,' I answered. 'And this is Mr Ambrose.'

The pince-nez fell off the man's nose and his eyes widened. 'Mr Ambrose? Mr *Rikkard* Ambrose?'

'Yes.' Mr Ambrose nodded, curtly.

'Oh dear Sir, please forgive me for not recognizing you on sight. Please forgive me for not properly welcoming you to my humble establishment. You honour me with your presence here!'

'Yes.' Mr Ambrose nodded curtly again.

'Once more I beg a thousand pardons. Everything I have, everything I am is at your disposal. What do you wish to see? I have some very fine waistcoats, just came in yesterday from France. Very expensive, but the best, the very best. Please, let me show you...'

'I'm not here to buy waistcoats,' Mr Ambrose cut him off. 'I am here...' He paused for a moment – gathering his strength, I would imagine. 'I am here to pay for a dress for this man's sister. One dress. As pretty and inexpensive as possible.'

The dressmaker blinked, surprised. I would have wagered that not one of his clients had ever before placed an order for a dress they wanted to be cheap. He dealt comparatively well with the new circumstances though, springing up from his stool and bowing deeply.

'Of course, Mr Ambrose, Sir. Please follow me, Mr Linton. What should the dress be made of? Muslin? Brocade? Silk?'

'Silk would be perfect. With plenty of lace at the sleeves and the cleavage, and gold embroidery, and little diamonds everywhere.' I smiled at him. 'Don't pay attention to what Mr Ambrose said. The dress needs to be spectacular. Make it demure but... alluring.'

The little dressmaker winked at me and nodded like an overexcited woodpecker, determined to make a new home for himself. 'I completely understand, Sir. I think I know just the thing. Do you have your sister's measurements, Sir?'

'No, but she is about my build. You can use me as a model.'

Half an hour later we emerged from the shop, and Mr Ambrose was carrying a large package.

'If this is going to be a waste of my money, you will be deeply, deeply sorry, Mr Linton,' he said, his voice as cool as ice.

'Don't worry. The onions will be cheap, I promise.'

~~**~*~*

'This is in contradiction to our agreement!' Mr Ambrose told me, quiet menace in his voice.

We were back at Empire House. All of us – Mr Ambrose, Karim, Warren and his cronies were assembled in the hallway in front of Mr Ambrose's office. Mr Stone, who normally occupied the desk here, was nowhere in sight. Maybe Mr Ambrose had given him the day off. More likely though, he'd sent him to slave in some other part of the building while we conducted our secret business here.

'It is not,' I said, cutting open the first string that held together the package containing the dress.

'It is. I only accepted you under the condition that you would pretend to be a man while working for me.'

'And I will,' I said patting the dress fondly. 'I will pretend to be a man pretending to be a woman.'

'You...' Mr Ambrose might have said something else, but for the moment he seemed lost for words. Then he demanded: 'And this is really necessary for that infernal plan of yours? You are not just doing this to anger me?'

I gave him my brightest, most happy smile. I was smiling a lot lately. But why the heck not? Thief hunting was fun! 'Now why would I do something like that, Sir?'

Before he could reply or try to throttle me, I vanished into my office and locked the door behind me.

'Err... Sir?' Warren's voice, muffled by the door, was as nervous as it was curious. 'What is he doing in there?'

'Apparently,' Mr Ambrose said, his voice as arctic as ever, 'Mr Linton's plan requires a female participant. Since we have none available, Mr Linton will impersonate one.'

'Will that work?'

'Oh yes. Take my word for it, Mr Linton is famous for his impersonations.'

Dear me. Mr Ambrose was capable of sarcasm? Wonder of wonders...

As quickly as I could, I stripped. Then I took out the dress Mr Ambrose had so ungraciously provided and proceeded to put it on.

Dressing took considerably longer than stripping. Not having Ella to help me this time, it took especially long to squeeze myself into the blasted corset. Finally, I was finished and took out a small mirror, about the only useful item ladies were allowed to carry.

My hair still looked a bit windswept, but that was not a problem. On the contrary, it would work to my advantage. The dress looked just as it was supposed to look. The tailor had really done a spiffing job.

Taking a deep breath, I stepped towards the door. Now for the first test. I opened the door, stepped out and did a little twirl.

'Well? What do you say, gentlemen?'

All of them were looking at me with interested expressions. Well, all apart from Mr Ambrose, who didn't have an expression on his stony face, and Karim, who had an expression but not one that I would like to describe.

Warren stepped forward and nodded slowly.

'I've got to hand it to you, Mr Linton, you know what you're doing. You look almost like a genuine girl.'

I raised an eyebrow. 'Almost?'

'Well, you know...' he waved a hand in the air. 'When one knows the truth one isn't as easily fooled as everybody else. One just sees those little signs that indicate something is not quite right about you.'

'You can say that again.'

That nice comment came from Mr Ambrose. 'Now, can we get on with this?'

We did get on. Or rather out, of the building to be exact. Then, to our employer's severe displeasure, we got into another cab and drove away. Our first stop was the Brown's Hotel in Albermarle Street. When the cabbie stopped his horses, I got out but held up my hand when Mr Ambrose moved to follow me.

'No. I'll go in alone.'

'What? Do you intend to catch Simmons all on your own?'

'No, of course not. I'm just going to inquire if he's here.'

'And they're going to tell you just like that, are they?'

'Yes, actually they are.' I winked at him. 'Could you hand me my sack of onions please?'

He didn't. Instead he said: 'You can't go in there alone. It's much too risky.'

'Risky?' Did he actually sound worried? Worried for *me*?

'I mean,' he added hurriedly, 'if Simmons should hear your questions and decide to flee before we can catch him.'

'Don't worry. I won't let that happen. My onions, please?'

He hesitated a moment – then handed me the sack of onions, looking as though he had just bitten into one.

Wordlessly, I turned and entered Brown's Hotel.

~~**~*~*

Ten minutes later I was out again and climbed into the cab.

'He's not here,' I proclaimed. 'Let's go try the next one.'

'How do you know?' demanded Mr Ambrose. Yet this was a demand I was not very disposed to comply with.

'You mean you can't guess, *Sir*?' I purred, smiling at him. 'Surely you are more intelligent than an insignificant little girl.'

The others laughed, thinking I had made a joke. Then they saw Mr Ambrose's expression and stopped laughing.

Soon we stopped at another hotel. I entered, and ten minutes later I left again.

'Not here,' I stated. 'Let's go on.'

'How,' Mr Ambrose asked, his voice dangerously low, 'do you know?'

We stopped at another hotel, and another, and another. After eight failures, Mr Ambrose's expression had turned from stony to steely. His hands were balled into fists.

I climbed into the coach again, just returned from my latest excursion.

'He's not here either,' I said. 'Let's try the next one.'

'How,' Mr Ambrose inquired, putting emphasis on each word, 'do-you-know?'

I smiled.

'Oh, it's just my female intuition.'

~~**~*~*

Stepping into the foyer of the Elderberry Hotel, I concealed myself behind one of the columns near the entrance, took the onion I had brought with me out of my pocket and cracked it in half. The strong smell immediately bit into my nose and brought tears to my eyes. Only with difficulty did I keep from sneezing.

It took a while for my eyes to become significantly wet. Two or three times I checked in the large mirror on the wall. Did I look distressed enough yet? No, not quite. I needed to be really distraught. Overwhelmed. Terrified.

When I was finally satisfied with my appearance, I let the onion drop and kicked it into the nearest corner. With an audible sob I staggered out from behind the column near the entrance as if I had just now come in.

It wasn't easy to stumble and stagger like a real damsel in distress on my way to reception. This rather silly behaviour was somewhat annoying. But I did a great job, if I do say so myself. By the time I had reached reception and clutched the counter in an apparently desperate effort to keep myself upright, the man at reception had noticed me. Oh yes, most definitely he had noticed me.

'Um... Miss... Are you unwell?'

In response, I gave him a pretty impressive heartbroken wail and tottered precariously.

'Err...'

The receptionist was desperately trying to find a spot where he could grip me to support me without being improper. His eyes were wild, showing his panic and complete puzzlement about what to do with this female who had suddenly appeared in front of him. Finally, he hit on the perfect solution.

'Sarah! Hellen!' he called. But unfortunately, the female staff seemed to be out of hearing range.

'I... no, don't call anybody else, please,' I begged him in a low whisper. Compassion and panic mingled in the face of the young man. My, my, I was pretty good. If Mr Ambrose kicked me out some day I could always try a career as an actress. 'The shame is too great. Please, Sir, don't'

'Of course not, Miss, if it will distress you,' the receptionist answered warmly. 'Only tell me what is the matter with you and how I can help you. Do you wish a room to rest? You look in need of rest.'

'No, I...' Shaking my head, I pressed my clenched hands to my face, half-concealing my features and wiping away a few of the tears that were running down my face. 'I don't need a room. I came... I came to...'

'Yes? Yes?'

'Oh no!' I half turned away from the young man, once again swaying from right to left as if I were about to fall. This was starting to be fun! 'I can't reveal the secret to another living soul! What he has done... it is too shameful. My lips will not form the words. What he has done... No, I cannot tell you. Even if he is here...'

'Who, he?' demanded the young man. 'Has somebody harmed you?'

'Please! Do not force me to speak of it!'

'You said he was here. It is one of our guests who has harmed you?'

'Please, Sir... have pity...'

'Miss,' he said gently, coming around the counter to stand directly in front of me, 'if one of our guests has behaved dishonourably to such a fine young lady as yourself, the honour of our house is in question. I must beg you, please, tell me who this man is and what he has done to you.'

I made a smile flicker across my face, with just the right amount of feminine feebleness and a pinch of sadness thrown in.

'You are too clever, too persistent for me, Sir. You are right. There is indeed a man I am looking for, a man who has done a grievous wrong. I have heard that he might be in this hotel, and have come in the hope of finding a gentleman willing to aid me. And now I have. Oh Sir, you have no idea how great a pleasure it is for a weak girl such as myself to find that there are still strong and honourable men in the world willing to stand up for what is right.'

The receptionist's narrow chest swelled. I fluttered my moist eyelashes at him and it swelled some more. I briefly wondered whether he had a balloon and a pump hidden under his shirt.

'Whatever wrong this man has done to you,' he promised, his voice a bit deeper than it had been before, 'I shall see to it that he gets what is coming to him.'

'Thank you, Sir, thank you!' I clutched his hand with both of mine and gave it a gentle, grateful squeeze. As if I had squeezed a trigger, his chest puffed out a little more. Interesting. This seemed to be a reflex reaction with the brain playing no part in the decision. Well, in what part of the male decision-making process did the brain ever play a part?

'Thank you,' I repeated. 'I shall be eternally grateful to you. But it is not to me that the wrong was done – it is to my sister.'

'Oh.' The receptionist looked slightly crestfallen at this news, so I quickly ploughed on, giving him another sad smile. 'Oh yes, my poor, innocent little sister. Dear Ophelia.'

I had heard the name in a play once. It seemed to fit, because immediately, the concern on the face of the receptionist returned.

'She... Oh, I can't bring myself to say it. You must understand, Sir, she has been educated in a convent. She does not know the ways of men who are no gentlemen, who are not like you. You must not judge her too harshly.'

I sniffled a bit more.

'What happened?' he gently enquired.

'She... she eloped. A man staying in the village of the convent enticed her with honeyed words, sweet words of love and eternal devotion. He said he would marry her.'

The receptionist's mouth dropped open.

'How shocking!'

'Oh no, Sir, the shocking part is yet to come. As I said – my sister is young, only sixteen years of age. She was deceived by his words.'

'Deceived? Do you mean that when...'

'When they had run away together, he... he...' I closed my eyes at this point. It seemed the right thing to do. After all, I was in such terrible pain about my poor little sister Olivia. Or was it Olga? No, Ophelia, right! 'He used her and then threw her away like a soiled handkerchief, left her at the first inn where they stopped and disappeared into the night.'

'The devil!'

'Oh please, Sir, your language.'

'I beg your pardon, Miss,' the receptionist said, his face reddened, 'but you must agree that only a demon in human guise, or perhaps a Frenchman, not an English gentleman, should be expected to behave in such a manner.'

'I cannot argue with you, Sir. It is not in my power to offer anything in defence of that man. Even though I might not like the harsh terms in which you express your view of him, it is nevertheless justified.'

The receptionist, overcome with his emotions and his manliness for a moment, stood there mute, holding my hand in silent support.

'And what is to become of your sister now?' He asked after a moment. 'What will your father do?'

'That is just the thing.' Renewed tears sprang to my eyes – and I didn't even have to use another onion. I wasn't just good at this, I was top-hole![24] A natural talent! 'We have not a father nor a mother, not even an uncle. We are all alone in the world, Ophelia and I, and have only each other.'

'And your name is?'

That was something I had pondered for quite a while before starting to put this little plan of mine into action. I mean, Lilly Linton? That didn't sound very romantic. It clucked off the tongue, rebounded from the teeth and came shooting out of the mouth like cannon fire. No. I needed a name with weight. With romance. So why not let myself be inspired by romance?

'Juliet,' I said. 'Miss Juliet Desdemona Bennet.'

'Miss Bennet, you have my sincerest condolences.' He pressed my hand again, with all the masculinity he could muster. 'Both for the death of your parents and the misfortune that has befallen you since. I stand in awe at your bravery, for I can see what has happened since. For love of your sister, you went out in search of this man, did you not? You, who had no one in the world, dared to go after such a monster?'

'How could I not?' I asked, my voice wavering just right. 'Ophelia is my only sister. Her honour and happiness mean more to me than life itself.'

'And you suspect him of staying in our hotel, this man?'

Oh boy. This was really working out nicely. Apparently I had delivered the first part of my performance so well that he was doing the rest of the job for me. So I just gave a shaky little nod.

'He shall be brought before the magistrate!' the receptionist proclaimed.

'Oh no! No, Sir, I beg of you!' Quickly I pressed his hand, which immediately caused some more chest-puffing. Yes, apparently this was a male reflex and worked quite automatically. Fascinating. 'If that were to happen, if the whole matter were to become public, my sister's honour would be forever ruined!'

'Oh, I see.' Floundering for a moment, the receptionist enquired: 'But what, then, do you intend to do?'

'I intend to confront him. To force him to marry my sister after all.'

'You alone? Miss Bennet, that would be far too dangerous.'

'I shall not be alone. There is a man – an old acquaintance of my father – who has promised to assist me. He cannot aid me in the search because he has his sick wife to take care of, but once I have found the miscreant, he has sworn he will come and place before the man the choice: to marry my sister or fight a duel to the death.'

The receptionist nodded solemnly.

'Then all that remains for me to do, Miss Bennet, is to determine whether or not you are right in your suspicion that this man is staying with us.'

Wonderful! I couldn't have put it better myself.

---

[24] Old British English expression for 'excellent' or 'fantastic'. Another one of those dying British English words that deserves linguistic rejuvenation.

'Indeed, Sir,' I said, blinking up at him tearfully, 'that would be most kind.'
Most kind indeed. Now get on with it before the onion stops working.

The receptionist went back behind the counter and picked up the big book in which all the guests signed their names. 'If you would be so good as to tell me his name, Miss?'

'His name is Mr Simmons. But I doubt he would have used his real name to sign into your book. He knows he is being sought and will probably make use of an alias.'

'How clever of you!' the receptionist exclaimed. 'I would never have thought of that.'

That, I believed.

'But then how will we find out if he is here?' he asked.

'I can give you his description,' I offered. Finally we were getting to the interesting part. 'My sister has told me exactly what he looks like. He has quite a distinctive appearance.'

'Then please do.' The receptionist nodded eagerly. 'I see all the people who check into our hotel, and it is part of my job to have a good memory for faces. I will certainly be able to tell you whether he is here.'

'Oh, I am so relieved.' I put a trembling hand over my heart. 'Thank you for your kindness, Sir. The man I am looking for is tall and gangly, with a long nose, long blonde hair and a thin moustache, and a scar over his right eyebrow.'

A curious expression spread over the receptionist's face: a mixture of disappointment and relief.

'Well, that is quite distinctive, Miss, and I can tell you right away that we have no one of that description living under our roof.'

'Indeed?' I began to back up. 'Well... then I was wrong. Sorry for your trouble.'

'Wait a minute, Miss. What will you...'

'I suppose I will have to go look somewhere else now. Bye!'

And I was out of the door.

Outside Mr Ambrose awaited me, looking at his open watch and tapping his foot on the ground. His fingers were unconsciously tracing some pattern on the lid.

'And?' he asked as soon as he saw me.

'He's not here.'

'How do you know that?' he growled through clenched teeth.

I winked. 'Let's just say... by the use of feminine wiles.'

~~**~*~*

Twenty-five hotels later.

'... I don't quite see. If you do not want the man brought before the law, what then do you intend to do?' the receptionist asked, concern in his voice. Gosh, it really was amazing how similar male minds were.

'I intend to confront him. To force him to marry my sister after all.'

'All by yourself? Miss Bennet, that would be far too dangerous!'

136

Hey, he had actually said 'by yourself' instead of 'alone'! So men were capable of some variety after all!

'I shall not be alone,' I answered, sniffling. 'There is a man – an old acquaintance of my father – who has promised to assist me. He cannot aid me in the search because he has his sick wife to take care of, but once I have found the miscreant, he has sworn he will come and place before the man the choice: to marry my sister or fight a duel to the death.'

The receptionist nodded solemnly.

'Then all I can do is to find out whether or not you are right in supposing this man to be staying with us.'

'Indeed, Sir,' I said, blinking up at him tearfully, 'that would be most kind.'

The receptionist went back behind the counter and picked up the big book in which all the guests signed their names. 'If you would be so kind as to give me the man's name, Miss?'

Yes, if you would be so kind as to do a handstand and a few pirouettes for me! God, can none of you ever say anything really different? Men! All the same!

'His name is Mr Simmons. But I doubt he would have used his real name to sign into your book. He knows he is being sought and will probably make use of an alias.'

'How ingenious!' the receptionist exclaimed. 'I would never have thought of that. But then how will we determine if he is here?'

Well, the same way I did it in the last twenty-five hotels, you dolt!

'I can give you his description,' I offered, having to restrain myself to keep from yawning. This was getting old. 'My sister has told me exactly what he looks like. He has quite a distinctive appearance.'

'Then please do.' The receptionist nodded eagerly. 'I see all the people who check into our hotel, and it is part of my job to have a good memory for faces. I will certainly be able to tell you whether he is here.'

Yes, yes, of course you will... Now can you stop blabbering so we can get on with this?

'Oh, I am so relieved.' I put a trembling hand over my heart. 'Thank you for your kindness, Sir. The man I am looking for is tall and gangly, with a long nose, long blonde hair and a thin moustache, and a scar over his right eyebrow.'

Again I had to suppress a yawn. Here we go again.

A grim smile spread over the receptionist's face.

'Miss, I believe you have caught your villain! A man of just such a description is indeed staying under our roof at this very moment!'

THE THIEF

My sleepiness vanished in an instant.

'A-are you sure?' I stuttered, this time not having to fake my feelings.

I was floored. My plan had worked! It had actually worked! Of course I never doubted it would, in a theoretical, philosophical, let's-think-this-problem-through way, but to have it actually succeed – that was something else.

'Yes, quite sure, Miss. He's in room forty-five on the third floor.'

'Um… thank you.'

Suddenly, I realized that now I was going to have to go out and tell Mr Ambrose that I had found Simmons. All this time I had been so obsessed with finding the thief, with proving to my employer that I actually could be of some use, that I hadn't thought about what might happen when we finally did catch him.

Now we had. And I was going to have to go out and tell that to Mr Ambrose, a man who didn't seem overly shy about taking the law and everything else he could into his own hands.

I looked down at my own hands. Soon, I realized, I might have blood on them.

But then, if you thought about it, it was a thief's blood. And who knew, I might even get a raise out of it.

Before I could think better of it, I left the hotel and opened the cab door.

'We have him,' I said.

All of them turned and stared at me as if I had just announced that the Duke of Wellington was a French pussycat.[25]

'You… you mean to say Simmons is in there? In this hotel?' Warren asked.

I rolled my eyes. 'No, he's in Siberia. *Yes of course* I meant he's in this hotel! What else do you think I'm talking about?'

'Well, that's… That's quite impressive. Congratulations.'

Karim held up a hand.

'Do not give out congratulations, Warren *Sahib*, before we have proof of the truth. It is easy to *say* he is there.' He raised an eyebrow at me. 'But have you indeed seen the man we seek with your own eyes?'

'No,' I had to admit. 'But he is here.'

'It is easy for you to say so, but he may be indeed farther than the stars and the sky.'

I turned to Mr Ambrose. 'Where did you pick this fellow up? Does he always talk like this?'

My employer chose to ignore this. He was examining me carefully without saying a word. Finally he inquired in a low voice:

'He is really there?'

'Yes,' I said firmly. 'He is.'

'Then let's go.'

Mr Ambrose was out of the cab and halfway across the street in a flash. His arms came up, one of them holding a cane I hadn't noticed before. He gestured, and Warren's men were suddenly out of the cab, too, spreading out in a loose semi-circle behind him.

---

[25] Field Marshal Arthur Wellesley, 1st Duke of Wellington, who defeated Napoleon in the Battle of Waterloo and saved Britain from occupation by the French Army, was Great Britain's most revered military hero. To refer to him as a French pussycat would have been considered less than polite in Victorian Britain.

Six of them, together with Karim, remained at the entrance to the hotel while the rest, without needing any orders, followed him in. They seemed to be well accustomed to follow his silent commands.

Well, I sure as hell wasn't! Cursing, I hurried after them.

The doorman of the hotel seemed to be quite surprised at the company in which I was returning. His surprise, however, was nothing to that of the receptionist, whose mouth actually dropped open as we marched into the entrance hall. We passed him before he had a chance to say or do anything and were already up the first flight of stairs when we heard him call out.

'Where to?' Mr Ambrose inquired, completely ignoring the shout of the receptionist.

'Room forty-five on the third floor.' I called from behind. 'And slow down, will you? It's no easy job climbing stairs in this blasted corset!'

Will it surprise you to hear that he didn't slow down?

Muttering a very unladylike curse, I sped up and managed to catch up with them just as they reached the third floor.

Mr Ambrose stood on the landing like an admiral on the bridge. With his cane, he pointed at a door a little distance down the corridor bearing the large brazen number forty-five. Then he nodded to his men.

Again the men seemed to understand without needing to be given orders. Two of them positioned themselves on either side of the door while another strode up directly to the entrance and knocked on the dark wood barring the way.

There was a short silence. Then:

'Yes? What do you want?'

The voice was high and slightly arrogant. I could see it fitting perfectly to the man Mr Ambrose had described. Thin, blonde, and a bit vain.

'Room service, Sir,' Warren's associate replied in a perfect I-am-a-well-mannered-servant tone.

'Room service? I didn't order anything.'

'I know, Sir. Compliments of the house, Sir. We always present a bottle of the best wine from our cellars to guests who stay longer than three days.'

'Oh, if that's the case...' The scraping of a chair came from the other side of the door. 'Would be a shame to let it go to waste.'

Warren's man sprang to the side, and silent as a shadow Mr Ambrose took his place. I tried to move so that I could get a look at the door when it opened, but Warren held me back.

'Not yet!' he hissed. 'Wait until he opens the door!'

Steps approached from inside the room. I waited, counting my breaths in a futile attempt to calm myself. Suddenly I was wishing that I had changed back into trousers and a shirt before coming up here. Say what you will about the degradation and annoyance involved in pretending to be a man, it certainly gives you more freedom of movement.

The door opened.

Mr Ambrose nodded to whomever was on the other side.

'Hello, Simmons.'

I heard a startled yelp, and then the door moved to close so fast my eye hardly caught the movement. Mr Ambrose caught it, though.

His foot darted forward and wedged itself between door and doorframe. He gripped the doorknob, the desperate man inside still struggling to push the door closed, and thrust it back with surprising strength. The door flew open.

Then he stepped into the room.

'Now!'

Warren let go of my arm and I darted forward. I was in the room even before the six other men. Mr Ambrose was standing over a deathly pale Simmons, who lay on his back on the carpet.

Taking an empty wine glass from a table beside him, Mr Ambrose raised it to the man on the floor in a mock toast.

'Bottoms up. I'm afraid I haven't brought any wine. But I have brought a few of my friends.' The glass sailed out of his hand and crashed against the wall, splintering into a thousand pieces. Simmons twitched, but Mr Ambrose's face remained calm as an iceberg. 'Actually, it's not just the bottoms who are up,' he mused. 'It's the game, too.' His voice suddenly became hard, as impenetrable as a mountain of granite. 'Where is it, Simmons?'

'H-how... how,' stuttered the figure on the floor.

'How I found you?'

Mr Ambrose threw a look over his shoulder, and for a moment his dark eyes held mine, filled with an expression that was difficult to interpret.

'That is none of your concern,' he answered, returning his gaze to Simmons. 'I will ask the questions. Not you.'

'N-no, Sir,' Simmons mumbled, his eyes darting right and left. 'I mean... h-how can I ever thank you. Thank you for coming after me, I mean. There were these men... they entered your office and took some things and forced me to come with them and...'

'Simmons?'

'Yes, Sir?'

'If you utter another lie, you are a dead man.'

Mr Simmons' mouth remained open, but there didn't come one more sound out of it. He seemed to have gotten the message.

Without paying any great deal of attention to the man on the floor, as if he were just another speck of dust, Mr Ambrose went over to the bed and flipped open the suitcase that lay there. It contained a few neatly folded shirts and trousers. With a flick of his cane, Mr Ambrose threw them aside.

An involuntary gasp escaped me as hundreds of banknotes appeared beneath the clothes. I couldn't make out the numbers from where I stood, but I didn't really need to, to be able to tell that this was a lot of money. More than I had ever seen in my life.

All for a piece of paper...

What sort of paper could be worth that much?

'Strange baggage for an abducted man,' Mr Ambrose stated, calmly.

Out of the corner of my eye, I caught a sudden movement. When I turned my head I saw that Simmons was on his feet again and heading for the window.

At first I thought he had gone insane or something and wanted to jump to his death – but then I saw that there was a building outside. A building with a flat roof.

'No! Get him!'

I sprang after him, trying to grab him. Unluckily, I forgot I was wearing a crinoline, got tangled up in the legs of a chair and fell to the ground with an unceremonious crunching sound. The last thing I saw was Simmons jumping out of the window, then my head slammed into the carpet and suddenly my eyes, mouth and nose were filled with fluffy dustiness.

Crap!

I lay there for a few moments, seething and breathing in dust motes. Somebody cleared his throat above me. I looked up to see Mr Ambrose extending his hand towards me.

'Do you need a hand?'

Reluctantly I reached out and grasped his hand. Don't ask me why – but for some reason I had expected his hand to be cold and hard, just like his personality. It wasn't. Oh, don't misunderstand me, it was hard all right. But it also was warm and full of life. It felt strangely... good. Considering the rest of him was so undoubtedly bad.

With a sharp tug, he pulled me to my feet, and for a moment we stood very, very close to one another. I was standing again. And yet he didn't let go of my hand, and I didn't let go of his.

Then I heard a triumphant cry from outside.

'Oh my God! Simmons!' Roughly, I pushed Mr Ambrose out of the way and sprang to the window. From behind me, I heard a hollow thud and an 'ouch', but I didn't care. 'He's getting away!'

Now let me tell you, a hoop skirt is not the right kind of attire for climbing through open windows. But I was about to try anyway when a hand closed around my arm. A hard, familiar hand.

'Don't,' Mr Ambrose commanded. I looked back at him, confusion written all over my face.

'What do you mean, don't? He's getting away!'

'Yes, he is.'

'We have to catch him!'

'I appreciate your concern for the pursuit of justice, Mr Linton,' he said, as cool as a cucumber. 'Even though you did not really have to be so keen on that pursuit as to push me on my backside. However, we don't want to go after Simmons just yet.'

'But...'

'We,' continued Mr Ambrose unperturbed, taking his old but very efficient-looking pocket watch out of his waistcoat pocket, 'have to go after him in exactly one minute and twenty-seven seconds.'

'Huh?'

I stared at him, flabbergasted. He, for his part, completely ignored me. His eyes focused on the watch, he simply stood there, waiting. I got edgier and edgier with every passing second. What the heck was going on?

'Mr Ambrose... shouldn't we go?'

'No.'

'But... '

'No. Be quiet!'

'Blast it, I won't be quiet!' I balled my hands into fists. This was insane. 'I've gone to a lot of trouble to find this thief, *Sir*! And now we're just standing around here while he makes good his escape, and we are waiting for your one minute and twenty-seven seconds to pass!'

'Actually,' he said with another look at his watch, 'it's one minute and three seconds now.'

'What the hell do I care? It makes no sense for us to just be standing around here!'

'On the contrary, Mr Linton. It makes a great deal of sense. Now be quiet and wait.'

I was fuming. But what could I do? He was my master, not the other way around. I had to do what he said. That's what I got paid for, even if it didn't make any sense.

With a snap Mr Ambrose shut his watch – and for the first time, I clearly saw the design on the lid. The sight struck me light a thunderbolt: it was a family crest. The same family crest I had seen on the pink letters from the mysterious lady.

'All right. It's time.'

Gripping the windowsill, he vaulted out of the open window. In quick succession, Warren and the others followed him. I just stood there, trying to shake off my shock.

What did this mean? Was Mr Ambrose really a nobleman? But why wouldn't he use his... I shook my head. No. Not now. I didn't have time for this now.

Unfreezing, I started to follow the others through the window. It took me two or three attempts, and I probably broke half of the crinoline beneath my dress into pieces, but finally I managed to squeeze myself through the opening. With a crash of breaking hoops I landed on the neighbouring building.

'Very graceful,' Mr Ambrose commented from beside me. 'Now hurry up. We have a thief to catch.'

By the time I had managed to get to my feet, he was already striding along the roof towards the distant figure of Simmons. Striding, not running.

Simmons, however, was running. Oh boy, how he was running. He already was off the flat roof of this building and onto the next, built right beside it. What was Mr Ambrose thinking? He still hadn't sped up, and he would never catch up with the thief at this pace!

But Mr Ambrose didn't seem to mind. He strode along the roof, his cane in his hand, his six men flanking him, as though nothing in the world could escape him. Getting to my feet, I hurried after them as quickly as I could.

But it would be no use. They weren't going to hurry up, I could see that now, and I wasn't in the best condition for a chase, wearing a broken hoop skirt and bruises in various places.

With a cry of triumph, Simmons jumped onto the next building. There was some sort of structure on top – the entrance to a staircase that led down onto the street! He would do it! He would get away!

Then the men appeared.

They appeared as sudden as could be: from behind chimneys, gables and bay windows. They stood between Simmons and his escape. As soon as he saw them, he froze.

I didn't understand until I saw the giant turban-wearing figure right in the middle of the men, opposite Simmons. Karim. The pack of wolves had cornered their prey.

Catching up to Mr Ambrose, I hissed in his ear: 'You were planning this the whole time, weren't you? You sent Karim up on the roof before we went in!'

'Yes.'

'So why did you leave me stewing like this? Why didn't you tell me?'

His face remained completely expressionless. 'Hmm... I really can't think why I did that. I mean, you have always been so open and honest with me.'

'Oh ha, ha, ha.'

He threw a sideways glance at me and my hoop skirt, which now would have to be more appropriately described as a hexagonal skirt with severe sartorial malformation. 'By the way, Mr Linton, I like your new look. The dress looks exquisite on you. Those tears down the side and the broken whalebones – quite *haute couture*[26], I must say.'

'Thank you, Sir,' I hissed. If looks could only kill, he would be already decapitated right now.

Up ahead, Simmons had turned around and was chasing back over the roofs. Apparently he had thrown a look back earlier and seen nobody following and now expected the way to be clear. When he caught sight of the eight of us approaching, he stopped dead.

Mr Ambrose nodded to his six men. They stopped walking, just standing still and watching. He himself took a few more steps forward until only a few yards separated him from his prey.

'Simmons,' he said in a level tone. That was all. Just the name.

The thief looked around him with wild eyes, searching for a way to escape. But there was none. Then he looked down into the street. The few people who were walking down there in the fog had not looked up and noticed anything yet. They were totally oblivious to the goings-on far above their heads.

Simmons opened his mouth.

'I wouldn't do that,' Mr Ambrose warned. And there it was – that cool tone of superiority in his voice that solely belonged to old aristocracy. How come I had never noticed it before?

With great effort, Simmons swallowed. His eyes darted to Mr Ambrose, and away again.

'D-do what?'

---

[26] French for 'high dressmaking'. It is a term normally used to describe the most exquisite and expensive fashion, or, in this case, to utilize sarcasm.

'You were going to call out.'

'Mr Ambrose, I never...'

'Do you remember what I said would happen to you if I heard one more lie from your lips?'

The thin blonde man paled and took a step backwards.

'Mr Ambrose, Sir, please...'

With a few bold steps, Mr Ambrose stood in front of the quivering Simmons. He looked cold, hard, and implacable – a lord or even a king sitting in judgement over his traitorous subject. I didn't want to be in my predecessor's shoes right now.

'The file, Simmons. Where is it?'

The intensity in his voice... again, curiosity welled up in me as to the contents of that damned file. Maybe, if I asked Mr Ambrose again...

The other said nothing, but just continued to quiver where he stood.

'Where is the file, Simmons?'

No answer.

'For the last time – *where is the file?*' Mr Ambrose's voice had gotten colder as he spoke and now sounded sharp and dangerous as an iceberg. 'You will give it to me, or... or.... or maybe you cannot.' His dark eyes widened a little. 'The money on your bed... You have already been paid for your theft! You haven't got the file anymore. It is...'

Simmons dashed forward and tried to push past Mr Ambrose. He grabbed the ex-secretary's arm and Simmons whirled around. His hand disappeared under his tailcoat for a moment and reappeared holding a short but wickedly sharp-looking sword.[27]

I think I gave a shout or scream or something, I didn't really know. Everything happened in a blur of motion. The blade of Simmons' sword came up and would have stabbed Mr Ambrose in the gut, but then it smashed against something I couldn't see, and a metallic sound rang out over the rooftops.

Mr Ambrose sprang back, holding his cane defensively in front of him. His wooden cane? But then what had made that metallic sound?

Gripping its lower part with the left hand, Mr Ambrose pulled at the hilt of his cane with the right, and a slim blade shot out of the hollow wood. He raised it in a defensive position and waited.

Simmons came at him, giving a loud screech that sounded hardly human. Their blades met with a clang. Mr Ambrose held him in that position, blade to blade

'You're finished, Simmons,' he said, voice still perfectly cool.

'Really?' Simmons grunted. 'What makes you think you'll beat me?'

'He does.' Mr Ambrose nodded to something behind Simmons.

---

[27] Not a medieval sword, the like of which knights used in the Middle Ages, but something more akin to a sabre which was used during the 19th century by the fashionable Victorian gentleman for self-defence, duelling and murder.

Before the ex-secretary could turn around, Karim stepped up behind him and let the pommel of his sabre come down on his head with a resounding thud. Simmons crumpled to the floor like a marionette whose strings had been cut.

'Simmons, Simmons.' Mr Ambrose shook his head and looked down at the groaning man. 'You really are a simpleton.' Bending down, he pried the sword from Simmons' hand. 'That petty stash of money we found in your room – you should have asked three times as much. Considering the trouble you're in now, it would only have been appropriate.'

Grabbing Simmons by the neck he hauled him to his feet and more or less hurled the man at Karim, who caught him and delivered another blow to his head that knocked him clean unconscious.

'Let's go,' Mr Ambrose said. 'We're finished here.'

The unconscious ex-secretary slung over one shoulder, Karim strode to the staircase entrance that Simmons had been heading for. Apparently, he and the other men had come up this way and had made preparations for coming down again, for when we had climbed down the stairs and left the building, a coach was waiting for us. Not a cab this time, but a real, large coach, with one of those discreetly-dressed men, of which Warren seemed to have an infinite supply, sitting on the box.

The coach was parked directly in front of the entrance, so nobody could see us as we climbed inside. I glanced at Mr Ambrose. Or was he more than just a mister? Images whirled through my head... A noble crest... A suitcase full of money... Flashing swords...

You should have asked three times as much.

Heavens above. What could be worth that much money? What would be worth the risk of betraying this man?

'What an extravagant vehicle,' I remarked, trying to dispel my dark thoughts. 'I'm quite surprised that you would use something as expensive as this.'

'I did a cost-benefit analysis,' he replied, drily, pointing to Simmons limp body. 'And I decided the benefit of not getting thrown into prison for abduction was worth the cost of a coach.'

'Very wise, Sir.'

'Agreed, Mr Linton. Pull down the blinds.'

I rolled my eyes. 'You could at least say please.'

'I could, if I wanted to. Now pull down the blinds.'

The coach had dark blinds on all windows. Once they were pulled down, the interior was quite sinister. It brought back what I had seen on the roof – or at least what I had thought I had seen. Had Mr Ambrose really pulled a sword on Simmons? What kind of man was he to carry a concealed weapon in his cane? What kind of man was he to deny a noble title?

The same questions, over and over again.

No. That wasn't quite true. There was one new question I had, and one I didn't feel quite so apprehensive about voicing.

'What was all that about?' I wanted to know. 'That chasing him over the rooftops. Why didn't we just grab him there in the room?'

Mr Ambrose didn't look at me. Instead, he kept his dark eyes fixed on the unconscious Simmons. But he replied, in his usual curt tone: 'To make things easier for us.'

'I don't understand. How is having to chase him over the rooftops making things easier for us?'

Apparently not in the mood to give lengthy explanations, Mr Ambrose waved to his hired henchmen.

Warren cleared his throat. 'It's easier because if we had brought him out through the hotel's front entrance, or tried to drag him out of the window by force, he would have screamed for help. The guests or hotel staff would have heard and called the police. This way, he attempted to flee, believing that there was still a chance to make a quiet escape. We caught him without anyone being able to interfere.'

'Ah.' Slowly I nodded. 'I see.'

Mr Ambrose nodded, too. 'Exactly. And now...' He took a deep breath. If he were capable of something like emotion, I could have sworn it sounded satisfied. 'Now I can deal with him as I see fit.'

Deal with him as I see fit.

The sentence reverberated in the air with dark promise.

Mr Ambrose raised his cane and knocked against the roof of the coach. 'Take us to Empire House,' he called to the driver. 'The back entrance. We have something to deposit safely in the cellar.'

The cellar? What did he want to put in the ce– oh.

My eyes flicked to Simmons. Of course.

Unbidden, something I had once read in one of my father's old history books fluttered into my mind. What did earls and lords do when they discovered a traitor among their men? If I remembered correctly, after prolonged torture in some dark dungeon, the traitor in question would be hanged, drawn and quartered.

Oh my God. If Mr Ambrose really was an aristocrat, I fervently hoped he wasn't one to keep up old traditions.

Making Lieutenant-Pancake

My ear pressed against the solid metal door, I listened intently for any sound of torture. Not that I knew exactly what torture would sound like, apart from the screaming, of course, which was pretty much a given. Still, it couldn't hurt to try. *Not me, at least,* I thought with a tiny shiver.

Considering Mr Ambrose's words, and even more than that the expression of his eyes, I had no doubt that something terrible was happening in there right now. But I couldn't hear a single sound. Was something the matter with my ears?

But then I suddenly heard footsteps approaching from the other side and hurriedly stepped backwards. A key turned in the lock, and Mr Ambrose exited the room, a ring with a large assortment of keys in his hand.

'And?' I asked. God, I was becoming as monosyllabic as he.

'We've managed to get him awake, but he won't talk.' Looking down, I saw that Mr Ambrose's hand was clenched to a fist around the ring of keys. 'Whoever paid him to do this, they must be powerful and frightening.'

'How do you know this?'

He fixed me with his steely dark gaze. 'Because *I* am powerful and frightening, and he hasn't told me a single thing yet. But he will, eventually.'

How do you know that? How can you be so sure?

Yet those thoughts were not what I spoke out loud. Instead, out spilled the question that had been plaguing me the entire way back to Empire House, the question which I never thought I would have the gall to ask:

'Will you torture him?'

He looked at me, supreme disdain in his eyes. 'No. Of course not.'

A momentous weight, which I hadn't really known was there, dropped from my shoulders. 'Thank the Lord!' I breathed. 'I almost thought...'

'Why would I sully my own hands?' he continued, cutting me off. 'I have people who attend to tasks like that for me.'

'Oh.'

The weight slammed right back in place.

My mood swing had apparently gone completely unnoticed. He motioned towards the closed steel door behind him with a careless finger. 'I have put Karim in charge of the investigation, and he has his methods.'

'Methods like what?' I demanded. Darn, this was... frightening. Something inside me told me I should report this to the police. But if I did that, I would end up on Mr Ambrose's list of traitors, barring all chances of my independence. I was too selfish to risk my entire future on behalf of some greedy little thief I didn't know from Adam. All right, I know I'm not a very good person! But at least I'll get paid for it soon.

Mr Ambrose still hadn't answered. He was looking at me intently.

'Methods like what?' I repeated the question.

'That's nothing a lady such as yourself needs to concern yourself about.'

'Oh, I'm a *lady* now, am I?'

'Currently, it looks like it,' Mr Ambrose said, gesturing towards my dishevelled dress. 'More or less, at least. It's high time that you got back into your trousers though, Mr Linton.'

I narrowed my eyes.

'Why? Do you have work for me, Sir?'

'No. I'm sending you home early.'

I was about to protest when he raised his hands. 'I know. I agreed....' he paused to take a deep breath and with effort said: 'I agreed to let you work for me, just like any other private secretary. This is not an attempt to get rid of you early. I'm giving you half the day off because you've had an exhausting day so far. Trust me, even if you don't notice it now, you'll notice once the excitement

147

of the hunt goes away. You need to rest, and I need to stay with Karim for a bit longer, so right now I don't have anything for you to do. Tomorrow you will come back, and you will work for me as hard as anybody else.'

For a moment I searched his face, trying to determine whether or not he was being truthful. Of course it didn't work. Not with his standard stony expression.

'Promise?' I asked.

He nodded. 'I promise on my honour as a gentleman.'

'But...' I hesitated before asking the question. 'But I'll still have to come dressed up as a man?'

'Yes.' His voice was as hard as granite. 'I cannot and will not accept a female secretary. I will not be made a fool of in front of the entire city. Either you come dressed as a man, or you never return.'

I nodded. This was hard for me to accept, but it was unavoidable. I turned to leave, but Mr Ambrose called me back, and so I turned again.

'What is it, Sir?'

'You know very well what it is. I want to know.'

'Want to know what?'

'Your method, of course. Well?'

'What method? What are you talking about?' I asked, truly bewildered.

A muscle in his jaw twitched in an annoyed sort of way. 'Don't play games with me! How did you do it? Find out where Simmons was?'

Ah! That was what was eating him. I struggled mightily to constrain my grin but probably failed.

'How about a deal?' I said. 'I tell you my method, and you tell me what's in the stolen file?'

His silence was answer enough.

Once again, I saw that mountain of money in front of my inner eye. And he had said it was too little payment...

'I won't tell a soul,' I said. 'I promise!'

'No!' He shot a glare at me. 'I don't have to make any deals with you. You work for me. You will tell me how you did it. Now!'

I hesitated. 'Well...'

I told him. I told him everything, with probably a bit more embellishment and gloating than necessary, but accurately enough. It had worked after all, hadn't it? There was no harm in taking pride in my work.

When I was finished, his stony face was even stonier than before – but his eyes were slightly wider as he gazed at me, and his mouth stood open a fraction.

'Still sure you don't want a female secretary?' I asked.

Then, before he could answer, I curtsied and hurried away.

~~**~*~*

I had decided to change back into men's clothes in my office. It would mean that I would have to change again when I came home, but under no circumstances could I go home in the dress Mr Ambrose had bought for me. None of my family had ever clapped eyes on it before, and besides, it wasn't in very great

148

shape. I was a bit concerned about changing in my office – after all, I couldn't lock the doors, so what if anybody came in? – but there really wasn't anywhere else to go.

As it turned out, my concern was totally unnecessary. On the desk in my office I found a small package. A note was pinned to it, saying:

Dear Mr Linton,

Mr Ambrose instructed me to leave these for you. A friendly word of caution: It is very unusual for his secretary to be entrusted with these around the clock. Take good care of them.

Yours Sincerely,

Edgar Stone

My curiosity spiked. What was in there? Well, there was only one way to find out. I ripped open the paper around the package, and in a little cardboard box I found a ring of keys, not as large as the one Mr Ambrose had been carrying but still substantial. On it hung a key labelled *Secretary's Office* and another labelled *Head Office*.

Slowly, a smile spread over my face. He trusted nobody, hm? Well, maybe he was making an exception to the rule.

Then I noticed that there was no key labelled *Safe* on the ring. Well, it seemed as though he was starting to trust me, at least.

But then, why was he still refusing to reveal the contents of the file...?

I stood there, clutching the set of keys to my chest, feeling oddly emotional. Why, though? Why should it matter to me whether or not my master trusted me? He was just the man I was working for. A man who had yet to pay me my first wages at the end of the month. Whether or not he trusted me was immaterial, as long as I got the money, right?

Yet still, the fact that he was opening up to me touched something deep within me. I felt that maybe, just maybe, he might be starting to respect me. If not as a woman, then at least as an intelligent human being with a head on its shoulders, provided I wore trousers.

Taking the ring of keys, I locked both doors to my office and started the mind-numbing process of changing.

You don't think there's anything more difficult than getting out of a corset and crinoline? Try getting out of a corset and crinoline which are broken and bent in strange angles in at least a dozen places. I felt like a cat trying to squeeze myself through a labyrinth of rat holes.

When I finally stood only in my underwear, it was a relief. I was just about to reach for Uncle Bufford's trousers when a knock came from the door, and the door rattled as someone pushed against it.

I almost jumped out of my skin.

'Y-yes?' I asked, not sounding very manly at all. I cleared my throat and tried again. 'Yes?'

'Mr Linton? It's me, Mr Stone. May I come in?'

'Err... not as such, no.'

'Why? Are you busy?'

No, I'm standing around in women's underwear, which, apart from being pretty indecent, makes it more or less obvious that I'm a girl!

'Um... yes, that's it. Very busy. Very, very, very busy in fact.'

'I see. Well then, I won't disturb you any further. I just wanted to ask if you found the keys all right?'

'Yes, I did.'

Yes I did, thank God, or else my office door wouldn't be locked right now, and you'd be staring at me in my drawers!

'Very well. I understand you're leaving now, Mr Linton?'

'Yes.'

'And Mr Ambrose?'

'He's very, very busy, too, Mr Stone.'

'I see. Well, I'll leave you alone then. Till tomorrow.'

'Yes, goodbye, Mr Stone.'

I heard him moving away and let out the breath I had been holding. I'm not sure what Mr Ambrose's reaction would be to someone discovering my true gender, but he wouldn't be jumping up and down with joy, that much I could tell. Maybe he would be jumping up and down on me instead, wearing iron-shod boots.

Though he probably would shrink from such a display of emotion. He would get Karim to do it. The big fellow would be excellently suited for the task and all too happy to oblige. For some reason, the thought brought a smile to my face.

Grabbing Uncle Bufford's trousers, I dressed in my unusually usual outfit again and left the office, locking the door behind me. Not that I thought somebody might steal my fountain pen, it just was a good feeling. My space. My door. My key. Stuffing the keys securely into my deepest pocket, I began the long descent down to street level.

I didn't call a cab. Luxuries like that would have to wait until I actually received my first pay cheque. Instead I walked home slowly, enjoying for the first time in my life the feeling I had done something useful. No sitting around trying to knit or sew, no silly whirling around in a ballroom full of overdressed nitwits. I had been out there in the real, rough world. And I would return there soon.

My exultation lasted all the way home. As I went in through the garden door and into the shed to change, slowly my feelings of joy waned and I suppressed a yawn. God, my legs hurt from all that running over roofs. The real world was pretty tiring.

As I approached the front door, another concentrated wave of tiredness hit me. Mr Ambrose had been right, today had been exhausting. I needed some rest, and I needed it quick. Fortunately, nothing was likely to get in the way of that. My aunt was sure to be too busy with my other sisters to care if I was lazy and slept through the afternoon.

That was when I first heard the excited chatter from inside the house. Strange... It sounded like we had a visitor. But who would come to visit us? I had to be mistaken.

The moment I stepped into the house, though, the door to the salon flew open and my aunt appeared in the doorway. 'There she is!' She exclaimed, a triumphant smile on her face. 'And just in time. Lilly, my dear, I have a wonderful surprise for you!'

Oh-oh. That didn't sound good.

'What surprise?' I yawned, and blinked furiously to keep my eyes open.

'Look who has come to visit you,' my aunt replied smiling, and waved invitingly to somebody in the room. Footsteps could be heard, and then, directly beside my aunt's triumphant visage, appeared the arrogantly smiling face of Lieutenant Ellingham.

He bowed.

'Miss Linton. How delighted I am to see you again.'

I straightened, and my eyes narrowed. His arrogant smile widened.

Delighted, eh? We'll see whether you still feel like that in five minutes, Mister...

~~**~*~*

'... killed every last one of the savages with my own hands. They were fearsome enemies, but my superior fighting skills struck fear into their hearts which they could not overcome.'

Lieutenant Ellingham thumped his chest theatrically.

'At last, only the big grey beast was left, and so I charged forward and stuck my sabre right into its belly! It collapsed dead on the spot!'

The lieutenant finished his narration with a flourish of the arm, simulating a sabre thrust.

'Marvellous! Simply marvellous!' My aunt, Maria, Anne and Lisbeth applauded enthusiastically, and even Ella moved her hands together a bit, though by no means so forcefully that it could actually be heard.

'What an impeccable display of courage,' Anne proclaimed, fluttering her eyelashes at the lieutenant. 'To think that you all alone went up against a raiding party of twenty-one savages, and charged such a terrifying monster as an elephant! This is the kind of bravery that made the British Empire what it is today!'

'Yes, really amazing,' I yawned.

The lieutenant raised an eyebrow. 'Praise from you, Miss Linton? That is a rare gift indeed. Thank you very much. I am delighted to hear you appreciate my bravery in the face of danger.'

I had to work hard to keep a smirk off my face. 'That's not really what I was talking about. I think it's amazing that you're sitting here alive.'

'That *is* due to his bravery,' Maria pointed out, which the lieutenant acknowledged with a graceful bow of the head.

'More to a miracle,' I disagreed. 'You stabbed the elephant into its belly? From below?'

'Yes?' The lieutenant's voice was suddenly cautious. I had to say that up to this point the conversation had rather bored me. But now I was enjoying myself.

'You see, that's what I find so amazing,' I mused. 'The elephant collapsed, and you were standing right underneath. Yet you are sitting here alive on our couch and are not flattened to some part of the Indian soil as lieutenant-pancake.'

'Err... well... the elephant fell to the side?'

'To the side?' I asked sweetly. 'Onto the savages that you were still busy fighting off?'

'Yes.'

'The ones you said you had already killed before the elephant attacked?'

'Err...'

'Be silent, child,' my aunt chided me. Then, turning to Lieutenant Ellingham, she continued: 'You must excuse my niece, Sir. She has led a very sheltered life and knows little of the ways of the world. Certainly she is totally inexperienced in such manly activities as you have described.'

He nodded graciously. 'That is no problem, Madam. Maybe,' he said, throwing a suggestive glance in my direction, 'I could show her a few *manly activities*. Then she would not be so ignorant anymore.'

I thought I was going to be sick.

'Which brings me to the point of my visit,' Lieutenant Ellingham continued, rising and extending his hand to me. 'Which is to enquire whether Miss Lillian Linton would wish to go for a walk with me. There is a beautiful park outside your house, and I am sure there are some things she has not seen there before.'

There were various possible answers to that:

Oh yes, of course there are things I haven't seen yet in the park. I've only lived here for over a decade of my life.

Or:

Hey, you can talk to me directly, you know! I'm right here in the room.

Or better yet:

Go for a walk with you? I'd rather go for a walk with a drunken French sailor!

But then I saw my aunt's face over the lieutenant's shoulder and decided on the more diplomatic:

'Um... I don't know. I think I know my way around the park pretty well already. But thanks for the offer.'

'That is no matter,' he said, waving my answer away. 'It is not the park I wished to see when coming here, but you. It is not the lush green trees I wish to enjoy, but your company, Miss Linton.'

Ugh! So much for diplomacy!

He extended his hand farther. Over his shoulder my aunt glared at me, promising death and destruction if I made the wrong choice now. Wasn't there any way to get out of this?

Then I thought: *Come on, it's only a walk. It's not like he's asking you to marry him. Well, not yet anyway. What harm can a walk do?*

Preferring not to think about the answer to that question, I took his hand and faked as believable a smile as possible.

'I would be delighted to take a walk through the park,' I told him, neglecting to mention that the same wasn't true for having him along as company.

He took my hand. It felt moist and alien. Holding it was a repellent feeling, like having a bug crawl up your arm. But I smiled bravely as I let him lead me out of the room. At least this would keep my aunt happy.

As we left the room, I couldn't help a thought shooting through my head: how very, very different this hand felt from that of Mr Rikkard Ambrose.

~~*~**~*~*

'...and I was standing there, you see? Two hundred feet away from the Indian, and even farther away from the young lady he was running towards, knife in hand. I knew I couldn't reach him or her in time. Yet I also knew that I was a crack shot.'

Personally, I would have called him a crackpot rather than crack shot.

I was walking beside Lieutenant Ellingham through Green Park. His promise to show me new spots in the park was long forgotten. He was far too busy entertaining me with stories of his supposed adventures in India. So far, he had killed about three hundred seventy-nine so-called 'savages,' thirteen elephants, five lions and one giraffe. Quietly I wondered whether he actually thought me stupid enough to believe above one word in ten.

'I took out my rifle, aimed, and bamm! He lay dead on the ground, shot through the heart. The medicine man of his tribe had never seen a gun shot before. So he and all the other Indians believed I was a god of some sort and freed the young lady when I commanded it.'

'Excuse me?' I interrupted. 'Medicine man? Tribe? I thought you were talking about Indians that live in India, not the kind that live in America. Only those have medicine men, or tribes.'

'Oh, really?' The lieutenant shrugged. 'Well, maybe he was on holiday in India. These savages are strange people, you know?'

'I can think of some that are even stranger,' I muttered, but he either didn't hear it or wasn't very well-versed in sarcasm.

After that, he didn't start telling any adventure stories again. Well, he had talked for the last half hour pretty much non-stop. Maybe it was time I contributed something to the conversation. But what could I say apart from, 'You may have a square jaw and a whitewashed smile, but you are the most odious man I ever met. Get the hell away from me right now, because I never ever wish to see you again. And by the way, I don't like you, and you smell funny.'

The face of doom, otherwise known as the face of my aunt, appeared in front of my inner eye, staring at me ferociously. Oh well, I guess I could at least make a tiny effort to be civil.

'Err... you seem to have led a very exciting life so far. Rescuing ladies... shooting Indians... must be fun. I mean the rescuing of ladies, not the other part.'

He sighed like a wise, worldly man talking to a silly student.

'Actually, the shooting is the part that is more fun. The ladies get tiresome over time. They are always so overwhelmed by thankfulness. So many ladies have shown interest in me that I have really grown tired of what is called the fair sex.'

'Oh well, if that is so, you're probably very tired of my society,' I jumped at the opportunity. 'I should leave you immediately.'

'On the contrary.' Shaking his head, he turned to me with an arrogant grin on his face. 'It is that fact that made me come to you.'

What?

'You're so unlike the other ladies,' he continued. 'Other ladies sigh and whimper to get a man's attention. You on the other hand – you are feisty! You insult me and push me back – but I've figured you out! It's your way of saying you're attracted to a man.'

What the...!

'It's no great surprise, I suppose.' He took a step closer to me, his eyes gleaming with some dark emotion that made me shiver all over. I remembered my earlier thoughts about what could possibly happen on a walk in the park, and the unwelcome idea occurred to me that I might be about to find out first hand.

I didn't like the expression on his face, not at all. He no longer looked like the pleasant, if slightly arrogant, young man of a few minutes ago. He now looked like a very, very nasty arrogant young man. And his eyes were fixed on me.

Desperately I looked around for anybody, but we were standing hidden behind a clump of trees. No help was in sight.

'You've had no proper upbringing, aren't even a proper lady,' he was saying. 'But that actually could make you quite fun, you know? Ladies are very restrained, but I'm sure you would be more open to... amusement.'

Taking another step forward, he leaned towards me. I didn't even know where it came from. My hand just to seem to appear out of thin air and make contact with his cheek.

Slap!

'Don't you dare touch me!' I snarled.

I thought maybe he would be angry. Or he would back off. Instead, he laughed.

'That's what I'm talking about,' he chuckled, his eyes dancing. 'It's really been getting annoying, so many girls throwing themselves at me because of my good looks and my position as an officer. You're different. A challenge.'

'I'll give you a challenge if you don't back off!' I threatened, raising my hand again. Taking a leisurely step backwards, he cocked his head.

'Plus, you're from a good family. Most of those stuck-up mothers at Sir Philip's ball wouldn't have let a poor soldier like myself near one of their daughters. But your aunt... I think she'd be happy if she could convince a beggar to take you. If I made you mine, she'd be delighted – and so would I. Granted, you don't have money, and neither does your family, so the dowry won't be worth marrying for, but in the military a good name is more often of greater worth. You have that, so you'll suit me admirably. The only thing that remains is for me to make it official.'

'Official? What are you talking about?'

'Why, marrying you of course.'

My eyeballs almost dropped out of my head. 'Marriage? I'm not getting married to anybody! And most certainly not to you!'

He sneered. 'What? You'd prefer a covert thing between us? I wondered whether that might be more your style.'

Covert thing? What kind of covert thing? The glint in his eyes told he was talking about something dark, something far less innocent than my little sister's secret meetings in the back garden. I had no idea what exactly and, honestly, I didn't want to find out.

'But I'm afraid I can't help you there,' he continued. 'I'm a gentleman and unfortunately have to behave as such. I shall have to wait until we are married before I can start taming you.'

'Go now,' I said, making my voice icy in my best imitation of Rikkard Ambrose. 'Right now! Or I will scream until the entire city of London comes running!'

He hesitated – then shrugged.

'Very well, just as you like.' The bastard had the audacity to wink at me! 'But I will get you, make no mistake. And you know you'll enjoy it when I do.'

I wondered whether there were smaller, feminine versions of that handy cane-sword that Mr Ambrose had used the other day. If so, I was going to buy myself one with my very first pay cheque. Occasions like this required a weapon more effective than a parasol.

'Who do you think you are?' I hissed at him. 'You can't just say such things to me! Who the hell do you think you are?'

'I?' He raised an arrogant eyebrow. 'I am your suitor.'

'My what?'

'Your suitor. I want you, and I'm going to get you one way or another.'

'No you won't! Not when I tell my family what you dared to say to me!'

'Oh really?' His eyebrow wandered up another inch. 'I have witnessed how very, um... dear you are to your aunt. Whom do you think she will believe? Bright, brilliant young Lieutenant Ellingham or a niece who can't even behave herself properly at her first ball?'

He raised his hat to me and made a slight, mocking bow.

'Good day to you, Miss Linton. I look forward to seeing you again.'

And he walked away.

~~**~*~*

Blast! If only he hadn't vanished that quickly! I might have punched him! Or bitten him! Or...

All right. I admit it. The thoughts that ran through my head as I walked through the streets of London, towards home, weren't the most romantic ones for a girl to whom a man had just as good as proposed. But then, it hadn't been the most romantic quasi-proposal. In fact, even I, who was definitely not an expert on quasi-proposals, could say that it had been about as romantic as a bucket of vomit.

Which, by the way, was also a very fitting description of my suitor.

'Bloody bastard! Oh, the next time I see him, I'll... I'll...'

I couldn't even find the words. Maybe I would have to sneak into the room where Mr Ambrose was holding Simmons, to get some inspiration on torture.

'Something spiky... with wicked screws, maybe!'

Only when I got home and saw my aunt's delighted harpy-smile as she looked at the latest flowers Lieutenant Ellingham had sent did I fully realize the son of a bachelor had been right.

Bugger! She really expects me to marry him!

A shiver ran down my back when I also realized that I was not in a good position to do anything against it. I was still under age. My legal guardians could dispose of me however they wished – and my aunt was very efficient in the disposal of rags, hen droppings, penniless relatives and other garbage.

Even were I already an adult, what could I do? I was dependent on others to pay for the food I ate, the bed I slept in and the roof over my head. It was those people who ruled my life. I had no money of my own.

Or at least, the thought shot through my head, *that was true until very recently.*

'Thank the Lord!' I breathed.

Never before had I been so glad that I had run into a certain stone-faced businessman that day on the way to the polling station. Never had I been so glad that I had taken the leap towards my own freedom. And never ever had I been so grateful towards Mr Ambrose. He could have turned me away. In fact, there had probably been nothing he wanted to do more. Yet instead he had kept his word and given me a chance.

My fingers travelled into the folds of my petticoats where the ring of keys was artfully concealed. More than that: he had given me his trust.

And soon, hopefully, he would give me some money. I just had to hold out until then.

Head held high, I started up the porch stairs, past my aunt, ignoring her chattering. Now that my harrowing encounter with the lieutenant was over, my exhaustion returned with renewed force. I needed to lie down, and quickly, or I would just keel over and take a nap on the floor.

Up in my room, Ella was waiting for me with a half-anxious, half-happy expression on her face. I walked past her and let myself fall face-downward onto my mattress, not caring about the protesting squeak from my hoop skirt.

'So...' I heard Ella's hesitant voice from behind me, 'did you have a nice walk with Lieutenant Ellingham?'

'No,' I groaned into my pillow.

There was a pause. Then:

'Um... this might be a silly question... but is he the young man you went to meet the other day? The one you have feelings for?'

With a gargantuan effort, I raised my head from my pillow and turned to stare at my little sister.

'You're absolutely right.'

'Oh!' Ella's expression brightened.

I let my head slump back onto the pillow. 'That *was* a silly question.'

'Ah.' Her face fell again.

'Honestly, Ella! Me and that blighter? How could you possibly think I have any feelings for him whatsoever, apart from abject horror and disgust?'

'He wasn't that bad,' Ella tried to console me. 'Although I must admit... I was very frightened by the way he treated those people and that poor grey animal. What did he call it again? An elephont?'

'Elephant,' I corrected.

'Exactly.' Ella shook her head sadly. 'I mean, did he have to stab it? He could have tried talking to it or petting it. Grandmother's chickens always let me pet them when I visit, and they're perfectly friendly if you show them some affection.'

'Don't worry,' I moaned and rolled over on my side to face her. 'Do not let the poor elephant's plight torture your heart. There was no fight in India, ergo there was no elephant and no stabbing in the belly.'

'What?' A frown appeared on Ella's lovely forehead. 'But Lieutenant Ellingham said...'

I gave a sigh. 'I will tell you a great secret, Ella, if you promise not to tell anybody.'

'Oh... of course!'

'Not everything a man says to a woman must necessarily be true.'

I sank deeper into my pillow, snuggling into the soft down feathers. I knew it would take Ella a while to adjust to the concept of such a thing as a dishonourable or lying man – certainly enough time for me to get a nap. So I slowly drifted off into the realm of Morpheus, where I happily chased thieves over rooftops, cut onions into slices, and didn't have to worry about catastrophes such as an impending engagement to the biggest bastard of London.

..**.*.*

My eyes fluttered open. The first thing I saw was Ella, who was sitting beside me on the bed, staring down at her fingers in deep contemplation. When she noticed I was awake, she looked at me.

'You mean... you mean the lieutenant was *lying*?'

I sneaked a glance at the old grandfather clock in the corner of the room. Two hours and twenty-six minutes. Not bad.

'Exactly. You've figured it out. Bravo!'

'But... that's horrible!'

I shrugged. 'Well, depends how you look at it. Lying can be quite useful sometimes, you know. For instance when there's something going on in your life you don't want anybody to know.'

Ella's cheeks turned as red as a ripe tomato. I had been thinking of my new occupation when speaking, but it was clear that her thoughts were on something very different, or rather somebody.

'Um... I suppose so,' she managed.

'And? Tell any good lies lately?' I inquired lightly, propping myself up on my elbows to get a better look at her.

'No! I didn't. Definitely not!'

'I see.' As hard as I tried, I couldn't keep the grin off my face. Ella, who seemed desperate to change the subject, blurted out:

'But what will you do? I mean, if Lieutenant Ellingham isn't the young man you've been seeing, what will you do? If he continues to pay attention to you, Aunt Brank will expect you to marry him, you know.'

'Oh yes, I know. But then, that's no surprise since Aunt Brank would expect me to marry any willing creature in trousers who walked through the door downstairs, just to get me out of the house.' I rolled my eyes.

'What will you do?' Ella repeated, anxiously. 'How will you reconcile yourself to having to say goodbye to your true love and marry somebody else?'

Oh right! Ella was still convinced that every time I went to work, I was going on a secret rendezvous with my mystery lover. Opening my mouth, I was about to explain to her that I didn't have and never would have a love in my life when it occurred to me that this would raise a whole lot of questions regarding my frequent absence. So I just said:

'Believe me, I'm not going to marry that blighter.'

Once again, Ella seemed to have problems with grasping my thought processes. 'But... Aunt wants you to marry him!'

'Yes.'

'And you're not going to?'

'No! You can bet your best silk parasol on that!'

'But... that would mean... *defying Aunt*.'

I clapped my hands. 'Bravo! You didn't even need two hours to figure that one out.'

'Tell me, my dear sister.' Eagerly, Ella knelt down on the bed beside me and clasped my hands. 'How would you do it? How would you bring yourself to walk up to her and say: "No! I do not want to marry this man, for my heart belongs to another!"?'

'Err... well, I would just do it.' *Apart from the my-heart-belongs-to-another part.*

'Oh Lilly!' Ella embraced me with all the strength and sisterly affection she was capable of. And while she didn't have much of the former, she had plenty of the latter. 'You're so brave. How I wish I had your courage. And you will truly rebel? Set yourself against this marriage with everything you have?'

I simply nodded and held her tightly, wishing so much that I could help her in her predicament. But unfortunately, she would have to find the strength herself.

'Yes,' I said. 'I will not marry Lieutenant Ellingham.'

'Oh Lilly!' She hugged me once more. 'Tell me about him, will you?'

'About who? The lieutenant?'

'No, not him! About your young man! The one you see on your rendezvous! The one whose love inspires you to such bravery!'

My mouth dropped open. Never in a million years had I expected that my brilliant excuse would backfire like this. What the hell could I tell her? I had absolutely no idea. I had absolutely no interest in men. What were women supposed to find attractive in men? Why would they lose their mind and fall in love with one?

Dear Lord, I had to tell her something, but what? Who from my acquaintance could I pick as my supposed lover? The only men I'd known for more than a couple of moments were my father, who was dead for years, and my Uncle Bufford, both of whom were, for obvious reasons, not good candidates. Should I pick one of the men from Sir Philip's ball? But to be honest, I couldn't remember a single one of them. Men just never seemed very important to me. They slipped my mind as soon as I left their company.

Well, except perhaps for one. A face appeared in front of my eyes.

'Um... well...' I began.

'Come on,' Ella urged. 'Don't be shy.'

'Err... he's tall, with dark hair and dark, sea-coloured eyes, almost black.'

She clapped her hands eagerly, like an excited little girl. 'Oh, that sounds so dreamy and mysterious.'

'You can say that again!' Too mysterious for my liking... he still hadn't breathed a word about the contents of that infernal file. Could there be something government-related in it? But if anything, Mr Ambrose struck me as the type who did what he wanted without reference to any government, his own or anybody else's.

'Is he good-looking?'

'W-what?' I resurfaced from my thoughts. Caught off guard, the words escaped me: 'Yes, he is, definitely.'

Oh God! What have I just said?

But if I was being honest, it was true. Blast!

'He... he has a chiselled face, and I mean literally chiselled: angular, and hard as stone. Maybe good-looking isn't even the best word to describe him. Beautiful would be better. A harsh beauty.'

The image of the face in front of my inner eye intensified, and an unwilling smile crept on my face.

'As for the rest of him... He has a figure like an antique statue, you know? A bit like Myron's Discus Thrower[28], though he would never dream of assuming such an undignified position.' I giggled. 'He walks around most of the time as if he has an iron rod up his behind. He's very serious, cool and distant, and about as free with his money as Uncle Brank. He always does what he wants, and nasty things happen to people who get in his way.'

Hmm... Perhaps I wasn't doing a very good a job of portraying him as the fellow I was desperately in love with. Shouldn't a lovable man have *one* good quality, at least? So I hurriedly added: 'But I think he actually may have a good heart, very, very, very deep down.'

Who knew, it might actually be true. He had taken me on, after all.

But not as a girl, said a nasty little voice in the back of my mind. I shook my head, trying to concentrate.

---

[28] A famous antique statue of a (quite impressively muscled) Olympic athlete, by the ancient Greek sculptor Myron – one of the most famous statues of antiquity, in spite of the fact that the broken-off arm was put back on wrongly during restoration.

159

'Oh Lilly!' Ella gripped both of my hands with hers. 'I'm so happy for you! He sounds amazing, like a modern-day Mr Darcy.'

'Hardly,' I muttered, smirking at the comparison. '*He* wouldn't spend ten thousand pounds on anybody, let alone me.'[29]

Ella's smile only widened. 'It sounds like you're very fond of him.'

'Does it?'

My eyebrows shot up. Apparently, I had done a better job than I'd thought. I had completely fooled her and made her believe I was in love with Mr Ambrose. I had no idea my acting skills were this developed. It seemed that male impersonations weren't the only thing I did well in that regard.

'And his name?' Ella continued eagerly. 'Tell me, who is he?'

Oops...

WHAT TO DO WITH PINK?

And his name? Tell me, who is he?

For just a moment, Ella's question hung in the air between us like a big, wet elephant on a washing line.

'Please, don't ask,' I blurted out. 'I, um... promised him to tell nobody. Yes, I promised!'

This was such a lousy excuse that no little sister in England would have accepted it. Other little sisters would have dug and bored and drilled until they had uncovered every last bit of the truth. But all those little sisters probably didn't have a secret lover.

Moisture sparkled in Ella's eyes, and the words 'just like me and Edmund' practically blinked on her forehead for all the world to see.

'Of course.' Nodding eagerly, she enfolding me in her arms. 'I understand. Of course you have to keep your love's secret. I understand more than you can ever know.'

Somehow I doubted that. I knew perfectly well why she was feeling so deeply for my supposed plight, and it didn't have anything to do with her general compassionate nature but rather, I suspected, with a certain young man who would soon be waiting for her at the garden fence.

'I really hope you two will find a way to be together,' she breathed into my ear, her voice sounding tearful.

Well *I* sure as hell didn't. I had to work hard to keep myself from laughing at the idea of my marrying Mr Rikkard Ambrose. It would perhaps make an interesting tragedy for the theatre, with all the participants ending up strangled within the first five minutes, but in reality? No, thank you!

---

[29] A reference to Jane Austen's famous romance novel 'Pride and Prejudice', in which the hero, Mr Darcy, spends ten thousand pounds to save the heroine's sister from disgrace, although his love for her has been rejected. His generosity, coupled with a good dose of romancing, ultimately leads to a happy end.

However, I didn't think that was what Ella wanted to hear.

'I'm sure we will. I think he's getting really attached to me, and it's quite likely that we will spend more time together in the future.' That last part at least was true. 'But enough of my problems,' I continued, holding Ella away from me with both hands. 'Let us talk about you and the man prowling around you. What about Sir Philip?'

Ella's face paled. 'He was here earlier today,' she muttered.

'To visit you?'

'Yes.'

'Did he bring flowers?'

'Quite a lot of them, yes.'

'And what do you think of him?'

'He... is a very pleasant gentleman,' Ella replied, doing her best to sound enthusiastic and failing miserably.

'That is wonderful! Simply wonderful!'

I was testing my newfound acting skills. Of course I knew Ella's interests lay in another direction, but I couldn't tell her that I had overheard her and Edmund pledging their eternal, epic and everlasting love. She would vaporise from embarrassment. And I wouldn't get another chance to eavesdrop on her and her lover, which was essential both for my plans of furthering the happiness of my little sister and as my favourite evening entertainment.

'So you want to marry him, do you?' I asked with a fake, bright smile.

What little colour had remained in Ella's cheeks vanished. 'Um... maybe not as such.'

'Why not?' I pressed. 'If he likes you and you like him, why wait?'

'Well, we're both so young. Too young, I think, to really think of marriage.'

'There are girls who get married at fifteen. That is two years younger than you.'

'True, but still... there's no need to rush things and... and I...'

She was desperately groping around for another explanation. I had to say I was impressed with her. Of course her flimsy little lies wouldn't even fool a cocker spaniel with severe concussion, but I was amazed that she even made the attempt. For Ella to lie to anybody, let alone me, was an impressive achievement. She really had to like this fellow Edmund.

~~**~*~*

The confirmation of this very theory I received not three hours later. After my nap and an oh-so-delicious meal of porridge and cold potatoes, which I consumed with more relish than usual, I took up my usual post behind the bushes in the garden and waited for the two lovebirds to arrive. Just in case, I had taken the masterpiece of my favourite author with me: Mary Astell's *A Serious Proposal to the Ladies for the Advancement of their True and Greatest Interest, by a Lover of Her Sex.*

Hey, I said she's a great author. I didn't say she was great at coming up with snappy titles. Secretly, I thought that *How to Squash Chauvinists* would have been a much better title, since that was what this fabulous book was all about – but I never dared to voice that opinion. If I had a heroine, Mary Astell was it. She had lived over a hundred years ago and already tried to grind the oppressive patriarchy of Great Britain into dust.

Today though, I didn't get any new tips on man-to-dust-grinding. I had just opened my battered copy of *A Serious Proposal to the Ladies* when the lovebirds made their appearance. One fluttered in from the direction of the neighbours' house, and it was not long after that Ella flew out of the back door and towards the fence.

'Oh Edmund!'

'Oh Ella!'

They both clutched the fence in their hands. Their eyes were drawn to the other's as if by some magnetic force.

'My love,' Ella breathed, moisture in her eyes – and *she* didn't need any onions for it. 'How I have longed to see you again.'

'And I you, my love. I have longed to see you again even more than you have longed to see me! Your sweet voice is to my ears as honey to my tongue.'

'Impossible!'

'I assure you, it is. The cadence of your speech...'

'No, no, I don't mean the bit about the honey! I mean the bit about you longing for me more than I longed for you! I have definitely longed more for you than you for me. How could I not? You are my pillar of strength in the midst of my woe, Edmund. My sole reason to continue living.'

That was laying it on a bit thick, wasn't it? Nice walks in the park, reading, fighting for women's rights... I could come up with half a dozen good reasons to continue living off the top of my head. And they most certainly were better reasons than some stupid man!

'I assure you, my dearest Ella, that I have longed for you more than you for me. That is the only way it could be. For who am I? Nobody but a simple merchant's son. You are the light of my life, queen of my heart, infinitely more important than me.'

You got that right mister. Satisfied, I nodded to myself. At least the fellow knew his place.

Apparently though, Ella didn't. 'You are not a nobody!' she protested. 'And I'm not more important than you!'

What the... of course you are! Through a gap in the foliage, I shot a glare at my little sister. She should squash this fellow until he was her willing slave, not try to build his self-esteem! Men's heads were big enough already.

Ella seemed to think otherwise. 'You are everything to me, Edmund,' she declared. 'Everything!'

'As are you to me.'

'Oh, Edmund.'

'Oh, Ella, my love.'

For a few more minutes they continued their protestations of love and debate about who had missed whom more in the unimaginably long twenty-two hours or so that they had been separated. Finally though, they seemed to run out of sweet compliments and flowery similes for the passionate strength of their love.

The first pause ensued, and then, in a voice as tense as could be, Edmund asked:

'How do things stand, my love? What of Sir Philip?'

Ella took a moment to answer. Peeking through the bushes, I saw that she was clutching the fence for support.

'He came to visit me today,' she whispered.

Edmund's eyes slid shut, and he let himself fall against the fence. 'Oh fearful harbinger of doom!' he groaned.

'He brought me flowers.'

'What agony!'

'They were pink roses.'

'This is unbearable! Please, God, strike me down with a bolt of lightning!'

I glanced up towards the night sky. It didn't look like God was in the mood to oblige Edmund. I wished he would. Then at least the moaning and groaning would stop.

'And he said I was more beautiful than any flower he had ever brought me.'

'Enough! Enough!' With another groan, Edmund slid down the fence until he was on his knees in the grass. 'Have mercy on me!'

'He also said I was the most beautiful girl he had ever laid eyes upon,' Ella continued, blushing. 'I asked him how it was he had met that few girls, and he laughed.'

'Please! I beg of you, stop! You are killing me! Stop!'

'Dearest Edmund!' For the first time, Ella seemed to realize that he was on the ground, unable to stand. Her face filled with horror, and she raised a hand to her mouth. 'What are you saying? I would never dream of hurting you!'

Personally, I thought she had done a splendid job of ripping his heart into tiny little pieces, but if I cheered her on, that would probably alert them to my presence. So I kept quiet and just pulled a branch aside to see better.

'And yet you are,' Edmund moaned. 'You are hurting me more than anyone has ever hurt me in my life! The way you speak of Sir Philip showering you with gifts and compliments... I cannot bear it!'

'But my love, you wished me to tell you everything! You expressly demanded it.'

'I know, I know. And yet it tortures me to hear it. Especially to hear the tone in which you speak. You sound as if his attentions are very welcome to you. Oh, I see how it is. Your new suitor brings with him a great name and honourable rank, and I shall soon be forgotten. Winning your love has only been a dream. Oh Eros,[30] why do you torture me so?'

'A dream?' Not caring if her dress got dirty, Ella dropped to her knees in the muddy grass to be at eye level with Edmund. My, my, she really had to love him.

---

[30] Greek god of Love, often depicted in modern times as a baby-like figure with wings, and armed with a bow that shoots arrows with little hearts attached to the tip. Known also by his Roman name of Cupid, his name is often used as synonymous for 'love'.

I remembered very well the talking-to I had received from my aunt the last time I had gotten my dress dirty.

'Edmund, if my love for you is a dream, then the sun is a phantom and the moon an illusion. My love for you is just as indestructible and everlasting as those two giants of the sky. Yet it is by no means as distant. It is right here.'

With a tender gesture she touched herself right above her heart.

'It is?' Edmund whispered. 'It truly is?'

Oh, come on already! She's already told you it is, hasn't she?

Honestly, I was a bit frustrated with the fellow. She had told him she loved him about three dozen times now, and he still didn't seem to have gotten the message. You would have thought once would be enough. How dense could he be?

'I swear on everything that is holy,' Ella responded with fervour. 'I love you.'

'But the way you spoke of Sir Phillip...'

'I may have been flattered, Edmund, I do not deny it.' Shamefully, she let her eyes sink to the ground. 'It is the first time in my life that I have been noticed by such a great and powerful man, and the strange feeling might for a moment have gone to my head. But that is all it is, Edmund. I swear. I love you, now and forever.'

Edmund wet his lips. He opened his mouth, and when he spoke, his voice was hoarse:

'But what then will you say when this great and powerful man asks you to become his wife?'

Ella rocked back on her heels. The question had hit her like a kick in the stomach.

I, for my part, was feeling an urge to kick Edmund in the stomach.

'Edmund, I...' Her words trailed off into nothingness. She seemed not capable of forming a response.

'This is what it all comes down to,' Edmund persisted, his eyes burning with passion – or maybe hay fever. I wasn't exactly an expert in the different nuances of burning eyes. 'Last time we could wait and hope. Last time we could imagine that it was only a passing fancy on his part, hope that Wilkins would be gone soon and we would be safe. But now? I tell you, my love, my darling, he intends to marry you. Sooner or later, he will ask you. The question that remains now is: what will be your answer?'

'Please, Edmund, don't!'

'Will you answer yes?'

'I... I...'

'I see reluctance in your eyes. I see tears streaming down your face. It is enough. I see, you do not wish to have him. Will you do the only other thing possible, then? Will you save our love? Will you deny him?'

Burying her face in her hands, Ella gave an anguished wail. Tears spilled right and left, and she still wasn't using any onions. Really impressive. This 'love'-thingy really had to be something if it could make people act this crazy.

'My aunt spoke of the wedding as a certain thing,' Ella whispered through her fingers. 'She told me how great a match it would be for me and how happy

164

she was for me, knowing that I would be provided for, and happy, and safe for the rest of my life.'

Slowly, her hands fell from her face, which was stained with salty moisture.

'Tell me, Edmund, how could I disappoint her hopes? How could I be that ungrateful a child?'

Hm... maybe by taking a leaf out of the book of your favourite sister?

But I knew that this solution wouldn't appeal to Ella. She and I lived in different worlds and by different rules, with her rules being pretty ridiculous and problematic. Edmund seemed to realize the same thing at this very moment.

'Ella... you don't mean... you don't mean you're going to say yes?'

Ella didn't reply anything, just sprang to her feet.

'Goodbye, my love,' she whispered, and with another sob she ran off, back towards the house.

Bugger!

~~**~*~*

I pretended not to notice Ella crying herself to sleep. But I noticed. Oh yes, I noticed all right. Not even a bedtime chapter of Mary Astell could comfort me that night.

My dreams were full of evil lords with oversized ears trying to snatch my little sister away from me and choke her under a mountain of flowers. For the umpteenth time I regretted that I, as a girl, didn't have the same rights as a man. If I had, I would have learned how to handle a weapon long ago, and then I could just go to Wilkins and challenge him to a duel.

One bullet right between the eyes. That would do the trick!

As things stood, though, the only thing I could do was get to work. Despite my worry for my sister and my determination to figure something out to help her, I had to admit I was also curious as to whether Simmons' night in the cellar had yielded any results.

Oh yes, you are. And you're even more curious whether one of these results is Simmons' ice-cold, mutilated corpse, aren't you?

I shook my head. Mr Ambrose would never do something like that!

Well... probably.

Before I left, I sneaked over to Ella's bedside and wiped the remaining tears from her cheeks as best I could without waking her. It would do no good for my aunt to see them. Although she was probably delusional enough to imagine them to be tears of joy, I was sure Ella had rather not let them be seen. Finished with my demoisturization, I stroked my little sister's cheek one final time affectionately and then hurried down the stairs and out the back. It was time to get going, or Mr Ambrose would skin me alive!

At Empire House, Sallow-face let me pass upstairs without comment. I couldn't suppress a tiny, triumphant smile.

Yay! He had accepted me. I only hoped Mr Ambrose had done the same and not decided to change his mind.

Exchanging friendly nods, I passed Mr Stone in the upper hallway and entered my office. I had hardly sat down at my desk when, with a little *plink*, a message plopped out of the pneumatic tube.

Oh dear... Here we go.

Mr Linton,

I have been waiting for you for hours. Where have you been? I do not tolerate tardiness, as I believe I have told you before.

Rikkard Ambrose.

What the heck...? *Late*? I could have sworn that I arrived on the dot!

Rising from my chair along with my temper, I looked around the room – but Mr Ambrose was too stingy to even buy a clock for his secretary's office, and I still didn't have a watch. So I marched to the door and flung it open.

'Excuse me, Mr Stone, what time is it?'

A bit startled, he looked up from his papers and, being confronted with an angry fury in baggy striped trousers, hurriedly fished his watch out of his pocket. 'Eight o'clock exactly, Mr Linton. Um... Why?'

'Nothing! Thanks.'

'Oh, Mr Linton, wait!' He held out a hand with a couple of envelopes. 'I almost forgot to give you these. The correspondence of the day.'

'Thanks again.'

Grabbing the letters out of his hand, I marched back to my desk like the wrathful angel of justice, and snatched up pen and paper to scribble furiously:

My dear and most beloved Master,

It is exactly eight o'clock, the time I usually arrive at your palatial office, which, by the way, doesn't even have clocks in its rooms

Yours ever

Miss Lilly Linton

The reply wasn't long in coming.

Mr Linton,

Yes, it is eight o'clock. You may remember our discussion from the day before? The discussion during which you gained the concession from me to be treated like a full employee? You are facing the consequences of that concession. Yesterday, I gave you the afternoon off to recuperate. When I give my employees time off, I expect them to put in longer hours at some later date. I was expecting you at five a.m. this morning.

Rikkard Ambrose

Was he kidding?

A brief image of his stony face flashed in front of my inner eye. No. Of course he wasn't. My answer was short and to the point.

Dearest Mr Ambrose,

How the bloody hell was I supposed to know?

Yours Sincerely

Miss Lilly Linton

There! That would show him!

I had already shoved the message into the tube when I remembered that now I had a key to his room. I could just have stood up, gone to him and told him to his stony face!

Or could I? If I were face to face with the tyrant, I might very well use the phrase 'sincerely up yours' instead of 'yours sincerely'. Probably not good for my career prospects. Also I had to admit... this way of communicating was kind of fun.

I shoved the message into the tube. His answer popped onto my desk only a minute later.

Mr Linton,

Mind your language. I will let your tardiness pass once, since you were not familiar with my office policy. Do not let it happen again.

Rikkard Ambrose

I had an idea – a rather delicious one, and I caught myself grinning as I wrote the reply.

Dear Mr Ambrose,

So... were you up in your office at five a.m. this morning, waiting for me?

Yours truly

Miss Lilly Linton

The reply was as quick as it was short.

Mr Linton,

Yes, I was. Bring me file S37VI288. The key to the safe is under the door.

Rikkard Ambrose.

He had been waiting for *me*! For *three hours*!

Whistling, I skipped off to get the safe key, imagining a grouchy Mr Ambrose at five in the morning, sitting in the office and twiddling his thumbs with stony ferocity. The image held a great deal of appeal. I found the file in record time, shoved it under the door and went back to my desk to examine his correspondence of the day.

A few advertisement letters from some firm or other quickly landed in the bin, so did several charity requests. I very well remembered his reaction to my letting those pass the first time. Then I fished a familiar pink envelope out of the remaining pile.

What? Another one of those? Yes. The sender read, in curly feminine handwriting: *Samantha Genevieve Ambrose.* Just like last time. And there was the same coat of arms stamped on the envelope, a lion and a rose, with the rest of the crest, as I now noticed, filled out by stormy waves.

Whoever she was, you had to give the lady her due; she was persistent. But honestly, I wished she wouldn't be. What should I do with her letter? Mr Ambrose had given the first one back unopened. I presumed that meant he wouldn't want another. Was I supposed to throw it away? Or was he just returning the first letter unopened out of principle and would relent to whatever the lady was writing?

Somehow I didn't think so. Mr Ambrose wasn't the relenting kind. Especially if the message came in a pink, scented envelope.

Still, I couldn't just destroy the letter. For all I knew, he might want this one, even though he hadn't wanted the first. I hadn't forgotten the crest on his watch, exactly like the one on the letter, and was reasonably sure by now that there was some deep connection between the letter-writer and Mr Ambrose.

But what kind of connection? Not knowing drove me insane! And it made it impossible to decide what to do with the cursed pink thing.

Well, what are you waiting for, Lilly? The problem of not knowing what's in there can be solved easily enough!

Hesitantly, I reached for the envelope.

Should I? I had to admit, I was more than a little curious to read what was inside. Was it from a relative? Or... maybe from his *wife*?

I swallowed. Up until now I had just assumed he was single, but you never knew. Maybe he was a romantic soul and deeply in love with his wife and was just hiding it very, very, very, very, very well. Maybe... maybe the letters even had something to do with the mysterious stolen file! Oh, the suspense of not knowing was killing me! Literally!

Surely, opening the letter couldn't really be wrong if it meant saving me from death by acute Nosystic curiositis?

I reached out for the letter opener – but my hand stopped in mid-air.

Mr Ambrose had taken me on. He had given me a job when many others wouldn't. I was his secretary and should behave like it. A professional wouldn't pry, and I intended to be a professional. That was the whole idea behind getting a job. Agonizingly slowly, my hand drew back from the letter opener.

Blast! A conscience can be such a nuisance, sometimes!

But the problem of what to do with the letter still remained.

Then I had an idea. I was a secretary, right? My job was filing things. And I still had the key to the safe.

Quickly I got up and searched the shelves until I found an empty file box. I put the letter inside and marched to the safe. Unlocking the safe-room, I entered and stowed the file box in the remotest, darkest corner I could find, where Mr Ambrose himself would hopefully never find it. Then, satisfied with a job well done, I left, closed the safe again and returned to my desk.

Two messages were already waiting for me.

The first read:

Mr Linton,
Where are my letters? I do not pay you to dawdle.
Rikkard Ambrose.

The second read:

Mr Linton,
Perhaps I was not clear enough regarding my intolerance towards dawdling. Where are my letters?
Rikkard Ambrose

Quickly, I looked through the rest of the letters. They all seemed to be strictly business-related, which was sure to be a balm for the soul of Mr Ambrose. No dealing with frightening pink personal letters today!

I scribbled a note, went over to the door, and shoved the letters under the door, together with the safe key and a note which read:

Dear Mr Ambrose,
Forgive my unforgivable dawdling. There were a lot of letters to sort through.
Yours always,

Miss Lilly Linton

It didn't take him long to send a reply through the tube.

Mr Linton,

Please correct your address of me to coincide with the truth. I am not 'dear' to any-one, least of all, I am sure, to you. Also, it is my ink you are wasting by writing unnecessary words. A bottle of ink costs 3 pence apiece. Therefore, I order you to refrain from all endearments in the future.

Rikkard Ambrose

I cocked my head.

Oh, particularly grouchy this morning, are we? I wonder why...

I quickly scribbled a reply.

Dearest most honoured and beloved Mr Ambrose,

Courtesy hasn't killed anybody yet. By the way, has Simmons given any information?

Your ink-wasting

Miss Lilly Linton

He couldn't have been very absorbed in his letters yet because his reply didn't take long.

Mr Linton,

Courtesy might not have killed anybody yet, but it has ruined quite a few people who didn't realize how much money it costs. Mr Simmons has not yet divulged anything. I am displeased, to say the least. We will talk about this more later. Now bring me file 28V214. And be quick about it.

Rikkard Ambrose

For some reason a smile tugged at the corners of my mouth.

Here we go again. Another normal day with Mr Ambrose.

Getting up from my desk, I made my way towards the shelves in a leisurely stroll.

I should have known better, I guess. I should have realized by now that no day with Mr Ambrose ever would turn out to be normal.

PROBLEMS? WHAT PROBLEMS?

Remember how I said life with Mr Ambrose would never be normal?

Don't get your hopes up. Nothing particularly exciting happened.

There wasn't another theft. No two villains staged a sword-fight in the middle of my office or anything like that. Oh no. What happened was far more mundane and far nastier:

For the very first time, Mr Ambrose did not get rid of me early. For the very first time, I ended up having to working the entire day. The *entire day*, do you hear me?

Now, don't misunderstand me. I'm not lazy or anything. It was simply that staying at the office the whole day meant that, for the first time, I had to deal with some basic needs that I hadn't been concerned about before. The half hour Mr Ambrose allowed us for lunch took care of one of those needs: I ran out of the building and purchased something to stuff myself with. With what money, you may ask, since I hadn't received my first pay cheque yet?

All right, I admit it. I was a bad girl. I had pawned Uncle Bufford's walking cane. Since he hadn't gone out walking for years, I figured he wouldn't miss it. And I'd get it back as soon as I had my first wages. I had promised myself that.

So I wasn't hungry when I returned to work. Yet over the course of the afternoon, another more pressing need made itself known to me. You could stay alive for several weeks without eating anything, I'd heard, but *this* need in the lower half of my body required more immediate release. Especially since Mr Ambrose kept me on my feet, hurrying around the room, fetching files, which didn't exactly combine well with the building pressure *down there*.

Another message landed on my desk with a *plink*.

Mr Linton,

Bring me file 29IV229.

Rikkard Ambrose

I stood up – and suddenly knew that file 29IV229 would have to wait a little longer. I hurried out of the room into the hallway. Mr Stone looked up from his paperwork as I approached.

'Excuse me, Mr Stone?' I squeaked. Quickly, I cleared my throat. 'Excuse me?' That was better, though my voice was still slightly higher than befitted my role as a gentleman. 'Do you know where the bathroom is?'

'Certainly, Mr Linton.' He pointed down the hall. 'Two floors down, then take the first door on the left.'

Ugh! Stairs. Would I survive that? I could only hope.

'Thank you!' I squeaked, and hurried off.

Shortly afterwards, I returned, my steps a lot more measured and careful. My voice was still unnaturally high when I inquired:

'Err... Mr Stone?'

'Yes, Mr Linton?'

'Are there any other toilets in the building? Maybe some that actually have cubicles?'

He frowned. 'No, I don't think so. Why?'

'Never mind!'

Back in my office, I saw two messages on my desk. Just as I closed the door behind me, a third landed beside the other two.

Mr Linton,

I refer back to my previous message. Bring me the aforementioned file.

Rikkard Ambrose

And the second one:

Mr Linton,

I'm waiting.

Rikkard Ambrose.

And the third one.

Mr Linton,

I am becoming impatient. Do not try me. Bring me file 29IV229. Now.

Rikkard Ambrose.

Bugger! What was I going to do? I couldn't fetch the file! I probably wouldn't get to the shelves without... well, I might not be a very polite lady, but even I wouldn't mention *that*. Quickly, I considered the roads which were open to me. Could I get through the entire day like this? No, definitely not. That left two options:

A) Do it in the waste paper basket

B) Talk to Mr Ambrose

It said a lot about the personality of my dear master that option A actually sounded like the better alternative to me. However, checking the waste paper basket I discovered that, although once made of solid cast iron, it was now so old that it had rusted through at the bottom, making it unsuitable for containing fluids of any kind. There was nothing for it. I had to gather up my courage and confront the monster in its lair.

~~**~*~*

I knocked.

'May I come in?'

'Do you have the file?' asked a voice from inside – that terse, cool voice which I already knew so well.

'No, but there's something else.'

'Important?'

'*Yeees!*'

'Then come in.'

Slowly, I entered. The office hadn't altered much from the last time I'd seen it. The big map had disappeared off the desk and, instead, heaps of paper were lying on it. I was a bit surprised that I recognized most of them: they were the files Mr Ambrose had told me to bring him, and he was working through them diligently. So he wasn't just ordering me around to annoy me. Good to know, if slightly unexpected.

I stepped in front of my employer's desk and cleared my throat.

No reaction. He didn't even look up. Instead, he picked up his fountain pen and began writing on a piece of paper.

I cleared my throat again. And again.

'Do you have a cough, Mr Linton?' he asked without looking up. He continued writing.

'No, Sir. I have a question.'

'Then put it and leave. I have work to do.'

'Well, err... it's a bit delicate.'

'Then put it delicately and leave.'

Ordinarily, his ice-cold manner would have gotten my dander up. But at the moment, my thoughts were fully occupied by a certain pressing matter.

'Err... yes, Sir. You see, I have to do some urgent... business.'

He tapped the stacks of paper with his free hand. 'So have I.'

'I'm sure, Sir. It's just that my business is somewhat more personal than yours. I, um, need to powder my nose.'

That was the first time he looked up. With his dark, sea-coloured eyes, he stared at my face intently.

'Why? Your nose looks fine to me.'

'Um... thanks for the compliment, but...'

'If you absolutely must,' he continued, bending his head again and continuing his writing, 'you can do it here. I don't mind.'

I nearly choked.

'Err... Mr Ambrose?'

'Are you still here, Mr Linton?'

'Yes, Sir. I wanted to ask – have you been out in society much?'

He didn't look up again. His fountain pen flew over the paper. Blue lines of ink spread over it with graceful ease. 'No. I detest society. Ever since I've returned to England I've been far too busy with my business, anyway. Why?'

'Because you seem a bit behind on social idioms. You see... to "powder your nose" is a phrase that ladies use when they want to indicate to gentlemen that they need to pee.'

There was a loud snap. When I looked, I saw that Mr Ambrose's fountain pen had snapped in half under the sudden pressure of his fingers. Ink dripped out of the half he still held.

'Then,' he said in a very measured, calm voice, 'please do *not* do it here.'

I nodded. 'That's what I thought.'

'Why don't you just do it somewhere else, then?' Mr Ambrose's voice wasn't quite as calm and collected as usual anymore. My, my. Was the great businessman at a loss? I had to hide my smirk.

'Well, Sir, I checked, and there's a bathroom downstairs. But it's only a *pissoir*, with no separate cubicles. And well, I know you think of me as a gentleman, Mr Ambrose, but I think some of the other staff members might disagree once I let my trousers down.'

'I see your point.'

Still not looking up, Mr Rikkard Ambrose, one of the country's richest and most powerful businessmen, pondered the question of where I might pee this afternoon. If I hadn't been so literally *filled* with anticipation, I might have burst out laughing. As it was, I preferred standing still.

Finally, he said:

'You can use mine. It's in there.'

And he pointed toward a small door at the back of the office that I hadn't noticed before.

'Err... your what, Sir?'

'My toilet. Go do what you need to do, and then get back to work. I don't pay you for standing around.'

I wasn't sure I had heard correctly. 'You want *me* to use *your personal*...'

He looked up, sharply.

'Mr Linton?'

'Yes, Sir!'

'What did we talk about in the last five minutes?'

Suddenly I got the feeling that an awful lot depended on me making the right answer.

'Err... business, Sir?'

'Very good. What kind of business?'

'For the life of me, Sir, I can't remember.'

'Very good indeed. Now bring me a new fountain pen. For some reason this one doesn't seem to be working anymore. And then get on with your *business*, and leave me to mine.'

'Yes, Sir! Immediately, Sir!'

I managed to bring him a new fountain pen without wetting myself, then ran to the little door, slid inside and shut it behind me. Quickly, I let my trousers drop. Thank the Lord I was wearing trousers and not a hoop skirt! I would have emptied my bladder three times over by the time I had gotten rid of that. With a sigh of relief I closed my eyes and sank down on the toilet.

As anyone will understand, I'm sure, for the next few minutes I was quite busily engaged. It was only after the pressure had appreciably decreased that I could open my eyes and look around at Mr Rikkard Ambrose's personal bathroom.

I was in largish chamber with – naturally – bare stone walls. The only thing that could maybe be counted as decoration was a small mirror hanging on the door. Maybe. The plain, ungilded frame and small size of the mirror, however, made it appear more likely to me that it was an object of daily use, in typical Ambrosian style.

My eyes did not rest on the mirror long. They were drawn to an object on the wall to my right. There, over a basin set into the floor, a shower head protruded from the wall.

On seeing this, I suppose I know what my reaction *should* have been. It should have been some mundane thought like 'Of course! He's too stingy for a bath, so he had a shower installed to save water' or 'I wonder where he gets the water from. Surely not out of the filthy river'.

Instead, all I thought was: *Oh my God, oh my God, oh my God! He showers here! He showers here, in this very room where I am right now, naked! Which would mean without any clothes on. Which would mean you could see all of his...*

For some strange reason, I took a little bit longer than usual to conclude my business in the bathroom that day. When I left, Mr Ambrose looked sideways at me. His granite expression didn't change.

'Something wrong, Mr Linton? You look a little flushed.'

'N-no, Sir. I'm very well, thank you.'

'Good. Then bring me file 291V229 now.'

'Yes, Sir! Immediately, Sir!'

~~*~**~*~*

I worked as hard as I could throughout the day. Yet the longer I worked, the more my thoughts wandered from my work and to Ella and my own men-problem. Well, *man*, really, not *men*. I probably wouldn't be able to think straight anymore if I had more than one of those creatures hounding me. Lieutenant Ellingham was quite enough.

How the devil am I supposed to get rid of him? I demanded of myself while puffing under the weight of a hundred heavy files.

He didn't seem to mind that my family didn't have much money or that I didn't have ladylike manners. He only seemed to care for my family's respectable name, which would help him in his advancement in the military.

Hm... Can you get rid of a respectable family name?

Well, short of changing my name or committing suicide, neither of which seemed a very good idea, I would have to do something so humongously stupid and dishonourable that it would disgrace my entire family.

Then why not do that? Sounds easy enough for someone as talented as you.

True, I had no trouble of thinking of possibilities – I could ride through the marble arch, which only the Queen was allowed to do. I could dance naked on top of the marble arch, which not even the Queen was allowed to do. I could make a handstand in Hanover Square and start singing the French national anthem. I could rob the Bank of England.

The last idea sounds nice. Then you can quit this bloody job and go lead a life of adventure, going to see the rain forests and the Great Wall of China!

But, alas, I was afraid that even dressed up as a man, nobody would take me seriously as a bank robber. You probably had to be six foot five for that, with a mask and a pistol.

Plink!

Surprised, I looked down and saw three messages lying in front of me on the desk. I had been so consumed with my own thoughts that I hadn't noticed them coming in. The first two were the usual missives from His Mightiness, reminding me to bring him file number 35X119 and hurry up about it. The third one was different.

Mr Linton,

Taking into account your negligence in answering my messages, I must assume that something is the matter with you. Is it the same business as earlier today, the business we are never ever going to talk about anymore?

Rikkard Ambrose

I couldn't suppress a grin as I answered:

Dear Mr Ambrose,

No, that business we are never ever going to talk about again is not a problem - at least not yet. I am sorry for my negligence. I will bring the files immediately.

Yours Sincerely

Miss Lilly Linton

But before I could rise, another message plopped onto my desk.

Mr Linton,

If it is not that problem bothering you, what is the matter?

Rikkard Ambrose.

My jaw dropped. Was I reading correctly? I reread the message. Then I turned it on its head and tried to read it like that, thinking I might be able to put a different construction on the words. Finally, I closed my eyes for ten seconds, yet when I opened them again, the impossible words were still there.

My hand shaking slightly from the shock, I quickly composed an answer.

Dear Mr Ambrose,

Careful, Sir. People might start to think you actually cared if everything goes well in my life.

Yours Sincerely

Lilly Linton

The reply to that came just as quick.

Mr Linton,

Care? Do not be ridiculous. I simply need you to work efficiently, without distractions.

Rikkard Ambrose

Of course. And there was I thinking that maybe he had asked just to make me feel better. Ha! I had forgotten who I was talking- err, writing to.

Yet regardless of his motivations, he wanted to know what was the matter. Panic began to well up inside me. How could I tell somebody I was being pursued by a man I detested? More terrible still, how could I tell that to Mr Granite-Face All-Businesslike Ambrose? The concept alone filled me with unimaginable horror! And what about Ella? I could never tell him about Ella's secret romantic rendezvous. To mention the word 'love' in his presence would be like trying to explain bicycles to an eel.

It's really nothing, I scribbled on a piece of paper. *Really, really nothing. Don't concern yourself with the matter. I am sure you have more important things to do.*

Hurriedly, I shoved the message into a container and the container into the pneumatic tube – only then realizing that I had forgotten my usual teasing salutation. Well, that could only be good, right? He had complained of my teasing him all the while, after all, and right now I wouldn't want to rile him up any more.

Twenty seconds later, a message returned.

It consisted of two simple words.

Tell me.

Oops. Maybe I had been wrong. Again I took up pen and paper.

Dear Mr Ambrose,

As I said, it is nothing. Please do not concern yourself with my petty troubles.

Yours Sincerely

Miss Lilly Linton

I shoved the message into the tube, pulled the lever and waited anxiously. When, after a minute or so, no reply had come, I dared to breathe again. He was going to let it go. So now I'd just have to find those files he wanted...

I was just about to get up when a noise from the room next door froze me in mid-movement: The scrape of chair legs over a stone floor. Then, quick, hard steps approached the connecting door and a key turned in the lock.

Holy Moses! He was coming over!

~~*~**~*~*

175

He stood in the doorway like a statue of some Greek god about to pass judgement on a poor mortal and maybe throw a thunderbolt or two.

'Tell me,' he ordered.

'I'm not obliged to tell you anything about my personal life,' I mumbled, and thought: *I'm looking down at the floor! Why the hell am I looking down? I'm a strong, independent woman!* 'That's not part of the job description of a secretary.'

'It's also not part of the job description of a secretary to tour the hotels of London in a dress and with a sack full of onions at the ready, but you did it anyway. Tell me. Now!'

I stayed silent.

'If you will not tell me, I'll deduct the time we spend arguing from your wages.'

I gasped. That was a low blow.

Well... maybe I could just tell him about me, personally. I couldn't tell him about Ella, of course. That wasn't my secret to share. There was only one thing left to tell. I took a deep breath.

'Well...'

'Yes?'

'I'm being pursued by a man.'

'*What?*' With three long strides, Rikkard Ambrose was at my desk and had grabbed hold of my hands. Startled, my eyes flew up to look at him.

Hey! He was supposed to be calm and immovable as granite! I wouldn't have thought him capable of an emotion such as this. True, his face still was as impassive as ever, but his eyes... His dark eyes were emitting sparks of fury.

'Why didn't you tell me about this earlier?' he demanded.

'Why should I? It was none of your business!'

I tried to free my hands from his grip. It felt disturbing, having him hold my hands in his strong grasp after the episode in his personal powder room. I tried to shove that from my mind and concentrate on the moment.

'None of my business?' he repeated, coldly. 'A man has been chasing you through London, and it's none of my business? Tell me, is he connected with Simmons? What did he want? Did he mention the file or threaten to harm you? How far did he pursue you? Was he on foot or on horseback? How did you escape?'

It all clicked into place then: his reaction, the grip of his fingers on mine, even the cold fire in his eyes. I almost started to laugh. Almost.

'Err... Mr Ambrose? When I said he's "pursuing" me, I meant he wants to marry me.'

Mr Ambrose's grip on my hand slackened, and he blinked.

'What?'

'He's trying to get me as his wife, not chasing me through town with a knife in his hand.'

'Oh.' There was a pause. 'Are you sure?'

'Am I *sure*?' I glared up at him. 'What's that supposed to mean? Of course I'm sure! Even I know the difference between a bouquet of flowers and a butcher's knife!'

'Err... of course you do. Well, that's good to hear. That's really...'

I stared at his face. A muscle somewhere in his cheekbone twitched, and his eyes went from side to side as if looking for an escape. Dear me. Had I managed to get Mr Rikkard Ambrose flustered?

Suddenly, an unpleasant thought struck me.

'How come the first thing you thought of when I said I was being "pursued by a man" was that somebody was chasing me to get information out of me about *you*?'

'Well, um...'

'Do you think I'm that uninteresting? Do you think I'm a shrivelled old hag, that I could only attract men who want to stab me, not ones that want to marry me?' As hard as I could, I tugged at my hands to free them from his grasp – but his fingers were too strong. 'How dare you! Do you really think that I am that ugly?'

'Of course not,' he snapped, not looking at my face, which was good, because my glare would have burned holes into him. I was so angry with him, I would have slapped him if the thought of my pay cheque hadn't stayed my hand. 'Of course not, Miss Linton, you're lovely.'

'It is abominable that someone like you can call himself a gentleman. You should know better than...'

My voice trailed off.

'Wait just a moment... *What did you say?*'

Belatedly, my ears registered his last spoken words. The ears delivered them to my brain, where they were turned around and examined carefully. Then they were submitted to an authenticity test somewhere in the dark depths of my mind.

You're lovely... Miss Linton, you're lovely...

The results of the test weren't long in coming. On the whole, it was extremely unlikely that these words could have really, as I imagined, come out of the mouth of Mr Rikkard Ambrose. Unlikely? Scratch that. Impossible!

'What did you say?' I repeated, my voice so weak I didn't recognize it anymore. Suddenly, having my hands in his felt completely different, and for some reason I stopped struggling to get them free. From my sitting position, I looked up at Mr Ambrose, who looked as though he had just been forced to swallow his own top hat.

'What did you say?' I repeated once more, though I remembered perfectly well. I just wanted to hear it again to make sure I hadn't gone temporarily insane. Rikkard Ambrose thought I was *lovely*? Nobody had ever told me I was lovely! Not even my own mother! And what kind of lovely exactly? The 'Oh-that-was-a-lovely-job-Mister-Secretary'-kind of lovely, or the other kind of lovely? The kind that involved him calling me Miss instead of Mister.

'I said...' Mr Ambrose hesitated. Then, straightening, he suddenly let go of my hands and glared at me, his cool expression recovered. 'I said bring me file 35X119.'

He turned on his heel and marched into his office, slamming the door behind him.

Luckily, fetching files is not really an intellectually taxing task. If it had been, I would have had enormous difficulties completing the day's work.

I was just about to leave my office at the end of the day when the door to Mr Ambrose's office opened, and I caught a glimpse of his dark, ramrod-straight silhouette in the doorway.

'Would you mind stepping into my office for a moment, Mr Linton?'

Oh, we are back to 'Mister,' are we?

Well, I wasn't exactly sure I had heard right that time he'd admitted my real gender earlier today, anyway.

'Yes,' I said, curtly. 'I would mind.'

Ha! You see? I can be rude and cold, too; it's not just you who has that extraordinary ability!

'Nevertheless,' he persisted, his dark eyes flashing, 'I would like it if you came into my office for a moment.'

'My work hours are over.'

'Consider it overtime to make up for your tardiness today. Come in. Now!'

From the tone of his voice I knew he would brook no further argument. Sighing, I followed him into his office, where he settled down into his chair and regarded me over top of his steepled fingers.

'The man who wants to marry you...' he stated. 'You don't like him.'

'Oh boy, I wonder how you figured that out,' I sighed, rolling my eyes. 'Sir,' I tacked on at the end quickly, as his eyes flashed again.

'You don't want to marry him.'

'No, I don't, Sir. And?'

'And nothing.' He looked down at his papers and waved a hand. 'You're dismissed. I hope tomorrow you'll show a better performance than today. Good day, Mr Linton.'

Bewildered, I left the office. What had that all been about? As hard as I tried, I couldn't figure out the answer. Neither could I figure out Mr Ambrose himself. Impolite, honourable, ruthless, moral, stingy, randomly considerate – filled with all these contradicting attributes, he was the strangest man I had ever met. Hardly anything like society's idea of a perfect gentleman, who was supposed to be moderate in all things. And yet, I realized, as I entered the garden through the back door and sneaked into the shed, although he might be the strangest man I had ever met, he was by far not the worst one.

Working for him was certainly not going to be boring. My thoughts strayed to Simmons, locked up in the cellar. Oh no, not boring at all.

Armed with my little clutch purse and parasol, which these days felt more like a disguise than Uncle Bufford's top hat, I approached the house. To my surprise, my aunt was waiting in the hall, her bony cheeks flushed with excitement.

'Guess who's just arrived,' she whispered so audibly that you could probably hear it three streets away.

Oh no. Not another visit from Lieutenant Ellingham. Please, God! Please let me have at least until tomorrow to recover!

'Sir Philip!' She exclaimed, ecstatic with joy, and I had to congratulate God on his ingenuity in giving me what I wanted and still managing to fill the rest of my day with privations to try the soul. 'He and Ella are in the drawing room[31] right now! I've already sent all the others up to their rooms, of course! The two lovebirds must under no circumstances be disturbed.'

'Certainly,' I said mechanically. 'That would be disastrous. After all, it might delay his marriage proposal for another two days or so.'

'Exactly! That's exactly my point! So you wouldn't mind going up to your room now, too, and leaving them undisturbed? For your little sister's sake?'

'I'd do anything for my sister,' I replied, completely truthfully.

'Good! I have to go now to prepare some snacks in case he stays longer. Be off with you!'

And she hurried into the kitchen.

I sighed. Well, at least I hadn't been obliged to lie to my aunt again. I would do anything for Ella. Including what I was about to do.

Twirling my parasol like a master swordsman swinging his weapon before a battle, I marched up to the drawing room door and thrust it open.

En Garde,[32] Sir Philip!

AMBROSIAN WASTE DISPOSAL SQUAD

'Ah, Sir Philip!'

Both of them looked around as they heard the voice of the unexpected intruder – sweet little me. When Ella realized who it was, I saw startled relief on her face. When Wilkins realized who it was, I saw startled startledness on his face. I marched over to the thin young man with the big ears and more or less shoved my hand into his face, so he was obliged to press a kiss on it.

'Oh, err... Miss Linton?'

I nodded graciously, and then let him have it.

'Sir Philip, I'm so delighted to meet you again! I can't say how happy I am to be able to thank you in person for that wonderful ball you gave the other night! The ballroom looked so beautiful, all those exotic potted plants, and the little table with the exquisite snacks! There was even solid chocolate! Did I tell you that I only had solid chocolate once before? It is one of my favourite things! As I was saying, it was simply wonderful – and I mean the ball, not the chocolate, although that was pretty nice too. Such wonderful decorations, and delightful

---

[31] A term still used today, this room is not called by its name because people like to draw pictures in it, but with*draw* to it. Sometime after the seventeenth century, the 'with' in 'withdrawing room' was lost in the labyrinth of linguistics.

[32] The call employed by fencing partners before beginning the duel, to warn their opponent of its beginning. It is French for 'Attention!'

music, and such incredibly mindless baboons for guests, and the chandeliers glittered so pretty, I thought I might faint!'

Sir Philip stared at me nonplussed. He was probably still trying to figure out how to fit the 'mindless baboons' into the long line of compliments. I wasn't going to give him enough time for that, though.

'And the music – It was simply so enchanting! But I already said that, didn't I? Dear me, my memory sometimes isn't the best one. You know, Sir Philip, I was particularly impressed with the architecture of your beautiful house. I have always had a passion for architecture,' I lied smoothly. 'Can you tell me who was responsible for such a monument to the modern science of building?'

'I believe a man called Bartley did the main design, Miss...'

'How wonderful! How interesting. How old is he? Has he designed any other buildings? Where does he live? Does he have any children? Did he design his own home? How long did it take him to build yours? It is so large and majestic, it must have taken him at least five years. I was so impressed by it.'

'I... can see that.'

Looking at me strangely, Sir Philip edged away from the window where he had been standing, towards the only empty seat beside Ella on the sofa. Maybe he was thinking about protecting her from her seemingly deranged sister. Maybe he was thinking *she* could protect *him*. But I wasn't having any of that! Quickly, I slid into the seat beside Ella before he could, and smiled up at him.

'You *must* tell me all about him. Please, I have a ravenous desire for knowledge. Please oblige me.'

A peer of the British Empire couldn't just ignore a plea from a lady, could he?

~~**~*~*

Approximately three hours later, I, Ella and Sir Philip left the drawing room, the latter with a slightly dazed look on his face. My aunt was just coming down from my uncle's room, looking disgruntled. In all probability, she had just been refused money to buy sweetmeats for Sir Philip, after having discovered that we had no ingredients for proper snacks in the house.

Her face lit up instantly when she saw caught sight of the three of us standing in the hallway.

'Oh, my dear Sir Philip,' she trilled. 'Are you leaving already? I'm so sorry for that. I was just getting something ready...'

'Do not make the effort, Madam, I beg of you,' he cut her off – and he actually sounded as if he were begging. 'As you have noted, I am just about to leave. It has been a charming evening. Thank you so much for your hospitality. And thank you, Miss Ella, for your time.'

'It was my pleasure,' mumbled Ella.

'And, um... thank you, Miss Lillian, for that... um... very interesting talk.'

'It was my pleasure,' I said with a smile. So what if it was slightly sadistic?

While Wilkins hurried away to snatch his hat and overcoat off the hanger, my aunt sidled up to me. 'And? Were you near enough to the door to hear something?' she asked in a low voice, not aware that I had been in the room the entire time. 'What was the topic of conversation?'

'Height, beauty and proportions, mainly, I think,' I said.

My aunt's eyes flicked to Ella, going up and down her figure proudly. 'Oh! That is good, very good indeed! And what feature did he find particularly appealing? Her eyes? Her form?'

'I think the chandeliers and windows were what he found most beautiful.'

'Chandeliers? Lilly, what are you talking...?'

Quickly, she cut off as Sir Philip returned to us and performed another bow.

'I take my leave of you, Madam. But I hope soon to return for a tête-à-tête with your beautiful niece.'

That remark wiped all annoyance from my aunt's face and plastered it on mine instead. Darn it! I would have thought my three-hour intensive treatment might be enough to put him off. Apparently not. It wouldn't be enough for Ella to have annoying relatives to chase him away. He would have to discover that she herself was deficient in some major way...

Doubtfully, I glanced at Ella's beautiful face and demure demeanour. That was going to take some work.

When the door had closed behind him, my aunt clapped her hands, my comment about chandeliers long forgotten.

'Girls!' She exclaimed. 'We have him! Ella, this man will be your husband as sure as grass is green and the sky is blue!'

Ella paled and grasped the wall to support herself. My aunt noticed neither.

'When it rains, the sky is grey,' I pointed out. 'And when it's hot in the summer, grass can grow brown.'

'Oh, don't be a stick-in-the-mud, Lilly! The two of them will get their happy end, I'm sure of it! Just as will you and Lieutenant Ellingham. Did I tell you that he's going to come around for a visit, too?'

'*What?*' I turned to face her, horror written all over my face.

Of course, my aunt didn't take the trouble to read it. Or maybe she was an emotional illiterate.

'Yes, yes. Isn't it exciting?' She threw her arms up into the air. 'My two favourite nieces, married in one go!'

I started to object to this, wanting to point out that firstly, I wasn't married yet, not even engaged, and secondly, I had never been her favourite niece, but she rushed off before I could say anything, probably to make some preparations for the arrival of Lieutenant Ellingham.

I didn't know what she did.

I didn't really care.

But I soon found out that she needn't have bothered.

The lieutenant didn't arrive. We waited for an hour. Still he didn't arrive. We waited for another hour. Still there was no sign of him. At Aunt Brank's supreme command, I sat at the drawing room window, forced to look out for him. Only once did I actually see a flicker of movement out on the dark street – but when

I looked, it wasn't the lieutenant, but a rather large gentleman in a turban, stooping over something on the ground. Funny... from this distance he looked almost a bit like Karim.

The lieutenant, however, never came. I would have been ready to leave for a long time, but my aunt insisted Ella and I stay in the drawing room to greet our guest. After three hours, even she finally gave up hope and marched out of the room, muttering things under her breath that were definitely not ladylike.

Ella looked after her uncertainly, then peeked back at me.

'What do you think could have prevented him from coming?' She whispered as if he was in the room with us and could hear her if she spoke too loud.

'I don't know,' I said, the beginnings of a disbelieving grin on my face. 'God's mercy? A miracle? A nice, bloody train accident?'

'Lilly! You shouldn't say such things!'

I grinned at her.

'Why? What's wrong with God's mercy?'

'You know what I mean. Stop teasing me.'

'Why, when it's such tremendous fun?' I sprang up from my seat and did a little twirl around the room, more graceful than I had ever done in a ballroom. 'Can it be that I am free? What joy is this, what wondrous joy?'

Ella let out a little laugh.

'Dear me, Lill, I had no idea you were so poetic.'

'I'm not. Not when I'm sane, at least. But tonight I feel a mad happiness coming over me! Is this just a dream, or is he really not here?'

'It's one hundred per cent real.'

'Really? You promise?'

'I do, Lill, I do.'

Quickly, I went to her and knelt in front of her, grasping her delicate hands. 'Do you think he's gone for good? Do you think it's possible I might be free of him?'

She shrugged, still laughing. 'How should I know?'

'Or maybe he's just been detained somewhere this once,' I fretted. 'Maybe he'll show up here tomorrow morning, just as obnoxious as ever!'

'Maybe,' Ella admitted.

'You're not helping! You're supposed to soothe and encourage me! You're my sister, after all!'

'Or maybe not,' she hurriedly added. 'He's in the army, after all. Maybe he's been stationed in some colony. Gibraltar, maybe.'

'Gibraltar? Why so near? Why not the Caribbean? Or better yet, India! Somewhere in the jungle where he can get eaten by tigers!'

We started to giggle like little girls. We couldn't help it.

'I don't know what has happened,' Ella said finally, when we had control of ourselves again. 'But although I definitely wish him no harm, I wish he's out of your life forever.' She encircled me in her slender arms and hugged me. 'Then you can maybe find true love and happiness.'

'Love? Me?'

'Of course! With that young man of yours you told me of.'

'Oh... yes! Of course, with him! I had nearly forgotten how much I am in love, sorry.'

That night, I went to bed exhausted with happiness, still wondering what could possibly have happened to Lieutenant Ellingham. To some extent, I was also afraid. Was it unreasonable to hope he was gone for good? Would he return and try to catch me in the eternal trap of matrimony? And finally, the most intriguing question: Why had he vanished at all? Was it an accident? A miracle? Or had someone done this? What, or who, could have that much power?

After a while I stopped my useless wondering and, as my mind drifted closer to sleep, the worries over Lieutenant Ellingham fell away, and unconscious thoughts drifted to the forefront of my mind. Thoughts of another man who had been there all along, hidden beneath the surface.

You are lovely.

He had said that, hadn't he? It hadn't just been my imagination?

My eyes fell closed, and I began to dream of showers. I had no idea bathroom appliances could be that interesting.

Neither the next morning nor the next few days after that did Lieutenant Ellingham put in an appearance. He did not write, he did not send a message through a friend, he did nothing. It was as though he had vanished from the face of the earth.

Lucky earth! In my opinion, her face was a lot prettier now.

I was still worrying about what exactly had happened to him, and especially if it was something from which he would return alive and in one piece. But with time, my worry eased. You can't worry too much about problems that apparently have disappeared by themselves when you have ones to deal with that are still very much present. And I had one of those every single day of the week from eight o'clock onwards.

If I had thought Mr Ambrose had been demanding and short with me before, he was reaching new heights now. He was pressuring me so hard, I was almost surprised I wasn't squashed and turned into Lilly-puree. From having me bring him single files, he went to have me bring him entire boxes, and let me tell you, those are heavy!

Did he have any helpful suggestions? Oh yes.

Mr Linton, start working on your musculature so you can carry several boxes at once. That would be far less time-consuming.

Mr Linton, walk faster.

Mr Linton, learn to open doors more quickly.

Mr Linton, I'm not paying you for tardiness! Get a move on!

I was absolutely sure now that me hearing him call me 'lovely' had been my imagination. Maybe he had said 'puffy'. That seemed a far more likely explanation.

As time went by, I noticed that all the files I carried into his office dated from the same year as the one that had been hidden in his safe. Slowly I realized: He was reading up on something. Preparing. Had Simmons spilled the beans yet, or the potatoes or artichokes, whatever secret vegetables he was hiding from Mr Ambrose?

Finally, I resolved to ask him about it. In person. This was actually possible now. The file boxes being too thick to be shoved under a closed door, the connecting door between his and my office was open all the time now.

I knocked.

'Yes. What do you want?'

The customary friendly greeting. Oh, what a joy it was to have a kind and warm-hearted employer.

I entered.

'Mr Ambrose, I was just wondering...'

He listened to my question and took his watch out as he did so. When I was finished, he stated:

'You have just wasted thirty-one seconds of my valuable time with unnecessary speech, Mr Linton. Simmons has divulged nothing yet. Now bring me the file box I asked for.'

'But what's the sense in keeping to question Simmons?' I persisted. 'It's been days since the theft. Whoever has it must long have made use of the information it contained.'

Which you still haven't deigned to share with me...

Mr Ambrose's dark eyes flashed menacingly.

'Do you think I am a half-wit, Mr Linton? I'm sure they would have made use of it, if they could. However, the information is heavily encrypted. We have some time left yet.'

'Encrypted? You mean... you invented your own secret language?'

'It is normally referred to as a "code" by specialists of cryptology, but yes, a secret language, if you wish to put it that way.'

I looked down on the files at the desk. 'Do you do this for all your papers?' I asked, knowing the answer.

'No. The file was a... special case. Now get me the file box I want!'

'Mr Ambrose?'

It shouldn't be possible for a man to narrow his eyes while not moving one muscle in his face, but somehow Mr Ambrose managed it. 'I notice you're still here, Mr Linton.'

'Yes, Sir.'

'I told you to go.'

'I know, Sir. I stayed anyway.' Swallowing, I tried to gather my courage. 'What is in the stolen file? What have they taken from you?'

His eyes flashed again. They looked more like the sea than ever. But if before they had been stormy, now there was a thunderstorm in progress. 'I already told you that you will never know. I do not appreciate my time being wasted with unnecessary questions.'

'Why won't you tell me?'

'It may surprise you to hear this, Mr Linton, but as your employer, I am in charge, and you have to do what I say. So if I do not wish to tell you something,

I am perfectly well within my rights. Your incessant questions are wasting valuable time.'

I gave him my most charming smile. 'Then why not just tell me anyway? It would mean I'd never have to waste your time again.'

There were a few moments of silence. Nobody could be silent like Mr Ambrose. His silence invaded your ears and pressed on your mind, making you wish for a single word to relieve you of the freezing, cold emptiness.

'Because,' he finally said, his voice lower than usual, 'your life has been put in danger enough already.'

My breath hitched. What did he mean? He couldn't mean what I thought he meant, could he? He couldn't mean that to get that piece of paper, somebody might try to kill me?

And the more important question: Why the heck would he care if they did?

'And,' he added in a more usual, cool tone of voice, 'because my last secretary sold this secret to my enemies. Something I wish not to happen again. I have plenty of enemies left.'

Indignation rose up in me. 'Do you honestly dare to suggest that I might betray you like that?'

He pondered the question for a moment.

'Yes,' he finally decided, nodding dispassionately. 'Everyone has his price.'

'I would never betray you,' I said with a bit more force than was strictly necessary. He looked at me intently for a moment – then quickly looked down at the papers on his desk.

'Bring me the file box I asked for, Mr Linton.'

I didn't move. 'When Simmons gives up his information–' I began.

'I will inform you,' he cut me off. 'Go get the file box, Mr Linton. Now!'

Ouch. What crawled up his derrière and died?

I quickly cut off that line of thinking because it made me think about his derrière, and that wasn't a place I wanted my thoughts to go after the disturbing dreams I'd had last night.

Liar, a little voice in the back of my brain cackled.

I'm not lying! I assured myself. *I have no interest in Mr Ambrose's derrière. None whatsoever!*

Quickly, I hurried off to fetch the aforementioned box. And then the next. And the next. And for the entire rest of the day, I managed to keep my thoughts off Mr Ambrose's rather nice-looking behind. Yes, I did.

And how were things at home? Well, my aunt was pretty miffed about Lieutenant Ellingham's disappearance but was consoled by Sir Philip's frequent evening visits. They became so frequent, in fact, that Ella missed several rendezvous with Edmund and became increasingly agitated. She didn't even notice my frequent absence from the house while I was at work.

My friends did, of course. Since our last day out in the park, a considerable time had passed, and they were wondering how it could be that I had so little time on my hands these days – until Ella let slip that I had a secret lover. Then they laughed themselves silly.

Thanks so much, my dear little sister! Where is the nearest butcher knife for sibling-dismemberment?

~~**~*~*

'Mr Linton!'

'Yes, Sir,' I panted. 'The files are coming.' I burst through the door and let the boxes of files drop onto his desk.

'Almost acceptable pace, Mr Linton,' he said, sounding quite close to *not* disapproving and frozen. 'Almost.'

'Thank you so much for the compliment, Sir,' I huffed, clutching my sides with a grimace.

'Bring me that file from over there, will you?'

Luckily, the 'file from over there' was not a gargantuan monster with enough weight to break my back, but a rather slim file in a black folder. It wasn't numbered like the other files, but said in bold white lettering: *L.E. from L.L. Waste Disposal.*

I walked over to get it and hand it to Mr Ambrose.

'You seem no longer as distracted as the other day,' came his voice from behind me.

'Well, I have less dead weight to carry around,' I answered, distractedly. I was still focused on the black file. Waste disposal? I didn't know that belonged to the businesses Mr Ambrose was conducting. Strange. By now, I thought I had seen something of everything he did. 'Do you remember the man I told you off the other day? The one who wanted to marry me. He's gone. Poof. Vanished into thin air.'

'Indeed.'

Seizing the file, Mr Ambrose flipped it open and placed a big, black-ink check mark at the very bottom. For a moment I thought I saw a gleam of triumph in his eyes, but surely I was mistaken. After all, what could be so satisfying about getting rid of garbage?

'Well, I hope your performance won't be affected like this again.'

'Yes, Sir. Um... if you don't mind me asking, Sir..?' Taking back the file, I waved it in the air. 'Are you expanding your business, Sir? I didn't think you were in waste disposal. Are you branching out?'

'No. This was a special case I had to take care of. Definitely a non-recurring venture.' He fixed me with his dark eyes and sent a glare at me that was as cold and threatening as an army of banshees and hydras at the North Pole. 'At least I hope so for your sake, Mr Linton.'

For my sake? What the dickens was that supposed to mean? What did I have to do with his waste disposal? Wait a moment... The initials on the file...!

Before I could let myself think too deeply about those initials, my thoughts were rudely interrupted.

Thump! Thump! THUMP! THUMP!

Heavy footsteps of a man running came up the hallway and intruded into the office. We both stared at the door, distracted. A moment later it flew open and Karim stood in the doorway, panting.

'Mr Ambrose, *Sahib*!' he exclaimed, the accent in his deep voice more distinct than usual from his excitement. 'I have done it! He is ready to confess! Ready to confess it all!'

'Simmons?' One second Mr Ambrose sat behind his desk, the next he was on his feet, erect, ready to move. This time there was no mistaking it: there *was* triumph in his eyes.

'Let's go,' he ordered and was already out the door. Karim turned and followed, wanting to close the door to the office behind him. I put my foot in between just fast enough.

'Excuse me. You seem to have forgotten me,' I said, sweetly.

The bearded mountain grumbled something in some foreign language – probably 'I wish I could!' in Urdu or Punjabi or some other Indian language. Then he marched after Mr Ambrose, who was already charging down the stairs. We could hear the harsh staccato of his shoes on the stone steps.

'Wait up!'

Mr Stone looked up, surprised, as he saw Karim stomp past him. Then his surprise doubled when I flitted by, even faster than the large Indian. I got to the staircase just before Karim did and flashed him a charming smile. If his face hadn't already been so dark, it would have turned red like a tomato. This was just oojah-cum-spiff! Finally some excitement!

If only that bloody man would stop!

'Mr Ambrose! Wait!'

I ran down the stairs after him and, behind me, heard the Mohammedan muttering again. I caught the word *ifrit* mixed in with several expressions that, in spite of the foreign language, didn't sound very complimentary.

Oh well. I suppose there are worse things than being seen as a 12-foot-tall demon with fiery wings.

'Mr Ambrose, Sir! Wait, please!'

Did he wait? Did he slow? Well, let me put it this way: Are lions vegetarians? Probably not.

It took me forever to catch up with the basted man! He wasn't running, but he seemed to have the ability to march with military speed, even down a staircase. I just caught sight of him as he stepped off the last landing and into the great hall, which was buzzing with people.

I certainly hadn't expected what happened next.

The effect of his arrival was earth-shattering. Everybody stopped dead and turned, standing stiff and straighter. No, they didn't just stand straighter, they stood at attention, their eyes wide.

'Holy Moly,' I whispered, gazing at the silent crowd.

Mr Ambrose stood at the edge of the hall. He stood on the same level with everyone else. Still, with their stares fixed on him like that, he seemed to tower over everybody like some Greek god on Mount Olympus who wasn't above hurling a few lightning bolts at people who didn't worship fast enough.

His dark eyes met those of Sallow-face, whose face actually lost some yellowness, turning white at the eye contact. He gave a tiny, curt bow, and bent over his books again, back to work. He wasn't the only one. That flicker of dark eyes had been enough: suddenly, everybody was moving again, only now they moved at double speed.

And Mr Ambrose started forward again.

Blimey...!

I could almost feel it radiating out from him: the power, like a spider's web, that joined him to every person in this building, the ends of the web connected to his employees' brains, right to the part that was responsible for fear and obedience.

Maybe, that annoying little voice inside me said, *just maybe, in comparison, he hasn't worked you that hard after all.*

Mr Ambrose headed straight across the hallway. He didn't need to navigate through the masses of people: wherever he stepped, people made way for him. Not like they would for a king, forming a guard of honour or something, no. They were far too busy showing him how busy they were, working for him, making more money, to stand around doing nothing. But they never got in his way as he headed for a metal door at the other side of the huge room, marching along a line as straight as a ruler.

Taking a large ring of keys out of his pocket, he opened the door, stepped inside the corridor beyond and was just about to let the door fall shut behind him when I woke up from my daze. Bloody hell! I was supposed to go with him!

'Wait up!'

He was so intent on getting to his victim and starting to squeeze information out of him that he seemed to have forgotten all about me, and Karim, too, for that matter. But when I called, he looked up to see me dashing across the hallway. I was beside him in seconds, and after a moment's hesitation, he held the door open for me.

'I thought... it's only... ladies who go first,' I panted, not able to conceal my grin. 'Since when have you started acknowledging my femininity?'

'Since I want to have the door locked behind us and am the only one with the key,' he shot back. I heard Karim come up behind me, huffing, puffing, and grumbling things in Punjabi. 'Now shut up and get a move on!'

'Yes, Sir!' I smirked and stepped into the corridor beyond. After a few steps I stopped, for a very good reason:

The corridor had no windows and no lamps. Before me lay complete and utter darkness. Well, almost complete and utter. Through the open door a few rays of sunlight shone into the corridor, but they only reached a few yards, then failed. All I could see were these few yards of cold stone floor.

'Err... Mr Ambrose, Sir...?'

I heard Karim step into the corridor behind me, and the door slammed shut, bringing us from almost complete and utter darkness to utter complete and utter darkness.

'Well, that's just spiffing,' I commented, turning my head from left to right, which made absolutely no difference to the blackness I saw. 'Now it's even easier for us to walk into walls!'

'This corridor leads underground,' Mr Ambrose said. 'That makes it hard to have windows. And why should I expend money on wall lamps...?'

'Yes, why? I mean, the human skull can take a few concussions, no problem.'

'...why should I spend money on wall lamps, when it is perfectly possible to carry one single lamp and save a lot of money for oil?'

A spark flared in the darkness. It caught on something and, a moment later, a yellowish light grew a few feet away from me, at about my shoulder level. It fell on Mr Ambrose's classic features, and he jerked his head to the left, down the corridor.

'Come. Let's go.'

Holding the lamp over his head, he marched ahead of us. The little light was just bright enough to shine a few feet ahead. Luckily the stone floor was as even as a ruler, or I would have stumbled and broken my foot a dozen times. Probably he'd polished it himself with sandpaper, to save the builder's bill. Or he'd just willed it to be smooth by staring at it long enough. I wouldn't put it past him.

The corridor started to slope downwards into the earth, towards the cellars under Empire House. We went around several curves, and the angle downwards remained the same, yet we never came across any stairs.

'Why is there no staircase?' I asked.

'Sometimes, the things we have to carry down this corridor can't walk on their own,' Mr Ambrose shot back without slowing his pace or turning his head.

Can't walk on their own...? Blimey! What was he talking about? Bodies? Dead bodies? Anxiety washed through me once again as I thought of his threats to me, and of all the things that could happen to Simmons. Maybe I should go to the police after all...

'Cargo and papers, Mr Linton,' Mr Ambrose added as if he'd read my mind. 'You have an over-active imagination.'

And you have threatened to kill me and have a man locked up in your basement, which should be the job of the police with whom the Queen of England is so kindly providing us! That doesn't exactly inspire confidence!

But I didn't say that out loud. I definitely did not want to end up in the room next to Simmons'.

Finally we reached the end of the corridor. Under a massive brick archway, that indeed would be large enough to admit large crates of cargo, we stepped into a room I recognized: it was the room just in front of Simmons' cell. At the opposite end of the room was the solid steel door behind which Simmons was held. To my left there was another door. I recognized it as the one through which we had entered the basement last time, by the back entrance.

Karim strode determinedly towards the door, but Mr Ambrose touched him lightly on the arm, and the huge Indian stopped in his tracks.

'Before we go in – Tell me, how did you finally crack him?'

Karim shrugged. 'I am sorry, *Sahib*, that it took me so long. It was my failure. I failed to take into account the character of the English.'

'In what way?' I asked, interested. After all, I was English. I had no idea that I shared a character trait with other English people. So far, I hadn't found a lot of common ground.

The bearded mountain threw me a glare and shut his mouth. Apparently, he wasn't ready to answer any questions that came from me.

'*In what way?*' Mr Ambrose repeated my question, so now he had no choice but to answer.

Karim cleared his throat. It sounded like a volcanic explosion. A very embarrassed volcanic explosion.

'Well, *Sahib*, I threatened him with the usual European, Arabian, Indian, and even Chinese torture methods. Nothing seemed to terrify him. But that was the wrong approach. As I said, I failed to take into account the character of the English. Then it finally came to me. I...'

He cleared his throat again – and then the sneaky son of a bachelor bent down and whispered something in Mr Ambrose's ear! And Mr Ambrose, Mr Immovable Stone-Face Ambrose, actually lifted an eyebrow.

'Is that so? And did it work?'

'Did *what* work?' I demanded.

'Oh yes,' Karim said with grim relish, ignoring me completely. 'He is talking like a trader in the bazaar. Only he does not wish to sell, but give it all for free.'

'What did you do?' I demanded. 'Karim, what did you do to the poor man?'

This time, they both ignored me.

'Very well then.' Taking the keys from his pocket once more, Mr Ambrose unlocked and unbolted the door. 'Let us see who is behind this infernal intrigue!'

He thrust open the door and stepped forward, into the dark.

THE ADVERSARY

I followed Mr Ambrose into the dungeon, and even by the dim light of the oil lamp I spotted Simmons immediately. He was sitting on a chair in the middle of the room, his arms tied to the backrest, and over his head...

I blinked, not sure I was seeing correctly in the gloom. Finally, I leaned over to Karim.

'Why does he have a bucket of water with a hole in the bottom hanging over his head?' I asked him out of the corner of my mouth.

'I do not hear your voice, *Ifrit*! Allah is my strength and will protect me from thee!'

'Oh. Thanks for the helpful information.'

Mr Ambrose approached the thin, blonde man in the chair, whose back stiffened at the sudden sound of footsteps. He hadn't seen us until then, with his head sunk on his chest and his eyes closed, but when Mr Ambrose stepped closer, he raised his head to face his former master.

'Mr Ambrose, Sir.'

Simmons' voice was rough. It sounded like he hadn't used it for conversation in days.

Drip.

A drop of water fell out of the hole in the bucket and landed on Simmons' forehead. He shook himself.

'Could you...' His voice dwindled, and he coughed. 'Could you please tell your servant to get rid of that bucket? It is quite annoying, having water drip onto you all the time.'

He didn't seem afraid any more. I wondered why. When we had caught him, he'd been terrified. Then I abruptly realized why. What was the sense of being afraid? The worst was already behind him. He had been broken and made to confess.

'Please...' Simmons rasped. 'Please, get rid of the bucket.'

Mr Ambrose considered in silence for a moment – then he made a hand gesture to Karim. The Indian stepped forward and, with a speed that made me yelp in surprise, whipped his scimitar[33] out of its sheath, severing the rope that held the bucket. It fell, sloshing water in every direction, and with a resounding *thump* bounced off Simmons' head, drenching him in cold water.

Simmons' face contorted in a grimace. 'That's not exactly what I meant.'

'It's down, isn't it?' Karim growled. 'Now start talking, or I'll start doing things with this you'll like even less.' He held the point of his scimitar to Simmons's throat. 'Talk!'

'I believe Karim has voiced my expectations very succinctly,' Mr Ambrose said, crouching down so that his dark, sea-green eyes were on a level with Simmons'. 'Talk.'

'What do you want me to say?' Simmons asked in a voice that sounded very tired and, yes, now very afraid again, too. Looking into Mr Ambrose's eyes obviously made him feel there might yet be worse things in store for him. I knew the feeling.

'When did all this start?' Mr Ambrose asked.

'All this, Sir? I'm afraid I do not...'

'Don't play games with me, Simmons! With me, the stakes are far too high.'

Simmons swallowed.

'I know,' his former employer continued in a cold voice, 'that you must have been in the pay of one of my enemies for some time. They could not simply convince you to break into my private safe overnight. You are far too insecure and timid for that. So I repeat: when did this all start?'

'S-six or seven weeks ago, Sir.'

'I see.' Mr Ambrose didn't seem to be fazed by the information. But then, when did he ever seem fazed by anything? 'How did it happen?'

'Th-they came to my house one evening. They told me that they had a proposition for me, that they would pay much better than that miser Ambro–'

---

[33] A curved one-edged sword popular in the Orient from the Middle Ages to the 19th Century.

Simmons almost bit his tongue off, realizing a bit too late that it might not be very wise to relate the men's exact words. I had to stuff my fist into my mouth to keep from sniggering. Karim noticed and threw me a look that could have burned holes in solid metal.

'Is that what they said?' Mr Ambrose mused, his facial expression not changing a bit. 'Well, and did they pay much better than that miser Ambrose?'

'Um... well...'

'Let's assume from the suitcase of banknotes we found in your room that they did indeed. What did you do for them?'

'I... I gave them information on your daily routine, your correspondence, on what files and papers passed through my hands, Sir. At least at first.'

'And later?'

'Later they wanted more, Sir. They wanted me to start taking things. When I refused, they started threatening they would reveal to you what I had so far done for them.'

Mr Ambrose nodded. 'Of course. You are stupid, Simmons, do you know that?'

'Yes, Sir.'

Simmons lowered his eyes, but Mr Ambrose stepped closer and with his penetrating dark gaze forced the man to look up again.

'These things you took – what were they?'

'All manner of things, Sir. Business letters, tables of cargo, personal letters...'

The silence in the room was sudden, frigid, and cut Simmons' speech off more effectively than the loudest of screams.

'You,' whispered Mr Ambrose in a voice I had never heard him use before, 'gave my personal correspondence to these men?'

'Err... yes.' There was a squeak of panic in Simmons' voice now. 'But... that's not that bad, is it? It's not like you ever read it, Sir?'

'Letters written by a woman?' Mr Ambrose inquired, ignoring the question. 'Letters in pink envelopes?'

'Y-yes, Sir.'

Silence again. Then Mr Ambrose stated, as cold as Antarctica itself: 'You are lucky that Karim is the one holding the sabre right now.'

'Yes, Sir. I am sorry, Sir.'

'You certainly will be.'

Again Simmons tried to look down, and again Mr Ambrose held him with his dark gaze. 'Now tell me. Tell me about the day you stole the file.'

'Well... they told me to take it and... and I did.'

'How many days did they have to work on you before you agreed?'

'A w-week and a half. I didn't want to take it. I knew it was important.'

Mr Ambrose's eyes narrowed infinitesimally. Simmons winced as if he'd been hit with a whip.

That reaction told me more about the contents of the file than any of my wild guesses.

'Oh, you're right about that,' Mr Ambrose said in low voice. 'It's important all right. When and how did you leave the house the night of your theft?'

'I... I was just finished with work, Sir. I knew you were still working on the Emerson papers in your office. I locked the door to the hallway, went into the safe and took the file.'

'How did you know where to look for it? You had never handled that particular file.'

'They told me it had to be in the safe, and told me the time it concerned. I knew your filing system, and so knew what to look for.'

'I see. And your way out?'

'That was easy. I am – was – your private secretary. Nobody challenged me on the way out. I had the file concealed under my waistcoat, tucked into my trousers.'

'Trust!' It was a vicious growl, a sound unlike any other I had ever heard escape from my employer's throat. With surprise I saw that Mr Ambrose had both hands clenched into tight fists. 'Of course, it would have to be trust that brought me down! Again! Ah, but we will change that. No more! Karim!'

'Yes, *Sahib*?'

The huge Mohammedan stepped forward.

'Talk to Warren. Have him station one of his men at the exit to my offices' inner sanctum at all times. From now on, we will search everybody who comes in and everybody who leaves. Understood?'

'It shall be as you command, *Sahib*!'

Karim left the room. Something clicked outside, and after only a few moments he was back in the cell. How...? He couldn't possibly have run up the corridor and delivered the message *that* quickly, could he? Then I remembered: pneumatic tubes. Apparently, they didn't only connect Mr Ambrose's office and mine. They had to be running through the whole building!

My employer, meanwhile, had his full attention focused on his captive again.

'What did you do with the file next?'

Simmons wet his lips. He seemed to be getting more and more nervous, which I didn't understand. He had already admitted the worst – taking the file, right? So what was there about his story that could cause him greater anxiety?

'I took it right away to a house in Penrose Street.'

'Mr Linton?'

It took me a few seconds to realize that Mr Ambrose had addressed me. He was still staring fixedly at Simmons, his back to me.

'Um... yes, Sir?'

'I haven't been back in London long, and neither has Karim. We've spent years away in the colonies. What kind of street is Penrose Street?'

I cleared my throat. 'Not a very reputable one, I believe, Sir. It's one of the names that often comes up in police reports in the papers.'

Simmons nodded eagerly and shuddered. 'It was a dreadful place, full of coolies and other lowlife. I have no idea why they always wanted to meet there.'

'I can think of only one explanation,' Mr Ambrose mused. 'In case you were caught or followed there, they wanted everybody to think it was low criminals with whom you were consorting. Which makes me think that the exact opposite was the case.'

'They weren't criminals?' I asked, confused.

'Oh, they were criminals all right. But certainly not low ones. In fact I suspect they were rather high up the food chain. Am I correct?'

Simmons' shudder was more than enough answer.

'The address?'

'Number 12, Penrose Street, Sir.'

'What exactly happened?'

'They gave me the money and said this was our last transaction. When I asked them why, they said that unlike the other times, this theft would not go unnoticed. They advised me to get out of the country right away. The expression on their faces... I'll never forget it.'

'Now we come to the interesting part.' Mr Ambrose took out his cane and placed the end on Simmons' chest. I remembered, as no doubt Simmons did, that there was a sword concealed inside it.

'Who are those "they" you keep talking about? Who hired you to steal from me?'

Simmons paled.

'I d-don't know. They never gave me their names.'

'But you do know one name, don't you? It's useless to deny it, I can see it in your face.'

'No, I don't! I swear, I don't know anything, Sir!'

Mr Ambrose's head whipped sideways to glare at Karim, and the Mohammedan retreated under the force of his cold stare. 'What's this? I thought you said this man was ready to confess everything!'

Karim looked pretty uncomfortable. I tried not to smile, but it was kind of funny to see that mountain of a man shuffle around like a told-off school boy.

'He was. I swear to you, *Sahib*, he was.'

'Hmm...'

Mr Ambrose turned to his captive again, scrutinizing him intently.

'You're scared. That's why you won't tell me. You're scared of this man whose name you won't speak.'

'No, Sir! I swear, I don't know anything! I don't...'

Mr Ambrose's cane pressing against his throat cut off his words in a croak.

'Simmons, let me put it this way: who are you more afraid of – this man or me?'

The ex-secretary opened and closed his mouth like a stranded goldfish, but nothing came out, even when Mr Ambrose drew back his cane.

'Interesting... apparently it's a tie?'

Simmons nodded.

'Well, then think of this.' Mr Ambrose leant forward and whispered, in a tone so calmly threatening it made the hair on the back of my neck and on some other more delicate place stand up: 'I have you in my power. He does not.'

Simmons slumped.

'All right,' he moaned. 'All right, I'll tell you. But only under one condition.'

'Which is?'

'You let me go and give me a train ticket out of town. If I tell you that name, I'll need to get out of town, and my legs won't be fast enough.'

Mr Ambrose didn't hesitate.

'Granted.' He nodded curtly. 'The name?'

'I... don't think I was supposed to hear it,' Simmons said in a low voice, looking around as if he expected somebody to appear out of the air and strike him down. 'They were talking one day when I arrived early, and I heard it.'

'The name, Simmons!'

'The train ticket! You have to swear that I'll get the train ticket!'

'I swear! The name, Simmons! Now!'

Simmons looked around and wet his lips again. 'It's... It is...'

Suddenly, he stopped and shook his head, gazing at Karim and me out of heavily lidded, tired and very frightened eyes.

'No! I don't want anybody else to hear it.'

What?

Was he joking? I was on the tips of my toes here!

'I don't want *him* to find out,' Simmons murmured. 'If he does...'

Quickly he leant forward and whispered something in Mr Ambrose's ear.

Blast the man!

I had been waiting breathlessly all this time for the solution of the mystery, and now I wasn't going to hear it? I wanted to clobber Simmons over the head with something heavy, especially when I saw Mr Ambrose's eyes lighting up in recognition.

'*Him!*' His hands were balled into fists again. 'After all this time, *him!*'

For a moment his eyes flickered to me – then they were back on Simmons.

'Well,' he said, almost as if speaking to himself, 'at least now we know that the file is still in England. *He* wouldn't dream of having to run and hide. He probably thinks himself untouchable.' In a softer voice he added: 'And who knows... He might be right.'

Abruptly, he fixed his icy glare on Simmons. 'You will not speak of this to anybody else, understand?' The threat was there, hard and cold in his voice.

Simmons' lips twitched. There was no humour about it. 'Certainly not, Sir. I value my throat just as it is, without any decorative cuts or slashes in it.'

'Very well.'

Mr Ambrose rose and strode towards the cell door.

'What about my ticket?' Simmons called after him. 'When will I be released? I want to get out of here!'

Mr Ambrose stopped. Slowly, he turned. When he was facing the cell again, both Simmons and I couldn't help but gasp. He had a knife in his hand.

'No! Please don't!' Simmons croaked. 'I've done everything you asked! Please...'

'Be quiet and hold still, man!' Mr Ambrose commanded. 'I nearly forgot – there's something I still need from you.' With two quick steps he was back at Simmons' side and grabbed him by the hair. The knife flashed in the darkness as it shot towards Simmons' head.

And then it was over, and Mr Ambrose's hand came away holding a lock of blond hair he had severed from Simmons' head.

'That was all.'

I stared at him incredulously. For once, Karim seemed to share my feelings. He was looking at Mr Ambrose as if he'd grown three additional heads.

Pointing to the blond lock in my employer's hand, I hissed: 'What's that supposed to be? A memento?'

'In a way.'

He turned away again and said, sparing neither me nor the ghost-white Simmons another glance:

'Somebody will be along to bring you a change of clothes soon. You can't be seen coming out of my building in the filthy rags you're in right now. The man will show you to the street and give you everything you need. Our business is concluded, Mr Simmons. Our paths will not cross again.'

Without waiting for an answer, he strode out of the cell. Karim and I followed him, the former grim and silent, the latter, that is to say my good self, twitchy and curious to the point of madness.

'What did you do to him so that he'd spill the beans?' I blurted out as soon as the metal door had closed behind us. 'And who was it that ordered him to spy on you? And why should anybody want to spy on you anyway?'

Mr Ambrose had already started up the corridor again. He didn't turn around or, God forbid, stop to let me catch up.

'Mind your own business, Mr Linton!'

'I work for you, so your business is my business. What's the point of someone spying on you?'

'It is commonly referred to as "industrial espionage",' he called. Blast! That way of his to talk into the opposite direction of where you were standing was really annoying. 'It means the stealing of secrets of one businessman by another businessman.'

'What's that good for?'

'It's not only nation states that seek to discover each other's secrets. Secrets mean faster development and more money. Always remember: Knowledge is power is time is money!'

I frowned. Something seemed to be wrong with that sentence. 'I thought it's "knowledge is power" and "time is money".'

'I combined the two to save time.'

'Oh.'

I lapsed into silence again for a moment. But then I remembered.

'Wait! That wasn't my only question. I had others! You were trying to distract me.'

'Oh yes. Karim's innovative torture methods.'

That hadn't been the question at the top of my list, and I was about to tell him that actually I was more interested in the name of his mysterious enemy, but then... this was something I was pretty interested to hear, too.

'Tell her, Karim,' Mr Ambrose commanded.

Good God! Did he just use a feminine pronoun to refer to me? Whoever is behind all this, hearing their name must really have gotten to him!

'Tell her?' The bearded mountain's eyes bugged. '*Sahib!* You do not mean that!'

'Have I ever given an order that I have not meant?'

'No, *Sahib*, but...'

'Have I ever fallen into the habit of joking or making other kinds of remarks that were not of a serious and literal nature?'

'I must admit, *Sahib*, no, but in this case...'

'Tell he- I mean, tell him!'

Karim lowered his head.

'As you wish, *Sahib*.'

With a few longer strides of his massive legs he had caught up to me and was marching next to me. I looked sideways. His face was trying for impassivity, but I could see the wrath of seven hells burning under the surface.

'After I failed in my attempt with the Chinese water torture,' he said in a voice that was supposed to be detached, 'it came to me in a divine stroke of inspiration that a less classical approach might be more effective. So I stripped Simmons of all his clothes, including his undergarments, and threatened that if he would not divulge his information, I would drug him, dress him in a pink French ballet dancer's costume, and tie him to the fountain in Trafalgar Square for the crowd to discover in the morning.'

There were a few seconds of silence.

'He didn't seem to believe me at first. That's when I went out and bought a costume. I brought it back and showed it to him... and that broke him.'

There were a few more seconds of silence.

'A... ballet costume?' I finally asked.

'Yes. Pink, with a short silk skirt and golden lace trimmings.'

'I see.'

Cautiously, I looked sideways again and could see Karim's hand at his belt, gripping the hilt of his scimitar. His eyes found mine. 'Come on,' they seemed to say. 'Laugh. Come on. I'm the one with the huge sabre. Laugh, and we'll see if you're still laughing when I have separated your head from your body.'

'Um... a very interesting method indeed,' I managed. I was fighting an epic battle to keep a straight face. Let me tell you, Waterloo was nothing to it. I might have lost it after all, just like Napoleon, the poor chap, if a more serious thought had not invaded my mind, providing much needed reinforcements.

'You distracted me!' I exclaimed. 'Again!'

'I?' Karim's stare changed from threatening abrupt death to confusion. 'I didn't...'

'Not you! You... at Mr Ambrose. He couldn't see it though, because he was still walki... ad of us, his back to me.

'You've done it twice... I want my first question answered! I want to know that name! Who was spying on you, damn you?'

He didn't stop, didn't answer. Just held up one admonishing finger in an abrupt movement. What the blooming hell... Oh, right. Be courteous. Be respectful.

'Who was spying on you, *Sir*?' I asked, my voice sweeter than a pot full of honey.

He didn't even glance around.

'Can't tell you that.'

'Why the dickens not? Um... Sir?'

'It is for your own good, believe me.'

Oh, of course I believe you. Why would I ever doubt a word that comes out of your mouth?

'Who is he? Who is this chap who's hiring people to spy on you?'

Mr Ambrose gave a snort. 'I'm not sure that "chap" would be the right noun to describe him.'

'Well, what would describe him, then?'

He didn't fall for the trap.

'Adequate try, Mr Linton.'

Not even *good try*?

'Why won't you tell me?'

I looked sideways at Karim again, but although he tried not to let it show, he was just as nonplussed as I was. He didn't know who this mystery man was either. And if Mr Ambrose's motivations of not telling for our own good also applied to Karim....

Eyeing the large sabre at the Mohammedan's belt, I shuddered. Who in the world could be a threat to Karim? Who could be more dangerous than a sabre-wielding bearded giant? Maybe I really shouldn't delve too deeply into this. Maybe it would be wise just to let it go.

But then again, when had I ever been wise? If I were, life would be so very dull.

'We could better guard against him if we knew who he was,' I pointed out.

I could see he'd rather have bitten his tongue off, but Karim opened his mouth.

'She does,' he said in a slow tone of voice as if he had to drag every word forcibly from the pit of his stomach, 'actually have a point, *Sahib*.'

'No, he doesn't.' Mr Ambrose shook his head.

We turned a corner and suddenly stood before the door into the main hall again. There Mr Ambrose waited till we had caught up with him. He stood, silent and still as a statue, facing the door as if he could see images there that were invisible to anybody else. We stepped up beside him, but still he didn't move. Karim, who obviously – unlike me – didn't have the intention of arguing with his master any more, felt the need to change the subject. He cleared his throat and asked: 'Should I buy a ticket for Mr Simmons, *Sahib*?'

Mr Ambrose twitched, seeming to awake from a trance.

'What did you say?'

'The ticket for Mr Simmons. The train ticket out of London. Should I buy it and give to him when he leaves the building?'

I immediately knew what that had to mean. On his previous visits, when Wilkins had come alone to see Ella, he had arrived in a small carriage with an open roof. The arrival of his largest coach could mean only one thing: a ball. And, moreover, a ball which not only Ella would be attending with him. No. We all would go.

Including *me*.

Me! Sweet little me, exposed to the horrors and dangers of a ball!

Blast, blast, blast! Why hadn't I heard of this? Yes, last time he had given us a last-minute invitation, but something like that was far from usual. Normally invitations to balls were issued weeks in advance.

Why didn't I hear about this? I could have started my protest in time, or hidden in the London sewers, or burned the house down!

I saw my aunt step out of the door. Thank God I had already changed out of Uncle Bufford's trousers, because a moment later she spotted me and gave me a self-satisfied smile. A very bad word escaped me that I was sure a lady shouldn't use, especially to describe her own aunt. But I couldn't help it. I realized what had happened. Of course! That witch had deliberately not told me about the ball so I wouldn't find a way to get out of it!

For a moment I considered running. I could escape into the dark streets of London and spend the night under a bridge, where surely it would be more comfortable than in a brightly lit ballroom with people everywhere wanting to dance. Nobody would try to step on my feet under a bridge, for a start. But then I remembered Ella and felt ashamed of myself. Hadn't I promised myself that I would find a way to help my little sister get rid of Wilkins? And here I was shirking going to a ball along with her and her unwanted admirer.

I had to go! I had to protect her from Wilkins' attentions as best I could.

So, feeling as though I were walking towards my doom, I began to set one foot in front of the other, finally reaching the doorway.

'Ah, there you are, Lilly!' My aunt smiled a smile so devious it belonged exclusively to aunts and serial killers. 'Do you know what? I absolutely forgot to tell you that we received an invitation to Lady Metcalf's ball.'

I closed my eyes. My fate was worse than I had imagined.

'Lady Metcalf?' I whispered, my voice resembling the last desperate vocal attempts of a victim of pertussis[34] before the grave claimed them.

'Indeed. And Sir Philip is so nice as to take us all there in his coach. Isn't that just wonderful, Lillian?'

'I can hardly find words to express my feelings on the subject.'

'Probably.' She eyed me sharply. Suddenly, her voice became a lot less sweet and a lot more like that of a general. 'Go upstairs and dress! I've laid your ball gown out for you and will expect you down here in five minutes.'

'We'll be leaving that quickly?'

'No. But I'll need to keep an eye on you. And I have a few words to say to you before we leave.'

---

[34] An intense coughing sickness that even today can result in death. You really don't sound at your best when you have it.

Oh-oh... This can't be good.

I hurried upstairs to change, determined to do it in under five minutes. Unfortunately, Ella wasn't there to help me, so it took me over a quarter of an hour to squeeze into my ball gown. When I came down again, my aunt didn't look at all pleased. I could hear Maria's high laugh from the drawing room, and a door opening.

'They are coming.' Grabbing me by the arm, my aunt dragged me outside and shooed the servants away. She pulled me behind the coach and drew herself up to her full height.

'Listen, girl! I don't know how you managed to scare off Lieutenant Ellingham...'

I started to protest, to tell her that I had nothing to do with his disappearance, but she silenced me with one of those scary-aunt looks that made you want to put your head under a blanket.

'I don't know how you scared him off,' she continued in a low tone, 'but I'll wager it was by exhibiting the same appalling behaviour as the other night at Sir Philip's Ball. Refusing to dance, indeed! There will be none of that tonight, little lady, none of your incivilities, none of your foolishness, *nothing!* You will behave yourself like a true gentleman's daughter, or you will have to answer to me.'

'But I don't misbehave on purpose,' I said with rising desperation. 'It just... happens. I'm not very good at judging what is ladylike behaviour and what isn't. What should I do?'

'Oh that's easy.' My aunt let her fan snap open and waved it experimentally. 'Just do the exact opposite of what you'd like to do, and you'll be fine.'

Can I just say that remark miffed me more than a little bit? I wasn't *that* badly behaved, was I?

Was I?

Well, maybe sometimes. When I felt like it. Which was, admittedly, most of the time. Oh, blast it! Very well. I would do as my aunt wished. Fixing a fake smile on my face, I curtsied as deeply as I could without keeling over.

'Certainly, Madam. May I be permitted to withdraw from your presence? I wish to seek out my sister.'

My aunt blinked as if she were seeing and hearing a mirage and not her own niece.

'Um... very well. Go ahead. That was not bad, just now. Not bad at all.'

I curtsied again. 'Thank you very much, Madam. You are too kind, Madam. Your obedient servant, Madam.' Curtsying twice more just to make the point, I withdrew.

On the other side of the coach, I met my sister. Unfortunately, it was the wrong one. I smiled at Maria as brightly as the sunshine and did another curtsy.

'Dear Sister! How glad I am to see you. Might I enquire where I can find my dear, dear, dear sister Ella? I wish to speak to her, my dear.'

Maria stared at my bright smile with open eyes, her mouth forming a little 'o'.

'Have you been drinking from uncle's port wine?' she demanded.

I wish I had. I had never tried alcohol myself, but I'd heard it was pretty good for numbing the brain and lessening the pain of torturous experiences – like the one I was going through right now.

'Good heavens, no, dearest sister. Whatever can have given you that impression? I would never be so presumptuous! Moreover, why would a lady even think of drinking spirits? What an outlandish idea, my dearest sister.'

I smiled again, and curtsied again. And again. Maria was dumbstruck. Blimey, my acting skills were fantastic. I should really consider going on the stage.

'I shall depart now and go looking for dear Ella, my dear Maria.'

I was hardly around the corner when my smile flickered and went out. Blast! This would be difficult to keep up.

I met Ella as she was leaving our house on Wilkins' arm. Immediately, I switched my smile back on and positioned myself on her other side. From the still-open door of our house, I caught a whiff of exotic flowers.

'New bouquets?' I asked her in an undertone.

Ella turned her wide, pleading eyes on me.

'Half a dozen of them! He has told me that my lips look like rose petals, and my hair like sunflowers, and my skin like lilies, and he apparently thinks it necessary to bring me copious quantities of all that vegetation every time he makes a comparison. Please don't leave me, Lill!'

I patted her arm. 'Don't you worry. I'm right here.'

For a moment she closed her eyes in silent gratitude. She looked about ready to faint. And this time, I was ready to bet her anxiety had nothing to do with the fact that the man next to her wished to marry her against her will. A knight of the British Empire was leading her by the arm! That was enough to make Ella faint any day.

I, personally, didn't have such a high opinion of Britain's aristocracy. They didn't seem to have anything better to do than to roam their lands shooting pheasants and foxes. Not that I missed those – I had met a pheasant in Green Park once, and it had squawked at me in a most unpleasant manner, enough for anybody to want to shoot it – but still, they didn't seem to be a very productive sort of bird[35]. The aristocracy, I mean, not the pheasants.

We all walked to the coach, Wilkins taking the place on one side of her while I squeezed myself in on the other side, in easy slapping distance of his face. With his long nose and over-large ears, he didn't seem like the sort of chap who would suddenly start ravishing a young lady, but then, you could never be sure. I wanted to be close so he wouldn't get any quick ravishing done while I wasn't looking.

'Well,' Sir Philip said, beaming widely. 'Isn't this cosy?'

Not for the first time I wondered whether there was something wrong with his brain.

The others climbed in after us, the driver jumped onto the box and off we went. The coach wheels rattled on the cobblestones as we moved towards Lady

---

[35] For some strange reason, in British English, you can use the word 'bird' to refer to a man, although they generally don't have wings.

Metcalf's residence at a brisk pace. Needless to say I didn't know how long the drive was going to be. I was not a regular visitor there.

Just before we turned around the first corner, I looked back and saw a figure standing in front of our neighbour's house. Even at this distance I could see the anguished look on Edmund's face. My, my. The chap had really got it bad. I was so glad I didn't have anything to do with this stuff called love and never would be stupid enough to. It never seemed to work out right.

Suddenly, Ella turned her head to look back, and I quickly turned forward again, fixing my new official ball-grin on my face. It was hard to keep up. The expression on Ella's face as she gazed at her love disappearing in the distance was like a poisoned dagger to the heart of a loving sister.

'What are you looking at, Miss Ella?' enquired the blasted Wilkins, turning to follow her gaze.

'Oh, nothing, nothing,' she said hurriedly and, thank the Lord, it was at that exact moment we turned the corner and Edmund vanished from sight.

'Well,' Wilkins chuckled nervously, turning around again, 'I guarantee you that anything we might be leaving behind is not half as interesting as what we are driving towards.'

'Indeed?' Ella's voice was polite but indignant; disbelieving love-light shone in her eyes.

Anne leant forward, her curiosity peeked. 'Is Lady Metcalf's ball going to be that spectacular, then? Do you know something we don't?'

'No, I fancy the ball will be pretty much like any other ball in London, though I do by no means intend to demean Lady Metcalf's hospitality.'

'Then what are you talking about?'

'Forgive me.' He smiled at us in a manner he obviously intended to be mysterious. For most of the inmates of the coach, it actually worked. 'I should have expressed myself more clearly. It is not *what* we are driving towards that is extraordinary, but *whom* we are driving towards.'

Now he definitely had Anne's and Maria's attention.

'Are we to understand that there will be a personage of special importance present at the ball tonight?' Leaning forward even farther, Maria lost no time in asking the central question: 'Is it a man?'

'Yes, Miss Maria.'

The twins' eyes gleamed, and even Lisbeth's seemed to flicker. Mine slid shut in desperation. I knew what the next word out of their mouths would be. It started with an 'm'. And the one after that with an 'o'. And the one after that... hmm.... let me think... with an 's'.

'Married or single?' Anne demanded.

I'm good at guessing, aren't I?

'Single, I believe.'

Opening my eyes again, I took a peek. If the twins' eyes had been shining before, they were ablaze now. They had sniffed prey and were preparing for the hunt.

'You're being very coy, Sir Philip,' Maria accused him, giggling. 'You're giving us answers of one or two syllables.'

Four or five syllables, actually, Maria, but who's counting.

'What is so special about this man?'

'Yes, tell us! What's so special about him?'

Sir Philip raised an eyebrow. 'Apart from the fact that he's just about the richest man in the city of London?'

My eyes, which had just been about to close again, flew wide open. My heartbeat picked up and so did my breathing. Good God in heaven! The last person of whom I had heard that said... no, that couldn't be! He couldn't be at a ball, could he? What would he be doing at a ball? He'd told me himself he hated any and every kind of social event!

Anne's and Maria's eyes were blazing like bonfires now. 'And his name? His manner? His looks?'

Sir Philip shook his head with a smile.

'No, Ladies. You will not be getting any more information out of me. It wouldn't do any good. He has to be seen to be believed.'

Oh my God, it's him! I know it! It's him!

Dear Lord, no! I was going to meet *him*? In a dress? With my family there, and people laughing and dancing everywhere? What the bloody hell was I going to say? What was I going to do? And most important of all, *where would I hide*?

TWICE SURPRISED

By the time we arrived at Lady Metcalf's, I was a nervous wreck. And I didn't mean some figurative-speech kind of wreck. I meant an old Spanish galleon with broken masts, a rotting hull and missing canons – and possibly with the rotting skeleton of the captain in the master cabin.

Blast, blast, blast! What am I going to do? Lord help me, what am I going to do?

The coach crunched to a halt on the gravel outside Lady Metcalf's residence, and Wilkins leaned over to my little sister with a look in his eyes as though he'd just been hit over the head with a heavy cudgel. Or maybe he was in love.

'You look so beautiful tonight, Miss Ella.'

'Um... thank you, Sir Philip. You are too kind.'

'No, I tell you nothing but the truth. And to further enhance your beauty, I wondered if you would do me the honour of wearing this in your hair tonight?'

He pulled a single white rose from behind his back. Ella paled. I could see what was going on in her head as clearly as though she had told me herself: she had accepted his attentions, even his gifts, because it was what courtesy demanded. But openly wearing a sign of his affection and thus accepting it? I could tell something in her was screaming that it would be a betrayal of Edmund, her love.

Silly, of course. It wasn't a betrayal – it was only a ruddy flower! But there it was.

'I... feel honoured–' she began haltingly.

'But then,' Sir Philip interrupted her, 'I reconsidered. I thought that maybe this flower would fit the colour of your hair better!' And letting go of the white rose, he pulled out a sunflower as big as my palm. Ella's eyes widened.

'And then, Miss Ella, I again thought, no. Nobody would see it. We need contrast to show off your beauty in the best light, it is what you deserve. So I brought this.' And he pulled out a red rose. With an uncertain smile, he looked at Ella. 'I simply cannot choose; they are all so beautiful! Could you perhaps pick one for me? Or maybe just wear them all? That would be the simplest solution. We could put the sunflower here, and the roses–'

I had heard enough.

'My sister is a lady and not a flower-arrangement,' I cut him off briskly. 'You forget, Sir, that she has to dance, and those beautiful flowers might fall out of her hair and get trampled underfoot. We wouldn't want that, now, would we?'

'Oh... oh, I suppose you're right.' The knight looked crestfallen, like a little puppy that had been denied his stick to play with, and for a moment I almost felt something like pity. Then he perked up. 'But she could always wear them after the dance, or maybe...'

I pulled Ella out of the carriage before he could finish the sentence. The others were already out there, enjoying the attentions of servants who were bowing, taking coats and opening doors, something which in our house happened very seldom.

'Quickly, quickly, take my coat!'

'You there! Open the door!'

I sighed, trying to shut out my twin sisters' voices. At home, if you wanted to wait until Leadfield had opened a door for you, you'd probably die of old age, and if you wanted him to take your coat, he'd collapse under the weight. So this was a very welcome change, especially for Anne and Maria.

The swarm of buzzing servants escorted us to the ball room, where Lady Metcalf was already awaiting us. I looked around anxiously. But the lean, dark figure I feared to see was nowhere in sight. Just Lady Metcalf.

'Ah! Mrs Brank! Miss Linton, Miss Linton, Miss Linton, Miss Linton, Miss Linton and Miss Linton! Thank you very much for coming. I am delighted that you could make it.'

I must say, I was impressed. Lady Metcalf's smile was even more fake than mine, and she lied like a professional politician. But then, her father had been Foreign Secretary, so maybe it ran in the family.

'Lady Metcalf,' my aunt trilled. 'I was so excited when we received your invitation. It was very nice of you, considering you have never before deigned to include us in one of your festivities.'

Ouch! I could see where this was leading. Poisonous fumes already hung heavily in the air between the two older ladies.

'I simply could not resist,' Lady Metcalf purred. 'Sir Philip was so... enthusiastic. And I simply had to invite the young lady who has been so fortunate as to attract the affection of one of London's finest young men, despite her... err... regrettable social position.'

If looks could kill, Lady Metcalf would have been a red blot on the wall right then, and my aunt would be hauled off to Codbath Fields Prison faster than you could say Jack Robinson. Unluckily, though, looks couldn't kill, and my aunt remained a free woman.

'Remember,' she hissed at me while curtsying to Lady Metcalf. 'Behave yourself!'

This was going to be a very long night. And *he* would be there!

~~**~*~*

The young man approached me with vigour in his step. He wore a bright waistcoat, a carnation in his buttonhole, and a bright, confident smile on his handsome face. I disliked him immediately.

'Miss Linton?' He bowed deeply. 'Will you do me the honour of granting me your hand for this dance?'

I smiled back at him one hundred times as brightly. 'Why certainly! How could I refuse to dance with *you*, Sir?'

Now if I could only remember your name, so I could put you on my list of murder victims...

'Thank you, Miss.'

Stretching out his fingers, he clasped them around mine. Blast! I knew I had agreed to dance with him, but did that mean he actually had to touch me? Working hard to keep my fake smile on my face, I let myself be led onto the dance floor. From the edge of the crowd I could see Anne and Maria ogling me with incredulity. I smiled at them, too. Tonight was smiley night! Argh!

As the first notes of the quadrille[36] began, the young man put his arms around me and began to shove me across the dance floor. I believe officially it is called steering, but that word implies that the steerer actually knows what he is doing, whereas my dancing partner evidently did not.

'Enjoying the dance?' he asked me with a cheerful smile.

'Why yes, of course,' I replied with an even more cheerfuller smile.

Curse you! May the furies of hell hound you to pandemonium and back!

'Me too. What a wonderful ball.'

'Oh yes. So wonderful.'

And gouging out your eyes would be great! Yes, they should definitely gouge out your eyes, pickle them and eat them for breakfast!

I would have dearly loved to grab the bugger by the collar and see how he liked being 'steered' himself, but my aunt was watching. So I smiled until my face hurt and only contrived to step on my partner's feet now and again. Finally

---

[36] A dance, the predecessor of square dance, that was popular in the Victorian Era. Amusingly enough, the first quadrilles were not dances, but military parades, where soldiers would perform formation riding. Apparently, the riding gentlemen enjoyed this so much that they decided to swap the horses for ladies and take the pastime to the ballroom as a kind of dance. Which goes to show that male intelligence is sufficient to recognize the superiority of women over horses as dancing partners. Hurray!

209

I had discovered an advantage of hoop skirts: nobody could see what my heels were doing. Not even my aunt.

I danced with partner after partner. Most of them were actually quite good dancers, and those who were, went away with their feet still intact and an annoyingly good opinion of yours truly. In passing, I heard somebody say: '... and that Lilly Linton.... such a nice, quiet, charming girl. Always smiling so brightly, it really lights up the evening. And so very...'

Mercifully, I was swept away by my partner then, so I didn't have to hear any more of my false accomplishments. Nevertheless, I knew that my aunt had been right. If I just said, 'Yes, Sir, of course, Sir,' to every question asked and smiled prettily, gentlemen who before would have been running in the opposite direction at the sight of me were suddenly delighted with this blasted charming new Lilly. It made me want find an umbrella stand in which to vomit.

All this play-acting took considerable concentration. Not enough, though, to make me forget about the special guest to whom Wilkins had promised to introduce us tonight. Continuously, my eyes scanned the ballroom for any sign of Mr Rikkard Ambrose. They never found any. My anxiety grew with every minute.

What's the matter? Why isn't he here? Or... maybe he is here! Maybe he is watching me, gazing coldly at my dress, my fan and any other articles that screamed 'female!', getting more determined to get rid of the girl in his office with every passing minute!

From the moment the idea first entered my mind, I felt an itch on the back of my head as though he was standing behind me, his cold gaze drilling into the back of my head – which of course was a load of cobblers because I was dancing the quadrille, ergo twirling continuously around the room, seeing everything.

Blast! He can't be here! And he certainly can't be watching me from behind if I'm always pirouetting!

Still, I fretted through three dances over Mr Rikkard bloody Ambrose! Only when I caught sight of Wilkins and Ella dancing a few paces away did I remember that I had other worries tonight as well. Remorse shot through me. For the moment, I had completely forgotten about protecting my little sister from Wilkins' overdone attentions.

Well, if I wasn't going to saw a hole in the ballroom floor through which Wilkins could be disposed of, I couldn't do anything while they were dancing. Afterwards, I swore to myself, I would become the most steadfast buffer in the history of womankind.

But my kind sisterly plans were cruelly dashed. By the time the dance had finished and I had manage to disentangle myself from my partner and rush to my sister's side, the evil flower-presenter was nowhere to be seen.

'Where's Sir Philip?' I asked.

'I don't know.' Closing her eyes, Ella sighed and leaned against my shoulder. I let her. I had originally come to serve as a sisterly buffer, but I might just as well be of use as a support column. 'Somebody told him something, and he excused himself. Honestly, I don't care. I only care that he's gone for the moment. Oh Lill!'

Her eyes fluttered open again, and I saw moisture glinting in there as she looked up at me imploringly. 'What should I do? What in God's name should I do?'

I was about to answer her (and a very clever answer it would have been!) when Sir Philip appeared out of the multitude around us, an eager smile on his face. I noticed that the sunflower he had brought along for Ella was sticking out of his buttonhole, rather clashing with his green and red waistcoat.

'My dear Miss Ella... oh, Miss Lilian, you're here, too? How wonderful! Where's the rest of your family? Ah, there!'

He waved them over eagerly, and they came, interested to see what he was so excited about. I was starting to have an idea and felt a dark pit of dread opening up in my stomach.

'What's the matter, Sir Philip?' Maria asked, breathless – maybe a bit more breathless than absolutely necessary. 'Is something wrong?'

'On the contrary, my dear, something is right.' He beamed at all of us. 'Remember that I told you of this special guest who would be here tonight?'

They all nodded. The black pit in my stomach grew by leaps and bounds. My knees wobbled.

'Yes, of course we remember.' Anne's eyes had become very large. 'You don't mean...'

'...He's here!' Sir Philip triumphantly finished. 'I have just bumped into him. I've known him for some years, and I'm sure he'll sacrifice a few minutes of his valuable time for my sake. Ladies, it will be my pleasure to introduce you to one of the most wealthy and eminent personages of the British Empire.'

I cleared my throat. 'Um... do you really think we should waste the valuable time of such a man?' Cautiously, I started edging backwards. Maria threw me a venomous look. Apparently, she was already determined to conquer the heart of this mighty, mysterious man.

Oh my dear sister, if you only knew....

'I'm sure he'll be delighted to meet all of you. Come, come.' Without further ado, Wilkins took me and Ella by the hand and started leading us towards the windowed front of the ballroom. In his boundless enthusiasm he didn't even notice that I was digging my heels into the ground and he more or less had to drag me across the ballroom.

Bloody hell! Let go of me! I don't want to see him! I can't! Not in a dress! He'll... Blast, I don't know what he's going to do, but he's going to do something!

But for a weedy man with a flower fixation, Sir Philip was surprisingly strong. In spite of my resistance, I was towed forward.

Others were not so reluctant. Lisbeth, Anne and Maria were giggling and whispering with each other, hard on our heels. Even Ella and Gertrude displayed a modicum of excitement. And as for my aunt... she was practically bursting! Golden coins were shining in her eyes instead of pupils.

'Please, Sir Philip...' I tried to wrest my hand from his grip. 'I would feel embarrassed, meeting such a great man.'

'Nonsense. Whyever would you?'

Because unlike you, I know what he keeps chained up in his cellar!

'Because... because I am a very modest person, that's why! And very shy!'

Turning her head towards me, Ella gave me a look of pure incredulity. She almost forgot to look where she was going and stumbled over the hem of her own dress. I suppose I couldn't blame her. She was my sister, after all, and knew me well.

'Oh, if that's the only reason, you do not need to worry,' Sir Philip assured me. 'My friend's manners are perfectly unassuming and charming.'

What?

I was so surprised by that description that I actually stopped struggling for a moment, and my knightly tugboat was able to drag me the rest of the way.

We arrived at a tightly-packed group of individuals. Mostly they were men – the most expensively dressed men I had ever seen, in midnight-black tailcoats and brilliant waistcoats with golden embroidery. They were centred around somebody we couldn't see, all talking excitedly.

For one last time I tugged at my hand, desperately trying to get away. But that blasted Wilkins held my hand firmly. There was no escape.

Wilkins tapped the shoulder of one of the men who were barring the way.

'Would you be so kind as to step aside for a moment, please?'

No! Don't be kind! Be mean! Be rude, please! Be bloody impertinent and stay where you are!

'I would like to introduce these ladies to my honoured friend.'

No! Bloody hell, no!

In spite of my internal pleading, the men in front of us parted. Out from between them stepped another man. I blinked in surprise. He was lean and he was tall, just like Mr Ambrose – but there was no way this man could be mistaken for my employer. He had longish blonde hair that was combed back in elegant waves, a slightly curvy, hawk-like nose and light, steel-blue eyes.

Even if all this could have been faked and underneath that inviting exterior somewhere lurked the brooding self I had suspected to find here, there was one characteristic which definitely identified this man as somebody other than Mr Ambrose: he had a broad, inviting smile on his face.

'Ah, good evening, Wilkins. What a pleasure to see you again.' The blonde man bowed to Ella's admirer, who in turn bowed back. 'And who, if I may ask, are these lovely ladies you have brought with you?'

His voice, too, was nothing like Mr Ambrose's. It sounded smooth and eloquent, like a public speaker who could move whole crowds, or maybe a young, dashing general who by his voice alone could persuade men to follow him into battle. For some reason I felt a blush creep up my cheeks.

'Of course, where are my manners?' Wilkins let go of my hand so he could point us out in turn. 'Lord Dalgliesh, may I present Mrs Brank, Miss Linton, Miss Linton, Miss Linton, Miss Linton, Miss Linton and Miss Linton. Ladies, this is Lord Daniel Eugene Dalgliesh.'

He bowed to each of us in turn, slowly and elegantly.

'I am charmed. Who knew that such bewitching company would await me at this ball.'

It hadn't escaped my notice that Wilkins had introduced us to him and not the other way around. Normally, men were introduced to women. For it to be done in reverse, the man must be presumed to be ten times more important than any woman.

With any ordinary man, this would have sent me into a fit of rage. Yet as Lord Dalgliesh bowed to me and for a moment I met his steel-blue gaze, I knew without doubt that this was no ordinary man.

There was an aura about him, a presence that bespoke greatness. I felt as though those steel-blue eyes could analyse every bone in my body and gaze into the darkest recesses of my soul. Which was complete bilge, of course. My soul didn't have any dark recesses! Did it?

I was ripped from the contemplation of my soul by my loving sister Maria, who shoved me out of the way to be closer to her target.

'It is I who am charmed to meet you, My Lord. Tell me how it is that, though I have been a frequent visitor to many balls in the city, I have never yet had the pleasure of making your acquaintance? Such a great lord as yourself should surely be the life and soul of every ball.'

Bravo, Maria, bravo! I really had to admire her. She had flattered him, depicted herself as a worthy object of his undying love, fished for information, and flattered him again, and that all in one sentence. She really knew how to catch her fish. Only I had a suspicion this one would prove to be a little bit too big for her nets.

Lord Dalgliesh gave a light, pleasant laugh. 'The matter is susceptible of a ready explanation, Miss Linton. I assure you that I am no recluse or social outcast. In fact, I have been away from the metropolis, even from Britain, for a long time now, looking after various matters in the colonies.' He shrugged apologetically and smiled a smile so charming, it could maybe even have charmed a fairy queen. 'It was very unfortunate, considering what I was missing here.'

My sister wasn't a fairy queen. She didn't have a hope.

'Oh, Lord Dalgliesh,' was all she managed to whisper.

'What brought you back?' Sir Philip wanted to know. 'I would have thought you had enough out there to keep you busy for a lifetime.'

Seeing our questioning looks, he added with a smile, 'Lord Dalgliesh is the main shareholder of the East India Company.'

Maria's eyes lit up. If she hadn't been determined to grab this man for herself before, she was now. Anne seemed to experience similar feelings. I must say, I was pretty floored myself.

The East India Company... Did such a conglomerate even deserve to be referred to as only a 'company', when it owned and ruled most of the Indian subcontinent, along with its own army and state apparatus? If this man truly was in charge of the East India Company, he was as close to a king as you could get without actually wearing a crown.

'What brought you back?' Sir Philip repeated the question.

For a moment, just a moment, the smile on Lord Dalgliesh's face flickered. It looked almost like what had happened to me not too long ago. But that was hardly likely, was it? What reason could Lord Dalgliesh have for only *pretending* to smile?

'Oh, no great matter,' he said, smoothly. 'Just a little unfinished business with an old friend. There's a game of chess we need to finish.'

I frowned.

'You came to England, travelled thousands of miles... just to finish a game of chess?'

Turning his head towards me, he cranked his smile up a notch. But his steel-blue eyes didn't lose their cool, assessing look. Blimey, he *was* faking! A darn sight more convincingly than I, but he was faking.

'In a manner of speaking,' he said, nodding. 'Though we may use no actual board or figures made from wood.'

My frown deepened. 'You've lost me, Your Lordship.'

'Do not worry. I can always find you again.'

He turned his head and started a light, flirtatious conversation with Anne, who leapt at the chance of overtaking her sister. I just stood there, shaking my head. This man was... disturbing. As soon as I could manage without seeming offensive, I excused myself. I wanted to get away from him. He was a darn sight too fascinating for me to want to be anywhere near him. I wanted to be alone – maybe find a quiet refreshment table and a chocolate bar. Gripping Ella by the hand, I started to tug her away with me.

'Come!' I whispered. 'It's time we made ourselves scarce!'

She threw me a grateful look and let herself be dragged away. On her own, she would never have had the nerve to run from that bloody Wilkins. But being forcibly carried off by her sister, that she could manage all right.

'Can you see where the refreshment tables are?'

Standing on my toes, I tried to determine a safe route through the jungle of people in evening wear barring our way. But it was no good. As soon as we detached ourselves from one group, we were swallowed up by another and welcomed with friendly voices.

Blast! It had all been so much easier when I had been impolite to everybody and scowled instead of smiled. Back then, nobody had given me a second glance.

Oh well, the good old days...

'Miss Linton! And another Miss Linton,' a gentleman with a huge waxed moustache greeted us. I couldn't for the life of me remember his name. 'Hello and welcome. Join our little group.'

'Oh no,' said another gentleman. 'I'm sure *ladies* wouldn't like to listen to our topic of conversation.'

'Nonsense,' Gentleman A overrode him. 'These are no modern, unladylike females. I danced with this young lady,' he inclined his head towards me, 'myself, and she was a model of charm and modesty.'

How nice of you. And you were the model of arrogance and idiocy.

'Why, thank you, Sir,' I said, curtsying. 'If I may ask, what is it that you were talking of before we came?'

Gentleman A leaned closer, and so did his companion. 'Now, I normally wouldn't be mentioning this in the hearing of any ladies. But I can see you two are sensible, demure and well-bred young girls. So it's all right.'

I must admit, he had peaked my interest. I was always interested to know what a person like me wasn't supposed to know.

'Go on,' I encouraged.

'Do you know what is going to happen next Wednesday?' Gentleman A whispered.

'No. What, Sir?'

'There's going to be a meeting about this confounded nonsense called *women's suffrage*.'

'Indeed, Sir?'

'Aye. A few influential gentlemen with press contacts are going to meet with sympathetic scholars and scientists at Speaker's Corner in Hyde Park, and try to put a stop to this codswallop once and for all.'

'Indeed?'

'Oh yes.' Gentleman B nodded gravely. 'Imagine, ladies, that there are actually mad creatures that call themselves women and want to *make decisions in politics!*'

I shook my head solemnly. 'You are joking? Can such individuals really exist?'

Ella stared at me, her eyes wide. Then she blinked and quickly turned back to the men. 'As for my part,' she ventured demurely, 'I find politics incredibly complicated. I am very glad that I do not have to deal with them.'

Gentleman B nodded energetically and smiled at Ella. 'Exactly! That is exactly what I was talking about. I can see you are sensible young girls who know their God-given place in the world, just as my friend said. So, no word about this to anyone, hmm?' He gave us what was supposed to be a fatherly smile. 'It will remain our little secret.'

I smiled at him brightly 'You mean it would be bad if somebody found out about it?'

'Oh yes.' Gentleman B gave a vigorous nod. 'If those infernal suffragists found out, they could use the meeting to spread their insane message.'

'Ah, I see. Well, every sensible person can see that such a thing must never happen.'

'Exactly,' Gentleman A entered the conversation again. 'Women's brains aren't big enough for politics.'

'Plus,' added Gentleman B, 'they do not have the potential for violence that men have, and that is the basis for all stable political systems, a fact that I have pointed out to Parliament on numerous occasions.'

My eyes flicked to Gentleman B.

'So it was *you* who came up with that idea, was it?'

'Yes, indeed.' He nodded proudly. 'Why, have you heard of my theories on female vulnerability?'

'You could say that...' My eyes narrowed infinitesimally. He didn't notice. 'I wonder, Sir, if you would mind stepping into this side-room with me for five minutes. I have something important to demonstrate to you in regard to your theories.'

'By all means. After you, Miss.'

Five minutes later, I re-entered the ballroom, my hair a bit ruffled, but otherwise perfectly fine. Ella was waiting for me.

'Where is the gentleman who went with you?' she asked.

'He experienced a sudden desire to leave through the back door.' I gestured to the side-room from which I had just emerged, a smile turning up one corner of my mouth. 'I believe something in there might have scared him a little.'

My smile widened. All that was missing now was a feast for the victorious warrior! Not far away, I spotted a refreshment table with something brown on it that might be chocolate. Yum!

'Come,' I said, grasping Ella by the hand. 'We could...'

'Miss Linton? Miss Lilly Linton?'

I turned and stiffened. In front of me was standing none other than Lord Daniel Eugene Dalgliesh, smiling at me as if I were another continent to be added to his empire.

'It is Miss Lilly, isn't it?' The charm-factor of his smile went up another level or two. 'I'm afraid I might have confused all these lovely Lintons.'

'Yes, um... yes,' I muttered. 'My name is Lilly.'

'Very well, Miss Lilly. Would you do me the honour of granting me the next dance?'

You could have struck me down with a feather. A piece of fluff would probably have sufficed as a cudgel, too. I stood there, mute, staring up at him.

'Lill? Lill!'

Somebody was tugging on my arm and whispering in my ear. 'Lill, answer him! For goodness' sake, please answer him!'

Who... oh yes. Ella. That was my sister's name, wasn't it? Lord Dalgliesh. Dancing. Hell's whiskers! Had he just really asked me to dance with him? The owner of an entire continent wanted to dance with *me*? Something was wonky in this world!

From somewhere I heard a voice that sounded suspiciously like my own say: 'Certainly, Lord Dalgliesh. I would love to dance with you.'

A hand grasped mine. It was firm but smooth. The skin of an aristocrat who had never done manual labour. As if in a dream, or maybe a nightmare, Lord Dalgliesh led me onto the dance floor with small, elegant steps.

I heard it around us: voices hushing, then whispering, the clatter of my aunt's jaw as it hit the floor. But I didn't see any of it. I only saw my own feet, and thought: *In half a minute, those will have to start dancing.*

Then the music started. Lord Dalgliesh gripped my hand, and suddenly we were whirling around each other with unearthly grace. He was tugging on my hand, throwing me this way and that, too fast for me to do anything about it.

Ha! I had thought the other men on the dance floor tried to lead when dancing? I had known nothing. This was real leading. Not pushing me forward, but pulling me into following him with masterful moves. I was powerless to resist. Part of me didn't even want to.

We went through the forms of the dance, stepping away from each other, marching down the line of dancers. He passed out of my sight. But in passing, I saw the look in his eyes as he gazed at me. In that look was something I hadn't seen in the face of this paragon of power: curiosity.

At the end of the line I turned, facing him again. Normally, I went down the line slowly. I was a careful dancer. But he rushed towards me, so I had to follow. Grasping me by my arm, he whirled me around once again.

I met his curious gaze.

'Why did you ask me to dance with you, Lord Dalgliesh?'

The question, uttered low but distinctly, was out of my mouth before I knew I had opened it. Some central, unchangeable, nosy part of me must have shoved it past my teeth in spite of the mesmerizing effects of his presence. It was good to know I was still myself somewhere in there.

We danced another turn.

'Why on earth should I have a special reason?' he enquired as we passed again. 'Is not the pleasure of your company enough?'

'Not really, no.' And he actually gave a little laugh. It rang like bells, pleasant to the ear.

'You do not think much of yourself?'

It's not that. It's just that I think you think a lot more of yourself than you do of me.

'Oh please.' I looked down, demurely. Tonight was play-acting night, after all. 'I am only a simple gentry[37] girl, not such an exalted personage such as yourself, My Lord.'

He flashed his brilliant smile again and began pelting me with a hundred little compliments, all perfectly arranged to melt the heart of any maiden. The compliments themselves did not get to me. The skill which with they were delivered, on the other hand, did.

What does this bloody fellow want with me? He could have dozens of women mooning at his feet!

Of course, there was always the possibility that he had fallen madly in love with me at first sight. But that was the kind of thing Ella might have believed, not I. And even if he had, he'd better fall out of love again right speedily!

Slowly, the flow of niceties ebbed. We continued to dance, and I had to admit he was an excellent dancer. Lord Dalgliesh led in a way that made me not even feel I was being led: it was effortless, graceful, and enthralling. And that was exactly why I hated it. He didn't make me feel like being led – but in fact I was, very skilfully. And I didn't take kindly to people trying to fool me.

Oh really? a tiny voice inside me asked. *Not even when it's done as magnificently as this?*

Finally, after three more turns and several more compliments, he got to the point. As we passed each other, he whispered:

---

[37] The gentry were (and still are) a class of landowners in England who have managed the astonishing trick of being treated and seen as nobility without actually having a noble title. On the social ladder, they lie between the real nobility and the middle-class. Elisabeth Bennet from Jane Austen's *Pride and Prejudice* is an example of a gentry girl.

'I must make a confession, Miss Linton.'

'Oh?'

He turned on the spot in a perfect pirouette. Grabbing my hand, he pulled me towards him, past him, and launched me into the movement alongside the other ladies. When I returned, he said in a low voice:

'Yes. I did have a motive to dance with you, other than your charms. Although I assure you,' he added, smiling again, 'that no other motive would have been needed.'

I faked a smile back at him. Now we were talking business! 'But there was one?'

Taking hold of my arm, he led me into another smooth turn.

'Yes. I was curious. When we first met, you looked at me rather strangely. As if you expected to see somebody else. I am used to how people react around me, and your reaction was startlingly different. So, as I said, I am curious. What was going through your mind when you saw me?'

Hm... How about 'Thank God, it's not him!'?

I hesitated. But I had already fulfilled my quota of lies for the day. And anyway, why shouldn't he know?

Fixing my gaze on his mesmerizing steel-blue eyes as the ballroom turned around us in a blur, I said:

'Sir Philip hinted to us that we were going to meet a person of great importance at the ball. From what he said....I was expecting somebody else.'

'Oh?' One of his brows rose in interest. 'Whom, if I may ask?'

I opened my mouth to speak.

At that precise moment, three heavy, loud knocks came from the large door leading into the ballroom. The music stopped. The dancers stopped. Everything stopped. I nearly stumbled over Lord Dalgliesh's feet, and only grabbing onto his shoulder kept me from falling. Quickly, I steadied myself again, letting go of his shoulder.

I looked around. I could see the same question on every face: Who on earth would be daring, impatient, bad-mannered and arrogant enough to interrupt a ball in the middle of a dance?

Oh no...

The doors swung open and, as I knew he would, in strode Mr Rikkard Ambrose, his face harder and more stunning than ever.

Everybody stared at him as he stood there, facing the motionless dancers. Everybody except me, that is. I was too busy staring at the tall, ravishingly beautiful woman who had entered the room on his arm.

Duelling on the Dance Floor

She was slim and fair with delicately curved lips, deep green eyes, and black hair that tumbled in rich curls down her back. She held herself regally, and it was clear that, unlike me, she felt perfectly at home in a ballroom. Her luxurious green and black ball gown, perfectly complementing her eyes and hair, fell down in elaborate folds over an elegantly sweeping crinoline. In short, she was very beautiful, and obviously knew just how to accentuate that beauty to attract a man's attention.

I hated her at first sight.

Well, what do you expect? I am a proud fighter for women's rights and independence. Of course I instantly despised somebody who conformed so absolutely to the female stereotype of the damsel in distress that I was trying to fight.

You despise her for being unfeminist, do you?

Yes, of course I did.

And the two hundred and fifty other women in the room, who are just the same kind of unfeminist, lily-livered cowards? You don't despise them, do you?

Well...

Might the intense loathing that you feel specifically for her have something to do with the fact that she is clinging to Mr Ambrose's arm like a limpet?

Sometimes I really wished that inner voice of mine would shut up!

My eyes flicked from her to Mr Ambrose and back again. Could he... could they be...? No. They couldn't be, could they?

Mr Ambrose strode over to Lady Metcalf, who stood at the edge of the crowd, gaping at him in a rather unladylike manner. In this, I noticed, she was mimicked by almost every female in the room. Blast! Why did that annoy me so much?

He made a quick, curt bow.

'Please forgive this intrusion, My Lady. I changed my mind about not accepting your most recent invitation. I hope I'm not too late and that the ball hasn't already started?'

Since the floor full of frozen dancers around him made it quite blatantly obvious that the dance had indeed started, this remark was rather redundant. It was also as impolite as one could get. Colour rose to Lady Metcalf's cheeks. Her mouth closed. And opened. And closed again.

Was she thinking of letting her servants chase him out with hunting crops? That's what she would have done if I or anyone else had pulled off something like this. But Mr Rikkard Ambrose wasn't just anyone.

'N-no, of course not, Mr Ambrose.'

My mouth dropped open. The voice coming out of Lady Metcalf's mouth wasn't the usual vulture's croak. It was soft, uncertain, almost demure. Under Mr Ambrose's cold gaze, she lowered her eyes.

Good God! Is she possessed or something?

'Of course we haven't started yet, Mr Ambrose. You've come just at the right time. May I introduce you to my family?'

'You may,' Mr Ambrose granted with infinite generosity.

The raven-haired beauty stepped up beside him.

No... not raven-haired. Crow-haired! She's a crow! She's just the sort to pick at rotting carcasses. She's probably just waiting to sink her beak into Mr Ambrose.

She smiled. And it was an artificial smile that didn't reach her eyes. I knew it! I knew she couldn't be trusted. You could never trust females – they were so bloody conniving! Apart from unfortunate young secretaries and other kinds of feminists, of course.

She directed her smile at him, and he, although he didn't smile, nodded graciously. More graciously than he had *ever* nodded at me.

A thousand questions buzzed through my head. Who was she? Why was she here? Why had he brought her? Was she rich? Was he in love with her? Were they engaged? And most important of all, why the blazes were all of my questions about *her*?

I forced my eyes back to Mr Ambrose. It was *him* I should be concerned about.

Should be.

But wasn't.

I was concerned about her. Or, more specifically, her and him in combination.

My eyes snapped back to her. Heat welled up inside me. The heat of some dark unnamed emotion. Was it possible to want to claw a stranger's eyes out? Well, people said there was such a thing as love at first sight. Why not hate at first sight, then?

'Um, Miss Linton? My hand, if you please?'

Blinking in surprise, so suddenly ripped from my thoughts, I looked up at Lord Dalgliesh, then down at his hand, which I was clenching so tightly that it was white from lack of blood. I let go as if I had burned myself. 'Oh, excuse me!'

'No matter,' he said, took his other hand off my arm and stepped back from me. His attention seemed to be on something else. He was looking towards the two newcomers.

Well, if he wasn't interested in me any longer, all the better. Quickly, I stepped back and ducked into the crowd.

Just in time: Mr Ambrose had spotted Lord Dalgliesh.

There was a moment suspended in time. The two men's eyes met, and it was as if they were two lions meeting at a Sahara watering hole. They were the kings, the rest of us were just so many zebras and antelopes.

Mr Ambrose prowled forward. Lord Dalgliesh, ignoring Lady Metcalf, who was still trying to engage the newcomers' attention, shook out his mane of golden hair and started to advance as well. People in their way stood aside hastily, as if they felt the tension in the air. I certainly did.

Finally, they stood facing each other. I watched from behind the shoulder of a bulky military gentleman who didn't realise he was being used as cover.

The two of them stared at one another, waiting for the other to bow first. After seemingly endless seconds, they both inclined their heads about half an inch, at the same instant.

'Lord Dalgliesh,' Mr Ambrose said.

'Lord Ambrose,' Lord Dalgliesh said.

A shiver went down my back? *Lord Ambrose? What the...!*

'*Mister* Ambrose, your Lordship.' Mr Ambrose's tone was arctic, but Lord Dalgliesh didn't flinch. He just smiled a friendly smile. A fake friendly smile. 'Of course. My mistake.'

There was a spell of silence so intense it pressed against my eardrums.

'It has been long,' Mr Ambrose said.

'Yes, it has,' Lord Dalgliesh said. 'Quite some time since last we met.'

The air between them seemed to crackle. Lord Dalgliesh started to say something else, but I didn't catch it because at that very moment the evil crow descended on Mr Ambrose, grabbing his arm again.

'Come, my dear Rikkard,' she said with the broadest of smiles. 'I wish to dance a reel or two.'

Rikkard? *Rikkard?* She was allowed to call him by his first name? Who was this creature? The writer of the pink letters?

Well, if so, he seemed to pay a lot more attention to her in person than he did to her correspondence. With a last dark look at Lord Dalgliesh, he took her by the hand and led her onto the dance floor.

'What was that?' I heard some lady whisper beside me. 'Between Mr Ambrose and His Lordship, I mean. I've seen a lot of important people taking the measure of each other, but that...'

'That was eerie,' agreed another in whispered tones. I was inclined to agree.

Lord Dalgliesh still followed Mr Ambrose with his eyes. He had his back turned to me, so I couldn't see his expression. But I didn't really want to.

Then suddenly he turned, again with his charming smile on his face. 'Miss Linton,' he began. 'I apologize for the interruption. Shall we finish our....'

His smile flickered and went out when he saw that I was no longer there beside him. I didn't wait to see what he would do next. By the time the music had started up again, I was already halfway across the room, trying to locate my little sister Ella.

I had to find Ella! It was essential that I found her again and helped her through the evening as well as I could. It was also essential that I occupied myself with something, anything which could keep my mind off the fact that Mr Rikkard bloody Ambrose was dancing in this bloody ballroom, probably only a few yards away from me, with some bloody female I had never seen in my life!

I felt like hitting something. Preferably Mr Ambrose. Or her. Oh yes, he could snap at *me* and even continue to deny the fact that I was a girl, but present him with a girl with long lashes, a demure smile and a pretty dress, and he was suddenly dancing and going to balls and whatnot. Typical man!

Or is he? whispered that tiny voice inside me. *You heard Dalgliesh call him Lord. It's not every man who has a noble ancestry but chooses to deny the fact. Why do it?*

No matter. Nobleman or common man, he was still a man! Self-centred, arrogant, infuriating!

I should just ignore his antics the way I had learned to ignore most men's chauvinist behaviour over the years. But... but... there was this possessive way in which the black-haired girl had linked arms with him. For some reason I could *not* ignore that.

I spotted them in the distance, twirling over the dance floor, and a stab of envy shot through me. No, I could not ignore that at all.

But why?

Fuming, I whirled around and left in search of Ella.

Bloody hell, *why*?

~~**~*~*

'There you are!'

I swooped down on my prey like a hawk on an unsuspecting field mouse. Well, maybe not quite. For one thing, I didn't grab Sir Philip Wilkins by the neck, but by the hand. For another, I didn't carry him off to my nest on a distant, rocky crag to devour him, but simply dragged him over to a chair next to the closest refreshment table, away from an exhausted-looking Ella.

'I have been looking for you,' I said with a reproachful little smile and more or less forced the lanky, long-nosed lord into a chair beside me. Ella, an expression of sublime relief on her face, dropped into a chair on my other side, out of range of his romantic attentions.

'All this dancing can be so exhausting, can't it?' I asked cheerfully as the first notes for the next dance sounded. 'I'm sure you've been *longing* for a break.'

'Well, actually I was rather enjoying-' Wilkins began, his gaze wandering with dreamy longing between Ella and the dance floor.

'So terribly exhausting!' I cut him off. This was the perfect time to test a very handy technique for talking with men I had recently discovered: if they were gentlemen, and a lady intimated there was something she might like them to do, they were usually too polite to refuse. Of course, nobody ever used this technique because it was ruthlessly impolite. But then, nobody had ever accused me of politeness. 'I'm sure you would *love* a little conversation for a change, wouldn't you?'

He hesitated. 'Um... well, yes, if you think so, but...'

It works! It works, it works!

'I must admit I found our discussion of your house in town extraordinary,' I cut him off again with a bright smile. 'So exciting, in fact, that I was wondering: Do you have any estates in the country, too?'

'Well, yes...'

That was all I needed. I let him have it – a full broadside of verbal cannonballs!

'Wonderful! That is so interesting. How many manors are in your possession? Are they large? Is there good hunting there? Not that I myself hunt, of course, but I find the noise of guns so soothing. Reminds me of good old English traditions, and that an excellent supper will soon be on the table, don't you know? Do you yourself hunt? Oh, forgive me for even asking! You are a true gentleman, of course you hunt! I'm sure you're an excellent sportsman, and that is so important in a man, especially an Englishman, since it's really so central to our national character. I mean, if a German or a Frenchman don't know how to shoot, that's all right, they can drink beer or think up poems and philosophy

222

and everybody will say "Here we have a true example of our Nation", but with us English, and the British in general, hunting and sportsmanship are so important. Rather demanding, don't you think? But then, our nation is the greatest in the world, I suppose that it is allowed to make demands of its subjects. What were we talking of again? Now I forgot. Oh yes, your family estates! I must ask you, do you have a library? For I am very interested in...'

And so I went on, and on, and on, until Wilkins' eyes became glassy, and Ella had settled into a comfortable nap. Let me tell you, it wasn't easy to come up with boring subject after boring subject. Dull things to talk of aren't as common as you might think.

Why don't you talk about flowers and greenhouses, or romantic love? He'll probably be happy to talk to you for hours then!

I snorted. But that was just it: I didn't want him to be happy. I wanted him to finally see what a horrible family he intended to marry into, and run away screaming. So far, though, from the looks he gave me, the only result I seemed to be getting for my efforts was that he intended to marry Ella as quickly as possible and remove her to one of these country estates of his, as far away as possible from her deranged sister.

'Of course,' I said brightly, 'Ella and I are *inseparable*. Wherever she goes, I go. Isn't that so, Ella?'

I elbowed her in the ribs as discreetly as possible. Abruptly awakening from her nap, she mumbled: 'What...? Oh yes. Inseparable, yes, of course.'

'I believe that even were one of us to *marry*,' I said poignantly, 'the other could *not survive without her sister*. We would *always* have to be *together*.'

Horror washed over Wilkins' face. Like a drowning man stretching out of the water to grasp a cliff, he jumped from his chair and tapped a passing gentleman in a black tailcoat on the shoulder. In the background, the music of the last dance faded as it came to an end.

'Excuse me, my friend.' The words tumbled out of Wilkins' mouth into the sudden silence. He couldn't get them out fast enough. 'The next dance will be starting soon, and this lady here has held me captive... um, I mean, has had to sit down for several dances, lacking a partner. Would you be so kind as to oblige?'

'If you wish it, Wilkins,' said a horribly familiar, cold, curt voice. 'You were most obliging in our recent dealings, I owe you a favour.'

'It is too kind of you to say so,' Wilkins sighed, relief breaking out all over his face.

'No. I'm never too kind.' Turning, Mr Ambrose nodded to Sir Philip. 'Now, where is this lady of yours?'

Then he saw me.

Slowly his eyes wandered up and down my figure, as if he could not believe what he was seeing. He opened his mouth a fraction of an inch. I *swear* he was about to make a cutting remark about me wearing no trousers! Then his eyes met mine, and he remembered who and where we were.

'Ambrose, may I introduce Miss Lilly Linton.' Wilkins' voice was a distant buzz in the background, his gestures meaningless. 'Miss Lilly Linton, this is Mr Rikkard–'

'We know each other,' Mr Ambrose cut him off. His dark eyes didn't leave my face, boring into me with searing intensity.

The music had started playing. Around us, people were busy chattering. Nevertheless, in our small portion of the ballroom you could have heard a pin drop.

'Y-you do?' Sir Philip looked from me to Mr Ambrose and back again. So did Ella, who was suddenly completely awake again. There was a pause.

'*Where from?*' Wilkins inquired added in a tone of undisguised curiosity and scepticism. As if I didn't exist on the same level as His Mightiness Mr Rikkard Ambrose!

Well, I didn't, monetarily speaking, but still. It was pretty cheeky coming from a chap who went about London bombarding innocent young ladies with flowers!

'We bumped into one another in the street,' Mr Ambrose explained, still not taking his eyes off me. His gaze wasn't just dark and intense, there was something else in it. A promise...

The promise of retribution. That's what's in his eyes – a threat! Is he afraid I'd give him away? Shame him in front of London society by revealing I worked for him? Yes, blast him, that's it!

Well, he'd just have to learn that I could keep my mouth shut!

And he's supposed to dance with me, is he? To hold me lovingly in his arms and sweep me over the polished floor in a passionate whirl?

To judge by the arctic look on his face, it was obvious that nothing was further from his mind, so I did him a favour. Not acknowledging his presence in any way, not even nodding to him, I rudely turned my head away. Soon enough, the crow in her green dress would probably appear and whisk him off.

There was a heavy silence. No footsteps. He did not move away. He was not whisked off. Blast him, why didn't he leave already? My rudeness was giving him the perfect excuse!

'Well, Miss Linton?'

Miss! He called you Miss! He admitted you're female!

Well, it was rather hard to ignore, considering the ball gown I was wearing. Still, that little admission tugged at my heart – and my head. Reluctantly, I turned it towards him.

'Well what?' The retort was abominably rude, but that was all right since it came from me.

Those dark, sea-coloured eyes of his were still fixed on my face. I made the mistake of looking into them and was caught. Blast!

He held out his hand for me to take. 'Miss Lillian Linton, will you do me the honour of dancing with me?'

My mouth fell open slightly. Was he joking? But then I remembered who this was. No, he wasn't joking. Dear Lord in heaven, how was I going to get out of this?

And then something utterly incredible happened – something more horrible than the Napoleonic Wars and the Black Plague put together.

'Yes, thank you,' I heard myself say in a shy, breathy voice.

What? What the heck was the matter with my vocal cords? How could they betray me like this? It wasn't fair!

A hand closed around mine. It was both lithe and muscular, and the grip it exerted was a little too hard for someone asking you for a dance.

For a dance! Argh, no! Not with him!

There was a slight tug on my hand. Not harsh, but insistent. Dazed, I started to move and followed Mr Rikkard Ambrose as he led me onto the dance floor. In my stunned state, I still noticed he moved very differently from Lord Dalgliesh: not like a born dancer, but with a harsh, precise force that went beyond dancing. They were the movements of a born fighter. It almost felt like marching beside an elite soldier on a victory parade.

No! Don't let this happen! Flee, you fool, before doom is upon you!

My insides were writhing in panic. But before I could turn and run, before I could do anything, we suddenly were in position on the dance floor, and I felt arms around me. Mr Ambrose's arms.

Blast! Why do they have to feel so hard and firm and... right? It's not right!

My heartbeat picked up, and I hardly dared to look up. I felt like an elephant who had been ordered to dance with the ringmaster. Would I squash his feet? Would I fall over? And what would happen when this madness was over and we returned to our normal routine of work, if that ever happened?

The music began. The four-four time lent itself to Mr Ambrose's way of moving. He went towards and away from me as the music required, grasped me when the music demanded, and let go when the music said so. Not once did he look at me or speak to me.

We turned. And turned again. And again. And again.

Blast, this is maddening! Isn't he going to say anything at all?

Apparently not. Nobody could be silent like Mr Ambrose. Not even a grave, or a whole graveyard for that matter, could compete with him. And as for looking at me, he didn't seem to have any intention of doing that either. Oh no. He was staring fixedly at something in the distance. When we turned again, in time with the music, I saw where his gaze led.

Of course. Her! He is looking at her!

The crow was standing near a window in the east wall, an infuriating smile on her face, chatting with Lord Dalgliesh, who stood right beside her. Rage, mixed with an infuriating curiosity, rose up in me.

Who the devil is she? The writer of the pink letters?

The possibility gripped my heart like a claw of ice. And Mr Ambrose still wasn't saying a single word! God, the silence was killing me! Somebody would have to say *something*. And if it wasn't going to be him, it would have to be me.

'I thought you didn't like social functions,' I blurted out.

There was a momentary pause.

'I don't,' came his curt reply, finally. Still he was staring into the same darn direction. 'But this one was special. I had to come. I needed to spend some time with an old acquaintance whom I had not seen for some time.'

I sniffed. 'So you've known the lady long?'

Is it she? Is it she who wrote you those letters? What did she say? What does she mean to him? And why the heck are you asking yourself that question?

'The lady?' His voice was absent and a little confused. He didn't seem to be paying any attention to me at all. Gritting my teeth, I nodded in *her* direction.

'What? Oh, Miss Hamilton?'

Hamilton. So finally, I had a name to put to the evil temptress! I relaxed infinitesimally as I realized that her name was not that of the writer of the pink letters. However, that relaxation vanished the instant I saw again the way he looked at the crow beside Lord Dalgliesh: so intently you might have thought there existed nothing else in the world for him but her.

'Yes,' I nodded. 'Miss Hamilton. You've known her long?'

He actually deigned to glance down at me then. If his face hadn't been carved from stone, I was sure there would have been a frown on it. His eyes narrowed a fraction. 'No. Whatever gave you that idea? I've only known her for a couple of days.'

Why the heck did you call her an old acquaintance then?

'Well, she must have made quite an impression on you.' *Considering you came out of your fortress for her sake and subjected yourself to the nameless horrors of a ball.*

He shrugged and looked away from me again, resuming his staring.

'So,' I continued doggedly, 'I assume you'll see more of her in the future, attend more balls than before, now that the situation has changed?'

His left little finger twitched. I had noticed this was his way of demonstrating extreme annoyance – the way someone else might scowl or curse at you. 'Hmm. I suppose. It will be unavoidable for what I have in mind.'

Oh yes, I'm sure it's very inconvenient to one as mighty as yourself that you can't just order a woman to marry you. You actually have to spend time with her first! How terrible!

Really, I should be feeling pity for this poor creature who would fall into the trap of marrying this man. A great deal of pity.

So why the bloody hell did I feel so angry instead?

He looked down at me sharply, the first time during the dance he had given me his full, undivided attention.

'How do you know I will be spending more time at social events?' His finger twitched again. 'You cannot have... No, you simply cannot have guessed my plans!'

Oh dear. He was just as self-centred as all other men. He couldn't hope to rival a woman's intuition.

'Actually, I think I have,' I said as sweetly as possible.

He looked up again, staring at Miss Hamilton and Lord Dalgliesh, who were still engaged in conversation.

'I must say I'm surprised, Miss Linton. I didn't think you would figure it out so quickly. In fact, I didn't think anybody could figure it out on their own.'

I had to work hard to conceal a snort.

Please! With your staring at her the entire time? What sort of silly guffin do you take me for?

'I think it is pretty obvious,' I retorted, my tone not a bit sarcastic. Honest, maybe, but not a bit sarcastic,

'Indeed? Well, if I were you, Miss Linton, I'd keep what you know to yourself. If it comes out that you know, you will be in terrible danger. You might end up with a knife between your ribs.'

My eyebrows shot up. 'That's going a bit far, don't you think?' A derisive snort escaped me. 'She can't be *that* jealous.'

'She?' Abruptly, he stopped turning. The neighbouring couples almost crashed into us, and only because I stirred him into motion again was a collision avoided. 'She? What are you talking about, Miss Linton?'

'Your...' I swallowed. For some reason it was hard to say out loud. Avoiding his eyes helped, so I looked down. 'Your *romantic interest* in Miss Hamilton, of course.' A frown crept onto my face. 'What were *you* talking about?'

He didn't answer me at first. Looking up, I saw that his beautiful statue's face was even more emotionless than usual. Whereas normally it just looked stony, now it looked completely vacant. He looked as if he was readjusting the gears of his brain.

'Well...' He cleared his throat. 'I was talking of my interest in Miss Hamilton, of course. You're right. I am very romantically interested. Indeed you could say, pining with love for her. That would be a very accurate description of the situation.'

'I see,' I mumbled, looking down again, so I didn't have to look at his chiselled face anymore. For some reason my eyes started stinging. 'What was it that caught your fancy? Her figure? Her eyes?'

'Her eyes. And her figure, too. And her dress, her manners, and her... well, she does not have anything more to catch fancies with, but all that she does have is very fancy-catching. You could say that I have passionately fallen in love with the entirety of her, not just the individual components.'

'But you like her eyes.'

'Yes, indeed.'

'What is so special about them?' I demanded to know, still not daring to look up. I had a suspicion why my eyes were stinging, and if it was correct I wanted nothing less than for him to see my face right now. 'I saw nothing extraordinary about them!'

He cleared his throat again. 'Well... they look very... very ocular, for one thing.'

'What is that supposed to mean?'

'Pardon?'

'This word, "ocular". What's that supposed to mean?'

'It is Latin. It is a word denoting everything that refers to eyes.'

'So... what you're in fact saying is that what's special about her eyes is that they look very much like eyes.'

Now I simply had to stare up at him suspiciously. He wouldn't see my face anyway. He would still be staring at *her*.

I was right. He was. His gaze was still firmly fixed on the lady and Lord Dalgliesh.

'Her nose is very lovely, too,' he added, sounding more like a salesman at the London market praising a fish of whose freshness he wasn't convinced than like a passionate lover. Maybe he always sounded like that when he was in love. If so, God have mercy on any poor creature who ever developed real, deep feelings for him! Not that something like that was ever likely to happen.

'Does it, Sir?'

'Yes, indeed, her nose has many excellent features. It is straight, not overly long or crooked like those of some other ladies in the ballroom; it has two holes at the bottom, and there is no hair growing out of them. Her teeth are adequate, too – none missing or falling out. I checked. You should always check the teeth first.'

'I believe that's when you're buying a horse, not when you're looking for a prospective bride,' I pointed out.

'Indeed? Well, it certainly cannot hurt to check. In any case, what all this boils down to is that I am in love with Miss Hamilton. Passionately in love.'

'Yes.' I bit my lip. 'You already mentioned that.'

'And that's the only reason I came to this ball. To spend time with the woman I am passionately in love with. There was no other motivation.'

Still he wouldn't even look at me. His words were like sharp pinpricks. I knew they shouldn't hurt, but they did. With all my might, I avoided looking up into his dark, sea-coloured eyes, staring at the floor instead.

'Yes, Sir. I understand.'

The dance ended just at that moment, and I had never been so happy about the end of a dance in my life. For once I had no desire to hound him about the contents of the file, or demand equal treatment with men, or do anything else. All I wanted was to be far away from him.

I am in love with Miss Hamilton. Passionately in love.

His words echoed in my head again and again, refusing to leave me alone. The moment he released me from his grip, I stepped back, not wanting him to touch or hold me any longer. I just managed a brief curtsy, then I turned and ran away through the crowd, wishing that in this ballroom there was just one quiet corner where I could hide!

SECRET PLANS AND POLITICS

There's no reason to be angry! No reason to be upset! I told myself, chewing savagely on a bar of solid chocolate I had found at one of the refreshment tables. *Not in the least! It is typical male behaviour, valuing a pretty doll in a ball gown more than a girl who actually chose to go out into the world and do something with her life. And there's no reason why that should make you angry! Not in the least!*

It didn't help. The chocolate did to some extent, soothing my nerves a bit, but I was still fuming when I reached a table with free chairs and slumped down onto the nearest one.

And do you want to know what the most infuriating part was?

I couldn't even figure out *why* exactly I was so angry! I mean, it wasn't as though I were entitled attract Mr Ambrose's attention or even had any reason to wish it. I was his secretary, no more and no less.

It's the inequality of the thing, I finally decided. *It wouldn't bother you at all if Miss Hamilton were a sensible female who actually worked for a living and stood up to men and their unjust laws. It is the suffragist in you that has taken a justified dislike to her, that is all.*

Satisfied with my findings, and very happy about my noble disposition which wouldn't stoop to something such as petty jealousy, I took another bite of chocolate and moaned as the piece melted in my mouth.

Ohhh...

The chap who invented this was surely the only decent man living! A true genius and benefactor to the whole world. The solid chocolate did wonders for consoling me. I sat at the table, slowly finding my calmer self again and wondering what step I should take next regarding Ella and her unwanted admirer. Maybe if I just pestered him a little more...

'Lilly, my dear!'

I froze. The voice that had come from behind me was unmistakable. It was the chief fury of hell! Turning, I saw my aunt rush towards me. But for once, she wore no angry scowl directed at me. Instead, her arms were wide open and there might have been actual tears of joy in her eyes.

'Come into my arms, most beloved niece of mine!' Before I could run for the hills, she had enfolded me in her arms and was pressing me to her meagre bosom. Startled, I hugged back reflexively. What was this? Could it be that this wasn't my aunt, but her not-so-evil twin? Or a moving wax replica? Those were the only explanations for the abnormally chummy behaviour of the being in front of me which I could come up with.

'I saw you dancing with Lord Dalgliesh!' she exclaimed, and suddenly everything became clear to me. This was still my aunt, as she lived and breathed. 'What did you talk about? Did he seem interested in you? Will you see him again? Oh, Lillian, don't just stand there saying nothing. You are always so quiet, girl! You will never get anywhere if you do not learn how to properly express yourself!'

'We didn't talk about important things really,' I murmured, choosing my words with care. I was well aware that I was walking a mine-field here. 'We just talked about, um... mutual acquaintances, that is all.'

'Wonderful! Wonderful! You have made a great start with him. Now don't lose sight of him, do you hear me? If you can secure him... Good God! That would probably be the most eligible match in all of England!'

I waited with bated breath, wondering if she would make any remark about my dance with Mr Ambrose, too. But she was so full of my dance with Lord Dalgliesh that she apparently hadn't even noticed what I had done once that had been over. I had to admit that after a while her profusions on the subject got a bit boring. Not that I had anything against Lord Dalgliesh – no more than against any other person in trousers on this planet – but I definitely did not entertain the thought of marrying him! Instinctively I knew that to him, I was no more than a marionette, just like all the other people in this room and all the people of his company. No more than an instrument to be directed according to his will. That was definitely not the kind of person I wanted to be linked with for the rest of my life.

My aunt was just in the middle of a hymn of praise on Lord Dalgliesh's taste in dressing, when I had had enough. Rising, I told her with a more than convincingly faked smile:

'Forgive me, Madam, but I think I am tired of sitting. I will look about and maybe find a pleasant partner to dance with.'

'Oh yes, my darling, do that, do that! And let it be the right one!'

'You mean the richest one?'

'Finally! Finally, you understand my concerns! Oh, Lillian, that I would live to see this day...' She seemed about to succumb to tears of happiness again. But then, with great restraint, she collected herself and waved me off. 'Go, go! The next dance is starting, don't miss your chance, my dear!'

'Certainly, Madam.'

As quickly as possible, I made my escape. In a corner of the room I spied a nice, big potted plant.

Wonderful! Just what you need to hide behind and take a few minutes' break before you have to face the ballroom crowd again!

Moving inconspicuously towards my target, I looked left and right to make sure no one was watching and then slid behind the large, dark green plant – only to discover that somebody else had apparently had the same idea.

Ella stumbled back against the wall, giving a little shriek, which immediately cut off when she recognized me.

'Oh Lilly, thank God it's you,' she whispered, leaning against the wall and closing her eyes. 'He isn't lurking somewhere, is he?'

I took a peek around the potted plant. Wilkins was nowhere in sight.

'No. At least I don't see him.'

'Thank God,' she repeated. 'I swear to you, if he tries to stick another flower in my hair, I will collapse.'

'Oh?' I raised an eyebrow. 'I thought you told me... what was it again? Yes, that was it! You told me it was an honour to be courted by such a great noble, didn't you?'

She blushed. 'Of course it is! I only meant... I mean... I am very honoured, very honoured indeed. He is paying me an enormous compliment, singling me out like this, and I really, and I... I really am flattered that I among all the ladies should be chosen to be the object of his–'

'Put a sock in it,' I told her with a goodly dose of sisterly affection. Ella hung her head, still blushing.

'You... I...'

'You don't have to pretend. Not where I'm concerned. Tell me honestly: do you want to marry Sir Philip Wilkins?'

She squirmed. 'Well... maybe not very much?'

'So you want to marry him just a little, do you? Maybe just his ring finger and his left foot, and the rest of him can stay a bachelor?'

Ella suddenly seemed to have an intense desire to inspect her feet. She looked down, avoiding my eyes.

'Um... if you put it that way... no. I don't think I do.'

'And what about the rest of him?'

She made a minute movement. Among immovable pillars of salt, it might have passed for a headshake.

'Say it,' I encouraged her. 'Do you want to marry Wilkins?'

'N.... n...'

'Go on! You can do it! Do you want to marry him?'

'No!'

'Bravo!' I rubbed my hands, grinning from ear to ear. 'Excellent!'

'*Excellent?*' Ella looked up at me, desperation in her face 'What's excellent about it? Aunt Brank wants me to marry him!'

'I mean it's excellent you have admitted it to yourself. You normally don't do that. It's the first step to problem-solving.'

'Err... and the next one is?'

I waved my hand dismissively. 'We'll cross that bridge when we come to it. Just at the moment you look like you need something to restore your nerves.'

'To be absolutely honest... I think that's true.'

'Well then, my dear little sister...' I put an arm around her and steered her from behind the potted plant. I already felt better. It had always been that way for me. When I was busy solving Ella's problems, my own suddenly didn't seem as important any more. 'I have just the thing for you. It's called solid chocolate. Let's see how you like it, shall we?'

Ella accompanied me willingly. We were about half the way towards the re-freshment tables when somebody roughly grabbed me by the arm and whirled me around. When I saw who it was, I gasped in surprise.

'There you are, strange lady!'

'Patsy!' I exclaimed, and then was swept up in a vice-like hug, ten times more forceful than my aunt's had been. With complete disregard for our hoop skirts, which should have kept us at a respectful distance, Patsy crushed me to her, and from the region of my legs, I heard whalebones[38] groan and crunch.

'Patsy,' I gasped again, pushing her back and looking at her solid figure, her broad, gruff, oh-so-reliable face. For the moment all dark thoughts about Mr Ambrose were forgotten. 'Is it really you? What are you doing here? How did

---

[38] In case anybody is wondering what whalebones are doing in Lilly's attire – that is what hoop skirts were often made of.

you manage to get invited? I thought old Lady Metcalf can't stand you and your modern ways!'

Patsy grinned.

'Well, she can't, actually, but she is an old friend of my mother's and has to pretend to like me. More to the point, what are *you* doing here?'

'Well you know how my aunt is, she always drags me to balls...'

'Not here at the ball, silly! I mean what are you doing here in London, here in England even? I thought you had emigrated to Timbuktu or something! I haven't seen you in ages! And don't tell me you've been driving around the park presenting yourself to the eyes of eligible bachelors. I know that's what you've told your aunt, because I came by your house to visit when you were out. But I and the other girls have been in the park often enough and haven't seen hide nor hair of you! What are you up to?'

I bit my lip.

Hell's Whiskers, what to tell her?

I couldn't tell her that I was working for a living, could I? Not that Patsy would have anything against it. On the contrary. I was certain she would wholeheartedly approve. But if I told her about my work, I would also have to tell her about Mr Ambrose. And for some reason I didn't want to do that. I didn't want to do that at all.

I opened my mouth, not knowing what I was going to say. Maybe a clever explanation would have come to me at the last moment. Yet before I could say anything, the decision was taken out of my hand by a very simple, very common event:

Beside me, Ella blushed.

'Aha!'

Patsy pounced on her.

'You know something, don't you? Out with it, Ella! Go on!'

Ella's eyes flickered from side to side like those of a frightened deer. I sighed. Ella was no liar, and under the unconquerable force that was Patsy Cusack, only one result could ensue.

'Lilly, um... Lilly is...'

'Yes...?' Patsy encouraged.

'Lilly is seeing somebody. But don't tell anybody. It's supposed to be a secret.'

'Yes, a *secret*,' I confirmed throwing a dirty look at her. 'That's why I asked *you* to keep it secret, by which I meant *not tell it to anybody*.'

With those adorable blue damsel-in-distress eyes of hers she threw me an apologetic glance. 'I'm... I'm sorry Lilly, I just can't... can't lie about....'

My anger was snuffed out like a candle flame under a wet towel. Nobody could stay angry at Ella. Not even the chief of avenging angels.

'All right,' I grumbled with a shrug. It was to be expected. And it wasn't like it had been the truth in the first place.

Turning my attention away from my little sister, I scrutinised Patsy. She hadn't yet said a word in response to Ella's disclosure. Her mouth stood slightly open, her lips were moving without producing any sound, and her eyes were unfocused. She looked like she had tried solving a complex mathematical equation and had ended up with 1009 = 0.

'Seeing somebody?' she echoed. 'As in... a member of the opposite sex? A *man*?'

'No, a hippopotamus,' I snapped. 'Yes, a man! What did you think?'

'Frankly, I would have thought a hippopotamus would have been more likely!'

My fingers flexed. 'Do you want me to clobber you with my fan?'

'No need to get violent. I'm just shocked.' She shook her head, dazed. 'A man. Fancy that. Lilly Linton going over to the enemy.'

Reflexively, my chin shot out. 'I'm not "going over to the enemy"!'

'Really? Hasn't your sweetheart asked you to shed your extremist political views about voting, working women yet? It'll happen, just you wait. And next you'll get all silly and soppy and start knitting and sewing and saying that a lady's proper place is inside the home.'

She shook her head in mock disgust, smirking.

'And I had such a promising future in the movement planned for you. You could have gone far, my young friend. Too bad you throw it all away for a simple life of marital bliss.'

I knew that she was joking, of course – but in a way, she wasn't. She really thought I was straying from the path and sacrificing my ideals.

Well, I'd show her!

With no work tomorrow, I would have plenty of time. Leaning towards her so that nobody else could hear me, I whispered: 'Meet me with the other girls at ten o'clock tomorrow morning in Green Park, and I'll tell you what I think a lady should be doing.'

She looked at me, a smile slowly spreading over her broad face, mingled suspicion and interest twinkling in her eyes.

'What have you got planned?'

'My secret for now.' I winked. 'Suffice it to say that I have overheard something which might be of interest to our little group of suffragists. We have work to do!'

~~**~*~*

The rest of the ball went by quickly, mostly because now I had something with which to occupy my mind. What the loose-lipped gentleman had told me about the meeting against the women's suffrage in Hyde Park kept reverberating inside my head. Ideas were fermenting inside my busy bean. Soon they would develop into plans.

I spent the rest of the ball plotting the downfall of mankind and the rise of womankind. Most of my plotting happened together with Ella and Patsy in Lord Dalgliesh's vicinity. This had multiple advantages:

The group around the lord was one of the thickest in the ballroom. Thus, whenever Sir Philip came in sight, we could shove Ella behind a fat duchess or broad-shouldered admiral, and she would be saved from another dance.

Whenever my aunt looked my way and saw me, right there, next to Lord Dalgliesh, she beamed as if it were Christmas and Easter put together. At least she wouldn't be able to say I wasn't trying.

For some reason, Mr Ambrose stayed far away from the group. This I found strange, because earlier he had made such a particular point of greeting Lord Dalgliesh as if they were old friends. But who was I to look a gift horse in the mouth?

By use of this clever method of unpleasant-people-avoidance we were able to keep the nasties out of our hair for quite some time. Everyone else pretty much left us alone, too. I was rather startled when somebody coughed beside me, thinking that it was Wilkins who had seen through our ruse at last – but it was only a servant, who bowed to me politely.

'Forgive me, Miss? Could you step aside? I have to deliver a message to His Lordship.'

Promptly, I did as he asked, and so did everyone else in the vicinity. I noticed, though, that they didn't step back too far to hear what this mysterious message might be. It consisted of a letter the servant bore on a silver tray.

Arriving at His Lordship's side, the servant gave another discreet cough.

'I beg Your Lordship's pardon? I have a message for you, My Lord.'

Lord Dalgliesh turned from the group of friends with whom he was laughing and joking and, seeing the tray, picked up the letter and eyed it over his aquiline nose.

'Who gave this to you?'

'Another servant, who would not divulge the identity of his master or mistress, My Lord. But he said you would know the identity of the sender once you opened it.'

Lord Dalgliesh's gaze quickly flicked from right to left. Feeling all eyes upon him, intent with curiosity, he snatched up the silver letter-opener on the tray and cut open the envelope. He grabbed whatever was inside and pulled.

Out came not a sheet of paper, nor a card, nor anything else with writing on it. No, out came a lock of hair – blond hair to be precise. For a moment, everything was still around the little group, then discreet chuckles broke out among the gentlemen, and the ladies fanned themselves.

'By Jove!' a colonel in the Royal Dragoons[39] exclaimed. 'I think it's rather more likely this letter came from a lady than from a gentleman, don't you think so, my friends?' This was greeted by affirmations and laughter from all sides. 'Come on, Dalgliesh, tell us who the lucky lady is!'

For a moment. Lord Dalgliesh stood stock-still, not seeming to see or hear the world around him, concentrating only on the lock in his hand. Then, quick as a flash, he stuck it back into the envelope and stuffed it into his pocket. Turning to the others, he smiled brilliantly and said: 'Now, now, my friends, you would not want me to compromise a lady's honour, would you? Besides, I assure

---

[39] A heavy cavalry regiment in Britain during Victorian times. My advice: not get in their way while they're galloping.

you. This is far from being a token of affection. You might rather call it a declaration of war.'

The colonel laughed again.

'A declaration of war, eh? On you? Then whoever sent this must be rather a formidable creature!'

Lord Dalgliesh's smile broadened, yet at the same time I noticed it seemed to harden.

'You never spoke a truer word, my dear Colonel.'

I shook my head. Somehow, I didn't think the hair came from a woman. It had looked far too short for that. To be honest, I had no idea what to make of it, though I had the strange feeling that I should have been able to. All in all, it was far too strange an occurrence for my personal taste. As charming as he was, I vowed to stay far away from Lord Daniel Eugene Dalgliesh in the future.

Then and there, I didn't know how short a time it would take until that vow would be broken.

~~**~*~*

The evening was drawing to a close. Lady Metcalf was standing at the door, curtsying to her dear friends and to people she couldn't stand but had to be polite to anyway. My aunt was in high spirits. She was so pleased about my dance with Lord Dalgliesh that she hadn't even noticed that Ella had only danced three times with Wilkins during the entire evening.

Anne and Maria, on the other hand, were in a very bad mood. They had been forced to listen to a prolonged lecture by my aunt on how I was doing better than they with seeking out prospective husbands. I did not relish the thought of getting in a coach with them but reasoned that there were five other people in the coach, so they could hardly try and beat me to death with their parasols.

I was just about to sneak past Lady Metcalf and get some fresh air before the coach ride when, suddenly, a gentle but firm hand placed itself on my arm and held me in place.

'A moment, if you please, Miss Linton?'

It was Lord Dalgliesh. Over his shoulder I could see my aunt, making frantic gestures of encouragement. I would have to disappoint her. Somehow I doubted that the enigmatic nobleman wanted to discuss an engagement.

'What is it, Lord Dalgliesh?' I enquired, letting myself be steered into a small niche, where we were cut off from the view of all others in the room, including my aunt – to her severe disappointment, I was sure. Lord Dalgliesh placed himself between me and the rest of the room so I could not leave without his stepping aside. Suddenly, I felt a tiny twinge of unease. I would have felt more unease if not for the fact that the nobleman's smile was so very reassuring.

'I wish to ask you something, Miss Linton.'

'Again?' I raised an eyebrow. 'You are getting brazen, My Lord. This time you are not even offering to dance with me.'

He smiled brightly, seemingly pleased by my reply.

'Indeed I am. Yet I have an excuse: the music has stopped, the musicians are gone. Will you still grant me my heart's desire and assuage my curiosity?'

'That depends on what your question is. Ask, My Lord, and we shall see about the answer.'

'Very well.' He leant forward. His steel-blue eyes bored into mine with a hypnotic intensity. 'Whenever I looked up earlier this evening, I knew I was being watched. Watched closely. The name of the one who watched me should be familiar to you, I think. It was one Rikkard Ambrose.'

I almost felt like laughing. *He wasn't watching you*, I wanted to say. *He was watching his dear darling Miss Hamilton.*

But then my thoughts screeched to a sudden halt. *Had* he been watching Miss Hamilton? Whenever I saw them, Lord Dalgliesh and Miss Hamilton had been standing right next to each other. Could it be that Mr Ambrose had been watching the former and not the latter? But why? He couldn't very well be in love with Lord Dalgliesh, now, could he?[40]

A maelstrom of confused thoughts roared in my mind. I tried not to let any of them show, though. Instead I asked: 'And what has that got to do with me?'

'Simply this: Whenever Mr Ambrose happened not to watch me, his gaze was drawn to you.'

What?

'A- are you sure? In such a large room as this ballroom...'

'Trust me, I am sure.' His Lordship stared at me, keeping his face carefully clean of any emotions. But I could see them in his eyes: mingled curiosity and incredulity. 'He looked at you more than at any other person in the room, myself excepted.'

I felt a surge of triumph rise inside me and beat it down with everything I had. As nonchalantly as I could, I shrugged.

'That may well be. I didn't notice.'

His eyes narrowed.

'Most young ladies notice when Mr Ambrose looks at them.'

'Perhaps I'm short-sighted.' I stepped to the side, seeking to go past him. But there wasn't enough room. 'Your question, Lord Dalgliesh? My coach will be leaving soon.'

'Ah yes, my question.' He nodded. 'I wish to know: What is Mr Ambrose's interest in you?'

I wet my lips and, forcing my voice to be calm, said: 'I was not aware that he had an interest in me.'

'Let me assure you, he does. And I wish to know what it is.' He concealed it well, but I could still read it in his eyes: the part of his sentence he would not

---

[40] For any homosexuals among my readers, I should perhaps point out that Lilly's incredulity is natural, considering the time she lived in. Back in Victorian England, only very few people displayed homosexual tendencies in public, which was quite understandable, considering the fact that until 1861, homosexuality was a capital offence. Fortunately, that particular law has landed on the rubbish heap of history.

speak aloud. *Why on earth would one of the richest men of London be interested in somebody like you?*

I felt my spine stiffen, and instinctively crossed my arms in front of my chest. 'Should you not direct that question at Mr Ambrose?'

Ignoring my counterquestion, Lord Dalgliesh stated:

'He danced with you tonight. He singled you out, in fact. All the other young ladies he danced with were ladies introduced by his host or ladies he could not help dancing with without giving offence. You on the other hand... You danced with him without being introduced. You had to have met before. Where was that? What happened?'

'I do not recall. I think I might have met him at some other party or in the street, maybe.'

Damn! Why couldn't I keep my voice steady? Maybe it was the way he was blocking my way out of the niche. It was bloody annoying! More than annoying, actually. It started to be slightly worrying.

'Most young ladies,' Lord Dalgliesh observed, leaning a little closer, 'would remember their first meeting with Mr Rikkard Ambrose.'

He still wore his charming smile, and to anyone listening, his questions might have sounded like nothing but idle curiosity. Yet I didn't think that anything about this man was idle. Still he was blocking my way.

'Well, I have a very bad memory,' I snapped. 'Especially for people I don't care to remember! Now step aside, please! My aunt will be leaving, and I have to join her.'

His eyes narrowed. 'Miss Linton...'

'Step aside, I said!'

For one moment he hesitated – then stepped back, giving me just enough room to pass.

'You're an intriguing young lady, Miss Linton.' His eyes were sparkling like moonlight on cold steel. 'I will look forward to meeting you again.'

Ha! When hell freezes over!

'Until then, My Lord.'

Keeping my back ramrod-straight so I could always look him in the eye, I gave a quick curtsy. Then I marched away at a measured pace and, using the fact that Lady Metcalf was just saying goodbye to a large group of burly army officers, ducked past her and out of the ball room.

Only when I was in the hallway and he couldn't see me anymore did I start to run. The slaps of my shoes sounded harsh on the marble floor, and servants stared at me as I rushed by, but I didn't care. Some instinct told me to get out of there as quickly as possible.

I stumbled out into the cool night air. Fog from the river Thames was wafting towards me. Yet neither the clammy moisture nor the cold air did anything to clear my mind. A thousand questions where whirling around inside my head. Only they weren't the same ones as a few hours ago, when Mr Ambrose had entered the ballroom, that hag on his arm.

Had Mr Ambrose really been interested in Lord Dalgliesh, not his beautiful partner? What did the lock in the envelope mean? Where did it come from? And why, of all people in the ballroom, should Mr Ambrose have been looking at *me*?

I hurried over to the coach, which had already been brought to the door by the driver, and hurriedly climbed up the steps. I needed a quiet place, shut off from all the noise of the ballroom. A place where I could think.

I sank onto the seat and breathed a sigh of relief. Alone, finally!

Then I looked up – and saw Wilkins sitting on the opposite bench. A rose and an enormous sunflower were sticking out of his tortured buttonhole, and he had a dreamy expression on his face which I immediately mistrusted.

'Ah, Miss Lilly,' he said, smiling at me with a smile like a seasick baboon. Or, maybe, like a man in love. It was difficult to tell the difference sometimes. 'How fortunate that you are the first to arrive. I wonder if I might have a word with you. It is about your sister, Ella.'

WOES OF LOVE

I eyed Wilkins cautiously. 'What about my sister Ella?'

'I... I have confession to make.' He pressed a hand to his heart, either overcome by his feelings or having a heart attack. Unfortunately, the chances for the latter seemed slim. 'A secret that I have borne in my heart for a long time but now must reveal to somebody, or else my heart will burst.'

Well, things are looking up. Maybe the chances aren't that slim after all.

'I see,' I said.

He had obviously hoped for a response like, 'What is your secret? I'm dying to know!' or something equally dramatic. When I didn't oblige, he floundered. But soon enough he found his voice again.

'I have chosen to confess my secret to you,' he whispered conspiratorially. 'If for now you promise you will reveal it to no living soul.'

'Go on.' I waved my hand. 'I promise I will reveal it only to vampires, ghosts and other members of the undead community.'

'Um... good. Very well, then.' He took a deep breath. 'I... am in love. I am in love with your sister, Miss Ella Linton.'

My left eyebrow rose about a millimetre. 'You don't say.'

Again he had apparently hoped for a more dramatic reaction. But he seemed to cope well with the disappointment, more than ready to supply all the necessary drama himself. He leant forward so far that the sunflower almost fell out of his buttonhole.

'The reason I tell you this,' he said, whispering, 'is that throughout the entire time I have had the pleasure to know your sister, I have noticed you have taken a most lively interest in the progression of our relationship. You have always been there, trying to help me...'

What?

'... and although your failed attempts at furthering conversation show how innocent you are, how inexperienced with romance, they are greatly appreciated.'

This man definitely could never be allowed to marry my sister! There was insanity in his family! There had to be! *Me* helping *him*?

'Miss Lilly,' he said in a fatherly manner, which might have worked better if he hadn't been just about three years older than I. 'I am a seasoned man of the world. I have no problem with striking up a conversation with your sister on my own. Have no fear. What you hope for is true: I am indeed pursuing your sister. I am so deeply in love with her I can hardly express it. Soon, after an appropriate courtship, I will ask her to be mine, and your sister Ella will marry one of the most eligible bachelors of London.'

He pressed my hand.

'Have no fear. Soon we shall be family.'

Argh!

~~**~*~*

Somehow I managed the ride home without getting hysterics. The situation was far more dire than I had imagined. My only consolation was that Ella still wasn't aware of the fact. But as we rode towards home, even that consolation began to disappear. The love-struck smiles which Wilkins sent in Ella's direction at regular intervals could hardly be misinterpreted, even by one as innocent as she. In addition, Wilkins had begun to suggestively wink at my little sister. Since he did this repeatedly and without great talent, he looked like somebody desperately trying to get a fly out of his eye, but still, she probably got the message.

The others were no help either. Lisbeth was sad because nobody at the ball had danced with her, Gertrude was quiet, Maria and Anne were shooting angry glances at Ella, and my aunt was still making hints about how well Lord Dalgliesh and I seemed to be getting along. It was only Sir Philip's presence that stopped her from pestering me for the date on which our engagement would be announced.

Finally, we stopped in front of my uncle's house and alighted from the coach. Wilkins didn't remain sitting, but got out after us.

'Do you wish to come in for a minute, Sir Philip?' My aunt enquired sweetly. She was always sweet to prospective nephews-in-law. The rich ones, anyway.

'No, madam. I wouldn't wish to inconvenience you.'

'It would be no inconvenience at all, I assure you, Sir.'

'That is kind of you, Madam, but I really must be getting home. I just wanted to say goodbye to your charming nieces, particularly to Miss Ella.' Taking her hand, he bent and placed a long, lingering kiss on it. 'Thank you, Miss Ella. Goodbye, for now. I look forward to seeing you soon again. Tonight was the best night of my life. May we spend innumerable nights like it, and may they each be brighter and happier than the one before. That is the deepest desire of my heart.'

Ella paled, and my aunt took on the blissful expression of an opium addict dancing in a field of poppies. It was almost as good as a proposal. If she'd had a chain and collar on her, my aunt would probably have chained Sir Philip up in the hallway until he had delivered the real thing. Unfortunately for her, she lacked that equipment and so could only curtsey and wave after him as he got into his coach and drove away.

While she was busy waving, I made myself scarce. I didn't want to hear any more profusions on the subject of Lord Dalgliesh or Sir Philip. Besides, I knew now with absolute certainty what my little sister was facing. I needed to take up my post so I was in position when the drama began. Grabbing a book from the library, I sneaked out into the garden and settled down comfortably behind the bushes. Only a few minutes later the backdoor creaked open and a white-clad figure stepped out into the garden.

~~**~*~*

Regretfully, I put my book aside. It had been a really interesting colonial adventure story, and I had just gotten to the best part – the bit where the hero is tied to a stake and the natives prepare to cook and then eat him alive. But I told myself he was sure to be rescued soon, and then a wonderful story would be ruined. Better to stop now and enjoy the drama that was beginning to unfold in front of me.

Edmund had appeared on the other side of the fence. He didn't look very well: his face was pale, his hair unkempt, and his shirt and waistcoat had seen better days. My gaze drifted to Ella, only to observe that she was in no better condition. Her blonde hair was hanging in wild tangles down her back, and her dress had obviously been put on in a hurry. Of course she still looked innocent as the new day and stunningly beautiful, but then, she was Ella.

I settled into a comfortable theatre seat provided by a patch of moss from which I could see everything through a gap in the brush. This performance was going to be pivotal for my further plans. On it would hinge everything I would try to do to further Ella's hopes and dreams and smash Sir Philip into smithereens!

The two of them stood on either side of the fence for a long while, simply staring at each other with desperate longing, trying to bridge the distance between them with their gazes. Or at least I figured that's what they were doing. With the moon having disappeared behind clouds, it was pretty dark in the garden, so I couldn't actually be sure about the staring-at-each-other-with-desperate-longing part. They might just have fallen asleep standing.

'Ella, my love,' Edmund said in a raw voice.

Ah. Not asleep. So I had been right. And if that wasn't desperate longing in his voice, I didn't know what desperate longing was.

'Edmund, my love,' my little sister whispered. Apparently, she was very much awake as well.

'How do things stand?' he demanded.

When Ella said nothing in response, he pushed on: 'What is the matter? Why do you not speak? Why do you not step closer to me? Speak, my love! I can no longer live without the sweet honey of your voice sustaining me!'

I suppressed an urge to gag.

How would you like the honey of my fist in your face, fellow?

But his mushy-gushy mush seemed to hit the spot with Ella. She opened her mouth and took a breath, preparing to speak.

'I... I danced three times with Sir Philip,' she answered timidly. I noticed she didn't step closer to the fence, made no move at all to approach her beloved with the messy hair.

'Only three times during the entire evening? When he is supposedly courting you?' Edmund's face brightened. I thought dancing three times with the same person was quite a lot, but I didn't doubt if he had the chance, he'd spent the entire evening glued to her. 'Oh Ella, you give me hope. Tell me, has he lost interest in you, the fool? Has he withdrawn his affections?'

My sister gave a little shake of the head.

'No.'

'Then why on earth would he not...'

'It is my dear sister.' *Dang! She's talking about me!* 'My dear, dear sister who protects me. It is amazing. Though she knows not a thing of how things truly stand, of where my affections truly lie, she instinctively seems to be able to sense somehow that I do not welcome his attentions. Not just tonight at the ball – whenever he comes, she is there, between him and me, helping me, protecting me. Sometimes I ask myself whether she is clairvoyant, so clearly can she read what I feel. It is as if she could hear every secret word I speak to you!'

Um... Well, about that...

Deeply moved, Edmund nodded. 'I have heard of this – a strong emotional bond between siblings who cherish for one another the deepest affection can have such remarkable effects. She must be a remarkable girl. I wish I could meet her someday.'

No problem. Just come around the bush and wave.

Ella shook her head vigorously. 'You cannot! Remember, she must never know of us.'

'You're right. She must never know.'

I rolled my eyes. *Really? Gosh...*

There was a pause. Then Edmund added: 'But we have strayed away from the heart of the matter, dearest.'

Ella's lower lip began to quiver.

'Which is?'

'Sir Philip Wilkins still pursues you.'

'Oh, cruel, cruel Edmund! How can you remind me?'

Edmund reached through the poles to squeeze her hands, and she immediately ceased her lamentations.

'I *must* remind you,' he persisted in a gentle tone of voice. 'I must, because we must form plans and find an escape, find some way to forge a future for ourselves.'

Her eyes tearing up again, Ella suddenly stumbled forward and sagged against the fence.

'No plans can save me,' she whispered. 'I have no future!'

Now that's just not true! I shook my head disapprovingly. If people only could be more accurate about such things. She might have a future wherein she would be absolutely miserable, married to a man she couldn't stand and separated from her one true love – but she would definitely have a future. One should always be accurate. Ten hours a day and six days a week of sorting files for an office tyrant teaches a girl that much.

'That is why I said we would *forge* a future, Ella. You may not have one now, but we will find a way.'

'How, Edmund, my love? How can we possibly find a way?'

'I do not know yet. But take heart, my love. With time, we will surely devise a plan and...'

'With time?' More tears running down her delicate face, Ella stared through the fence in desperation. Now the moon was out from behind the clouds and I could actually see the mournful expression clearly. It made me wish for darkness again. 'With time? Edmund, you do not understand. We do not have time. I... I believe...'

'What?' Edmund stepped closer to the fence and grabbed the metal poles. 'What are you keeping from me? Tell me! I beg you, my love, tell me!'

'I believe,' Ella said in a breathless whisper, 'that Sir Philip will shortly propose matrimony.'

'No! Say it isn't so!'

'Yes, my love.' Reaching up, she swiftly touched his pallid cheek with her fingertips. 'Yes, it is. I wish it were not so, but I cannot change it. I cannot change my fate.'

There were a few moments of heavy silence. Edmund was staring at the ground, his fists clenched at his sides. Curious, I leaned forward, trying to get a look at his face, but it was impossible to see from here.

Blast! And this is the best part of the drama!

I should have gotten a seat closer to the stage.

Then, suddenly, he raised his head again, and I blinked in surprise. I hardly recognized him. All the despair was gone from his face, replaced by a look of iron, immovable determination.

'Yes, you can,' he said in a hoarse voice. 'You can change your fate, my love. Run away with me! Run away with me and become my wife!'

You could have knocked me down with a feather. Actually, half a feather might have done it. Or maybe a very small piece of yarn?

Ella, I could see, was equally taken aback. She wasn't gaping open-mouthed at Edmund like I was – proper ladies don't do that sort of thing – but she had definitely turned an even whiter shade of pale than she normally was.

'M-marry?' Her voice was almost inaudible over the soft wind that had picked up and that rustled the leaves in the trees as well as the soft folds of her dress in an appropriately romantic manner. 'But how... Aunt Brank would never agree!'

242

'I asked you to run away with me, my love,' Edmund reminded her, his voice gentle but firm, his gaze never leaving her face. 'That means she wouldn't have to agree.'

'But... go against the wishes of her and all my family...?'

'Yes.'

'Shame them before all the world? Hurt them in such a way?'

'Yes, my dear. For love, it must be.'

Hell's whiskers! He's really going to do it! He's really going to take advantage of your poor, innocent little sister and whisk her away.

Getting stealthily to my feet, I prepared to launch myself from the bushes if he made even one tiny move towards her.

A rake! That's what he is! A dastardly rake!

I knew what was coming next, of course. I had heard Anne and Maria discuss romance novels often enough. Next he would grab Ella and carry her off into the night. But he didn't reckon with me in that equation! The moment he touched her, I would be ready to take up the chase!

Of course, there's the small matter of the fence between them, so you probably won't have to hurry that much.

'Are you in earnest, Edmund?' Ella whispered. 'Do not toy with my heart. Would you really make me your wife, if you could?'

Grasping her hand, he stepped forward. I prepared to jump out of the bushes, but he didn't move to touch any other, strictly restricted, parts of her. Instead, he fell to his knees, bowing his head over her hand and kissing it softly.

'How could you ever doubt it?' he demanded. 'For years I have admired your beauty, your charm and your loving nature. My love for you has grown and blossomed ever since it first sprang to life. Now that is has come to full bloom, nothing will stop me from making you mine. Will you do me the honour...?'

With a small sob, she pulled her hand from his grasp. I could see her face as she turned from him, towards my hiding place, her arms wrapped around her slender body as if to protect herself.

'This,' she said in a quivering voice, 'has gone far enough.'

The words may have been weak, but on Edmund they fell like a hammer blow. I was almost disappointed not to see a substantial bump swelling up on his head.

'W-what?'

'I said, this has gone far enough.' She turned back to him, and as she did I could see the moisture on her face glittering in the moonlight. She seemed to have an endless supply of tears tonight. Dear me... This love thing seemed to require an enormous quantity of bodily fluids.

'Please,' she continued, 'do not torture me further by actually asking me. I could not bear it.'

His voice in return was broken. Utterly defeated. 'You no longer love me then.'

Ella twitched as if she had been hit by a whip. Rushing forward, she grasped the poles of the fence.

'Of course I love you, Edmund. More than my own life!'

His face came up, displaying a whirling mix of hope and despair.

'Then you will come with me?'

'No! I cannot!'

'But Ella, my love... I... I do not understand. If you love me, if you really, truly love me...?'

Ella leaned her head against the fence. She didn't seem to have the strength to hold it up anymore. The wind tugged at her hair, pulling a few loose strands through the iron poles and onto Edmund's side of the fence, as if everything in her was straining to go to him.

How come the weather is so bloody romantic? Why isn't it raining buckets out here?

'Edmund... I cannot find the words to answer you. But I do not have to. The poet has already given me my lines, which I tell to you now: Yes, I do love you. Desperately, with all my heart. But *I could not love thee, Dear, so much, Loved I not honour more.*'[41]

Behind the bushes I cocked my head, trying to find the logic in her last statement. I thought it was pretty darn daft, myself. Somebody had written *that* down, and been published? I would never fall in love myself, of course, but if I did, I didn't think honour would enter into the equation in any major way. Honour, respectability - they were mostly nicely sounding terms for means of curtailing a girl's freedom. Really, I loved my little sister, but sometimes she really could be a silly goose. She should just say yes to the fellow and-

Hey! What are you doing? You're supposed to not want her to run away with him.

Oh, right. No! I definitely didn't want that!

---

[41] This ingenious line is taken from the 1649 poem *Going to the Wars* written by Richard Lovelace and addressed to a lady named Lucasta. It runs like this:

Tell me not, sweet, I am unkind,
That from the nunnery
Of thy chaste breast and quiet mind
To war and arms I fly.

True, a new mistress now I chase,
The first foe in the field;
And with a stronger faith embrace,
A sword, a horse, a shield.

Yet this inconstancy is such
As thou shalt adore;
I could not love thee, dear, so much,
Loved I not honor more.

Translation: 'Sorry sweety, but a man's gotta do what a man's gotta do. I love you and all, but I have to go to war and kill a lot of bad guys before I can get back to you. (I actually managed to make my translation rhyme!) The line quoted in the text above has been applied to all sorts of situations where duty comes before love.

'Don't you see?' She reached out to tenderly touch the hair of the broken man kneeling in front of her. 'I'd rather cherish my love for you as a tender, secret memory, than do what I know to be wrong. Yes, I could go with you now and spend the rest of my days in bliss, but where would be the good in that? Far better that I marry Sir Philip, knowing that I have done right, preserving the honour of my family and of yours, than that I destroy them for earthly happiness. I might spend the rest of my days in misery, but at least I will do so with a clear conscience.'

Um... All right...

I had always suspected that my sister was, on some level, completely off her rocker. It was gratifying to have one's suspicions confirmed. Besides this purely intellectual gratification, though, I could not receive much satisfaction from the fact.

Though he might in general have a higher opinion of her degree of sanity, in this case Edmund seemed to share my views.

'I'd prefer the earthly happiness,' he told her outright.

A weak little smile appeared on her face.

'That is your warm heart overwhelming your better nature, Edmund, and I love you for it. But please, do not tempt me any further. It pains me to refuse you.'

'You can still say yes.'

'No, I cannot. We must not see each other again, Edmund. I will become Sir Philip's wife... and you...'

She closed her eyes for a moment, and I could see the next words would be the hardest for her.

'... and you go, find yourself a girl who is not bound. Do not let yourself be dragged into misery. Find love, be happy. Maybe I can continue to live, as long as I know that you are happy.'

'But I cannot be happy without you, Ella! Not ever!'

'Do not say such a thing, Edmund! It pains me!'

Then why the heck is she smiling through her tears?

I scratched my head, nonplussed. This love thing was obviously more complicated than I had thought. Oh, I was so glad I didn't have anything to do with it myself.

'I will ask you one final time, Ella.' Slowly, Edmund rose to his feet. Her hand slid into his, and he held it firmly. 'Will you elope with me?'

She shook her head.

'No.'

'You refuse to go against your aunt's wishes in the matter of Sir Philip?'

'I beg you, Edmund, understand. I cannot!'

'Shh. Don't be anguished, dearest. I understand. I understand, my love. You cannot go against your gentle nature.' He sighed. 'Then there remains only one thing for me to do.'

'Y-you will do as I ask? You will move on?'

In spite of the fact that she was trying to affect a cheerful manner, I could see the fear in her eyes.

Pressing her hand again, Edmund shook his head.

'No. I shall go out and buy myself a pistol. In the morning I shall call at Sir Philip's residence and challenge him.'

Any feathers available with which to knock me over? For the second time this night, I was completely taken by surprise. This tradesman's boy was turning out to be a regular Casanova! Had I heard correctly?

'W-what?' Ella stuttered. 'What do you mean, challenge him?'

Apparently, she hadn't yet understood what he meant. Or she would not let herself understand, maybe.

'I mean, challenge him to a duel,' Edmund replied calmly. 'To the death.'

She took an involuntary step towards him. Or maybe it was voluntary. You could never tell with these love-struck people

'Edmund, you must not jest about such things,' she whispered, her hands clasping the iron poles of the fence tightly. 'You must not.'

'Who says that I am jesting?'

'Please, Edmund, stop. You worry me sick.'

'I am sorry for that. But it cannot be helped. You say you will not refuse Sir Philip, nor stand up to your aunt, so I have no choice.'

'No choice but to contemplate violence?' Letting go of the poles, she threw her hands up in the air. 'What mad demon possesses you, Edmund? I beg you, relinquish this mad scheme!'

'It is not mad. Indeed it is highly logical. You will not rid yourself of Sir Philip, very well, then I shall do it for you. I shall acquire a pistol, go to his house and challenge him. Do you think I should explain the situation to him? How things stand between us?'

Ella almost fainted right then and there. Only Edmund's quick hands, which shot through the gaps in the fence and caught her around the waist, prevented her from falling.

Wait just a minute!

I was on the point of charging in. Now he definitely was touching areas he wasn't supposed to be touching on a lady, and I had to look after my little sister, after all. But then, he had only prevented her from falling. I decided to not kill him for his insolence just this once.

'Tell him?' Ella whispered, obviously in no hurry to get out of his arms. 'Are you mad?'

He smiled at her. It was a boyish, excited kind of smile that looked new on his face, which I had seen so often anxious and sad, yet it suited him well. He looked like a different person, and for the first time I began to understand what Ella saw in him, just a little.

'That's the second time you've accused me of insanity tonight, my love. Don't let it become a habit.'

'Be serious, Edmund!'

'I'm absolutely serious. I don't want you to suspect me of a mental disorder.'

246

'You know what I mean!'

'Yes, I do. And I'm serious about that, too.'

'But telling Sir Philip? After all the hundreds and hundreds of times I have begged you to keep our love a secret?'

Edmund's smile became a trifle wistful.

'Ah, but what is there to keep secret anymore? If I go to him tomorrow and vanquish him, then it will not matter whether or not I have told him, will it? I need to explain it to him, Ella. I cannot simply march up to him and insult him to make him fight me. I would smudge the honour of my family, which, as you so diligently pointed out, is a bad thing to do. No, I need to go to him and say: "Sir Philip, I love the girl you have set your sights on, and she loves me. I will fight for her with my last breath." He is a gentleman. He will understand and allow me the opportunity to fight for you. Once I have put a bullet through his heart, the way will once again be free. So you see, Ella, I am not mad. I have thought this through very carefully.'

I nodded approvingly. For once, it seemed, somebody had been using their brains instead of their heart. The plan was indeed highly logical – except for one point. With unusual quickness, Ella realized it too.

'And what,' she whispered, trembling in Edmund's arms, 'if it is he who kills you?'

There were a few moments of silence. Well, almost-silence, anyway. In the distance, a dog barked with total disregard for the romantic drama unfolding in front of me.

'I wouldn't worry about that, love,' he said, dismissively.

'Not worry?' she exclaimed, and suddenly it wasn't just his arms around her – she was clasping him now, too. That was more like it! Finally, she was taking some action of her own.

'Edmund, he is a gentleman! You're a tradesman's son. He's been raised to shoot with guns, hunts every year and knows what he's doing. Have you ever handled a pistol before in your life?'

'I'm a quick learner.'

'Edmund, tell me! Have you ever handled a pistol?'

'Not actually, no,' he admitted. 'But I've seen other people do it,' he added as an afterthought.

The groan that originated from Ella indicated that she thought about as much of this excuse as I did.

'Edmund, please don't, I'm begging you!'

He shook his head.

'I would give you almost anything you want, love, but in this I must deny you.'

'But why?' Reaching up, she clutched his shirt and, through a gap in the fence, buried her face in his chest. 'Do you want to die? Are you truly mad?'

Encircling her with his arms, he drew her even closer towards himself. I was debating again whether or not to intervene – but somehow I couldn't bring myself to interrupt them. And there was still an iron fence between them, so things couldn't really get very intimate. 'I have no wish to die, Ella.'

'Then why? Tell me, for heaven's sake!'

'Don't you see?' Pushing her away a bit, he raised her chin and forced her to look into his face. 'I have to free you. I have to believe that you and I can be together. If that cannot be, life would not be worth living anymore. Not for me, anyway.'

Atta boy! I had to admit, part of me really liked this plan. If it worked, Ella would be rid of Sir Philip. If it didn't, she'd be rid of this silly fellow. A win-win situation.

'Isn't it enough to know I love you?' She asked, her voice thick. 'To know that I will never, ever love anybody else, no matter what I shall be forced to do?'

He shook his head. 'I'm afraid I'm not that noble, my dear. I need to feel your love, to feel you in my arms, safe and warm. I need to know that you can say to me "I love you" without blushing in shame. I need to know that I am yours and you are mine, now and forever.'

'That can never be!'

'It must and it shall be.'

Slowly, he began to untangle himself from her and from the fence. The latter took longer than one might have thought. In order to passionately embrace her, he'd had to squeeze his arms through some pretty tight spots. Apparently, he still hadn't thought of using the ladder that still rested peacefully against the Conways' garden shed.

'What are you doing?' Ella cried as he slipped from her grasp.

'Going,' he returned. 'The time for talk has passed. Now it is time for action.' His face took on a grim expression. 'I am going to have to be fit and alert tomorrow. I had better call it a night.'

'Edmund, you don't... you don't seriously mean you'll go through with this?'

'I have never been more serious about anything in my life. Except maybe once – when I first told you I loved you. And what I shall now do is practically the same – the only difference is that I shall translate the words into deeds.'

'Edmund, no!' She tried to stop him as he stepped away from the fence and turned, but he was too strong for her. He set out across the lawn, and I felt a lump in my throat. From the back he looked nothing like the cheerful tradesman's son I had known him as throughout the time we had lived in this street. He looked like a tragic hero going towards his final end.

'Please, Edmund! You can't go! You can't challenge Sir Philip. Please don't! Please!'

Halfway down the garden, he stopped and turned his head to look back at her wistfully.

'I have to,' was his only reply.

'But what if he kills you?' she wailed.

He smiled sadly.

'Then I will die in the knowledge that I have done everything in my power to keep us together. It will be a comforting knowledge when the darkness closes in.'

Turning away again, he continued through the garden, towards his parents' house.

'Edmund, wait!' Ella reached through the fence, as if she could grab him and drag him back to her side. But there were yards of distance between them. 'Edmund, please! Don't go!'

This time, he did not stop.

'Edmund, my love, I'm begging you!'

She sank to her knees. By now the volume of her voice had risen considerably over the usual careful whisper she used for her secret rendezvous in the garden. I threw an anxious glance back at the house, but so far, nobody seemed to have heard.

'I'm begging you, please, come back! You can't do this, please!'

Still he did not stop. If I'd had a rock of the right size to hand, I'd have lobbed it at his silly receding head. Nobody made my sister cry like that! But simultaneously, another part of me wanted to hug him fiercely. He was willing to risk his own life to free my sister from a marriage she feared and despised. I couldn't help respecting anybody who was ready to do that, even if I did want to throw rocks at his head.

'Please, Edmund,' Ella tried once more. 'By your love for me, I beg you, stop! Don't go! Don't die!'

When this final attempt failed, she slumped to the ground and knelt there, weeping, her face hidden in her hands.

'All right!' she whimpered. 'I accept! I will... I will do it.'

Edmund, just about to reach the back door of his parents' house, froze in place.

'What?' he asked, without turning. His voice was barely audible. 'What did you say?'

'I... I said, I'll do it,' repeated Ella, taking deep breaths as though she had run miles and miles. 'I accept your offer, Edmund Conway. For you, to save your life and give you happiness, I shall forsake my family. I will run away with you. May God forgive me.'

~~**~*~*

I sat behind the bush for quite some time. I suppose it had to be quite some time, because when I wandered back into the house, everybody was already asleep. Even Ella, up in our room, had stopped crying by now, though I could still see the moisture on her cheeks twinkle in the moonlight which streamed in through the window.

Only when I lay in my bed, the warm blankets over me, did I realize that if I didn't do something really quickly, I would lose my little sister.

Suddenly, in spite of all the blankets, I felt cold inside.

When I woke the next morning, I fervently hoped that last night had been a nightmare. But when I saw Ella's red-rimmed eyes, I knew that was wishful thinking.

Last night had been true. My sister was going to elope – and not even with a romantic rake of a Scottish laird or something similarly adventurous, but with the tradesman's son next door. I wasn't sure what trade his father actually practised. I thought I had heard somewhere that he was a piano tuner.

Sadly, I shook my head. Constantly going around making sure that everywhere you went things sounded the same had to be about the dullest occupation there was. His son didn't seem a lot more exciting to me, generally speaking. All right, he was a nice enough fellow, for a man, but still, nothing to write home about. And he was the man for whom my sister would lose her honour.

Now don't get the wrong impression – I wasn't all too keen on honour and virtue myself. If you're willing to walk around in men's clothes to work for a living, you have to be able to bend a few social norms and customs. I myself wouldn't mind getting a few stains on my non-existent good reputation. But I knew that Ella would mind. Very much so, in fact.

Maybe she loved this man enough to run away with him and be happy. But she also would be sad on a deeper level, a level she wouldn't let anybody see. It would break her heart to disappoint her aunt, silly, compassionate soul that my little sister was. This solution would make Edmund happy – but it would save Ella from one misery only to plunge her into another.

Unless, that is, I could prevent it.

Full of purpose I jumped out of bed. This was no time to dawdle! My sister's happiness was at stake, and I only had one day to take action before I had to go back to slave for Mr Ambrose. Quickly, I dressed – or as quickly as I could, considering the multitude of petticoats I had to put on – and slipped out of the house without anybody noticing. It was Sunday, and after the tiring dance the other night, the household was sure to sleep long and not notice my absence.

As I ran down the street, the beginnings of various plans were already forming in my mind. Somehow I had to get rid of Wilkins. That was the heart of the matter. No Wilkins meant no threat of marriage, no threat of marriage meant no elopement, no elopement meant no unhappy Ella.

For a moment I considered carrying out Edmund's plan – getting hold of a pistol and just shooting the blasted Wilkins. Yet I discounted that for various reasons. Firstly, wanting to marry my sister was, according to the laws of England, not yet a crime that deserved the death penalty; secondly, I didn't have money for a gun; and thirdly, even if I did, I would most likely miss.

Hmm... That last bit will have to be rectified in the not-too-distant future. Now that you are regularly running around in men's clothes you might as well claim male privileges, such as shooting anybody whose face you didn't like.

Back to planning... how to get rid of Wilkins without shooting him?

By the time I had reached Green Park I had hit on quite a promising idea.

I needed only to find out something, something strange or disreputable or otherwise horrible about Wilkins, which could be revealed to my aunt. With her snobbish ways, she would cut off the connection faster than you could say Jack Robinson. I had no doubt there was *something* to Sir Philip's detriment that could be discovered. An over-romanticised, flower-fanatical guffin like he was bound to have some skeletons hidden in his closet.

And I knew exactly who could help me find some of those.

I raced through Green Park, people right and left throwing me disapproving looks. I was running far faster than was seemly for a young lady; that was clear for all the world to read on their faces. But in the distance I could see three figures who did not look disapproving. On the contrary, they looked delighted to see me, waving at me energetically. One of them nearly brained a passing gentleman with her parasol.

Unable to stifle a grin in spite of how worried I was, I picked up my pace. It had been ages since I last saw all my friends together, and now I needed them more than ever. They would be my company of spies, who would help me find a chink in Sir Philip's armour. They would help me save Ella.

And in spite of my private troubles, I had not forgotten the original reason because of which I had called them together: the anti-suffragist meeting which was soon to take place here in London. With these two topics, we were sure to have more than enough to talk about.

I came to a stop only a few yards away from them, gasping for breath.

'Listen,' I said. 'I... I have something really important to tell you. I have–'

'So it's true?' Eve demanded, skipping forward eagerly. 'You do have a lover?'

I blinked at her, taken aback.

'What?'

'I knew it I knew it I knew it I knew it!' Eve started a little dance around me that would have been more fitting for a Cherokee medicine man than for a proper young English lady. Some part of my mind wondered how the heck she was managing those acrobatics with a hoop skirt on. Most of my mind, however, was wondering what the heck she had been talking about.

'I knew it was true the minute Patsy told us what Ella had told her,' she babbled, and it all became clear to me.

The ball. Patsy grilling Ella for information, and Ella spouting out the ridiculous excuses I had told her.

No. Oh please, God, no! Don't let Patsy have told everyone!

As usual, God didn't listen.

'Flora didn't believe it, but I knew right away it was true. You were away all the time last week and not one of us had the slightest idea where you had disappeared to and oh isn't this exciting, girls? Lilly has found herself a man! You must tell us all about him!'

'Well, really I came to talk about something el–' I began, but that was about as far as I got.

'Is he tall?' Eve demanded. She had stopped dancing around me and was now bobbing up and down in front of me like an overexcited puppy. 'Is he handsome? Is he rich? Will you marry him and go live on a vast estate in the country somewhere?'

'Eve!' I said, shocked. 'Where's your pride as an independent woman?'

'Right here,' she said, indicating her head. 'Now will you tell me whether he's rich and handsome?'

'Look,' I said, crossing my arms defiantly, 'this isn't what I came here to talk about!'

'Too bad.' Patsy grinned at me over tiny Eve's head. 'Because it's apparently what you're going to have to talk about.'

'But–'

'What's his name?' Eve interrupted me eagerly. 'Does he live in London? Well of course he does, or you wouldn't have been gone all that time. You were with him, weren't you? Were you two up to anything, you know... special?'

She winked, and then winked a couple of times more in case I hadn't gotten it. I had, and so apparently had everybody else in the vicinity. The looks from passers-by had become a good deal more disapproving.

I would have to stop this. Ella I could deal with, but these three were of another calibre entirely. I would have to placate them somehow. Inspiration struck me!

'I haven't got a lover, all right?' I hissed. 'Now stop it, you're making people stare.'

'Oh.' Eve stopped bobbing up and down, obviously deflated. 'But... but Patsy said...'

'Patsy said what Ella told her.'

'And what you told Ella wasn't one hundred per cent true?' Patsy guessed, her grin having widened after a momentary flicker.

'Actually,' I corrected, 'it's not even one per cent true. But I couldn't correct Ella at the time. She mustn't know.'

'So what is it you have been up to these last few weeks?' Patsy sounded quite demanding, and when Patsy Cusack demanded, you didn't deny her. She might be inclined to back up her demands with a swipe of her mighty parasol, the destroyer of worlds.

'You mustn't tell a soul,' I whispered, grabbing the three of them by the arms and dragging them away from the people in the park, who were still muttering about loose morals in this modern age and unladylike behaviour. 'Especially not Ella. She mustn't know what I'm doing.'

We ended up by the same bench behind the discreet clump of bushes where we had sat before. It was our favourite spot. Nobody ever bothered us there.

'So it has something to do with Ella?' Eve enquired eagerly, sitting down beside me, her disappointment at my lack of romantic entanglements already forgotten. 'What you've been doing all this time, I mean?'

'Yes, very much so. She's in danger.'

All their faces became more serious instantly, especially Flora's. They all liked Ella, and Flora recognized in her something like a kindred spirit, somebody so gentle and meek she made a dove look like a hunting hawk in comparison.

'Explain,' she said in a quiet voice, regarding me with large eyes full of worry.

'Well...' I bit my lip, thinking. 'I'm not quite sure how to explain. Um... do you know a Sir Philip Wilkins?'

Patsy snorted. 'What? That flower-obsessed nincompoop?'

Surprised, I turned towards her. I hadn't actually expected any of my friends to know him. Just like me, they weren't all that fond of male society.

'You know him, Patsy?'

'Sure I do! About a year back I met him at a ball. He started showering me with flowers and calling me stuff like "Delight of my heart" and "Summer Rose" and worse things I wouldn't want to repeat with ladies present. I made it quite clear that I didn't appreciate such behaviour.'

For a moment I wondered how Patsy had made herself 'quite clear'. Then, looking at her big, meaty fists I thought it best to stop wondering.

'Well,' I continued, 'it's him that Ella is in danger from.'

Patsy stared at me, her face blank.

'You're joking.'

'No, I'm not.'

'What has he done? Threatened her with a bouquet of tulips or something?'

'Worse. He wants to marry her.'

Patsy barked a laugh. 'So he's up to his old tricks again. Well, what a terrible danger!'

She stopped laughing when she saw the look on mine and Flora's faces.

'I'm sorry,' she said, pulling her face into the best imitation of contriteness that was possible for Patsy. 'He's really after her?'

'With a vengeance,' I affirmed. 'And tons of green stuff.'

'But I really don't see the problem,' Patsy mused, frowning. 'He's after her. So what? Why doesn't she just say no?' I opened my mouth to answer, but she had already held up her hand, understanding flashing in her eyes. 'Don't bother, forget I said that. I forgot it was *Ella* we were talking about.'

'It... it isn't always easy to say "no" when people want something from you,' Flora interposed. 'Especially men.'

'I beg to differ,' Patsy said, firmly. 'It's very easy indeed. But I admit there are those unfortunates who don't seem to have understood that fact yet.'

'So if she won't say no to him what happens now?' Eve asked. 'Will that mean she'll have to marry him and have a whole lot of babies and grow fat and mopy because she really wanted to do something else with her life but she never said it out loud and so she'll die a tragic death from sadness and nobody will know why?'

'Well...' I said, carefully, 'I was hoping to avoid that kind of thing. I spent the last few weeks trying to find a way out for her.'

'Daft of you not to ask us,' Patsy said with her typical talent for delicacy. 'It's always better to have help.'

'I didn't want to burden you with my problems.' I lowered my head. That much was actually true.

'That's what friends are for, you dolt! You have to burden them with all kinds of problems, so they can unload their misery on you in return.'

Looking up again, I gave them a tentative smile. 'I'll remember that in future, Patsy. Will you still help me?'

They all nodded – Eve about three times as fast as the others and Flora rather hesitantly, but they all nodded.

'So what should we do?' Patsy lifted her parasol and let it smack several times into her palm. A thug with an iron crowbar could not have looked more threatening. 'Do you think I should have a talk with this Sir Philip Wilkins? Just him and me and my parasol?'

If only things could be so simple. Shaking my head regretfully, I said: 'I'm afraid that wouldn't be a good solution. Wilkins always has heaps of servants around him wherever he goes, except in ballrooms. And you can't just haul off and let him have it in the middle of a ballroom. Besides, I think your mother got suspicious after that incident with Mr Wright last summer. I don't think she entirely believed your story about your parasol having been chewed up by a rabid spaniel.'

Patsy shrugged. 'Yes, but the man lived. So even if she had found out, it wouldn't have been that serious.'

'But don't you see,' I insisted, 'in this case, in Ella's case, nobody must even suspect, let alone find out for certain, that I had a hand in this matter. Either my aunt or Wilkins must drop the acquaintance of the other of their own accord. If we were involved in the matter, Ella would feel mortified to find out what you were doing! She might marry the fellow just to prove it wasn't necessary and show everyone what a good, sweet girl she is.'

Slowly, Patsy nodded, though she still looked regretfully at her parasol.

'I see what you mean. If anybody could be that silly, she could.'

With indignation I crossed my arms in front of my chest. 'My sister is not silly!'

Patsy gave me a searching gaze. I relented.

'Well, maybe a tiny little bit. But it's not nice to say it.'

'I'm not known for being nice. That's why I'll never have to worry about an unwanted matrimonial arrangement.' She thought for a moment. 'So what are you going to do if you're not going to act directly?' she finally enquired.

'Well, I had an idea. Listen.'

I explained. At first they looked doubtful, but by the time I was finished Patsy was nodding thoughtfully.

'It's not a bad idea. A fellow like Wilkins has got to have something about him that would make him an undesirable son-in-law. And your aunt *is* the biggest snob in the world.'

'Thank you very much.'

'You're welcome. So, where do we start?'

I gestured beyond the bushes.

'I thought we could start by talking to the people in the park. People here do nothing but talk all day. That's why they come out here: to hear the latest gossip and make up some more.'

'Some of them come here to walk and feed the cute little ducks in the pond,' Flora pointed out shyly.

'Those are the worst,' was Patsy's reply. 'Have you ever listened to those old ladies who stand around feeding ducks? They chatter worse than the ducks do.'

I smiled. They were on the wagon. 'Which will suit our purpose excellently, my dear friend.'

'Quite right, Lilly. So, let's go!'

They were already standing from the bench and about to embark on their secret spying mission when I waved them back.

'Wait! There's something else I've got to tell you.'

'What?' Patsy raised an eyebrow. 'Does Ella have another suitor? Dear me, that girl is busy these days.'

'No, no! It hasn't got anything to do with Ella.'

In concise words, I explained to them about the anti-suffragist meeting. By the time I was finished they were all smiling. Patsy might even have had a demonic glint in her eyes.

'So they don't want anybody to show up, do they?' she asked. 'Afraid of opposition, are they?'

'So it seems,' I confirmed, smirking.

'I wonder...' Eve said. 'Maybe we should do something about that. What do you think?'

We looked at each other – and smiled again.

'This is getting better and better,' Patsy grinned. 'Looks like we're going to have a busy morning.'

~~**~*~*

My spies on their secret mission were less successful than I had hoped.

'Nothing!' Frustrated, Patsy stamped towards me, one hand on her hip, one stabbing her parasol into the air as if she could stab the unobliging passers-by who hadn't been able to offer any useful gossip about Sir Philip. 'They told me nothing! And I bet they knew at least something about him worth knowing, something really bad. They looked frightened when I brought the subject up and kept looking from left to right in a very shifty way.'

'That might have been because you stared at them like an inquisitor in a hoop skirt,' Eve pointed out. 'You should have been more relaxed and easy-going, and everything would have been worked wonderfully! I met some people who were quite eager to talk, actually, and we conversed about him for a long time.'

'Really? And what did you learn?' I asked eagerly.

'That... he is rich, has a long nose and is fond of flowers.'

'What blasted good will that do? We already knew that!'

'Yes, well... I suppose we did.'

255

'Let's face it, girls,' Patsy said gloomily, slumping down on the bench again. 'The chap has a clean slate. An abnormally long nose and a flower fixation are hardly grounds on which one can convince an aunt to reject an affluent nephew-in-law.'

'So what does that mean, Patsy?' Eve wanted to know.

Patsy shrugged miserably. 'It means that Ella is doomed to a life of matrimonial misery, doesn't it, Lilly?'

When I didn't answer, all of them looked up at me. They had all settled on the bench again by now. Only I was still standing, looking down at their inquiring faces.

'Doesn't it?' Patsy repeated.

I thought of Ella on her knees in the garden, weeping, accepting Edmund's proposition to run away.

'Actually, it means something much worse,' I said, darkly.

'Oh my God!' Eve clapped a hand over her mouth and stared at me wide-eyed. 'She's not going to poison him, is she? Arsenic in his bacon and eggs, right after the marriage?'

'Eve!'

'Sorry! Sorry, I forgot. Ella would never do such a thing.' She looked down, and for a moment I thought she was actually ashamed of her outburst. Then she looked up again. 'So *you* are going to poison him, then?'

'You read a great deal too much Edgar Allan Poe, Eve,' I said, pulling a face. 'Nobody is going to poison anybody.'

'But then what did you mean?'

For a moment I hesitated. Should I? They looked so eager, so helpful. But I couldn't. Deep inside I knew Ella would have died rather than have this particular secret revealed to anybody. I myself could listen in – that was all right, after all, I was her big sister and had absolutely altruistic motives. But I couldn't tell a soul.

'Sorry.' I shook my head. 'I can't tell you.'

I saw the hurt on their faces even before all the words were out of my mouth. 'It's not because I don't trust you,' I assured them. 'I would trust you with my life! It's just... well, this is not my secret to share.'

They exchanged looks with another. Finally, Patsy nodded. 'All right... Let's file that under "very mysterious".'

I jumped. The word 'file' made me edgy these days, evoking the urge to jump up and run for the nearest shelf full of boxes. Fortunately, none of them noticed.

'The question isn't really *why* Ella needs to get out of this so desperately,' I reminded them. 'You know she does. We have to figure out *how* to do it.'

'So what's our next step?' Eve asked. 'If poisoning is out of the question, which I still think is not...'

'Think,' Patsy said firmly. 'We go home and think. We're exhausted from running around all morning. We need a good meal and rest. After all, this Sir Philip hasn't proposed to her yet, and even if he did, there's still the time of the engagement before things become final. We have time to figure out a plan, and now we have four brains to do it instead of one.'

'I could ask around in the neighbourhood if people know anything,' Eve suggested. The rest of us exchanged a look. Eve lived in a rich neighbourhood and had a virtual army of acquaintances among her neighbours' daughters. If gossip was to be found anywhere, it was there.

'I could re-read a few of my romantic novels,' Flora offered timidly. 'Maybe there is something in there not only about how people get engaged and married, but also about how they could avoid it.'

'Great idea.' Patsy nodded. 'And just in case that doesn't work, I'll go and buy an especially hard and spiky parasol.'

~~**~*~*

We discussed our plans for the anti-suffragist meeting and then disbanded not long after. I arrived home late for dinner, but so many flowers from Sir Philip had arrived in my absence that my aunt didn't even make a sharp comment. She was in heaven. When Ella sprang up after dinner, I was ready and followed like the watchdog I was.

Our Romeo on duty was waiting just beyond the fence, an incandescent smile on his face, his arms held out at his sides as if to catch Ella when she would come rushing towards him. Only when she had crossed about half the distance did he seem to realize that because of the metal barrier in the way, that wouldn't be quite possible, and he lowered his arms.

His smile didn't become any less incandescent, though.

'Ella, my love!' He breathed, gripping the poles of the fence with both hands.

'Edmund, my love,' she breathed back. 'Finally! I've nearly been driven to distraction, waiting all day! Not knowing what will happen and when is pure torture! When will we leave?'

I leant forward as far as I could. This was the question I had come to hear the answer to, the question the answer to which would determine whether I could work on a plan to get rid of Wilkins or whether I would have to take Patsy up on her offer of parasolical violence. My heart started to pound faster in my chest as I stared at Edmund, the man who held my sister's fate in his hands.

Why wasn't he saying anything?

Why was he just standing there?

Finally, he took a deep breath and leant forward until his lips were almost at her ear – and whispered something in a low voice I couldn't hear!

I couldn't believe it! He had whispered! The whole evening they had conducted their secret affair   in the back garden in perfectly audible voices, and now, when it would actually had been useful for something to be audible for a change, that son of a bachelor decided to whisper!

Ella's eyes went wide.

'So soon?'

Soon? What does that mean, soon? Tomorrow? The day after?

Or did she have a different conception of 'soon'? Could it be weeks still? Edmund had said it would take time to procure a marriage license, so it couldn't just be a few days, could it? But then why had she said 'soon'?

The anxiety tortured me. I wanted to run over to the man who wanted to steal my sister away from her family and shake the truth out of him, but that would kind of have given the game away. So I stayed put and tried to take deep, calming breaths.

'It's not really that soon,' Edmund replied.

Wait? What's that supposed to mean? Is it soon or isn't it?

'I think it's quite soon,' Ella said. 'I have to pack, remember?'

'Yes, but remember, we will travel light, my love. We have to, in order to get away quickly.'

She bit her lip. 'You're right. Yes, if I don't have to pack too much, it's not that soon. I think I can manage.'

Argh! This is maddening!

'If I could, I would leave tonight with you,' Edmund whispered. 'I've done the best I can, but it still will take so long to get a marriage license. I only hope Sir Philip does not make his intentions clear before then. If he does, if all our hopes and dreams are smashed...'

'Hush!' Ella raised her slender hand, gently touching his lips with her forefinger and silencing him. 'Everything will go well. I have no doubt. I trust you, my love.'

His answering smile was melancholic.

'I only wish I had that much faith in myself.'

'And do you know the exact time of day when we will leave?' Ella asked, clearly in an effort to distract him from his dark mood.

I perked up. This was something! Maybe I'd know this much at least! Maybe I could lie in wait every day and make sure they didn't get away without me noticing!

Edmund shook his head. 'No, my love, I'm sorry. It depends on when I can get an inconspicuous coach to bring us out of town.'

This couldn't be happening. It just couldn't!

'So how will I know when it's time to leave, Edmund, my darling?'

'That is the very best part of my plan,' he whispered conspiratorially. 'When the time is upon us to flee, I shall change the curtains in the window of my room.'

He pointed up to a small rectangular window in his parents' house that pointed towards their back garden. 'You see that now they are white? I shall change them to red curtains when the time for our elopement has arrived.'

'Oh Edmund! You are so clever!'

'Well... actually I got the idea from a book...'

'Clever and well-read! My dream man!'

'Am I really?'

'Of course you are! Let me show you. Come closer, my love.'

'Oh, my love! Only if you do, too.'

After that, the conversation was pretty much over. I turned discreetly away and, listening to the noises coming from the fence, did my best not to vomit into the rosebushes. It wasn't easy. This was my *sister* we were talking of, after all.

Well, those were the burdens you had to carry when you were trying to save your sister from disgrace. Once this was over, I would really deserve a medal for my efforts.

Not that I had actually discovered a way to save her yet. And this problem had now abruptly become even more urgent than before. I had no idea how much time was still left before our piano-tuning pseudo-Casanova carried my sister off to parts unknown. The thought sickened me. Despite her brave speech from earlier, I knew she would be devastated to disappoint my aunt. She wasn't like me, she was considerate of other people's feelings. Some people were mad like that.

But what could I do? What could anyone do to prevent this disastrous turn of events? There didn't seem to be anything that could make my aunt dislike Wilkins, and as for scaring him off in some way, I hardly believed it would be possible. His infatuations with Maria, Anne and even Patsy seemed to have been just passing fancies, but he appeared pretty stuck on Ella.

The question was now – how to unstick him in time. Was that even a verb, unstick? I would have to look that up in a dictionary. After I had saved my sister's honour and reputation, of course.

I remained quite a while behind the bushes while Ella and Edmund exchanged sweet nothings at the fence. Fortunately, I had brought a book with me: one of my favourites, a historical retelling of the story of Jeanne d'Arc, the woman who had almost single-handedly thrown the English out of France during the Hundred Years' War. I did my best to plunge myself into the narrative. I admired Jeanne d'Arc deeply and felt a deep spiritual connection to her – not because I was secretly French, but because I, too, often felt the urge to chase after English men with a sharp sword in my hand. If I were Jeanne d'Arc and had a sword of my own, I wouldn't have any problems with disposing of Wilkins!

Finally, the two lovebirds at the fence seemed to remember that there was such a thing as sleep, which was usually accomplished at nighttime, and parted from one another with many apologies and promises to see each other again soon. I waited until Ella had passed my hiding place, shut the book upon my heroine's story with a regretful sigh, and followed Ella into the house. When I entered our bedroom upstairs, Ella had already curled into a tight ball under her blankets.

I lay down in my own bed and recapitulated my to-do list for tomorrow:
- bring back two books to the lending library
- refine plans to foil the masculine plot to undermine women's suffrage
- save Ella from eternal shame and dishonour

I frowned. Hadn't I forgotten something? Something I had to do tomorrow?

Then the memory dropped back into my mind like a red-hot piece of coal. Of course. Tomorrow was *Monday*. And on Monday I had to go back to the office. To Mr Ambrose.

Other memories returned. Mr Ambrose entering the ballroom, Mr Ambrose whirling me around and around on the dance floor with the grace and precision of a clockwork dancing master, strong and contained. Mr Ambrose staring at Miss Hamilton with an intensity with which he had never looked at me...

Wait just a second! Where had that thought come from? Why would you want Mr Ambrose to look at you? You want him to employ you, and that's it! Looking at you has nothing to do with it!

Only, maybe it had. If he couldn't even bring himself to look at me, how could he bring himself to accept me as a female and one of his employees? Yes. I wanted his acceptance as an independent lady, that was all.

Angrily, I punched my cushion and turned onto my other side. Damn the man! Why did he have to pop into my head now? My mind belonged on saving Ella, and maybe also on saving the future suffrage of women from men's chauvinism, but not on him. Most certainly not on him.

So why was it that as I drifted off to sleep, all I could think of was the feel of his arms around me as he danced with me at yesterday's ball?

~~**~*~*

The fact that I had still not discovered the answer to the question by next morning didn't exactly improve my mood. I got up at an unearthly hour, went through the routine of switching clothes and left the house. I needed to clear my head, and the cold morning air was just the way to do it.

Besides, maybe I could force Mr Ambrose to look at me at least once by turning up three hours early.

I turned into Leadenhall Street and marched towards my destination. This early in the morning, the foggy streets were pretty much empty of people. Thus, the two huge shapes that dominated the street were even more overpowering than usual: On the left, the stark, towering Empire House; on the right the broad, elegant façade of East India House. The two buildings facing off over the street like that reminded me of Mr Ambrose and Lord Dalgliesh shaking hands in the ballroom. Just as they had back then, this confrontational stance looked almost... threatening.

Shaking my head, I looked away from East India House and started up the stairs of my workplace. I was being fanciful.

Only when I reached the door of Empire House did it occur to me to wonder how I might get into the building. As yet, it seemed to be deserted. The door was firmly locked, and when I peered in through one of the high, narrow windows, I couldn't see a soul inside. I couldn't even see somebody without a soul inside – a condition, I was sure, that applied to many of the men who normally occupied its bustling halls, especially the one who paid all the others.

As I walked back from the window to the front door, something clinked in my pocket. Of course! The ring of keys Mr Ambrose had given me. How could I have not thought of it before?

Well, if I thought about it, it wasn't that surprising. There surely wouldn't be a key to the front door on the ring, not after the defection of Mr Ambrose's last secretary and considering the fact that I didn't have the right gender. He wouldn't trust me in a million years!

But it can't hurt to try, right? After all, you're already here.

I stuck the first key into the keyhole, although I had already seen that it was much too small. Of course, it didn't fit. Neither did the second, nor the third, although they seemed to be of more appropriate shape. I shoved another one into the keyhole, knowing already that this, too, wouldn't work, although it looked deceptively fitting. I tried to turn it.

There was a *click*, and the lock snapped open.

I stared at the door in disbelief.

Cautiously, I stretched out a hand and pushed against it. It swung open a few inches with an eerie squeak, then stopped. I pushed again, and it opened far enough for a human being to enter. Maybe I was hallucinating? Maybe the door had already been unlocked? Quickly, I slipped inside and faced a vast hall of empty silence. No Sallow-face behind the desk, no multitude of clerks hurrying about, doing Mammon only knows what. I hadn't been mistaken: the door had been firmly locked.

The key had worked. Could it actually be that Mr Ambrose *trusted me*?

Not letting myself think about this too deeply just now, I turned around, pulled the door shut hurriedly and locked it after me. Then I began the long ascent to my office, my stomach churning all the way. How would Mr Ambrose treat me after what had happened at the ball? What would he think of me? Did he think even less of me now, because he had seen me in a dress and been reminded of the fact that I was female?

My hands balled into fists at the very thought. It just wasn't fair that he would stare at this Miss Hamilton like she was the most precious thing on earth to him, while treating me like a piece of dirt! She was just as female as I was! In fact, a darn sight more obviously female, considering the rather revealing nature of her dress. Just because I wanted to be independent and earn my living, I wasn't supposed to be entitled to the same treatment as she? I wouldn't allow that! I would force him to respect me. And I would start by giving him a nice surprise.

Since you're so early... How about waiting in his office and, when he arrives, making some very smart remark about him being a bit late for work?

I grinned. That would nettle him to no end, I was sure!

With light steps I crossed the length of the hallway and stuck the right key into the keyhole when I reached the door to his office. I couldn't wait to see his face when he arrived and I was already there, waiting for him.

The door swung open – revealing a Mr Rikkard Ambrose, sitting straight as a ruler behind his dark wood desk, studying papers. He glanced up briefly from the papers he was reading, his cool expression not altering in the slightest.

'Ah, Mr Linton. You are here, finally.'

BLOODY WORK

Looking down at his papers again, Mr Ambrose gestured to a pile of files and a box beside him on the desk. 'Deposit these in that box over there, will you?'

I gaped at him, speechless. It was *five in the morning!*

When, after a few moments, he noticed that I still hadn't moved, he looked up again. Mr Ambrose would never go so far as to actually raise a questioning eyebrow, but he didn't need to.

'You are still standing, although I gave you an order. Any particular reason?'

'Do you *sleep* here or what?' I demanded indignantly.

He looked down again.

'Why so interested in my sleeping arrangements, Mr Linton? Were you thinking of joining me? If so, I must disappoint you. I do have a bed here, but it would not be wide enough.'

Several things ran through my mind at the moment which I could throw at him, none of which were fit for polite conversation and all of which were likely to get me sacked on the spot. I swallowed my anger and hoped it wouldn't give me indigestion.

Instead I said: 'I am *three hours early*, Mr Ambrose.'

He nodded.

'Yes, I noticed. Now stop dawdling and take care of those files. Return to me when you are done. Since you are here, I have something else for you to do.'

I went and got the files, praying vehemently that the 'something' he wanted me to do involved a sharp sword and the severing of his head from his body. In no time at all I was back in front of his desk, and I still had not exploded or run to get sharp weapons. I was rather impressed with myself.

'The files are stored as ordered, Mr Ambrose, Sir,' I said in as sweet a tone as I could manage.

'I see.'

No 'Well done' or 'Thank you'. He didn't even raise his head from his papers.

'Sir? What is it you wished me to do?'

'To wait until I have finished reading. Then I will give your instructions.'

I closed my eyes and slowly counted to ten to calm myself. Unfortunately, it didn't work, so I continued to fifteen and then to twenty. But when I reached fifty, I was still just as infuriated as I had been at one. Did he have to be so... cool? So distant?

51, 52, 53...

Well, he was Mr Ambrose, so he was naturally about as warm and welcoming as a freshly calved iceberg, but still. It aggravated me more now than it had before, having seen, in contrast, his infatuated behaviour towards that bloody female the other night at the ball.

64, 65, 66, 67...

And of course he had to have horrible taste in ladies! I wouldn't have minded if she had been a halfway decent creature, but this Hamilton person was a femme fatale and would leach all the life and money he had out of him.

'Mr Linton?'

79, 80, 81...

I was incredulous that he couldn't see it or that he couldn't find a better woman.

'Mr Linton!'

He should be able to find another. After all, he was, I had to admit, abominably handsome. Very, very handsome...

97, 98, 99...

'Mr Linton? Mr Linton, I am talking to you!'

'What?' My eyes flew open and I blinked at Mr Ambrose, who was staring at me coolly over the top of his business papers.

'Mr Linton, I have called your name about five times now and you have been just standing there with your eyes closed. If you are not fully awake yet, I had rather you return home and waste your own time sleeping there than waste my time here. There is work to do.'

I raised my chin and met his gaze unflinchingly.

'I am completely awake, Sir.'

'Indeed? Then go and fetch a small leather-bound volume out of the left part of the lowest drawer of your desk. And keep your eyes open while you are walking, will you? I would hate for you to walk against a wall by accident.'

I managed a smile, though I doubt it was very polite.

'Thank you for the concern for my welfare, Sir.'

He had put his papers aside now, but still he hadn't looked up. Instead, he was methodically arranging them into several small piles.

'Who said anything about your welfare, Mr Linton? Stone walls are quite expensive, and I would not like to have to spend money on repairing any cracks.'

I got out of there before I committed a justifiable murder, and marched through my office towards the desk. Of course he had been right, blast him. There was indeed a small, leather-bound book in the lowest drawer of the desk, in the back left corner. I retrieved it and opened it out of curiosity.

'Bring it directly to me,' his voice sounded from the other room. 'There's nothing in there that would interest you particularly, I can promise you.'

I did not blush as easily as Ella, but my face might have just been a tiny bit red when I returned to Mr Ambrose's office, the book in hand. Stopping in front of the large, dark wood desk, I held it out to Mr Ambrose. He waved me away.

'Keep it. It is your responsibility now.'

'But... you didn't want me to look inside?'

'I didn't want you to waste time on idle curiosity. Remember: Knowledge is power is time is money.'

'I would have gained knowledge if you had let me read it,' I pointed out, my rebellious spirit flaring.

He considered this, the coldness in his eyes for a moment replaced by thoughtfulness. Then something sparked there. Surely I was mistaken, but for just a fraction of a second, it looked almost like... humour?

'True. You may take it home with you and study it in your leisure hours. I shall expect that you have fully familiarized yourself with it by tomorrow morning.'

My mouth popped open in astonishment.

'What?!' I demanded. He wanted me to work even after I was out of here?

He looked at me, not a trace of humour in his face anymore. 'First you stand around with your eyes closed, now your ears don't seem to be working? I must say, I am quite disappointed in you, Mr Linton.'

I straightened.

'There is no call for that, I assure you, *Sir*. I shall have the book memorized by tomorrow, *Sir*.' I don't think that anybody had ever managed to make the word 'Sir' sound so much like 'slug'. Mr Ambrose, though, didn't seem to notice.

'Then we can proceed immediately. Go to the current week.'

'W-what?'

'I am becoming tired of hearing that word, Mr Linton. Go to the current week in the book you are holding. It is an appointment book. It holds my appointments over the year, which is divided into months, which again are divided into weeks. You do know what a week is, Mr Linton?'

'Yes, Sir. I do, Sir.'

'How fortunate. Go to the current week.'

Quickly, I flitted through the volume until I had found the appropriate page.

'It is your task to enter and keep track of all appointments. If I forget, it is your duty to remind me in time.'

I looked up, raising an eyebrow.

'*You* forget appointments?'

'No. In fact I have never forgotten a single appointment in my life. However, better safe than sorry.'

'Is that one of your principles, like the knowledge-power-money thing?'

'You could say so.'

'Maybe I should start a list to keep track of all the wisdom you impart to me.'

'What you should keep track of, Mr Linton, are my appointments. Now, can we return to the matter at hand?'

'Yes, Sir! Of course, Sir!'

He started rattling off dates at an incredible rate, detailing when and where he was to go exactly. The list went from various factories to places at the harbour, several banks, business associations and meetings. Whatever his business interests were, exactly, they were many and varied. I did my best to take all the dates down in a legible manner, and did pretty well, I think, until he dropped the bomb.

'At three pm on Saturday, I shall be attending the opera.'

I left a blot of ink on the page.

'*What?*'

He looked up at me with those cool, sea-blue eyes of his.

'There is that word again. Are you particularly fond of it, Mr Linton?'

'Don't change the subject,' I accused him. '*You* attend the opera?'

'Yes.'

'You do not consider such a frivolous activity to be a waste of your time and money?'

'No.'

'And why not, if I may ask?'

'Because I own it.'

'Oh.'

'I like to keep the management on their toes. And the ballet dancers as well.'

I blinked. Had he just made a joke? His face told me otherwise. It was as stony as ever. But nobody could be that serious, could they?

The opera...

Suddenly, a thought shot through my mind. A very annoying thought in a green ball gown.

'Will anybody be going with you?' I enquired suspiciously.

Like Miss Hamilton, for instance? Or the writer of the pink letters? Or... both?

'Is that any business of yours, Mr Linton?'

'It is if you want me to procure tickets for you.'

'I see.'

He thought for a moment, tapping with his fingers on the desk, looking away from me, out of the window and over the city of London. I waited with bated breath.

'Yes,' he said finally. 'I think *somebody* will be going with me. Procure two tickets for the opera.'

Somebody? *Somebody?* Was he torturing me on purpose? Did he know that I was dying to know? There wasn't the slightest indication of it on his face. But then, when was there ever any indication of anything on his face? He was as easy to see through as a brick wall and just as friendly.

'Anybody in particular?' I asked, and immediately regretted it. After all, he shouldn't be thinking I was... interested in him in any way, which I clearly was not.

He swivelled around and fixed me with his cool gaze again. 'Why do you ask? Do opera tickets have to bear names nowadays?' If it hadn't been Mr Rikkard Ambrose, I could have sworn there was a hint of sarcasm in his voice. Blast it! Blast me! And blast the opera! Who needed Mozart and Meyerbeer anyway?

I hid my face behind the appointment book and wished it were larger. 'Just curious.'

'Undoubtedly.'

'Any more appointments, Sir?'

Mercifully we moved on from the subject of opera, and he kept me busy enough writing down more appointments that I didn't even think too much about Miss Hamilton. When I was finally finished with the thirty-sixth appointment, he nodded curtly.

'Give me the book and let me see.'

Handing him the book, I waited for his judgement. I knew my handwriting wasn't very good, and he had talked with the speed of a Spinning Jenny.[42] His face was, as ever, indecipherable as he studied the page, giving me no clue as to what he might be thinking. Finally, he closed the book with a snap.

---

[42] Not the name of a circus artist famous for her fast cartwheels, or anything like that. No, the 'Spinning Jenny' is one of the first industrial machines invented during the Industrial Revolution in England, by James Hargreaves.

'Adequate,' he said. 'You managed to take it down without leaving anything out, which is more than I can say of my last five secretaries.'

It took me a moment to realize that this had actually been a compliment. When I did, a ridiculous grin spread over my face. What was wrong with me? Why did his approval give me this warm, fuzzy feeling inside, like drinking hot chocolate on a cold winter morning?

Except hot chocolate didn't stare at me so disapprovingly. Not ever.

'If you're quite done exhausting your facial musculature needlessly, Mr Linton, then perhaps we can move on with work?'

'Yes, Sir! Just as you say.'

'Put this away again.' He handed me the appointment book. 'Remember, you're responsible for it.'

Still exhausting my facial muscles in what I thought was a definitely not needless expression of satisfaction, I hurried back into my office. As I bent to open the drawer, the appointment book slipped out of my hand and fell to the floor, opening at the previous week. Picking it up, I saw that the week was covered with appointments: Mr Ambrose must have left his office without telling me. All the appointments were written down in a familiar neat and precise hand.

He had been keeping track of his own appointments! It had been silly of me not to think of this, really. After all, it was a secretary's job to take care of appointments, so why had it not been part of mine?

The answer was evident: because he didn't trust me to handle them! Had he been afraid that – silly, overexcited female that I supposedly was – I would send him to a brothel-house in the east end instead of the Bank of England? A storm of indignation began to brew in me, and the barometer of my temper slowly rose. But then I suddenly remembered that *now* he *had* entrusted me with the appointment book.

Did this mean he was finally coming around? Was he beginning to accept me? Maybe soon I could drop this ridiculous charade of pretending to be a man, and he would stop calling me 'Mr Linton'.

An image flashed in front of my eyes: I, entering the big hall downstairs, in an undoubtedly feminine dress, my head held high, going up to work for one of London's most powerful businessmen. The first ever lady to earn her own way in this world...

'Mr Linton!'

Blast!

Just like that, a cold voice from the neighbouring room shattered my daydream. Quickly, I put the appointment book away and made my way back to my employer's office. Not quickly enough for his taste, though, apparently.

'What did I tell you, Mr Linton?'

I straightened, knowing exactly what he wanted me to hear.

'That knowledge is power is time is money, Sir!'

'Which means you have to be what...?'

'Quick and efficient, Sir!'

'Indeed. Now go to your desk, get notepaper and a pen.'

Wondering what the heck he wanted me to do now, I fetched the required items and returned, receiving no admonishment this time.

'I have a business letter to write,' he declared when I had taken up my station beside his desk, a notepad in hand. 'Obviously, you are not what I wish for in a secretary and have very limited abilities, but my handwriting is not elegant enough for official letters, and I need somebody to do this. It might as well be you.'

I tried my best not to look at him. Having just seen a sample of his handwriting, I knew there was nothing whatsoever wrong with it. In fact, his clear, precise script was one of the most beautiful hands I had ever seen. A smile tugged at the corners of my lips, and I hid behind the notepad. I had been right. He *was* beginning to accept me, even if he'd rather die than admit it.

'The letter is to a very important business partner of mine,' he warned. 'Make one mistake, and I shall be *very displeased.*'

I couldn't help remembering what had happened to the last guy that had 'displeased' him: hauled off by Karim into the misty alleys of London, never to be seen again. But surely he wouldn't do something like that to me simply for making a mistake in a business letter, would he?

Um... *would he?*

He went off before I had a chance to ponder this further. If I'd thought his listing of appointments had been fast, it was nothing to how he raced through that letter. He seemed to have it all perfectly written out in his head already, and was just reading off a wall in front of his inner eye. Not once did he stumble or think in enumerating figures, trade routes, factories and a million other things I had never even heard of before.

By the time we had finished, I had filled five pages and my hand was screaming for a relaxing bath in hot water. With my left hand, because my right one was on strike right now, I picked up the handwritten pages and offered them to Mr Ambrose.

He let his cold gaze wander over them. I held my breath again.

Please, God, no mistakes, no mistakes, no mistakes...

'Passable,' he allowed.

Thank the Lord! It had to be faultless. If there had been any mistakes, I was sure he could not have resisted pointing each one out to me before dismissing me for failing in my duty.

'Try to remember next time that you are a human being writing, not a hen with inky feet running all across a sheet of paper,' he added.

I pursed my lips, suppressing the urge to go for his throat.

'Any other constructive criticism, Sir?'

'No, that is it for now.'

He grabbed a piece of paper and scrawled something which he then handed to me. 'Here. Address the letter to this address and put it out on Stone's desk. Stone will take care of posting it.'

'Yes, Sir.'

Taking the letter from him, I hurried back into my office and did as I had been told. Inside of me, conflicting emotions were fighting a fierce battle. The appointment book, the letter... was he beginning to trust me, or was I reading too much into this?

Yes, a nasty little voice inside me said. *You are.*

Bloody hell! But I wanted so much for him to trust me!

You may want anything you like – that doesn't mean you'll get it.

After his parting words last time we had been at work together, when he had practically threatened to find an excuse to get rid of me, I had been plagued by anxiety. I remembered so well our words before we had parted.

'I have my own empire and consequently must deal with my own espionage and fight my own wars, Mr Linton. Right now, a war is coming.'

'A... war? Over one piece of paper?'

'Yes. A war. Possibly the biggest I've ever fought. I don't want you to be caught in the crossfire. I cannot have a girl being in danger!'

But did these words still count? Somehow, after what had happened today, I felt a strange mix of hope and fear inside me.

But it's fear that's the biggest part, isn't it?

Bloody hell! Sometimes I really wished that inner voice of mine would shut up! I *needed* this position, more than ever now, and not just for myself. I didn't know how things were going to go with Ella, but there was always the worst possibility of all: that she would end up alone and disgraced, forsaken by her family and her so-called lover, and maybe even with child. Things like that had happened before. Now and then you read about such a scandal in the papers. Young love run mad...

If it came to that, I would be there to save her, with enough money to take care of her. That, I had sworn to myself.

Angrily, I stepped out into the hallway and slammed the letter onto Mr Stone's desk. I shouldn't think like this! I shouldn't give up hope. There was still time to discover a way to scare off Wilkins. Yet with every second that passed, I felt the darkness circle closer around my little sister. I needed this job! I had to keep it!

But it's not really up to you, is it? It's up to that stone-faced bastard in the office over there. Do you think he'll ever really accept you for who you are?

Well, there was one way to find out. One way to see whether his earlier doubts about me had been laid to rest.

Swallowing my apprehension, I returned to his office and made a little bow, which he didn't seem to notice.

'Letter deposited as ordered, Sir.'

'I see. Then I have another task for you. I–'

'Sir?'

He looked up, and I might actually have detected a miniscule morsel of surprise on his face. Surprise that anyone, even such a despicable creature as I, dared to interrupt him.

'Yes, Mr Linton?'

'I have a question, Sir.'

Carefully he put down his papers and intertwined his fingers, regarding me over them like a sharpshooter taking aim.

'Indeed? Well, then fire away.'

I swallowed.

'Have we found out where the stolen file is, yet, Sir? When are we going after it?'

Mr Ambrose's intertwined fingers clenched hard.

'*We?*' His cool voice had a dangerous undertone – and overtone and middle tone, if I was being absolutely honest. '*We* have not found anything nor will *we* find anything, because in *we*, a *you* would be included, Mr Linton. And you will have no further part in the search for the missing documents. I thought I already made that abundantly clear.'

This was what I had been afraid of.

'Not clear enough for me,' I shot back, matching his cold tone with fire. 'Why shouldn't I help?'

'Because you will only be a liability. Keep to office work, Mr Linton, and leave the darker parts of this life to real men.'

The words hit me like a fist in the stomach. I didn't know exactly why – I mean, he was right, of course, that underneath the trousers I was still absolutely female. It wasn't the words so much as the way he said them – *real men*, as if men were something special, something stronger, something better than women.

So this was how things stood. Nothing had changed. He was prepared to keep me, to let me work for him, but not as he would let another work for him. He was being charitable to the poor, mad girl who wanted to earn a living. Rage welled up inside of me!

'There is no need to concern yourself in any case,' he continued. 'Clues have been discovered as to the whereabouts of the mastermind behind the theft. Warren and his men are out on the streets searching for his hideout as we speak. They will soon discover it and this will be taken care of.'

'Why won't you let me help?' I demanded. 'You did last time, in the search for Simmons.'

'That was different.'

'Different how?'

His eyes took on a whole different level of coldness. They seemed to be staring off into icy distances, over the endless expanse of the Arctic, or some similarly desolate place I couldn't even imagine.

'That, Mr Linton, was before I found out who is behind this.'

'Well, who is it then? Who is this mystery man you are so scared of?'

His eyes snapped back from the distance onto me, flashing.

'I am not scared, Mr Linton. I am cautions. There is a difference.'

I bit back a comment. Men and their egos. 'Very well, then. Who is this man you are so cautious of?'

Silence.

'Why won't you tell me?' My voice grew louder as my anger rose.

Silence.

'Will you at least tell me what's in this file that is worth killing for?'

Silence.

'Will you tell me anything at all?'

Silence. Really extraordinary silent silence.

He sat there, glowering, and I stood in front of him, fuming. How quickly things had turned from a relatively companionable work mood into a fierce battle.

'Um... excuse me?'

Both our heads jerked towards the door. We had been so consumed by our argument that neither of us had noticed how Mr Stone had poked his head into the room. He was nervously playing with his bow tie, his eyes flicking from one of us to the other.

'I am deeply sorry to disturb you, Mr Ambrose,' he hastened to assure his employer, 'only I needed to deliver this memorandum.' He held up a piece of paper. 'I knocked twice, but you probably did not hear me over all the... err... shouting.'

'Well, don't just stand there like an ape, man, give it to me!' Mr Ambrose snapped, his voice not so devoid of emotion as usual. Mr Stone rushed forward, deposited the memorandum on his master's desk and got out of the danger zone as quickly as possible. The door fell shut behind him.

'Why can't you accept me?' Strangely, my voice was soft now. Soft and muted. 'Why can't you let me do the work that needs to be done, whether harmless or dangerous?'

He met my eyes without flinching.

'You know why.'

'Because I am a lady?'

Silence.

'Talk to me!'

Silence.

'The search for the file...' I began again, but a raised hand from Mr Ambrose stopped me in mid-sentence.

'You want to work for me?' he snapped. 'Really, seriously work for me? All right. If it's work you want, it's work you're going to get. Bring me file 38XI201.'

'The search...'

'I said *bring me file 38XI201!*'

What could I do? He was my employer, it was his prerogative to tell me what to do. Honestly, I wondered as I went searching for the appropriate box, maybe Ella and I should just move into the workhouse voluntarily. Surely, the tyranny of the workhouse foreman and the tyranny of Mr Ambrose would be much the same?

Well, I was wrong about that. As I was about to find out, the tyranny of Mr Rikkard Ambrose could be much, much worse.

˷˷**˷*˷*

'Bring me file 38XI205! Take this note to stone! Hurry! Here, the safe key! Go and fetch the steam engine model from the safe. No, not that one, the one with two pistons and the larger exhaust outlet. Move faster! If you dawdle so much you'll never get your work done. Where is that file?'

That's how it went on all day. He harried me like a pack of vengeful harpies, chasing me from this task to that, and when that was done to these and those and numerous others. It wasn't long until my feet began to ache and I had numerous paper cuts on my fingers from hastily leafing through files. When I got bloodstains on one of them, he accused me of wilfully damaging company material and ordered me to stop bleeding.

'How about if I bandage my finger?' I hissed at him.

'Too time-consuming. Just stop bleeding, and that's the end of it!'

I could see exactly what he was doing, but I wasn't giving in. No matter how much he hounded me, I wouldn't collapse and admit it was too much, or he was being unfair! I would give him no leverage, no reason to throw me out!

Without pause, I worked as long as I could, but at some point came the time when I had to step up to his desk and say: 'Um... Mr Ambrose? I have to powder my nose again.'

'You nose looks fine. Continue working.'

'Mr Ambrose, do we have to have another talk about euphemisms?'

He hesitated for a moment.

'Oh. *That* kind of nose-powdering?'

'Yes, Sir.'

'Fine!' he snapped. Motioning with his hand to the door of his private bathroom, he gave me a curt nod. 'Go. But be quick about it!'

'I shall do my very best, Sir,' I answered sardonically.

The rest of the day continued pretty much the same. About mid-day, when he had sent me into   the file section to retrieve a box, I devoured a sandwich I had brought with me for lunch. It wasn't much, but it kept me going until the sun finally began to sink and the moment was approaching when I could finally stop this torture and go home

The moment arrived and went away. Mr Ambrose gave no indication of wanting to stop. I heard Mr Stone outside in the hall pack up and leave, but Mr Ambrose stayed behind his desk, shooting orders at me in rapid succession.

The storm clouds of my temper rumbled dangerously. He had no right to do this! I had worked the whole day, in fact three hours longer than I was supposed to, and he was still making me work overtime for no reason.

Well, that wasn't exactly true. He had a reason: wanting to get rid of me. It just wasn't a very nice one.

Finally, when, over an hour after Mr Stone had left, he still showed no sign of wanting to leave, I snapped. Marching up to his desk, I dumped the last box of files onto it with an earth-shattering thump.

'This isn't going to work, you know!' I announced, glaring at him in defiance. 'No matter how much work you heap on me, you can't make me quit!'

He looked up, regarding my angry face over the top of the box.

'Yes, I can see that.'

'So are you going to give up?' I demanded.

His eyes glittered dangerously. Rising from his armchair, he slowly leant forward until our faces were only inches apart, and his dark, sea-coloured eyes became pools beckoning me to drown myself in them.

'Give up?' he breathed. 'Hardly. I shall simply have to find another method to... persuade you.'

~~*~**~*~*

When I finally left the office, I still had goose bumps all over my body.

Another method to persuade me... to persuade me to leave... I wondered what that might be. Whatever he was thinking of, I wasn't looking forward to it – not after he said it in that tone of voice.

Really? You little liar!

I told myself most firmly to shut the hell up! At the moment I was just too tired to think much about it or anything else for that matter. I only wanted a nice, soft bed after a long day at work. Still, I had to go through the cumbersome process of changing clothes before I could approach the front of the house. Sighing, I finally stepped through the front door, wishing I were already upstairs.

'Lilly!'

My head whipped around to see my aunt standing right beside me. She had to have been waiting there, behind the door, ready to pounce on me the moment I came in.

'Where were you?' she demanded, her eyes glittering dangerously. 'You've been gone the whole day!'

Ah, so she had finally caught on to my frequent day-long absences, had she? Amazing what caring surrogate parent she was: it had only taken her a couple of weeks.

Lucky for me, I had a plan ready.

I winked. 'You remember the gentleman from the ball the other day?'

Her frown lifted a bit. 'You mean...'

'I won't name names of course,' I said, hoping fervently she wouldn't make me, because I didn't have any. 'But you know... I've been seeing a little more of *him* recently.'

'Oh.' Her eyes went wide. 'Oh, if that's the case...'

She smiled. She actually smiled. 'Good girl! Now, off to bed with you!'

Thanking God that I had gotten off so lightly, I scampered up the stairs. Beautifully! That's how it had worked, simply beautifully! I would have to come up with a new story soon, of course, as soon as she realized there were no flowers or presents arriving for me. But I'd cross that bridge when I came to it.

Up in our shared room, Ella was waiting for me. She sat on her bed and looked up at me with a timidly hopeful smile.

'Have you been out with your young man again?'

I didn't really see the point of saying no. I had been lying so frequently lately, it had almost become second nature to me. And anyway, this wasn't *technically* a lie. I had been with a young man. An incredibly rich, intimidating man whose

272

head I wanted to rip off and feed to piranhas at the moment, but he was still a young man.

'Yes.'

Ella's cautious smile bloomed into full radiance.

'Really? Did it go well?'

Well, he worked me over pretty hard, I bled a little, and he gave me permission to use his toilet. Nice, isn't he?

All true, but I didn't say that. Instead I plastered a smile on my face and told her: 'Yes, very well indeed. I think we're getting to know each other better.'

'Come and sit down.' Ella reached out to me pleadingly. 'Tell me about him.'

Oh Dear God...

Was this a good idea?

Of course not, you idiot! Of course not! Lie your way out of this right away!

I opened my mouth – but Ella was sitting there, all sweet and innocent and eager. 'Oh, Lilly, I know you can't mention his name or anything,' she assured me. 'I just want to know what kind of man he is, how you two get along, how you feel about him. Please.'

She looked up at me with big, pleading doey eyes. Damn! Sisters like that should be illegal! Without really meaning to, I took two steps forward and sat down on the bed beside her, putting my arms around her.

'All right,' I said, smiling encouragingly. 'What do you want to know?'

'Well... how long have you two known each other?'

Well, that was easy. I could just tell the truth.

'A couple of weeks, now.'

'And how many assignations have you had yet?' she whispered, leaning closer, an eager look in her eyes.

Darn! This wasn't so easy any more. What should I say? *I go to him every day because he pays me for it?*

If I said that, she would be jumping to conclusions about my relationship with Mr Ambrose that were even worse than the truth, and her screams of horror would alert the entire household.

'Um... assignations...' Desperately I grabbed for a number. My mind seized on Mr Ambrose's date book. 'Thirty-six,' I blurted out. 'Thirty-six assignations.'

'Oh. That is quite a lot.'

It was. And all in one day, too. The fact that I had only noted them down, not actually been there, I chose not to mention.

'And...' Ella leaned closer, lowering her voice as if now the really important part began. 'And how do you feel about him?'

Oh bloody heck! More lying. Well, I supposed it was unavoidable.

I bit my lip.

'I... care about him. But he's difficult, you know? Taciturn and cool, and not very free with his money. He keeps me at arm's length, which isn't easy to deal with sometimes. But underneath it all, he's really important to me.'

Goodness, was I doing an amazing job! My lies were delivered brilliantly, in just the right tone of voice with just the right amount of nervous hesitation. I could see on Ella's face that she believed me. Heck, I very nearly believed myself, although I knew of course it was all codswallop. Mr Ambrose was a source of income, nothing more, nothing less.

'Lill, I... I know you don't want Aunt to know about him.'

Darn right I didn't! If my aunt found out what I really was doing during my supposedly romantic escapades, she would have a coronary! Worse, she would recover from it and come after me!

'So I'm guessing,' Ella continued cautiously, 'that he's not very respectable or not very wealthy.'

I smirked. Ella had always lost guessing games. She couldn't have been more wrong in this case. From what I had gathered, half the mothers in London were out to get Rikkard Ambrose for their maiden daughters, and the other half was not similarly engaged only because Lord Dalgliesh was also in town.

'So... have you ever thought about running away with him?'

The question hit me like a steam engine. So that was what this was all about! I had wondered why, this late in the evening, she would be here in her room and not outside in the garden with Edmund. Now I knew! He was out forging his escape plans, and she was seeking reassurance. And who better to give her that than her big sister, who just also happened to have romantic troubles?

Or at least in Ella's imagination.

Curse my lies! They had turned out to be bleeding inconvenient!

I cleared my throat, trying to banish a mental image of Mr Ambrose slinging me over his shoulder and dragging me to the nearest altar. 'Um... not really. We aren't really quite that far in our relationship.'

Damn right you aren't! For example, you'll first have to get an actual relationship! One that involves more than me carrying around files and jumping at his every command, that is!

'But if he asked you,' Ella insisted, clearly determined to get an answer, her eyes looking large and forlorn, 'would you run away with him?'

Unbidden, the image of Mr Ambrose slinging me over his shoulder shoved its way back into my thoughts. Of course we wouldn't embark on our elopement in a comfortable coach – a chaise would have to do, if we wouldn't walk. Real carriages were, after all, much too expensive. And we wouldn't get married by special license either, for that cost money, too. Once we had gotten married in some country church by a young priest who didn't ask too much of a fee, we would return to London and spend our honeymoon sorting through the business correspondence that had arrived in our absence.

I shook my head at the absurd image, and a smile crept onto my lips.

'Of course.' The words had slipped out before I had even noticed. 'Of course I would run away with him.'

God! This was taking the convincing lying a bit far, wasn't it? After all, I wanted to *dissuade* her from eloping, not *encourage* her! What was I doing?

I was of course being sarcastic and insincere, but Ella couldn't know that, the poor girl! Somehow, when I spouted that outrageous lie just now, I had managed to make my voice sound horribly convincing!

'Oh.' Ella's shoulders slumped and she looked even more lost than before. I had been right. She had been looking for advice on her own situation, and this obviously hadn't been the answer she had been expecting. She had probably expected words of caution from her big sister.

'That doesn't mean that *you* should, though,' I added hastily. 'If you ever were in that kind of situation, I mean, hypothetically. What I would do isn't necessarily the best thing. You know I'm a reckless maniac who should probably be locked up for her own safety.'

'Oh, Lill!' Ella tried her best but couldn't keep a smile off her face. 'You shouldn't say such things!'

'Why not, if they make you smile?' I teased and drew her closer towards me. 'Don't worry. Everything will be fine. Everything will be just fine.'

I was really an excellent liar. Later, when I lay in bed and watched Ella sleep with a peaceful smile on her face, I wondered how I had managed to give her so much reassurance. I certainly didn't feel sure of myself or of my ability to help her. The unknown date when she would forever be snatched away from me was drawing closer.

What... what if I simply talked with her about it? Tried to talk her out of it?

But then I remembered the fire in her eyes when she had looked at Edmund, and I knew that talking wouldn't do any good. It might only serve to destroy her trust in me. I only had one chance: find a way to get rid of Wilkins before it was too late! And I would do so, *and* I would make Mr Ambrose fully accept me, *and* the day after tomorrow I would challenge British chauvinism and demonstrate for women's suffrage with my friends at the chauvinists' convention in Hyde Park. I had a lot of obstacles in my way, but none of them were going to stop me! Least of all a certain detestable, handsome, rich businessman!

~~**~*~*

Taking a deep breath, I walked down the hallway. In passing, I nodded to Mr Stone.

'Good morning, Mr Stone.

He smiled and nodded back at me.

'Good morning, Mr Linton.'

For a moment I hesitated, wondering whether I should enter my own office, not that of Mr Ambrose. His words rang through my mind again: *I shall simply have to find another method to... persuade you.*

No matter how morbidly curious a part of me might be, I didn't want to find out what that meant. I wasn't suicidal.

Don't be a chicken, Lilly! You know it's far better to face his next attack head-on. If you don't come directly into his office, he's bound to see it as another attempt at time-wasting.

So I squared my shoulders, marched past Mr Stone's desk and pushed open the door to Mr Ambrose's office, ready for whatever might await me.

'Ah, Mr Linton, there you are! How nice to see you! Come in, come in and make yourself comfortable.'

I was just over the threshold when the words and the scene before me registered, and I stopped in my tracks.

I had been wrong. I had not been ready for whatever awaited me. I certainly wasn't ready for a Mr Rikkard Ambrose standing in front of me with a broad smile on his outrageously handsome face.

THE IMPORTANCE OF BEING NICE

'Please, Mr Linton.' That broad smile still on his face, Mr Ambrose gestured for me to come in. 'Please don't just stand there. Close the door behind you and sit down, please.'

A smile.

He had a *smile* on his face.

Rikkard Ambrose had a *smile* on his face. And he had said *please!* I tried to remember whether he had ever said please to me before, and I couldn't recall a single instance. And now he had said it *three times in a row*.

Maybe I was still asleep. Maybe this was a dream and I would wake up soon.

'Won't you sit down, please?' He repeated, still displaying that dazzling smile.

Don't be a fool, Lilly! A tiger smiles too - but that's no reason to sit down next to it!

But Mr Ambrose's smile... It transformed his whole face. Where previously there had only been harshness, there now was splendour and magnificence. It nearly took my breath away. If I had thought he was handsome before, that was nothing compared to the sight that was now in front of me.

He gestured to a chair, again inviting me to sit.

Don't! Don't do it!

I was about to take a step back - when Mr Ambrose stepped towards me and, looking deep into my eyes, took my hand. At the feel of his touch, a shock shot up my arm. His touch wasn't harsh as I had expected, nor was it gentle. It was just right. My hand lay in his as if it had been made to be there.

Listen to yourself! You sound like Ella!

'Come,' he ordered. Only it wasn't the kind of order he usually gave. Not a 'Bring my file XYZ!' shouted in a voice like a sergeant major on mission in Antarctica. No, this time his voice was full of a darker, deeper meaning I couldn't hope to fathom.

My feet started to move without consulting my brain.

Oh well, if this was a dream, I might as well enjoy it while it lasted. A chance to sit down in the presence of His Mightiness Mr Ambrose the Cold and Terrible might not come so quickly again, even in a dream world. I let myself be led over to one of the empty chairs in an outrageously unfeminist manner, unable to take my incredulous eyes off his smiling face. When I sat, he didn't immediately take a seat himself, but instead just stood there, holding my hand, gazing into my eyes.

'Are... are you quite well?' I asked carefully. Maybe this was real after all, and he just had a touch of brain fever.

'Yes, I'm very well, Mr Linton. Thank you very much for your concern.'

The fourth 'thank you' in one morning! Something was clearly wrong with him!

'Are there no more files to go through?' Looking around, I saw that there was nothing on his desk. The door to my office, which yesterday had been open practically all day, was firmly closed.

'No, Mr Linton, no files today.'

He still hadn't let go of my hand. It felt as if it were smouldering. With his thumb, he started rubbing circles on my palm, heating the delicious burn to even higher temperatures.

'And...' My voice sounded a little off for some reason. 'And letters to write? Is there correspondence?'

'No, Mr Linton. No letters, either.'

Now his other fingers had joined the fun, caressing the back of my hand in a complex pattern that played havoc with the rhythm of my heart. This sort of thing surely wasn't part of my contract! What the hell was going on? I should wrench my hand out of his grasp and demand an apology! Yes! I definitely should!

Only... I didn't.

'I...'

That was all I managed. One syllable. That's how dry my mouth was.

I cleared my throat. 'I... I don't...'

Yay! Two syllables!

Again I cleared my throat. 'I don't understand.'

An entire sentence! Yes! I did it! Thank you, God!

Still smiling, he trailed his thumb up and down between my fingers, leaving flames in its wake. How could a man as cold as he set me on fire like this? It was unfair! And certainly unfeminist! I had to get my act together!

'Not understand, Mr Linton?'

'No, Sir.'

That was putting it mildly. My world was doing a handstand, everything was upside down. And Mr Ambrose was still smiling at me. His teeth were brilliantly white and even, flawless like the rest of his face that seemed to be hewn out of white stone by a master artist.

'What don't you understand?'

Letting go of my hand, he settled down comfortably in the chair beside me. Gasping with relief, I snatched my hand back and sat on it. Then, realizing that this might be construed as showing that he affected me in some way – which of course he did not! – I quickly pulled it out again and folded both hands in my lap.

'What don't you understand?'

A very good question. I could start with the furniture. The chairs we were sitting in hadn't been in this office the last time, and neither had the small table around which they were arranged adjacent to one another. Whenever I had spoken to Mr Ambrose before, whether sitting or standing, I had been facing him head-on. Now I was sitting beside him.

And more importantly: we weren't having an argument. It felt weird. Extremely weird.

'What don't you understand?'

'Well...' I hesitated. 'Why haven't we started to work yet? Why are we sitting here?'

And why the heck are you being so darn nice?

He shrugged. 'Well, I thought we should talk instead of work today.'

'Talk?' I echoed.

'Yes, talk.' He sounded as if it were his favourite hobby and there was nothing strange about us sitting down for a nice chat. 'In any working relationship, it is important to establish a friendly, comfortable atmosphere. To work efficiently together, it is indispensable to get to know and trust one another.'

I wanted to say 'So when did you reach that epiphany? Was it before or after you hounded me like a slave runner yesterday?'

But before I could get the words out, he leant forward and stroked one long, smooth finger down my cheek. Just one finger. 'I want to get to know you, *Miss* Linton. I want to get to know you much better.'

My heart stopped. I'm not joking. It literally stopped right then and there. What was I going to say again? Something snarky and not very nice. The words were suddenly gone from my mind.

He called you Miss! He called you Miss! He practically admitted you're female! And that finger on your cheek...

I cleared my throat. Somehow it had gotten dry again already. 'Well... I suppose you're right.'

Cocking his head like a predator on the prowl, Mr Ambrose leant closer, almost blinding me with the shine of his smile. I could feel his breath on my cheek, right next to my finger. I had never felt anything like this before in my life – mostly because I had always stabbed a man in the gut with my parasol before he could get so close to me. But somehow I didn't feel like doing this to Mr Ambrose.

'So glad to hear you agree with me,' he murmured into my ear. 'Here, have one of these.'

Something white drifted into my line of sight. A plate of biscuits. Mr Ambrose was offering me a tray of biscuits! And by the looks of them, not cheap ones either!

This has to be a dream!

But the biscuits looked tasty, and I never said no to a tasty morsel, especially if it was sweet. Never mind that I was only dreaming it. I took one of the biscuits and carefully bit into it. It was sweet and delicious, almost as good as solid chocolate. I leant back with relish and didn't close my eyes only because I was too busy watching Mr Ambrose. He took one biscuit for himself and, leaning back away from me, bit into it with delicious slowness. Even while leaning back, though, his posture still seemed like that of a tiger ready to spring.

'We never really got around to having a nice chat,' he said. 'The start of our relationship was a little... stormy, if you recall.'

'You mean you shouting at me a lot? Yes, I recall that.'

For a moment his smile seemed to flicker. But it was over so quickly that I wasn't sure. I had probably just imagined it.

Lifting the rest of the biscuit to his mouth, he swallowed it whole, his eyes trained on me.

'Ah...' he sighed. 'A tasty morsel.'

I felt an involuntary shiver run down my back. His voice alone was more seductively sweet than all the biscuits in the world. And from the way he looked at me, he knew that. What was going on here?

'I'm actually not referring to the day when you first came into my office and we had our first altercation, Miss Linton. I'm talking about our very first meeting in the street. Do you remember?' He sighed nostalgically. 'You did me a singular service that day, Mr Linton – saving me from my own folly. And then you went into that building and later were forced out of it by two policemen. Do you remember that, too?'

I took another bite of biscuit and nodded absent-mindedly. 'It's not the kind of thing you're likely to forget.'

Before I could try to flee, before I could even tense or start to think, he had leant forward and taken my hand again. His fingers were trailing over mine, reigniting the fire.

'What kind of building was it again those cads dragged you away from? A polling station?'

'Y-yes, it was.'

'I see. Another biscuit, Miss Linton?'

'No, I...'

Before I could finish my sentence, he had picked up one of the biscuits from the plate and was lifting it to my mouth. The sweet little thing tickled my lips, enticing them to open. They did.

'And?' Mr Ambrose asked, his eyes boring into mine, his fingers still setting my hand on fire. 'Everything to your taste?'

'Y-yes. Very much so, Sir. Thank you.'

He lifted his hands in a deprecating gesture, and I quickly tucked my tingling hand away again. To hell with looking unfeminist, it was simple self-preservation!

'No need to thank me.' There was that smile again. 'By the way... why were you at the polling station? Are you interested in politics, Mr Linton?'

I couldn't suppress a smirk. 'You could say that.'

Suddenly he clapped his hands together. 'Of course! You were wearing the same attire then as you are wearing today, weren't you? Your masculine attire. And I remember the policemen saying something about what you had attempted. I didn't pay much attention at the time because, honestly, I was rather startled, but now I understand! You were trying to vote, weren't you?'

'Yes, I was.' My smirk grew into a full-blown grin – but then it abruptly turned into a grimace. 'Didn't turn out that well, though.'

'Do not be disconsolate,' he said, leaning forward, actually having a kind expression on his face. *Kind? Mr Ambrose?* This dream got weirder and weirder by the second. 'In any fight, there's always another day. And from what I know of you, you have hardly given up.'

'Well, you're right about that.'

'Is that issue something you feel passionately about? That women should be allowed to vote?'

I was touched. He really sounded interested, and his smile was so friendly... Maybe he had finally gotten over his irrational aversion to having a lady working for him. Maybe he regretted his outburst of yesterday and wanted to make it up to me. Maybe this was real after all.

'I feel passionately about living my life as I wish to,' I told him earnestly. 'And I don't care for people telling me I cannot simply because I am a girl, and not a man.'

He regarded me with shrewd eyes. 'So your quest for free will and independence – it's not just political?'

'Would I be sitting here if it were?'

'I suppose not.'

His shining smile faded a little, and his eyes became more questioning. 'Why do you do it? Why did you come here and seek work?'

Strangely, although his friendly smile was waning, he sounded even more interested than before. And so I answered: 'I don't want to be dependent on anybody. I don't want to wear chains.'

'You could marry,' he suggested, touching my hand again and sending sparks all the way up my arm. 'I'm sure that there would be many interested gentlemen.'

Not bothering to point out the unlikeness of that, I shook my head.

'Chains of gold are still chains, Mr Ambrose. I want to decide what to do with my life.' I hesitated, and then enquired: 'Why are you so interested?'

Abruptly, the beaming smile was back in full force.

'I am simply trying to get to know you a little better,' he said, spreading his arms in a gesture of innocence. 'I find that it is always much easier to achieve one's aims if one knows about people.'

I had to admit, some part of me was flattered. Suddenly, I couldn't really meet his eyes, but had to look down at the floor, abashed. He was being so... nice. I knew how to shout at nasty Mr Ambrose. I didn't really know to say to nice Mr Ambrose who touched my hand and gave me biscuits. My eyes fell on the biscuit in my hand. It was the fifth I had consumed so far. They really were excellent.

'And what about you, Sir?' I asked, feeling the need to be polite and show interest in him just as he had shown in me. 'Why do you do the things you do?'

His smile seemed to flicker once again.

'Never mind about me,' he said with a wave of his hand. 'Here, have another biscuit. And tell me more about the efforts of the suffragists. It all sounds very interesting.'

I spent the easiest day at work ever. Mostly, we talked a lot, and he smiled a lot. A very, very great lot. Sometimes I ate another biscuit. He only had me write down a single appointment: a new one for tomorrow, which he said he hadn't known about previously. I was kind of surprised he would squeeze an appointment into his timetable at such short notice, but with the brightest smile ever he told me it was very important, and I didn't like to pry.

'And by the way,' he said, 'I would like you to accompany me to this particular appointment.'

I nearly dropped the appointment book.

'But... it's after working hours,' I stammered.

'Yes it is, but it's really very important. Please? I need someone there I can rely on.'

He thought he could *rely* on *me*! And his smile was so convincing...

'Yes, of course, Sir,' I said, growing about two inches, a proud grin on my face. 'I will be there.'

'Thank you very much, Miss Linton.' His smile almost blinded me with its brilliance. 'I promise, it will be an unforgettable experience.'

After that, he didn't require much more from me. It wasn't long before he told me I could go home.

'But it's not time yet, Sir,' I protested.

He waved my protest away. 'Oh, tush! You've had a tiring day, and you're going to need all your strength for tomorrow. Turn in early and catch a good night's sleep.'

'Well... if you say so, Sir. Thanks for your concern.'

A bit flustered, I packed up my things and left the office. Was he going to keep up this behaviour? If so, things would really change around here. I could certainly use one change for the better in my life, the way the rest of it was going.

I almost ran home. My friends and I had agreed to meet in the park for some last-minute discussion and preparation before the big event tomorrow – our plan to sabotage the efforts of those evil, diabolical chauvinists who were going to meet in Hyde Park. I had told them I might be a bit late to our meeting, but now, since Mr Ambrose had let me go early, I might be able to make it in time.

Through the back door I slipped into the garden and quickly changed from male into female outfit in the garden shed. Back on the street, I wasn't quite as quick as before; apparently trousers were better suited to running than hoop skirts. But still I made pretty good time. I had almost reached Green Park when the realization hit me.

The big event was *tomorrow* – our demonstration for women's rights. Our protest action against chauvinism. Tomorrow, after working hours. Which was exactly when I had agreed to go on a special appointment with Mr Ambrose.

Blast!

I stopped in my tracks. Blast! Blast! And blast a few more times, preferably with loud explosions! What was I going to do?

For a moment, I considered going back to the office and telling Mr Ambrose that I couldn't go with him. But I discarded that idea quickly. He had been so friendly today, so accepting – I couldn't just throw that in his face. I needed the work and had to do what was necessary. My friends would understand.

Will they? Oh, sure, they'd understand if they knew your reasons. Unfortunately, though, they don't. And you can't tell them.

I really couldn't. Or could I?

For a moment, I considered the possibility. But immediately an image came into my mind of Eve jumping up and down excitedly, shouting 'What, Lilly? You run around all day dressed up in trousers?' loud enough for the entire park to hear.

I shuddered.

That image was followed by one of Flora regarding me with wide, fear-filled eyes. She wouldn't be able to sleep at night if she knew what I was up to during the day! I could tell Patsy, maybe, at some later point, but there was no way of tipping her off while the others were there.

I made my decision.

Squaring my shoulders, I started off again and, soon after, had reached our little bench by the pond where we always met. The others were already there, passing around several large cardboards and chattering excitedly. Eve spotted me first and started waving like mad. The others turned and beamed at me.

'Ah! Our general has arrived!' Patsy proclaimed. 'Ready to inspect your troops before our attack on the chauvinists of the United Kingdom of Great Britain and Ireland?'

'Well, yes... but...'

'Look here,' Patsy continued, interrupting me. 'We made signs! This is mine.'

She held up a large cardboard sign on which she had painted in large, bold, red letters:

VOTES FOR WOMEN **NOW!!**

'And this is Flora's,' she said, holding up another sign. It read, in elegant cursive script:

Please consider granting votes to women at the earliest opportunity. Thank you.

My lips twitched.

'I think I would have been able to tell which of you made which. Patsy...'

I swallowed. Now was the time. There was no way around it. 'Patsy, there's something I have to tell you all.'

'Yes, what is it?'

'I... I have to...' I stopped, not knowing what to say.

The smile slowly disappeared from her face.

'What's wrong? Has something happened to Ella? Has that fellow Wilkins...'

'No, no,' I hastened to assure her. 'It's nothing like that. Ella is fine.'

'What's the matter, then? You look strange.'

I swallowed again. Why did my throat have to be so darn dry? It wasn't like I was planning to commit a murder.

Only, it was nearly as bad. They had all looked so happy a moment ago. Now they looked at me with anxious faces. My friends – the best friends in the world. The people I was going to have to disappoint.

'Well... not to beat around the bush... to come straight to the point... I can't come tomorrow.'

'I don't understand,' Eve said, a puzzled frown on her face.

'To the demonstration. I can't come to the demonstration in Hyde Park tomorrow.'

'*What?*'

Patsy had a sergeant major's voice, and when she used it to full effect the result was deafening. Wincing, I took an involuntary step back.

'Look, it wasn't my choice. I didn't mean to...'

'You can't mean that, Lilly! You can't possibly mean that!'

She advanced on me, hands on hips, a thunderous expression on her normally so cheerful face. With relief I noted that her parasol was leaning against the bench a few yards away.

'After all the preparation we did, all the planning we put into this? Now you want to draw in your tail and run?'

'It's not like that, Patsy, really. I never...'

'And it was you who came up with the idea in the first place! I thought you were a rebel! I thought you despised oppression just as much as we do!'

'Well,' Flora dared to venture, 'I don't exactly despise op–'

Patsy shot her a steely look. 'Shut up! You'll despise oppression if I say you despise oppression, understand?'

'Yes, Patsy. Of course, Patsy.'

'Look,' I tried to reason with her. 'It's not like the demonstration won't happen. I mean, you will all be there, right? Goal achieved.'

'But *you* won't.' Eve's voice was much more quiet than usual. She was looking at me, her eyes large, and if I wasn't mistaken I could see a bit of moisture shimmering in them. 'It'll feel like a defeat if you aren't there!'

The words touched me – they *more* than touched me. They cut me to my very core, sharply and mercilessly.

'I'm sorry,' was the only thing I could think to say. 'I'm really sorry.'

Seeing that I meant it, the moisture in Eve's eyes spilled over. 'You can't do this!'

Patsy stomped over to the bench. At first I thought she was going for her parasol and retreated a few steps, but she picked up a piece of cardboard which had been leaning next to the parasol.

'Here!' She held out the cardboard to me. 'That's the sign we made for you!'

My throat felt suddenly dry. The sign read in letters even bolder than hers:
VOTES FOR WOMEN, FELLOWS... OR ELSE!

I could hardly hold back my tears. How could I desert them at a time like this? But I couldn't do anything else.

'I'm terribly sorry,' I repeated, feeling tears sting my eyes. One of them rolled down my cheeks and fell on the sign and smeared the paint. 'But I can't. I simply can't be there.'

'Why? Is something the matter with Ella?'

'No, not with Ella.'

'Then what is it?' Patsy demanded. 'What is so terribly important that you would abandon us?'

'I... I can't tell you.'

It took me about two seconds to see that that had been the wrong answer.

Patsy's eyes flashed. 'Oh, of course. Of course you can't tell *us*! Because we're only your best friends in the world. Why would we deserve your honesty or your confidence?'

'Patsy... It's not like that. I...'

But it was no good. Patsy turned away from me, towards the others.

'Come, girls,' she said to them, her voice hard. 'Let's go somewhere else, where there's no unpleasant company around.'

~~**~*~*

I cried myself to sleep that night. I, who never, ever cried.

Stupid, I told myself. *This is not the first time people have been angry with you or argued with you. Why start crying now when you never have before?*

I suppose it was that whatever trouble I had faced in the past, I always knew that I could count on my friends. Now I wasn't so sure. Maybe my friends weren't my friends anymore. Remembering the expression on Patsy's face as she turned away from me made my heart ache.

Sometime during the night, exhaustion must have overpowered me and pulled me into sleep, for I woke up the next morning, curled into a tight protective ball against the evils of the world. I had to force myself to get dressed and leave for work. If not for the fact that today was Mr Ambrose's special appointment, I doubt I would have gotten up at all.

Get a move on, I ordered my lazy limbs. *If you don't go to work and show up at that appointment, the fight with Patsy will have been for nothing!*

Somehow, I managed to drag myself to work. Through some merciful miracle, Mr Ambrose had retained his bright smile and easy manner of the previous day. He didn't put me through much work and didn't seem to notice my bad mood.

As the day progressed, thoughts of Patsy slowly retreated to the back of my mind and I began to feel hopeful. It really seemed that Mr Ambrose had turned over a new leaf. He was warm and friendly towards me in a manner I wouldn't have thought possible two days ago. I considered bringing up the matter of the search for the missing file again – I really wanted to help! But in the end I decided to wait until after his special appointment. If it went well, maybe he would be in a good mood and listen to my arguments.

'Mr Linton?'

I looked up from the files I was sorting to see Mr Stone at the door of my office. He had a nervous look on his face, but since he looked nervous pretty much all the time, I didn't pay too much attention to that.

'Yes, Mr Stone? I know it's almost closing time. I'm just putting these away and then I'll be right out.'

'I know, I know. That's not why I'm here, Mr Linton. Mr Ambrose sent me to tell you that he has ordered a carriage and is awaiting you downstairs. He says the two of you are going to a special appointment this late in the day?'

My face brightened. 'Yes, that's right. I'll be on my way down right away.'

'Good. Good.'

Mr Stone didn't leave, but hovered in the doorway. I continued putting the files away. When I was closing the box and he still hadn't moved, I asked: 'Is something else the matter, Mr Stone?'

'How kind of you to ask, Mr Linton, very kind of you. Yes, there is something, indeed. I wanted to ask... did you notice anything odd about Mr Ambrose lately?'

'Odd?'

'Yes. I couldn't help notice he has been behaving a bit... strangely. I thought you might have noticed it, too.'

'Can't say I have. In my opinion, he has been behaving like a perfectly amiable gentleman recently.'

Mr Stone cleared his throat. 'Um... well... that is kind of what I meant by "strange".' His ears reddened, and I had to fight to conceal a smile.

'Don't worry, Mr Stone. I'm sure he's perfectly fine.'

'Good, good. That's very good to hear. You've put my mind at rest, Mr Linton, thank you.'

With a quick bow of his head he hurried out of the room, and I left after him, crossing the hallway and starting down the stairs.

It was true, for Mr Ambrose, being well-mannered and smiling was strange. But good manners hadn't hurt anybody – except for me getting arrested that time because I curtsied. So why not rejoice at the change? Some small part of me was beginning to hope that maybe, just maybe, I was the reason for the improvement. Maybe I had managed to get under his granite-hard skin. The thought made me feel hot and fiery inside for some reason.

'Ah, there you are,' Mr Ambrose greeted me when I pushed open the doors of Empire House. He was standing at the foot of the stairs, smiling at me. A coach stood behind him – not a cab or a chaise, but a large and maybe even luxurious carriage such as many of the wealthy gentlemen of the city used to get around. I blinked in confusion. Again I got the uncanny feeling that something was going on here which I didn't understand. Mr Ambrose couldn't just have turned so nice by accident, could he?

'I have been eagerly awaiting your arrival,' he told me with a small bow of his head as I came down the stairs, my steps cautious, as if approaching an unknown wild animal.

'I'm sorry, Sir, if I took too long. I had a few files to put away and...'

'Don't apologize, don't apologize. After today, all these petty matters of business won't seem like much to you, I assure you.'

What did he mean by that? That the rest of my employment would be one continuous tea party?

My bewilderment grew as he opened the door and gestured for me to get in.

'Since when do gentlemen open doors for other gentlemen?' I asked archly, gesturing to my male attire.

'They do not, in general. But soon enough the perspective on what you are might shift.'

His words left me reeling. Did he mean what I thought he meant? Was he really considering to accept me as a female employee, dress and all? I hardly managed to get into the coach, my head was so full of questions. Why this sudden turnaround? How was it possible? Why now? The day before yesterday he had still been adamant about getting rid of me, adamant that I should not be involved in the investigation of the theft because this matter was too dangerous for a lady. And now... Had he changed his mind?

Somehow though, although his words seemed to indicate a change of mind, the tone made me hesitant to rejoice. There was something behind the words, some dark intent not yet revealed, that made me shiver.

Nonsense! Shaking my head, I settled down at the right window of the coach, facing the horses. *You're imagining things! Stop and enjoy the moment!*

Mr Ambrose took the seat beside me and tapped the roof of the carriage with his cane.

'You know our destination, driver. Go!'

Without a word in reply the coach started to move.

We drove in silence. There were many things I wanted to say – questions I wanted to ask, thanks I wanted to give – but something held me back. He for his part was still smiling the same brilliant smile he had worn all day yesterday and today. For the first time I had leisure to study his smile in more detail and was surprised by what I found. It somehow looked... unnatural.

I remembered the small quarter-smile he had once deigned to give me, long ago. That had seemed much more natural, much more himself. This iridescent show of teeth... If you studied it long enough it put you in mind of the smile a drowning man might see in the ocean, topped by a dorsal fin and approaching fast and hungrily.

Oh, don't be such an old worrywart! You should have a more optimistic outlook on the future!

To distract myself I looked out of the window – and jerked upright in my seat! We were going down Oxford Street, the street that led away from Leadenhall Street in a westerly direction. The direction of Hyde Park.

This had to be a strange coincidence. Surely, we would soon turn away to the left or to the right, to wherever this mysterious appointment of Mr Ambrose's was.

No, we didn't. Instead we kept going straight down Oxford Street. I was no longer lost in thought. I was hanging out of the window, gripping my uncle's old top hat with both hands to prevent it from being blown off by the wind.

'Something interesting to see, Mr Linton?' Mr Ambrose's voice came from within the coach. I didn't reply. There were indeed a great many things to be seen: the closer we got to Hyde Park, the more people were milling in the streets. Apparently they were heading towards the park. A great event seemed about to take place.

He calls you Mister again. Something is happening here.

Over the heads of the crowd, I could see the black iron of Cumberland Gate in the distance. The gate stood wide open, and loud voices drifted from the Park in our direction.

Naturally they did. This was the northeast corner of the Park, after all: Speaker's Corner.[43]

There were several people there, standing on wooden boxes or on the ground. But nearly all of them had given up trying to catch the crowd's attention. The focus was clearly on a group of important-looking men standing on a large podium right behind Cumberland Gate.

Then I saw the large banner suspended over the podium.

'MEETING OF THE ANTI-SUFFRAGIST LEAGUE – UNITE IN THE STRUGGLE FOR THE NATURAL WORLD ORDER AND WOMAN'S GOD-GIVEN PLACE IN THE WORLD'

My head whipped to the side to stare at Mr Ambrose – just in time to see the smile drain from his face like wet paint from a wall in the middle of a hailstorm. And I realized that was all it had ever been: paint, over a perfect, cold, merciless granite statue.

The coach stopped.

'Come, Mr Linton,' he ordered, meeting my eyes with his icy gaze and pushing open the door. 'Or else we shall be late for this very important event.'

AM I A CHIMPANZEE?

'What is this?'

My voice didn't sound like my own. It sounded as if it were coming from very, very far away.

Mr Ambrose sprang out of the coach and looked up at me. 'What do you think it is? It is me expressing my cherished political opinions for the good of Britain and the Empire.'

His voice sounded exactly like his own. In fact, it sounded more like his own than it had done during the entirety of the last two days. Gone was the friendliness. Gone was the interest. Gone was the politeness. Gone was all the pretence.

And I suddenly understood what this was all about. His words rang in my head like a great brass bell:

You can stay – until and unless you leave of your own free will. And I will find a way to persuade you.

---

[43] Speaker's Corner in Hyde Park, London, is an area where for a long time in English history, anybody has traditionally been allowed to publicly speak and debate on important political and social issues. Many important events, meetings and demonstrations have taken place there, and the idea of a speaker's corner has been taken up by a lot of other countries and cities.

This was his way. His way to get rid of me. His way to make me hate him so much that I couldn't stand to be in his company anymore, let alone in his employ. I threw a glance at the banner over the podium and shuddered. So he wanted to make me hate him, eh? Well, he was going about it right. Whatever else you could say of him, he knew me well.

I stole a glance at his immovable marble face. He... he couldn't really believe that, could he? He couldn't really be on the same side as those blasted chauvinists?

But then my eyes wandered to his dark, ice-cold eyes.

Are you kidding? Of course he can! Look at him! He's probably spearheading their movement!

And as much as I hated my inner voice right at that moment, I had, for once, to agree with it. If there ever was a man who crushed anything in his path, it was Rikkard Ambrose. Arrogance and raw masculinity rolled off him in waves that were almost tangible. The bastard!

Anger surged up inside me.

So what? So what if he was in cahoots with them? I would be damned if I let his intrigues deprive me of this once-in-a-lifetime opportunity! I didn't care whether he thought I couldn't handle the dangers of my job, I would prove him wrong! And I would begin proving him wrong by surviving this humiliation! How bad could it be? I only had to stand beside him, after all.

Yes. Stand beside him and listen while he defiles the most sacred beliefs of your heart.

Oh, thank you very much for pointing that out. Thank you!

Leaving the coach in the capable hands of the driver, Mr Ambrose strode towards Cumberland Gate and the park beyond, myself close at his heels. In spite of the masses of people gathered at the northeast corner of the park, we had no problems finding our way towards Speaker's Corner. People made way for Mr Ambrose as if he were the King of England. Well, in a sense he was the king of his personal empire. Did the people around us know that? Or did they just feel the iron aura of authority that surrounded him?

'... have developed a theory which rests on my study of the female brain. Though spurned by my colleagues at Cambridge University, I, Professor William H. Anstruther, am wholeheartedly convinced of this theory. It may be years ahead of scientific thinking today, but that only adds to its brilliance.'

Looking up, I saw that there was a man at the front of the podium, speaking to the crowd. He was a thin fellow, with a thin moustache and thin voice. Nevertheless, the crowd seemed to be listening intently.

'Based on my measurements of female head circumferences,' the man continued, 'I have concluded that their capacity for logical thought is far behind that of any man. Throughout my studies, this empirical conclusion was supported by behavioural evidence: a great many of the females I approached as potential test subjects frankly refused to have their head shorn in order for me to be able to take their measurements.'

I opened my mouth to laugh – however, then I took a look around and saw other people nodding and exchanging looks of satisfaction. Bloody hell! The people here were actually taking this seriously!

By now, Mr Ambrose and I had approached the side of the platform, where a staircase led upwards. A young underling in a too-big suit waited there and almost fell over himself when he recognized the man who was coming towards him.

'Mr Ambrose!'

If he had bowed any deeper, his nose would have brushed the ground. I threw him a disgusted glance he didn't notice. His attention was fully focused on my loathsome, conniving, cold-hearted bastard of an employer.

'W-we are t-terribly honoured that you could join us here t-today, Sir,' the young man stuttered. 'It is not often that we have the good fortune of a man of your stature lending his support to our venture. We cannot thank you enough...'

'Mr Cartwright is waiting for me?' Mr Ambrose cut him off.

'W-well, yes, Sir,' the young man answered, not seeming in the least offended at this gross violation of good manners. 'He has been eagerly a-awaiting your a-arrival, Sir. He was so thrilled w-when we received notice of your intention...'

'Lead me to him!'

'W-why, yes, of course, Sir. F-follow me.'

The stutterer started to stumble up the stairs, and we followed with enough distance so as not to run into him, should he trip over his own feet.

'Why so abrupt, Mr Ambrose?' I hissed at the broad, ramrod-straight back in front of me. 'Don't you like to be flattered?'

'I don't like wasting my time, Mr Linton – which is, essentially saying the same.'

'If you don't like wasting your time, then why are we here?'

'Because this is a very important event which will further one of the most important aims in my life.'

I clenched my teeth together.

Don't say anymore! Don't say another word to him, or you will start screaming and cursing, or try to attack him!

So stopping women from getting the vote was one of the great aims of his life? He was very lucky that, unlike Patsy, I didn't carry a parasol around with me wherever I went!

Thinking of Patsy made my heart ache again. What had I done! Betraying my friends, forsaking them in their hour of need, and for what? For *this*? For having to stand idly by and do nothing while Professor William H. Anstruther propounded his theories about female head circumferences? And let me tell you, he was still very busily propounding.

'And refusing to take part in my experiment was not the only manner in which females exhibited strange behaviour,' Professor Anstruther proclaimed with a raised finger. 'Oh no. Furthermore, completely insensible of the vast contribution to scientific progress they might have made, several of the females I approached about shaving their head even started to exhibit unnecessarily emotional behaviour, screaming for help and doubting my mental health, in very strong language. Through such irrational behaviour, they only confirmed my belief that their mental capacity is vastly inferior to that of men in general.

It is now up to you, lords, ladies and gentlemen, to use the results of my work and implement...'

'Mr C-Cartwright?'

My attention snapped back from the professor to our stuttering companion. We had reached the top of the stairs by now. A group of well-dressed men was waiting there, at the back of the podium. Doubtless they would all take their turns smashing the aspirations of modern womanhood. I let my eyes wander over them. Lords, industrialists, priests and scientists... it seemed the powerful of this world were out to trample my dreams. Well, since it was me, what else was to be expected?

Stuttermouth had lead us to a portly figure with a neat black beard, before whom he bowed nearly as deeply as he had done in front of Mr Ambrose. The other man nodded back.

'Mr C-Cartwright? I have b-brought you our special g-guest. May I introduce you to Mr R-Rikkard Ambrose, who has kindly agreed to s-support us in our efforts t-today? Mr Ambrose, this is Mr C-Cartwright, the organizer of this little initiative.'

Mr Cartwright's face split into a delighted smile, and he bowed deeply.

'Mr Ambrose! Welcome! I must say, I was most pleasantly surprised when I received your message yesterday that you had decided you would support us. It is not often that a man of your stature involves himself in politics.'

Mr Ambrose eyes remained as cold and distant as ever. He did not smile. He did not bow. 'When there is a good cause to be aided, I cannot simply stand back and do nothing, Mr Cartwright.'

'That is a very admirable quality in you, Mr Ambrose. And who is this gentleman, if I may ask?'

The fiend gestured to me.

For a moment I thought the ghost of a smile flickered over Mr Ambrose's face. But no, I had to be wrong. Mr Ambrose did not make use of something as wasteful as a smile – unless he was utilizing it to manipulate people, of course! Bastard!

'That is my private secretary, Mr Victor Linton. He has a keen interest in matters of gender-politics and so I brought him along. I'm sure it will be a valuable lesson for him.'

Gah! Go on! Strangle him! It'll be worth the life-long prison sentence! Just do it!

Valuable lesson my foot! I hardly noticed when Mr Cartwright bowed to me as well and said, brightly:

'I'm delighted to make your acquaintance, Mr Linton. I hope you enjoy our little gathering.'

I didn't quite know what to answer to that. Making his acquaintance created several powerful feelings in me – delight was definitely not among them. So I just bowed and muttered something unintelligible. He smiled and directed his stuttering assistant to lead us to an empty place in the row of waiters at the back of the platform, right beside a deaf old duke. We were right among the nobs, apparently.

'So I have a keen interest in gender-politics, do I?' I hissed into Mr Ambrose's ears as soon as stuttermouth had vanished.

'Well, you do, don't you?'

'Do you know what I have a keen interest in right now? Bashing your face in!'

He didn't flinch.

'Calm your overexcited feminine temperament, Mr Linton,' he advised. 'No one is threatening to shear *your* head. Not yet, at least.'

'You...!'

But before I could specify my opinion of Mr Rikkard Ambrose, a roar of applause went up from the crowd. Either Professor Anstruther had just reached a very convincing argument in his theory, or his place had been taken by a stand-up comedian from the nearest music hall.

I took a look and sighed with resignation. No, it was still Anstruther, propounding his opinions. By now he had reached a detailed analysis of the differing head circumferences of females and males, and was comparing female human skulls to those of various apes.

'The most similarities I have observed are to be found between women and chimpanzees,' he was just saying, to another round of applause from the crowd. 'Their heads show about the same growth pattern.'[44]

'Interesting theory, don't you think?' Mr Ambrose commented, in a voice so low only I could hear. 'Especially considering their comparable intellectual capabilities.'

I balled my little hands into fists. They felt so insignificant. If only they were larger and stronger. If only *I* were. Strong enough to withstand this.

'You are despicable,' I informed Mr Ambrose. 'I really ought to teach you a lesson!'

'Really?' He cocked his head, looking at me with calculating cold eyes. 'I am quite sure that an assault on your employer would be in contradiction of our agreement and that I would be perfectly within my rights to release you from my service. But if you think it is worth it...' His cold gaze wandered to my clenched fists. 'Do not let me stop you.'

Taking a deep breath, I tried to relax my fingers.

You can do this, I told myself. *You can do this!*

My fingers didn't relax. But I didn't punch him either.

'I know what you're doing,' I informed him. 'And it is not working.'

'Indeed?'

'Yes. You're trying to get me to give you a reason to sack me.'

'I see.'

---

[44] Professor Anstruther is a product of my imagination. However, he is based on scientists of the Victorian Age who propounded similar theories, connecting head size or facial features to intelligence and character traits. For instance, Cesare Lombroso, an Italian criminologist and physician, came up with the theory that criminality is not a character flaw, but an inherited trait, and that it can be recognized by studying a person's facial features. Nice, isn't it?

'But I will not. You're trying to get rid of me because you don't think I can do my job properly, but I will prove you wrong!'

'So that is my sinister motivation? How deplorably easy I am to see through.'

Was that sarcasm in his voice? No, it couldn't be. After all, sarcasm was a form of humour.

I didn't reply to his words, choosing instead to lapse into silence. So did he. I simply stood there and endured, while Mr Ambrose waited for me to crack.

I did not.

Maybe he was surprised by my endurance as I listened to Professor Anstruther droning on and on about women and chimpanzees. But there was something I knew that he didn't. I had something to look forward to. Maybe, just maybe, this event wouldn't go quite as Mr Ambrose had anticipated.

It was during a particularly long-winded sub-speech on chimpanzee mating practices that what I had waited for finally came. A shout went up from the back of the crowd, and a waving sign appeared over the heads of the assembled people.

The sign read:

VOTES FOR WOMEN **NOW!**

'Forward, girls!' A familiar voice rose up, drowning out Anstruther without much difficulty. 'For the oppressed women of Britain!'

~~**~*~*

People made way for Patsy & Co extremely quickly. That might have been partly because of the menacing way in which Patsy wielded her parasol, but her mere presence would have parted the masses as Moses had parted the red sea. Only that the red sea had probably not been that afraid of Moses.

'Down with chauvinist oppression! Votes for women now! Votes for women now!'

I was so proud of my friends, as I watched them marching through the crowd, chorusing their beliefs for all the world to hear! Unthinkingly, my feet moved forward to join them – but then I remembered: I was in men's clothes!

I wasn't Miss Lilly Linton, dedicated suffragist, I was Mr Victor Linton, private secretary to Mr Rikkard Ambrose. If only I had known more swear words! I would have dearly liked to curse my trousers and the man who had forced me to put them on with every existing expletive in the world!

'Votes for women now! Here, educate your mind, Sir. Take this leaflet! Broaden your horizons, madam. Do you really think you are unfit to make decisions that men can make? Here, take a look at our pamphlet.'

They had now started handing out flyers among the crowd. I had never even known they had prepared any! That served me right. I had been so caught up in Ella's problems and my work for Mr Ambrose that I had totally neglected my friends. And the worst thing was: I couldn't even tell them why!

'This is outrageous!'

Mr Cartwright had appeared at our side. The portly man, who had looked so friendly just a moment ago, was glaring at Patsy with an intensity I hadn't thought him capable of. 'How dare this lady interrupt our event! Oh, what am I saying? Female, not lady! You cannot with a clear conscience call such a wanton creature a lady!'

Mr Ambrose nodded. 'I agree.'

'What do you think, Mr Ambrose? Should I have her removed?'

Without meaning to, I shook my head. Have Patsy removed? 'I don't think that would be a good idea.'

'Bad press, you mean, manhandling a woman?' Mr Cartwright snorted. 'Unfortunately, you're probably right, Mr Linton.'

It wasn't easy to suppress my smile. That wasn't what I had been thinking of, actually. Patsy had her parasol with her. If some men attempted to 'remove' her, I wouldn't like to be in those men's shoes.

Hm... why not let them try?

'Miss! Mind your manners!' Professor Anstruther waved imperiously at Patsy and rustled with his scholarly papers. 'Surely you do not intend to disturb my speech?'

'Oh yes, that's exactly what I intend! Votes, ladies and gentlemen, votes for women!'

'I beg your pardon?' The professor was turning red in the face. He sounded as if he wished a quick disappearance from Patsy, rather than her pardon. 'It is the right of every Englishman to freely speak his mind on Speaker's Corner! How dare you interrupt me?'

'Oh, you can talk as much as you want,' Patsy agreed, not stopping with the flyer distribution or even bothering to look up. 'That doesn't mean, though, that I can't talk back to you. Votes for women, ladies and gentlemen! For equality between the sexes and a bright future for Britain!'

'The head circumference of the chimpanzee...' Professor Anstruther continued, raising his voice – but to no avail. Patsy raised her voice, too, to heights he couldn't hope to reach.

'A bright future,' she called, 'where no women will be pestered to shave their heads without good cause!'

There were snickers from the crowd, and a few of the ladies present surreptitiously grabbed one of the flyers, studying with interest.

'...circus dance... no, circumference, I beg your pardon, lords, ladies and gentlemen, circumference, of course.... yes, the head circumference of the chimpanzee is similar to that of females from the age of...'

'Women contribute to life in Great Britain just as much as men do,' Patsy proclaimed. 'Why should they not have the same rights? Read the pamphlet, make up your own mind.'

'...the age of seven is equal to the male head circus tents, as my thesis has proven and... Blast it!'

Professor Anstruther had dropped his notes and was now on his knees, trying to salvage as much of his marvel of anthropological science as he possible could. All that remained of his speech against suffragism were a few very unscholarly curses.

'A disaster! A downright disaster!' Mr Cartwright was wringing his hands now, and it was a joy to see. 'Mr Firth, the next speaker, is supposed to arrive in only half an hour! What am I supposed to do? Curse these infernal suffragists!'

It was becoming increasingly difficult to keep a sombre and worried expression on my face. All I wanted to do was run to Patsy, hug her and congratulate her on her glorious victory against the masculine forces of evil! It took all my willpower to stay still and pull the corners of my mouth down.

'Are you having facial cramps, Mr Linton?' Mr Ambrose enquired out of the corner of his mouth.

'No, Sir. I'm just enjoying myself.'

'Is that so, Mr Linton?'

'Yes, it is, Mr Ambrose.'

'Well, let us see what we can do to change that.'

With two swift motions, Mr Ambrose removed his gloves and his top hat. Then he handed both, along with his cane, to Mr Cartwright, who took it all, too surprised at being treated like a common footman to refuse.

'Hold these for me, will you?' Mr Ambrose flexed his fingers. Suddenly, I felt a cold pit opening up in my stomach. No. Oh no. 'I have work to do.'

He strode towards the front of the podium, shoved the kneeling Professor Anstruther aside none too gently and built himself in front of the crowd. Shouldn't I have said planted himself? No, he was too hard, too cold for a plant. He built himself like a monument of stone and metal.

I watched, dread welling up inside me, as the crowd whispered excitedly, my friends stopped moving and all eyes went to him. Especially the female ones.

Mr Ambrose took a deep breath and opened his lips to speak.

Memorable Speeches

'Silence.'

The word wasn't shouted. It wasn't even loud. It was simply spoken with such chilling precision, with such power behind it, that all went silent instantly. The crowd, the birds, the other speakers in the distance, even – I could hardly believe it – Patsy closed her mouth and stared up at Mr Rikkard Ambrose. When she took in his six foot six of poor, hard masculinity, she nearly dropped her sign, and for a moment, 'VOTES FOR WOMEN **NOW**!' was upside down.

Placing his hands on the balustrade, Mr Ambrose leaned forward, towering over the crowd.

'My lords, ladies, gentlemen.' He gave a curt nod. 'I do not pretend to be as well-versed in scientific knowledge as our friend the professor here.' With a derisive movement of his head, he gestured to his red-faced predecessor on the podium, who was backing away now, the remnants of his speech clutched against his chest. 'I am no scientist. I am just a simple entrepreneur who has made it his business to own as large a portion of the world as possible.'

Chuckles rose up from the crowd. They thought he was cracking a joke. I knew better.

'My name,' he continued, cutting through the chuckles like a sword through silk, 'is Mister Rikkard Ambrose.'

The chuckles died abruptly. Eyes widened, mouths dropped open. Some people took a step backward. Aghast, I watched as he transformed the crowd. It was obvious he was far better known and his wealth far more legendary than I had imagined. They all knew of him. He had hardly had to say a word, and already he had them in his hands. A mountain of money combined with his magnetic and menacing presence was all that was needed.

'So far,' he told his loyal audience when he was sure his words had taken their full effect, 'I have met with not inconsiderable success in this venture to enlarge my power. And that is what I am going to talk to you about today, my lords, ladies and gentlemen: success and power. Trust me, I am an expert on the subject.'

He let his cold gaze wander across the crowd, at last fixing it on Patsy as if daring her to contradict this. She did not.

'I would be the last one to deny, my lords, ladies and gentlemen, that if women and men were equal, they would deserve equal rights.'

There were gasps from the crowd. Patsy grinned.

Abruptly, he held up a single finger. 'However...'

Her grin vanished.

'However, this is not the case. Women are weaker than men.'

My hands, which had relaxed a little up to this point, formed fists again. They ached to find a target to practise on, and the lean, black-clad man at the front of the podium looked deliciously tempting. His cold, gorgeous face seemed to be downright begging to be punched!

'Wonderful,' that slug, Cartwright, murmured beside me. 'See how he commands the audience? Simply wonderful! Did you know your employer was such an accomplished orator, Mr Linton?'

'No,' I managed to get out between my grinding teeth. 'Usually he's rather terse. This seems to be... a special occasion.'

'I see. Well, if I should not get the opportunity, please do give him my thanks for exerting himself for our sake.'

'I will, Mr Cartwright. And don't worry, I won't hold back my feelings on the subject.'

'That's very kind of you.'

'You may now justly ask – how do I know this?' Mr Ambrose called, pointing at the audience. He seemed to be reading the question out of their eyes. 'How do I know of women's weakness? Have I scientific evidence?'

He gave a derisive snort and swept his arm around in one large gesture, including all around him.

'I say to you, lords, ladies and gentlemen, that all I need is the evidence of my own eyes! Do you see any women as prime ministers? As generals of our army? As admirals of our navy? As leading entrepreneurs in our country's industry? No! Women have not been fighting and working alongside men for hundreds, for thousands of years. Why then, I ask you, should they be granted that equality right now, only because they are seized by a sudden fancy?'

The men in the crowd were muttering their assent. Women were lowering their eyes demurely, as if afraid to meet his cold, implacable gaze. I could hardly believe it! Even Flora and Eve had cast their eyes down. Only Patsy was still staring at him, the expression of hate on her face the second most intense one in all of London.

Guess whose was first?

Yeah. You guessed right.

If my hate had been fire, Mr Ambrose would have been a smouldering pile of ashes by now. *Women are weak?* So that was what he thought of me? That was why he was trying to get rid of me? After all I had done, all the effort I had put into convincing him that I was loyal, trustworthy and reliable, he still saw me as a weakling, a shadow of the man he could have working for him.

The crowd was getting more excited now. Mr Ambrose raised his voice, and his fist along with it, hard as stone.

'Women have shown us for hundreds of years that they are weaker than men, that they require protection – protection which we have given them, because they are weak and we are strong! This world is about the survival of the strong. How can we grant political rights, the rights to govern our very own nation, to the weak when our enemies would leap at the chance to exploit any weakness?'

With a swift, cutting gesture, he brought down his fist diagonally, cutting off the mere notion of such foolishness. Even through my rage I had to admit – he was good. Infuriating and chauvinistic and exactly what I despised in every other possible way – but he was good at what he did.

'I tell you, we cannot afford it! And I tell you that in all my travels around all the colonies of the great British Empire and beyond, I have never encountered a woman who would deserve to be called strong, who would deserve to be called my equal!'

It was then that Patsy decided she had had enough. She stepped forward, holding up her 'VOTES FOR WOMEN **NOW**!' sign like a shield.

'Really?' she called to him. 'Maybe you should look over here!'

No! Here! I growled in my mind. If any girl was going to show this arrogant son of a bachelor what females were capable of, it was going to be me!

Mr Ambrose's cold gaze met Patsy's – and she took another step back.

'How much money do you earn, miss?' he asked.

Patsy blushed.

'Well... I don't, not as such...'

'How many battles have you fought in?'

'Battles? But I'm a girl, I...'

She stopped, biting her lip in fury. Around her, snickers rose up from the crowd.

'Ah.' Mr Ambrose nodded. 'So you don't want to have to fight in wars. You just want to vote, do you? Well, since you want to vote, I'm sure you're up-to-date on politics.'

'I... well...'

'Tell me, I'm curious: what is your opinion on our current political situation in regard to the French Empire?'

'I... I don't know.'

'Strange, for someone as interested in politics as you. Then tell me, what is our gross national income?'

'I don't know that either! I'm not–'

'What about all the cabinet ministers and their political affiliations and allies in the House of Commons?'

Patsy's hand were balled into tight fists around her sign. 'I–don't–know!'

With a sigh, Mr Ambrose turned from her and nodded, as if she were not even worth another look.

'I rest my case. Think on what I have said, my lords, ladies and gentlemen, for I am not a man to repeat myself. Success comes from power, and power comes from man. It always has. It always will.'

With a curt bow, he stepped back. The crowd was muttering and nodding. His speech was unlike any other they had heard so far, I could see that just from watching them. It also was a heck of a lot more effective.

As he walked back to me, an expression of cold superiority on his face, I glared at Mr Ambrose in pure rage. How could I ever have believed I could not hate this man? Well, now he had revealed himself for what he really was. I would not make the mistake of trusting him again.

'Wonderful! Simply wonderful!'

Stepping forward, Mr Cartwright grasped Mr Ambrose by the hand and shook it energetically, not seeming to notice that Mr Ambrose looked down at the hand clutching his as if it were the arm of a slimy squid that was smearing goo all over his black jacket.

'You were marvellous, Mr Ambrose! I don't know how to thank you! How you put that shrew in her place... I have never seen anything like it in my life. On behalf of our little community, let me offer you our deepest thanks.'

I could almost see the letters *wasted time* blinking in Mr Ambrose's cool eyes as he directed them at Mr Cartwright.

'It was nothing,' he said, curtly, and pulled his hand from the other's grasp. 'It was simply the truth.'

Just as he said this, he looked at me, and our eyes met.

Oh yes, I hated him. But if he thought that this was going to make me give up my position, he was in for a disappointment!

'What did you think of my speech, Mr Linton?'

I did my best to keep my voice steady.

'It was very... impressive.'

'Indeed? Was it, Mr Linton?'

'Yes, Sir.'

I wouldn't scream! I wouldn't attack him, no matter how much I might have wanted to! And I most certainly wouldn't leave his employment! Not because of something like this. I'd had to listen to chauvinist diatribes all my life. Maybe none quite so terrifyingly effective as his had been, but still. I had only had to stand there and listen. It wasn't as if I had to do anything.

'I'm glad to hear that,' Mr Ambrose told me in such a low voice that only I could hear. 'Because the fun is only just beginning.'

That didn't sound good...

Calm, I reminded myself. *You only have to listen. Just to stand still and listen.*

'Thank you for your appreciation, my dear Mr Cartwright.' Without warning, Mr Ambrose turned back to the black-bearded man. 'I'm very flattered that you think so much of my oratory skills – particularly since you will be in for another, similar treat today.'

Cartwright's eyes widened.

'You mean...'

'Yes!' Swift as a cobra, Mr Ambrose whirled to face me once again. 'Now, Mr Cartwright,' he said in a voice so cold and calculating that the devil would have been envious, 'my trusted friend and employee Mr Victor Linton would like to say a few words on the subject.'

For a few moments, his words failed to register. Then comprehension sank in, and as the comprehension came, the colour drained from my face.

'You can't be serious!' My voice was just a hoarse whisper.

'Do I,' he enquired, his gaze as arctic as the heart of an iceberg, 'look like I am joking?'

I stepped closer and leant forward so Cartwright couldn't hear us. As I spoke, there wasn't just anger in my voice. There was desperation and pleading. But I didn't care.

'You... you can't do this to me. You can't! I won't do it!'

'You will, unless you want to lose your position, Mr Linton.'

Taking me by the arm, he manoeuvred me forward. I tried to pull away, but his grip was like granite. Soon I was standing at the edge of the podium, facing the crowd. Hundreds of eager faces looked up at me, expecting me to betray my most cherished beliefs.

'Go on,' he whispered in my ear. 'Speak. And make it memorable, if you ever wish to receive your first month's wages.'

Hundreds of people were looking up at me expectantly. The silence stretched.

What am I going to say? What in heaven's name am I going to say?

I opened my mouth.

And I closed it again.

And opened it again.

And closed it again.

I can't do this. I can't speak out against everything I believe in!

Then I heard a gasp from one of the expectant people. Instinctively, I looked in the direction of the noise and, with a nasty shock, saw who it was: Patsy. And in her eyes I saw what she saw. All the other people might see a small young man with shoulder-long hair standing on the platform, opening and closing his mouth like a suffocating goldfish. But she saw her friend, Lilly, dressed in trousers and a baggy old tailcoat, standing amongst her worst enemies.

Our eyes met.

And suddenly, I had an idea. Suddenly, I knew what I was going to say.

Swallowing hard, I raised my chin and stared down the crowd with strength and nobility shining out of my eyes – or at least that's what I hope it looked like.

'I think,' I began, my voice not nearly as weak as I had feared it would be, 'that it is time for us to reconsider our antiquated prejudices. I think it is time that we grant women the rights that have too long been denied them. Political rights are rights of self-expression. Would you deny a woman the right to express her heart and her soul? To aid in the forming of the country which is as much hers as it is any man's? I stand here today to tell you: we need women's suffrage in Great Britain!'

There were cheers and claps from the women among the crowd. There were even a few claps and cheers from those men who were too slow to realize what I had actually been saying.

We *need* women's suffrage.

Not we *don't* need women's suffrage.

Out of the corners of my eyes I could see the happy smiles on the faces of Mr Cartwright and his cronies slowly dissolve. I saw Mr Ambrose, too. He, of course, had no happy smile to dissolve in the first place. But I noticed him stiffening, and a certain pallor creep over his features.

'Women and girls of Great Britain!' I shouted. 'You are not alone! Even–' I had to work hard to suppress a smirk, '–among the hardest conservatives such as Mr Ambrose and myself, there are those who have been secretly convinced of the righteousness of your cause; they are just too afraid to admit it!'

Turning my head slightly, I gave Mr Ambrose a small, meaningful smile. The eyes of every member of the audience followed the motion, mesmerized. His face... Oh my God, his face!

With difficulty, I managed to tear myself away from the sight and face the audience again.

'Do not give up! Eventually, the resistance shall crumble and the way shall be open to a Britain in which all people, men and women alike, are allowed to express their political opinions freely and without having to fear reprisals. Stand fast, and you will be victorious!'

In the midst of the crowd, I could see Patsy gesturing wildly to Flora and Eve, who had already started to retreat when Mr Ambrose had held his speech, terrified by his unforgiving glare. Now, they had turned around and come back to Patsy, who whispered excitedly to them. She kept pointing up at the podium, up at the speaker.

The two girls looked up at the speaker – and their eyes went wide. I smiled at them, and their mouths dropped open.

Mr Cartwright was now shaking his head in confusion, looking between me and Mr Ambrose. Other members of the assembled anti-suffragist organization had stuck their fingers in their ears and started cleaning them, as if they were sure that what they were hearing would change once they had gotten rid of residual earwax. Only the deaf old duke beside Mr Ambrose was looking just as cheerful as before, probably because he couldn't understand a word I was saying.

'I heard a story the other day from one of my closest acquaintances,' I continued, marvelling at the fact that I was holding a speech I had never actually rehearsed. Apparently my acting skills went beyond simple lying. 'She had decided to take it upon herself to fight the unfair laws of her country, to rebel, and dress up as a man in order to vote. And can you imagine what happened? When discovered for what she truly was, the poor young lady was dragged off like a criminal and put into prison! Into prison, ladies and gentlemen! And people wonder why there are no female politicians and generals, when the mere attempt to speak your mind can get you thrown in jail?'

My fist slammed down on the lectern.

'And do you know what is the most outrageous? People who allow this dare to call themselves gentlemen, and dare to say that women's suffrage would put an end to chivalry! I say the contrary – *men's suffrage* puts an end to chivalry! It already has put an end to it for hundreds of years! No true gentlemen would allow a lady to be treated thus!'

There were calls of agreement from the crowd, both ladies and gentlemen. Three ladies in the midst of all were leading the way, clapping and yelling enthusiastically: Patsy, Eve and Flora were all grinning like lunatics on a field trip to the circus. Eve could hardly hold herself upright, she was laughing so hard. Patsy met my eyes again. There was a fiery glow in hers that spread over her entire, broad, apple-cheeked face, and in that moment I knew that I was forgiven. Or rather, that there was nothing to forgive at all.

'Women deserve suffrage! So we have no prime ministers who are women, nor generals, nor admirals, nor entrepreneurs! What does it matter? For, let us not forget,' I said, raising my finger, 'let us never forget, that they all rank beneath one individual, one mighty sovereign who eclipses them all in her glory – our sovereign, Her Majesty, Queen Victoria, a woman! Long live the Queen! Long live suffragism!'

All over the square shouts of 'Long live the Queen!' rose up. Even the sour-faced men behind me started to fall in with the rest of us. You had to. It was practically built into the English national character to want the queen to live long, and to say so at every available opportunity. Never had I heard anybody say 'Short live the Queen!' or 'Gruesomely die the Queen!' My words were the perfect thing to say, at just the right moment. They united my audience. Mixed in with the royal shouts, I could even make out one or two yells of 'Long live suffragism!'

I was on a roll! I would have continued bewitching the masses, and no doubt started a revolution in the middle of Hyde Park that very day, but before I could continue my speech, rough, manly hands grabbed me from behind. A few of the anti-suffragists had finally grasped what I was actually saying. They started to drag me backwards, away from my audience. At least I got out a last shout of 'Long live suffragism!' before I was towed off the podium. Out of the corner of my eye I saw my friends whooping and waving their signs in support for the best speaker of the day.

The door slammed open when he kicked against it. None too gently, he pushed me into his office and strode in after me. Staggering backwards, I managed to right myself again just in time to face him as he whirled towards me.

'You!'

Have you ever heard the phrase 'chilling contempt' before? Well, you don't know the full meaning of the phrase until you've heard a few words out of the mouth of Mr Rikkard Ambrose when he's really cold under the collar. Burning cold.

'You,' he whispered, and his voice sent chills down my back. 'You will regret this. You will regret this very much.'

I raised my chin defiantly.

'Indeed? What will I regret? Speaking the truth?'

'You will regret making fun of me in public. It is not something I tolerate.'

'Making fun?' Now my voice turned cold too. 'I couldn't see anything funny about the proceedings at Speaker's Corner today. I was dead serious.'

He raised a threatening finger and, almost against my will, I took a few steps back, retreating until his desk stood between him and me. In the park, he'd had two other man grab me and drag me to the coach, and back to Empire House. Inside, he had driven me indoors and up the stairs simply by the icy force of his eyes. Only as he had reached the door to his office had he touched me, once, a sign that his walls of cold control were finally starting to crack beneath the strain.

I was afraid. Afraid what might happen if that wall broke down and the creature beyond the façade of the cool businessman broke free. And yet, I was also strangely fascinated. There was tension between him and me that made me want to grab that threatening finger he was waving in my face, pull it towards me, pull *him* towards me and... do what exactly?

I didn't know! But something inside me screamed for some kind of release.

He took another step closer. He was close enough to touch now, although the desk was still between us. Somehow, I both felt safer behind it and wished for it to be gone.

'You made a laughing stock of me in front of the entire city of London,' he growled.

'Indeed?' I raised a sceptical eyebrow. 'Several million people live in the city of London. I didn't see that many at that silly event.'

'You know perfectly well what I mean, Mr Linton! There were reporters there!'

Oops. Actually, I hadn't noticed that. Oh well, I had been busy holding speech.

'Tomorrow, the entire city will know about this disgraceful charade! Soon, it will be on the front page of *The Times*! Maybe there will even be a semi-humorous image of the episode in the *The Spectator*!'

For a moment, I imagined a comical drawing of the sinister Mr Ambrose being chased around Hyde Park by Patsy swinging her 'VOTES FOR WOMEN NOW!'-sign appearing in London's most widely read illustrated magazine. The image made me feel warm inside and conjured a smile on my face.

'That sounds good.'

'Not good for you!' Raising his arm, he pointed to the door of his office. 'Get out! You are dismissed from my service.'

The words fell like an axe. I stiffened. My smile was gone as quickly as it had come. 'On what grounds?'

'You dare to ask that? You disobeyed a direct order!'

'I did not!'

'You have an hour to pack your things, and then I want you go–' His voice cut off. Only now did he seem to register that I had spoken. *'What did you say?'*

Stubbornly, I repeated: 'I did not disobey any direct order.'

'But you–'

'When we stood on the podium and you leaned over to whisper into my ear, you told me to go and say something memorable. You didn't specify what exactly it was I should say. And no matter whether or not you liked it, I'm pretty sure what I said was memorable.'

I gave him my sweetest smile. 'But if you want, we can wait and see what *The Spectator* has to say on the subject.'

He moved so quickly I hardly saw him coming. In a flash he was around the desk and had grabbed me by the arms. An instant later he had pushed me back and up against the wall.

'Do not dare to make fun of me,' he hissed, his quiet voice colder than ever, his eyes shards of furious ice. 'You would not like the consequences!'

For some insane reason, the smile on my face didn't vanish, but widened into a reckless grin. His fingers were digging hard into my flesh, but I didn't care. I had finally managed to rattle him, to get under that granite skin of his!

'Ah, so you're *manhandling* me now, Sir? Does that mean you have decided I am enough of a *man* for you?'

He didn't answer. Instead, his grip tightened and he pressed me harder against the wall, his sea-coloured eyes darkening to the depths of the ocean.

I suddenly realized how tightly his body was pressed against mine. I could feel every muscle in his chest as it heaved in an effort to steady his breathing, could feel the hardness of his lean body as he held me in his arms. His heart hammered against mine, beating out a frantic rhythm. And for a moment, just a moment, I *didn't want* the same things as a man. In that moment, I *didn't want* to be as good as man for him. I just wanted to be a woman.

'Miss Linton, I...'

His voice was rough, his face stonier and more unreadable than ever. I tried to read the emotions behind the granite façade, but to no avail. He was impenetrable.

Only...

Only I imagined that maybe his eyes weren't quite as cold as they had been a moment ago.

'Y-yes?'

Why was my voice suddenly unsteady? I was in the middle of having an argument with him, for heaven's sake! I had never been afraid of arguments, or afraid of men. What was the matter with me? Why were my legs feeling so weak all of a sudden?

He called you 'Miss' Linton, said a tiny voice in the back of my mind. *Not Mister. Miss. Maybe that's why.*

'I...' He stared at me, searching for words – then he abruptly let go and stumbled backwards, the momentary fury that had taken hold of him gone, his demeanour back to cool, calm self-possession.

I just leaned against the wall, too weak-kneed to stand on my own.

For a moment or two, there was silence between us. Then he took a deep breath.

'I... am sorry if I acted inappropriately. I should not have touched you.'

Part of me wasn't so sure about that. For some strange reason, being touched by him, touched that roughly and demandingly, had felt exciting. But I nodded anyway, accepting his words. To get an apology out of Rikkard Ambrose was such a rare opportunity that you simply had to take it.

My mouth felt dry – too dry for speaking. Yet I had to ask a very important question. I wet my lips, not taking my eyes of Mr Ambrose.

'So what about it?' I asked.

'About what?' he shot back.

He had to be joking. Surely he couldn't have forgotten what we were talking about, could he? But he was looking at me so oddly that I almost thought he might. What on earth could he be thinking about instead right now?

'Am I still one of your employees?' I clarified.

That brought him back down to earth. His mouth thinned into a line. 'No!'

It was no more than I had expected. But I dug my heels into the ground. I was not prepared to give up yet!

'I told you,' I repeated, crossing my arms defiantly in front of me, 'I was not disobeying your orders! I did exactly what you told me to do. You cannot dismiss me for that!'

'Don't you play the innocent! You deliberately interpreted my words in such a way as to humiliate me!'

'Oh yes? And you, *you* didn't try to humiliate *me*? To hurt me in the worst way you could imagine, by making me speak up against what I believed in?'

I felt scalding hot moisture at the corners of my eyes. Driving it away by pure force of will, I took a step forward, making my voice strong and steady.

'You tricked me! You made me believe that you had accepted me, only to spring your worst attempt ever on me in your accursed quest to get rid of me! So don't you dare be angry at me now just because I was cleverer than you and came out on top!'

Silence. Well, at least he didn't deny it.

'Why did you do it, anyway?' I asked after a moment, my voice quieter. 'Why did you drag me up on that podium? Why are you so desperate to send me packing?'

Silence.

'*Tell me*! Why? Am I that bad a secretary?'

To my surprise, after a moment, he shook his head.

'No,' he told me. 'In fact, your work so far has been quite acceptable. For a female, you have an astonishingly unmuddled mind.'

'Well, thank you *very much* for that ringing endorsement! If it's not my work that's the problem, then what is it? Is it...' I hesitated. We were back to the old subject. The old battleground. 'Is it that I am a girl?'

He nodded.

'You bastard! I'd like to throw something at your head!' I told him.

'Be my guest,' he said, 'and you'll be out of here faster than you can say "assault charges".'

I was seething with fury. But behind his cold words I could sense something – something that wasn't clearly expressed, and yet I felt it, in his eyes, his voice...

He wanted to get rid of me because I was a girl? But he had said that I did my work well enough. So why would he still want to get rid of me? Why did men think women shouldn't work? Because they were a distraction, because it was unbecoming, because they were in too much danger–

My thoughts screeched to a halt.

'It's because of *him*, isn't it?'

'Who?'

'*Him*! This mystery-man behind the theft of that all-important file! You said he was dangerous, and that you wouldn't let me be in on the chase, because you couldn't put a *lady* in harm's way!' I loaded the word 'lady' with as much disgust as I could manage. 'It *is* because of him, isn't it?'

Silence. But this time, the silence told me all. Yes. It was because of him.

'Who is he?' I demanded. 'What is in the file? Who is this mysterious mastermind that makes even you think twice about taking him on? Tell me!'

Silence. Thickening silence.

'I just don't understand!' I exclaimed, shaking my head. 'Who could be that powerful, that evil, that he would give even you pause? He would have to be a king, a ruthless killer or... or...'

It was only a flicker of movement, but I noticed it: Mr Ambrose's head turned, almost imperceptibly, for just a split second to look out of the window, across the street – and at the façade of East India House.

...or a man who owned an entire subcontinent and his own private army.

'No,' I whispered. 'No. It couldn't be!'

I Realize I Danced with a Criminal Mastermind

His head jerked up and around to look at me, but I didn't see him. Instead I saw a dozen images, whirling in my head, connecting together for the first time:

Mr Ambrose shaking Lord Dalgliesh's hand with enough force to whiten his knuckles.

Mr Ambrose staring across the ballroom to a table where only two people stood - Miss Hamilton and Lord Dalgliesh.

Mr Ambrose cutting a lock of hair from Simmons' head in the dark cellar beneath Empire House.

Lord Dalgliesh opening the envelope that contained a single lock of golden hair - hair of exactly the same shade and texture as that on Simmons' head.

'But...' I steadied myself against the wall. 'But he's one of the peers[45] of England! One of the most wealthy and respected gentlemen of the Empire! He wouldn't be involved in something like this!'

'He?' Mr Ambrose asked, his face expressionless. 'Who?'

'Don't play dumb with me!'

'Mind your language, Mr Linton!'

'Fine! Don't play dumb with me, *Sir*! You know exactly who I am talking about.'

The only answer to this was silence. That is, outside of my head. Inside, a multitude of voices and pictures were clamouring for attention. Rapidly, I went through everything I had seen that night at the ball, when I had first met Lord Dalgliesh.

'You went there to meet with him,' I whispered. 'That's why you came to the ball! To meet with him and let him know that you knew what he was up to. To warn him off!'

'I went to the ball to court Miss Hamilton,' he said with a facial expression that was about as passionate as a piece of dried cod. 'I went to be with the pearl of my heart, the girl for whom I feel the most ardent love which ever a man has experi–'

'Oh, put a sock in it!' I cut him off with a hand gesture. 'We both know you have no romantic interests whatsoever!'

'Do we indeed?

'Yes! They would waste too much of your precious time and money.'

He almost nodded in agreement but caught himself and suggested, almost defiantly: 'Love could have overwhelmed my defences and made me weak with longing.'

'No it couldn't.'

'Yes it could!'

---

[45] A 'peer' in the ancient British English sense is one of the most of the most important and powerful lords, who is a member of the House of Lords and thus, in times gone by had considerable political influence.

'No it couldn't!'

'You don't know that for certain. I could feel the most ardent passion–'

'No you bloody well couldn't! Not for *her*, anyway!'

His eyes narrowed infinitesimally. 'And why is that, Mr Linton?'

'Well... she... she... she's obviously not the right girl for you! Much too impractical and time-wasting. She's probably after your money, too.'

'Thank you for the warning.' I might have been mistaken, but I thought I saw the corner of his mouth twitch. It wasn't a smile. It wasn't even half a smile. He was far too miserly with his facial expressions for that. It was about a quarter of a smile, at the most, but it *was* there. 'Though I seem to remember that back at the ball, Mr Linton, you seemed quite convinced of my attachment to Miss Hamilton, in spite of her many defects. If my memory serves me right, it was even you who originally suggested the idea that I might have feelings for her.'

I flushed guiltily.

'In fact,' he continued, 'you seemed quite extraordinarily interested in the subject – and not very pleased by it. Very interested indeed...'

'I wasn't *interested*!' I snapped. 'I was being impolite and nosy, which is normal for me!'

'That is certainly true.'

Wishing desperately to get off this subject as quickly as possible, I made a dismissive hand gesture.

'Anyway, we weren't talking about Miss Hamilton! We were talking about your reason for going to the ball!'

'She *was* the reason.'

'No!'

His eyes narrowed another fraction of an inch. Impressive! Together with the miniscule motion of his mouth, this was the closest he had come to having a facial expression since I had known him. He had to be boiling inside.

'Strange, Mr Linton, how you seem to know my motives and feelings better than I.'

'Yes it is, isn't it? But if *you* don't know them, somebody has to. You went to the ball to confront Lord Dalgliesh. It was *you* who sent him that letter!'

'What letter?' His voice was so smooth, so cool, I could almost have believed he didn't know what I was talking about. Almost.

'*That* letter. It had a lock of Simmons' hair in it, as a sign that his man had been caught. Remember? You cut off a lock of hair from Simmons' head when we were down in the cellar with him. I didn't understand that at the time, but now I do.'

Silence. Frozen, ice-hard silence from the centre of the arctic wasteland.

His eyes were dark, the dark green-blue of the sea, and totally unreadable. Still, I had a feeling he knew exactly what I was talking about. I, for my part, hovered somewhere between exhilaration, doubt and fear. I had figured it out, finally! I knew who was behind the theft, without a doubt. Everything fit together.

And yet... and yet... it couldn't be. It was insane. Lord Daniel Eugene Dalgliesh was, by all accounts, one of the wealthiest men of the British Empire. He didn't have need of petty theft. He had armies at his command, an entire sub-continent under his control. What would he want with one miserable piece of paper?

'The only thing I don't understand,' I continued, my eyes lit still by my epiphany, 'is why the lock? Why send him a lock of hair, not just a simple letter warning him off?'

I expected him to deny it again or to once again be silent. He actually was silent for some time. But then, just as I opened my mouth for the next attack, he raised his chin and said:

'A letter could have incriminated me. A paper in which I accused him of theft, even in the vaguest terms? He would have found some way to use it against me! A lock of hair on the other hand – that was a message only he would understand. A message that needed no words or signature.'

A wave of cold swept over me. He had admitted it. He had finally admitted it. My exciting theory was no longer just a theory.

'It can't be him.' How come my voice suddenly sounded so small? 'It simply can't. I mean... He's so wealthy. So powerful. And it's just a piece of paper. It's not important.'

He regarded me coolly. Not for the first time, I had the feeling that he was assessing me. And not for the first time, I had no idea what the result was.

'The American Declaration of Independence was just a piece of paper, Mr Linton. It lost us most of our American colonies. In retrospect, do you think it was "unimportant"?'

'Um... well... no, I suppose not.'

'Indeed.'

I lifted an eyebrow. 'The pen is mightier than the sword? Is that what you're driving at?'

'It very much depends on the context. I would prefer a sword to fight a duel, but a pen to plan a war.'

He said 'to plan a war' as if it were something he did on a regular basis. Looking into his calm, emotionless face, I could believe he did. Another shudder ran down my back. But it was no shudder of revulsion. Oh no. I remembered his powerful body pressed into me, all that tightly contained energy only a fraction of an inch away. What could he unleash, if he wanted to?

More importantly: what would be unleashed when he pitted himself against his arch enemy?

'Lord Dalgliesh,' I muttered. 'Lord Dalgliesh is a thief.'

Before I could blink, Mr Ambrose had crossed the distance between us. He didn't grab me this time. He just stood very close in front of me, one finger touching my lips. The feeling was electric, sending tingles from my mouth all through my body.

'Don't ever,' he mouthed, 'say that aloud again. Not ever. Not if you want to live to see your next birthday. Do you understand me?'

That did it. Anger welled up inside me, pushing my fear to the side.

'No, I don't understand!' I snapped, nearly biting off his finger. 'You two are *businessmen*, or financiers or whatever you call yourselves – not cold-blooded killers! If he is guilty of this theft, why should I be afraid of him? Why shouldn't I simply go to the police and tell them what I know!'

'Which is?'

'That he's guilty!'

'Based on what evidence?'

'Based on... well...' For a moment I floundered, but it wasn't long. 'Based on Simmons' word, for one. We could make him a witness!'

In answer, Mr Ambrose simply turned and walked away from me. I was about to protest, when he stopped and snatched up a newspaper from his desk. A paper? I frowned. What did he want a paper for?

He came back and held out the paper, opened at a particular page. One section was outlined in blue ink.

'Read it.'

'What is this?'

'Read it, Mr Linton!'

Grumbling to myself, I took a closer look at the paper. It was open to the obituaries page. My eyes travelled to the outlined section.

Died, at London, 15 September 1839

Mr Walter Simmons

After having been most brutally attacked by two members of the criminal classes and robbed of all he possessed, he succumbed to severe wounds in St Christopher's Hospital. Our hearts go out to his poor parents, whose only child he was.

I read it, and I read it again. Then I read it a third time. Still, I couldn't quite process it.

'Dead?' I whispered. 'Simmons is dead?'

'Why so surprised, Mr Linton? I told you this would happen.'

'But how... how did this happen? Why did two people attack him? You took his money away, why would they want to rob him?'

His steady, cool gaze was unnerving.

'Do you really need to ask that question?'

The way he said it, it sounded like there was an 'I had thought you were cleverer than that!' attached at the end – which was silly, of course. Mr Ambrose didn't think me clever at all! He thought I was a girl, and that all girls were stupid and weak.

Well, my bones certainly agreed with him on the last part right now. Stumbling over to the chair in front of the desk, I fell into it and put my arms around me in an unusually vulnerable gesture.

'And if we went to the police...' I managed to say.

'... they would probably not be very eager to investigate a personal friend of the home secretary and relative of Her Majesty the Queen on an unsubstantiated allegation of murder,' he finished my sentence. 'In fact, one might even say they would be strongly averse to the idea.'

'And if we just brought up the theft, Sir?'

'The one for which you've just lost your only witness, Mr Linton?'

'Oh.'

'Quite.' Mr Ambrose shook his head, looking down at me. 'You have to believe me when I tell you that there's more to business in the British Empire than signing papers and building machines. Oh, here in the metropolis it's all glamour, smiles and handshakes. But behind the façade, things are not so pretty.'

'So... what will we do now?'

'We?' He gave a little derisive noise. 'We will return to our original discussion: the subject of your impending dismissal.'

My head shot up, and I stared into his eyes disbelievingly.

'What? You really meant that?'

His eyes were very dark.

'I do not say things I do not mean, Mr Linton! You made a fool of me in front of the entire city. I do not take such things likely. And you're mistaken if you think you can sidetrack me. Who stole the file, whether it was Lord Dalgliesh or Queen Victoria or Father Christmas for that matter is no concern of yours!'

There were noises from outside the room – the footsteps of a heavy man, coming closer. But neither of us paid attention to them. We were too intent on each other.

'But... of course it is of concern to me if I'm going to help in the search for the file,' I protested.

He made a move towards me – then stopped himself in mid-movement. Slowly, as if he had to drag himself back, he removed himself from my vicinity and retreated behind his desk, where he sat down so he was on a level with me and could stare directly into my eyes.

'No.'

The footsteps were still coming closer. They were as loud as drumbeats now, pounding down the hallway outside. But still, neither of us cared.

'Yes, Sir, I will!'

'No, you won't.'

Behind Mr Ambrose, over the city, the sun was setting. Its last red remnants of light streamed directly into the room, casting Mr Ambrose's shadow towards me and making him look more like a stony, sinister statue.

'You,' he said, slowly and precisely, 'will not have anything to do with the search for the file, whether you stay or go, and let me tell you, at the moment the latter is far more likely. You will not come within a hundred leagues of Lord Dalgliesh! You won't even hear a whisper of any trail or clue my men and I will discover! I'll make sure to keep you far, far away!'

The footsteps outside came to a sudden halt and the door was thrown open. We both turned to stare. Out of the corner of my eye, I saw a rebuke form on Mr Ambrose's lips about how anyone could dare to disturb him without knocking – but his lips froze when he saw who stood in the doorway.

Karim was breathing hard, leaning against the doorway, triumph flashing in his eyes.

'We have found it!' he exclaimed. '*Sahib*, we know where the file is!'

~~**~*~*

'Why did you do it?' I demanded. 'Why did you try to make me believe that you were in love with Miss Hamilton?'

Silence. Icy silence, which filled the space around us completely and absolutely.

There wasn't much space to fill, in any case. We were stuffed into a chaise, Karim, Mr Ambrose and I. Or rather, Mr Ambrose and I were actually *in* the chaise, while Karim's huge form sat, perched precariously at the edge. He was propelling us forward, yelling and wielding the whip, making the little chaise jolt and swerve insanely.

Why? Why have we taken such a miserable little ride?

I had dared to ask that question before we got in, and it turned out that this, apparently, was the only coach actually owned by the unimaginably rich Mr Ambrose: a creaky old chaise, drawn by one shaggy little grey beast of a horse.

'Why do you own this? Why not a proper coach?' I had asked.

'Because it's cheap and fast. But if you prefer to wait for the Queen's carriage, by all means, stay here.'

Ignoring him, I had clambered into the chaise and Karim, not paying the slightest attention to the light rain that had begun to fall, had swung himself onto the precarious strip of wood that, in a bigger coach, would have been a real box to sit on. Besides being his loyal bodyguard and sabre-carrying scarecrow, Karim appeared also to fulfil the function of Mr Ambrose's coach driver.

Now we were rattling through the darkening streets of London at an alarming speed, swaying from right to left in a way that never let me forget we only had two wheels under us, and the beast of a horse at the front was all that was keeping us upright. I hoped with all my heart it wasn't as mean as it looked.

The chaise swerved around a corner, and a shower of rain hit me in the face. I shuddered. The thing had only half a roof and one wall. It was meant for driving through the park on a nice Sunday, not racing through the pouring rain in the middle of the night! But did that stop Mr Thick-headed Stinginess Ambrose? Of course not!

'Why did you try to make me believe that you were in love with Miss Hamilton?' I asked once again. I had already asked that question about half a dozen times since we left Empire House. So far, I hadn't gotten an answer. Mr Ambrose just sat in his corner of the chaise and brooded, silently. Say what you will about his other traits, but he was an expert at silent brooding. Disapproval at my incessant questions, and at my presence, gender and existence in general radiated off him like heatwaves. Unfortunately, unlike heatwaves, it did nothing to warm my soaked clothes.

'Tell me!' I insisted. 'You're about as likely to be in love as the doorknob of my privy door back home! Why did you pretend to be in love with her?'

With a cold look in my direction, Mr Ambrose leaned out of the window. 'Karim!'

The big Mohammedan shifted, turning around. His weight made the little vehicle lean to the side in a dangerous way, and I had to work hard to stifle a scream. Only the knowledge of the way Mr Ambrose would look at me if I screeched like a silly damsel in distress kept my teeth firmly clamped together.

'Yes, *Sahib*?' our driver enquired calmly, not at all bothered by his master's cold look.

'Karim, is there any particular reason why this... individual is accompanying us?' He pointed to me.

Karim shrugged. 'She wanted to get in the coach. So, she got on into the coach, *Sahib*.'

'Just in case you didn't notice, I'm sitting right next to you,' I pointed out, staring daggers at Mr Ambrose.

He ignored me.

'I know she got into the coach, Karim. I want to know *why*. Did I give orders for her to accompany us?'

'No, *Sahib*.'

'In fact, I remember distinctly saying that she was not to be involved in the search for the file, correct?'

'Yes, *Sahib*.'

'So, I repeat, and trust me, I won't do it again: why is she here?'

'It is rude to talk about people as if they weren't there!' I snapped. 'And even ruder not to answer their questions! What about Miss Hamilton?'

Again I was ignored. Karim shrugged, and it was a mystery to me how he managed to do that without falling out of the coach. The chaise swayed again, and the horse whinnied.

'A shrug?' Mr Ambrose's eyes narrowed infinitesimally. 'That's all? Why didn't you stop her?'

'Why did not you, *Sahib*?' Karim asked, deadpan.

Silence.

'She wanted to get in the coach,' he repeated. 'She is the woman that is worse than *Ifrit*. I do not disagree with a woman that is worse than *Ifrit*.'

Mr Ambrose gave his servant another cold glare, which the Mohammedan dutifully ignored. From Mr Ambrose's stonier-than-stone face, long past granite and transcended into the realms of fossils, I gathered he didn't like to be ignored.

Well, neither did I!

'Excuse *me*!' Impatiently, I tapped on his shoulder. 'Will you answer my question now? Why the heck did you pretend to be in love with that shrew?'

Immediately, Mr Ambrose switched targets. His frostbite-inducing stare, before directed at Karim, now turned to me.

'Have you forgotten what I told you, Mr Linton? As long as you are in my employ, you will speak respectfully to me and refer to me as "Master" or "Sir".'

Swallowing the answer I would have liked to deliver, I gave him a tight smile.

'Yes, of course, *Sir*. I thought you said earlier, *Sir*, that you had decided to dismiss me, so I no longer considered a formal address necessary. I am so glad you have changed your mind and will allow me to continue to work for you, *Sir*.'

'Mr Linton?'

'Yes, Sir?'

'I've changed my mind. Be as rude as you want to me. You're dismissed.'

'Oh no, *Sir*. I couldn't possibly forsake you in your hour of need.' I pointed out the window at the wet houses rushing past in the gathering darkness. 'Besides, we're already on our way to get the stolen file back. You can't stop now, when that might mean that it could slip through your fingers.'

He studied me, his eyes narrowing the fraction of an inch.

'I'm not going to get rid of you, am I?'

'No, Sir.'

'I am the master here! I can decide to dismiss you whenever I want.'

'You gave your word, remember? Your word that I would get this position.'

'Get it, not keep it.'

'Did I do anything to deserve to lose it?'

Silence.

'Well, Sir? Did I? Really, honestly? On your honour as a gentleman?'

Silence.

Then, speaking as if every word was a painfully pulled tooth, he said: 'No! Congratulations! You managed to disobey me and ridicule me by following my instructions to the letter! I cannot dismiss you!'

With a happy little smile on my face, which I made sure he couldn't see, I snuggled into the moth-eaten old upholstery of the chaise bench, creating my own little corner of warmth.

'I'm very gratified to hear it, Sir,' I mumbled. 'So I suppose this means I'm still in your employ?'

It was impressive how he managed to sound both displeased *and* grudging, while at the same time maintaining a perfectly cool, aloof voice. 'I suppose that is correct.'

Maybe I even heard a little admiration there. But no, I was probably mistaken.

'Good. Then perhaps *now* you can answer my question: Why pretend to be in love with Miss Hamilton?'

His left little finger twitched minutely. For him, that was the equivalent of an impressive scowl.

'You don't give up, do you, Mr Linton?'

'No, Mr Ambrose.'

He sighed. It was such an unusual thing for him to do that it made me come out of my little protective corner of warmth and turn towards him. But he had turned away from me and was looking out of the chaise window. For a minute or two he didn't say anything. I had almost opened my mouth to ask once again when he suddenly began:

'When I spoke to you at the ball – you remember, when we were dancing?'

'Oh yes, I remember.' I suppressed a snort. Rotating around the ballroom with the granite statue of London's richest businessman holding me close – I wasn't about to forget that in a hurry! It surely had to have been one of the most awkward moments of my life. And yet, I realized suddenly, in retrospect, a moment oddly dear to me. Strange.

'When I first saw you at the ball, I was... quite disturbed.' His jaw twitched, betraying the roiling tension under his stony façade. 'To see you like that, so feminine and vulnerable, in the same room as *him*, the very man I had tried to keep you away from as much as possible – it was... not pleasant.'

He paused for a moment, then continued.

'Why were you there? I had no idea, and the question didn't stop hounding me. I decided I had to get you alone, to find out how much you knew – get you to leave, if possible. So I asked you to dance and struck up a conversation. And then you told me that you knew why I was attending the ball.'

He shook his head.

'I would never have thought that you would guess Lord Dalgliesh's involvement in this dark affair and my resulting interest in him. It meant that you were in considerably greater danger than I had previously imagined. I was starting to run through emergency plans, when you continued to speak, and I realized that you thought I was there not for Lord Dalgliesh but for *Miss Hamilton*.' He gave a derisive noise that made it quite clear how absurd he thought such an idea. 'I was... quite relieved.'

'You still haven't answered my question! Why pretend to be in love with Miss Hamilton, *Sir*?' Nobody would be able to accuse me of not being focused on my target.

'I am coming to that, Mr Linton,' he snapped.

'Yes, Sir.'

'Don't interrupt me again!'

'No, Sir. I'm sorry, Sir.'

I waited.

He took a deep breath.

'As soon as I realized your misconception, my mind was dominated by the thought of trying to keep you from realizing the true reason for my presence. I could only keep you out of the path of danger by keeping you from seeing the true identity of my enemy. The best way I could think of doing that was to further foster your fallacy and pretend a romantic interest in Miss Hamilton.'

'Oh.'

I thought for a moment, then asked: 'And why did you want to keep me out of danger so badly?'

Immediately as I spoke the question, I saw the answer. Holding a hand up I said: 'No, don't bother to answer that. It was because I'm a *girl*, because I am *weak* and I have no business meddling in men's affairs, right?'

He hesitated, his face still turned towards the window, away from me, so I couldn't read his expression. What did it matter? He never had one, anyway.

'Yes. Yes, Mr Linton. That was the only reason.'

'I see. Well, let me tell you, you didn't do a very good job. Pretending to be in love, I mean. I could see right through you!'

He turned then and looked at me.

'Could you indeed? Can you?'

'Yes!' I flushed. 'Of course I could! It was obvious you weren't interested. She's such a boring, superficial creature.'

'Oh really? Some men might find her quite charming.'

'Nonsense! Did you hear her conversations at the ball? All she talked about was dresses and dancing and the right way to hold fans! She has nothing in her head but stale air and dead flies!'

Mr Ambrose shrugged.

'What of it? Some men prefer their brides unintelligent. After all, women are supposed to do housework and little else. You do not need much intelligence for that.'

'Only stupid men would want stupid wives! Marriage is supposed to be a union between two equals who love and support each other, not a master-slave relationship in which the man commands a docile woman.'

'There's something to be said for docile women.' He leaned forward, spearing me with his dark gaze. 'They don't argue with you, for one!'

'And there's something to be said for progressive men. *They* don't normally have such thick heads that women *need* to argue with them! *They* have learned to listen to what women have to say.'

'I pity them thoroughly!'

Angrily, I turned my head away. He was impossible! Why I made all this effort to get accepted by him was becoming more and more of a mystery to me. He obviously would never learn to see me as more than a temporary annoyance.

Why was I doing this? Why was I in this coach? I could be going home right now, looking forward to another boring, safe day at the office tomorrow. Instead I was in this miserable little chaise with him, on my way to God only knew where, to deliberately put myself in danger. And for what? The acceptance of a man! Bah!

'So... are you really?'

The question was out of my mouth before I knew it.

'Am I what, Mr Linton?'

'Interested in her. Romantically, I mean.'

I sneaked a look at him out of the corner of my eye. He, too, wasn't looking directly at me. He was pretending to stare out of the window. But his dark pupils betrayed him. They were watching me out of the corner of his eye, just like mine were on him.

He said nothing.

Why the dickens did I ask that? Why would I even be interested in Mr Ambrose's romantic life or, more likely, the lack of it? The man was as romantic as a block of wood! A very attractive block of wood, certainly, but still a block of wood! He wasn't interested in anyone.

And still, the thought of him being in love with that Hamilton wench...!

I shook my head, trying to ignore the heat that was rising in my cheeks.

Still I had gotten no answer.

'Well, Sir?' I repeated my question. 'Are you interested in her?'

This time, I hadn't sounded angry. For some reason, my voice had been low, and softer than I had ever heard it.

Slowly, he began to turn towards me. His sea-coloured eyes met mine, and they seemed darker than usual, the colour of storm.

'Not in her, no.'

What? What was that supposed to mean?

Wetting my lips, I opened my mouth. It suddenly felt very dry. 'Mr Ambrose... Sir...'

'*Sahib?*'

Karim's face appeared only inches away from us. Let me tell you, it's rather disturbing to be staring into Mr Ambrose's eyes and then suddenly have a bushy black beard shoved into your face.

'It's rude to interrupt!' I snapped. 'Can't you see we're having a conversation?'

Karim didn't seem perturbed. 'Yes, I can. I just thought you would like to know...'

The Mohammedan pointed straight ahead. Only then did I realize something which I hadn't noticed before because I had been so intent on Mr Ambrose: the coach had stopped moving.

'We've arrived,' Karim said. As he swung down from the chaise, I could see he had his hand at his belt, around the hilt of his sabre. 'Shall we go?'

I Mash and Bend Myself

'This is it?' I stared incredulously at the building down the road which Karim had pointed out. '*This* is where the wealthiest man of the British Empire keeps a document that is so important he has killed people for it?'

'*Second*-wealthiest,' Mr Ambrose commented coolly. '*I* am the wealthiest man of the British Empire, not that reprehensible individual who calls himself a lord.'

'Oh, who cares?'

'*I* do.'

Rolling my eyes, I turned to Karim, ignoring my employer. 'This is it?'

With both hands, I gestured towards the house. It was a two-story brick building, slightly slanted, with dark stains on the front wall. The noise of cheap piano music came from inside, and over the door hung a sign which designated the establishment to be *The Plough and Anchor*.

Karim simply shrugged. Lord, I just had it up to here with men who couldn't open their mouths to give me a straight answer!

Looking around again, I got a fuller impression of my surroundings. The place might not look like what I expected Lord Dalgliesh's fancy headquarters to look like, but it certainly seemed evil enough to be the lair of a lord of the criminal underworld. The houses around us were dilapidated. Black smoke hung over the area, although none of it actually came from the houses' chimneys, which were cold empty. Washing lines criss-crossed between the roofs, or at least I assumed they were washing lines. The things that hung from them didn't look much like clothes to me, but I didn't think anybody would bother hanging old rags up to dry.

In a doorway not too far down the street sat a thin figure, wrapped in just such rags. It didn't move. I shivered.

'Where are we?'

My voice wasn't nearly as forceful as before.

Mr Ambrose looked around, his eyes coolly assessing the neighbourhood. Nobody's eyes were better for cool assessment than his.

'Norfolk Street,' he said finally, pointing to a dirty street sign I couldn't for the life of me decipher.

'Where's that, Sir? I've never heard of such a street before.'

'It's only natural that you wouldn't have. It's near the docks – in the East End.'

The East End.

Every child in London knew that name. The worst fear of every wealthy citizen of London was to get lost and end up right here: in the stinking, rotting liver of London, where all the refuse its heart didn't want to deal with was dumped until further notice. It was a labyrinth of small streets and dirty houses where poor people crowded together because they had no money to go anywhere else. They looked for work at the docks or at one of the numerous factories. The smoke, unending hard labour and poisonous food slowly killed them off, one by one.

And when they happened to stumble across some unlucky member of the upper classes in their home territory, they weren't shy about expressing their displeasure at these circumstances. Sometimes with the help of knives and cudgels.[46]

Shuddering, I took in my bleak surroundings once more, then looked back the way we had come. Maybe...

'Do you wish to return to Empire House?' Mr Ambrose asked curtly. 'Karim can drive you back, Mr Linton.'

I hesitated. A scream sounded in the distance. It wasn't the kind of harmless little scream that came from a sleepwalker just having put his foot in a puddle of water, either. Wind howled through the street, driving the fog past us. It seemed thicker here, somehow, than in the rest of the city. Darker. As if a thousand sinister things were hiding in its depths.

Mr Ambrose seemed to sense my hesitation.

'It is no problem,' he said, and there might actually have been something akin to compassion in his voice. 'You can leave if you are afraid.'

Immediately, I raised my chin and met his eyes.

'I? Afraid? Of course not, Sir. What do we do now?'

A muscle in Mr Ambrose's jaw twitched. It seemed, just for a moment, as though he might be going to argue. In the end, though, he turned towards Karim.

---

[46] My sincere apologies to anybody living in the East End. Please keep in mind that this book takes place over a hundred and fifty years ago. I know perfectly well that today, its residents are not smugglers and cutthroats – well, at least most of them aren't... **evil author grin**

'Where in this building is the file?' he snapped.

'I do not know, Sahib. Warren told me that they had found what we had been looking for, and I rushed to you without delay.'

'I see. Then call Warren. Now.'

Not taking his right hand from his sabre, the Mohammedan raised his left to his lips and put two gnarled fingers in his mouth. He blew twice, and the whistle-tones echoed from the dilapidated houses.

Suddenly, Warren appeared out of the darkness. He was dressed in dockworker clothes and had a man on either side of him.

'Sir.' He gave a little bow to Mr Ambrose.

Mr Ambrose didn't waste any time on social niceties. 'The file, Warren. Where is it?'

'I do not know, Sir.'

'But you said–'

'I said we had found what we had been looking for. But not the file. Not exactly. We found the man who bought the file from Mr Simmons. The middle man of the deal.'

Mr Ambrose took a step forward.

'I dislike inaccurate reports, Warren,' he said, pinning the other man with his eyes of dark ice. 'I know you have not been in my employ long, so I tell you now: I dislike them intensely.'

Warren swallowed and hastily bowed again, while I tried to hide a grin. I could have told Warren that much. 'Yes, Mr Ambrose, Sir. Of course, Mr Ambrose, Sir.'

'This man... He's in that pub now?'

'Yes, Sir. *The Plough and Anchor*, Sir. We have the place surrounded.'

'By how many men?'

'A dozen.'

'Only a dozen?'

Mr Ambrose's mouth, normally a thin, exquisite line, turned into nothing more than a scratch on his chiselled face. Other people might not have noticed the minuscule change in expression – I, however, had learned to read the signs foretelling of approaching storms.

'Tell me, Mr Warren, how often have you conducted investigations in the East End before?'

'Um...' Warren nervously tugged at his collar. 'Never before, to be honest, Sir. I was mostly employed in the more reputable parts of London, seeing as my clientele were wealthy citizens. To be honest, I expected that in your employ, too, Sir, I would not be venturing into these–'

'Your expectations do not concern me, Mr Warren!'

'No, Sir! Of course not, Sir.'

'Indeed. Now listen to me. I know this kind of place.' He indicated the shady street with a sweep of his arm. 'As soon as we try to grab the man we're after and drag him out in the street, fifty of his cronies will be on us with knives and broken bottles.'

Knives and broken bottles? Unconsciously, I moved a little closer to Karim and the safety of his large sabre. I was too preoccupied by the mental image of a grinning thug with a broken bottle in his fist to wonder how on earth a phenomenally rich financier would know *this* kind of place.

'Is that so? But then what should we do, Sir?' Warren asked.

'There's nothing for it.' Mr Ambrose, his narrow mouth still nearly invisible, held out his hand. 'Give me your jacket and cap.'

'W-what, Sir?'

'That grimy little jacket and that disgusting cap of yours. Give them to me. I'm going to go in there in disguise and see what I can squeeze out of our friend by means of friendly conversation.'

Warren started at this, flabbergasted. 'You? *You* are going to have a *conversation*, Sir?'

'Yes! You, meanwhile, go back to headquarters and get backup. Pray that you return in time, before our prey decides to leave!'

'B-but Sir,' Warren stuttered, 'you can't... I mean... you're a gentleman of good family. You couldn't possibly go into a place like this and pretend to be part of that scum in there!'

The look Mr Ambrose gave his subordinate could have frozen lava.

'I've had a lot of practice in dealing with scum. Now *give me your clothes.*'

Warren was out of his cap and jacket before you could say "God save the Queen!".' He handed them to Mr Ambrose, who in return gave him his carefully folded back tailcoat.

'I don't want to see a single stain on it when you give it back,' he commanded. 'It is only ten years old and still in mint condition.'

'Um... yes, of course, Sir.'

Warren took the jacket, which in my opinion was definitely not in mint condition, handling it like a newborn babe. Mr Ambrose shrugged on the workman's jacket and placed the cap onto his neatly trimmed black hair, drawing it deep into his face. I had expected the workman's clothes to look odd or unnatural on him, expected that everybody would be able to tell immediately that this was Mr Rikkard Ambrose, one of the richest men of the city.

I could not have been more wrong.

What the heck...?

My mouth fell open and I stared. I blatantly stared.

The filthy cap and jacket transformed him as if they were a second skin: All of a sudden, he looked darker, rougher around the edges. He looked like a delinquent who would beat the stuffing out of you if you even looked at him wrong. A man who lived hard, and by his own rules.

I had to admit, the look suited him, suited him very well indeed.

At a motion of his hand, Warren and his two associates hurried off down the street. Mr Ambrose looked after them, shaking his head.

'Were did you find him, Karim?' he asked, grimly. 'He has no clue what he is in for.'

Karim shrugged. 'He had good references, *Sahib*. This is not the colonies. This is the city. It is not easy to find people good with their guns and their brains.'

Mr Ambrose gave a curt nod of acknowledgement. 'You two, wait here,' he ordered. 'I'm doing this on my own.'

'But Sahib-' Karim began, yet one glance from Mr Ambrose cut him off. I, for my part, knew better than to argue. Without hesitation, Mr Ambrose marched off towards *The Plough and Anchor*, leaving Karim and me behind.

I waited until the door had closed behind him and Karim was looking after Warren, disappearing in the distance. Then I stole away from the giant bodyguard and followed Mr Ambrose into the pub.

I indeed knew better than to argue. Simply disobeying was so much easier.

~~*~**~*~*

Inside, it took a few seconds for my eyes to get used to the dim lighting. But it would take even longer for my nose to get used to the stench. Coughing, I covered my mouth and nose with my hand. Sweat, cheap drink and other fumes I didn't care to identify formed an aroma in the air that could have knocked out a world champion boxer.

My eyes began to water from the stench. Hastily, I blinked the tears away. I had to keep my eyes open if I didn't want to get my throat cut here. Quickly, I took in my surroundings.

Several dirty tables stood against the back wall, grouped around a half-open door. A number of dirty sailors and dirty factory workers in dirty clothes sat there, together with a couple of dirty women with very dirty, low-cut dresses, playing dirty cards, and from time to time joining the even dirtier song played by a dirty piano player to my left. To my right, there was a dirty, long bar with large, dirty barrels of drinks behind it, and a bartender whose largeness and dirtiness could easily compete with his barrels. He was polishing a dirty metal tankard with an even dirtier cloth. Several people were sitting at the dirty bar. They too – surprise, surprise – were dirty, and staring into dirty tankards. Only a few, who didn't have dirty tankards to drink out of, were staring in the direction of the women. But I bet at least their thoughts were dirty.

So, on the whole, the establishment was not really clean as a spring shower, if you catch my drift.

And there, lounging against the corner of the bar as if he were a regular patron of this den of iniquity, was Mr Rikkard Ambrose, one leg leisurely crossed over the other, an elbow resting on the bar, a tankard in his hand. As I watched, he emptied the tankard in one large gulp and slapped the surface of the bar.

'Aye, this ain't half bad! Another one, me good fellow!'

I blinked, stunned. Had I just heard correctly?

It was Mr Ambrose's voice, and it came out of Mr Ambrose's mouth, but... Mr Ambrose would never in his life call anybody 'My good fellow', let alone commit the gross grammatical incorrectness of substituting a 'me' for the 'my'. This kind of behaviour was reserved for the lower strata of society, the people who weren't the second-richest, or maybe even richest, man of the entire British Empire!

Maybe you're dreaming, Lilly. Maybe this is a nightmare.

'Didn't ye hear me?' The Pseudo-Ambrose roared like a drunken lumberjack. 'Another drink!'

A really, really strange nightmare.

'Don't you make no fuss,' the barrel-bellied bartender growled. 'I'm coming, I'm coming.'

'You'd better!' The person at the bar with Mr Ambrose's voice and looks growled back. 'I'm dying for a few pig ears!'

Correction: a completely crazy dream!

When the landlord turned his back on the Pseudo-Ambrose – or was it him? It had to be! – to fill a tankard, I sidled up to him.

'Pig ears?' I hissed into his ear. 'What the heck do you want with pig ears? I thought we were here for the file.'

He jerked.

'You!' Mr Ambrose's usual, cold, cultured voice came out of the corner of his mouth and let me tell you, I had never been so relieved to hear it! Hooray! This was not a nightmare, and not a body-snatching double either! Mr Ambrose was still alive and right in front of me!

He, however, didn't seem so overjoyed to see me. Dark, sea-coloured eyes bored into me. 'What are you doing in here?'

'Don't try to change the subject! What do you want with pig ears?'

He growled. 'I do not want pig ears. It is cockney rhyming slang for "big beers". I was ordering a drink whilst trying to fit in with the natives. Now tell me, what are you doing here, Mr Linton?'

I drew myself up to my full height – which, unfortunately, was nowhere near his. 'I'm coming with you, Sir.'

'I specifically ordered you to stay outside!'

'Yes, Sir. That's why I came in. I find it very hard to be docile and obedient.'

About one hair of his left eyebrow twitched, betraying a desire to rise. 'Indeed? I hadn't noticed.'

He eyed me coolly.

'I have the feeling that it will not do any good to argue with you about this.'

'You're right.'

'And of course you know I can't argue with you, really, because it would draw attention to us.'

'You put it succinctly, Sir.'

'You are a devious individual, Mr Linton.'

I dipped my head courteously, doing my best to conceal a grin.

'Thank you, Sir. So can I stay?'

'Agreed. You can remain.' He leant a bit closer. I had to strain to hear him now. 'But if you value your life, behave inconspicuously. I will see if I can find our man at the tables.' With his head, he motioned over to the dirty tables, where the patrons were just now singing a song that seemed to include a lot of ale, men, women, and combinations of the latter two elements. 'You stay at the bar and mingle with the patrons. Talk like they do, do what they do, and listen.'

At that moment, the landlord turned around with a tankard of ale in his hand. Mr Ambrose grabbed it and was gone before I could answer.

So I turned to the bar and eyed the patrons suspiciously. They were a motley crew – cab drivers, sailors, factory workers, and some shady individuals whose profession I would prefer not to learn. All of them looked even more dishevelled and dangerous up close than they had from afar. The only one who looked even more disreputable than all of them put together was the bartender. He was eyeing me suspiciously, which didn't really surprise me. In his eyes, I had to be a small, beardless youth in baggy, middle-class trousers. Not his usual customer at all.

Talk as they talk, do what they do...

Well, at the moment, the others at the bar weren't doing much of anything except slouching. I was wondering whether I should just try to imitate their general silent sullenness when, suddenly, one of the patrons held out his tankard and the bartender turned his suspicious gaze from me and started filling it with a glistening amber liquid. As soon as it was full, the man drank it down in one gigantic gulp.

Do what they do...

Inspiration struck me.

'Ey, landlord!' I pounded the bar with my fist. 'I want some great big pig ears! The fattest, rosiest pig ears you have! Lots of them!'

NAPOLEON AND ALL THE LITTLE PIGGIES

A hand tapped on my shoulder. With some difficulty, I turned around to see Mr Ambrose standing before me, his face as cold and expressionless as ever.

'I believe I have discovered our man,' he hissed, and made an inconspicuous hand gesture. 'His name is Thomas Gurney, a factory worker who now and again seems to like doing work not quite legal to improve his monthly earnings. He's sitting at that table over there, engaged in gambling activity. I believe I can...'

Suddenly, he stopped. His voice turned lower and darker as he asked: 'Why are you grinning, Mr Linton?'

'Because p-pig ears are w-wonderful,' I declared, my grin widening. 'Truly, they are. I must remember to congatel... concattle... congratulate a farmer the next time I see one. It is really worth raising all those pigs and fattening them up and whatnot, just to get such wonderful pig ears to d-drink.'

I frowned.

'The only thing I d-don't understand is how they end up liquid in a tankard. I c-could swear somebody told me, only I c-can't remember...'

'Mr Linton?'

'Y-yes, Sir? I'm here, Sir! Ready to obey your every command, Sir!'

'Lower your voice, Mr Linton! And do not call me "Sir" while we are here incognito.'

'Yes, Sir! Of course, Sir!'

'Mr Linton, I have a question.'

'Shoot!'

He leaned forward until his granite face was only a couple of inches away from mine.

'Are you intoxicated?'

I blinked. That word had too many syllables for my current mental capacity to cope with.

'Intoxiwhatsy?

'Intoxicated. Inebriated. Lashed. Mashed. Tiddly. On a bender. In other words, Mr Linton: *are you drunk?*'

Slowly, the frown on my forehead deepened.

'D-don't know. I've never been drunk b-before. How do you... How do you tell, Sir?'

'Well, the inability to speak correctly is generally considered a reliable indicator of intoxication.' I may have imagined it, but his reply sounded a tiny bit sarcastic. 'And I told you to not call me Sir!'

For a moment, I considered complying. But he had hounded me for so long to call him Sir, it was too good an opportunity to get back at him by doing what he'd actually demanded of me.

My grin returned.

'I owe you p-proper respect as my s-superior, Sir. I could never be so d-disrespectful as to forget that, Sir.'

His eyes narrowed infinitesimally. 'Or at least while you're drunk you can't be, apparently.'

'Yes, Sir! Exactly, Sir!'

He gave me his coldest glare yet this evening. But then, suddenly, his eyes shifted upward, looking over my shoulder. Turning my head, I followed his gaze and saw the grimy landlord watching us with suspicious little eyes.

'Over here,' Mr Ambrose commanded in a low voice and, without waiting for an answer, grabbed me by the arm and dragged me into a quiet corner.

'I can't believe it!' There really was disbelief in his voice, mingled with exasperation and wonder and... well probably a lot of other things I was too intoxiwhatsicated to notice. 'I can simply not believe it. You have been *drinking*. And not just drinking any drinks, but *drinks containing alcohol*!'

'What's so strange about it?' I mumbled. 'People do it every day.'

'*Men* do it every day! But you are... you are...'

'Yes?' I smiled up at him. I felt like smiling. I felt like it was a happy world. 'I am what?'

'A girl!'

'Really? Gosh. I hadn't noticed.'

He drew a deep breath.

'When men gather after dinner to consume alcoholic beverages, Mr Linton,' he pointed out in a very tight, controlled voice, 'it is the custom of civilized society that women leave the room, because women have no interest in alcohol and no business drinking it. It is not within their nature.'

'Very interesting, I'm sure.' My grin grew wider. It was getting a bit easier to talk without stumbling over my syllables. 'But since, as you're so often kind enough to point out, I am *Mister* Victor Linton while in your employ, what do those poor, alcohol-deprived females have to do with me?'

'Why in heaven's name did you drink?'

'You ordered me to.'

'I never...'

'You said to behave like everybody else. Everybody else was drinking. *You* were.' I nudged him playfully in the ribs, something that I vaguely knew I normally wouldn't have done with a ten foot pole. 'Don't you remember? *Another one, me good fellow*, hm?'

From the look Mr Ambrose gave me, he didn't appreciate being nudged playfully in the ribs very much. Nor did he apparently appreciate vocal impersonations.

'You,' he told me in a tone that could have frozen the Sahara, 'are a disgrace to your sex.'

'Which one would that be?'

From freezing the Sahara, his eyes went right on to the Kalahari.

'That is a discussion we will have at a later time. Right now, Mr Linton, I have to go interview the man we came to look for, before he decides to leave.'

'How may I be of assi... assissi... assistance, Sir?'

'You may go into that room there,' he said, pointing to the door which led to the pub's back room, 'sit quietly in a corner and not touch another drop of alcohol until I come to get you. Understood?'

'Y-yes, Sir... I understand.' Damn! I was stumbling over syllables again. 'But how will that help you f-find the file?'

'By having you out of my way. Now go!'

With that, he turned and strode towards the tables.

I scowled after him. That hadn't been very nice. And I didn't like it when people weren't nice to me, particularly not him! Still scowling, I moved towards the door he had indicated. It took me a few moments to get through it, because it was rather difficult to determine which of the three doors that kept dancing around in front of my eyes was the one I wanted, but eventually I managed it. In the back room, there were more tables, and a maid was running around, taking orders.

Most of the men here were drinking from mugs or glasses that were a lot smaller than the ones out front. I slumped down at one of the tables, where another man was already sitting, and waved the maid towards me.

'I'll have what he's having,' I'll ordered. 'And there'll better be no donkey's hoofs or bull's horns or other animal parts in there!'

The maid blinked at me in confusion. 'Sorry, Sir?'

'Oh, forget it! Just get me a drink!'

'Aye, Sir.'

I watched her bustle away and gave a derisive snort. Blast Mr Ambrose! Don't drink any more my foot! I would show him!

'Here, Sir.'

Ah, my mug had arrived. I took the tiny little thing, sniffed – and broke out into a coughing fit. By George, that smelled sharp! But I had already ordered it now, so I might as well drink it. And anyhow, it wasn't as if it could do much harm. The mugs were much smaller here, after all...

~~**~*~*

I had to confess, after a while I got rather fond of the stuff that came in small mugs. Admittedly, at first it made your throat burn and your eyes water, but in the long run, it had the most interesting effects. For instance, not so long ago, a troop of jolly little yellow pigs had come out of the chimney and started to dance on the back wall. They were performing quite excellently, all thanks to this amazing liquid that had opened my eyes to a new world.

I pounded the table with my fist.

'Another one! Another cow's ear... or was it pig's tail... Darn it! Another cup of this stuff!'

The maid hurried to my table and deposited another cup in front of me with an anxious expression. Was she afraid of me? Maybe it was this miraculous substance that I was consuming, making my voice all rough and manly, that made me more intimidating. I grinned. I liked the idea.

Swiftly, I grasped the metal cup and gulped down its contents. Yes, I could really grow to like this drink. It made you feel pleasantly woozy.

'Ey there, little fellow! Are ye planning to drink the whole River Thames in one night? Leave something for the rest of us.'

Somebody laughed. I looked up from my empty cup and saw that the words had come from the other chap sitting at the table. He hadn't said a word before, but now he was grinning at me.

I gave his question a few moments of serious contemplation.

'No,' I finally decided. 'I don't want to drink the Thames. There's too much crap swimming in it.'

That got another laugh from him and a few of the other people around us.

'Blast it,' my table partner told me, raising his cup to me, 'I'm impressed. Ye 'old your licker well, considering.'

'Considering? Is that supposed to mean that wom- that little people can't drink as much as a big fellow like you?'

He grinned, displaying several missing teeth that gave his gnarled old face a jaunty look.

'No. They just usually end up unconscious under the table if they give it a go.'

'Well, I'm not nearly drunk enough for that yet!'

'Let's drink to that.' He raised his cup. 'Bottoms up!'

'No,' I told him, raising my cup but shaking my head. 'Bottoms down. I won't take my bottom off this chair until I am completely intoxi... intoxiwhatsy.... well you know what I mean.'

'No, I ain't got no clue, to be honest, lad.'

'Doesn't matter.'

We sat there and drank for a few minutes in companionable silence. I studied my counterpart as I did so. He was an old chap, sixty years or more, a sailor's cap covering his bald head, and his wiry figure wrapped in an old, faded jacket. I liked him. He didn't seem to be in a very good mood, though. He was staring into his cup dejectedly, and whenever he showed his charming toothless grin, there was a tinge of melancholy to it.

'The world just ain't what it used to be no more, lad,' he said, smiling sadly and raising his cup again.

'We can agree on that,' I said, and we clinked cups and drank. After all, I was sitting in the back room of a disreputable pub in the East End, getting thoroughly and royally drunk. If somebody had told me a few months ago I would be doing this, I'd have suggested they see a doctor.

'No honesty, you know,' he added dejectedly. 'Nowhere.'

'Quite right.'

We clinked cups again. We drank.

I wondered what would happen if I told him that he was having this conversation with a girl in disguise. Maybe he would be angry about my dishonesty? Though something about the glassy look in his eyes made me think that maybe he'd laugh at the good joke, or maybe just not understand what I was saying.

'Makes me really want to get drunk,' the gnarled old sailor said.

I nodded.

We clinked cups. We drank.

'So... why do you want to get drunk?' He asked.

I scowled.

'Because somebody I despise told me not to.'

He laughed. 'Is that so? You don't despise him, little fellow!'

'And how would you know? You don't even know who I'm talking about!'

'Because if ye despised him, ye wouldn't care what he told you to do. Ye'd just ignore him for the puddle of piss he is. Ye respect him. And ye want him to respect ye. That's why ye ain't doing what he's told ye. So ye can show him ye've got your own 'ead on your shoulders!'

'What are you? A doctor or gipsy fortune-teller or what?'

The sailor's shoulders slumped. 'Nay, lad, just an old man who's seen too damn much of the world.'

'So what about you?' I asked, eager to change the subject. 'Why are you getting drunk?'

The shoulders slumped even farther.

'I told ye. Dishonesty.'

'Yes, but what kind of dishonesty? Were you tricked?'

'Aye, tricked, lad. Tricked as surely as ever a fellow was.'

He gave a deep sigh.

'So you really want to 'ear my sad story, lad, do you? I warn ye, it's as sad a story as ever you 'eard.'

'As I said,' gesturing to the chair I was sitting on, 'Bottoms down. I'm not going anywhere for a while. You might as well unburden your heart while we get drunk.'

'You're a good lad.'

The old sailor sighed again. 'Oh, well... I've got this partner, you know? 'ad him ever since I came to London. When times are tough, we... do jobs together, ye know? The world ain't what it used to be. Surviving can be 'ard, sometimes.'

I had the feeling that the 'jobs' he alluded to weren't exactly legal. But I wasn't feeling particularly judgemental tonight. He seemed like a nice old fellow, for a man, and besides, the yellow piggies were still performing so delightfully at the back of the room – I just couldn't be in a bad mood...

'We were real pals, this fellow and me,' the old man continued sadly. 'Did everything together, shared everything together. If one of us found a job, we always got the other, and we split the cash. But then, the other night, he came in 'ere, drunk like the dickens, and started playing at cards, ye know. And he starts wearing fancy stuff he ain't got the money for. So I go and asks him where the money's coming from, and he tells me he's got luck at the tables. But ye see, I know he's not telling the truth. I know he's found a good job and don't want to share. So I follow him, and what do I see? Him going off to meet some posh geezer. Gives him something, and gets a bag full of cash in return, the little weasel!'

He took another large swallow from his cup, and gave a big, big sigh.

'The world really ain't what it used to be. I wouldn't never have expected that of 'im. Not of old Tom Gurney.'

I nodded philosophically. Only a few seconds later did the name register in my befuddled brain.

I choked on my next mouthful of the burning drink.

'W-what did you say his name was?' I gasped, coughing.

'Tom. Thomas Gurney, the little weasel. Can't imagine he did that, and to me, who looked after him ever since his mum died. Aye, the world ain't what it used to be no longer...'

'Yes, yes, I'm sure it aintn't... um... isn't. Tell me... where exactly was this house where your partner met this "posh geezer"?'

~~**~*~*

I had a nice, long talk with my friend, the old sailor, and afterwards sat and watched the amazing visions produced by the burning drink. The dancing piggies at the back of the room had performed about half of a Russian ballet when I heard a familiar arctic voice from the main room.

'Mr Linton? Mr Linton!'

'Ah.' I sighed and nodded to my drinking companion. 'Duty calls.'

He grinned at me.

'Don't be too hard on him, lad.'

'I?' I demanded, outraged. 'Hard on *him*? He's my superior, not the other way around.'

'Exactly.'

Shaking my head, I stumbled towards the door. The old fellow was nice enough, but strange.

326

Out in the main room, Mr Ambrose awaited me, displeasure evident in every unmoving line of his face.

'We're getting out of here,' he stated. 'The lips of that man Gurney are sown shut! I cannot get a single word out of him. This was a waste of time. We'll have to try something else.'

I raised an eyebrow. Or maybe both. Control over my facial muscles was rather difficult to maintain at the moment.

'Really?'

'Yes, of course!'

'You got nothing at all, did you?'

'No.'

'Not the tiniest-winiest tiddly bittly bit of information?'

'I am not in the habit of repeating myself, Mr Linton. No, I got nothing. Now let's go.'

'Tut-tut...' I smirked at him. Or maybe I drooled at him a little. What did it matter? This was great! The little yellow piggies were doing pirouettes, just for the special occasion of my triumph. 'N-not so fast, Sir. I think I have some interesting news for you...'

~~**~*~*

'...there was this drunk old fellow, you know, really drunk, you could really, really tell from the way he spockle– spak– spoke...'

Mr Ambrose listened to my account with his usual facial expression – or lack thereof. In fact, *both* Mr Ambroses did. There seemed to be two of him at the moment. Sometimes there were even three, but most of the time there were only two. They were swaying slightly and going in and out of focus.

'...and I totally conned him! Just like that! And he started bubbleabable...babbling...and... what was I talking about again? Barman? Another round of pig's snouts... no... eyes...? Oh, to hell with it! So I got him talking and...'

The blurry, stony-looking Ambrose in front of me morphed into two again, neither looking very pleased. Under normal circumstances, I might have been terrified – I mean, *two* Mr Ambroses to hound me all day, trying to drive me insane? Please! Every girl has her limits! But right now, there was this warm, fuzzy-glowy-gargantuan-greatly-gubbledly-wobbledy-wonderful feeling inside, and not even the thought of two Mr Ambroses to deal with at once could faze me.

Why should it? I was a strong woman! Strong and brilliant and all-powerful! Ha! Let all men cower before me! Right now, I knew I could squish them all like bugs and conquer the world – even if it did seem slightly blurred.

'...and he said he followed him there,' I finished my account, 'and saw him there, because he went there, and he followed him. And he told me, and now we know. Isn't that just peachy, slug? Um, I mean... Sir? We know what we wanted to know. Although I can't for the life of me remember why exactly we wanted to know. Bugger! Well, I'm sure it'll come back to me once I've conquered the world. Do you think I should start with Spain, or rather France?'

His facial expression didn't change. Somehow, he still managed to suddenly radiate twice as much cold disapproval. 'Mr Linton?'

'Yessir!'

'You neglected to mention where this man you were conversing with actually went.'

'Oh. Really? How strange. Um... well...'

'Yes?'

I tried to sort through my foggy mind to find the answer to this conundrum. It wasn't easy. Finally, the answer popped out of the mist.

'Duck Road!' I exclaimed. 'He went to Duck Road, number 97!'

'Mr Linton, there is no such place as 'Duck Road' in London.'

'Sure there is! It wasn't a native duck, though. Some kind of foreign little beast... from the East, I think.' I snapped my fingers, or at least tried to. Somehow, my twenty-seven fingers got tangled up in each other. 'East India Duck Road! He went to a large house on East India Duck road! Number 97!'

Mr Ambrose gave me a long, long look. Even in my current conquer-the-world mood, I felt that look.

'Mr Linton... is it possible that you are talking about East India *Dock* Road, not *Duck*?'

I put my plans for conquering France and squashing all men like cockroaches aside for the moment and considered this. 'Possible,' I conceded.

'Of course!' Mr Ambrose's eyes flashed, and he looked past me, half-speaking to himself. 'East India Dock Road! The East India Company!'

'I still think it was "Duck", though,' I told him. He didn't pay any attention to me.

'Yes, the East India Company... and Dalgliesh is the main shareholder. One more piece of the puzzle.'

I blinked up at him. 'I always get those wrong. I always try to use the piece with the blackberry as the nose for the dog in the background. Are you going to help me conquer the world now, Sir?'

His gaze snapped back to me.

'Mr Linton?'

'Yessir! Right here, Sir!'

'I again have a question for you.'

'Shoot! But please not me.'

'Mr Linton, did you consume even more alcohol?'

'Certainly not, Sir! I never drink on dudelty... dudley... on duty.' A burp escaped me, and I quickly covered my mouth with my hand. 'That's what the soldiers in novels always say when they've been drinking, anyway.'

'You *did* drink even more!'

'How did you know that?' I demanded. 'I told you no, like any good little soldier!'

He ignored my question, taking a threatening step closer. 'Why did you consume even more alcohol? I gave you express orders not to!'

I nodded sagely. I remembered that.

'Yessir! But then I remembered that I simply love disobeying your orders.' I grinned. 'I suppose I'm not a soldier, am I? Not so good with following orders.'

'No, you're not.'

'Blast! Well, I'm still going to conquer the world. Want to help me?'

'No.' He sounded terse for some reason, and not at all eager to help me with my big project of world domination. Strange... Very strange...

'At the moment, what I want to do, Mr Linton, is to go to number 97 East India Dock Road, and to tear it down brick by brick. But considering the state you are in, that will have to wait. Come on.'

A firm hand grasped my elbow and started to lead me towards the exit, away from the suspicious innkeeper and the dancing yellow piggies on the wall. I waved goodbye to them and smiled brightly.

'Nighty night!' I called over my shoulder. 'Thank you all sooo much for your performance! You were mesnesmeresizing...mesmerizing.'

'Will you hold your tongue!' Mr Ambrose hissed.

I shook my head.

'No, I don't think so. It's too wet, I don't want to get my fingers wet.'

We were out of the pub now and walking down the street. Our progress was rather slow, though. For some reason, the world kept wobbling, and the two Mr Ambroses insisted on walking with one arm around me. Amazing how they both managed to use one and the same arm.

'You see,' I said, gesturing at the swaying houses on either side of us, 'that's why I want to conquer the world. If I could tell the world what to do, I'm sure it would sit still and not be moving around like this.'

'Assuredly, Mr Linton. Come along.'

'Plus, there's this whole thing about equality of the sexes. I could fix that once I'd conquer the world, and kick all the chauvinists out of government, and make them tie the shoelaces of passing schoolgirls and clean public latrines.'

'Very sound policy, Mr Linton. Now if you could walk a little faster...'

I was touched. I never would have thought a Mr Ambrose would actually agree with me. I just wish I knew which of the two it was. Maybe at least one of them would help me conquer the world after all, and we could rule it together – although he would act in a solely advisory capacity, of course. The power had to stay with women, where it belonged.

'I'm so happy you agree with me,' I said, snuggling up against him. I could feel him stiffen beside me, and his steps, which up to that point had been regular as clockwork, became uneven. 'I mean... you normally act like the most cold, callous, cruel, dogmatically domineering bastard in the world, but sometimes... sometimes, like now, I get this crazy idea and I start thinking you could actually be quite nice. You know, if you wanted to.'

'I... am gratified to hear that, Mr Linton.'

The world swayed again, and I put my arm tighter around him. 'Yes,' I murmured. 'Quite nice. You feel nice, too.'

Mr Ambrose missed a step and stumbled. The swaying world must have started to put him off balance, too.

'I-indeed?'

Had he gotten drunk, too? For a moment, it had almost sounded as if he had stuttered.

'Feel nice, look nice... you'd think you'd have more brains.'

'More brains?'

'Yessir!' I nodded vigorously, glad at the chance to explain to him what a humongous dickhead he was. 'I mean this whole business with Miss Hamilton, for example. I mean, how could you be so stupid? If you really had to pick somebody, why somebody like that, so shallow and effeminate and... boring?'

The fingers which held my shoulders twitched.

'Do feel free to air your views on my bad taste in female companions, Mr Linton,' he said. Did I imagine it or did his voice sound slightly strange. 'Don't mince your words on my account.'

'Don't worry,' I assured him, glad to put his fears to rest. 'I wasn't going to. I mean... Couldn't you at least find somebody intelligent? No, no. You had to show up with the first pretty face you could get hold of. That's shallow of you. Made me angry.'

'Angry, Mr Linton? Why?'

Stored away somewhere in my befuddled brain, I might have had an answer to that. But I thought it was time to come back to my overarching theme.

'And that's why I am going to conquer the world,' I concluded. 'To prevent such horrible things from ever happening again!'

'My going to a ball with a young lady? That is why you intend to conquer the world?'

'Yes! And to end the oppression of womanhood, of course, and the sad lack of solid chocolate and beer in the pig ears of an average English girl. These are all grave injustices which it is my duty to put to rights!'

'No doubt. Now, if you could just take a few more steps... There's the coach, over there.' And indeed, he was steering me towards a blurry, vaguely coach-like form. 'Soon, we'll be with Karim, and you can tell him all about how you want to conquer the world.'

'Do you think he would help?'

'I'm certain he would.'

'Napoleon and Alexander the Great will, you know. I think I saw them with the dancing piggies, inside the pub.'

'Of course you did. They'll help you, and they'll help me put you into the chaise, and we will drive away to somewhere where we can make plans for world domination.'

'Spiffing!'

'Yes, Mr Linton. Very... "spiffing", indeed.'

We were about halfway to the chaise now. My eyes had gotten used to the darkness outside the pub by now, and I could see the fuzzy figure of Karim advancing towards us.

'Were you successful, *Sahib?*'

A muscle in Mr Ambrose's temple twitched. 'No, I was not.' He shot me a look. 'But we still know where we have to go next.'

'Forgive me, *Sahib*, I do not understand...'

'And I'm not in the mood to explain right now! We're leaving.'

'Of course, *Sahib*. As you command.'

I would have to learn that commanding tone, I thought, if I was going to conquer the world. Maybe Mr Ambrose could teach me...

Karim was just about to start back towards the chaise, when he suddenly tensed and held up his hand. Mr Ambrose froze, and I stumbled right into him, getting a mouthful of his jacket collar.

'Mpf! Wtf ftif?'

'Silence!' Karim hissed. 'I could have sworn...'

He cut off as, suddenly, men appeared out of the darkness around us in a semicircle. There was a glint of sharp metal in the gloom.

'Look what we've got here,' said a sneering voice out of the shadows. 'We've been looking for you, gents.'

FIGHTING SPIRIT

One of the men stepped forward. Or maybe two or three. It was all kind of blurry to me. But there was something sharp glinting in his/their hand(s), I could see that much. The sight sent a cold chill through me which, for now, brought me back to earth. For the first time, I realized these men might possibly not be here to join the little yellow piggies in their dance routine. But what else could they be here for?

The man with the knife smiled at Mr Ambrose, who was still wearing Warren's dirty jacket and cap.

'Hm. Can't say I can see what's so special about you. Can you, men?'

There was a round of guffaws from the other dark shapes. Even my befuddled brain realized – the man who had spoken was the leader. The others were his henchmen. And they were all carrying knives. Bloody heck! They hadn't come to slaughter the dancing yellow piggies, had they? If so, I would defend them with my last breath!

'You look like something that's crawled out of the gutter, apart from that pretty face of yours,' the man spat. 'Well, pretty boy, I think you've stepped on the toes of some high and mighty people hereabouts. We was told by some posh bloke you needed a reminder of who was in charge.'

Mr Ambrose regarded the other man as if he were a cockroach not worth stepping on. Ha! He apparently wasn't pleased that they had come to kill the dancing piggies, either. My heart went out to him with a warmth that I didn't know it possessed for any man. He would save the cute little yellow ones, I was sure!

'Indeed?' His voice was as cold as ever, and I revelled in it. 'And what was the name of that gentleman who thought I required such a reminder, if I may enquire?'

'My, you talk mighty fine.' The piggy-murderer smirked. 'Well, as I sees it, you won't have no need to know his name. You'll be dead soon enough.'

Laughing again, the men came closer. On some level I knew that should worry me. But the dancing yellow piggies, completely unaware of the danger, had suddenly appeared on the wall of the house opposite me, and I couldn't stand for them to be so near the danger! Anger boiled up inside me. Who cared about some men with thingies... knives! Yes, that's what they were called. Who cared about some men with knives, anyway, while artistically talented, cute little animals were in danger?

The men stepped closer again. The knives glinted.

'Karim?'

Mr Ambrose's voice was so low I hardly heard it.

'Yes, *Sahib*?'

'On my command.'

'Yes, *Sahib*.'

Mr Ambrose concentrated on the leader, wielding his voice like a whip.

'So... this "rich bloke", as you choose to call him... did he give you any information about me besides my description? Any indication who he was sending you off to attack?'

The man's step faltered for a second.

'No. Why?' His voice was suspicious.

'Ah.' Mr Ambrose nodded curtly. 'That explains it.'

'That explains what?' the leader spat.

'Why you came with so few men,' Mr Ambrose told him. '*Too few.*' He brought his hands up and together, and a sharp clap echoed through the alley. 'Now!'

More shapes appeared out of the darkness all around us, behind the thugs. At first I thought they might be Napoleon or Alexander the Great, coming to help me conquer the world, but they were men in workmen's and sailors' gear, with grim, determined looks on their faces and knives in their hands. Several of them held glinting objects that weren't knives. I didn't realize what they were until one of the men raised his weapon and a thunderclap tore the air between the dirty East End houses.

Yay! The cavalry of piggy-protectors had arrived!

Light flashed as the gun went off, and I stumbled backwards against Mr Ambrose, startled by the light. Two hard arms gripped me around the waist and swung me around, depositing me behind somebody's back, as more gunshots went off.

'Who...?' I mumbled.

'Warren's men!' A familiar, cold voice hissed next to my ear. 'Now be quiet! You don't want to draw attention to yourself!'

Mr Ambrose? It was Mr Ambrose who had shoved me behind his back? Was he... protecting me? Surely, that was not an efficient use of his time and resources. After all, a disgustingly rich financier was surely worth more pounds sterling than a rebellious little female such as myself. And anyway, there were others who needed protection more than I! I looked around searchingly for any of the yellow piggies, but they seemed to have gone for now. Very wise.

'Warren's men...?' I mumbled drowsily, trying to make sense of what was going on. I had thought this was the official piggy-protection squad, arrived just in time. 'But... you sent them away.'

'I sent Warren away. The men stayed. Standard security procedure. Now belt up!'

He was half-dragging, half-pushing me away from the fight and towards the chaise. I dug my heels into the ground, looking around for my piggy dance troop. Maybe there were some stragglers we had to bring with us.

'What are you doing? We have to get out of here!'

'I'm looking for the yellow piggies,' I explained, my voice a little slurred for some reason. 'Have you seen the yellow piggies?'

'*What?*'

Suddenly, a figure appeared in front of us. I grinned broadly, thinking it was one of my little yellow dancers – but it was just a thug with a revolver in his hand. Dang!

'Look what we 'ave here,' he leered. 'I think–'

Without pausing, Mr Ambrose brought up his knee and drove it between the man's legs. Gasping, he doubled over and dropped the revolver.

Throwing him aside like a dirty dish rag, Mr Ambrose pulled me behind a dysfunctional lamp post that stood halfway between the entrance to the pub and the waiting chaise, which he seemed to be intent on getting to for some reason. I wondered why. We had to stay here and fight and die bravely in defence of the piggies, didn't we? That's what Alexander and Napoleon were doing. And from what I'd just seen, Mr Ambrose could give those two a run for their money.

Interestedly, I looked back and forth between Mr Ambrose, intent on the chaise, and the man who lay a few feet behind us, groaning on the ground.

'You just kicked those men in the... in the...' I hesitated. To be honest, I wasn't absolutely sure what parts of male anatomy lay in this particular spot. I just knew that kicking them was generally a very good idea.

'Yes, I did.' Mr Ambrose voice was unconcerned. He didn't take his eyes off the chaise for a moment, waiting for his opportunity.

'But... but you're a gentleman!'

'Yes. In *all* parts, Mr Linton.'

'Um... I see.'

I didn't really. But I would never have admitted that.

'When I tell you to run,' Mr Ambrose hissed, 'you run.' His eyes roamed the darkness as if they could pierce it by sheer force of will. 'Three... two... one... *Run!*'

We darted from behind the lamp post, racing across the street towards the dark silhouette of the chaise. The beast of a grey horse was still standing where we had left it, apparently completely unconcerned by the fact that bullets were flying around its ears.

Around us, men were fighting and dying. The chaise came nearer and nearer. Twenty yards. Fifteen. Ten...

Another man appeared in front of us, and I sprang forward immediately. I wasn't about to be outdone by Mr Ambrose! Quickly, I raised my foot and kicked out.

The figure ducked away, and I heard Karim's deep voice, cursing. '*Kī naraka!* What are you doing, *Ifrit?*'

'Oh. It's you. I'm s–'

Before I could finish, he pushed me aside and reached for the sabre at his belt. I saw a glint of metal and heard a scream out of the darkness. Something wet sprayed my face.

Strange, I mused. *It isn't raining, is it?*

Then another flash of gunfire illuminated the alley and I saw that it *was* raining. It was raining red stuff. How funny. That meant the yellow piggies would have red spots at the end of the evening. That would look really spiffing!

'Quickly, *Sahib!*' Karim had drawn his own gun now – a longish thing of glinting metal and dark wood, and he was firing quickly and precisely. 'Go! There are more coming!'

'Then let us face them!' I yelled, waving a fist in the air. 'My strength is as the strength of ten because my heart is pure!'

Somebody grabbed me again and dragged me away.

'Let go of me!' I yelled and struggled.

'Have you gone completely insane?' I heard Mr Ambrose's burning cold voice in my ear. 'Be quiet, and we may get out of this alive!'

Ignoring my protest, he dragged me farther towards the coach. Behind me, I heard Karim shouting war cries in a language I didn't know. Well, at least he would stay behind to protect the piggies. That might be enough.

We had almost reached the chaise when the gang leader jumped out from behind the horse and raised his gun to point directly at Mr Ambrose's chest.

'Who the 'ell are you?' He snarled. 'Where did these buggers come from?' There was fear flickering in his wild eyes, and they didn't stay trained on his target like they should have. His men were more numerous, but Warren's so-called 'associates' were fighting like trained soldiers. Maybe that's what they were. A private army trained for the defence of dancing animals! I was so proud of them.

'I see your employer failed to inform you who you are dealing with.' The cold in Mr Ambrose voice was so intense that I was surprised not to see the gang leader freeze on the spot.

The leader cocked his gun. 'Tell your men to stop fighting, or I'll put a bullet through your chest!' He snarled. 'Now!'

Mr Ambrose shrugged. 'Very well. I'll give the signal.'

He raised a hand and gave a short, sharp wave. The gang leader smiled.

Suddenly, the giant grey horse behind him reared up on its hind legs, kicking out wildly. With a strangled scream, the gang leader was thrown forward onto the cobblestones. A red puddle formed around his head.

'Just not the signal you want,' Mr Ambrose told the corpse.

In a flash, he had dragged me past the dead man and to the chaise and pushed me inside. 'Good boy.' He patted the horse on the neck, and for a moment I thought I saw the hint of a smile on his face. But no... that couldn't be.

'You there!' He yelled. 'On the box! Now!'

One of Warren's men, who had just finished off another of the thugs, rushed to do his master's bidding and swung himself onto the box. Quickly, he grabbed the whip and cracked it over the horse's head.

'Gee up!'

Mr Ambrose managed to jump into the chaise just in time. It took off down the street at an alarming speed. Dark houses rushed past us, and the screams behind us grew fainter and fainter. Slowly, I sank back into the old upholstery. Through the dreamy haze that surrounded my brain, I began to realize something.

'I've just been in a gunfight,' I said lazily. It was getting really hard to keep my eyes open.

'You certainly have,' a cool voice said next to me. There was a short silence. Then the cool voice continued: 'I suppose you now understand what kind of situation you signed up for. I shall of course understand that you wish to leave your post. I shall have all the necessary resignation papers prepared for you in the morning. You will have to come to sign...'

'I've just been in a gunfight,' I repeated, not really listening to whoever was speaking. Listening was so difficult.

'Yes, you said that already. About the resignation papers...'

'A gunfight! That's... That's spiffing!' I giggled.

Another pause.

Then, the cool voice said, not quite so cool anymore: 'It is *what*?'

'Spiffing. Top-hole. You might even say... ticketyboo.' I giggled again. 'I just wish I'd had a gun, too! That would have been even more top-hole. I could have put some holes into other people. Top-hole holes! The little piggies would have been proud!'

I nudged the fellow with the cool voice in the ribs. What was his name again? I couldn't remember right now.

There was a stifled groan from the dark. Hm... Wasn't I supposed to know this groaner with the cool voice? If only I could remember his name... his name...

Of course! Mr Ambrose! He had dragged me through the gunfight! Mr Ambrose, who had fought in defence of the little yellow piggies! How romantic...

I giggled again.

'My hero,' I drawled, leaning against him. 'You rescued me.' A frown spread over my face. 'Although, now that I think about it, I actually didn't want to be rescued. I wanted to stay there and join the fight.'

'Exactly why you needed rescuing,' he responded drily. Suddenly, I noticed that his arm, which had been around my shoulders the whole time he dragged me towards the chaise, was around my shoulders still. Why? And why was it suddenly gripping me so tightly?

'You are incorrigible, Mr Linton,' he told me, his voice low, tight, controlled. 'Why didn't you do as I told you to? Why, once in your life, didn't you do the sensible thing and run?'

My frown deepened into a scowl. 'The men didn't run. *They* fought.'

'Because that's what they're paid to do! You're paid to stay alive! To stay safe!'

'I'm no coward!' I growled. 'I'm as good as any man! And the little piggies needed me!'

'Excuse me... the *what*? What pigs?'

I rolled my eyes. He was incapable of grasping the simplest, most logical concepts. He didn't even understand dancing yellow pigs. Typical man!

But for some reason, leaning against this annoying man also felt comforting. Somehow, I had slipped sideways, and my head had come to rest against his chest. It felt firm, and oh so warm. But that couldn't be, could it? It was Mr Ambrose. Mr Ambrose was as cold as ice. Surely he would feel icy and hard, not so warm and reassuring.

'Do you think the little piggies will be all right?' I murmured, my eyes drifting closed. I felt very drowsy all of a sudden, and so comfortable...

'I'm sure they will,' he whispered reassuringly, his hand squeezing my shoulder. 'I'm sure they will.'

The last thing I felt before darkness swallowed me up was a hand on my cheek, stroking gently.

HALLUCINATION MANICURE

'Mr Linton.'

'Hmm?'

'Mr Linton, wake up. We have to go inside.'

'Why?' I mumbled, unwilling to open my eyes.

'Because... Well, because I say so!'

I chuckled. I knew that voice. Cold. Commanding.

'Not good enough,' I murmured.

'You are still in my employ, Mr Linton. You have to do what I say.'

'Not after hours, Sir.' A yawn escaped me. Talking was tiring business. Maybe I should just go back to sleep. I was lying on something so comfortable...

The comfortable thing shifted and grabbed me.

'If you don't get up, Mr Linton, I'm going to carry you. Either way, you will get out of this chaise.'

Oh. Mr Ambrose. It was Mr Ambrose I was lying on. How had that happened? I was sure he hadn't volunteered to be my personal sofa.

'Did you hear me, Mr Linton? I will drag you out of here, whether you want to or not.'

For a moment I considered letting him do it. Truth be told, I felt too warm and fuzzy to think about walking. Being carried might actually be nice. However, the moment that thought of weakness popped into my head, the vigilant feminist inside me reasserted herself. I might utilize men as a couch, I might even allow them to pay me wages. But the day I allowed a man to carry me in his arms because I felt too unsteady on my poor little feminine feet would be the day I publicly confessed to being a chimpanzee.

Never.

Ever.

Blindly I groped around, grabbing Mr Ambrose and pushing myself into a sitting position.

'Be careful with my coat, Mr Linton! It's only ten years old and–'

'...still in mint condition.' I nodded. 'Yes, I know. You've told me before. I'm not stupid, you know.'

'Maybe not. But you *are* drunk.'

'Drunk? Me? Of course I'm not drunk!' Outraged, I staggered out of the chaise. How dare he suggest such a thing? I was stone-cold sober! And I had plenty of witnesses to the fact. Grasping the carriage wheel to support me, I pointed with my free hand at the yellow piggy sitting beside the driver. 'Ask him over there, if you don't believe me.'

'Me?' The driver looked taken aback. 'Well, Sir, I could not hazard a guess as to–'

'Not you! The Pig.'

'Pig? What pig?'

The driver's nervousness seemed to increase. What was the matter with him? A yellow pig wasn't something you could miss easily, was it?

'Forget it, Godwin.' Mr Ambrose appeared beside me. With a jerk of his head, he indicated to the driver and the yellow piggy that they should leave. 'Take the chaise away and care for the horse.'

He was obviously bent on ignoring my logical arguments! So typically male!

'Yes, Sir, only...' the driver hesitated. 'What about the other men, Sir? I should go back and–'

'Warren will have reached the tavern by now with all the reinforcements he could muster,' Mr Ambrose cut him off. 'Do as you're told. I and Mr Linton will go inside now.'

'Yes, Sir. As you wish, Sir.'

Climbing from the box, the driver and the yellow piggy started doing Mr Ambrose's bidding, leading the horse and carriage away. The power of this man was unbelievable! Even little yellow animals were under his power, even though I was sure they weren't on his payroll!

'Come along.' Mr Ambrose strode ahead, gesturing for me to follow with a flick of his fingers. Taking a cautious step forward I lifted my head – and my eyes widened in shock. Before me stood the vast, gaunt façade of Empire House. The chaise had deposited us in Leadenhall Street, right in front of Mr Ambrose's business headquarters. Like the bow of a gargantuan wreck in the dark depth of the ocean, the two-columned portico loomed up in front of me, white and ghostly. Ornate gas lanterns were spread out all along the street, throwing their yellowish light across the empty street. The whole scene looked even colder now than it had in daylight.

What were we doing here? Why wasn't I at my own home? I was sure I had one of those, tucked away somewhere in London.

My eyes flicked to Mr Ambrose. Honestly, surprisingly enough, he had not strode ahead, ignoring me – instead, he was waiting for me at the foot of the stairs, tapping his foot on their foot in impatience.

I smiled. His foot on their foot. That sounded funny.

Leisurely, I strolled towards him. With fuzzy curiosity, I gestured up at the towering monument of mammon above me.

'Why here?' I asked, directing my unsteady smile at Mr Ambrose. 'I don't live here. Not that I'm aware of, anyway,' I added, as an afterthought. Nothing seemed to be too sure, lately. 'Do I?'

Mr Ambrose's face was hidden in shadow, his voice as terse as ever.

'No, you don't. But I thought I would bring you here first and give you the chance to clean up. Unless you want to go home in blood-spattered clothes, that is.'

'What?'

He gestured, and I looked down at myself. Even in the pale light of the gas lamps, it was undeniable that the upper part of my uncle's old tailcoat had distinct signs of red on it. If they weren't blood spatters, they were the experiment of a deranged tomato-enthusiast.

'Hell's whiskers!' A giggle escaped me. 'That looks dashed nifty!'

'*Nifty*, is it?' The dark figure of Mr Ambrose took a step towards me. 'You consider blood spattered all over your clothes *nifty*? Maybe even *chic*? You have interesting fashion tastes, Mr Linton.'

'Why, thank you, Sir.' I bowed and nearly toppled over. Strong arms caught me and put me upright again.

'Still,' his cool voice continued, 'I doubt your aunt shares your tastes in that direction.'

Thoughtfully, I tugged at my lower lip. He might be right about that. Aunt Brank was often completely unreasonable in regard to modern fashion.

'Might be interesting to see her reaction, though.' I giggled again. 'The look on her face...'

'...would undoubtedly be a sight to be seen. Still, in the interest of secrecy, I would advise against it.'

'Oh, all right! Don't be such a stick-in-the-mud.'

He turned. 'I assure you I am not in the habit of sticking sticks into mud, Mr Linton. Follow me.'

Marching up the stairs, he pulled a ring of keys out of his coat pocket. I had never before met anyone who could truly march on stairs, not without breaking their toes, anyway, but he managed it just fine. He reached the door well ahead of me and had unlocked it in a jiffy.

The huge wooden doors squealed like the tortured souls of the undead as they were pushed open. I looked around with interest, just in case some of the tortured souls of the undead happened to be around and wanted to swap recipes, but there was only Alexander the Great, atop his horse, winking at me from the other side of the street.

'Nighty night, Alexander! Conquer Persia for me!' I called, waving to him energetically – until Mr Ambrose grabbed me and pushed me towards the door.

'Hey! There's no need to be so rough,' I protested, resisting his grasp. 'I was only being polite.'

'To a hallucination. And you were waking the whole street up in the process, which is not a good idea. Or have you forgotten that the headquarters of the East India Company is right across the street?'

I furrowed my brow in concentration. For some reason, I was sure that was important, but I couldn't for the life of me remember why.

'Well, no,' I explained, and started grinning again. It was easy to grin right now, and very difficult to frown. 'Actually, I hadn't forgotten. I just don't care. I mean... Alexander the Great conquered parts of India, right? He's surely not afraid of some stuffy old company board members.'

'Mr Linton?'

'Yessir?'

'We need to get you inside.'

'Yessir! Why, Sir?'

Without answering, he renewed his grip and began to push me forward again. This time, I didn't react fast enough, and he managed to manoeuvre me through the entrance into the darkness of the hall beyond.

'Why do we have to go?' I demanded, trying to push my heels into the ground. But it was no use. My shoes just slipped on the polished stone floor. 'I was talking to Alexander the Great!'

That didn't seem to make Mr Ambrose want to let me go, the ill-bred lout! Didn't he know you couldn't behave like that to an Emperor?

'We have go back. I didn't get to say goodbye properly.'

'We can't go back. We have to go upstairs, and you have to sit down.'

'Why?'

'Because you are drunk, Mr Lin–'

'I'm not! Just ask the yellow piggies!'

There was a pause.

'Well... then let's just say that I'm not on the best of terms with Alexander the Great. I wish to avoid him, if possible.'

'Oh.' Now this was interesting news, and my curiosity spiked immediately. 'Why's that?'

There were a few moments of contemplative silence.

'He kicked my favourite dog once.'

'Really, Sir?'

We had reached the other end of the hall by now. There, the floor suddenly vanished, and instead there were these angular thingamies... what were they called again?

'Yes, really, Mr Linton. And a very harsh kick it was.'

Oh yes. Steps! Pride flooded through me! I had actually managed to remember what steps were called! And Mr Ambrose thought I was drunk. Hah! I'd show him.

I took a confident step forward – and a hand shot out to grab me.

'No, not those stairs, Mr Linton. Those lead to the cellars, that's why the steps go down. We want to go to my office and need to find some stairs that go up.'

I pondered this. He might actually be right, I finally decided.

'How clever, Sir! I would never have thought of that.'

'Indeed.'

Somehow, another staircase appeared in front of me. Had he pushed me around again? I decided, just this once, to let it go without protesting. My mind was engaged on a much more serious and enthralling topic than stairs, anyway.

'You have a pet dog?' I asked, the incredulity clear in my voice.

He hesitated. I could feel it: he didn't like to give anything away, be it money or personal information.

'Two,' he finally snapped. From what I could see of his face in the dark it was as impassive as the stone I set my feet on.

'But... aren't dogs expensive, Sir?' I nudged him in the ribs, grinning. 'Really expensive, from what I heard. Why waste money on pets that don't do anything useful?'

'They *do* do something useful. They bite people I don't like.'

'Oh.'

He gripped my arm again. 'Stop! Don't try to go any higher, there are no more steps.'

'Oh really?' I blinked into the gloom. 'I hadn't noticed.'

'Yes. Now we have to go down the hallway. Here, down this hallway, you see. We're almost there.'

'Down? No problem... no problem at all, Sir.'

'I didn't mean *lie* down, I mean *walk* down! My office is over there. You can rest there.'

He stopped me in time before I could rest my head on the floor of the hallway. Honestly, had I lain down there, I would not have been able to get up again. Despite the fact that I was definitely not drunk, I felt effects which, to the amateur eye, might look considerably like drunkenness.

With unusual gentleness, Mr Ambrose helped me up again and manoeuvred me to his office door. There, he took me by both shoulders and looked sternly down into my eyes.

'I have to unlock the door now, and for that I have to let go of you, Mr Linton. Do you think you can stand upright on your own long enough for me to do that?'

I blinked up at him, deeply curious. I would never have thought that he cared whether I keeled over or not – except perhaps that he might regard me bashing my head in on the stone floor as a very beneficial occurrence. But here he was, looking down at me with... well, it wasn't exactly *concern*. It wasn't as if he looked at me like I was someone he cared for – instead, he stared at me like

I was a priceless object in his possession, and he was expressly forbidding me to damage myself and thus lessen my value.

'I must admit,' I muttered, bracing myself against the doorframe, 'I feel a tiddly little bit unsteady on my feet.' I looked around for help and smiled. 'Hey, Napoleon! Come over and help me, your Imperial Menagerie, while he gets the door open!'

For some reason, my application for help to the emperor, who was leaning against the wall next to me, cleaning his nails with a dagger, didn't seem to alleviate Mr Ambrose's concerns. He just doubled his efforts to get the door open as quickly as possible. Hmm. Maybe he had a beef with Napoleon, too, not just with Alexander. These powerful tyrants were always at each other's throats.

'There!' The door swung open, and Mr Ambrose grasped my arm again. 'Get in and sit down, will you?'

'Why not lie down on the floor out here?' I asked, blinking back longingly at the hallway. For some reason its stone floor looked a lot more comfortable than stone floors usually did. It felt soft, too, and was wobbling under my feet like a mattress. 'I could keep the Emperor company.'

'He'll manage just fine without you. Come in, please? You need to rest.'

My ears needed cleaning. Did I just hear Mr Ambrose say *please*? And that in what could almost be described as a gentle tone of voice, compared to the deep-frozen tyrant's voice he usually employed?

A moment later, he squeezed my shoulder. 'Please?'

Holy moly! Miracles did happen!

Almost involuntarily, I started forward. Under his firm but gentle guidance, I stumbled into the room. This was becoming a very strange night... Maybe I really had drunk a tiny bit too much of that burning stuff.

Inside, the office was dark. Mr Ambrose reached to his left. There was a soft noise, and the shimmering light of a gas lamp illuminated the room with a warm, golden glow, throwing long shadows against the walls. Suddenly, the office, so stark in daylight, looked totally different.

'Well, will you look at that?' A broad smile spread over my face as I spread my arms in an attempt to hug the room. Mr Ambrose ducked just in time to not be cuffed around the ears. 'It looks almost cosy! Now all you need is a carpet on the floor and a couple of nice pictures on the walls.'

Mr Ambrose rose out of his crouch again. 'Which, Mr Linton, would be a needless waste of time and money.'

'Oh, come on! Don't you ever feel the urge to make this place a little less... cold?'

'No. I have a very warm cloak, should I need it.'

'I was speaking metaphorelly... metareferain... metaphorically!'

'I was aware of that.' Half-turning to the door, he kicked it shut behind us. 'Metaphors, Mr Linton, are also a waste of time and money'

'Bah! With your attitude, I'm surprised you have gas light in the house. It's supposed to be pretty expensive.'

'Much less expensive than the hospital bill for running headlong into a stone wall in the dark, I assure you.'

He sounded as if he had made the experiment. We were still standing at the door. Neither of us seemed to know what to do, where to go next, now that we had reached our destination.

Suddenly, the floor gave a lurch and threw me to the side. I knew it! I knew that the floor out in the hallway would have been much nicer to me than the evil floor in here! The floor in here seemed to have it in for me, personally. It didn't stop, but kept quaking underneath my feet, while Mr Ambrose seemed to have no problems whatsoever remaining upright. Quickly, he was at my side and had an arm around my waist. I could feel his strong muscles brushing against me, pulling me close –

Then he stiffened.

'Excuse me.' His voice was oddly strained. 'I shouldn't be touching you like this. I only meant to... well, I'll let go soon. Only let me help you to a chair.'

'Don't let go,' I muttered, groggily. 'Feels nice...'

And it did feel nice, having his arm around me. It wasn't like we were the only ones doing it, either. Two yellow piggies on the other side of the room had their arms (or were those legs?) around each other.

'Mister Linton... I...'

'You can call me Lilly, if you want,' I offered, not managing to keep a grin off my face. Funny. I didn't usually smile this much. 'But if you did, you'd admit I'm a girl, which you don't want. So maybe Victor? No, I have it!' A giggle escaped me. 'Call me *Ifrit*!'

I heard a strange noise. A noise I would have never expected to hear in this place. Was it really...? Was that a chuckle? From *him*? Had Mr Ambrose, Mr Rikkard Don't-waste-time-with-idle-frivolities Ambrose actually *laughed*? Or had it been one of the yellow piggies?

'My little *Ifrit*,' he murmured almost inaudibly, tightening his grip around me. I could feel the reverberations of the chuckle through my whole body. It felt really nice, being held by him like this. I felt safe and warm and, for once, not at war with the rest of the world.

'Yes, I'm an *Ifrit*,' I confessed to him in a whisper. 'You were quite right. I didn't really believe you in the beginning, but now, well... you can see for yourself.'

'See what?' For some reason, he sounded confused.

'Why, my huge fiery wings of course! Aren't they beautiful? So sparkly and pretty.'

I pointed up to where my wings almost brushed the ceiling. They were a marvel to behold. It was nearly incomprehensible that I hadn't noticed them before tonight. Maybe it was because I had never much been interested in how I looked before. But tonight, alone in this room with him, I was suddenly glad there was something undeniably beautiful about me, even if I remembered vaguely that a pair of huge fiery wings wasn't exactly a traditional sign of female beauty.

'Don't you think they're pretty, Sir?' I sighed.

'Um, well... yes, of course. Very pretty.'

He thought my wings were pretty! He actually thought my wings were pretty!

'I should jump off the roof to see if I can fly with them,' I suggested eagerly. 'Wouldn't you like to see me fly?'

Abruptly, his grip around my waist became tight as a vice.

'Err... maybe not right now. You're surely tired from being up the entire night. How about tomorrow, if you still feel like jumping off the roof then?'

I pouted. 'But I want to do it now! It'll be fun!'

'Personally, I'm not quite sure about that. Would you sleep on it? Please?'

There was that word again... that word that Mr Ambrose never used.

'All right.' Sighing contentedly, I wrapped my arms and also my huge fiery wings around him. The little piggies in the corner had started to dance tango. 'I'll do anything for you.'

'Ehem... I am gratified to hear it. Now... how about sitting down?'

'If you want...'

He led me to the middle of the room, to where the visitor chair stood in front of the desk. As I moved closer to the desk, the light of the lamp fell on me, and Mr Ambrose's eyes widened.

'Wait just a minute,' he exclaimed. 'Don't sit down just yet. Your coat...'

But he had already let go of me, and my legs somehow were unable to support my own weight. I was about to fall into the chair when his hands shot out and held me back.

'Are you insane?' He hissed. 'I said wait! Look at yourself! You can't sit down like this! Take your tailcoat off, first. It is spattered with blood and street dirt. Have you got any idea how much it costs to clean the upholstery on a chair like this?'

I blinked up at him, confused. 'Not really, no.'

'Too much for me to be willing to pay it.'

'That doesn't say much,' I pointed out.

'My point, Mr Linton, is that if you try to sit down on that chair again, I will bring you back outside into the hallway and dump you on the floor, just like you asked me to earlier.'

So he felt more concern for the upholstery of his office chair than for me. It was nice to see he hadn't changed that much.

I realized that in stopping me from sitting down, Mr Ambrose had grabbed onto me a lot more generously than before. He had both arms around me now and was pressing me to his chest with the fervour of a man determined to avoid a large bill from the cleaner's.

He must have been really anxious to avoid that bill, because instead of letting go of me when my legs had steadied a bit, he pulled me even tighter against him. Though my vision was slightly blurred, I could see the hard lines of his face perfectly well. His jaw was taut, which only accentuated the noble harshness of his features. His eyes were boring down into mine, full of dark intensity.

'Do *not* sit down.' His voice was actually hoarse. Dear me, cleaning the upholstery of a chair had to be more expensive than I thought if he could get this worked up about it. He didn't let go.

343

'But... then what am I supposed to do?' My voice wasn't too steady either. And... I didn't want me to sit down any more than he did. I didn't want him to let go. Odd. I didn't have to fear a big bill from the cleaner's, did I?

He cleared his throat. 'You can take off your tailcoat. Then you can sit down... Mr Linton.'

The 'Mister' came over his lips with no slight hesitation. Was that because he was still calculating the cleaner's bill? Or did it have something to do with the way we were pressed together, so closely it had to be evident that 'Mister' was not the correct address for the person he was holding in his arms?

I, for my part, felt enough so I would never have called him 'Miss Ambrose'. The hard muscles of his chest, his arms, his abdomen... they all pressed into my softness in a way that made it all too clear what he was.

A man.

A really manly man with a lot of mannishness in his manliness.

As if of their own volition, my arms snaked up behind and around him. My head found a comfortable spot on his chest and came to rest there. All of a sudden, I didn't care about any cleaner's bill. I certainly didn't care to sit down. To sit down, I would have had to let go.

'Hmm... take it off,' I mumbled. Beneath my ear that lay on his chest, I could hear his heart. I wondered why it was beating so fast. 'Take my tailcoat off... Good idea. Only... I'm not sure I can stand on my own. I feel so tired...'

Gently, hesitantly, he reached up to unwind my arms from behind his back. 'I'll help you. Don't worry.'

He stepped back from me, and somewhere inside me I felt a tug of disappointment. Disappointment? Why? What did I care whether he was close to me?

But then he started unbuttoning my tailcoat, and the disappointment vanished. It was replaced by a surge of heat up from my toes to the tips of my ears. What was the matter with me? It had to be the drink. Or terror of the the cleaner's bill.

Gently, his fingers travelled up my belly, popping buttons as they went. His fingers were unlike any other fingers that had ever touched me there: smooth and yet firm, light and yet insistent. I realized suddenly that they weren't just unlike any other fingers that had touched me there before – apart from my sisters' and my own, they were the *only* fingers that had ever touched me there. They made me wish for more buttons on my coat, for something to prolong the feel of this. The feel of him.

Then, the tailcoat slid off my shoulders and landed on the floor with a soft, velvety noise. I stood before Mr Ambrose in nothing but trousers and a thin linen shirt. Drowsily, I looked down at the shirt.

'Oh,' I mumbled, and pointed to the left side of the shirt, where a few specks of blood stained the white material. 'The blood must have seeped through the coat. Do you want to take the shirt off, too?'

From somewhere, I heard a strangled groan. When I looked up, Mr Ambrose was standing before me, his face as composed as ever, but his jaw seemed to be a bit tighter than usual.

'I don't think,' he said, 'that will be necessary, thank you.'

344

'But it's got blood on it!' I protested. 'I should take it off! The upholstery on your chair–'

'...will be perfectly fine, Mr Linton! Now sit down!'

For once, I did as he said. My legs didn't feel all too steady, and even Alexander the Great, who had sneaked in behind us unnoticed, was sitting down in a corner of the room. Surely, if a world-famous conqueror was sitting down, that meant that I could, too.

Mr Ambrose bent to retrieve my tailcoat from the floor. Straightening, he said: 'I will give your clothes to the night porter. He will have them washed and dried soon enough.'

I squinted at him, doubtfully. 'He's a porter. Does he know how to wash clothes?'

'Probably not. But I demand ingenuity and dedication of all my employees.'

Turning, he marched towards the door without another word. Was it just my imagination, or did he walk just a little faster than usual, almost as if he were running? At the door, he hesitated. 'I'll be back soon,' he said. Then he fled, slamming the door behind him.

Suppressing a yawn, I nodded to Alexander in the corner. 'I think he really doesn't like you,' I told him.

The Macedonian conqueror shrugged and started cleaning his fingernails.

LOOKING FOR TRUFFLES AND BUTTER-FLIES

Mr Ambrose's porter apparently was no instant-cleaning wizard. I soon grew tired of waiting for my tailcoat's return. To tell the truth, I felt tired in general – tired and battered and dirty. What I really needed was not just to get my clothes cleaned, but to get myself cleaned, too. To wash the dirt off my skin, and all the confusions of the night along with it.

Didn't Mr Ambrose have a powder room? With a shower? I thought I remembered something of the sort from when I had needed to powder my foot. Or had it been my nose?

I got to my feet and waited until that nasty, ill-tempered floor had more or less stopped trying to buck me off. It took some time, but finally it seemed to accept I wasn't just going to be thrown out of the window.

With all the authority I could muster, I pointed a finger at the floor.

'Stay!' I told it. 'I'm going to go to powder my little toe now, and you're going to stay right where you are. Understood?'

The floor nodded, and I raised my chin in triumph. There! I had gained a complete victory. The little yellow piggies cheered and applauded as I paraded past the desk to the little door behind it.

The powder room was just as I remembered it. One toilet, one shower, and no powder at all. Not even gunpowder. But then, I had come to shower, not to blow things up, so maybe that was just as well.

It was a little darker in the room than the last time I had been in here, though. For a moment I wondered why, until I remembered.

Of course! It's nighttime, and that bright thingy in the sky is missing. What's it called again?

The sun! Yes, that's what it was called.

So... you need those other thingamies now. Those whatyemaycallit... lamps!

Dear me! I was really quite impressed by my vast memory and intellect. It even led me to suspect that there might be some sort of switch for the lamps beside the door – and voilà, I was right! My fingers found the switch and turned it.

Bright light exploded from my left and I gave a little gasp, shielding my eyes from the sudden invasion. After a few seconds of familiarization, I took my hand from my eyes and saw that the room was now bathed in a soft yellow light. Now all I needed was for me to be bathed, too – only with water instead of light.

The shower head protruded from the left wall, over a broad, white, ceramic basin. Of course, it had absolutely no gold ornaments or other adornments like any other decent upper-class British bathroom. This was Mr Ambrose's shower, after all. At the moment, though, I didn't care about ornaments. All I cared about was that water would come out of the pipes.

Closing the door behind me, I strode over to the shower. For some strange reason, I felt as though I had forgotten something, but the prospect of the shower was so alluring I put it out of my mind.

The floor in here seemed to be friendlier than the office floor. It only wobbled slightly once or twice as I made my way across the room.

'Good floor,' I mumbled. 'Nice floor. That's right. Just stay where you are.'

The floor obeyed, and soon I had reached my destination and could grab one of the pipes for support.

I noticed there wasn't just a shower, there were towels, too. Perfect! Though a bit strange, admittedly. Who kept bath towels in his office?

He probably practically lives here.

Well, all the better. I wasn't in the mood to drive miles to our bathtub at home, and I needed the calming feel of water on my skin. Maybe my head would feel a little clearer after I sprinkled a little water on it.

Humming contentedly to myself, I slipped out of my remaining clothes, getting it done much more quickly than usual. Trousers were really handy things to wear, compared with hoop skirts. I grabbed one of the towels, all of which, of course, weren't made of embroidered terry cloth, but simple white linen. They felt so smooth and cool that they reminded me of *him*. Wrapping myself in them was almost like wrapping myself in him. It felt nice.

But... wasn't I supposed to do that only after the shower? I felt a bit confused. Oh well, it couldn't hurt and, as mentioned before, it felt *so* nice. I was so engrossed in the task of wrapping the towels tightly around me that I didn't hear the approaching footsteps outside.

Only when the door swung open and I heard a gasp behind me did I realize I was no longer alone.

'Mr Linton!'

Drat! I knew I had forgotten something. Nobody was supposed to be able to come in, right? Though I couldn't remember how or why exactly…

I turned, towels pressed against my chest, just in time to see Mr Ambrose back out of the room, his eyes tightly shut. The door slammed behind him.

'Mr Linton?' His voice came from the other side of the door. Was it just my imagination, or did he sound just a little bit not his usual cool self?

'Yes, Sir?'

'The next time you decide to use my private bathroom, would you be so kind as to *bolt the door?*'

Bolts! That's how you made sure the door didn't open. I remembered it now. With effort, I squinted at the door.

'I can't, Sir. There's no bolt on it.'

'Of course there isn't!' he snapped. 'Do you think I would waste money having a bolt installed on the door of a bathroom which only I ever use?'

I nodded gravely. 'Of course not, Sir. Time is money is pumpernickel, right?'

'*Power*, Mr Linton, *power*. Not pumpernickel.'

'Oh. Right you are, Sir!'

'Next time you go in there without informing me, wedge a chair under the door! Understood, Mr Linton?'

I nodded again. That sounded like a sound policy.

'Yes, Sir. As you say, Sir. And by the way… I think you can stop calling me "Mister" Linton now.' I giggled a little. 'You've probably seen enough evidence to the contrary.'

'*Mister Linton!*'

'No, no. Not *Mister*. Didn't you hear what I just said?'

There was a silence from the other side of the door.

'Mr Ambrose, Sir?' I asked. 'Are you still there?'

'I am counting to ten to calm myself. Do not disturb me, Mr Linton.'

'As you wish, Sir.'

I tried to count along, to know when it would be all right to speak again, but it didn't quite work. Every time I got to three I sort of stumbled and couldn't remember the number that came next.

'Mr Linton?' His voice finally came from the other side.

'Yes, Sir?'

'Tell me when you are done in there. I, too, am not completely clean and wish to freshen up before retiring for the night.'

'You can come in now, if you want,' I offered generously. 'There's room enough for both of us here.'

'No!'

He sounded quite adamant. That was strange. Confused, I looked around the bathroom.

'Yes, there is. Don't you know the size of your own bathroom? There's plenty of room, believe me.'

'I am not disputing that. However, I still cannot come in.'

I frowned. He was so stubborn sometimes. 'Why not?'

'Because,' he explained to me, his voice painfully calm, 'persons of different sexes do not shower together. Society generally frowns on that kind of thing.'

My frown deepened as I tried to concentrate. If I tried very hard, I vaguely seemed to remember something of the sort.

'But Napoleon is in here with me, too,' I pointed out, waving at the Emperor, who was leaning against the opposite wall, playing chess with one of members of the piggy dance troupe.

'Err, well... he's a Frenchman. That's different.'

Before I had a chance to argue, I heard hurried footsteps receding on the other side of the door. Strange. Why had he run away?

Pouting, I removed my towels and stepped under the shower. It would have been a novel experience taking a shower with somebody else. For some reason I couldn't recall at the moment, I had never done it before. Thoughtfully, I eyed Napoleon on the other side of the room, but he didn't seem interested. He was much too engrossed in his game of chess. The yellow piggy appeared to be winning, and the Emperor's face was set in grim lines of concentration.

Ah well, it would be a new experience anyway. To be honest, I had never stood under a shower before. They were a pretty new and fancy invention – expensive, too, by all I had heard. Much more expensive than the traditional bathtub. Mr Ambrose probably only had installed one because he had calculated that in thirty-seven years or so, the water he had saved would justify the additional investment.

Money is power is pumpernickel, right?

Oh well, there couldn't be that much difference between a hot bath and a hot shower. Shrugging, I grasped the tap and turned it.

A banshee-like scream echoed through the halls of Empire House. Outside the door, I could hear the sound of running footsteps, and then Mr Ambrose's voice, calling: 'Mr Linton? Mr Linton, has something happened?'

'Yes!' I yelled back. 'Yes! A bucket full of ice water, that is what has happened! Where the dickens does the water in your pipes come from? Antarctica?'

I heard something from the other side that sounded very much like a wall being punched with energy. Or maybe the floor. I hoped it was the floor. He deserved it more.

'Well?' I demanded. 'Where the heck do you get your water from?'

'A rainwater tank on the roof,' came the cool reply. 'Why?'

'You use *rainwater*?'

'Yes. You don't honestly expect me to pay for water when I can get it for free, do you?'

'Mr Ambrose, Sir?' I asked, as sweetly as I could.

'Yes?'

'Is the water in this tank per chance *heated* in any way?'

'No, of course not. Why would I waste money on that?'

I proceeded to explain to him exactly why. My explanation might have contained an expletive or two, or maybe a dozen, most directed at him, his ancestry to the tenth generation, and most especially his architect. When I was finished, his cool voice came from outside:

'Mr Linton?'

'Yes, Sir?'

'Do not make any unnecessary noises again. I am trying to work.'

And with that, he was gone.

Quivering with cold, I stood under the shower, cursing the icy water running over my skin, and cursing Mr Ambrose. If he were in here with me, damn him, I was sure I would not be half as cold. He could be surprisingly warm considering how icy he was all the time.

Closing my eyes, I imagined him here with me, wrapping his arms around me, holding me tightly against him. For some reason, I was sure it would feel very nice having him here. He would be much more interesting company than Napoleon, who was still standing against the wall, bent over his chess game.

When I opened my eyes again, I saw him.

He had come after all! Mr Ambrose had entered the room. I wondered briefly why he was dressed in a red hunting costume, but who cared. I smiled a wide smile.

'You came,' I mumbled.

He smiled back at me, opened his mouth, and growled like a tiger. Hmm... that wasn't something he did normally, was it? And normally, he wasn't so fuzzy around the edges. But you couldn't expect everything, could you? He was here, that was the main thing. Who cared if I got tiger growls instead of intelligent conversation. It wasn't as if he was a great talker under normal circumstances.

He stepped closer, his cold eyes raking up and down my body in a way for which any man deserved a slap in the face. Yet, strangely, I felt no urge to slap him. I felt an urge to draw him closer. Maybe then the cold water would be easier to bear. Heat already began to simmer in my belly...

'Mr Ambrose, Sir...'

My words were cut off as he took another step forward and reached out for me.

~~**~*~*

Sometime later – insofar as time still had a meaning for me – I stumbled out of the powder room in a shirt and trousers, my feet still bare and my hair damp from the shower. Mr Ambrose awaited me outside, attired in his usual black tailcoat, bow tie and icy expression. How odd. I could have sworn that he'd just been wearing red, and then... well... significantly less.

'What exactly did you do in there, Mr Linton?' he demanded icily. He held his silver watch open in his hand. 'You spent thirty-one minutes, four and a half seconds under the shower. The average time people require to take a shower is eight to fifteen minutes.'

I blinked at him owlishly. 'How do you know the average time people need to make a shower? Do you spy through people's windows with a telescope?'

He chose not to honour that with a reply.

'*I* only require three and a half minutes,' he informed me instead.

'I'm sure you do, Sir.'

'People are too lazy.' He let the watch snap shut and strode past me into the powder room. 'This room is now occupied, and since there is no lock on the door, you had better remember not to come in.'

'Say hello to Napoleon for me,' I called after him. 'And tell him, if he's planning a rematch, to start with the ruy lopez, e4 e5! Classic opening move!'

The door slammed shut without a reply. How rude! I had liked him better under the shower.

Remembering, heat flushed through my lower body. Much, much better.

Oh well, you couldn't expect people to behave the same when they were dry as when they were wet, now, could you? Disconsolately, I wandered over to the straight-backed visitor's chair and was just about to sink down on it when it occurred to me that Mr Ambrose probably wouldn't like water stains on it any better than bloodstains. So I leaned against the wall and tried to dry my hair as best I could with the towel I had brought with me. It didn't go very well. The floor had it in for me once again, rocking from side to side, making it nearly impossible to find my own head, let alone get it dry.

'Blast!'

I tried to throw the towel over the back of my head so I could rub my neck dry. But somehow I managed to throw it over the front of my head instead, to rub my face wet. I got a mouthful of towel, and tried in vain to dislodge it from between my teeth.

'Blaft, blaft, blaft... pfft! Blast!'

Finally! But by now I had managed to wrap the towel around my throat. Could one strangle oneself with a towel, I wondered? It would certainly make an interesting headline:

Sparsely dressed young lady found strangled with a towel in office of London's richest businessman! The scandal thickens! Mr Rikkard Ambrose unavailable for comment!

Mr Ambrose would not be pleased – and neither would Napoleon or Alexander. They'd prefer it if I died bravely in battle, I was sure. I should probably try not to strangle myself.

Tentatively, I tugged at one end of the towel again. The beastly thing constricted around my throat, with total disregard for the wishes of two famous historical emperors.

'Blast!'

'Here, let me.'

My hand jerked when somebody touched it, and I really would have strangled myself had not this other hand gripped the towel firmly and unwound it from around my neck. Wait just a minute – I knew this hand!

It was Mr Ambrose. He had returned and appeared beside me without my noticing. Well, I suppose strangling oneself is a rather engrossing activity.

He wasn't wearing his red hunting costume this time, or his black tailcoat, though I saw that hanging over the visitor's chair nearby, next to a piggy that was looking through the pockets, in the hope of finding truffles, presumably. This Mr Ambrose was simply dressed in a white shirt and black waistcoat and, of course, his icy expression, which he probably hadn't taken off even under the shower.

His hands weren't icy, though. They were gentle and warm as he unwrapped the towel from around my neck and pulled it over my hair, which he seemed to have no difficulty finding.

'Hold still a moment.'

His fingers worked too quickly for me to tell what exactly he was doing, but when he was finished, the towel was wrapped up and around my head in a complicated knot, keeping the cold air out and my wet hair in place.

'Now you can sit down,' he ordered tersely. 'When the towel has soaked up most of the water from your hair, get a fresh towel and dry your hair again. Don't even think of starting to rub, just take a bit of hair at a time and pat it dry from both sides.'

He led me to the visitor's chair, and I was so surprised I let him do it.

'How do you know how to towel-dry long hair?' I asked him, once I was seated beside the truffles-seeking yellow piggy. 'Don't tell me you used to work as a hairdresser's assistant.'

'No. The explanation is somewhat simpler than that. I used to have long hair, once.'

'*You?*' My voice probably contained a bit more incredulity than was proper, but then, I had an inkling I had been doing a lot of things lately that were not entirely proper, and so far I was having lots of fun. I eyed Mr Ambrose's neatly trimmed black hair with suspicion. '*You* had long hair?'

'Indeed.'

'*Why?*'

'Because I did not have enough money for a knife or scissors to cut it with.'

He was out of the room before I could think of a reply. And really, thinking of replies was so exhausting...

~~**~*~*

'Mr Linton? Mr Linton, you have to remove that damp towel.'

'W-what?'

Blinking, I sat up straight. The world seemed very fuzzy again. There was a man standing in front of me... White shirt, black waistcoat and bow tie... stone-faced... Mr Ambrose! Mr Ambrose with a fresh towel!

'Here. Take this.' He handed the towel to me.

'But you said to wait,' I protested.

'You have been waiting. Sleeping, to be exact. But five minutes is long enough. My office is no home for passing drunkards.'

He unwound the damp towel from my head, and I, luckily able to find my head again, began to rub vigorously.

'I said *pat* your hair dry,' he reminded me. 'Pat. Gently. Not rub like you want to rip it out of your head.'

'Why don't you go write a brochure on hair care?' I grumbled. 'I can dry my hair however I want, thank you very much.'

After a few minutes, I let the towel sink with a sigh.

'I can't get it really dry with this,' I complained. 'You wouldn't happen to have a hairbrush, would you?'

He was standing at the dark window by now, looking out over the lights of the city. He didn't turn around at my question.

'Why on earth would I possess such a useless item? Use your fingers. That's perfectly good enough.'

Why was he suddenly being so antagonistic? He had been so nice just a minute ago, saving me from strangling myself, and even nicer before that, in the shower... and now? Now he was cold as stone again, and staring away from me. I didn't understand it. Didn't understand him.

'I liked you better in your hunting costume,' I grumbled.

'What did you say?'

'Forget it.'

I did my best to dry my hair with fingers and towel. Beside me, the piggy had switched to the inner jacket pockets, still searching for truffles.

'Try the upper left one,' I whispered to it. 'Take his wallet and you can buy all the truffles you've ever dreamed of.'

The piggy squeaked excitedly and proceeded to take my advice. I leaned back in the chair with a contented sigh, imagining how it would find Mr Ambrose's wallet and sneak off with all his money to buy truffles in Brussels. Suddenly, my hair felt much drier, and I myself better in a general way, though my feet were still a bit cold.

I sneaked a peek at Mr Ambrose, to see if he had taken notice of the piggy's activities. But he was still standing at the dark window, his back to the room, looking out over the city. In the distance, beyond the glass, one could just see the lights glowing at the docks. Work went on there, even through the night.

'Mr Linton?'

Exasperated, I tapped on the armrest of the chair. 'You still persist in calling me that? Even after what you've seen?'

Maybe it was a trick of the light, but I could have sworn his ears turned a tiny bit red. So, this creature of stone actually had some blood in him.

'*Especially* after all I've seen, Mr Linton.' His voice was as frosty as the heart of an iceberg. 'Not,' he added immediately, 'that I actually saw anything. I turned away and closed my eyes very quickly. I saw nothing at all.'

'Mr Ambrose, Sir?'

'Yes?'

'Don't lie.'

'Mr Linton!'

He started to turn – then thought better of it and folded his arms in front of his chest. So I folded my arms in front of my chest, too, in defiance. And for the sake of gender equality, of course. Peeking at him out of the corner of my eye, I saw he was still glaring out of the window, trying to freeze the city of London with his gaze alone. I didn't have a window to stare through belligerently, so I had to make do with the wall, but my stare was nevertheless a match for his.

For a while we just remained like this, glaring in angry silence. Finally, he spoke again:

'I wanted to ask you something, Mr Linton.'

'Well, why didn't you?'

'You distracted me.'

'I'm quite skilled at that,' I admitted.

'Yes, you are.'

'So ask now.'

There was another moment of silence. Then, abruptly:

'Why do you do it, Mr Linton? Why work for me? Why insist on doing work that is meant for men? You saw that it is dangerous. If you didn't believe me before, you cannot doubt it after tonight. Why do you do it?'

It was the first time he had asked me this question – outright, without cold disdain, sounding as if he really were interested in hearing the answer. For a moment, I considered giving a smart reply like 'because of the cheerful working atmosphere at your office' or 'because I like gun fights', but... I was feeling strangely drowsy and unprotected, robbed of my usual defensive layers of sarcasm against the masculine world. The truth slipped out of my mouth before I could help it.

'I want to be free.'

He whirled around, and I jerked in surprise. I had not expected my simple statement to get such a reaction. His eyes were like shards of dark ice.

'That is it? That is all? You *are* free. England is a free country. Nobody can hold you against your will!'

I wanted to laugh out loud. But the subject really wasn't anything to laugh about.

'Once I'm married, my husband can,' I hissed. Anger was rising inside me, burning away the tiredness that had clouded my mind. What did he know of freedom? What did any man know? They took for granted what women could never have. 'I *must* work to make a living. The only other choice is to give myself to a so-called "eligible" man, Mr. Ambrose, Sir. For life.'

In three steps he was around the desk and in front of me.

'And would that be so detestable? To belong to a man?'

I shot up to face him, not knowing where the energy came from. I was bone-crushingly tired. But I suddenly ran on anger now, and I always had a good supply of that at hand. My mouth tightened, the tired smile disappearing. Woozy or not, tired or not, seeing little piggies or not, I had an absolutely clear opinion on that one particular question.

'I'd rather die!'

A muscle in his beautiful, mask-like face twitched.

'Even if the man... harboured feelings for you?'

At that, the yellow piggy stopped searching for truffles and started snickering. I wanted to throw something at it, but didn't see any ammunition in the vicinity.

'And how likely is that?' I scoffed.

For a moment he just stood there. His jaw moved; he looked like he wanted to say something. But then, why didn't he? Instead, he just stood there in silence.

Finally, he said in his most icy voice: 'How should I know? I am certainly no expert on bridegroom choice. Still, it would seem a safer option to marry than to do what you are doing.'

'Life is not about living the safer option,' I told him sleepily. 'Life is about living a life worth living.'

'You won't get to live a life worth living, or any life, if you go on like this!' Grabbing my upper arms, he pushed me backwards until my back slammed into the wall. 'Don't you understand, Mr Linton? You could have died out there tonight! Died!'

And he shook me, as if he could get his point across by treating me like a salt shaker. All it did was make me angrier! All right, I admit it also made me feel the hardness of his body grinding and bumping against mine, but I tried my best to ignore that and focus on the being angry part.

I remembered another time not long ago when we had stood like this, pressed close together, my anger boiling like a volcano in me, his freezing cold in him. I remembered what it had felt like to feel every line of his sinuous, statuesque body pressed against me. Statuesque – that was normally a word you used only for women, if you wanted to say they were tall and graceful. But as I felt him now, I knew it described him perfectly. It described the hardness of his muscles. It described the lack of motion on his face. It even described his taciturn and stony manner. Like a statue. Statuesque.

The only thing it did not describe was the anger I swear I could feel underneath the stony exterior, in his deep, dark eyes.

What was there for *him* to be angry about? What was it to him if I died? He'd finally be rid of me, something he had been trying to achieve by a multitude of methods for weeks now. He should be glad if a stray bullet did the work for him.

'You could have died,' he repeated. Behind him, Napoleon, who had left the bathroom by now, the chessboard under his arm, nodded solemnly. Blast! Even the Emperor agreed with him. I had to swallow.

'I know,' I said softly. 'I know I could have died, but so could you. So could any of the men who were there, fighting.'

'But you are not like them, Mr Linton.'

The unspoken spoken words hung like the sword of Damocles in the air over our heads: *You are a girl. You are weak.*

My chin rose up in proud defiance.

'I can be like them, in all the things that matter.'

His icy, sea-coloured eyes wandered from my face then, went down my body, slowly, lingeringly, and up again. I could feel the breathing in his chest, still pressed against mine, quicken as he did so.

'No.' The word was absolute, brooking no contradiction. 'You could never be.'

He leaned forward until I could feel his breath tickle my skin. What was he doing? His hands, his body, his breath, all melted together into a frightening, exciting melee of sights, feelings, smells and sounds. Suddenly, I could feel butterflies dancing in my stomach.

Butterflies? What the heck were butterflies doing down there? I hadn't eaten any this morning, had I?

His silent, stony face was only inches away now. He was so near, so terribly near – and then he moved to close the last bit of distance.

SEEING STARS

I pushed.

It wasn't a very hard push. Somehow, when pushing away Mr Ambrose's hard body, my arms didn't want to move as determinedly as I had ordered them to. But the push caught him by surprise, and he staggered back, letting go of my wrists.

'Who do you think you are, telling me what I can and cannot be?' I shouted. I was angry. Boiling hot volcano angry! 'I can be anything I want! I could decide to be a member of a yellow piggy dance troop, and I could make it work if I wanted to!'

The yellow piggy removed its snout from Mr Ambrose's coat pocket and shook its head vigorously. I ignored it.

'You can never be a man,' he repeated, not retreating an inch from his position. His eyes raked up and down my body once more. I was very conscious of how, without my tailcoat, the fabric of the shirt barely concealed my form, which, while lacking upstairs, was definitely feminine in the butt department.

But... that couldn't be what he referred to, was it? He couldn't possibly think of me in *that* way, could he? He was talking about women's rights and liberties, not about me and him doing...

No!

Definitely not.

Oh God.

'I don't want to be a man,' I somehow managed to say. *Especially when you're looking at me like this, with eyes as deep and dark as the Atlantic Ocean.* 'All I want is to be *treated* the same!'

'Where's the difference?' he demanded.

The difference is the way I feel right now. The way the blood is pumping through my veins twice as hard.

'The difference,' I said, with clenched teeth, 'The difference is... it is....'

He regarded me like a scientist would regard a strange, undiscovered creature, while I searched for words that I could speak aloud. There were none to be found. All I could think about was how fast my heart was hammering and how hot my face felt.

Well, what if it did? I was angry at him! So *of course* my heart was hammering and my face was flushed. And of course his being such a chauvinistic bastard was the reason. It had nothing whatsoever to do with how his deep, sea-coloured eyes were boring into me right there and then.

'You see?' he said coldly. 'You can never be like a man.'

I glared at him with all the force I could muster.

'Will you ever give me anything but scorn?' I demanded.

'Yes.' My hopes flared – until he continued: 'I will give you your salary at the end of the month. If you do your work properly, that is.'

The flare of hope I had felt extinguished.

Why? Why did disappointment flood through me? After all, money was all I wanted from him. The money to give me my freedom. What else would I want from him?

He was still looking at me like that. In that way that made my knees feel weak.

'Good.' I raised my chin and, ignoring my knees, turned away from him. Marching over to the visitor's chair I sank down on it. 'That's all I want. Money enough to be free.'

'Oh, you'll have money.' His eyes glittered. 'You still won't be free, though.'

My head whipped towards him. 'How so?'

He marched back to his own chair and sank into it with a grace I couldn't hope to match. From behind his desk, projecting paramount, cold power and authority, he looked at me over his steepled fingers. 'Just like in marriage, you'll still be tied to a man – to me.'

My eyes narrowed. 'Yes. But unlike in a marriage, at the end of the day I can go home and recuperate. And unlike in a marriage, if I ever get sick of seeing your stony visage every day, I can resign.'

Abruptly, his hands tightened into fists again. 'But nobody else would give you a position.'

'True,' I mumbled. 'Seems you're stuck with me for now.'

Was it my imagination or did his hands relax again marginally when he heard that? We glared at each other for a moment or two, at a silent stalemate. I didn't know what the heck he wanted, what would make him stop hating me so much! God, when he was looking at me like that, I didn't even know what I wanted anymore! But whatever it was, it had nothing to do with him!

I sat there for a while. But after a few minutes, something intruded upon my befuddled brain. A feeling... something about my feet...

Did they feel colder?

Yes, they did. Colder, and colder and colder. And I couldn't quite figure out why. Glancing down, I saw they looked perfectly normal. Two feet, with five toes each. But wasn't there something missing?

Shoes! Shoes and socks, you idiot! I had left them in the bathroom.

Of course!

Carefully, I rose. The floor seemed to be peaceable right now. Should I dare dash across the room to the bathroom to get my shoes and socks, or would the evil beast try to buck me off again? Thoughtfully, I regarded the stone tiles. They seemed to be solid and still.

On a sudden impulse, I took a step forward, then another. Yay! The floor was apparently asleep and not intent on making trouble for me! I reached the bathroom door in no time at all, and without falling down once.

Mr Ambrose turned towards me as I passed.

'Is something the matter, Mr Linton?'

'My shoes,' I growled. I wouldn't be polite to him. Not now. Not after he made me feel so... so strangely alive just by looking at me. That was too damn peculiar! 'I forgot them in the powder room, and my feet are getting cold.'

He nodded, coolly. 'Be careful. You didn't look too steady on your feet, earlier, and it would be a shame if you survived the gunfight only to break your neck in my office.'

'I was perfectly steady! The floor was attacking me!'

'Pardon?'

I just shook my head, not wasting my time on an answer. Unbelievable that a man who was supposed to be clever enough to have amassed an immense business empire couldn't even understand that his own office floor was conspiring against unsuspecting visitors. Though I had to admit, it seemed to be quiet enough right at the moment. I had probably frightened it into submission with my implacable courage and determination.

I found my shoes and socks under the sink and returned to the office carrying both with me. Mr Ambrose was standing at his desk, turned towards me, a strange look on his face. He was probably finally considering the conspiracy of the office floor – as well he should! But at least I was safe. It wouldn't dare attack me, seeing as I was so courageous and determined.

It was when I had crossed about half the distance to the visitor's chair that the evil floor struck!

I felt my bare foot slipping on an unusually slippery piece of polished stone. My socks and shoes went flying, and I fell backwards, my arms flailing – until another pair of arms caught me in their strong hold. I gasped as they hauled me up. Not all the way up. Just far enough so I could feel my body pressing against that of the man who held me.

'What did I tell you?'

Blinking, I tried to dispel the layer of mist that seemed to cloud my vision. Sparkly lights danced in front of my eyes. When they slowly disappeared I looked up into the dark, sea-coloured eyes of Mr Rikkard Ambrose.

'What,' he repeated very slowly and clearly, 'did I tell you, Mr Linton?'

Once again his face was only inches away from mine, and suddenly my shoes and socks didn't seem quite so important anymore.

I gulped. What was happening? 'T-to be careful. You told me to be careful.'

'Yes.' His eyes darkened further, until they resembled the deepest abyss imaginable. 'Too bad I don't ever listen to my own good advice.'

Then he plunged down.

For a moment, all my fuzzy mind could manage was the thought: *What is he doing? Is he going to butt heads with me?*

A second later that question was answered with a resounding negative, as his lips reached mine and enveloped them, soft as velvet and yet unyielding.

They started to move, pushing my mouth apart and my conscious self out of my body.

What... wait, this couldn't be right, could it? If somebody was touching his lips to mine, that would mean that they were... kissing me?

So he was.

Waves of heat raced through me as the realization hit my befuddled brain: Mr Ambrose was kissing me! His lips moving against my mouth, caressing, demanding. How... curious. For a moment, I was just numb.

Then, I remembered the world again, and I felt rage flood through me. How dare he? After treating me so abominably for the last few weeks, after humiliating me in public and insulting me again and again, after trying to rid himself of me a dozen times and wrecking my dreams, how dare he take such liberties with me? First he conspired with his office floor to trip me, and now he was kissing me!

And worse, far worse – he wasn't just *kissing* me. He was making me *like* it! And he was somehow, by some nefarious chauvinistic manly trick, managing to make me *kiss him back*!

How dare he make me do this? How was he able to force me to respond to his kisses in a way I had never even imagined? I was sure it had to be *his* fault. Under no circumstances would *I* ever consent to let a man knead my lips like this, least of all him! The idea alone was abominable! Horrible! Horrific!

Though... now that I thought about it, the reality of it was actually... not... quite... so... horrific...

Somewhere along the line, the thought dissolved and vanished. The clarity of my mind was gone in the blink of an eye. Not drowned in alcohol this time, no. Drowned in the soft touch of his mouth.

His lips on mine felt so soft yet so strong, moulding themselves to the shape of mine, as if they had been meant to be there. As if on their own volition, my teeth opened and bit down on his lower lip, drawing it and him closer towards me. My hands grabbed his waistcoat lapel and pushed and pulled, venting my anger and frustration and... something else. Something I couldn't name or define. I heard a strangled moan as if from a distance and realized, startled, that it came from my throat.

Suddenly, he broke away from me, leaving me gasping and weak-kneed. I was still in his arms, looking up into his chiselled face for the first time since our lips had touched. I could see something in his eyes, something dark and dangerous. They had widened, and I could see to their utmost, darkest depths.

'Now do you believe me?' His voice was still cold as ice, but rough now, as though covered with fresh frost. 'You could *never* be like a man. Trust me, I would not have done that if you were one.'

Before I knew it, we were kissing again. My hands wandered from his lapels, over his rock-hard chest and onto his arms. My small hands weren't large enough to fit around the muscles of his arm, so I grabbed hold of his shirt sleeves to... what? Push him away? Pull him closer? I seemed to be trying to do neither and both at the same time.

I was shaking him. That's what it was. Shaking him like he had been shaking me, forcing all my anger onto him and into him. I wanted to punch him, to pay him back for all the ways in which he had hurt me, for all the times he had tried to get rid of me, again and again. And now he was kissing me, as if all he wanted was to possess me and never let go – and I was kissing the chauvinistic son of a bachelor back!

Why the heck was I kissing him back? And why was I bloody enjoying it? That wasn't fair!

The world had stopped making sense.

His lips moved from my own then, to the side of my mouth. Another sound escaped me – not a groan this time, but a growl, like that of a feral beast.

'Let... go... of... me!' I managed with enormous effort.

My hands, though, seemed to have other plans: they grabbed him by the lapels again and pressed my lips forcibly to his. Traitors!

We were clenched together like this for I knew not how long. Finally, we broke apart. 'Why?' he rasped. His voice was a winter storm. 'You don't seem to mind.'

His hold tightened around me. I fought against it, fought very hard. When I broke free, I grabbed his collar and pushed him backward until we both rammed into the desk.

'I'm a girl!' I growled. My anger was burning like a furnace. The world around me seemed to be lit in colours brighter than the sun, and he was brightest of all. Damn him! 'I'm not supposed to be in control of my emotions. That's your job! So stop the hell touching me!'

'Why don't you stop?'

I traced my fingers down the side of his hard, chiselled face. 'Because I don't bloody want to!'

'Well, I'm similarly disinclined.'

Oh, bloody hell! If he wouldn't stop making me feel this treacherously good, I would have to force him! Drawing back my hand, I prepared to slap him.

'Oh no, you don't.'

He caught my hand in mid-air. Drawing back the other one, I let it fly! He caught that one, too. Before I knew how, my hands were on his face and I was drawn down towards him. Our lips collided.

On the rare occasions that I glanced between the covers of a romance novel, I had chanced upon an expression that seemed to be a favourite with romantic writers – lips 'melting together'.

Well, our lips didn't melt. They collided. They collided like a ship and an iceberg. They collided like two stars, one red hot, one icy blue. They collided like two wolves, bent on devouring each other. And so did we.

I nearly knocked him over backwards and rammed his head into the desk. He didn't seemed to mind, though. He was too busy pulling me down towards him. His hands had found their way to the small of my back. The feel of him there, his fingers skimming over me, holding me close... it was like nothing I had ever felt before.

Oh, I had been touched there before – by insolent fellows at some ball or other who didn't know how to keep their hands to themselves. But those touches had only ever made me want to reach for a bucket to puke into. His touch had quite a different effect. It made me just want to touch him back. Maybe not even by punching him. Just... touching. Softly.

What was wrong with me? Help!

Slowly, I sank forward until I came to rest on his chest. I was resting against a man's chest. And I didn't want to cringe away in horror! What the bloody heck was wrong with me?

This is what you've always worked so hard to avoid, a small voice in my head whispered. *Get away! You don't want this! You didn't ever want a man to touch you like this!* But the voice was getting smaller and smaller, until I could no more hear the *want a man,* and all that was left was an echoing *touch... touch... touch...*

Something touched my face. I jerked back, breaking the kiss, and gasping. His fingers! He had his fingers on my face, stroking my cheeks.

Dear God! How could I have ever thought him cold? The tips of his fingers on my face were like torches, sending sparks racing down my spine to somewhere deep, deep inside me, a place I had never known about before. A place that only waited to be kindled.

'Come.'

It was an order. But this time one I didn't mind. His fingers grasped my face tightly, pulling it back towards his. I had never seen it this close: his smooth, raven-black hair – how had I never noticed how shiny it was? – his classical, chiselled features – beautiful, simply beautiful – and above all, his mouth. His mouth. The word suddenly held a whole new meaning for me. No longer was it just the origin of curt, demanding orders and misogynistic balderdash. It was the source of a touch that was so intimate, so inflammatory, that it was beyond anything I could have imagined.

His arms were still around me, holding me tight. His eyes didn't leave mine for a moment. Was this, I wondered, what it was like for Ella when Edmund was holding her? What it was like to be close to a man, to open yourself and let all barriers fall?

It was an unearthly thing, in the truest sense of the word. I could even see bright stars dancing at the office ceiling, behind Mr Ambrose's chiselled face.

My head felt strange. What was happening? The fire was slowly burning out. And the stars... the stars were no longer dancing behind Mr Ambrose. They were also dancing *in front* of his face. And they were multiplying, obscuring my vision. Mist came, flooding in from the edges of my sight, and I slowly sank into the darkness. From very far away I heard a voice calling out: 'Miss Linton! Miss Linton!'

Now, who could that be? I wondered. *Mr Ambrose never calls me Miss.*

Then the darkness swallowed me.

A Trace of Fire Brings the Winter

When I awoke, I was slumped in the visitor's chair, my head resting on my shoulder. My eyes didn't want to open, but I knew where I was sitting without looking. No one in London except Mr Rikkard Ambrose owned a chair this hard and uncomfortable. A soft groan escaped my mouth.

'Ah. You are finally awake.'

The voice was cool, and as distant as Timbuktu. I didn't need to open my eyes to recognize it, either.

'What... happened?' I moaned.

'You went to the bathroom to get your shoes. On the way back you stumbled and passed out. I believe you hit your head.'

Slowly, memories started coming back. The memories he spoke of came first – but there were faint images of others, too. I had bumped my head? Some part of me did feel as if a bruise was likely to develop, but it wasn't the back of my head. Almost unconsciously, I reached up and touched my lips. They felt unusually warm and swollen.

Could one knock oneself out by falling on the mouth? I wasn't sure. And shouldn't I have knocked my teeth out in the process? I felt my jaw. All teeth were still firmly attached. But my lips... My lips felt different, somehow. Not really in a bad way. Tingly and hot. If that's what keeling over did to you, maybe I should do it more often.

Mustering all my energy, I forced my eyes open. Mr Ambrose stood over me, looking even more like the statue of some Greek god for the fact that he was towering above me. Any moment I expected him to start throwing thunderbolts.

Touching my lips again, I met his gaze. For a moment, something in his eyes flashed, something that was gone so quickly that I had probably imagined it.

'Did... anything happen?' I mumbled. 'Anything else?'

Not a muscle in his face moved. 'Other than you falling and nearly cracking your head open on the floor, Mr Linton? No. I must inform you that if you wish to remain in my employ, you will in the future have to refrain from such effeminate displays of clumsiness. I have no time for them. Do we understand each other?'

'Y-yes, Sir.'

'Good. Then maybe you can finally leave now. I wish to have my office to myself. Your presence here is distracting.'

I got to my feet. Apparently, the floor still wasn't interested in a peace treaty. It wobbled threateningly under my feet as I made my way to the door. Mr Ambrose, though, who walked beside me, didn't have any problems, which confirmed my suspicion: he had been in cahoots with the floor all along! They had worked together to do... something.

Yes, something had happened.

But what?

If only I could remember. Yet the memory was just out of my reach.

Had they collaborated to knock me down? But why would they hit me on the lips to do so? Surely it would have worked better if they had tried the back of my head. Besides... I couldn't believe that Mr Ambrose had anything to do with my silly accident. The yellow piggies would have warned me if they saw him sneaking up on me.

'You would have, wouldn't you?' I asked the one that was standing in the corner and playing with the long tails of Napoleon's army uniform. It nodded solemnly.

'What?' Mr Ambrose asked.

'I wasn't talking to you. Come on. I want to get out of here before the floor tries to eat me.'

~~**~*~*

The whole way down the stairs Mr Ambrose kept a tight hold on my elbow for some unfathomable reason. Only when we had arrived in the cavernous entrance hall did he let go of me. But when I started towards the front door, he shook his head.

'Not that way.'

'But that's the way we came in, Sir.'

'Still, it will not be the way we leave.'

'Why not?'

He stared at me pointedly.

'Why not, *Sir*?' I amended, exasperated.

'Lord Dalgliesh is sure to have this place watched. It is of no matter whether his men saw us enter – but they must not see you leave. Not when your next stop is your family home, from which he might infer your true identity. Have you any idea what Lord Dalgliesh would give for the news that I have lowered myself to employing a female as my private secretary?'

'You think he'd be interested?' I asked curiously.

'*Interested* is too mild a word for it. Come.'

He led me straight across the hall, past the receptionist's desk and towards a large door at the back of the vast room. Though it was only illuminated by the scant moonlight that filtered in through the narrow windows, the hall was behind us in a matter of seconds. He seemed to know his way around perfectly, and never reduced the tempo of his long, rapid strides. The door where we ended up was large and double-winged, almost as impressive as the entrance. I wondered why one would need such a large door inside a building. The question was answered only a second later when the double-door swung open and revealed what lay beyond.

'Bloody...!'

We stood at the entrance to a large courtyard, surrounded by high, Doric columns[47], which gave the yard a stark appearance in the cold moonlight. Under

---

[47] On buildings with classical Greek/Roman or neo-classical architecture, there are three kinds of columns. Doric columns are simple, straight and austere, Ionic columns are curly-

362

a portico at the far end of the yard stood Mr Ambrose's chaise, the grey beast of a horse already attached to it by an assortment of leather straps the names of which I didn't care to know. A driver already sat waiting for us.

'Mr Ambrose!' A portly little man with a reddish nose came hurrying forward, wearing an anxious expression and a uniform-like tailcoat on which several buttons were missing. Mr Ambrose's night porter, I deduced. Only Mr Ambrose would be stingy enough not to replace missing buttons on his employees' uniforms.

'I'm honoured, Mr Ambrose, so very honoured.' The little man bowed, and then bowed a second time for good measure. 'So honoured that you would come down to give me your orders personally, Sir, I can hardly–'

'Yes, yes, you said that when I came down earlier,' Mr Ambrose cut him short. The porter swallowed and froze in the midst of his third bow. It was obvious he had taken the night shift in the hope of never ever coming across his formidable employer – and now his worst nightmares had been realized.

'Is all ready?'

'The coach is prepared, Sir, all is prepared, Mr Ambrose, Sir. I have seen to everything myself. The horse has been watered and fed, the coachman awaits your orders, Sir, Mr Ambrose, Sir.'

'Adequate. And where is Mr Linton's tailcoat?'

The porter paled.

'I... I don't know that it's dry yet, Sir. I will have to go and check.'

'Then do so. Now!'

'Of course, Sir, of course. I shall go immediately. Just you wait, Sir, I shall run like the wind, Mr Ambrose, Sir!'

And he was off, as if the hounds of hell were after him, or maybe even Patsy jabbing him with her parasol.

Mr Ambrose strode over to wait beside the carriage, and I followed him. There was something weighing on my mind. To be honest, there were several things weighing on my mind, all of which were feeling distinctly unpleasant and started giving me a headache. But this particular thing was weighing even weightier than the other weighty weights.

I gathered all my strength to speak.

'Um... Mr Ambrose?' My voice sounded slurred, even to my own ears.

'Yes, Mr Linton?'

'I have a question, Sir.'

'Indeed.'

I waited, but he didn't say anything. Then I remembered that I hadn't actually asked the question yet. By Jove, I was a tiny bit confused tonight, wasn't I?

I cleared my throat.

'Are you... are you sure that nothing else happened? Up there in your office? Nothing else but me passing out?'

---

twirly, and Corinthian columns are extremely curly-twirly. Guess which kind is Mr Ambrose's favourite?

363

He hesitated. I saw his hand tighten around the walking stick that concealed his sword. His lips parted.

'I...'

'Here, Mr Ambrose, Sir!' Like a fat little ball of lightning, the porter shot around the corner, and I mentally cursed the man and all his descendants to the seventh generation. Or maybe the eighth. 'Here is the gentleman's tailcoat! Dried and cleaned as requested!'

Although it was my tailcoat he carried, he handed it to Mr Ambrose, an action that didn't endear him to me any more than his sudden appearance had. I added a few curses for the ninth and tenth generations. They probably more than deserved it. And I was sure my good friend Napoleon would see to it that they were adequately tortured if I asked him.

Mr Ambrose nodded to the man.

'You're dismissed. Take up your post again.'

'Yes, Sir! Immediately, Sir!'

Emitting relief like a beacon did light, the man hurried off, and Mr Ambrose held out my tailcoat to me.

'Here.'

'About what I said,' I tried to return to the earlier subject. 'About what happened up there in your office... I'm pretty sure I can remember something about you and me–'

I didn't get any further than that. Suddenly, I was cut off by a violent hiss. Mr Ambrose's fingers had clenched into the material of the tailcoat, around a lengthy tear in the black cloth. He stared at the damaged garment with eyes like icicles.

'Look at this,' he told me, his voice matching the coldness of his eyes. 'Look at this, Mr Linton. Now!'

Uncomprehendingly, I stared at the tear in the coat.

'Yes? I see it. And? I must have ripped it somewhere. Maybe on a nail or something like th–'

'That's no tear,' he interrupted me with deadly calm. 'Do you not see that the whole is round? Do you not see the blackened edges of the cloth where it is ripped open? Those are gunpowder stains!'

My fuzzy brain tried to grasp the meaning of his words. It needn't have bothered. Stepping so close to me that our faces were almost touching and I could see the darkness of his eyes, Mr Ambrose told me:

'A bullet grazed you and ripped your coat open! Another inch and it would have buried itself in your flesh!'

The way he said *your flesh* sent shivers down my back. Shivers of fear, anger and... something else I couldn't quite grasp.

He wasn't shivering, though. He was colder and harder than I had ever seen him.

'You could have died.' He seemed to be speaking to nobody in particular. His icy eyes were staring right through me. 'You really could have died.' They were looking so far into the distance, those eyes of his – as if he was seeing some other world, another reality altogether. Suddenly, they refocused on me again, and he thrust the tailcoat into my arms.

'Here. Let it be a reminder, Mr Linton.'

I staggered back, clutching the coat in my arms.

'A reminder of what?'

His hands, empty of cloth now, once again curled tightly around the handle of his hidden sword. 'A reminder to *never, ever cease to be careful.*'

He turned in the direction of the chaise and started towards it.

'You're right.' I swallowed. Somewhere on the edge of my consciousness was hovering the knowledge that a piece of lead could have buried itself in me tonight. But my mind was so exhausted, it wasn't quite ready to let that realization in. Not yet. Hurriedly, I started to follow him. 'Now... about that thing in your office... I could swear that you–'

'Nothing happened in the office!' His voice cut through the air like a blade of ice. Without looking back at me, he swung himself into the carriage and slammed the door shut behind him. 'You fell, you hit your head, no more. Nothing happened. Nothing at all. Let's go!'

~~**~*~*

Nothing happened. Nothing at all...

Those were the last words he had spoken to me that night. Leaning out of the chaise, he had flung a command at the porter, who'd hastily opened the large outer gate of the back yard. I had yanked open the door on my side and clambered in. The driver hadn't needed prompting after that, he appeared to be well familiar with Mr Ambrose's distaste for wasted time.

'Gee up!'

The cry of the coachman was followed by the crack of the whip. Seconds later, the coach lurched forward and we were rattling over the cobblestones, out under the massive archway, into the street. The blurry shapes of gas lanterns rushed past us like ghosts on their way to the underworld. I wondered if any of them could be bothered to stop and haunt us, maybe rattle their chains for a few minutes or something like that. Mr Ambrose certainly looked like he could use the company.

He was staring out of his window, his face turned away from me. He was even more cold and taciturn than usual. What was the matter?'

'Mr Ambrose?'

Silence.

'Mr Ambrose, Sir?'

More silence. Really quite extraordinarily silent silence.

But then, why should that surprise me? This was Mr Ambrose I was trying to talk to, after all. Still, for some reason I had expected him to be more talkative. I had expected him to want to talk about *something*... something important. The memory hovered on the edge of my consciousness. Once more, I reached up and touched my lips. In his icy, silent corner I saw Mr Ambrose shift, almost imperceptibly.

Had I... had we...?

No. I just couldn't remember.

The streets rushed past as if in a dream. The houses shrank, the streets narrowed. No more palatial mansions and memorable marble façades, we were now driving past honest middle-class homes, the comfortable little brick houses of greengrocers, shoemakers and probably also piano-tuners and their sons who had illicit affairs with young blonde ladies.

'Oh gosh,' I mumbled. 'I almost forgot about them!' My gaze wandered to Napoleon, who was sitting between me and the ice-cold statue in the corner that was Mr Ambrose.

'You couldn't take care of that for me, could you?'

The Emperor shook his head sombrely. I sighed.

'I thought so. Blast! You're an abominable slacker, you know that, don't you?'

Mr Ambrose slowly turned his head towards me. His gaze cut into me like a deep-frozen razor.

'I didn't mean you,' I clarified. 'I was talking to Napoleon.'

Mr Ambrose turned his head slowly away from me again. He didn't speak.

'Where to exactly, Sir?' called the coachman from the box. It seemed Mr Ambrose hadn't given him an exact address. I perked up. Surely, now he had to open that stubbornly silent mouth of his.

Wrong. He sat in the corner, staring silently out of the window, just as before.

'Err... Sir? I ain't got no idea where to go!'

Nothing but perfect silence came from the granite monument at the window.

Raising my hand, I knocked against the roof of the chaise.

'Driver?'

He turned around to face me.

'Yes, Sir?'

A strange feeling ran through me at having somebody else call me 'Sir' – the same hated respectful address I had been forced to give Mr Ambrose day after day, week after week. I felt a surge of power rush through me at hearing the word.

'Do you know St James's Square?' I yelled over the rushing wind.

'Yes!'

'Take us there. I can find my way from there.'

'Yes, Sir!'

He turned towards the street again, and I settled back into the seat, a contented smile on my face. Napoleon nodded at me, approvingly.

Not long after, the chaise began to slow down, and we then came to a halt. Looking out of the window, I saw the familiar three- and four-story houses around St James's Square, looming up out of the darkness. Only in a few windows was light still visible.

I turned to Mr Ambrose.

'Well... I guess that was it, then,' I mumbled.

Silence.

'I don't suppose you want to congratulate me on my excellent work? You know, finding the place where the file is for you, and all that?'

More silence.

'That's what I thought.' Sighing, I pushed the door open and clambered out of the carriage. I was careful when I set my foot on the cobblestones of the square. St James's was familiar, a friend – completely unlike the floor in Mr Ambrose's office. Still, you never knew. Tonight, all flat surfaces seemed to have it in for me.

I already wanted to walk away, but then I hesitated one final time.

'Mr Ambrose?'

Silence.

'Good night, Si–'

'Driver!' he cut me off. 'Get moving!'

Behind me, the whip cracked, the grey horse whinnied. I jumped out of the way, just in time to avoid getting sprayed by the chaise as it drove through a puddle. It raced across the empty square and out of sight as it plunged into the darkness of nocturnal London.

~~**~*~*

Said darkness of nocturnal London proved a not inconsiderable hindrance in reaching my uncle's house. It wasn't far away, of course – most of the streets were lit by gas lanterns and I knew the area well – but I had never considered how different things might look at night. For example, there were all those pretty lights dancing in the air around me. Were they there every night? If so, I should be out this late more often. London seemed much more interesting at nighttime.

There was a strange pounding in my ears, getting louder as I stumbled forward. It was probably Napoleon and a regiment of cavalry, riding off to conquer the world. Oh well, I wished him luck with all my heart. I probably had to abandon that particular project. I felt so tired... Conquering all the world seemed too exhausting an idea.

Maybe you could take over just half the world? Or only Eurasia?

Yes, that sounded acceptable. But the rest would have to wait until tomorrow.

Finally, I found my way to the little wooden door in the wall surrounding my uncle's back garden. After some groping around in my pockets, I managed to unearth the key and insert it into the one of the three fuzzy-looking locks that proved most substantial. Safe inside the garden, out of sight of prying eyes, I slipped into the shed and changed my clothes. Taking the garden ladder with me, I approached the window, gazing up at the mountainous height I had to climb.

Ha! I would climb this peak! And if I was going to perish like all the brave explorers before me, who had boldly ventured where no man (or woman!) had gone before, then so be it! I had been planning on conquering the world, after all. Climbing a ladder would be easy.

Well, it didn't turn out to be, really, but I managed to hit the first rung with my foot after only three failed attempts. After that, things got a bit simpler. I climbed higher and higher until suddenly, there loomed an opening before me. What was this again?

Your window, you idiot!

Oh yes! Quite right. I wanted to climb through the window into my room. That was why I was up here in the first place. Funny how that had almost slipped my mind.

Through the window, I could see Ella. She was sitting in bed – in *my* bed, to be precise –anxiously twisting the sheet on my empty mattress between the fingers of her small, ivory hands and staring down at my rumpled pillow.

'Lill,' she sighed, again and again. 'Oh Lill!'

Strange... Why was she trying to talk to me, when from what she knew, I wasn't even there? And why was she up in the middle of the night? She should be in bed, recuperating from an evening of tiring love affairs at the garden fence. But there she was, sitting, awake, and for some reason, apparently quite upset, too.

Taking the last few rungs, I swung my leg over the windowsill. When Ella heard a sound coming from the window, she sprang up and whirled around, clutching her hands to her chest. Her mouth opened to scream as she saw a sinister figure climbing in through her bedroom window.

The sinister figure, that is to say I, sprang forward and clamped a hand over her mouth.

'Be quiet, silly! It's no burglar, only me!' I hissed into her ear. 'If you scream, you'll chase the little yellow piggies away!'

Her whole body relaxed in my arms.

'Mmpf! Mgmpf nmm mpf.'

'I suppose that means "Hello, Lilly, how nice to see you"?'

'Mmmpf!'

'I see. It's nice to see you, too. If I let you go, do you promise not to scream?'

'Ympf!'

Seeing as that was the closest approximation to a 'yes' I was likely to receive, I took my hand from her mouth. She turned to face me, grabbing me by the shoulders. Her eyes were large and moist with panic.

'Dear God, Lilly! Where have you been? I was expecting you to come home hours ago, and I waited and waited, but you never arrived. I've had to tell the most dreadful, fiendish lies to explain your absence to Aunt. Where have you been?'

'I?' A small laugh escaped me. 'I was with the little yellow piggies. Alexander was there, too.'

'Little yellow... what? And who is Alexander?'

'Alexander the Great. Haven't you heard of him? Spiffing chap, absolutely spiffing.'

Ella sniffed.

'Lilly? What is that smell?'

'Smell? I don't smell anything. What do you mean?'

'That smell... It smells like the tables at balls where the drinks for gentlemen... are... served...'

Her voice dwindled. Slowly, the colour drained from her face.

'Lill! No, you can't have! Lill!'

I smiled broadly. She remembered my name! It was so nice that someone did. Mr Ambrose never called me by my first name, let alone a sweet nickname like Lill.

'Yes, my delightful, dear little sister?'

'Lill, have you...?' She lowered her voice until it was only a hushed whisper, deserving of a dark and dingy crypt, where human sacrifices were conducted by some strange oriental cult. 'Have you been *drinking*?'

I pondered the question carefully.

'Yes,' I finally decided, nodding to emphasize the point. 'I have. In fact, I have it on the reliable authority of a professional drunkard that I have emptied the entire River Thames. I must confess, I had no idea my belly could contain that much liquid.'

'Lill!' A moment later, I was in Ella's arms and she was rocking me from side to side as if I were a small child who needed comforting. 'Oh my dear, dear, sister, tell me, who is the man who has done this to you, the rake who has led you off the path of virtue and intoxicated you? I will help you, I promise!'

She continued to rock me like a baby, making cooing noises all the time. By Jove! I had no idea she felt so strongly about me. That was gratifying. But I was also slightly irked by the fact that she thought I needed a man to lead me astray. I was perfectly capable of straying from the path of virtue on my own, thank you very much!

'Don't be afraid. Don't be afraid, Lill! I will go to him, make him leave you alone. He will never bother you again, I promise!'

There was a lump in my throat. Oh dear God. Was this really happening? My little sister Ella, sweet, innocent, shy little Ella was willing to face down a dastardly rake for my sake? She had hidden emergency reserves of courage that she had tapped now, for my sake, to protect me from the villain that was dragging me into a cesspool of iniquity. Never mind that the villain only existed in her imagination – this was touching.

She truly was the best sister one could wish for.

Yes, she is, but maybe she could stop this infernal rocking!

Very true. The motion made me feel woozy all over again, and once more, stars started dancing in front of my eyes. Ella's voice seemed to be coming from a distance now...

'Who is he? Oh Lill, please tell me. Who is the man? I know it may be hard for you to concentrate right now, but you really need to tell me. Can you tell me anything? What he looks like? His name?'

'Napoleon...'

'Napoleon? Dear Lord, he is a Frenchman? No wonder you're in such a state! Did he touch you? Did he hurt you? Lill, you poor thing, do you remember his last name?'

'Bonaparte,' I mumbled, gazing at the stars dancing across my bedroom ceiling. 'You know, the Emperor? The little chap with the funny hat and the hand glued to the inside of his jacket.'

'Merciful God, Lill, you're hallucinating!'

'Am not!' I protested. 'He was there! He was! Ask the little piggies if you don't believe me.'

'Lill?'

My head slumped to the side. The world around me shrank until all I could see was Ella's anxious face.

'Lill, stay with me!'

Now there was only the anxious tip of her anxious nose, surrounded by darkness.

'Lill!'

And then there was nothing.

Unreal Dream of a Really Wonderful Nightmare

I woke in a torture chamber that bore significant resemblance to my bedroom. It couldn't really be my bedroom, though. In my bedroom, my head was never filled with such agonizing pain, nor did my tongue dare to feel so much like an inflated badger's tail in my private sanctum.

This was a torture chamber. Now, I only had to wait for the torturers to arrive, and the fun could begin.

I waited.

And waited.

And waited a little longer.

The badger who had substituted his tail for my tongue wiggled his behind, and I groaned as pain lanced through my head. Desperately, I tried to think of any ways I had ever learned to make badger tails vanish from one's mouth. None came to mind.

I waited some more.

Slowly, the piercing pain in my head began to recede a little. As it did, memories of the previous night started to trickle back into my consciousness.

The drive to the East End... Dear me, had I really visited that horrible part of the city? It seemed so, the images were there all right, if a little bit jumbled. The dirty pub... the old sailor... the fight... by Jove, a real gunfight! Pity I didn't have a nice, daring scar to show for it that would put any suitors off for the rest of my life. The drive back to Empire House in the dark... the office... the kiss...

My mind froze in mid-thought.

Wait just a minute!

The *kiss*?

I sat bolt upright, and regretted it immediately as a searing surge of pain shot through my skull. Clamping both hands on my eyes in an attempt to shut out the world, I pushed the pain aside and grasped desperately for the vague images of last night. No! Dear God, no...!

My hands slipped from my eyes, over my face, down to my parted lips. I was sure they had to be hideously swollen, about twice their normal size. Nothing less than such a gruesome disfigurement would do as a punishment for forsaking all my feminist principles and giving myself, even if just for a moment, willingly over to a man.

Shivering, I remembered Mr Ambrose's mouth on me... The memory was demanding and gentle, cold and fierce all at the same time. It had been like nothing I had ever felt before.

In a totally disgusting way, of course, I reminded myself!

Ha! As if having Mr Ambrose kiss me could ever excite any feelings other than horror in me. It really had been horrifically horribly terrible, the way his lips had caressed mine, had asked me to open up, to give myself to him and just for a moment forget my aims, my dreams, the world and everything else for the sake of a hot feeling in the pit of my stomach that had rapidly grown into a firestorm. His arms around me had been like iron vices, his eyes dark as the deepest wells, and full of secrets I couldn't hope to fathom. The fire that spread through my body seemed to be drawn to them, to him, out of my body into his, heating us and moulding us together in a silent cyclone of feelings.

I realized I was staring dreamily off into the distance, and hurriedly snapped my thoughts back on the here and now, where they belonged.

As you said before, I reminded myself once more. *Frightfully disgusting and horribly terrible! That's what it was like. Definitely. Absolutely.*

My hands were clenching the sheets in a steely grip, and only now did I realize that they were shaking. How could I have let myself go like this? How could I have let go of every cherished principle of female independence for the sake of a few seconds of hot, immensely blissful...

No, not blissful, I corrected myself hurriedly, *awful! Awful, understood? Awful!*

How could I have forgotten myself like this, just for a few seconds of immensely *awful* kissing in the arms of a man?

Not just any man, mind, but Mr Rikkard Ambrose! The man who had humiliated me, who had made my life hell for the past few weeks, the man who was determined to get rid of me.

But... wasn't he also the man who had let me stay because he had given his word, even though he didn't like it? The man who had given me a job when nobody else would have? The man who had brought adventure and independence into my life? The man whose kiss roused feelings in me that had never, ever before...

No! Stop it!

I had to stop right there. If I sank into those memories again, I would start thinking thoughts I wouldn't like... or rather would like too damn much.... and would despise... and desire... oh, this was all so confusing!

Grabbing the pillow on the bed that most resembled Mr Ambrose's head, I drew back my arm and gave it a good right hook. Unfortunately, the pillow didn't have a great resemblance to the original. I knew, because if it hadn't been before last night, now his chiselled face was branded into my mind forever.

No surprise, considering the lengthy opportunity I had had to study it at close quarters. Once more, the scene from last night flashed in front of my eyes: he swooping down towards me, pressing his lips on mine, hard, demanding, so incredibly...

Blast him!

How dare he! How dare he want me? And how dare I not want him to not want me?

Dash it all!

I had to face the facts.

It had really happened. Mr Ambrose had kissed me, kissed me passionately. I remembered it distinctly.

I sank forward onto the bed. This was probably the time when I should have started to cry in shame, like a good little lady. Ella probably would have. Personally, I thought my head still hurt too much to make the effort, but I punched the Mr-Ambrose-pillow a few more times for good measure.

Blast, blast, blast!

Was there no way it could *not* have happened? No way I could get out from under the weight of this horrible catastrophe, and could have imagined the whole thing?

No. I distinctly remembered it.

But then... I also remembered Napoleon playing chess in the powder room and a dance troupe of little yellow piggies. Maybe my memories of last night weren't quite as reliable as I had thought. A ray of hope broke through the darkness of despair around me.

Please, I prayed. *Please let them be unreliable, please!*

Calm down, I told myself. *You have to think about it logically.*

Easier said than done. Every time my mind strayed back to those few heated moments in the office, every kind of logic simply vaporized, leaving in its place a hot shiver that usurped power over my brain and tried to have my common sense executed by guillotine.

Slowly. Do it slowly. Think back to what happened first, before the kiss...

Well, I got drunk. Royally. Epically. The thrumming pain in my skull could attest to that. A smile tugged at the corners of my lips.

Don't get me wrong – I didn't exactly enjoy the pain. But the realization that I had done something that proper young ladies definitely were not supposed to do gave me great satisfaction. Plus, while doing it, I had actually had fun. I could understand why men drank. There was a certain liberating effect to it, if you didn't mind yellow piggies too much. I might actually drink again some time –

though maybe not quite as much. And not the same rotgut they'd sold in that tavern.

What next...

Oh yes. The fight. My smile widened. Most of that was a blur, a red and black blur. On some level I knew that I hadn't been of much use, and that irked me a bit, but the thrill of the experience made up for it.

Hmm... Could you try and learn how to shoot a gun?

Why not? Soon enough, at the end of the month, I would have money of my own. Money with which I could buy anything I wanted – even firearms. Or perhaps solid chocolate. My smile widened even more.

What next...

The drive to the office. I didn't remember much of that.

And then...

The shower.

My smile disappeared, whisked off my face like chalk off a board.

I had been in the shower – which had been much too cold, by the way – and Mr Ambrose had come in, dressed in a red hunting costume, and he had...

Heat flooded my cheeks, and I hurriedly buried my face in my blanket. Dash it, no! I... we... we couldn't have, could we? I mean... how could he even...? That wasn't really possible, was it, that a man and a women could... like that? Dear me! And after he... Oh gosh, that was even more... No, he couldn't possibly, we could never have... no! I refused to believe it! It had to have been a dream. I would never have done anything like... well, like what I remembered us doing. Not with him, anyway!

And even if I had been persuaded to engage in such elicit activities by some underhand method, Mr Ambrose would never, ever wear a red hunting costume. He probably didn't own a stitch of coloured clothing. This last point consoled me a great deal. A really great deal. I had actually been wondering whether he and I had, after all... no!

Laughable. It hadn't happened. It couldn't have happened.

But did that mean the kiss hadn't happened, either?

Almost against my will, I reached up to touch my lips again. They didn't feel swollen. If anything, they felt... warm. Surely, after touching the lips of that silent, cold master of Mammon they would be cold as ice. But I remembered his lips on mine so fiercely! Could all that have been a dream?

I thought of Mr Ambrose – of his arctic manner towards me, his attempts at getting rid of me. It must have been a dream. How could this coldest of men, this block of ice, ever feel something for anybody? The warmth of the feeling would surely melt him away and just leave a puddle of meltwater for Mr Stone or Karim to clean up.

I couldn't suppress a giggle at the mental image.

Him? Feel something? Let alone feel something for *me*? Never!

He couldn't want me for my money, either. I had none, and he had all he could ever wish for. Well, knowing him, he probably wished for a lot more still. I should have said he had all the money a sane person could ever wish for.

Last but not least, the last possible motivation: him wanting me not because of some silly romantic feeling, or for pecuniary reasons, but because he had been overcome by irresistible desire at the sight of me, like the villain in a penny dreadful.

I looked up from my blanket into the mirror that hung on the opposite wall. In the glass, I could see my reflection: round cheeks, a perky nose, wild tangles of brown hair and equally chocolate brown eyes, and skin that was turning tanned from all the time I had spent outdoors. No, I was pretty sure that sight wouldn't instil irresistible desire to put their hands on me in anyone, except perhaps a hairdresser with a serious work ethic.

I sighed. I was now quite sure the kiss hadn't happened. Well, that was cause for rejoicing, wasn't it? And I *was* rejoicing, I was definitely rejoicing *a lot*. I wasn't feeling *the least bit* sentimental or regretful that it all had turned out to be a hallucination. Now that I knew there had never ever happened anything between us, I could go back to the office and face Mr Ambrose with my head held high, knowing that I had not succumbed to this supposed weakness of my sex that men propagated, suggesting that we needed men to take care of us.

Ha! I was proud of myself. Once more, I knew I was an independent and rational human being and perfectly capable of taking care of myself. How wonderful. Absolutely wonderful.

In the mirror on the opposite wall, I caught sight of my reflection. It was looking quite dejected, considering how wonderful everything was. Grabbing the Mr-Ambrose-pillow, I hurled it at the wayward image.

'Smile!' I commanded. 'Smile already, will you? Everything is spiffing. Just spiffing!'

Apparently, my reflection didn't quite agree. I grabbed another pillow, convinced it needed persuading, but then, suddenly, a bolt of pain shot through my head again.

'Ohhh!'

With a groan, I sank back onto the bed and used the pillow for its conventional purpose instead of as ammunition. The pain in my head receded only slowly. Blimey, was this normal after drinking? Surely not. If it were, not so many people would be doing it. I resolved to make the experiment to test my theory at the earliest opportunity.

But not right now. Right now, I was trapped in this torture-chamber facsimile of my bedroom, with no hope of escape. At least there still were no torturers in sight, but that didn't do me much good. My head felt as if it were full of red-hot coals, anyway. Maybe I would get lucky, and Ella would show up instead of the torturers. Lying buried under the blanket, I touched the sleeve of my nightgown. She must have put me in it, I realized, since I didn't remember changing into it last night. My heart swelled with love for my dear little sister. She had taken such good care of me. Surely, she wouldn't leave me here alone for long, in my terrible state of ill health? No, she would come and fight off any torturers who dared to approach me.

From somewhere downstairs, screeching and yelling met my ears. I wondered whether I was starting to hallucinate again. Well, at least there were no yellow piggies this time. Why piggies? Why in God's name had I hallucinated little yellow *sus domestica*? I didn't even like piggies! I didn't even like any animals in general. They either peed on the carpet or bit you. And pigs? I only liked them in slices on a dish, which unfortunately we never got in this stingy household.

Oh, my head... My eyes slid shut. Forget hot coals, this was an inferno!

'Is she in there?' The commotion downstairs was getting louder, and was now joined by an exuberant voice I knew very well. 'Well, Leadfield, is she? Get out of my way, man! We have to see her! No, I don't care what hour it is, or what day or week or century for that matter! We have a victory to celebrate and are missing our general!'

Footsteps thundered up the stairs. More than one pair of them. A moment later, the door to my bedroom burst open. I squinted at the doorway, and there she stood: Eve Saunders, a huge grin plastered on her face. Over her shoulder I could see two other figures, one large, one slight. Patsy and Flora.

'Lilly!' Eve yelled in triumph. 'There you are!'

'Oh, fabulous,' I groaned. 'The torturers have finally arrived.'

VICTORY PARTY?

With a cry like a hunting-hawk, Eve burst into the room and jumped onto my bed with a force that jarred my teeth and made little fireworks of agony explode in my aching skull.

'Lilly, where have you been? We waited for you, hours after the event yesterday, and searched all over the place for you, and asked people, but they told us you left in a coach and we didn't know where you were so we came back here but then you didn't come home and so we didn't know where you were again and waited some more but you still didn't come so we decided to go home when it got dark but we were so worried and you must never do anything like that to us ever again, understand? We're all so terribly angry with you!'

She hugged me as if I were her favourite kitten and pressed a kiss on my forehead.

'Yes,' I told her. 'I can see how terribly angry you are.'

'Shut up! You're a genius! A bloody genius! Did you know that? Well, you probably did, but just in case you didn't, I'm going to tell you: you're a genius!'

She hugged me again. Over her shoulder, I could see the figure of our ancient butler, Leadfield, as he hobbled down the landing and respectfully stopped at the open door, not daring to enter a lady's room.

'Forgive me, Miss, but these... females simply forced their way into the house and insisted on seeing you. Should I...'

'It's no problem, Leadfield,' I assured him, while attempting to duck out of the way of another of Eve's hugs. They were more than my head could take right now. 'They're my friends. You remember Patsy, don't you? She came by last month to tea.'

The old butler opened his mouth to give a reply, but you had to be quicker than that to be part of the conversation while Eve was in the room.

'You're a genius!' She burst out again. 'An absolute genius. You know, at first we were so angry with you after you left us standing in Green Park – Patsy was foaming at the mouth!'

'She was?'

'Yes, and I didn't know what to do, take her to be checked for rabies or go after you and try to bring you to your senses or something else; there were a million ideas flying around in my head at the same time, you know how it is.'

'I can guess.'

'But we had already made the signs, and we couldn't just not go through with it because you had the jitters.'

'Very admirable. But Eve...'

I should have known any attempt to stop her was in vain.

'And then we showed up there, and you appeared up on the stage, all dressed in men's clothes, and gave a speech! A *speech*! And everybody listened! And cheered! Long live suffragism! Oh Lilly!'

She hugged me again, but this time, I wasn't trying to fight her off. My attention was focused on Leadfield, who was still standing at the door. There were two red patches on his normally pallid face, and his eyes were about to pop out of their sockets.

'Dressed in men's clothes?' He gasped. 'Miss Lilly! What in the Lord's name...!'

'Not in public,' I groaned, hurriedly planting a hand over Eve's over-eager mouth to shut her up. 'It was charades! We were playing charades.'

'Oh! I see, Miss.' The old chap's eyes retreated into their sockets, his frame visibly relaxing. He shook his head with all the bewilderment a sensible servant could muster at the upper classes' strange habit of dressing up in all sorts of insane clothing for fun. 'Well, far be it from me, Miss, to begrudge you and your young friends your amusement.'

'Thank you, Leadfield.'

'Do you require anything? Master's old hats and coats? His Indian turban? The old cook's apron?'

'No, thank you, we're not planning on playing charades right now, Leadfield.'

'I see, Miss. Well, I'll leave you to it, then.'

'That would be nice.'

The old servant turned with geological velocity. When he was almost facing the door, he tried to look back over his shoulder and almost toppled over in the process.

'By the way, Miss, breakfast is almost ready. I shall begin serving in a few minutes, so you won't have long.'

'I'll be down directly,' I assured him.

When Leadfield was outside and the door was closed, Eve couldn't hold it in any longer.

'Vlt? Rrrrmt? Yrntnng dwnn tbrkfst tst dt ths gstl tmts...'

I removed my hand from her mouth, and she grabbed me by the collar of my nightshirt.

'Lilly! Are you mad? You're not going down to breakfast to sit and eat those ghastly tomatoes your uncle puts on the table! You're staying here with us to celebrate, do you hear me? If you try to leave, I'll personally tie you up and gag you!'

'Which would rather get in the way of my celebrating,' I pointed out, squeezing my eyes shut and massaging my skull for a second. Ah! That felt good. My headache was much better already. Apparently, I had the right stomach for this sort of thing. I felt a tinge of pride. 'You needn't worry, by the way. When Leadfield says he'll serve immediately, that means he needs ten minutes down the stairs, another fifteen to reach the kitchen, and another twenty to get to the dining room table with all the plates, bowls and platters. We have plenty of time.'

'So... we can celebrate now?'

'Yes.' Sighing, I let myself fall back into bed. 'We can celebrate.'

'Topping!' Two hands took mine in an iron grip and more or less wrenched me out of bed. Three seconds later I was dancing around the room in my nightgown, a trilling Eve as an over-energetic dance partner.

'We showed them! We showed them! We showed them! Well, technically it was you, but who cares! We showed them! We showed those chauvinist sons of bitch... sons of bachelors! Huzzah! Huzzah!'

All I saw of the room were a few whirly impressions as Eve spun me around like a top. Occasionally, I would catch a glimpse of Flora's anxious, but happy, face, and Patsy's smile from where she stood in the background, leaning against the window, watching my impromptu dancing lesson. All this twirling around wasn't doing much good for my woozy head, though. I saw lights beginning to flicker at the edges of my vision.

'Eve? Eve, stop!'

'We showed them! We showed them! We showed them!'

'Eve? Hello, Eve!'

'We showed them! We showed them! We showed them!'

'Eve! I said stop!'

With all the force I could muster, I dug my heels into the ground. Unfortunately, the force I could muster after a night out on a bender wasn't all that great. Eve rammed into me and we landed on the floor in a confused heap of cotton gowns, shawls, hats and shouts of 'We showed them!' You had to give Eve credit for being determined.

Spitting out the end of a silk shawl with purple peonies printed on it, I sat up.

'What the dickens did you do that for?' I challenged Eve. Sitting on her derrière, her crinoline flattened underneath her, she grinned up at me broadly.

'We showed them! We showed them! We showed them!'

Apparently, she wasn't quite ready for sensible conversation yet.

Scrambling to my feet, I turned to the other two. Flora gave me a shy smile, and Patsy... Patsy just stood there, leaning against the wall beside the window, in the background, where she was normally least likely to be found. The smile on her face was small, but unmistakably there.

Our eyes met.

She came forward. I came forward. The rest of the room didn't exist anymore. We met in the middle, and she caught me up in hug so fierce it could have squashed an elephant into mincemeat.

'Lilly!' She said.

'Pfft!' I said.

'I never should have doubted you.'

'Plss let ggg!'

'Oh. Sorry.' Relaxing her grip, she stepped back, but I held on to her arms.

'Don't be,' I gasped. 'I needed that.'

'Oh Lilly, Lilly.' If I hadn't known better, I would have said there were tears twinkling in the corners of Patsy's eyes. But I did know better. She was much too tough to cry, right? 'Lilly! You mad, ingenious, wonderful girl! Why didn't you tell us what you were planning to do?'

Planned? Planned what? Why were they all so pleased with me? And then it struck me. She was convinced I had deliberately called off my participation in the demonstration, to go up on that stage and hold that speech for women's suffrage.

Actually, I hadn't planned a single little thing in the last week the way it had turned out, but I couldn't tell her that. I could see in her fiery eyes that she had gotten it into her head that all had been part of my master plan. And to be honest, it would have been an ingenious plan – definitely worthy of me!

'It was risky,' I said, with an apologetic shrug. 'I... well, if I'd told you, you all would have felt obliged to take part, and there was a much greater chance of success if only one of us tried to get up there on the podium. In any case, as soon as one of us started her speech, all would be discovered and the others forced to leave along with her. So, a solo operation just made more sense.'

'Eve's right.' Patsy hugged me again, softer this time, but with undeniable warmth. 'You are a genius.'

I looked up into her broad face with wide, searching eyes. 'So, I'm forgiven?' I asked, and wasn't able to keep the quiver totally out of my voice. This very question had been torturing my mind ever since my quarrel with my biggest, bestest friend. Not to have Patsy watching my back would be like not having a hat on my head – a cold and unprotected life.

'There's nothing to forgive,' she told me. 'You're my best friend, and always will be. Nothing will ever change that.'

'Hey! And what about me?' Eve protested from floor level.

'You,' Patsy told her, 'are my most annoying friend, and will always be. Nothing will ever change that, not even an excellent governess hired to educate and restrain you.'

Eve beamed at the compliment and clambered to her feet. Then she suddenly slapped her hand with her forehead. 'Oh, where did I leave my head this morning? We brought you something!'

'A present?' My face lit up, and it only hurt a little bit. The day was getting better already. 'I love presents! What is it?'

Maybe a piece of solid chocolate...

'No, not a present as such...' Patsy waved at Flora, who retrieved something from behind her back, where she had stashed it along with her hands for the last few minutes. 'More a memento of sorts. A trophy of a victorious battle.'

Taking the object from Flora, she handed it to me. I stared down at the blank piece of cardboard in my hand, and confusion must have been evident on my face. Patsy smirked.

'Turn it over.'

I did. And there, in large, bold letters were the words:

VOTES FOR WOMEN, FELLOWS... OR ELSE!

I didn't know what to say.

But I didn't need to, really, because Eve did all the talking that was humanly possible.

'You didn't answer me before,' she accused me, tapping on my cardboard. 'Where were you? We waited ages and ages and ages for you to return, and you never did? Where did you go? What did you do? We wanted to celebrate with you so badly, and to knock you on the head for doing something like that without telling us, but we couldn't! Where did you go? Were you abducted? Held prisoner?'

My mind flashed back to the events to the previous night. A shiver shot down my spine, and I had to restrain myself from touching my lips again.

'Um... no. Neither of those.'

'Well, what happened, then?'

Rikkard Ambrose. That's what happened.

'Nothing, really. It just took me a frightfully long time to get away from those men. They had a lot of questions, none of which I answered. Then I went away.'

I shrugged.

Eve gave me a disapproving look. 'Is that all? I expected, at least, that you were held captive in some dark dungeon miles under the city, where a group of conspirators determined to prevent the suffragist movement from rising up against the corrupt world of men tortured you into swearing off all unladylike behaviour forevermore!'

'Err... no. Sorry to disappoint.'

Not that I thought she would be disappointed if she knew the truth. I had something a lot better in store than an anti-suffragist conspiracy: a mystery surrounding stolen documents, drunken revels, a street fight in the East End and a mind-blowing, toe-curling encounter with Rikk–

No! Don't think about it! That part was a hallucination. It was all completely imaginary. And even if it wasn't, under no circumstances are you ever going to reveal that to Eve!

'Thank you. Thank you so very much for this.' Holding up the sign, I gave them all my most sincere smile, already edging towards the door. It was time to get away. 'Now, if that's all... I think it's about time for me to go down to breakfast.' I started towards the stairs in earnest, but Eve was quicker. She blocked my way before I could make my escape.

'Oh no, it most certainly isn't all. You aren't getting away as easily as that. Do you know how many unanswered questions we still have?'

She indicated the other two, who surrounded me like a pack of jackals.

'One? Or maybe two?' I suggested hopefully. Crap! I had to get out of here before I started stumbling over my own lies.

'At least a thousand! For starters, who was that man?'

'What man?' I asked, hoping to hell they wouldn't notice my guilty ears burning.

'*That* man.' Using both her hands, Eve grabbed her face and pulled a threateningly stony grimace. If there had been any doubt in my mind as to whom she meant before, it was gone now. 'The one everybody treated as if he were the emperor of China, France and India put together. The one who gave that monstrous speech. He had a face like *this*!' With her fingers, she pulled her mouth even farther, until it was almost nothing but a straight line. 'And he stared at you like he had icebergs for eyes, and would headbutt you if you didn't agree to every single little thing he said!'

'Oh. Him.' I coughed. 'Um... yes, now that you mention it, I seem to remember a man like that.'

'I don't think he looked like that, though,' Flora dared to point out, doubtfully regarding Eve's facial contortions. 'I think he looked much more handsome. In fact,' she added with a slight blush, 'I found him quite ravishing.'

A second later, she quailed under the punishing glare Patsy gave her.

'Shame on you, Flora Milton,' she proclaimed sternly. 'That man is an enemy of the cause! No true suffragist would think him anything but an ugly monster!'

Flora's cheeks reddened – though not half as much as mine did. Blast! Why was I blushing? I had nothing to be guilty about, did I? Well, did I? He was misogynistic, and arrogant, and cold...

...except when he's kissing you.

Luckily, Eve was still too firmly on the trail to notice anything wrong with my face.

'You still haven't told us who he is,' she said, narrowing her eyes at me. 'And up on the platform, he introduced you as his secretary. How on earth did you pull that off?'

I opened my mouth – and no convenient lie came to mind.

Of all the times my creative talents of creative truthbending could have forsaken me, they chose *now*? When I most needed them? Bugger! Nothing was reliable anymore, nowadays.

'Well?' Patsy eyed me curiously. 'How did you manage it?'

I was standing with my back against the door, the three of them surrounding me, with no escape in sight. Not just Eve and Patsy were burning with curiosity. Even Flora had stopped blushing and was staring at me. She never stared at anyone. She thought it was rude, and that this was enough reason not to do it. But now she was staring at me.

I wet my lips.

'I... um...'

Suddenly, there came a knock from the door behind me.

'Lill? Lill, are you in there?'

Ella! My angel, my darling sister, my life-saver! I love you!

'Yes! Yes, I'm in here.'

Something pushed against my back.

'Why won't the door open?'

'Because I'm standing against it.'

'And why are you standing against the door?'

'Good question. Have been asking myself the same thing.' Like a fox between a regiment of red coats, I slipped between Eve and Flora. Turning, I saw the door open. Ella stood in the doorway, looking from me to Patsy to Flora to Eve and then to me again. When her eyes fell on me, an expression of quiet gravity appeared on her face which I had seen only once before: when our neighbours' cat had gotten squashed by a coach and she had gone to deliver the news to the bereaved family.

'Patsy, Ella, Eve,' she said without removing her gaze from me, 'would you mind leaving me and my sister alone for a few minutes? There is something we have to discuss in private.'

'Sorry, Ella, not right now. We were here first, so we get to talk first.' Patsy waved Ella off. 'Go off and play, we've got serious things to talk about.'

At this, Ella did not quail and shrink back, or hurry off with an apologetic 'I'm sorry to disturb you' as I expected – she raised her chin and met Patsy's eyes.

'So have I, and what I have to say cannot wait. I have to discuss something of the *gravest* importance with my sister. You will please leave now. You can talk to her after I'm finished.'

Patsy's mouth dropped open. She was so surprised that she did something which she had never, ever done before: what she was told. Her feet started moving towards the door, while her eyes were fixed with utter disbelief on the little wisp of a blonde girl ordering her around.

'Err... I see. All right, Ella. We'll see you outside, Lilly.' And with a last look at Ella, like a bulldog would look back at the chicken that has just chased him off his yard, she left the room, Eve and Flora in tow.

Closing the door behind them, Ella advanced towards me. She was smaller than me, but still she made me feel like a naughty child as she looked at me with those wide, blue, sincere eyes of hers. Her gaze could have made an archangel confess his secret sins.

'Lill,' she said, shaking her head.

I waited for more, but nothing was forthcoming. It seemed she expected me to know what she meant without actually saying it. Clairvoyance, however, was not yet among my many talents.

'Ella,' I said, hoping to encourage some further explanation through reciprocal brevity.

'Lill,' she said again, with another very graceful and sad shake of the head.

'Ella.'

This was getting a bit tedious. I wondered if I should broach a different subject or, for that matter, any subject. But then, it was taken out of my hands.

'Lill, please tell me nothing happened.'

Ah! Finally, a variation.

Not that I understood what she meant, but still, it was progress.

'Fine. If you really want me to: Nothing happened. Nothing at all.' I rubbed my head, which was still throbbing a bit. 'Now, can you please tell me when and where nothing was supposed to have happened?'

'Lill!'

'And while you're at it, tell me what kind of nothing happened that was supposed to have actually happened. I am a bit fogged, to be honest.'

'Lill, don't joke about this! This is serious!'

'Are you sure? I'm not, because I still don't have the foggiest idea what you're going on about.'

At last some life flooded into Ella's face. She stepped forward, grasped me by the arm and shook it.

'Lill, pull yourself together! You were with a man last night, weren't you? *That* man!'

Actually, I had been with several dozen men, about half of whom had been trying to kill me at one time or another. I didn't think it prudent to share this with my little sister, though. For some strange reason my aching head couldn't figure out, she seemed to think that the company of one man was already inexcusable. So I just said: 'Yes, I was. What about it?'

Ella sucked in a breath.

'Oh God, Lill! Do you know what could have happened last night? Or... dear merciful Lord, what if it actually did?'

'Certainly I know,' I mumbled. The pain wasn't getting better from the shaking. 'I could have caught my death in that powder room. Showers without boilers for hot water should be prohibited by law.'

'Showers? Lill, what are you talking about?'

'What are *you* talking about? I still don't have a clue. You look at me as if you're not sure whether I should be confessing my sins in a month-long session, or thanking God on bending knees for escaping the jaws of hell. What's the matter with you?'

Ella bit her lip, hesitating. Whatever was biting her butt, it was something not easy for her to say.

'Did... it happen last night?'

'It? What it?'

'You know! *It!*'

'No, I don't know "it". I would be happy to make the acquaintance of "it" and shake its hand, but only after you've explained to me what "it" is.'

'Well... it is... *it!* You know! *It!*'

'Thank you for that elucidating explanation, my dear little sister.'

Ella bit her lip again. 'Just... just tell me... what happened last night. Please.'

I groaned. 'I'm not actually very sure, you know. My memory of last night is a little vague.'

'Oh.' Again that lip-biting. This apparently came as an unpleasant surprise to her. No wonder. When you were about to preach to somebody about the grievousness of his sins, it's preferable that the sinner still remembers them. It saves quite a lot of confusion.

'Well... when you came home last night, you were intoxicated. Do you remember that?'

I pressed my hand to the left side of my head. The ache was particularly acute there.

'Oh yes. I remember that.'

'And I undressed you and put you to bed. Do you remember that, too?'

'No. I think I might have been unconscious at the time. That sort of thing usually impedes my memory a little.'

Ella was immune to sarcasm. It was a very useful skill at times.

'And before that, my dear sister? Do you remember anything of what passed before you returned home?'

'It's all a little hazy,' I said evasively. My quota of good lies had already been used up for the day. Plus, my head wasn't feeling its best today.

'You went to see *him*, didn't you?'

I blinked in confusion. 'Him? Him who?'

'You know perfectly well who I mean! You went to see *him*! The young man you have been seeing.'

'Oh, him!' Right! I had given Ella some vague hints about Mr Ambrose hadn't I? She thought he was an admirer of mine. Sometimes it was really hard to keep track of one's own lies and fibs.

'Don't try to deny it,' Ella told me, looking up at me with those big, blue, sincere eyes of hers. 'You went to see him, and he... and he... oh Lilly!'

Suddenly, her arms were around me and she was crushing me to her with all the force she was capable of. Luckily, she was no Patsy.

'I can't bear it any longer! Please! Simply tell me, Lill! You have to tell me! I won't judge you, I promise! I know you would never, before marriage... Not willingly! Just, please! Please tell me! I mean... he... you... did he... did you... did the two of you...?'

My eyes went wide. Abruptly, it began to dawn on the excuse for a mind stuffed into my aching head what exactly Ella was talking about.

'No! No, no, nonononono! No, not ever! Never! Not in this lifetime or a thousand others, or if I were a bee and he a spring flower full of yummy pollen! No, no, nonononono *No!*'

I shook my head so vigorously my brown hair bounced around like chocolate come to life, and I was in danger of head-butting Ella. I didn't care! The idea of Mr Ambrose and me... doing *that* – well, it was too horrible to think about!

Really? Are you sure about that? asked a little voice at the back of my mind.

I told it to shut up.

Ella pushed me away a few inches, just enough to be able to look me in the face. Hers was shimmering with tears.

'Really? Are you sure?'

She sounded eerily like that little voice in my head.

'I think I would have noticed, Ella. I wasn't that drunk.'

'Oh. Um... well, good.'

We stood there for a few moments, not knowing what to say – then Ella suddenly pulled me against her and started sobbing again.

'Hey! I told you! My virtue is safely under lock and key!'

'I know!' Ella wailed. 'I'm crying from relief!'

'Oh. You could have fooled me.'

'Shut up!'

'If you insist.'

'Never do anything like that to me again!'

'All right. Next time I get drunk I'll be sure to be much more promiscuous.'

'Oh Lill! Shut up!'

I could count the number of times my little sister had told me to shut up during my lifetime on the fingers of one hand. Anne and Maria were doing it constantly, but Ella? If she was being bossy, I really must have upset her. Tentatively, I put my arms around her and pulled her close.

'What did he do to you?' She sobbed.

'I told you. Nothing,' I soothed, patting her head.

'I don't mean *that*! I mean what else happened to you? What about the drink? What did that vile man make you consume?'

'Ella, it's not like that. He didn't make me, I...'

'Don't you dare defend him!' Letting go of me, she stared up at me, her face wet with tears. 'You didn't see yourself last night. You didn't see what had happened to you. Oh, Lill!'

'Ella, I...'

'I know you love him–'

O really?

'–but you can't defend what he has done.'

Don't intend to while you're glaring at me like that, trust me.

'I thought he was good for you, Lill, I thought he loved you, but a man who can do that to a girl is not worth a grain of feeling. Please, Lill, I know it must be painful, but try to rid yourself of those feelings. They will only hurt you. *He* will only hurt you.'

I felt almost like laughing. Poor Ella! If she only knew that all her concerns were for nothing. If she only knew that there was no special man in my life, certainly no man who could do anything to hurt me.

An image of Mr Ambrose's hard, chiselled face flashed across my inner vision. Suddenly, I didn't feel so much like laughing anymore.

'Please, Lill! Won't you try to forget him? For me? Please?'

She looked so forlorn, so torn apart by anxiety. What could I do?

'Of course.' Tightening my arms, I pulled her towards me. For some reason, tears started to prick my eyes, too, and as our cheeks touched as we hugged, our tears mingled. 'I've learned my lesson. Don't you fear. Everything will be all right. Everything will be just fine.'

'Oh Lill!'

'Shh.'

Gently, I held her in my arms and rocked her from side to side until her sobs had subsided. The Rocking made my head ache, but seeing her like this made my heart ache, and that was far worse.

Reaching around me, Ella gently stroked my hair.

'I... I'm sorry. I know I'm asking a lot of you. I know it can't be easy to give somebody up, when you feel about them this strongly.'

Feel strongly? Did I feel strongly about Mr Ambrose? I had, on more than one occasion, wanted to take him by that short, shiny black hair of his and slam his head into a wall. But those probably weren't the kinds of feelings to which Ella was referring.

'Yes. It will be very difficult to stay away from him.' *Particularly since I want to see a pay cheque from him at the end of the month, and he isn't going to cough it up if I'm not there, doing my job.* 'Almost impossible. But I'll try.'

And I'll fail. But you don't need to know that.

'Oh Lilly. Thank you!' Once more, she hugged me with a ferocity I would not have suspected could fit into her small, slender form. 'It may cause your heart terrible agony now, but you will see, it is for the best.'

She let go of me. Relief was shining out of her still watery eyes, but it was mixed with apprehension.

'You won't blame me for this, later, will you?' she asked fearfully. 'You won't say I was terribly harsh and robbed you of your love? Please, Lill, I couldn't bear it if you thought that of me. I'm only trying to look out for you. And it's not as if I don't understand what you're going through. I and Edm–'

Her lips clamped shut, and her eyes widened in shock.

I knew perfectly well whose name had almost escaped her mouth. Immediately, my headache was pushed to the back of my mind, my attention focused. Could it be that not all her tears were for my sake? Was she afraid of her approaching elopement? Had she found out when it was to take place? Dread flooded my chest. Imagining my life without my little sister... it was a barren prospect.

'Oh, you don't need to worry about anything like that,' I said with an airy wave. 'I know you were only giving me good advice – stay away from men. And why not? They are all beasts, anyway, the whole lot of them.'

Ella's cheeks flushed. 'Some are not so bad. A few can be really nice.'

Probably in particular if their names began with 'Edm'. But I didn't voice my thoughts out loud. Instead, I said:

'I won't ever start to hate you, Ella. How could I? You're my little sister, the one who has always been there when I needed someone to talk to, or to undress me because I was passed out drunk...'

'Lill!'

'You get my point. I could never, ever hate you.' I gave her a final hug – and inspiration struck me. 'I will heed your advice,' I continued. 'But you must promise me something in return.'

Curious, Ella looked up. 'What?'

'You must promise me to learn from my example. Never do anything rash or improper where a man is concerned. Never. Promise me.'

What little colour there was in Ella's ivory face drained away as if she'd seen a ghost.

'I...'

There was hesitation in her voice. I never would have thought it possible. Ella hesitating, where honour and propriety were at stake? Blast! Things with Edmund had to be even worse than I had suspected. Or better, from his perspective. But I wasn't very inclined to see things from his perspective at the moment.

'Promise me,' I said, putting emphasis on both words.

'I... Lill...'

Behind us, there came an interrupting knock from the door. I wasn't remotely as pleased about this as I had been the last time.

'Yes!' Ella called in an eager voice. 'Yes, enter!'

Slowly, the door opened, and Leadfield stuck his bald head into the room. 'Breakfast is served, Miss Ella, Miss Lilly.'

Ella was out of the room before I could demand her word again.

I remained alone in the room where she and I had slept, laughed, cried and simply spent time together for years and years. For the first time, I asked myself whether, soon, I would be alone here.

TOILET SECRETS

Eventually, I followed Ella out of the room and down the stairs. The torturers weren't far away. They were waiting to pounce on me on the landing.

'Finally! There you are!' Eve was in front of me like a flash. 'What have you two been talking about in there? Never mind, never mind, I have more interesting questions right now, I can be nosy about Ella later. You have to tell us now! Tell us everything about how the heck you managed to get up on that platform!'

My mind was still on alcohol-induced headaches and back-garden romances. I couldn't find a single, plausible lie to put forward. Maybe I should just tell them the truth... but no! I couldn't. Out of my mad visit to a financier's office some weeks ago had arisen a real chance for me to forge myself a life of independence. I couldn't risk that by telling Eve. I loved her dearly, but she had the loosest mouth this side of the Thames.

Bloody hell! What can I do?

'Excuse me?'

We all turned to look. My aunt was standing a few steps below us, an expression on her face that could have been used to pickle cucumbers.

'Will your friends stay and join us for breakfast?' she asked me, letting her cool gaze sweep over the group of girls around me. 'They didn't say they were coming beforehand, but I'm sure there will be enough boiled potatoes for three more people.'

For the first time in my life, I would have liked to kiss my aunt.

'Oh no, Mrs Brank,' Patsy said hurriedly. 'Don't exert yourself on our account. I, um... had a very filling dinner yesterday. And we were just leaving, weren't we, girls?'

'Oh yes,' Eve nodded quickly. 'We were. Most certainly.'

'What?' Flora, who was a bit slower on the uptake, asked. 'But I thought we... ouch!' She winced as Patsy stepped on her foot. 'Yes, of course we were. Just leaving, right now.'

'Come along, girls.' Like a general gathering her troops, Patsy waved the other two to her flanks, just in case any boiled potatoes or disgusting bowls of gruel would suddenly launch an attack. 'We've got places to be. And as for you-' At the bottom of the stairs, she turned a final time and gave me a significant look. 'We'll have a talk with you later.'

Oh dear. It didn't seem as though I was off the hook. But at least I would have time to think up a convincing cover story. With relief, and with thankfulness for the fact that I and the girls were fast friends again, I watched Patsy and the others depart.

'Well?' my aunt snapped. 'Why are you standing around gawking like that? Come down to breakfast, or do you expect the rest of us to wait for you?'

'No, Aunt, I do not expect that.'

'Then come down! The potatoes are already getting cold!'

If they had been served with Leadfield's usual speed and alacrity, they had probably been cold long before they reached the table. Yet I didn't say anything, simply followed my aunt down and to the breakfast table.

Everybody was already seated, apart from Uncle Bufford, of course. The head of the table, where he was supposed to sit, remained conspicuously empty, as always. My aunt could have sat there, but she preferred not to, as a demonstration that my uncle was grossly far behind in the performance of his social duties. Sometimes I wondered whether before we had come to his house, he had already had the habit of dining up in his study, or if that habit had developed to avoid an overdose of female company.

'Sit,' my aunt told me, as if I were a misbehaving puppy – which, when I came to think about it, probably was exactly how she thought of me. I took my place at the table directly opposite Ella. She didn't meet my eyes.

Leadfield started limping around the table, doling out potatoes as he went. The potatoes turned out to be still lukewarm, not cold as predicted. Yet this overwhelming culinary advantage didn't much increase my motivation to dig in. It seemed that, along with the headache, the inability to eat potatoes was another symptom of excessive alcohol consumption.

Maybe it wasn't just restricted to potatoes, either. I didn't feel as if I could have eaten much, even had there been a roasted pheasant in front of me. Any pheasant in the room would have been squashed, anyway, by the elephant in the room that was Ella's and Edmund's secret plan. She didn't know that I knew she was going to flee, and I didn't know when she was going to flee. I only knew something had to be done about it.

Again, I tried to catch her eye. She kept her gaze firmly fixed on her plate of potatoes as though they were the most fascinating work of art she had ever seen. I knew for a fact they were not. She liked going to the museum or to art galleries, and not to look at potatoes.

I hated seeing her like this, anxious and uncertain. I wanted her to be care-free and happy. I wanted him out of her life. And yet... a tiny part of me suspected that having him out of her life would not exactly contribute to her happiness. She cared for him, and he for her, probably. It was the one thing that had prevented me from going to him and threatening him with exposure, or just disclosing his conduct to his parents. They had to be together to be happy. Yet I couldn't just let them run off together. I knew Ella, knew the value she placed on honour and propriety. The scandal would follow her everywhere, it would ruin her life.

Still, the alternative... her marrying that nincompoop Sir Philip...

I shuddered from head to toe. She would drown in flower bouquets and be forced to look at that silly grin and over-large nose for the rest of her life. What a hideous prospect.

'It is a beautiful day, today, girls,' my aunt initiated the conversation with a glance out of the window, her voice cheerful, which probably meant that she had momentarily forgotten both me and the plate of potatoes in front of her. 'The sun is shining, for a change. Do you have any special plans?'

'Maria and I planned to go out for a picnic with the Hendersons,' Anne piped up. She shot a sideways glance at Gertrude. 'Want to come? Young Master Charles Henderson will be there, and I'm sure he would be enchanted to meet you.'

She giggled, and not in a nice way. I knew it, because I prided myself on hav-ing brought the art of nasty giggling to perfection.

'No, thank you,' Gertrude replied quietly, not looking up from her plate. 'He is five years younger than I, if I am correct. And I would much prefer to stay at home and work some more on my needlework.'

'I'd like to come,' Lisbeth put in, her eyes shining eagerly.

Anne chose to ignore that.

'And the rest of you?' My aunt's eyes went from the window, through which sunshine streamed into the room, to me. Her expression soured. 'What do you plan to do, Lillian?'

My hand, in the act of piercing a piece of potato with my fork, froze in mid-air.

Hell's whiskers!

What did I plan to do? Up until a second ago, I had planned absolutely noth-ing. But in the back of my mind, I knew what I had to do, whether I planned it or not. It was a weekday. A workday. If I wanted to keep my position as Mr Am-brose's private secretary, I would have to go to work. I would have to face him, after everything that happened last night.

But... nothing happened last night, right? It was all just my imagination. The more... intimate parts, anyway. Not real. Imagination. Only imagination.

Ha! Really?

'Lilly?' For the first time this morning, my aunt didn't sound like a shark out for blood when talking to me. 'Lilly, are you all right? You look pale.'

Out of the corner of my eye I saw Ella quickly glance up from her meal. She looked down again so fast that I couldn't read anything in her expression except her concern – concern for me.

She thinks I'm going back to the man who has me in his hold, it shot through my head. *And the fact is: I am.*

I shook my head. No! Mr Ambrose didn't have me in his hold. Not in any sense, and certainly not a romantic one! I had chosen to work for him of my own free will. I could quit any time I wished to. I could quit today. I could stay at home and not leave the house, and ... and... and never find out if last night had really only been a dream.

Angrily, I speared the potato and shoved it into my mouth.

'I'm fine,' I lied gruffly. 'Perfectly fine. I think I'll take a walk in the park. As you said, it's fine weather. There ought to be a lot of potential suitors hiding in the bushes, waiting to pounce on the first likely girl to come along.'

'Very good, girl, very good indeed. But suitors don't hide in bushes. They ride carriages or horses. The good ones, anyway.'

'I would never have guessed. What would I do without your wise advice, Aunt.'

'You would be destitute, of course, child. Don't ask such silly questions.'

'Yes, Aunt.'

I was getting quite accomplished at playing obedience. However had that come about?

Oh yes. My practice with the tyrant king of London finance.

I chomped down on my potato a bit too hard. Ruddy hell! Could nothing banish that man from my thoughts?

'W-will Sir Philip be calling today?'

The hesitant voice was Ella's. And it answered my question. Yes, something could banish Mr Ambrose from my mind, if only temporarily: my concern for my little sister.

'I do not think so,' my aunt sighed.

Good.

'But,' she added, brightening, 'we'll all see him at the ball tonight, of course.'

Oh. Bad. Very bad.

'Ball?' What little colour there was in Ella's face disappeared.

'Oh yes. Didn't I mention it? Another invitation arrived a few days ago. We are all to go to another ball at Lady Metcalf's, and Sir Philip has kindly agreed to accompany us.' She winked at Ella in so suggestive a way that a blind possum couldn't have failed to notice the message.

Ella went from white to translucent.

'How... nice of him.'

I stabbed my fork into the next potato, imagining it to be Sir Philip's head.

'We are all invited?' I asked. 'Me, too?'

My aunt looked at me in surprise. 'Yes, of course, but... do you want to come? I thought I would have to drag you there as usual.'

'Trust me, madam,' I told her, and bit down on my potato, severing it in the middle. 'I want to come.'

~~**~*~*

The mist sparkled in the early morning sunlight in all the streets of London. It parted before me as the ocean before the bow of a battleship as I marched towards Leadenhall Street. In my mind I was going over things I could do to Sir Philip Wilkins if he didn't leave my little sister alone. Boiling alive was quite high up on the list.

This ball might be my last chance. Things were coming to a head, I could feel it! Considering all Wilkins had said to me the last time we had met, it wouldn't surprise me if he intended to propose to Ella tonight. That could never happen, I knew. She would not have the courage to refuse him.

Sweet, mad, little creature! She had the courage to offer to face down a drunken rake for my sake, but not the courage to stand up for the wishes of her own heart. If only Wilkins had fallen in love with me, instead! He would be in Inverness by now, on his way to charter a ship to the polar regions, in the hope of getting as far away from my wrath as possible.

I thought I would never be able to stop fretting about Ella. Yet the closer I drew to Leadenhall Street, the more thoughts of her and Wilkins were replaced by thoughts of another. Someone beside whom they seemed to pale into insignificance. Someone made of granite, iron and money. Soon I could do nothing but obsess over one question:

What the dickens am I supposed to say to him? How should I react to him after what has happened?

But no, I reminded myself. Nothing *had* happened. Nothing at all. Especially nothing that involved lips touching. It had all just been in my imagination. So I wouldn't need to say anything.

But...

What if *he* said something?

What if he started to talk about last night, and it turned out that all I remembered hadn't been some insane, alcohol-induced dream but, in fact, reality?

The world about me seemed to shiver and shimmer like a mirage. All of a sudden, I felt as if reality were a dream and dreams reality. What if... just hypothetically speaking of course... Mr Ambrose really did... want me in some way? What would I do if he indicated his intentions?

I really did not know. I had no idea what I would do.

And that was disturbing.

In the past I had always known what to do with a man who had declared his intentions and wanted to make me his. In most cases, a lecture on suffragism or a good, long dance during which I used his feet for target practice with my heels was sufficient to send the gentleman running. In tougher cases, a few good whacks with the parasol usually solved the problem. For some reason, though, I didn't think this would work as well on Mr Ambrose. Nor, I discovered to my horror, would I be likely to try.

What was wrong with me?

I didn't... it wasn't possible that I... no! I could never feel anything like *that*. Never, ever. Not for any man, especially not this one.

And besides, I didn't have time for anything like *that*. I was completely focused on forging an independent life for myself. Yes, I was totally concentrated and not in the least bit distracted.

Suddenly, the mist parted, and in front of me loomed the giant facade of Empire House.

Hell's Whiskers! How did I get here?

Confused, I looked around and saw the familiar houses of Leadenhall Street. Had I walked all this way without noticing?

But I was much too focused for that, surely.

Ha, ha, ha. You are?

Quickly, I made my way up to the front door and past Sallow-face in the entrance hall. He still gave me suspicious looks whenever I passed by, and I didn't like to subject myself to his scrutiny for too long, particularly when I was not at my best, performance-wise.

I climbed up the stairs.

They were very long stairs. I had noticed that already the first time I had climbed up to the higher realms of Empire House, but it impressed itself more particularly on my mind today. There were a lot of steps. And with every step, the question repeated itself:

What is he going to say?

What is he going to say?

What the bloody hell is he going to say?

By the time I had reached the upper landing, my head was ringing with the question. I hardly mumbled a 'Good morning' at Mr Stone in passing before I sneaked into my office and fled behind my desk. I wouldn't go to *him*. If he wanted to say anything, he would have to come to me. And I wanted some solid protection between us when, or rather if, he did.

I didn't have to wait long.

After only a few moments, I heard movement on the other side of the wall and tensed. My eyes snapped to the door that separated my office from that of Mr Ambrose.

I heard footsteps approach it from beyond. Sharp, hard footsteps. Footsteps with which I was, by now, very familiar.

Although I didn't want it to, although I screamed at it to behave normally, screamed that there was nothing to be excited about, the beat of my heart picked up. The footsteps came closer and closer, finally stopping right in front of the separating door.

There was a moment of silence, then a faint jingling as of coins or keys – then the footsteps turned and retreated back to where they had come from. A chair scraped across the door in the neighbouring room.

What's this? What is he doing, damn him?

He didn't leave me a lot of time for wondering, or for damning. Two minutes later, a small metal container shot out of the pneumatic tube and landed with a *plink* next to me on the desk. I jumped and grabbed the thing, pulling out the message. It read:

Mr Linton,

You are three minutes late. This will be deducted from your wages at the end of the month.

Bring me file 38XI301.

Rikkard Ambrose

All right. So, at a guess I'd say he wasn't pining with passionate love for me. So he didn't want me.

Ergo: the kiss never happened.

Well, so much the better. I wasn't even a tiny bit disappointed. No, I wasn't. After all, the fact that last night's more... intimate occurrences had just been a dream had been what I had been trying to convince myself all the time. Now that I knew it was true, I ought to feel nothing but deep satisfaction.

Ought to, yes, but...

Hurriedly, I stood up and marched to the shelves of files. In no time at all, I had discovered the required document and transported it to the door. I reached for the doorknob, turned it – and almost ran headlong into a closed door. A very unladylike word escaped my lips as I stumbled back, the file clutched to my chest.

What the...!

I tried the door again. I hadn't been mistaken. It was firmly and utterly locked.

'Hey!' With my free hand, I pounded against the heavy wood. 'What's the matter? Why is the door locked?'

Silence.

'Didn't you hear me? I said why is the door lock–'

A soft *plink* interrupted me. Turning my head, I saw that another metal cylinder had arrived on my desk. Mystified and annoyed, I stomped over to the desk and grabbed it. Now what would he have to say?

Because I locked it.

Rikkard Ambrose

I took a deep, cleansing breath, trying to calm my stormy temper. It didn't work.

Crossing out the original with maybe a little bit more force than strictly necessary, I wrote under his message:

Dear Mr Ambrose,

And why did you do that?

Yours faithfully

Lilly Linton

Ha! I wondered what he was going to say now. Was he going to claim you could work more efficiently with all the doors locked? I wouldn't put it past him, the stingy, stony old...!

Plink.

Ah!

Mr Linton,

It is a measure to further your abstinence and thereby the efficiency of your work. There is a liquor store only two streets away and a sweetshop selling solid chocolate right beside it. From your behaviour at the tavern, I deduced that keeping you locked up is the only way to prevent you from succumbing to irresistible urges.

Rikkard Ambrose

How on earth did he know I liked chocolate? Wait... *irresistible urges?* My eyes sparked!

I'll give him irresistible urges!

Not alcoholic ones, though – the ones I was feeling right now tended more towards homicidal!

Still... there might be other kinds of irresistible urges, too. I blushed as, unbidden, memories flooded into my mind... soft skin pressing against my lips, moving, caressing...

Dreams! Hallucinations! The whole lot of them! Things like that would never happen in real life. In real life, Mr Ambrose didn't go around kissing people. He went around bossing people around and locking them up.

I'd show him!

Fuming, I grabbed the next best bit of paper.

My very, very, very dear Mr Ambrose,

May I inform you that the strongest urge I feel at the moment has nothing whatsoever to do with alcohol, and everything to do with your disembowelment? OPEN THAT DOOR!

Your affectionate secretary

Lilly Linton

The answer wasn't long in coming.

Mr Linton,

You may say anything you like as long as it distracts neither you nor me from working. The door stays locked.

Mr Ambrose

The obstinate...! But why was I wasting my time like this, anyway? I was in a superior position.

Dearest Mr Ambrose

You might not recall, but I have the necessary keys in my possession to open the aforementioned door. You gave them to me yourself. Therefore, I shall see you in a minute.

Yours affectionately,

Lilly Linton

I stuffed the message into the tube, pulled the lever and marched off triumphantly towards the door without waiting for an answer. My triumphant march was somewhat impeded, however, when my keys wouldn't fit in the lock. I tried them again, and again. Still, they didn't fit. Marching over to the other door, the one to the hallway, I tried to open this one, but discovered that it, too, had been locked, and my keys didn't fit. By the time I had returned to the desk, another message had arrived.

Mr Linton,
I had the locks changed.
Rikkard Ambrose.
P.S. Affection is not among the services I require of you.

Heat rose to my cheeks on reading the last line. I had reached for the pen before I had started to think.

Dear Mr Ambrose,
I wonder you went to the expense of two new locks, simply for the sake of my absti-nence! How wasteful of you.
Yours
Lilly Linton
P.S: If you do not require it, I shall not offer it.

Only half a minute later, his response arrived.

Mr Linton,
They were not new, but second-hand. I am still waiting for file 37VI288. Shove it un-der the door.
Rikkard Ambrose

I'd like to shove it up his...

Oh no. I didn't want to have anything to do with his... Well, with that part of him. No matter how juicy it looked. Not even for shoving files up it.

Dear Mr Ambrose,
I demand to be let out immediately!
Yours
Lilly Linton

His reply was short and to the point. Who could have guessed?

Mr Linton,
You work for me, not the other way around. You cannot demand anything. Now bring me file 37VI288.
Rikkard Ambrose

What did I do? Yell? Hammer at the door in protest?

No.

I brought him the file.

I just managed it, all the while chanting in my head 'Think of the money. Think of the independence it will bring you. Think of what you can do for Ella if all goes horribly wrong. You must have that money. You must.'

My chant was interrupted by the *plink* of another message arriving.

~~*~**~*~*

'Mr Linton?'

'Yes?'

I resurfaced from a mountain of files I was sorting through and looked around. But there was no one there.

'Mr Linton? The door to your office is locked.'

It was Mr Stone's voice, coming from the other side of the door leading to the hallway.

'Yes, um... Mr Ambrose wanted me to lock it.'

'Oh.' From Mr Stone's bewildered tone, I could tell he wanted to ask why but didn't think it was worth the risk of arousing the wrath of Mr Ambrose. 'Well, I have his letters here. Sorry for the delay, the postman got here late.'

'I see. Can you just shove them under the door, please?'

'Of course. See you later, Mr Linton.'

'Yes, thank you, Mr Stone.'

Hurrying over to the door I grabbed the pile of letters and began to leaf through it. Business, business, business, charity (waste), charity (waste), more charity (definitely waste!), pink envelope–

My hands froze as I stared at the crest on the pink paper. Not another one of these!

Heat rushed to my cheeks as I stared at the name of the sender. Samantha Genevieve Ambrose. Already once before had I entertained the idea that this might be Mr Ambrose's wife. The idea had irked me back then. It drove ice through my veins now.

Flashes of last night again appeared in front of my inner eye. His arms around me, his lips on mine – no, no, no! It had all been a hallucination. What did it matter if he was married? He and I hadn't engaged in amorous c–

Well, we had certainly done *nothing* that non-married people weren't supposed to do. All this existed only in my head, it had been a dream.

Quickly, I ran over to my desk and stuffed the pink envelope into the drawer, to keep the others of its kind company. The old saying said 'out of sight, out of mind'. I slammed the drawer shut and took a deep breath.

And soon I discovered that the old saying was complete poppycock.

I would like to be able to say I worked like a slave that day, but it wouldn't be true. Slaves are shouted at, and probably whipped, too. I, for my part, was simply badgered to death with little bits of paper. The latter method turned out to be quite as effective as the former, though. He kept me at it for about three or four hours without one pause or break. And if that wasn't enough, thoughts of the letter tormented me ceaselessly. And the hallucinatory kiss! And... and... finally it started to feel like it all built up as a physical pressure, growing inside me. It built and built, waiting to be released–

Until I finally realized that it didn't just feel like a physical pressure. It *was* physical pressure.

Oops.

'Mr Ambrose?' Marching up to the connecting door, I hammered against the wood. 'Mr Ambrose, I have to use the powder room. Now.'

Silence.

'If you don't let me use it, I'm going to pee in the waste paper basket,' I threatened.

That worked. Footsteps approached, and keys jingled in the look. A moment later, the door opened and he stood before me: Mr Rikkard Ambrose in all his cold, stony glory. His eyes were like dark pools of unfathomable deep water. His mouth could have been carved from granite. And his lips...

Luckily, my bladder took my thoughts off that subject fast.

'Finally!' I hissed. 'What the dickens do you mean by locking me up like this? Are you–'

He interrupted me with a curt motion of the hand towards the powder room. 'Get in.'

I would have liked to stay and argue, but my pressing need was becoming ever more pressing. Oh well, I could always argue afterwards.

Two minutes later I sat on cool ceramic, sighing in contentment – probably the first time ever I had felt contentment within the walls of Empire House, 322 Leadenhall Street.

As my feeling of contentment slowly faded, my thoughts drifted to Mr Ambrose's behaviour. I couldn't make head or tail of it. Why would he lock me in like this? To prevent me from drinking and thus being distracted from my work? But that was preposterous! If I were in danger of becoming a drunkard, if I were to run away and succumb to alcohol during my work hours, then he would have the perfect excuse to dismiss me – exactly what he had been waiting for all along. So why should he try to prevent that? To want to keep me from drinking to excess, that wasn't the act of an employer for whom one employee was like another, easily exchangeable. It sounded more like the act of somebody who cared about my safety...

Who cared about me.

I slammed the door on that thought immediately. I slammed it so hard I almost thought I heard the sound of a door shut with my actual ears.

Then, when I heard Karim's voice from outside the powder room, I realized I *had* heard a door shut: the door of Mr Ambrose's office!

'*Sahib?*'

Mr Ambrose's reply was unintelligible. His cool voice was much quieter than the rumble of the mountainous Mohammedan.

Quickly, I jumped up and pulled up my trousers. This male outfit was pretty nifty. Had I been in a dress and crinoline, it would have taken me a quarter of an hour to get up from the toilet. As it was, I was up and across the room in a few seconds, my ear pressed against the keyhole.

'...perimeter is watched closely, *Sahib*. We have been asking questions – it seems, no unusual shipments have gone out.'

'So it might be that the file is still there?'

My ears grew to the size of bat ears. They were talking about the stolen file!

'Yes, *Sahib*.'

Yes! Dalgliesh hadn't gotten away with it yet, that slimy little... incredibly powerful peer of the British Empire.

'And what about the house itself? Number 97, East India Dock Road?'

That was it! That was the address I had discovered. I remembered that much from last night and knew that this part had not been a dream.

'It is better guarded than the Queen's hulks[48], *Sahib*. Men with swords and guns are everywhere, some even professional soldiers. Something is in there, that much is sure.'

'I see. We will go ahead as planned then.'

Go in? As planned?

Was there something planned? And if so, what? And most importantly, why hadn't I been told? It had been I who discovered the ruddy place, after all!

'Be ready in three days. I shall need all the things on list I gave you by then.'

Three days? And then... what? What were they going to do? Just march up to the doorstep and demand that they be given back the file? No, that couldn't be it. But the only other explanation could be...

A shiver went down my back.

Secret preparations. Scouting. These words sounded familiar. They sounded like something you would do when you were planning something illegal.

'*Sahib*... I must once more raise the matter of–'

'No! Karim, we discussed this.'

'Still, *Sahib*, going in there by yourself...'

Violently, I jerked away from the keyhole and stared at it in disbelief. But as soon as they started speaking again, I pressed my ear back against the metal. Surely I could not have heard right!

'I have always done what needed doing myself.'

He had? Damn and blast the arrogant bastard!

'Yes, you have, *Sahib*. In the colonies, when we were dealing with bandits, and gold-diggers and other fools who thought too highly of themselves. This is an operation of Dalgliesh's, *Sahib*.' Karim's voice hesitated. 'You know what happened the last time you faced him, *Sahib*.'

The silence that erupted on the other side of the door could have cut iron.

What? What happened? Lord Dalgliesh and Mr Ambrose have met before? Go on! What happened? I want to know!

Silence.

Speak up, blast you!

Silence.

Then, a voice. But not the one I had been hoping to hear.

'I... am sorry, *Sahib*.'

'I will go alone.' Mr Ambrose voice was as cutting and cold as his silence had been. 'Who else can I trust to do it right?'

'You can trust me, *Sahib*.' If I wasn't very much mistaken, I could hear something like hurt in the bearded mountain's voice.

'I know. Which is why I need you to say here to keep an eye on things.'

'I... Very well. As you wish, *Sahib*.'

---

[48] By 'hulk', Karim is not referring to an overgrown green monster who likes to smash things. In Victorian times, prisons were overflowing with criminals, and 'hulk' was a term for an old navy ship that was no longer fit for sea, and was therefore used as a temporary, floating prison. I don't know why the Victorians preferred to store their prisoners on water rather than on land. Maybe they thought the ship rats deserved some company.

To the dickens with the *Sahib*'s wishes! Mr Ambrose was not going alone! I was going to stick with him, if it was the last thing I did!

If there had been other men in the room, they might have exchanged a few pleasantries before breaking up the meeting. But I had learned enough about Mr Ambrose by now to know that he wasn't given to chatter. Karim left the room, and I hastily got up off the powder room floor, dusted off my knees and cracked the door open, peeking out.

Mr Ambrose was sitting behind his desk. When I entered, he looked up from the papers he was studying, meeting my gaze coolly. I had to catch my breath when I looked into his eyes. How come I had never noticed quite how beautiful their deep, dark depths were until this moment?

'You heard.' It was a statement, not a question.

'Yes, Sir.'

'Then forget what you heard.'

'I cannot do that, Sir.'

'Oh? I gave you an order.'

'You can take your order and stick it up your– um, I mean you can take your order and feed it to the ducks in Green Park! I'm coming with you!'

There was no need to say when and where. We both knew what I was referring to.

'No.'

'Yes, I am!'

'No, you are not.' His eyes glittered with frost. 'Mr Linton – believe me when I say that if we could recapture the file by excessive consumption of alcohol, you would be in the front lines. Unfortunately, this is not the case, and I therefore decline your request.'

'It was no request! I can't let you go in there alone!'

'You can, and you will.'

Dear God! Had he always been like this? Was this why his wife had left him and was bombarding him with pink letters? Were they living apart? But why would she be sending him letters if they were parted?

Although I had to admit to my shame that, in her place, I might be sending him letters, too, just to have him snap back at me.

In defiance, I shook my head. 'I won't let you go alone! I won't!'

'Yes, you will.'

'But...' For some reason my voice was unsteady. 'But Karim said... he said *armed guards*. You could be hurt out there or... or killed.'

Silence.

'At least tell me what it is,' I pleaded. 'Tell me what that damned file is! Tell me what is worth risking your life for!'

The silence stretched between us as we gazed at each other.

He swallowed.

'You want to know what's in the file?' he asked, his voice like a raw winter blizzard. 'You really want to know?'

'Yes.' My voice – small, tense, expectant – was nothing like his.

'In the file,' he said, 'is the centre of the world.'

I stared at him, uncomprehending. His words had registered, but I had no idea of their actual meaning.

The centre of the world.

'Forgive me, Sir, but I don't...'

His eyes narrowed infinitesimally.

'Get out.'

'What?'

'You understood me, I believe? I have told you what you wanted to know. Now get out! And shut the door behind you.'

'But-'

'This is an order!'

My hands opened and closed in helpless anger. I had no choice. I had to obey or be dismissed. And right now, I could see he was hungry for me to give him the chance. His words came back to me, ringing loudly in my head – *affection is not among the services I require of you.* What was I doing? Why was I arguing to risk my life alongside him? I whirled on the spot and stormed out of his room, into mine.

My room. The centre of my world. But not the centre of all the world.

The centre of the world... The words echoed in my head with ominous significance. What on earth could he have meant?

He didn't give me much chance to ponder his strange revelation. As soon as I was in my office again, the door firmly shut behind me, I heard him get up from his chair and lock the door from the other side. It didn't take long until I heard a familiar *plink* from the wall beside my desk.

The rest of the workday went by in a blur of fetching papers, and *plinks* and trying not to worry about the writer of the pink letters or what Mr Ambrose intended to do.

I shook my head. He couldn't really be planning to break into Lord Dalgliesh's...?

No!

I mean, he was a *businessman*, not the leader of some street gang. Though... he hadn't practised his business here in London, I remembered, but in some corner of the former colonies. The West of America, if I remembered correctly? There was something about that region... I seemed to recall having heard it called the 'Wild West' once.

Personally, I couldn't see what was so wild about it. From the few pictures I had seen, it was a country just like any other, with trees, rivers, mountains and people.

Though, now that I thought about it, most of the people in the pictures I had seen had carried guns.

Just like the guards at Lord Dalgliesh's headquarters.

Mr Ambrose couldn't be planning to do what I was thinking he was planning to do, could he?

Really? Not even for the centre of the world?

˷˷*˷**˷*˷*

It was about seven pm when the messages stopped coming though the pneumatic tube. Some minutes later, I heard keys rustling, and a slightly confused-looking Mr Stone unlocked the door to my office.

'Um... Mr Linton? Mr Ambrose instructed me to "let the Ifrit out of the dungeon", as he put it. Was he referring to you?'

Had I been in a better mood, I might have grinned. But now, only a scowl managed to make its way onto my face.

'Yes.'

'I see.' Mr Stone cleared his throat. 'Um... excuse me, but I still don't quite see what his words actually mean. Could you explain, perhaps?'

'No!'

'Oh. Very well, then... I suppose I'd better pack my things and go. Until tomorrow, Mr Linton.'

Grumbling a response, I rushed past him and down the hallway. Maybe, just maybe, I could still catch Mr Ambrose before he left the building. I raced down and into the main hall at breakneck speed. Just as I stormed into the giant stone monument that was the entrance hall of Empire House, I saw the end of a black tailcoat disappearing through the front door.

'Wait!' I shouted, and all eyes turned towards me as I ran across the hall. Over the slap of my footsteps on the polished stone floor I could hear the whispered words 'secretary' and 'new' and 'replacement' echoing from all around me.

Wait, I wanted to shout again. *What about the centre of the world? What is it? Where is it? How can it be on a piece of paper?*

But I knew better than to speak those words aloud. I might not know what the 'centre of the world' was – but I knew the words had power. If I let them become common knowledge, I was as good as dead. With a last burst of effort, I threw myself after him. He would not escape me! He would tell me everything! Finally, I was at the door and, pushing it open, jumped outside – only to see a chaise, drawn by a beastly grey horse, disappearing in the distance.

I uttered some very unladylike words.

But there was nothing to be done. For now, he was gone. And gone with him was the chance to convince him to explain his mysterious words, the chance to convince him to let me go with him. For now, I could do nothing.

But, I had to remember, I still had three days to convince him to let me in on the secret, and to make me part of his plans. There was another occasion coming for which the timetable was slightly more pressing.

Turning the other way, I started down the street, towards home.

Another centre of my world...

As soon as I turned into our street, I could see that the preparations for the ball were in full flow. Or perhaps it would be more accurate to say that I could *hear*, rather than see.

'Faster, faster, girls, the carriage will be here in less than an hour! What are you thinking, still running around only half-dressed? What if he should happen to arrive early? Maria, your hair looks like a haystack! Take it down again. No, here, let me. Someone fetch me a comb! And where in heaven's name is Lillian?'

Quickly, I glanced around, to see whether any of the neighbours were around to hear. None of them were outside, but my aunt's tirade was audible out here in the street, with all the doors and windows closed. What did a few additional walls mean to a shriek as impressive as hers?

'Leadfield! Go and look for Lilly, and bring her to me as quickly as your feet can carry you!'

Good. That meant I had plenty of time.

'And bring Ella, too, if you can find her. What she is thinking...'

Ella wasn't with them? My breathing quickened, and I hastened my steps. Soon I was past the front entrance and at the door to the back garden. Unlocking it and slipping through, I made my way to the garden shed and disappeared into the shelter of its darkness.

I was probably less than presentable when I did up the laces of my dress, but since I would take it off and exchange it for my makeshift ball gown as soon as I was in the house, I didn't think much of the fact. I was too concerned about the fact that my aunt hadn't been able to find Ella.

Dear God! She didn't... she couldn't just...?

No! Not without saying goodbye to me!

Don't jump to conclusions, I told myself. *It doesn't have to mean the worst.*

The worst.

What I had feared all along.

That she had run away.

In a dash, I crossed the last bit of distance to the door and pushed it open.

No. It didn't have to mean she had run away. She could be in a part of the house they hadn't thought to look in, or she could be on a walk, or she...

...could be hurrying across the garden right in front of me!

There she was! Even in the darkness, that white gown and golden hair were unmistakable!

Like a flash, I was back inside the shed, the door open only a crack now, just enough to allow me to see through. There could be only one reason why Ella would visit the garden at this hour, only one person she could have come to see.

As if my thinking of him had conjured him up, Edmund appeared from between the bushes on the other side of the fence. Ella gave a little cry and hurried towards him. She was already in her ball gown and not caring a bit if she got grass stains on it. I had to admit, this *was* real love. Or at least a very convincing imitation.

'Ella, my love!'

'Edmund, my love!'

They ran towards each other as if they wanted to jump into each other's arms. Fortunately, they remembered the fence in time and didn't crack their skulls.

Instead, they just clasped hands. A much wiser policy.

'Oh, Ella, my love, is it true what I have heard?'

'I don't know. What have you heard, my love?'

'That there is to be another ball at Lady Metcalf's this evening, and that Sir Wilkins is taking you. I heard something of that mentioned by Mrs Richardson, and now I hear that your house is busy...'

Busy. What a very diplomatic way to describe my aunt's forceful tones.

'Say it isn't so, Ella, my love!'

'Alas, I cannot, Edmund. For we are indeed invited to Lady Metcalf's ball, which is tonight...'

'And...?'

'...and Sir Wilkins is taking us.'

'Taking *you*, you mean to say.'

'We will all go. I, Aunt, Gertrude, Lisbeth...'

Edmund's eyes were aflame. 'But it is you he wants there. You he wants with him!'

Ella shuddered, her hands slipping from his.

'Don't you think I know this?' she asked. 'Don't you think I wish every waking moment it weren't so? But I cannot wish him away!'

Edmund's freed hands balled into fists. 'Neither can I. I have tried often enough.'

'But...' Ella hesitated.

'But what, Ella, my love?'

'But maybe I can wish myself away.'

He looked confused. Ella hesitated again, then suddenly set her small chin and looked up at him.

'Take me with you,' she said, her voice trembling, her eyes two shining pleas. 'I do not wish to go to this ball. I do not wish to dance with Sir Philip. I do not wish to be in any man's arms but yours. Take me away from the place, just as you said you would.'

'Tonight? Now? But Ella, the preparations...'

'I don't care about preparations! I only care that I love you, and that I want to be with you. Take me away, Edmund, please!'

Edmund closed his eyes.

'I am sorry, my love, but I cannot,' he whispered. 'I could not yet procure a marriage license. And I will not soil your honour by taking you without the knowledge that I can make you my wife, to love and to hold.'

There were tears in Ella's eyes.

'Then, it is *adieu* for us, Edmund. I shall go to the ball. You will procure a license as quickly as you can, I know that. Just... just don't take too long. And know that *whatever might happen*, my heart will always be yours.'

'*Whatever might happen?*' His eyes snapped open, hearing the weight of her words. 'You don't mean to say that... Ella, you don't think Sir Philip will chose tonight to ask you to... oh, I cannot even say the words! Tell me, darling! Tell me that it will not be tonight!'

Ella remained silent. I had spent enough time around Mr Ambrose to be able to distinguish different kinds of silence. Hers was the silence of someone who wished to speak, but could not.

'Ella!' With both hands, Edmund reached through the bars, attempting to grasp her shoulders. But she retreated a step, out of his reach. 'Ella, at least tell me that if he asks you tonight, you will not say yes! Please! I beg you!'

Ella's tears were rivulets now, streaming down both her cheeks.

'I... I cannot,' she whispered.

'Ella!'

'G-goodbye, Edmund. Goodbye, my love.'

'Ellaaa!'

His cry echoed through an empty garden.

On my way into the house I actually had to blow my nose. Had the scene in the garden moved me to tears? Or was I getting a cold? The latter possibility seemed much more likely to me.

I slipped quietly inside and made my way up to our room. As I entered, Ella, who was sitting in front of the mirror, jumped and tried to conceal her tear-stained face – until she saw it was me. Then she didn't bother. Our eyes met, brown to blue. There was a silent agreement in hers, which, I was sure, was mirrored in mine. She didn't ask where I had been all day, and I didn't ask why tears were running down her cheeks.

Without saying a word, I took my handkerchief out of my pocket and handed it to her. Hers was already too wet to be of any use. She took it with a thankful expression. Having dried her cheeks, she proceeded to help me out of my dress and into my ball gown.

Another kind of silence, I mused. *The silence of love, where no words need to be spoken, because the eyes say enough.*

My little sister had hardly finished tying up the laces of my dress when we heard a familiar screech from below:

'Come! Quick, girls, come! He is here! Sir Philip has arrived, I see his coach!'

Ella's knees nearly buckled. I whirled and caught her at her elbows just in time to steady her.

'I can go down alone, if you want,' I offered. 'I can tell them that you can't attend the ball because you are sick.' *You definitely look like it.*

'No.' Ella shook her head sadly. 'Aunt would never believe it, or she would insist that I go, regardless.'

That was probably true. Our aunt's world order was very clear and structured: social duties came first, sick girls second. Or maybe twenty-second.

Lifting the skirt of her ball gown, Ella took a deep breath and opened the door. 'Let's go, Lilly. Let's face this.'

She was so brave. I couldn't for the life of me understand how one could be so brave and so timid at the same time. Why couldn't she just wait until Wilkins proposed and then tell him, '*Thanks, but no thanks!*'?

Well, the day I understood Ella would be the day I achieved my doctoral degree in philosophy. Not ever.

Over our joined footsteps on the creaky wooden stairs, I could hear Sir Phillip's voice from below. My back stiffened. This was the voice of the dread foe I would have to meet and defeat before the night was out.

At the moment, the dread foe was talking about a new variety of tulips he had recently discovered growing near his country home.

'They are beautiful, the most beautiful flowers you have ever seen, but *so* delicate. I think I will have to rescue them before the winter comes.'

'I see. How very... considerate of you,' my aunt said, smiling one of her brightest and most fake smiles. Now, if they just could keep each other occupied for a few seconds longer, maybe Ella and I could sneak past unnoticed and get seats next to each other in the coach, with Ella in the corner. Then, at least, she would be save from tulips for the ride to the ball.

Catching her eye, I gestured to the door, and she nodded.

Slowly, we started towards the door, behind the backs of both Sir Philip and our aunt.

'Winter is such a harsh season, don't you think?' Wilkins sighed. 'All the little flowers dead and buried under snow. And in the house, too, it produces such a cold atmosphere. You know, I have long been wondering whether there isn't something I could do to counteract that, and I think I have found the solution.' He sighed significantly. 'I think it is time to make a permanent change in my home, if you understand what I mean.'

My aunt's eyes flew wide open, practically glowing with greed. From one moment to the next, all her attention was on Wilkins. So was mine – and Ella's. We both had frozen in place and were staring at our terrible enemy.

'A... significant change?' My aunt managed, her eyes gleaming.

'Oh yes, quite significant. I feel that I cannot go on as I have these past years. I need something that can warm my heart in the coldest of times. My own little sunshine.'

My aunt's hands were clasped together in eagerness, and at his last words, she almost fainted. 'Oh, *I see*, Sir Phillip. I understand *perfectly*.'

My eyes flicked to Ella. She was leaning against the doorframe, her face ashen. Apparently, she, too, understood perfectly.

'And when will you be initiating this change?' my aunt enquired.

'As soon as possible,' the accursed Wilkins said with a dreamy look in his eyes. 'Why postpone something that can bring so much happiness to one's life?'

'True, very true.'

Ella was in motion again, then, hurrying towards the door. I didn't know what she meant to do, run to the coach, or to Edmund, or to Ecuador, but she was too late. Just in that moment, Wilkins turned around and beheld her.

'Ah! Miss Ella! I have been looking forward to seeing you.'

~~**~*~*

It wasn't long before Aunt Brank shewed us outside and into the coach. No matter how eager she might be for a little love scene between Ella and Sir Philip in the hallway, she was even more eager for Ella to get to the ball and be proposed to. I did my best to insert myself between the couple, using my hoop skirt to great effect, but there was only so much I could do. I could not keep Wilkins from sending my little sister glowing looks and flowery compliments, no matter how much I wanted to punch him in the face.

What the bloody hell am I going to do? If he really proposes to her... How can I stop him?

It was only just as the last of my sisters took her seat in the coach that I glimpsed the possible answer, out in the street. An answer in human form.

By George!

He was standing at the little gate that separated the flowerbeds in front of his parents' house from the cobblestones. His face looked pale and gaunt in the light of the gas lamps, though I thought it might have looked pale and gaunt tonight in any sort of lighting. Edmund Conway stood erect, like a man about to be summoned to his execution, and stared over at the coach. I knew exactly whom he was looking at: Ella and Wilkins. Judge and Executioner.

All of a sudden, pity welled up inside me for this young man. I had no idea where it was coming from. It certainly wasn't usual for me to feel pity for any man, much less one who was conducting an illicit affair with my little sister in the back garden. But the feeling was there. And, as is always the case with these blasted feelings I have, it led to an impulsive action.

'Mr Conway!' I waved at him energetically, plastering a broad smile on my face. 'How nice to see you. What brings you out at such a late hour?'

I had called quite loudly, loudly enough so neither he nor anyone else could ignore it. Hesitantly, he detached himself from the garden gate and came towards us.

'I... was watching the stars,' he said, his gaze fastening on Ella's face.

I bet you were. Two particularly bright, blue stars, hmm?

'What a happy coincidence you're here,' I proclaimed, before my aunt, who looked like she'd eaten a wagonload of lemons, could say otherwise. 'I was just thinking about how we have an empty seat in our coach and how it would be a pity to waste it. We're all going to a ball tonight. Have you heard about it? A grand affair at Lady Metcalf's. Would you like to come with us?'

I might as well have hit him in the head with an iron cudgel. The effect would have been similar to that of my words. Maybe it would even have been kinder.

The colour drained from his face and he staggered back a step.

'C-come with you?'

'Tosh! Lilly, how can you talk such nonsense?' my aunt cut in. 'It is not our coach, it is Sir Phillip's. You cannot simply invite this...' She regarded Edmund with her nostrils. '...this young person into a carriage that does not belong to you.'

Sir Philip smiled brightly. 'Oh, but I would be delighted to take Mr... What was your name again, Sir? I'm afraid we haven't been properly introduced.'

'Mr Conway, may I introduce you to Sir Philip Wilkins, a friend of the family,' I said before anybody else could open their mouth. 'Sir Philip, this is Edmund Conway, one of our neighbours.'

'Delighted to make your acquaintance, Mr Conway.' Sir Philip gave an awkward sitting bow. The flower in his buttonhole almost dropped out.

'L-likewise, Sir Philip,' Edmund mumbled and returned the bow stiffly.

'As I was about to say,' Sir Philip said to my aunt and me, smiling broadly, 'I would be delighted to take Mr Conway. Lady Metcalf said I could bring as many friends as I wished, and such a charming young man would make an excellent addition to our party, don't you think?'

My aunt would have rather swallowed broken glass than admit that the son of a humble piano tuner could be charming company. But she also was not about to disagree with the only member of the nobility who was a potential nephew-in-law.

'Mhm,' she said, which left things pretty much open to interpretation.

'What do you think, Miss Ella?' Wilkins said, directing his smile at my little sister. 'Don't you think our friend here seems like charming company?'

Ella swallowed, hard. Her eyes met those of Edmund.

'Yes,' she whispered.

That was all.

Just the one word – but it was sufficient.

Sir Philip clapped his hands. 'Excellent. Get in, Mr Conway.'

'But... but I...'

'You don't have other plans, do you?'

'No, I...'

'Well, then, what are you waiting for? Let's go and enjoy ourselves!'

~~**~*~*

Let me say right now that on the ride to Lady Metcalf's residence, Edmund didn't look as though he were enjoying himself. He had mentioned once that it was one of his heart's deepest desires to attend a ball with Ella, his love – but I guess in none of his fantasies had his rival, Ella's probable future husband, sat with them in the coach.

I'm not an expert on romance, but I suppose something like that dampens the ardour of even the most determined Casanova.

'Tell me, Mr Conway,' Wilkins, who was completely oblivious to the icy silence in the coach, asked with a bright smile. 'Where are your family's estates?'

If he had wanted to pick a question to make the other young man despise him even more, he could not have chosen better.

'My family does not have any estates,' he said stiffly. 'My father practices a trade.'

'A trade? How interesting.' Wilkins' smile didn't waver. 'What kind of trade, exactly?'

'My father is a piano tuner.'

A snort could be heard from the corner in which Maria sat. And for the first time in my life, I saw my sweet little sister Ella throw somebody a murderous look. Wilkins, for his part, continued his babbling, completely unaware of the icy stares he received. He seemed to be fascinated by the whole subject of piano tuning. Apparently, before tonight he had thought pianos just sounded the same all the time by themselves.

'One never ceases to learn,' he remarked. 'Pianos seem to be like flowers, in a way. Flowers have to be taken care of regularly, too, or they shrivel.'

'But, unlike pianos,' Edmund pointed out, 'flowers cannot make music.'

'True, very true. A pity that is. If they could, they would be perfect.'

Ella sneaked a quick glance at Edmund, who was looking out of the window. 'Nothing in this world is perfect,' she said in a sad, quiet voice.

I thought she had hit the nail on the head with that. But Wilkins, the blasted son of a bachelor, leant forward, took her hand and pressed a light kiss on the back of it.

'Apart from your beauty, fair lady,' he said with a wink.

From the corner where Edmund sat, I heard a gagging noise. I was beginning to ask myself whether bringing him along had really been such an ingenious idea.

But when we drew up in front of Lady Metcalf's house and climbed out of the carriage, and I saw Ella looking at him as if there was no other man in the world, I knew I couldn't *not* have brought him along. From inside the house, I could hear the musicians try the first notes of music. On Ella's face, I could read her emotions as plainly as if they were written in a book: she was at a ball, and Edmund was with her. If only he could come to her, take her in his arms and dance till the night turned into morning...

Setting his jaw, Edmund took a determined step towards her.

'Ah, there you are, Miss Ella!' Smiling broadly, Wilkins appeared at Ella's right elbow, offering her his arm. 'Shall we go in?'

Edmund stopped in his tracks.

Ella looked at her lover for a moment longer, then she wrenched her gaze away from his and faced the house again.

'Yes,' she said. 'Let's go.'

At the door to the ballroom, Lady Metcalf awaited us.

'Sir Phillip,' she trilled, clapping her pudgy hands together. 'How wonderful to see you again!' She didn't mention that it was wonderful to see the rest of us. But then, considering that none of us was titled or rich, it probably wasn't, for her.

Suddenly, I realized that Wilkins, busy with greeting Lady Metcalf, had had to let go of Ella's arm. Quickly, I slipped in between them and took Ella's hand with a firm grip. She looked up at me, a world of thanks shining in her eyes.

'Please, come in.' With a false smile directed at all of us, the lady of the house waved us towards the open door. 'The first dance will start very soon, I believe.'

Sir Philip nodded and reached for Ella's hand – only to find that it had, by instant-sister-transfer, been moved to a safe distance, along with the rest of her. Confused, he blinked up at us, standing three paces away, then smiled his guffin smile again and started towards us.

'Please, Lilly,' a hurried whisper shot out of Ella's mouth. '*Please* don't leave me alone with him. I can't explain why, right now, but I don't want to be alone with him. Please...'

She didn't have to say another word. I was already dragging her through the door and into the ballroom.

Bright light exploded in a magnificent spectacle before us. After the dim light of the street lamps outside, we both had to pause and blink for a moment, until our eyes got used to the sparkling scene in front of us: crystal chandeliers shining in the candlelight, women in brightly coloured dresses, men in glossy black evening wear, and large windows which, with the black night outside, worked like mirrors and made the room seem twice as large, the guests twice as multifarious.

'...quite the society event,' we heard Lady Metcalf's voice from behind us. 'Important people from all over England have come, gentry, military, knights of the Order of the Garter... even one of the Peers of the Realm has been kind enough to accept my invitation.'

'Yes, Lady Metcalf,' came Wilkins' reply. 'I'm sure it's magnificent. Now if you will excuse me, I have to go after Miss...'

'Quick!' I hissed, and pulled Ella to the left, into a throng of people gathered around some painting, a recent addition to Lady Metcalf's collection. There wasn't a single flower on the painting, so I was inclined to think that Sir Philip wouldn't be likely to join the crowd of admirers.

Ella slid behind a column left of the painting and sank against it, not being able to support her weight anymore on her legs alone.

'Dear God, Lilly,' she sighed. 'Thank you! I... I don't know what I would do if he caught me alone. I...'

She watched me with wide, fearful eyes, unable to find the words to explain.

'It's quite all right,' I said, patting her shoulder with a reassuring smile on my face. 'I wouldn't like to spend all night in the company of such a nincompoop, either.'

She gave me a grateful smile.

'Yes, that's all. I just feel... uncomfortable with him.'

'Don't you worry. I'll keep you safe.'

Taking my hand, she pressed it, just for a moment, then let it go again.

'I know,' she whispered.

There was a moment of companionable, or should I say sisterly, silence. Around us, people discussed Dürer's particular style. I, for my part, had no idea what his style was, if he had one at all, and if he had, what he did with it. But I really didn't care. All I cared about was that Ella was with me, and for the moment, she was safe.

'Lilly?' Ella's voice was quiet.

'Hmm?' I answered, trying to peer over the heads of the crowd to spot whether Sir Philip was closing in.

'Why did you ask Ed– I mean Mr Conway to accompany us?'

I stopped trying to peer, and started trying to think of an answer very, very quickly.

'Well... I knew you weren't that fond of Sir Philip's attentions. So I thought if I'd ask somebody else along, somebody Sir Philip didn't know yet, maybe he would keep him busy for the night, and you wouldn't be bothered.' I shrugged. 'Sorry it didn't work.'

'Oh. That's all?'

'Yes. Why?'

Ella seemed to relax. 'Nothing. I was just curious.'

Nothing my foot!

'Well,' I added teasingly, 'I had hoped this Mr Conway might be fond of flowers. In that case, he'd certainly have distracted Sir Philip for the entire night.'

That actually brought a little smile to Ella's face. 'No, he doesn't like flowers, they give him hay fev-'

She clamped her hand over her mouth.

'What did you say?' I asked, pretending not to have heard her slip.

'N-nothing. Nothing, really.'

She looked away from me, to the left. I followed her gaze and saw Edmund standing with his back towards us, staring out of one of the enormous windows, into the black night. The yearning in Ella's eyes was so immense, it hurt to watch. Quickly, I looked away.

What would it be like, the thought shot through my head, *to care about another person so completely that you couldn't live without them? To care about a man?*

The image of a face appeared in my mind – cold, hard, forbidding and so completely unreachable. I shoved the image away with all my might.

To hell with it! To hell with *him*! What would it be like to care about a man? I didn't ever intend to find out! If this tragedy of Ella's had taught me anything, it was that men brought nothing but trouble. Trouble, and too many bouquets of flowers.

'Ah! Miss Ella! There you are.'

Blast!

My head whipped around. There he was - Sir Philip Wilkins, the evil one. Why had I let my guard down? Why had I let my thoughts wander? Now he had discovered us.

I started forward, to place myself before my sister. But then, something else started, quicker than I was: the music.

With a few steps, Wilkins was in front of my sister, and bowed.

'My dear Miss Ella. May I ask for the honour of your hand for the first dance?'

Was it only I who thought there had been a slight pause before the words 'for the first dance?'

Ella shivered like an aspen.

'Y-yes, Sir Philip. Of course.'

There was a thump and a muttered curse from the left. If I was not very mistaken, Edmund had just tried to punch through the wall.

Wilkins, oblivious to both him and me, took Ella's shivering hand and led her off onto the dance floor, as the first notes of a quadrille floated through the ballroom. Ella threw a look over her shoulder, a last, long, desperate look, in answer to which I could do nothing but look back, helplessly.

Then Wilkins spoke to her, and she looked away from me.

Rage thundering within me, I stared after the fiend as he led my poor little sister off to her doom. Why hadn't I thought of this before? I could protect her while we just standing around, put myself as a barrier between him and her – but as soon as the dancing started, that was over. I couldn't interfere on the dance floor, not without making a scandal that would ruin my little sister's reputation.

Was he going to propose now? Could you propose while dancing with a lady? You had to kneel down to propose, didn't you? I had to admit, I had little experience in the matter. Any man who had ever dared to fancy me had been chased away long before he got that far. Could you kneel down while dancing, or would the other dancers trip over you?

Such questions and a million more assaulted me as I tried to burn a hole into blasted Wilkins' back with the sheer force of my gaze. This man was going to ruin the life of my beloved sister! Oh, if only this weren't a ballroom. If only I were alone with him, and had a parasol with a nicely sharpened tip in my hands, I would...!

'Excuse me?' I heard a man's voice from behind me. 'Are you intending to murder him in a dark alley later on? If so, I'm afraid I will have to stop you.'

A WAIST OF TIGERS

I whirled around, my heart pounding.

'What? Who said that?'

Behind me, or rather in front of me now that I was facing him, stood a tall young man with long, curly dark brown hair. He wore an easy smile on his face and a triangular patch of beard on his chin that wasn't really a beard, just a statement: *look, I can grow hair here, if I want to.*

'W-what did you mean? Who... who do you think I was looking at?'

'Old Flip over there.' He nodded towards where Sir Philip and Ella were dancing. Did he mean Sir Philip? But I could have sworn that wasn't what he said.

'Who?'

'Flip. Well, Sir Philip to you, probably. Are you planning to assassinate him? You looked like you were. So I thought I'd ask. I'm his friend, you see, and friends usually try to prevent that sort of thing – their friends getting assassinated, that is. Always such a messy business, and funeral costs are steep these days.'

I shook my head, having no clue what to say to that – particularly considering I wasn't even supposed to talk to this man. You weren't supposed to talk to *anybody* unless you knew them, and had been introduced to them. That's how society worked.

'Who... who are you?' I finally managed.

'Oh, I am so sorry.' His smile widened and he gave a snappy bow that made his mahogany locks fly. 'My name is Carter, Captain James Carter to be precise. I apologize for accosting you thus without being formerly introduced, but when there is something important at stake, like the impending violent slaughter of a close friend, I tend to forget social niceties.'

I looked back and forth between Wilkins on the dance floor and this fine specimen of military manhood in front of me.

'You are a friend of Sir Philip's?'

'I believed I already mentioned that, yes.'

My eyes, which had been fixed on his face before, wandered down to take in the rest of him. He didn't look like the average man, exactly. For starters, he wasn't wearing a uniform – very strange for military men, who generally used their shiny red coats to attract silly girls like flies. Instead, he was wearing a dark blue tailcoat and beneath it a waistcoat decorated with...

Wait a minute!

'Your waistcoat has tigers on it,' I said. '*Golden tigers.*'

'Ah, yes!' His smile widened, as if I could not have hit upon a subject that suited him more. 'Do you like it?'

'Um... it's nice. The tigers look very... shiny.'

He thrust out his chest. 'Fabulous, aren't they? I've had a French dressmaker stitch one on for every tiger I killed on safari.'

My eyes snapped up to his face again, narrowed. 'Really?'

'No, not really. It's just some story I tell people when I first meet them, to see whether they fall for it.'

'And do they?'

'Generally, no.' He sighed. 'I have no idea why. After all, I am the image of a fierce tiger hunter.'

'Excuse me, Sir, but...'

'Yes?'

'Are you drunk?'

'Not yet. But I hope will change as the evening progresses.' Relaxing his posture, he rubbed his hands together. 'Now, back to business. We were talking about your plans to assassinate my friend.'

I took a step back. Either this man was drunk in spite of denial or, the more worrying possibility, he was absolutely sober. In which case he was probably stark raving mad.

'I don't have any plans to assassinate your friend!'

'Don't you? So, that look that said you'd like to ram a knife into his back, you give that to everybody?'

I promptly gave it to him, which seemed to amuse him to no end. He lifted his hand to his face to hide a chuckle.

'I see. May I have the honour of learning your name, Miss, so I can denounce you at Scotland Yard when the deed is done?'

'I,' I said, with as much disdain as I could pack into my voice, 'am Miss Lillian Linton.' Unfortunately, there wasn't as much disdain in my voice as I'd hoped, which probably came from the fact that some part of me was rather amused by the stranger and his waist full of tigers. 'And I assure you, I have no intention of murdering Sir Philip. Why would I? He is courting my sister.'

'Well, that alone would be a good reason,' Captain Carter said cheerfully.

My mouth dropped open.

'I- I thought he was your friend!'

'He is. He's also the biggest nincompoop between here and Yorkshire. I pity the lady who links her life with his. But fortunately, that's not going to happen any time soon.'

At that, my face suddenly became deadly serious again. For a moment, this strange man had distracted me, but now it all came rushing back – Ella, Wilkins, the approaching proposal.

'Did I say something wrong?' Captain Carter enquired, obviously noticing my dark mood.

'Not as such,' I mumbled. 'It's just that I think you're wrong.'

'Wrong? Wrong in what way?'

'In supposing that your friend would not marry for a long time.'

'Why? Has he finally found a victim?'

I scowled at him. His amused, cavalier attitude made my blood boil. 'Of course! Didn't I just say he was courting my sister? He wants to marry her!'

'You said he was courting her, all right,' he agreed. 'But the one doesn't necessarily imply the other. Not with him, anyway.'

I blinked, taken aback, the anger going out of me. 'What the heck is that supposed to mean?'

'That's supposed to mean that if old Flip had married every woman he'd ever courted, he'd have a harem to rival that of King Tamba of Benares.'

'Who?'

'King Tamba of Benares. He was a 6th century king in India, and, according to some of the Hindu legends, he had a city of sixteen thousand women available to fulfil his every–'

Hastily, I interrupted him before he could go into any more detail. 'I don't care about any King Tamba! Are you seriously suggesting that Sir Philip Wilkins does not intend to marry my sister, after courting her for several weeks?'

'Certainly.'

'But he has come to her house practically every day!'

'A man has to spend his time in some way, doesn't he?'

'He sent her flowers! Masses of flowers!'

'He is a passionate botanist. Maybe you have noticed he likes flowers in general?'

'*Likes* is not the word I would have chosen, Captain Carter.'

His lips twitched. Apparently, he really did know Sir Philip. At least well enough to know his interests.

'Quite. Well, it didn't take him long to discover that men don't tend to share his passion. He tried presenting a few men with flowers, and they either stared at him coldly or threw him out of the house. Women, on the other hand, are always delighted when he gives them flowers. Poor chap, I haven't brought myself to disillusion him about the reason. Better let him think that England is full of botanically-interested ladies.'

I shook my head. This just couldn't be. After all the worry, all the scheming, hope, despair... no. It just couldn't be!

'But he is in love with her!' I blurted out. What was I doing? One never was supposed to be this blunt with a new acquaintance – not even I. But I couldn't seem to stop myself. 'He told me as much! He told me he loved her.'

'Oh, he probably does.' Captain Carter waved his hand airily, as if this were of no great concern. 'He is rather fond of being in love, particularly if the lady in question has bright blue eyes. But after a week or two, he'll meet a new lady, and fall in love again, just as he'll find a new flower to interest him.'

My mouth popped open.

'That's why we – his old university friends, I mean – call him Sir Flip,' Captain Carter added with a nostalgic smile. 'We came up with the nickname when we were at Oxford together, and he used to turn his eyes on a different lady every five days or so. It was rather amusing to watch, though it could get a little confusing at times.'

'That... that is horrible!'

'No,' the Captain disagreed, cheerfully. 'It would be, if he were as stunningly handsome as my good self. But being such a colossal guffin, it's not really something to worry about. I mean, can you see any lady he falls in love with actually returning the favour? Be honest.'

I threw a dubious look at Sir Philip, and cleared my throat. 'It... it still isn't right!'

'Well, it's not as if he does it on purpose, Miss Linton. I assure you, he's perfectly convinced each time that he's found the woman of his dreams.' He shrugged. 'And then he wakes up. As I said, since he's not exactly a Don Juan, it's not really something to worry about.'

Again, I didn't know what to say. I stared aimlessly at the tigers on the waistcoat and thought: *For nothing. All my worry has been for nothing.*

Or had it? This was all so insane. It couldn't really be true, could it?

'Unless...' Captain Carter's voice was hesitant now, and not amused anymore. 'Unless your sister really *does* have true affection for my friend. In that case, Miss Linton, I'm afraid that your sister will have to prepare herself...'

'No!' Before I knew what had happened, my head had started to shake itself. 'No. No, no, no, no, and no again. She doesn't. Never has, never will. Not in this life or the next.'

He breathed out a sigh of relief. 'Thank the Lord. I'd hate for the old fruitcake to make the front page of the times for breach of promise.'

'Um... forgive me, but you don't speak very highly of your friend.'

'A friend's prerogative.' He winked at me, and I wanted to smile in return. Immediately, I clamped down on the feeling. This was no time for smiles!

'But you can't be serious,' I repeated my earlier doubts. 'You can't really mean that he doesn't mean to marry her.'

413

'He might, at the moment. But I assure you, the fancy will leave him soon enough.'

I should have been relieved. I should have been ecstatic. But to be honest, some part of me was actually insulted and disbelieving, not able to take it that anybody would so callously throw aside my little sister, even if being thrown aside was exactly what she wanted.

'No,' I insisted. 'No gentleman in his right mind could do such a thing.'

'Well, as to whether old Flip is in his right mind or not, that's a subject for debate,' he mused. 'But regardless, I tell you, he will not marry your sister. Didn't you see him lose interest in the last girl he bombarded with flowers, before he decided to target her?'

My mind flashed back a few weeks. Oh dear Lord! Could it be...?

'Well... yes.'

'So he was interested in another girl shortly before?'

'Um... two, in fact.'

'Even better. Who was the unfortunate pair?'

'My other two sisters.'

'Your family's house must be full to the attic with tulips.'

'It is.'

'Are they beautiful?'

'The tulips?'

'No! Your other two sisters, Miss Linton.'

'Oh.' I pondered this for a moment, conjuring up an image of Anne's and Maria's faces. Finally, I reluctantly admitted: 'I suppose so.'

'With long blonde hair?'

'Yes.'

'And shining blue eyes?' He fluttered his eyelashes in a way a man should not be able to. I just barely managed to stifle a laugh.

'Um... yes. Both of them.'

'No wonder poor old Flip was carried away. How long did it take for him to forget they existed?'

'Err... I think about a week.'

'You see?'

He rubbed his hands again, as if everything were resolved.

I did indeed begin to see. A part of me did, at least. That part wanted to burst out laughing and hug this strange stranger who had so simply dispelled the doom that had been hovering over my sister and me for weeks. But another part of me still couldn't believe. Carefully, I sniffed the air. There was no smell of alcohol. Could it be that Captain Carter really was not drunk? That he was telling the truth?

I suddenly remembered Patsy telling me how Wilkins had been pursuing her, even before Anne and Maria. Patsy had blonde hair, even though it was tied in a knot, and her eyes were definitely bright – bright as a blowlamp about to explode.

Could it be true? Maybe...

414

But of what use was it to me? I realized with a sinking feeling that, even if Sir Philip didn't mean anything by his attentions, Ella was still very much in danger of losing her honour.

For a moment, my eyes strayed to Edmund, who was glaring at the dancing couple with an intensity that could probably have incinerated the floor, had it been made of wood.

When my eyes went back to Captain Carter, I saw him studying me critically. 'You still don't believe me,' he accused me.

'No, no, it's not that... I...' My voice trailed off. How on earth was I supposed to explain things to him? To a complete stranger? Should I even try? Was it right for me to disclose secrets I wasn't even supposed to know myself?

'What?' he asked, and the gentleness in his voice surprised me. 'Miss Linton, I have no wish to cause pain to you or your sister. If there is some problem...'

'My sister,' I said, hurriedly, before I could think better of it. 'She doesn't want to marry Sir Philip.'

'Well, where's the problem in that?' He raised an eyebrow. 'Why doesn't she just send him packing?'

'Because,' I said, feeling angry that I had to explain my sister's motives to this stranger, 'she feels it would be her duty to accept him, since our aunt wishes it.'

He blinked, speechless for the moment. But the moment didn't last very long.

'That's silly!'

'No, it isn't!' I snapped, though privately I couldn't agree more.

'Oh? So you would do the same?' he asked, a mischievous grin tugging at the corner of his mouth – a place where there often seemed to be one.

I flushed.

'Well... not exactly.'

'I didn't think so.' The grin grew some more. 'But to be honest, I still don't see the problem. I told you, Flip won't propose to your sister. In a week or two, he'll spot another beautiful fair head, and all will be joy and jubilation.'

Looking around to see if anybody was listening, I took a step closer.

'I... I'm afraid in a week it might be too late.'

'Too late?' The grin on his face didn't waver. 'What do you mean, too late?'

'I mean that my sister might do something rash.'

'Something more rash than agreeing to marry a man whom she can't stand?'

'Yes!'

'Oh, I see. That's rash, indeed.'

He didn't sound nearly serious enough for my liking. I glared at him, and he grinned back, not perturbed in the least.

'You can't persuade her to... you know, maybe not be rash?' he enquired.

'No!'

'But as I told you, it's just a matter of time. Trust me, when Flip comes across the next lovely lady with big blue eyes, he'll forget all about your sister.'

And what good will that do, if Ella runs away with Edmund tomorrow night? Blast, blast, blast!

415

'If it takes a week for him to find one,' I said, 'that will be too late.'

'Hmm.' Thoughtfully, he stroked his jaunty little triangle of beard. 'Well, that leaves only one option, then. We'll just have to pick one out for him – immediately.'

I stared at him as if he'd spoken Chinese.

'What do you mean, "pick one out"?' I demanded.

'Well,' he said with a renewed grin and a sweeping gesture that took in the whole ballroom with all the dancing, chatting guests, 'There are a lot of ladies available here – a great many of them with blue eyes, I'd wager. We can pick one and shove her into his way. With luck, he'll fall in love with her on the spot and leave your sister alone. If it doesn't work, we can always try with another.'

It took me a few seconds to think of something to say.

'Captain... are you quite sure you're not intoxicated?'

'Quite. If I were drunk, I would be seeing two of you, but there is only one.' He bowed, just as snappy as before. 'And what a lovely one it is.'

Heat rushed up into my cheeks. 'You're trying to make me compliments when a few minutes ago you accused me of wanting to murder someone?'

He winked. 'Who knows, that might have been a compliment, too. For all you know, I'm the most abominable villain and murder people in their beds every night.'

'I wouldn't be surprised,' I said drily. And he actually had the gall to look amused!

'You have to be drunk!' I pronounced. 'Nobody could talk this much nonsense without at least *some* alcohol in them.'

He gave a sad little sigh. 'I always talk like this. My aunt tried to teach me manners, but it never worked. It's why I went into the army. In the army, you don't have to say anything, just do what you're told, so nobody has noticed what a colossal scoundrel I am, yet. I have hopes of keeping it up for another two or three years before I'm found out.'

'Will you stop gibbering and listen?'

'Yes, Miss. Certainly, Miss.'

'Look here, you can't be right. You simply can't be. It's not possible that anybody could forget my sister as easily as you say! Nobody could be that emptyheaded.'

'You've never looked into one of Flip's ears, Miss Linton. I swear, you can see the light from the other side.'

'You promised to keep your mouth shut!'

'Oh. Yes, indeed, I did. Sorry. I tried my best.'

'All you told me,' I said, shaking my head, 'is well and good, but it doesn't change the facts. Even if he hasn't wanted to marry any of the other girls before, he does want to marry Ella. He told my aunt so.'

Captain Carter's eyebrows went up so high they almost vanished into his curly brown locks.

'Really? What exactly did he say?'

'Something about needing his own little sunshine in his home...'

I broke off, because he had started laughing. He was almost bent double, and people were starting to stare.

'Captain Carter!' I hissed.

'I- I'm sorry,' he chortled. 'It's just... his own little sunshine... that's so... you know...' Slowly, he brought himself under control again – but there was still a broad grin on his face. 'He told me about that, too, you know. That he wanted sunshine in his home.'

'You see? I told you he wants t–'

'He'll build the place on the south side of his manor house, I think. Where the sunshine is most abundant. Though he might have problems, since the ground drops off rather suddenly there.'

I blinked. 'W-what?'

'He's planning to build a winter garden,' Captain Carter told me gently. 'He's always been heartbroken that all his lovely flowers die during the winter, and, well, he's just hit on this idea...'

'A... winter... garden...?'

'Yes. You know, one of those places with big windows where plants can grow all year round? They are very much the fashion at the moment. People are building them as house-extensions all over London, and even beginning to decorate them with tables and chairs, and have their tea parties there, I've been told. Though, personally, I prefer to take my tea beside a crackling fire in the har–'

'Shut up!'

'Yes, Miss. Of course, Miss.'

'I'm going to kill him.' Slowly, I turned towards Sir Philip, who was still whirling across the dance floor, my sister in his arms, a ridiculous grin on his ridiculous face. 'I'm going to drag him into a dark alley and strangle him to death!'

'I thought I had convinced you not to do that.'

'I've changed my mind. I'm not even going to bother with an alley! I'm going to murder him, right here, right now.'

Captain Carter cleared his throat. 'I'm not sure that is such a good idea.'

I whirled on him, for the moment forgetting about Sir blasted Phillip. 'Have you any idea what heartache this man put my sister through? What kind of tragedy he almost caused?'

'Yes, but I'm sure he didn't mean any of it.'

'And that's supposed to make it better?'

'No. It just means that maybe he doesn't deserve to be strangled.'

'We'll see about that!'

I turned again and started towards the dance floor, but immediately my way was blocked by a wall of black velvet with glittering gold tigers on it. I hadn't noticed before how tall and broad-shouldered Captain Carter was. Now I did.

'Get out of my way,' I growled.

'Miss Linton,' he said softly. 'Has it occurred to you that if you kill somebody in the middle of a crowded ballroom, you might be thrown into prison?'

'I don't care!'

He studied my face. 'Yes, you probably don't, at the moment. But what about your sister? I'm sure she would.'

I hesitated. He was right. Besides... I had never actually killed anybody before. I might not get it right the first time.

'May I suggest an alternative solution?' he said.

'You don't mean that silly plan of yours to just select a random blonde and throw her in his way?'

'It's not silly.'

'It is!'

'It's not. And I'll just have to prove it to you – if only to keep you out of prison.'

Grabbing my hand, he started pulling me towards one of the raised niches that overlooked the ballroom, on the opposite side of the room from the large windows.

'What are you doing?' I exclaimed, as he pulled me through a throng of noble ladies, who gazed after us with interest. It was not common for a man to hold a lady's hand at a ball, still less to pull her through the crowd.

'Helping you,' was his cheerful answer. 'We need to take up a position from where we can inspect our possible recruits. Then we can discuss candidates and pick the unlucky lady whose fate it will be to save your sister's life, love and honour.'

Before I could free myself, he had pulled me up the steps into the raised niche he had been heading towards. We could see over the heads of the guests and had a good view of the entire ballroom.

'Now, do you see any likely blue-eyed lady?' he prompted, sweeping his arm across the crowd.

Was he honestly asking me to look for someone I thought could replace my sister?

'No,' I growled, crossing my arms in front of my chest. I wasn't going to play this ridiculous game!

Even though it might be fun? asked a little voice in the back of my head. I ignored it.

'Not one, Miss Linton?'

'Well...' His smile was so coaxing, so charming... Reluctantly I pointed to one random lady. 'There's one over there.'

'No,' he decided. 'She has brown hair. Didn't I tell you Flip likes to fall in love with blondes? Don't ask me why he does it, I find brunettes much more interesting.' He winked at me! He actually had the nerve to wink at me! 'But for Flip, the ladies have to be blonde.'

'Any other requirements?' I asked, as sourly as possible. But I was hard-pressed to keep a grin off my face. 'Should she have a tiny waist? Or two noses, perhaps?'

'Well, one that isn't over eighty would probably have a greater chance of engaging his affections.'

Against my will, my lips twitched.

'What about her?' He pointed to another young lady.

'She has a face like a horse.'

'So does Flip. They should suit each other admirably.'

'In case you hadn't noticed, Captain Carter, ugly men are no less fond of pretty girls than others.'

'True,' he sighed. 'What a shallow sex we are. Now... what about her?'

'She looks nice enough, there is only one problem.'

'Which is?'

'The ring on her finger. She's married.'

Captain Carter waved a hand, dismissively. 'We don't need to tell Flip that. He's short-sighted, he probably wouldn't notice.'

'Captain!'

'Besides, we don't need her for long. We would only borrow her for one night. I'm sure she wouldn't mind.'

I hadn't thought there existed a man in England who could shock me. I had been wrong.

'Her husband might,' I pointed out, drily.

The Captain nodded earnestly. 'I bow to your superior knowledge of men, Miss Linton. So... on to the next one.'

'What about her?' I said, feeling a silly grin appear on my face. 'The one with the perky nose and big hoop skirt?'

'I don't think so. She looks rather like a fat woodpecker.'

'Hmm... maybe. And the one on her left?'

'She would be perfect,' Captain Carter admitted. 'Only, Flip already fell in love with her two months ago, and I'm not quite sure he has forgotten yet.'

'You talk about falling in love as other people would about a visit to the hair-dresser!'

'Not quite. Flip has his hair cut about once every fortnight, but he usually manages to fall in and out of love once a week.'

'Um... then maybe the most intelligent approach would be to first exclude all the ladies he has already fallen in love with once?'

'You're quite right!' His face lit up. 'How clever of you, I would never have thought of that. Well, let me think... there's Miss Alden, Miss Cokes, Miss Howard, Lady Darwin, Lady Caroline...'

'*Lady Caroline*? She's at least seventy years old!'

'Yes, he fell in love with the back of her head and changed his mind when she turned around.'

I squinted at him suspiciously.

'Are you making half of this up?'

'What do you think of me, Miss Linton,' he said with grave propriety. 'That I would joke when such serious matters are at stake?'

'Yes.'

'Marvellous. You already know me so well.'

Whipping out my fan, I gave him a sharp jab into the ribs. He flinched in a very gratifying way.

'Be serious, Captain! My sister's welfare is at stake here!'

Rubbing his ribs, he gave me a smile. His smile was quite charming, particularly with that perky little spot of beard at the bottom of his strong face, which made him look like a trickster out of some old northern legend.

'For you, I shall do my best to be serious, Miss Linton. Though I can't promise anything.'

'Very well.' Content, I turned to the crowd again and pointed with my fan. 'What about her?'

~~**~*~*

'Flip! There you are, my dear fellow!'

At the sound of Captain Carter's voice, Sir Philip turned around. 'Carter!' he exclaimed. 'I've been looking for you, to...'

His voice trailed off, as he saw who was standing beside Captain Carter.

The Captain nodded to the rather confused-looking blonde lady who was standing beside him. 'Philip, may I introduce you to Lady Katharine Rowntree? Lady Katharine? This is the man I said you simply had to meet, Sir Philip Wilkins.'

'But you said you wanted to show me a painting from Lady Metcalf's collec-' the young lady began.

'Anyway,' Captain Carter said hurriedly, and loudly. 'Now we're all introduced. Isn't that wonderful?'

'Wonderful is hardly the word for it,' Sir Philip breathed. He had an expression on his face I had seen only once before – when he had first beheld Ella at Lady Metcalf's last ball. 'Perfect would be more appropriate. Lady Katherine, would you do me the honour of the next dance?'

'Oh... why, certainly, Sir Philip,' she said, blinking in astonishment. 'But... don't you already have a partner? Your companion...' her eyes wandered to the place where Ella was standing. Ella opened her mouth reflexively.

I was beside her in a flash, grasping her arm in iron grip.

'She doesn't mind at all. I think she's a bit tired.'

'Oh. Well, if that's the case...'

Sir Philip's eyes hadn't left Lady Katherine. He extended his arm, and she took it.

Ella watched as the two of them departed.

'W-what was that?' she asked.

'Can't you tell? A miracle, of course.' Across the ballroom I could see Edmund. He was staring gloomily out of the window again. 'And,' I added, 'We might just have time for another, tonight. Look over there.'

~~**~*~*

'Ella.' Edmund's voice was hoarse. I could tell, because I was hiding behind a potted plant nearby. I was curious, all right? I had worried myself to death over this affair of Ella's. The least I wanted in exchange was to see the happy end!

The young piano tuner's son looked around the ballroom. 'I don't see Sir Philip anywhere.'

Ella took a step forward. Her eyes were glued to the young man opposite her. 'No.'

'So is it done, then?' he asked bitterly. 'Are you his now? He has proposed?'

Another step forward.

'No.'

Edmund's eyes flew open. Then his jaw muscles twitched. 'But he will.'

Another step. They were standing in front of each other now. I thanked God that they were in a quiet corner of the room, with nobody paying attention to them. The way they were looking at each other made things all too clear for anyone who cared to look.

'No,' Ella whispered.

'What do you mean, no?' His voice was just a whisper, too – desperation, pain, with a tinge of hope.

'It appears Sir Philip has lost interest in me. I... I cannot rightly understand it, but he was introduced to another young lady, and from one moment to the next seemed to forget I exist.'

The spark of hope in Edmund exploded into a fiery blaze. I could see it shining in his eyes.

'He is a fool,' he said in a quiet voice.

It was he who took the next step forward. They were standing almost close enough to kiss now.

But they wouldn't, here in the ballroom, would they?

Would they?

To keep myself from screaming a warning to the two lovelorn fools, I bit down on the sleeve of my dress.

'So, Miss Linton, it appears that you are still free.' Edmund's voice was casual, but his eyes weren't leaving hers for a moment.

'It appears so, Mr Conway.' Her eyes seemed fixed on his by the same unbreakable force.

'And will remain so? Or will Sir Philip appear at your door tomorrow morning, begging forgiveness?'

'Do not ask me how... but I know in my heart that he is gone. He will trouble me no more.'

Edmund took a deep breath.

'And don't you regret his leaving? Haven't all the flowers that he sent you conquered your heart?'

'If he were to send me a million red roses it would not gain him my love.'

I nodded approvingly. My sister might have very strange ideas about love, life and honour, but at least she wasn't mercenary. Never that.

'And his noble titles, his lands?' Edmund enquired. 'Are you not sorry to lose such grand prospects?'

'Were he the King of England and offered me all the riches of the Empire, I would not be swayed.'

Quite right! Oh, that's female rectitude for you!

421

'So you are truly still free,' Edmund breathed.

'I am,' she said, then, lowering her voice so only he – and I, behind the nearby potted plant – could hear: 'But my heart is not. It was given to another long ago.'

Love, adoration, yearning, relief: A symphony of emotions played on Edmund's face – or maybe it was a sonata, considering he was a piano tuner's son.

'Then,' he said, his voice trembling in vibrato, full of feeling, 'since you are still free, may I request the honour of your hand for the next dance, Miss Linton?'

She dipped her head in the chastest curtsy I had ever seen. 'You may, Mr Conway. I shall await you on the dance floor.'

And with that, she glided away.

May I say that, up to this moment, I had never looked forward to a dance as I did to this one? Which says something about my attitude to dancing, considering I wasn't even going to be involved in the actual exercise.

When, finally, one song ended and the musicians struck up the tune of the next dance, I stuck a bit more of my dress into my mouth, just to be sure I wouldn't make any noise and alert them to my secret hiding place.

There he was! Edmund was approaching Ella while in the background, the notes of a slow waltz sounded. The most romantic of all couple dances – I couldn't have planned it better myself.

He stopped in front of her and bowed.

'Miss Ella?'

She curtsied.

'Mr Conway.'

He extended his arm. She took it, her face composed, but her eyes shining with an inner light. I didn't fail to notice that instead of placing her hand against his so his fingers touched the back of her hand, as was custom for reasons of propriety, she slid her hand into his so that his fingers could surround all of her little hand and touch her palm. When her hand was in his, I could see a small shiver going through her body. It was as if she had finally come home.

He led her onto the dance floor to a place between the other couples. Most of them stood there, awkward, fidgeting, not knowing where to look. Edmund and Ella knew exactly where to look, and it wasn't at their feet. They stared at each other's faces as if beholding an angel from heaven. I had slight worries that they might trip during the first turn, considering how they couldn't take their eyes off each other – but somehow, they managed not to.

As the music began in earnest, they seemed to sink into each other's arms. Their movements were perfectly synchronized, fluid, and graceful. I stared in awe. This I had not expected. All right, Ella was not as bad a dancer as I – she was far too timid to step on any gentleman's feet. But I doubted the piano tuner's son had had much experience with waltzing, and there they were, waltzing away as if they wanted to win a dancing competition.

It couldn't just be their infatuation, could it?

Suddenly, I remembered that when dancing with Mr Ambrose, I hadn't stepped on his feet either, though I had been sorely tempted to. Why did I remember this now? I couldn't imagine that I was...

422

'They make quite a couple, don't they?'

I jumped about a mile high. Captain Carter had appeared next to me out of nowhere. It was an astonishing feat for a man wearing a waistcoat with glinting golden tigers on it that were visible from a mile away.

'Now I see what you meant when you said there might be complications if your sister were faced with marriage to Flip,' he said, smirking. The dance had just ended, but Edmund and Ella hadn't moved away from each other. They were still standing there, each locked in the other's gaze. 'Do you think if we go over there, you could introduce me to the complications? He looks like a nice young man.'

'Certainly not,' I hissed, grabbing him by the arm, as he was already starting forward. 'It's supposed to be secret! Nobody must know about them.'

He looked back at me, a quizzical expression on his face. 'They are conducting a secret liaison in the middle of a ballroom full of people?'

'Well, um... yes.'

'Not the brightest pair of candles in the shop, are they?'

'Oh, shut up! That's my sister you're talking about!'

He bowed his head. 'Yes, Miss Linton. As you wish, Miss Linton.'

'And... thank you.' I looked down, but not quickly enough to miss how he raised one of his eyebrows.

'Thank me? For what?'

'For helping Ella.'

'You mean for helping you.'

I moaned. 'Yes, if you must put it like that.'

'I must,' he said, nodding gravely. 'To help a lady get rid of a prospective husband – now that is no particularly honourable deed. But to help a lady save her sister's honour and happiness? Now *that's* something entirely different. Something I might confidently brag of when I next drink with my comrades.'

My eyes shot up to his. 'Don't you dare! If you breathe a word of any of this...'

'...You will hamstring me and subject me to the most terrible tortures you can devise,' he finished my sentence cheerfully. 'Don't worry. I know when to keep my mouth shut. It's only when it's already open that the wrong things come popping out of it.'

I eyed him, the doubt obvious on my face.

'Promise?'

He put a hand on his heart. 'I swear on the honour of my regiment,' he said. 'Except for me, its members actually have some.'

I couldn't help it. I laughed.

'That's better.' He smiled back at me. 'This is an hour for joy and celebration, Miss Linton.'

And he was right – it was. Ella was saved, or to be more precise, she had never been in danger. Later, I might rampage a little about the fact that all my worry and scheming had been for nothing. But for now, simple joy filled every part of me, and I was happy and secure in the knowledge that Ella would stay happy, her honour intact and her future once more in her own hands.

Captain Carter stepped closer and opened his mouth, as if he wanted to say something – but just at that moment, a man in the uniform of a colonel waved him over. 'Carter! Come over here, I've got to tell you something. I just got a memorandum about the Sinai situation.'

The Captain gave me an apologetic smile. 'I fear I have to depart, Miss Linton. Work calls me even in my leisure hours.'

'That's all right,' I assured him. 'You've already given me enough of your time. Thanks again for your help.'

'It was my pleasure.' He winked at me. 'If ever you should feel the inclination to go searching for a romantic interest again, I hope you'll come to me.'

Before his words had fully registered, he was already gone.

~~**~*~*

'There you are, Lilly!' My aunt and Maria appeared next to me, waking me from my stupor. 'Where have you been?'

'I... um...'

Doing my best to prevent the marriage that is your heart's desire.

'I... I've been dancing,' I fibbed. 'Yes, that's what I've been doing. Dancing all the time.'

'Really?' Her eyes narrowed suspiciously. 'I didn't see you on the dance floor. With whom were you dancing?'

'Um...' Quickly, I looked around for a suitable candidate. My eyes fell on a tigered waistcoat. 'That gentleman, over there.'

'Where? Who do you...?' My aunt trailed off as she beheld the muscular figure with his long mahogany locks.

'You have been dancing with *him*?' Maria said. 'You are joking, aren't you?'

'No,' I said, desperately hoping they would believe me.

They didn't.

'Well, if that's so,' Maria said, 'you won't have anything against introducing us to your friend, surely.'

'What a brilliant idea, my dear,' my aunt exclaimed. 'Lilly, go on, introduce us.'

By now, Captain Carter seemed to have finished his talk with his military friend. I had no other choice, though I would rather not have approached him, particularly after what he said to me last.

I approached, my aunt and sister behind me like a pack of hounds behind the poor little fox.

'Captain?'

He turned, and seemed surprised to find it was me.

'Yes, Miss Linton?'

'Captain Carter, may I introduce you to my aunt, Mrs Brank, and my sister, Miss Maria Linton,' I said, pointing them out in turn as they curtsied. 'Aunt, Maria, may I present Captain William Carter of the British Army.'

'Very pleased to meet you, I'm sure,' said my aunt with another curtsy.

'So am I.' Did Maria's voice actually sound breathy?

'No, it is I who am delighted to make your acquaintance,' the Captain said, bowing with the same snappy precision he had shown before. 'What can I do for you?'

'I was just telling them how we had *danced together for three dances in a row*,' I said, hoping he would understand.

He blinked, once.

'Indeed, and what marvellous dances they were,' he said. Thank God, he was quick on the uptake. 'I can hardly find the words to express my admiration of your charming niece's skill on the dance floor.'

I threw him a thankful smile. My aunt smiled, too. Maria didn't.

'That's wonderful to hear,' my aunt trilled. Again, she let her eyes roam over the Captain. 'That is an interesting waistcoat you're wearing, Captain. Don't most officers prefer to wear uniforms?'

'Most do,' he said, nodding gravely. 'But I had this specially made. I commissioned a French dressmaker to embroider it with one tiger for every one I killed while on safari.'

'Is that so?' My aunt's eyes widened in awe, and so did Maria's. 'You actually killed so many of these fearful beasts? Captain, you must be a man of tremendous courage!'

I ducked behind the nearest potted plant. If anybody noticed the snort of laughter that issued from behind it soon afterwards, they didn't connect it with me.

It wasn't long before I emerged again, my face perfectly straight. Captain Carter was regaling the wide-eyed Maria with tales of his tiger hunts. My aunt was still present, too, but she wasn't really listening. I recognized the look in her eyes immediately – a look somewhere between that of a shark and of an accountant of the Bank of England. She was sizing him up as a potential suitor, a task that consumed all her attention for the moment.

'...and then,' he was saying, 'the tiger sprang at me, and I grabbed for my rifle.'

'And did you shoot it?' Maria demanded, breathless.

'No. The rifle was jammed.'

'No!'

'Yes. Just in time, I managed to turn it around and let it come down with the blunt end on the tiger's head. I hit it with such force that the beast was knocked clean unconscious.'

Maria clapped her hand in front of her mouth.

Behind her back, I imitated her gesture, and Captain Carter's lip twitched.

He was by no means the first gentleman I had heard telling fake tales of bravery and adventure. But he was the first one who had let me in on the game. And somehow, because of that, I didn't mind. I exchanged a smile with him.

'Ah,' he said, smiling back and nodding. 'There you are, Miss Linton.'

'Were you so desperate for my company?' I asked, arching an eyebrow.

'Indeed I was. Did I not tell you before how much I enjoyed our dancing? I fear those three dances you have shared with me so far have only left me starving and craving for more. In fact, I can hardly remember them anymore. May I beg you to favour me with another?'

He extended his arm to me, his eyes sparkling with evil mirth.

The smile drained from my face.

'If you try very hard,' I said, 'I'm sure you'll remember the three dances we danced together perfectly.'

'Indeed, no,' he said, sighing regretfully. 'It already seems to me, somehow, as if they never happened. Which would be such a pity, wouldn't it?'

He extended his arm a little further.

'Well, Miss Linton?'

I took his arm, forcing a smile on my face. On our way to the dance floor, as the first notes floated through the air, I leant towards him and said: 'I'm going to murder you, Captain.'

He smiled.

'Will you wait till after the dance?'

~~**~*~*

It wasn't terrible.

I didn't step on his feet, he didn't step on mine. He was a considerate dancer, and didn't try to steer me across the ballroom like most other gentleman. Neither was he like Mr Ambrose, with every movement perfect and sleek. Instead, he was flamboyant, every note of the music expressing itself in the way he moved, he smiled, he held me.

Maybe he held me a little bit closer than other gentleman usually did.

When he let me go, a crowd of his military friends came and started talking about this place called Sinai again.

He bowed to me, an apologetic look on his face.

'I'm afraid I will have to leave you, Miss Linton. I hope that I will be able to have the pleasure of dancing again with you soon. Four times it has been now, and yet it seems only one.'

I couldn't suppress a tiny smile. It hadn't really been that bad...

'Well, maybe,' I murmured, 'If you promise to behave yourself, I'll dance with you again someday.'

I was rewarded with a cheeky smile. 'I shall look forward to it.'

'I said *maybe*!' I called after him as he strode off with his friends. But he didn't turn around again. He just walked away, a spring in his step.

Shaking my head, I turned away. How likely was it that we would ever meet or dance again? After all, now that his friend had dropped Ella like an Irish peasant would a hot potato, Sir Philip would likely cut off all acquaintance with us. It would simply be too awkward to spend time in his company. Surely, most of his friends would follow his example and shun us. I wasn't likely to see Captain Carter again. Well, good riddance. The less men there were in my life, the better.

Even if they do happen to be quite nice, in a crazy way.

I turned once more to watch Ella. It was clear that she didn't feel the same as I. She lay in Edmund's arms as though there was no place on earth she would rather be. The smile on her face could only be described as radiant. It was shining brighter than any of the chandeliers that hung from the ceiling and illuminated the ballroom.

Sighing contentedly, I retreated to a quiet corner of the ballroom, from where I could watch them quietly. It was joy to see Ella's joy, a balm for my soul that had been tortured for her sake over the last few weeks. How wonderful and simple the world suddenly seemed. All right, my working life still left a lot to be desired, an unlocked office door for instance, but as regards affairs at home, things were looking up, and I was feeling pretty chuffed as a result.

Everything had worked out to perfection. Ella was happy, I was happy, and even Edmund was, though this wasn't exactly on my list of priorities. Wonders had been worked within a few hours. All the perceived dangers and difficulties I had foreseen for the near future had dissolved into nothing tonight. I was sure that tonight, nothing could go wrong anymore. Absolutely nothing.

And then I heard *his* voice behind me.

A voice that sounded very familiar, although I had heard it only twice before... A cultured, voice. A voice of knowledge, power, and maybe... darker things.

'Ah, Miss Linton. I was wondering if you would be of the party when I saw Sir Phillip's name on the guest list. How marvellous...'

And I remembered Lady Metcalf telling us as we arrived: *Important people from all over England have come, gentry, military, knights of the Order of the Garter... even one of the Peers of the Realm has been kind enough to accept my invitation.*

Slowly, I turned, and was met by the penetrating, steel-blue gaze of Lord Daniel Eugene Dalgliesh.

'I have been wanting to meet you again,' he said, and smiled. 'How fortunate that I always seem to get what I want.'

BEHIND THE MASK

No, I told myself, *You cannot run away. You cannot run from him, or he will know that you know. And then you will be dead.*

But... was this really true? I could hardly believe that this suave nobleman, member of the House of Lords and uncrowned king of Britain's largest imperial enterprise, was supposed to be involved in dealings so far beyond the law that they had lapped it and kicked it in the derrière while it was concentrating on catching up. The man owned his own subcontinent, for heaven's sake!

Yes, but the question is: how did he get it? If it's by similar methods as Caesar or Napoleon... Well, they hadn't been squeamish, either.

'Lord Dalgliesh. How nice to see you again.' I forced my legs to stay where they were and to bend into a curtsy.

Remember the alley in the East End! Remember the attackers! It was this man who sent them.

But it was hard to remember. Lord Dalgliesh, in his exquisite black tailcoat and blue satin waistcoat, looked as if he had never so much as heard of a place like the East End, let alone paid a visit to some of its occupants.

He wouldn't have to. He could pay somebody else to pay somebody else to pay somebody else to pay somebody to do it.

'Indeed it is, Miss Linton.' Taking my hand, he lifted it to his lips and pressed a gentle kiss on the back of it. My reaction now was very different from when Sir Philip had done the same. A shiver went down my back, and my cheeks warmed. Thank the Lord my cheeks weren't fashionably pale. With luck, it wouldn't show.

Think of the alley! I told myself again. *Think of the blood!*

I tried. I honestly tried. But with images of the alley also came images of what had come after: the ride back, the office, Mr Ambrose, the kiss...

Had I thought my cheeks warm before? It was nothing to the explosion they suffered now. Yet if Lord Dalgliesh saw it, he probably couldn't deduce the reason.

Hopefully. Some part of me, though, was feeling as though it was written all over my face.

'Do you know, Miss Linton, why I have been desirous of renewing our acquaintance?' he enquired.

I swallowed, hoping the reason didn't have anything to do with knives, guns, or locked cells.

'N-no.'

Blast! Why was it that I couldn't keep my voice steady just when I needed to?

'I have been making enquiries into any connection of yours with a certain Rikkard Ambrose, with whom you seemed extraordinarily well acquainted at the last ball, where I had the pleasure of seeing you.'

What?

'And lo and behold, I have not found a single shred of evidence to connect the two of you.'

Oh. Good.

'Not a family connection, not a bank loan your family is overdue to pay back, not a previous social acquaintance, not even a romantic involvement with heartbreakingly sweet little notes secretly exchanged...'

He said all this in a perfectly conversational voice, as if there were nothing strange about digging into my family's financial affairs or my personal life. Not if *he* did it.

Once again, I felt in my legs the nearly uncontrollable urge to turn and run. I fought it, and stayed where I was.

'Interesting,' I said, meeting his gaze as steadily as I could. 'You know, some people might think those sorts of enquiries discourteous. Invasive, even.'

'Might they?' He looked royally entertained. 'It is an amusing fact, Miss Linton, but in my whole life not a single person has ever accused me of

428

discourteous or ungentlemanly behaviour.' He smiled again, spreading his hands. 'Not a single one. On the contrary, everybody always assures me how considerate and polite I am. Sometimes, they assure me three or four times in a row.'

He took a step closer to me.

Without moving my head, my gaze darted from side to side. I discovered that we were pretty much alone in our own private little corner of the ballroom. Indeed, if I was not very much mistaken, there seemed to be a literal wall of people who had their backs to us, separating us from the rest of the crowd. None of them appeared to show the slightest bit of interest in our conversation, although they were perfectly within hearing distance. They stood at attention, and several of them were in uniform. The uniform of the Indian Army – the strong arm of the East India Company.

Suddenly, I found myself wishing Captain Carter had not left my side.

'You could not see your way to tell me what connection exists between you and Mr Ambrose?' Lord Dalgliesh's voice was deceptively soft. 'I would really like to know.'

'I told you before,' I said, finding it increasingly difficult to meet those blue eyes that bored into me like drills. 'There is no connection.'

'Such a pity, such a pity.' He sighed, and smiled regretfully. 'Do you remember, Miss Linton, that I told you I always get what I want?'

Without sign or command, the men who separated us from the rest of the ballroom and who, until now, had been standing with their backs to us, turned and stepped closer, surrounding us, surrounding *me*, cutting off any way of escape.

Escape? Why would I want to escape? We were at a ball, for heaven's sake – a public festivity, hosted by one of London's most prominent noblewomen! He couldn't do anything to me here, surely, could he? And besides, he didn't even look as if he wanted to do anything to me. His smile was so friendly, so charming, he looked as if he desired nothing but good for the entire world.

With every step the soldiers took towards me, I felt less sure of that.

'Would you like to accompany me on a little stroll?' he suggested, brightly. 'I've heard Lady Metcalf's garden is truly beautiful at night.'

What should I do? Scream for help? But help with what? He hadn't done or said anything improper. There was nothing concrete to suggest danger of any kind. And still, something inside me screamed and clawed at my innards to get me to turn and run.

'I...' My voice was a mere whisper. What should I do? 'I... don't think so, Your Lordship.'

'Are you sure?' He looked crestfallen, then he suddenly glanced around, saw the soldiers, and his face brightened. 'Oh! There are a few friends of mine!' He turned to me again. 'Are you sure you wouldn't like to come for a stroll? I think my friends would love to accompany us. These military fellows spend so much time breathing in gunpowder fumes, they need a lot of fresh air.'

He laughed – a light, carefree laugh that expected nothing but my joyful acceptance. If anybody watching the scene saw me decline again, they would think me abominably rude. What should I do? Oh, if only some help were here, Captain Carter, or Mr Ambrose, or...

'Excuse me? Excuse me please, gentlemen, let me through please...'

And from between the beefy soldiers of the Indian Army stepped the figure of Edmund, the piano tuner's son. He gave the startled Lord Dalgliesh a polite smile and said: 'You will excuse us for a moment, I'm sure? I have to tell the lady something.'

And with that, he took me by the arm, leading me a few steps away without even waiting for an answer. Lord Dalgliesh stood where he had been standing, his face back to the perfect beneficent smile that seemed to be his favourite expression. Yet, in my time with Mr Ambrose, I had learned to read minuscule changes in facial expressions. Charming as his smile was, it didn't soften the steel in his blue eyes.

'Miss Linton,' Edmund began, and gave a little bow, 'I must thank you from the bottom of my heart for your initiative in inviting me to this ball tonight. It has brought me joy beyond what I can say. I cannot adequately express my thanks, but, as a gesture, I wondered whether you would do me the honour of dancing a reel with me?'

I could have kissed him.

Not *literally*, of course! I mean, my little sister was in love with him, for heaven's sake! And even if he weren't the apple of her eye and cherry of her heart, I would never kiss *him*. He looked just so... kind. Harmless. Conservative. Plus, I didn't have plans to kiss *any* man, of whatever sort, ever.

But figuratively speaking, I planted a big buss on his forehead.

'Why, thank you, Mr Conway,' I said, curtsying and extending my arm in the most ladylike manner I had ever managed to fake. 'A dance is just what I need right now.' *Yes, and please in the middle of the dance floor, far away from His Lordship and company!* 'I would be delighted.'

Over my shoulder I smiled at Lord Dalgliesh. 'You will excuse us, Your Lordship.'

'Certainly, Miss Linton.' He bowed, just a few inches. Was it a coincidence that, at the gesture, the wall of soldiers opened up to let us pass? 'Until we meet again.'

I shuddered as we passed between the uniformed men and they closed ranks behind us.

'Are you cold, Miss Linton?' Edmund enquired politely.

'No.' I shook my head. 'Let's dance.'

~~**~*~*

It was terrible.

He stepped on my feet a lot, but nevertheless, I tried not to step on his. I thought it was the least I could do, considering he may have just saved my life. I still wasn't too sure about that, to be honest. Lord Dalgliesh hadn't really said anything threatening. He had just invited me on a little walk, after all.

But now and then I caught his eye across the ballroom, and had the feeling that it would have been a pretty long walk to an unpleasant destination. I made sure that I stayed among plenty of people for the rest of the ball. Unfortunately, that meant having to dance almost every dance, with any partner who happened to be available. Sometimes, safety came at too high a price.

All that sustained me through the long hours of the ball was the sight of Ella and Edmund. Whether they were dancing or not, and no matter how far apart they were, their eyes never left each other. I had to admit I was beginning to warm to this Edmund chap. Maybe it wasn't so terrible that my little sister was in love, and she wouldn't end up miserable and oppressed like so many other women who gave themselves over to a man.

And if she would, Edmund would rue the day he was born!

As the evening dragged on, the music became slower, the crowd less excited, and finally, it was all over. Lady Metcalf stood at the door to say goodbye to all the guests. We were some of the last ones to leave. Yet there was one other behind us, surrounded by an entourage of figures in uniform.

Lord Dalgliesh nodded to me and smiled.

I could almost hear a voice whispering into my ear: *This is not over.*

I had assumed that, now he had dropped my sister like a hot brick, Sir Philip would try to get rid of us as soon as possible. I was mistaken. He took us home in his coach as planned and, the entire drive, did nothing but chinwag about the fabulous Lady Katherine he had met at the ball. However, other than you might imagine, this was not awkward in the least. Quite the contrary.

Why, you might ask?

I might have been angry with him for casting aside my sister like a used glove – but seeing as Ella was quite *delighted* to be thrown aside like a used glove, and looking happier with every word he spoke, taking pains to agree most energetically with his praise of Lady Katherine, it was rather hard. Especially since my aunt was shooting gazes of fiery anger at the poor Sir Philip, not one of which he actually noticed.

'...and her hair, as golden as the sunlight, don't you think?' he sighed, his eyes dreamy.

'Most definitely,' Ella concurred, nodding energetically. 'Golden sunlight on a summer morning. Don't you think so, Mr Conway?'

'W-what? Oh yes,' stammered Edmund, who had been too busy staring at Ella to hear one word in ten.

'I shall send her a bouquet of flowers directly in the morning. Or maybe two, or three! What do you think, Miss Ella?'

'Make it four.'

'What an excellent idea! My thanks.' He bent to her and gently kissed her hands. 'Only a good friend can give such good advice.'

At the word 'friend', my aunt nearly burst into flames from indignation.

It wasn't long till we reached home. Sir Philip's departure then happened a lot more speedily than usual. He needed to leave to buy flowers for Lady Katherine, and my aunt needed to retreat to her room to simmer with rage at the inconstancy of young aristocrats.

'Farewell, you all,' he called to us, sticking his head out of the coach window and lifting his hat in parting a last time, an excited smile on his face. 'I shall hope to see you all at my next ball. You are all invited.' And, turning to the coachman: 'Onward! Find me the nearest florist, man!'

'Yes, Sir!'

The whip cracked, and the coach rolled off down the street.

My aunt was already in the house, as could be deduced from the sound of crashing china from somewhere on the first floor. Lisbeth and Gertrude were on their way to follow; Edmund had excused himself. Only Ella, Maria, Anne and I were still standing outside, looking after the coach.

'Well,' Maria sneered, giving Ella a superior look. 'It seems you are one suitor short, little sister.'

'Yes!' Ella sighed, a happy smile suffusing her features. 'Will you excuse me? I have, um... things to do.'

Pirouetting around like an overexcited ballerina, she hurried off around the house, into the back garden. I thought I had an inkling what 'things' she had to do, and with whom.

'Is it only me,' Maria asked, confused, looking at Anne and me in turn, 'or did she seem not the least bit disappointed about losing one of the most eligible bachelors in London as a potential husband?'

'Of course she was disappointed,' I said. 'Couldn't you tell by the way her left little finger twitched? That always gives people away. Now, if you will excuse me, I think I have the sudden urge to take a late night stroll in the garden...'

~~**~*~*

'Oh, Ella, my love!'

'Oh, Edmund, my love!'

As sweet nothings fluttered through the holes in the fence, I settled myself comfortably down behind the bushes. Seeing as this might be a longer episode of the romantic Drama of the Back Garden, I had brought a copy of *The Further Adventures of Robinson Crusoe* with me. For now, though, it remained closed, and I peeked through the foliage towards the place where Ella was clinging to the fence and, through the fence, to Edmund. It had to be quite uncomfortable embracing somebody around several metal bars, but neither of them seemed to mind.

My eyes strayed to the ladder leaning against the garden shed. Still, neither of them seemed to have noticed it, or thought of using it.

'Oh, Ella, my love,' Edmund whispered. 'How can this be? How can I be so fortunate to be holding you in my arms tonight, when I thought that by now I would have lost you forever?'

'We must have a guardian angel watching over us from heaven,' she whispered, pressing her face into his chest as best she could.

From heaven? From behind the bushes, rather.

But otherwise, she had hit the nail pretty much on the head.

'Tell me this is true,' Edmund sighed. 'Tell me I am truly holding you right now, and it is not some phantasm I have dreamed up in my desperation of losing you to another.'

'It is true, Edmund, my darling. I am here. I will always be here. I love you!'

'I love you, too!'

'I love you more!'

'No, I do!'

I tuned out their conversation and immersed myself in *The Further Adventures*. I only resurfaced from my adventures in Madagascar when, out the blue, I heard my name.

'...Lilly!'

'Yes, my darling Ella. Your sister...' Edmund murmured.

I was up on my feet and listening intensely in an instant! They were talking about *me*? What the heck did they have to talk about me?

Edmund was smiling. 'So I finally met her.'

'What did you think of her?' Ella asked anxiously.

I leaned forward, pricking up my ears.

Yes? Yes? What did you think of me? And be careful what you say, you little piano-tuning bastard! I have a sharp parasol!

'What do I think of her?' Edmund laughed. 'Ella, if not for her, I wouldn't even have been at that ball. I would never have held you in my arms. Right now, after you, she ranks as the person I respect most in the world, more than the Queen, or, yes, even Ignaz Bösendorfer.'

Bösendorfer? Who the dickens is Ignaz Bösendorfer?[49]

The name sounded like someone you wouldn't want to meet in a dark alley, but from the reverent way he pronounced it, and the way Ella beamed up at him, the chap must have been royalty or maybe an ancient demigod. For some reason, I found myself grinning.

Blast! What did it matter if Edmund thought well of me? But I couldn't wipe the silly grin off my face.

'If only we could reveal all to her,' he sighed.

'I know, I know, Edmund.' Ella mirrored his sigh. 'I wish, too, that she knew how dear I hold you in my heart. I wish she could hear and see us right now! But it cannot be.'

Well, actually, my dear sister...

'Nobody must ever know! If our affections ever became known...!'

She trailed off. He picked up the meaning of her words without great difficulty.

'Your aunt didn't seem very fond of me,' he ventured.

---

[49] A famous Austrian piano builder whose pianos were preferred by pianist and composer Franz Liszt, because his energetic playing smashed all other pianos to bits.

'She can be... difficult, sometimes.'

'Do you think she might ever be prevailed upon to accept me as the man who loves you?'

'I... don't know. Maybe.'

One thing about my little sister... she is an eternal optimist. From inside the house, there came another crash of china, followed by a screech that sounded like Sir Phillip Wilkins' name, mixed with powerful invectives.

Ella jumped and guiltily looked back at the house.

'Your aunt?' Edmund asked.

She nodded. 'She had set her heart on this match. I would be sorry for her sake that it did not come about, but...' she smiled weakly at Edmund, 'somehow, I cannot seem to manage to be very sorry.'

He smiled back. But then, his face became solemn again.

'But you're not sorry that we didn't have to run away, either, are you?' he asked.

Ella sucked in air, sharply. She hesitated. Then: 'No, I'm not.'

Her voice was small. 'I... love you with all my heart, Edmund. But in my heart I also love Aunt, Lilly, my other sisters, even Uncle Bufford, though we practically never see him. My heart would have been broken, had I been forced to leave them. And with a broken heart, I could not have loved you half as well as you deserve.'

There were a few minutes of silence. Then, Edmund spoke again, and his voice was a little unsteady.

'Ella, I... I have to ask your forgiveness.'

'Forgiveness, Edmund? For what?'

He swallowed.

'For this... for my devious plans. For how I tried to lure you away from your home, your family, and trap you in a disgraceful union. Now that the weight of Wilkins is lifted off my mind, I can hardly comprehend what I was thinking, what I was doing. And I'm not just talking about my plans to run away with you. The way I've been acting, presuming to touch you where I shouldn't touch you, presuming to hold you like no gentleman should... I must have been mad! I... I only ever want to behave to you as a gentleman should behave, Ella. You are the sweetest, most gentle lady that ever walked the earth. You deserve nothing less, in fact, you deserve a lot more.' Again, he took a breath. 'So, I wanted to apologize for all I did. I wish you to know that, had there been any other way, had I been master of myself and my heart, I would never have suggested an elopement. If you can, forgive me, and forget all about it. We will go back to the way things were. I will behave with propriety towards you, and never again step out of line.'

'Of course I forgive you, Edmund.' Was something wrong with my ears or did she sound a tiny bit disappointed. 'And of course you are right. We should behave properly. We have been acting... foolishly, lately.'

He nodded.

She nodded.

Yet he didn't loosen his grip on her, still holding her in a manner that I, at least, would not have termed proper for a gentleman.

'Before we return to propriety and forget foolishness, though...' he muttered, his voice rough.

'Yes?' Her voice was tinged with hope.

'Could I hold you for just one minute longer?'

Tears sparkled in her eyes as she pulled him even closer. Unlike so often in the last few weeks, I knew that this time, they were tears of happiness.

'Yes!'

~~**~*~*

It was only next morning I realized that, during the latter half of the romantic interlude in the garden, I hadn't once got bored and reached for *The Further Adventures of Robinson Crusoe*. Did this mean I was actually developing an *interest in romance*?

If that were the case, I thought I'd better find a lake to drown in!

But no!

It had to be that I was simply happy to see Ella happy. Yes, that was a perfectly legitimate reason to stare at her from behind a bush. My reasons had nothing whatsoever to do with the fact that I was beginning to wonder what it might be like to have somebody care for me the way Edmund cared for her. Nothing at all like that.

And Ella was happy, incandescently happy. It was as though she was a flower that had been squashed by a heavy stone. Now that the stone had been lifted and the sun could reach her again, she stretched towards the sky, unfurling her petals and blooming like never before. She even had her own bee fluttering around in the form of Edmund, though I would biff him if he should try to pollinate her. Even metaphors should have their limits.

Apart from the happy time I spent in the garden each evening, listening to Ella's profusions of happiness, I tried to avoid home as much as possible over the next few days. My aunt was still in a china-chucking mood, and even though Uncle Bufford, by a message sent via the trusty Leadfield, had strictly forbidden her to indulge in such wanton waste of perfectly good crockery, she might still succumb, and my head was too precious to me to serve as a target.

Moreover, Patsy and the others frequently appeared at home to try and capture me for the purpose of questioning. I had no wish to be subjected to their inquisition on the why and how of my spectacular speech at the anti-suffragist rally, at least not until I had thought of satisfactory lies to give as answers.

So, you can see, I had all the reasons in the world to avoid home for now and seek refuge in another place that afforded me more peace and quiet. And the only other place available to me was number 322 Leadenhall Street.

Did I mention something about finding peace and quiet?

Well, it didn't quite work out that way.

~~**~*~*

Mr Linton
Bring me file 38XI201.
Rikkard Ambrose

Springing up from my chair, I ran towards the shelves containing the file boxes. I needed about two seconds to reach my goal, three seconds to grab the books, and another three seconds to return. By the time I reached my desk with the correct file in hand, another message had already landed beside the first one.

I didn't need to open it to know it said *Hurry!* or *Faster!* Mr Rikkard Ambrose was a tiny bit impatient and acrimonious these days.

I could guess why. A deadline was looming over us like the shadow of an evil giant – a giant with a hawk-beak nose, a golden mane of lion's hair, and piercing steel-blue eyes. Soon it would be time. Soon, Mr Ambrose would try to get back what was his, by force. And I would not join him in the venture.

That fact gnawed at me like a pesky rat, not willing to let go of its dinner. After all, *I* had found out where this precious file, the contents of which he still hadn't deigned to share with me, was being kept. And I wouldn't be part of the retrieval! If only he had, at least, kept his mouth shut about the file's contents. His vague, sinister statement was driving me to distraction.

The centre of the world.

Whose world? Surely, he didn't mean it geographically, as in the earth's core? Something like that couldn't be contained in a piece of paper. But then, what?

Not knowing was making me imagine all sorts of terrible things. What did Mr Ambrose consider the centre of the world? Money? Was the file, in fact, a deed signing his entire fortune over to another?

All of a sudden, I thought of Edmund and Ella. He was the centre of her world, and she of his. Could it be...? Could the file contain illicit notes revealing a romantic relationship with somebody who was the centre of Mr Ambrose's world?

Maybe... said a nasty little voice in my mind, *Maybe the writer of the pink letters?*

No. Mr Ambrose wouldn't go berserk over a woman. The possibility of losing all his money, yes, that would make him bite off heads. But I couldn't see him fretting over a lady's reputation. Not even that mysterious femme fatal who continued her pink missives with infuriating regularity. The pile of letters in my bottom drawer was growing larger. And Mr Ambrose was growing more persistent in keeping up my working morale every day.

I tried to talk to him, to get his permission to accompany him on the secret mission that loomed on the horizon, or at least get some information out of him about what the centre of the world might mean, might be – what centre of the world was worth risking his life for.

To no avail. He remained silent.

Now there's a surprise!

Well, it didn't mean I was giving up.

'Mr Ambrose?' I knocked against his door. 'I have file 38XI201 here, Sir. Don't you want me to bring it in instead of sliding it under the door? It must be tedious for you to always have to stand up and get it from the door. Won't you open up?'

I heard another *plink* from the desk. Without letting go of the file, I reached over and open the message container.

No. The file. Now.

You couldn't get much clearer than that, could you?

Sighing, I bent to push it under the door. I was just about to rise again when suddenly, an idea struck me.

For a moment, I froze where I was. Then, a grin spreading across my face, I rose and knocked against the door.

'Mr Ambrose, Sir? I need to talk to you. It's important. You should open the door.'

Silence.

'Really! I'm not just making this up. Something important happened, and you should know. Open up, please.'

More silence. A bucket full of silence.

I gave an especially dramatic sigh. 'Oh well, if you don't want to hear what Lord Dalgliesh said...'

There was a crash from the other side of the door. It sounded as if somebody had jumped up from his chair so violently that it had been hurled over and smashed onto the floor.

About half a second later, keys rattled in the lock, and the office door was ripped open. Mr Ambrose stood in the doorway, looking like a Beethoven bust on a bad day. Except for the weird hairstyle.

'Ah, Mr Ambrose,' I said, smiling at him with innocent delight. 'How nice of you to honour me with your presence. I thought you were too busy for poor little me this fine morning.'

My comment didn't improve his mood. With a sharp jerk of his hand, he directed me to enter his office.

'Inside. Now.'

'And so loquacious! My, I would hardly have known you if not for your customary cheerful smile.'

He didn't dignify that with a reply. As I entered his stark office, he shut the door behind me with a *click*. It wasn't loud, but somehow managed to sound like the gates of doom slamming shut behind a poor soul trapped in hell.

I sat on the visitor's chair, figuring that if I waited for the invitation to sit in Mr Ambrose's talkative mood, I could stand until kingdom come. Actually, I could probably stand until kingdom came, drank a cup of tea and left again.

I was right. Without a word, he walked around the desk, took a seat in his armchair and fixed me with his dark, sea-coloured eyes. Looking into those eyes, I felt a shiver go down my back. Not the same kind of shiver I experienced when looking into Dalgliesh's eyes – one of fear – or another man's eyes – one of revulsion.

No, this was a shiver of excitement.

Well, life as his secretary had been pretty exciting. So why shouldn't I be excited? It had nothing to do with him, personally, after all, so it was perfectly all right.

His eyes were so dark... they seemed to draw me in, somehow making it seem as though he and I were moving closer together, though our chairs hadn't moved an inch.

'Dalgliesh!' he ordered, his voice cold and hard. 'Tell me everything,'

And I did. Well, not *everything*. I told him how I had gone to Lady Metcalf's ball, and how Dalgliesh had surprised and questioned me there.

I *didn't* tell him about picking out a young blonde lady to distract my sister's suitor from the object of his adoration. I also didn't tell him about my meeting and dancing with Captain Carter, for some reason. It just didn't seem important enough to mention.

Anyway, it was Dalgliesh he was interested in, surely, not some army captain with a strange tiger-waistcoat and an even stranger sense of humour.

So I told all I remembered of my encounter with the suave aristocrat. By the time I had finished, Mr Ambrose wasn't looking at me anymore, but concentrating on a stack of papers in front of him. Strangely, however, although he normally was a fast reader, he had already stared down at one page long enough to read the complete works of William Shakespeare.

When the last words had left my mouth, he said, without emotion in his voice:

'You are fortunate that this young man, Edmund, appeared. Had Lord Dalgliesh succeeded in luring you into the garden, you would have gone on very long walk with him. One from which you would not have returned before you had answered all his questions, if at all.'

His words gripped my heart like a fist of frost. So I had been right in wanting to run. But...

'But he seemed so friendly,' I burst out. 'Not threatening at all.'

A muscle in Mr Ambrose's jaw twitched.

'Of course he did. He never threatens. He never strikes. He never says a word against the laws of England. And yet, wherever he goes, things happen. A wink from him means ruin, a twitch of his fingers means death. When he nods, wise men turn and run.'

'He nodded when he met you.'

'I've never claimed to be wise.'

There was a spell of silence, that complete silence that I only ever felt in the presence of Mr Ambrose. Shivering, I remembered Lord Dalgliesh's friendly, harmless expression, back in the ballroom. Could anyone really be that good an actor?

'I still can't really believe–' I began.

I didn't get any further. In a flash, Mr Ambrose was up and around his desk. Before I could move he had grabbed me by the shoulders and hauled me out of my chair. Forcefully, I was thrust against the wall of the office, cold stone pressing against my back.

'Believe!' he hissed. 'Believe anything and everything where Dalgliesh is concerned. He's the man who invented the word ruthless. If you get in his way, he will step on you and crush you like an insect.' His dark, sea-coloured eyes were burning into me with deadly intensity. Slowly, the grip of his right hand loosened and left my shoulder. He raised it, almost unconsciously it seemed, until it touched my cheek. 'Stay away from him!'

His hand fell.

Yes! a voice inside me screamed. *Yes, I will! I'll do anything! Just touch my cheek again! And maybe lean a little closer...!*

My inner feminist slammed shut the door on that voice.

'You can't make me do anything,' I whispered.

Why the heck did I whisper? My voice should be strong and independent!

It's those darn eyes of his! They're sapping the strength out of you, making you feel all gooey and weak-kneed. No man should be allowed to have eyes like that!

'I can,' he bit out. 'Stay away from him. That is an order, Mr Linton!'

I opened my mouth to argue – not because I really wanted to go near Dalgliesh; I mean, I'm not completely nuts – but because I refuse on principle to be ordered around by a man after working hours. But when Mr Ambrose's head moved forward, the words caught in my throat. What was he doing? Why was he moving so close to me? He was just inches away!

He couldn't possibly...

Could he?

For just one moment, it looked as though he was going to kiss me.

Then the moment passed, and he halted, his perfect granite face only a fraction of an inch away from mine. His hard body pressed into mine, a living threat, ready to deliver. His eyes narrowed infinitesimally, challenging me to dare and speak the words that were on my tongue. I swallowed.

Memories flooded my mind. Memories of him pressed against me, just like that – only back then, he had taken the plunge, and closed the last bit of distance that separated us. Today, he was in control – of himself and me. The hand that still gripped my shoulder, pressing me into the wall, was steady as rock.

But how long would he hold out? How long would he be able to refrain from reliving our memories?

They're not memories! I told myself, fiercely. *You imagined it! You imagined it all! You did not let yourself be kissed by Mr Ambrose! And you most certainly did not enjoy it more than you ever enjoyed anything else in your life, understood?*

'Will you stay away from him?' Mr Ambrose demanded. His breath tickled my skin as he spoke, momentarily robbing me of the strength to answer.

'Y-yes,' I managed.

He gave a curt nod. 'Adequate.'

'But,' I hurriedly tacked on, 'not because you said so. I'll stay away because I, as an independent, strong woman independently decided, on my own, to stay away from him!'

He cocked his head as if to say, 'As long as you do what I say, why do you think I care about the why?'

I glowered at him. He ignored me.

439

'Let me go!' I demanded.

He still ignored me. Taking a deep breath, he leant forward just a little more.

The sensation that hit me was shocking! Not his lips, no – they were much softer than this. It was his forehead, resting against mine. I could feel a few wild strands of my hair tickling his forehead, and... my God! He really was hard-headed! In the literal sense of the word. And bloody heavy! It was downright uncomfortable.

Really? If it's so uncomfortable, why don't you want him to pull away?

His eyes bored into mine.

'Swear!' He demanded. 'Swear to me you'll stay away from him!'

Swear. Not promise, not pledge, *swear*. And I had a feeling that an oath sworn to Mr Rikkard Ambrose had better not be broken.

So I quickly crossed my fingers behind my back, just in case.

'I swear.'

And suddenly he was gone. I swayed for a moment, used to the press of his body into mine. He was standing three feet away, standing tall and forbidding, as if we hadn't just been pressed more tightly together than two flounders in a printing press.

'Quite sensible of you, Mr Linton.'

Sensible? *Sensible?* I didn't feel very sensible right now! Or reasonable, or cautious, or prudent, for that matter.

I sucked in a deep breath, my eyes still fixed on Mr Ambrose, fumbling for something to say. Something that wasn't *Come back here! I wasn't finished with you!*

'But it doesn't make any sense!' Finally, some words had managed to find their way out of my mouth. And they sounded angry, not breathless. Good.

'Indeed?' Mr Ambrose regarded me coolly. 'What are you referring to, ex-actly, Mr Linton?'

'Lord Dalgliesh! Why would I have to try and stay away from him? What does he want from me? For some reason, at the ball he was determined to find out your reason for dancing with me. But it was just one dance! Why would he be interested in that? I mean... what's one dance?'

'He has been trying to find a weak spot in my armour for years now, Mr Lin-ton. If he had reason to believe that I had formed a romantic attachment to someone, this would give him the hold over me he has always desired.'

'But... why would he think that, after just one dance?'

There was a pause. Then he said, in voice so low I hardly caught it: 'I don't dance, Mr Linton.'

My heart made a jump. 'Not ever?'

'No. It's a waste of time.'

'But you danced with me.'

'Yes.' A muscle in his jaw twitched. 'Apparently, that one dance was enough to convince Dalgliesh that I might have formed a romantic attachment to you.' Abruptly, he turned and strode back to his desk. 'Ridiculous, of course, but there you are.'

Unconsciously, my hands closed into fists.

Ridiculous, is it?

'Oh,' I said pointedly, 'So he thought I was the *centre of your world*?'

He froze halfway to his desk. Slowly turning back towards me, he met my eyes with his own. Their dark force took my breath away.

'Probably.'

'What is it?' Why was my voice so low and breathy all of a sudden? 'What is the centre of the world for you?'

'I'll tell you what it is *not*, Mr Linton. It most certainly not a girl.'

Why this odd tugging sensation in my chest? Had I ever expected the centre of Mr Ambrose's world to be anything emotional?

'I asked what it is,' I told him, forcing my voice to be firm. 'Not what it is *not*.'

'I know.'

'So are you going to tell me?'

'No.'

'But–'

He cut me off with a jerk of his hand.

'You,' he said, 'are not in here to question me. You were in here to answer *my* questions. You have done so. You can leave. Now.'

'But–'

'That is an order, Mr Linton!'

Slowly, I got to my feet and walked away. At the door, I turned to look over my shoulder a last time. He was sitting there at the desk, with that unfathomable lack of expression on his face that belonged solely to him.

'The world is a heavy thing to bear,' I told him, 'whether at the centre or elsewhere. Why won't you let someone help you?'

Without waiting for a reply, I turned, leaving him behind.

~~**~*~*

The longer the day stretched, the more fantastic my imaginings became. In my mind, the centre of the world became the name of a priceless diamond, an heirloom of the noble house Mr Ambrose was a member of, though he refused to acknowledge it. A moment later, it turned into the title of an ancient script that revealed the lost location of Atlantis. In the next moment, it turned into Buckingham Palace, centre of the British Empire and home of its Queen, and maybe a plan to prevent her assassination.

Though, in the latter case, I couldn't see Mr Ambrose risking his own life willingly. Not unless there was a healthy reward involved, or... or unless he had a secret affair with the Queen, and *she* was the writer of the pink letters...

It was probably better that, at this point, another *plink* from a tube message distracted me from my own thoughts. I wasn't far away from imagining the missing file to contain a magical portal to Sleeping Beauty's castle. Or, more likely, to the seventh circle of hell.

The hours flew by as I worked ceaselessly, and thought ceaselessly, always asking: *What will happen? What will he do? What is the centre of the world?*

I didn't find any answers. The hours grew longer and turned into days. The closer the deadline came, the more insane became Mr Ambrose's idea of an appropriate workload. Working seemed to be his way of dealing with anxiety – if he truly was anxious. He seemed just as cool and collected as ever. Maybe it was simply his way of earning more money.

Maybe...

On the last day before the great day, I sat at my desk and gazed out through the window over the city of London. The sun was just sinking beyond the horizon, flooding the city with blood-red light, half-obscured by the black smoke that rose from thousands of chimneys. It seemed like an omen to me. Darkness and blood.

Quickly, I rose from my chair and went to Mr Ambrose's door. He hadn't called for a new file yet, in fact, he'd been suspiciously undemanding the last few minutes, but I knew he was still in there. If he had left, I would have heard the keys in the lock.

After a second of hesitation, I raised my hand and knocked.

'Mr Ambrose?'

No answer.

'Mr Ambrose, I know you're still in there!'

Silence.

'Mr Ambrose, Sir, please, open up. I want to talk to you again. Maybe I can convince you! If you'd let me help you...'

I heard a *plink* from my desk.

Turning, I saw another message had arrived. Carefully, I opened the container and read:

No. Go! Tomorrow, you can remain at home. I will not require your services.

Tomorrow – when he would put his plan into action and move against Dalgliesh. I knocked again.

'Mr Ambrose? Mr Ambrose, please!'

Silence. A tomb full of silence.

Well, if he wanted to ignore me, fine. He wasn't the only one who had secret plans for tomorrow!

TRAPPED

I woke up and thought: *The day has come.*

Today Mr Ambrose would go to number 97 East India Dock Road, and...

An excited shiver went through me. I didn't really know what exactly he was going to do – but I didn't think it would be very legal.

It'll be exciting, though.

Oh yes. It definitely would be exciting. And I was supposed to stay home like a proper little lady and do nothing! My hands gripped the sheets tightly, balling into fists. Quickly, I looked around. It was still very early in the morning, probably around six a.m. The sun was just starting to peek over the roofs of the houses, outside. Its rays fell on Ella, who lay in her bed, sound asleep, with a smile on her face.

Even in my current mood, I wasn't totally unaffected by my little sister's happy smile. But it could not soothe me for long. My thoughts returned to *him* all too soon.

How dare he exclude me? Hadn't I proved my worth, earned the right to have his respect? It was I who had discovered Dalgliesh's base, after all!

Admittedly, I had done it while I was as drunk as a lord, and rather accidentally, but still, I had done it. He owed it to me to take me along on this. When I thought of him, facing a host of heavily armed soldiers alone, delving into the dark to recover the mysterious file that was so all-important for reasons which I still did not understand, I wanted to scream in frustration.

Of course I didn't, because it would have woken Ella up. Instead, I punched my pillow, again wishing it had a greater resemblance to Mr Ambrose's head.

I won't! I won't! I won't allow him to do this!

Suddenly, having decided what I was going to do, I slid out of bed and towards the window. I didn't bother putting on my dress. Once I reached the shed, I was going to exchange it for trousers and a shirt in any case. If somebody saw me running through the garden in my pink lace nightgown with little embroidered songbirds, I would just have to murder that person before they could spread the word.

I had never dressed that fast in my entire life. Five minutes later, I was striding down the street, on my way to Empire House. There probably was no reason to hurry – if Mr Ambrose had any sense in that hard head of his, he wouldn't take action until nightfall. Still, the early worm catches the bird, or however the saying goes.

When I reached Empire House about a quarter of an hour later, I saw that arriving early had been a good idea: a familiar chaise, drawn by a shabby beast of a grey horse, was standing in front of the main entrance. Knowing that I would have to get past the grey monster, I approached carefully. It eyed me, with what I could only suppose was a mix of interest and appetite.

I raised a cautioning finger.

'If you bite me, I'll bite back,' I told him. Nobody would be able to say I didn't warn him.

The horse snorted and turned its head away derisively.

Quickly, I stole past the beast and into the main hall. It was completely deserted. Nobody was in sight. The gigantic man-made cave of Mammon was as silent as its master. My steps echoed from the wall as I hurried across the floor and towards the steps, wondering why he was going this early. Did he still have preparations to make?

Maybe he simply wants to avoid you. Isn't that nice?

On reaching the upper landing, I heard familiar voices from the hallway. One was especially familiar.

'...quicker, Karim! We have places to be.'

'Yes, *Sahib*.'

'And double-check everything.'

Cool? Check. Distant? Check. Forbidding and reserved? Check. Now, who could this possibly be?

Carefully, I peeked around the corner and there he stood: Mr Rikkard Ambrose, a motionless figure in white and black, overseeing Karim, who was packing a few scrolls of paper into a bag. They looked like maps to me. Or ground plans.

'...the main entrance. Soldiers will be stationed there.'

'Yes, *Sahib*.'

Mr Ambrose stood more like an Ancient Greek statue than ever, his body now as motionless as his face, his figure erect, his eyes distant, as if looking at something three thousand years away.

Well, it was high time to startle some life into him.

I stepped out into the hall.

'Hello, everybody.'

Mr Ambrose jumped in a most un-statue-like way. He whirled around, and his hand was already on its way to grip his sword cane when his eyes fell on me.

'You!'

'Yes, I.' I marched forward and stopped only a few feet away from him, my fists on my hips. 'What did you think? That I was going to stay home and miss all the fun?'

'It was probably too much to expect sensible behaviour from you, for once.' His eyes flashed, darkly. 'I certainly didn't expect you to be here this early.'

Ha! I knew it! He had known I would show up, but had hoped to be gone before I did so.

'Well, I'm a morning person,' I told him with a bright, fake smile.

'I told you to stay away!'

'Yes, well, I ignored you.'

'I can see that.' He took a step closer, bending forward a little. 'I am displeased, Mr Linton, to put it mildly. Leave. Now.'

'No.'

'Mr Linton?' He took another step closer. His eyes grew darker and stormier the closer he got. 'I am going to do something I have never done to an employee in my entire life.' Slowly, he bent forward, fixing me with his cold, sea-coloured gazes. 'I'm giving you the day off. Go!'

'No.'

'Didn't you hear me? You have a holiday in front of you! Enjoy it! It'll be the last you'll get out of me for the next five hundred years.'

'You can take your holiday and stick it where the sun doesn't shine! I'm coming with you!'

'You work for me! You have to obey me.'

I raised my chin, meeting his gaze without blinking. 'If you give me the day off, that means today I *don't* work for you, and I can do as I wish. And I wish to accompany you.' Gesturing to Karim. 'I can't let you walk into danger with only *him* around for protection.'

The Mohammedan's eyes bulged, and I fancy he would have said something pretty explicit, had not Mr Ambrose spoken first.

'And what,' he asked, his voice as cold as the North Pole, 'makes you think I am going to let you accompany us?'

'Oh you probably won't.' I shrugged. 'But I can hire a cab and follow you. It's as simple as that.'

'I see.' For a few moments, Mr Ambrose regarded me in silence. Then: 'All right. You have won, Mr Linton. You can come.'

I wasn't sure whether I'd heard correctly.

'Excuse me?'

'I said, you can come. I am not fond of repeating myself, Mr Linton.'

My mouth popped open.

'I... I was expecting you to fight me on this for about a hundred years.'

He shrugged. 'I know when to yield to superior forces. You have convinced me, Mr Linton. You should be there, you were right from the beginning. I need you.'

'What?' Karim demanded. '*Sahib*, you cannot be serious! She cannot–'

'Silence, Karim!' Mr Ambrose cut him off. 'You will speak when I say so, and not before!'

The mountainous man closed his mouth, his eyes burning with anger.

'As I said,' Mr Ambrose repeated, 'You should be there. You have a right to.'

'Well... thank you. I'm glad you've finally seen sense.' A timid smile broke over my face. At last! He was starting to be sensible. He was starting to accept me! 'Shall we go, then?'

'Soon,' Mr Ambrose said, looking out of the window, his face as immovable as ever. 'I just need one last thing. I think I've forgotten to take one of the ground plans I need. It's on the desk in my office. Would you get it for me, please?'

'Of course, Sir.' Quickly, I ran past him and into his office. If he was going to take me along, I would do anything! In my mind, I was already picturing the sinister silhouette of the villain's lair. My first ever real villain's lair! My first adventure!

I had thought that the visit to the polling station was my first adventure, but compared to this, it was nothing! I would be entering a new world. A world of mystery, money, power and strife that most people didn't even catch a glimpse of. I was so excited, that I almost didn't catch the click behind me.

Almost.

I whirled around, just in time to see the door to the office close.

~~**~*~*

Would it surprise anybody to hear that there was no ground plan on the desk in Mr Ambrose's office? No? I didn't think so.

'Let me out! Let me out, curse you!' My hand already hurt from hammering against the door. It was useless. The door was firmly locked, just as was the connecting door to my own office. He must have directed Karim to lock it while he was doing the same with the other, damn him!

'Let me out, or I will break this door down!'

'Don't excite yourself, Mr Linton,' came a cool voice from the other side of the door. 'The door is oak, reinforced with steel. It won't break. And don't bother calling for help, either. Nobody is here, and even when the other employees arrive, it won't be any use to call out. I sent Mr Stone to Newcastle on a matter of business, the hallway will be empty. Everybody else will be out of hearing range. This building has thick walls.'

I heard him turning away from the door.

'Come, Karim. We still have to collect the necessary supplies and scout the area one final time before the operation can begin.'

'Yes, *Sahib*.' Karim's voice dripped self-satisfaction. I wanted to pull his beard out hair by hair and throttle him, and then bash in his employer's head. Unfortunately, the door was in the way.

'Mr Ambrose! Let me out!'

In answer, I heard only silence. Silence, and the sound of footsteps retreating down the hallway. Then those were gone, too.

I beat against the door, again and again, not because I thought I would be able to break it, but simply to vent my anger. Anger at him, and at myself. How could I have been so stupid? Of course he didn't want to let me come along! Of course he had a hidden trap laid for me! This was Rikkard Ambrose we were talking about. And I had forgotten that fact, and walked right into his trap.

Maybe I didn't deserve to come along on the great adventure. Maybe I deserved to stew here, in this office, like an old piece of beef in an old pot the cook forgot to take off the fire. I felt appropriately disgusted with myself.

When my hands hurt so badly I could hardly feel them anymore, I stopped torturing the office door. Instead, I looked around, desperate for a way to get out. But there was nothing. The office was just as bare as I remembered, with no possibilities of... wait a second.

In the farthest corner, there was a niche I hadn't noticed before. Quickly, I crossed the room to see what it contained, and found myself in front of a door. My heart made a leap! Could it be? Could my escape be so easy?

I reached for the doorknob. My fingers clasped the cool metal, turned it, and – the door was locked.

Blast, blast, blast!

Of course, my escape couldn't be that easy.

Turning around, my gaze drifted to the windows. They, too, appeared to be firmly shut and locked. I could break the glass, of course, but what would that gain me? If I shouted from the top floor to people in the street that one of London's richest financiers was keeping me prisoner in his office, this surely would bring the police down on me. I would be lucky if I ever got away, let alone in time to join Mr Ambrose in his illegal endeavour.

Yes, but it would make a nice, juicy scandal and annoy the hell out of him, wouldn't it?

True. But in my heart of hearts, I knew the problem was I *didn't want* to annoy him.

I wanted to *help* him.

Blast!

446

Resigned, I dragged my feet over to Mr Ambrose's desk and slumped into his chair. Not even the thought of what he might say, were he to know I was sitting in the chair reserved for the master of the house, could improve my mood right now. I sat there, in endless anxiety, horrible images flitting through my head the entire time: Mr Ambrose faced by a platoon of the Presidency Armies, Mr Ambrose being led off to a firing squad...

The thought sent a shock of pain through my heart.

But why? Why did I feel pain? For the future I might lose if he died? My job? No. This pain was not for me. It was for him. Maybe... maybe I didn't detest him quite as much as I had always imagined.

This is getting you nowhere, you lazy idiot! Think of something!

My fist came down on the desk, hard. Curse him! Curse him and his chauvinistic ways! How dare he go without taking me with him! Hadn't I earned the right to be a part of his life, to go where he went and support him in what he did? And he left me behind simply because I was no man!

But then, whispered a nasty little voice in my head, *maybe, if you were a man, you might not want to go with him so badly.*

Angrily, I sprang up and marched over to the window. The sun had risen by now. I could see people coming down the street. It wasn't difficult to pick out the ones who were heading to work at Mr Ambrose's: they were the ones running like scared rabbits.

Suddenly, it occurred to me that some of those people might know me from sight. If I smashed the window, and called out to someone who worked here, telling them that I had locked myself in and couldn't find my keys...

Even before the thought was finished thinking, I started pounding on the glass. If I had managed to break it, I would probably have cut my hands to ribbons. Yet the glass held firm, no matter how hard I pounded it.

Of course it did. This was Mr Ambrose's office. His walls were hard, his chairs were hard, his head was hard, why shouldn't his windows be hard, too? Plus, they were next to his archive and safe. Whatever these windows were made of, I would not be able to break them, not even with a hammer.

I went back to the chair of the man who had locked me in here and sat down again. A humourless smile spread on my face. My entire life I had been afraid of being trapped by a man. Most of my imaginings had contained such gruesome horrors as engagements, wedding bells and a honeymoon in the south of France followed by a slow death by domesticity. Never had I imagined being *literally* trapped by a man, in a room, high up in London's largest monument to Mammon. And, also, unlike in my imaginings, where the man himself would have been my prison and I would have wanted nothing more than to get away from him, now the room was my prison and I wished nothing more than for the man to be with me, or for me to be with him.

But not because I felt anything for him, of course! I was a strong, independent woman and would never have any sort of silly, soppy feelings for any man, least of all Rikkard Ambrose. I just...

My eyes slid shut, trying to keep the tears in.

Well, I just wished I were with him. That was all.

If only there were a way to have someone come and open a door...

Slowly, my eyes opened again – and fell on the pneumatic tube with the basket of message papers right beside it.

Slowly, as if I feared they might run away should I approach them too quickly, I stretched my hands out in the direction of quill and paper. My fingers were only a few inches away from the pen, my way to freedom. It didn't seem to want to make a run for it. My fingers closed.

Yes! A way to get out. A way to get to *him*.

But one thing after another.

Putting one of the little squares of message paper right in front of me, I dipped the quill into the ink. For a moment, the quill hovered hesitantly over the paper. I thought of the pale man who staffed the desk downstairs. What was Sallow-face's name again? Mr Ambrose had mentioned it to me once, not appreciating the accuracy of the nickname I had come up with...

Ah yes: Pearson!

Quickly, I wrote in my best imitation of Mr Ambrose's neat, precise handwriting:

Dear Mr Pearson,

Be so kind as to bring me a list of all last week's visitors, which I require for a project I am currently working on. I may not be in my office when you arrive. If that is the case, unlock the door and leave the list on my desk. Thank you.

Yours Sincerely,

Rikkard Ambrose

For a long moment, I stared down at what I had written. Then I crossed it out, grabbed another piece of paper and wrote:

Mr Pearson

Deposit a list of last week's visitors on my desk immediately.

Rikkard Ambrose

'There,' I murmured. 'Much more realistic.' My heart fluttering excitedly, I put the message into its metal container, shoved it into the tube and then examined the control board right beside it. This one was much more complicated than the one in my office, with innumerable dials, levers and buttons to reach every part of the vast complex which served Mr Ambrose as his headquarters.

I selected a lever labelled 'E.H.' and hoped fervently it stood for 'Entry Hall' and not 'Excrement Hatch'. Why did men have to make all technical devices so infernally complicated? With bated breath, I sat and hoped for a result from my wild plan.

Only two minutes later, hurried footsteps approached from outside. *Very* hurried footsteps. A grin spread over my face. Yes, my plan *had* worked. Whoever was coming did indeed believe the message to originate from Mr Ambrose.

It didn't take the runner long to reach the office door. He tried to turn the doorknob and, finding the door locked, hesitated. A moment later, I heard the sound of salvation: the jingling of keys. The lock made a clicking sound, and the door swung open, revealing Sallow-face, standing in the doorframe.

'Mr Ambrose,' he began, holding up a sheet of paper, 'I have your...'

Then he noticed that the figure he was facing had little resemblance to his master.

'Mister Linton!'

'Mr Pearson!' My smile widened into a joyous grin. 'You don't know how glad I am to see you.'

'Mr Linton,' the pale bureaucrat managed, obviously having to struggle hard in order to contain his tumultuous emotions, 'why, pray, are you sitting in Mr Ambrose's private chair?'

'Oh.' Looking down, I saw he was absolutely right. I had completely forgotten that I was reposing on my employer's official chair with my feet propped up on his desk, something that secretaries were probably not supposed to do. 'Well, I just thought I'd give it a try, you know?' I wiggled my behind for emphasis. 'To see it if is comfy or not.'

Sallow-face's features turned a little more yellow, which seemed to be his version of getting angry red blotches on the cheeks.

'It is no concern of yours how "comfy" this honoured seat is, Mr Linton,' he informed me, glaring at me as if I had sat on a king's throne and committed high treason. 'You shall never have another chance to sit there! Where is Mr Ambrose?'

'Oh, he... he is in the safe, checking something,' I lied and, when Sallow-face turned in the direction of the safe, hurriedly added: 'And he doesn't want to be disturbed.'

'I see.' Sallow-face turned back to me. I, by now, had risen from my traitorous position on Mr Ambrose's throne and was thus not quite as fiercely glared at as before. 'Mr Linton, Mr Ambrose told me to bring him this.' He held out the list of visitors. 'Should I wait here for him, or...'

'Leave it with me,' I told him. 'I'll see that he gets it.'

He narrowed his eyes mistrustfully. 'On your honour as a gentleman? This is very important business material. Mr Ambrose trusts me with the most important tasks of all his employees. He told me himself that he needs this information as soon as may be.'

'Of course,' I replied, trying my best to keep a straight face. 'I swear on my honour as a gentleman that he shall receive it as soon as possible.'

'Very well, then, Mr Linton. Here. I shall trust you with this important document. Do not fail me, or Mr Ambrose.'

'I shall not.'

He nodded stiffly. 'Until later, Mr Linton.'

'Yes, until later, Mr Pearson. And...'

'Yes?'

'Leave the door open behind you, will you?'

~~**~*~*

Five minutes later I was out on the street, hailing the nearest cab. The very important business information Mr Pearson had delivered was crumpled up in the waste paper basket in Mr Ambrose's office.

A cab drove up beside me, and at exactly the right time! Just as I climbed in, I saw Mr Ambrose's chaise approach from the West End. Whatever arrangements he'd had to make before embarking on his secret mission lay in the opposite direction from his destination in the East End. Quickly, I ducked out of sight, peeking over the top of the cab's window frame. From this hidden post I watched, while the cabbie regarded my antics with interest.

There he was! Karim was driving, and Mr Ambrose, his face colder and more distant than ever, was sitting straight as a rod, two large bags and a small chest beside him.

'Follow that chaise!' I hissed at the cabbie, without resurfacing from my hidden position.

'Are ye from Scotland Yard, guv?'

'Yes,' I said boldly. 'This is a criminal investigation of the highest level. The fate of the British Empire, maybe even the world, is at stake!'

'Blimey!' The cabbie seemed very impressed. 'Well, we'd better be going then, ain't we?'

I was in hearty agreement. The cabbie was about to spur on his horses, when my hand shot up. 'Stop! Don't!' I had just remembered something. Of course! 'Don't follow them. I've changed my mind.'

The cabbie's face fell. 'No chase, guv?'

I smiled. 'Only because I already know where they are going.'

~~**~*~*

On the entire way to number 97, East India Dock Road, the cabbie mumbled and complained. Apparently, he had read enough about the adventures of Scotland Yard detectives to know that this was not how things were done. Detectives of Scotland Yard were supposed to chase after their prey in an exciting race, not leisurely drive to wherever it was their prey was going because they already knew the place. Such a thing was apparently simply not done.

On arrival in East India Dock Road, still some distance away from number 97, I paid him with the last money I had left over from pawning my uncle's walking stick and got out of the cab, promising myself again to retrieve the stick with my very first earned money. Well, maybe *after* I had bought a really big piece of solid chocolate. A girl has to have her treats in life.

The cabbie took the money and looked around curiously. 'This is where ye wanted to go, guv? But there ain't nothing close to 'ere except the docks.'

I winked at him, in what I hoped was a mysterious manner. 'Exactly. Things being brought in and out of the country... maybe not as they are supposed to be.'

'Oh, I see,' the cabbie said, though this obviously wasn't the case. 'Well, good luck to you, guv!'

Turning his coach around, he cried an encouragement to his horse and drove off towards the western, safer parts of the city. Looking after him, I suddenly wished I could follow. But I had made my choice.

With a sigh, I turned to face my destination. Not that I could see very much of it – it was mid-day, and the broad street was crowded as could be. Carts loaded with goods and large omnibuses packed full to bursting with dockworkers drove up and down this broad way of British Commerce, and people stood on all the street corners, waving their wares and yelling at the top of their voices to get the attention of potential customers. I supposed they thought yelling would give them an advantage over the large, but completely silent, billboards and posters which spread over many of the exterior walls.

I probably should have been grateful for all the noise. Nobody paid attention to me as I wandered down the crowded street. While in the West End of London, people had given my baggy trousers and loose-fitting old tailcoat strange glances, here, nobody looked twice at the strange little figure wandering down the street. A lot of people here wore clothes that didn't fit them well, probably because they had originally not been theirs. It was quite liberating in a way, swimming in a sea of people who didn't pay any attention to me and wanted nothing from me but that I returned the courtesy. It made me feel... free.

Of course, the aforementioned sea of people also blocked my view of number 97.

I slowly made my way down the street. As I got closer to my destination, I started to draw more curious glances from the surrounding people, as if they found me unusual to look at. I had to admit, I returned the feeling: the farther down East India Dock Road I went, the more the faces of passers-by changed in shade and form: from glances I caught of their faces, I thought noses were broader than usual, and their eyes strangely slitted. I thought I was imagining things, until one of the street-hawkers approached me, starting to address me in a strange tongue I had never heard before. At the sight of his face, I jumped back in shock.

Holy Hell! Who plucked me up from the earth and put me down in Peking?

Then it came to me. Of course! I had heard once that, in the some parts of the East End, there lived a large group of workers from China. This must be it. Chinatown.

Looking frantically from one strange face to another, I tried to remember what else I had heard about this area of my own city that was a foreign country. Only now did I see the colourful ribbons suspended over the street, the dragons painted on house walls, and the strange cuts of people's clothing.

Think! Think! Isn't there anything you recall about this place?

Vaguely, I seemed to remember somebody calling it the filthiest, most disreputable rat hole in all of London. Who had this information come from again?

Ah yes, my aunt.

So, hopefully, it's actually a quiet neighbourhood with nice, well-behaved people.

I caught the gaze of a particularly slant-eyed youth, who was staring at me over a knife he used to clean his fingernails.

Hopefully.

Making some apologetic gesture to the hawker, who had now taken something strange-smelling and steaming from his tray and was waving it in front of my face, I retreated hurriedly. Pressing myself as closely to the walls of the houses as I could, I made my way down the street without any further delay. As if it could protect me from the strange environment, I turned up the collar of my tailcoat and buried my too-European face in the depths of Uncle Bufford's old, moth-eaten Sunday best.

I went down the street as quickly as I could manage without running, counting the numbers on the opposite side as I did so.

Number 89, a butcher's shop...

Number 91, an apartment building...

Number 93, an... an...

Well, I wasn't exactly sure what it was. It was some kind of unidentifiable building, with a few ladies around the entrance whose clothing seemed to be even more loose-fitting and considerably more revealing than mine.

Number 95, a liquor store...

Number 97, a... Hell's whiskers!

Quickly, I jumped back into the nearest alley. The man I had spotted on the opposite side of the street turned his head; he must have caught my movement out of the corner of his eye. As he turned, I saw I had been right in thinking I had recognized him.

Warren.

Warren was here. And where Warren was, Mr Ambrose would not be far behind.

He looked around once more, then, shrugging, started to haggle again with a Chinese hawker over the price of some oriental artefact he was apparently trying to purchase. Or, more likely, *pretending* to purchase. He wasn't here to buy something exotic for the mantelpiece. He was here for the same reason I was here. The building right across the street from the alley in which I was hiding.

It was an impressive brick bulk: a broad façade, at least forty yards, with higher portions of the building rising threateningly up out of the roof in the centre and at every corner. Originally, it must have had many windows, but now it was obviously a warehouse, since most of the windows had been bricked over.

Or... was it? Behind the few, narrow openings in the brick walls, I could see movement. Not what you would expect in a warehouse where tin plates and cotton trousers waited for weeks before they were shipped to God only knew where. And the narrow, high parts of the building at each corner, connected by walls and walkways... they looked almost like watchtowers.

On the highest of the towers, I saw, blinking in the mid-day sun, the brass number 97.

Over the top of the building, in the distance, I could make out tops of masts, swaying in the breeze. The street wasn't called East India Dock Road for nothing. The docks of the East India Company, the centre of its web of power extending over half the world to the distant, tropical sub-continent of India, were only a few dozen yards away. Right next to this building.

There! There it is again!

Once more, I saw something move through one of the narrow windows, and caught the flash of a red uniform.

This is no bloody warehouse!

I waited, hidden in the shadows of the alley. After a while, Warren disappeared. In his stead, other men appeared, some European, some Chinese, some an unidentifiable mix. All lingered in front of number 97 for a little while before disappearing, only to reappear some time later, hovering and watching. Nobody would have noticed. Nobody, that is, who hadn't seen many of these faces before in Mr Ambrose's office.

I had.

Slowly, the sun began its descent towards the horizon. As it did so, people started to disappear into their houses. Nobody seemed to want to stay out in the street at night in this neighbourhood. Doors closed, and little could be heard from inside. Only from number 93 you still heard sounds. The scantily dressed ladies who lived there seemed in no hurry to go to sleep.

As the last vestiges of sunlight dwindled, lights were lit inside of number 97. Squinting, I concentrated on one of the narrow windows, high, high above me. It wasn't long before my earlier observations were confirmed: a flash of red and gold passed the window. And again! And again! Red and gold – like on the uniforms of a soldier of the Presidency Armies.

Suddenly, I heard a rattle and jumped, whirling around. But the rattle was not coming from behind me, nor was it coming from the main street. Rather, it sounded as if it was coming from a side street, parallel to the one in which I was hiding.

Quickly ducking into a narrow path between two brick houses, I made my way towards the origin of the sound. I thought it was somehow familiar – and I was not mistaken.

Looking around the corner of the house, I saw Mr Ambrose's chaise coming up the street. It stopped, well out of sight or hearing of the guards in the towers of number 97. Mr Ambrose slid out of the passenger compartment with one fluid, precise movement. The tails of his black tailcoat fluttered around him like dark wings.

'Warren?' he called in a voice no louder than a whisper.

The black-clad figure of Warren stepped out of a doorway, where he had concealed himself. He bowed to Mr Ambrose.

'We've been watching the place, observing the soldiers just as you instructed, Sir.'

'Adequate.'

'Thank you, Sir. Here is the report with their duty roster.' He handed over a piece of paper to his master, who nodded in acknowledgement. 'But...'

Warren hesitated.

'But what?' Mr Ambrose's voice was cool and distant as ever.

'But we think the soldiers are not the only guards, Sir. We have caught glimpses of movements on the roof. Understand me, we didn't actually see anybody, we only caught a flash of dark brown and grey here and there.' He shook his head, looking over his shoulder at number 97 nervously. 'I've never seen anything like it.'

Mr Ambrose's jaw muscles twitched, and Karim let out a long string of foreign words that were better not translated.

'They are here!' Mr Ambrose hissed.

'They?'

'A squad of special riflemen in the Presidency Armies who are at Lord Dalgliesh's disposal alone.' Mr Ambrose's voice could have frozen lava. I gathered he had met this special squad before, and did not have fond memories of them. 'They use a native plant to die their coats in mottled tones of brown and grey, which makes them hard to see in daytime, and helps them to disappear almost into nothing during the night.'[50]

'But why should one wish for soldiers not to be seen during a battle?' Warren asked, his mouth slightly open.

'These special riflemen are not intended for open battles. Dalgliesh employs them for... different purposes.'

His tone of voice made it clear that nobody who wished to continue to sleep at night should ask what those purposes were. Warren looked slightly sick. Mr Ambrose didn't seem to care. He said no more, but started to study the paper Warren had handed to him. After a while, he nodded.

'Whether Lord Dalgliesh's personal commando is here or not, this will have to suffice.'

Karim looked worried. And if I could see that from where I was standing, in the dark, and through the vast amount of beard blocking my view of his face, he must have been *really* worried.

'*Sahib*, maybe we should...'

Mr Ambrose threw him a look, and the Mohammedan stopped in mid-sentence.

Warren was not as wise, however. He cleared his throat.

'Um... Sir, forgive me for asking, but why exactly have we been noting down the guard changes and been keeping watch on this house?'

Mr Ambrose was studying the list again. He didn't look up. 'As preparation for a break-in, of course.'

'*What?*' At an angry gesture from Karim, Warren lowered his voice, but it sounded no less stricken than before. 'Sir! You have to be joking!'

'No, I do not have to be. In fact, I have never in my life felt any irresistible compulsion to joke.'

Warren swallowed. He seemed to realize with whom he was arguing here.

'Sir... I ... I'm afraid I cannot in good conscience be a part of an illegal activity.'

Mr Ambrose now had exchanged the list of guard changes for a ground plan he had taken out of his leather bag. He still didn't look up.

'Then do it in bad conscience, Mr Warren. I don't care, either way.'

'Mr Ambrose...'

---

[50] Squads like this did indeed exist in the armies of the East India Company. It is here that camouflage gear for soldiers is said to have originated.

'You didn't seem to care about bending the law when we laid our hands on that snake Simmons.'

Warren bit his lip. 'That was different.'

'Because,' Mr Ambrose concisely stated, 'he was a private secretary, not a Peer of the Realm, like the owner of that building over there, correct?'

To this, Warren didn't seem to have anything to say.

'Don't worry.' Mr Ambrose exchanged one set of plans for another. 'What you have done is quite enough. I won't require your services further tonight.'

'You won't?'

Mr Ambrose gave a derisive jerk of his head. 'You don't think I would entrust *you* with a task as important as this? No. One thing I learned early in life is: If you want something done well, do it yourself.'

If possible, Warren paled even more.

'Mr Ambrose, you cannot mean... You are a gentleman, not a criminal! You cannot mean that you are planning to break into...'

At that, Mr Ambrose looked up, his eyes flashing icily.

'Dalgliesh took something that belongs to me, Mr Warren. If that happened in the colonies, and if he were any other man, I wouldn't hesitate to put a bullet in his head. Here, business practices are slightly different. But I will get back what is mine, and you'd rather not stand in my way.'

Warren swallowed again. He retreated a step, and bowed. 'No, Sir. Of course not, Sir. Your word is my command, Sir.'

'Indeed it is.' Mr Ambrose stuck the ground plan back into the bag, slung it over his shoulder and took out of the coach another one, which he handed to Karim. 'Stay here, Mr Warren. Guard the coach, and wait until at least one of us returns.' He turned away from Warren, towards the entrance of the alley and number 97. 'Karim, we're going in. Stay behind me and watch my back.'

'Yes, *Sahib!*'

I thought it was about time to make my presence known.

With a little smile, I stepped forward, out of the shadows, and raised a hand. 'And where do you want me, Sir?'

A Man's Work

To see actual surprise on the rock-hard face of Mr Rikkard Ambrose would have been too much to hope for. But I had the satisfaction of seeing one of his eyelids twitch about half a millimetre when he caught sight of me.

'Mr Linton...!' he breathed.

Karim jumped back, uttering another incomprehensible curse.

'She really is *Ifrit, Sahib!* She can walk through walls and appear out of thin air!'

'Actually,' I remarked, smiling at him, 'I drove here in a cab. Sorry to disappoint you.' My eyes flicked from Karim to Warren. Apparently, he was too startled to have noticed Karim's slip of referring to yours truly as 'she.' But really, it was not Warren's reaction to my appearance, or Karim's, that I was interested in. Slowly, my eyes drifted back to Mr Ambrose.

His face was still devoid of anything akin to emotion. But there was a muscle twitching in his chiselled jaw.

'A *cab*?' he said, as if it were the dirtiest of words.

'Yes, Sir.'

'And this cab, I suppose, is not in the vicinity any more to take you right back to where you came from?'

'No, Sir.'

'I didn't think so.'

Stepping closer to me, he lowered his voice to a chilling whisper that only I could hear.

'I am not commonly given to expletives, Mr Linton, yet under the present circumstances I find myself justified in enquiring what the bloody hell you think you are doing here!'

'Coming with you,' I said cheerily, though the tone of his voice made my whole body quiver.

'Did I or did I not tell you to stay away from this, Mr Linton?'

'You did, Sir. But it is after hours. You cannot tell me what to do now.'

Thunderclouds full of lightning flashed in his dark eyes.

'Did you or did you not hear what I discussed with Warren, Mr Linton?'

'Yes, Sir. I did.'

'And? *Well?*'

'Well what, Sir?'

'Tonight's operation will be deadly dangerous. The moment we are spotted, we will be shot down like animals. Our corpses will be thrown from the docks and never again see the light of day!'

His words sent a cold shiver down my back. To die... to actually die. I had never contemplated it before. I was nineteen, still so young, and had hardly seen anything of the world. And I could die tonight, if I continued on this mad course. Why not turn back? Why not turn away from him, let him go alone? He surely wouldn't fault me for it.

'Never see the light of day again? My, my.' I shook my head. 'I'm sure that would worry me a lot, once I was dead. Terrible fate for a corpse.'

What was I doing? This was no time for sarcasm? This was serious!

Yes, it is, a tiny voice in the back of my mind said. *Deadly serious - which is exactly why you have to go with him.*

'Never, ever joke in my presence again, Mr Linton,' Mr Ambrose said in a voice that could have frozen an erupting volcano. 'I do not appreciate it.'

'Really? I would never have guessed.'

'The same goes for flippancy, Mr Linton.' He stepped forward until we were almost nose to chiselled chin. Damn, he was tall! 'I meant what I said. This is dangerous.' For a moment I saw a flash of something in his eyes that I think I was not supposed to see. Anxiety, maybe? For what? For the recovery of his lost file?

456

Or for you?

No! Impossible!

It was gone too quickly for me to see, in any case. Again, a coating of frost closed the brief opening in his armour.

'I know that it is dangerous,' I said impulsively, reaching out to touch him. 'That is why I have to come.'

Hell's whiskers! Why did I just say that? What if he interpreted something into it that I hadn't meant? Or worse, what if he interpreted something into it that I *had* meant? I snatched my hand back before it made contact with his face.

Quickly, I added, trying for a lighter tone: 'After all, I can't let you go in there with only *him* for protection.' I gestured at Karim. 'You'll be dead before you take two steps.'

Though my words had been too low for him to have heard, Karim seemed to have guessed the general message of my gesture. He gritted his teeth, and his massive right paw closed around the hilt of his sabre.

Mr Ambrose took another step forward. We were now standing almost close enough to touch.

'And what,' he hissed, 'makes you think that I will take you along? I could have Warren take you and hold you here until Karim and I have returned. He might be afraid of Dalgliesh, but even he should be capable of restraining someone like *you*.'

Heat rose to my cheeks. I knew what he meant – someone like me: a girl.

'Don't count on it,' I growled, putting my hands on my hips and returning the cold glare he shot at me with fire in my eyes. 'I'll bite the first man who dares to touch me! And I'll scream bloody murder, too!'

Mr Ambrose, who had just been about to signal Warren, froze.

'No, you won't,' he said in a low, threatening voice. 'You won't make a sound, understood?'

Immediately, I saw I had found my perfect weapon. 'I won't if you take me with you,' I offered. 'Otherwise...' I let the sentence hang in the air with dark promise.

Mr Ambrose's hands clenched into fists. His eyes flicked from me, to the exit of the alley and his goal beyond, and back again. I knew exactly what he was thinking. If I screamed, the guards would hear. His precious operation would have to be postponed.

'If you scream, I will sack you,' he threatened.

'You can't sack me for something I do after hours. I could paint Buckingham Palace in pink, and you wouldn't be allowed to throw me out. So, what is it to be?'

Silence.

I quirked an eyebrow at him.

'Well, Sir?'

More silence.

'Oh well... as you wish.' Opening my mouth, I took a deep breath.

Before I could utter a single syllable, Mr Ambrose was on me. His hand clamped down over my mouth, his hard arm shot around my waist, pulling me towards him. Suddenly, my back was pressed against a hard wall of sinews and muscle. I struggled, but it was in vain. His arms held me as tightly as iron fetters. Only that iron fetters would probably not have felt quite so interesting. After a few moments, my resistance waned. I became very aware of his fingers on my lips, almost as if I were...

'You,' he said in a tone imported straight from Iceland, 'are an insufferable nuisance.'

His arms tightened even more for a second or two, holding me closer than iron fetters ever could. Besides, iron fetters could never make my heart rate pick up like it did just then.

'You also,' he continued grudgingly, 'have some courage and loyalty. More than I would have expected from a–'

He cut off.

Yet I knew what he had been going to say.

All of a sudden, he released me, and I stumbled away from him, turning as I did so. He was staring at me with his totally unreadable, sea-coloured eyes, the gloom of the alley making them appear even more dark than usual.

'You can accompany us,' he said. 'But if you get us caught, you are dismissed, no discussion! Understood?'

'Um... I thought if we were caught, we would be shot.'

'I will dismiss you *before* we are shot, Mr Linton.'

'Yes, Sir! I understand, Sir!'

Turning away, he motioned to Karim. Suddenly he was all business again.

'Show Mr Linton the plans, Karim.'

Karim's beard bristled in outrage.

'But *Sahib...!*'

'If he does not know where we are going, he is likely to get us caught. Show him the plans of the building, Karim. Now!'

Karim clenched his teeth. His master's tone brooked no discussion. Reluctantly, he unslung the bag from over his shoulder and pulled out of it a large roll of paper, which he unrolled and held against the side of the coach in a spot where the moonlight shone into the alley and illuminated all in its path. By the cold, blueish light I was just able to make out thin lines on the paper, forming what looked like the intricate plan of a large complex.

'We got these out of the city records,' Mr Ambrose explained curtly. 'They're decades old, and probably not up-to-date anymore, but Dalgliesh has made sure that any more recent versions have disappeared from the face of the earth.'

He pointed to a spot at the eastern side of the complex.

'We will enter the building here–'

'Why on the east side?' I asked. 'That's between the building and the docks, Lord Dalgliesh's centre of power. Isn't it likely that there will be many of his men, there?'

Mr Ambrose threw me a look. 'Which is exactly why we will come from this direction. He will not expect it. Do not interrupt me, Mr Linton. I don't wish to have to repeat myself.' He tapped the point on the plan. 'As I said, we will enter here–'

'How exactly?' I demanded. 'In case you hadn't noticed, there's a wall in the way.'

His finger stopped tapping.

'What did I say about not interrupting, Mr Linton?'

'Excuse me, Sir. Carry on, Sir.'

'The guards will be drawn off by a distraction on the western side of the building. We will have to climb over the wall, and thus penetrate into the inner courtyard.'

I still couldn't see how we would be able to climb over a wall that was at least 24 feet high, but I held my tongue. From the way Mr Ambrose's left little finger was twitching, I surmised this was not a time to rile him.

'There will be guards on and in the inner building, too.' His finger moved across the courtyard to a central, U-shaped building consisting of a large central part flanked by two wings. 'They might not see us against the dark brick wall, but the courtyard is brightly lit. As soon as we attempt to cross it, we will be spotted.'

'So what do we do?'

Instead of my receiving another rebuke for having interrupted His Mightiness, it was Karim who answered this time.

'Disguise ourselves,' he grumbled, opening a bag and pulling out something bright red. It took me a few seconds to recognize uniforms of the Presidency Armies.

Suddenly, Mr Ambrose whirled around to face me.

'But that's it! Karim, you only brought two uniforms! So sh- *he* can't come with us. Mr Linton, you...'

His voice trailed off as he saw Karim's embarrassed expression. Then, his gaze wandered to the uniforms, of which, there was no doubt, there were three.

'I thought,' Karim growled, throwing a venomous look at Warren, who retreated a step or two, 'that *he* would be coming with us.'

Mr Ambrose's little finger twitched again, overcome by uncontrollable rage.

'Fine,' he said coolly, and turned back to the plans. 'We will descend from the wall and hide behind this shed here, where brooms and tools are being kept, according to my information. There, we will change into guard uniforms, so we can cross the courtyard unmolested.'

With his forefinger, he tapped a spot marked with a longish rectangle and a question mark.

'The door to the main compound may or may not be locked. My sources have not been able to determine that. But from what I know of Dalgliesh, it will be locked thrice and bound with chains. That, however, is no insurmountable problem.'

It seemed to be, to me, all right. I was just about to open my mouth when Mr Ambrose looked up from the map to throw me a cold glare.

I closed my mouth again.

'Once inside, things will become more difficult,' he continued.

Oh, so they've been easy up until now?

'We do not know exactly where the file is. We believe it to be somewhere in this area.' His finger moved to a red circle that centred on the upper left corner of the building. 'This is where the office of the overseer was, back in the days when this was still a factory. It is, in all probability, where Dalgliesh's office is situated now, and where the file is kept.'

He traced a route from the front door to the red circle. I could see faint lines on the old paper, marking a narrow hallway. 'We will follow this corridor here, and hopefully will not encounter any guards. Yet, even if we do, they should take us for comrades and let us pass. The corridor will lead us straight to where we suspect Dalgliesh's office to be. When we are there, we will take the file and leave the same way we came.'

'But... won't the file be behind locked doors?'

Mr Ambrose patted one of his mysterious bags. 'Doors are not impenetrable, Mr Linton. What did I say about interruptions?'

'So sorry, Sir.'

'Karim?'

The Mohammedan stepped forward. '*Sahib?*'

'Since you were so obliging as to provide three uniforms, you surely have also brought three of the cloaks?'

'Certainly, *Sahib.*'

From his bag, Karim withdrew three mottled brown-and-grey cloaks. A strangled gasp came from Warren, and I remembered what Mr Ambrose had said about the special unit of riflemen under Lord Dalgliesh's command.

Mr Ambrose threw Warren a look. 'Yes. It is not only Lord Dalgliesh's men who can steal up on you unsuspected, Mr Warren. Remember that. Remember it well.'

He threw one of the cloaks at me, wordlessly. As I caught it, he threw the second around his shoulders and, a moment later, seemed to melt into the darkness. I saw only a vague shape moving away.

'Come, Mr Linton,' his voice called out, cold and imperious.

I made a move to follow him. Suddenly, Warren, who had watched the whole scene from the background, his mouth slightly open, was stirred into motion. Quickly, he took two steps forward and grasped me by the arm.

'Mr Linton! You are not truly going to accompany them, are you?'

I looked down at his hand. Quickly, he removed it.

'Yes,' I said. 'I am.'

'I hope you do not think I am speaking out of term, Mr Linton, but I would strongly advise against it. The man they are going up against...' Warren drew his coat closer around himself, as if he were suddenly feeling the cold night air more strongly. 'Let us just say, you hear rumours when you serve the members of London's high society like I do. I council you, Mr Linton, desist. Go home. It is nothing any man would have to be ashamed of.'

I gave him a scathing look.

'Yes,' I said. 'Any *man* wouldn't have to be.'

Then, without staying to explain my words, I turned and, drawing the cloak around me, followed Mr Ambrose into the darkness.

I nearly had to run to keep up with Mr Ambrose as we passed through the dark streets of Chinatown. We circumvented number 97, always keeping a great distance between ourselves and the wall. Not once did he or Karim slow down, his long legs swinging as regularly as a pendulum, the strange, mottled cloak fluttering around his shoulders.

'Why... are we... in such a hurry?' I gasped, out of breath.

His voice as he answered was, of course, perfectly calm and collected. 'Your unexpected appearance and the necessity for an explanation of our plans has cost us time. Time we do not have. The distraction for the guards is scheduled to occur in exactly...' Fishing his watch out of his pocket, he let it snap open. For a moment, I saw the coat of arms on the lid shining in the moonlight. '...six minutes and thirty-seven seconds.'

'What is this distraction?' I panted.

'Wait and see.'

Apparently, he was not in a talkative mood. What a great surprise.

By the time we stopped behind a cart parked on the side of the street that ran along the eastern side of number 97, my lungs felt fit to burst. I leaned against the cart, and for the next few minutes concentrated fully on getting my breathing under control again. I really had to find some way of building up my stamina if this sort of thing would come up regularly in this job.

Out of the corner of my eye, I could see Mr Ambrose glancing around the cart. My lungs feeling normal enough by now to allow some movement, I followed his example and saw the bright red figures of Presidency Army soldiers, parading on the walls. Decoys only, as I now knew. The real guards were hiding in the shadows.

'We can thank God this cart is standing here,' I whispered. 'Or else we would be clearly visible – perfect target practise for Lord Dalgliesh's personal team of pheasant hunters.'

'Thank me instead of God,' Mr Ambrose told me without taking his eyes off the roof of number 97. 'I had one of my men park the cart here this morning.'

'Hm.' It had been a clever idea. But if he expected a compliment from me, he would have to wait for a long time. Besides, I was much too interested in something else. 'What is this mysterious distraction you keep not talking about? How will it direct the attention of Lord Dalgliesh's guards away from us?'

Retreating behind the cart again, he let his watch snap open a second time.

'You shall find out in exactly two minutes and fourteen seconds, Mr Linton.'

'Why not tell me now? Are you absolutely sure it will get the attention of *all* the guards?' I persisted. 'I'm not anxious to get my head perforated, you know. What if your distraction isn't distracting enough?'

'I am certain that they will not have eyes – or ears for that matter – for anything else. We will have about a minute before they focus their attention back on the street again.'

Once more, I opened my mouth to ask what was going to happen. But before I could speak, he pointed around the cart towards the corner of number 97's outer wall.

'When the distraction occurs, we will head for the corner, understand? I suspect that the gunmen aren't actually sitting on the roof. More likely, they are looking out through dormers or even lifted roofing tiles. This will mean they will have a blind spot at the corner, where the sides of the roof meet. Once we are across the street and at the wall, they should not be able to see us, and won't shoot.'

Oh, good. I breathed a sigh of relief.

'But we should be quick anyway, just in case I am mistaken.'

Not so good.

Mr Ambrose nodded to Karim. 'You know what to do once we're there?'

The mountainous Mohammedan nodded, patting the bag slung over his shoulder. Not for the first time, I wondered what was inside.

'Yes, *Sahib.*'

'Adequate.' Mr Ambrose raised his watch again. 'Brace yourselves. It will begin in ten... nine... eight... seven... six... five... four... three... two... one... *now!*'

Nothing happened.

With an angry snap, Mr Ambrose shut his watch.

'They're late,' he complained. 'You can't rely on anybody to be punctual anym–'

Suddenly, there was an almighty clash from the other side of the building. Screams pierced the night over the city. For a moment, I thought that some sort of street brawl had broken out.

Bloody hell! Has he hired people to attack Lord Dalgliesh's guards? They'll all be shot down!

But then the clash came again, and it didn't sound like swords or guns – rather, like a cymbal.

An orchestra attack?

'What the bloody hell...' I started to whisper, but was cut off by more screaming. It didn't exactly sound painful. If I had to choose an adjective, I would have said 'enthusiastic'. But that couldn't be, could it?

Curiously, I peered around the cart. Coloured lights were visible around the corner of a house. It sounded like people were approaching. But... the sound of the footsteps wasn't right. It didn't sound like normal traffic, or even soldiers marching – more like people at a ball, dancing to a rhythm. But who would be crazy enough to stage a ball on a street in the middle of Chinatown, in front of a house with professional gunmen on the roof?

Who do you think?

The sound came nearer – and then, without warning, the head of a giant, red-golden beast appeared in the street. It was at least two yards high, with thick spikes on its forehead and snout. A livid red tongue protruded from its horrifying maul that could surely swallow a girl whole, and as it reared up into the air, a roar and renewed clashing cut through the dark night again.

The monsters eyes fixed directly on me.

I opened my mouth to scream – and a hand clamped down on my lips. 'I said,' I heard a very cool, controlled voice at my ear, 'brace yourselves. That means no horrified screaming.'

'Bmm! Hmpff!'

My attempts to warn him of the approach of the giant monster went unheard. He pressed down harder.

'Look,' he told me. 'Look closely.'

No! I don't want to look! I can't even stand to look at that grey beast of a horse you own, and this – this is a thousand times worse! Run! Run for your life, you granite-headed idiot!

What apocalyptical demon had he set loose in the streets of London, while the unsuspecting public slept in their beds, and the police were nowhere to be seen?

'Look, Mr Linton. That is an order.'

Unwillingly, I moved my eyes to rest on the red-and-golden monster. For a moment, I just stared in fear as the wild eyes moved from left to right and the head jerked in wild contortions. Then...

Then I saw the pair of legs protruding from the lower part of the head.

Dear, merciful God! Has the monster already devoured somebody?

But no. Those legs weren't sticking out of the beast's mouth. They were just protruding from the bottom of the head, as if a man were standing inside it, holding it up. For the first time, I noticed that the face of the beast was hard and immovable as wood, and that its tongue did not move, and neither did its jaws. I saw the glint of paint on its features, and it dawned on me that I might have slightly overreacted.

My body relaxed.

Mr Ambrose's arms, still around me, did not.

And, for the second time in half an hour, I realized that I could feel his fingers on my lips, and his stone-hard, sinuous body pressed against my back. Suddenly, the fake monster was only a dim memory. Suddenly, I was wondering whether he remembered the last time, too, and what it felt like to him. My derrière was pressed very tightly against him, soft flesh against hard muscle. More soft flesh than was probably advisable. I found myself wishing that I had tied my corset a bit more tightly in that area.

Don't be ridiculous, I chided myself. *Why should you care what Mr Ambrose thinks about how you feel, or that he probably thinks your bottom is too fat?*

Not that it was, mind you. A little on the generous side, maybe, but not fat. No, definitely not.

Mr Ambrose cut short my posterior musings by releasing me and stepping back.

'Be quiet, Mr Linton,' he warned me, his voice as cool as ever. No. He definitely hadn't been thinking of anything... down there.

Quickly, I tried to push all thoughts of the feel of his body out of my mind. It wasn't too difficult, considering the circumstances. My eyes were drawn once more to the giant beast, of which now, not only the head, but a long, snake-like body was in view, each part of it supported by another pair of legs. The snake-like thing had by now started advancing towards the western side of number 97.

'What in St George's name is that?' I panted, pointing at the wagging head of the fake monster.

'Chinese New Year celebrations,' Mr Ambrose said, his face as straight as a ruler. 'The performance is called "The Dance of the Dragon", I believe.'

'*Is* it the Chinese New Year?'

'No. But I doubt Lord Dalgliesh's guards know that. They are not Chinese.'

'Well, fortunately, neither am I,' I said, watching the head of the monster with trepidation. 'Real animals are scary enough. I have no idea why any people would want to dream up even more monstrous creatures, and for a celebration, to boot. Give me a nice, quiet suffragist demonstration any day...'

'If you're quite finished, we should get going.' Mr Ambrose jerked his head in the direction of number 97. 'Or we will get shot in spite of the performance of our Chinese friends, and I'd hate to have spent enough money for an entire dragon and twenty-four pairs of legs for nothing.'

Without waiting for my response, he whirled. Drawing his cloak in closely around himself, he started across the street. Crouching low, he stayed out of the light of the street lamps, jumping from shadow to shadow. Karim followed without hesitation.

I gazed at the thirteen steps or so that separated me from number 97 with trepidation. At any one of the thirteen steps I would have to take, I might get shot. I wondered what it would feel like, having a bullet pierce my flesh. Yet – the longer I stood here wondering, the more likely I would be to find out. And *he* was already halfway across.

You don't really have a choice, do you?

I threw myself forward.

When I had just taken my first step, I thought I saw a glint on the rooftop of number 97, and my heart almost stopped. The barrel of a gun! I expected the crack of the shot, the bullet hitting me – nothing came. It must simply have been a drainpipe, glinting in the moonlight.

Ten steps left.

Inwardly, I cursed the London authorities for making this road so damnably wide. Couldn't they have reduced the size a bit? Couldn't they have felt compassion for poor girls who were running across the street in the darkness, hoping not to get shot by villainous assassins? I was sure if there had been a woman on the planning committee, she would have thought of it! It was such an obvious point to consider in city planning.

Seven steps left.

Every time one of my feet hit the ground it sounded like a drumbeat in my ear. I wondered at the fact that the men on the roof hadn't heard it yet and put a nice, round hole into me. But in reality, the clash of the cymbals and dozens of thundering feet on the opposite side of the building were probably more than covering the noise of my advance.

But they could still see me, if they were not looking the other way. I drew the mottled cloak tighter around me, though I could not really believe in its powers of disguise. It was only a cloak, after all...

Three steps left.

I surged forward with renewed effort. In front of me, I could see Mr Ambrose and Karim appearing out of the gloom. They were pressed against the brick wall of number 97. Closing my eyes, I leapt forward. If I was to get shot at the last moment, I didn't want to see the blood.

I slammed into something hard – much harder than a brick wall! From above me, I heard a sharp exhalation, and then, suddenly, a set of arms was around me, pulling me to a chest that felt wonderfully familiar.

Well, maybe that's because you've been pressed up against it twice already in the last hour!

This time, he wasn't holding me to shut my mouth, though, and my back wasn't to his front. Instead, the hard muscles of his chest were pressed more tightly against mine than they had ever been before. He was holding me so tightly, I thought he didn't ever want to let go again. I would not have minded if he never did. I felt so overjoyed to still be alive, and here, and with him...

A strange feeling flooded my body. A feeling of heat and weakness and wanting... something. From one moment to the next, I went limp in his arms, collapsing against his chest with a faint sigh.

What the hell is happening? Lilly to legs: start working again, now! Right now, do you hear me?

Above me, I heard him catch his breath. And then, something happened which I would never have thought possible, certainly not here. Not now. His hands started roaming over my body, expertly probing my face, my neck, my arms, my... oh my!

My heart beginning to beat a frantic rhythm, my legs wobbled and almost gave way. His hands travelled farther down, over my waist, down my hips and to my legs... wait a minute! What did he want down there?

My eyes fluttered open, just in time to see him straighten and give me a cold, questioning glance. 'Why did you sag against me?' he demanded in a low, burning cold voice. 'I have checked everywhere and cannot detect a single sign of a shot wound! Have you sprained your ankle?'

Checking for shot wounds? He was *checking for shot wounds*?

'Um... no.' Hurriedly, I straightened, hoping that with my tanned complexion and in the gloom of night, nobody could see my furious blush. 'I was just exhausted from the run, I suppose.'

He made a soft noise in his throat that combined a minimum use of his vocal cords with a maximum of male scorn. Then he turned to Karim, who had been watching everything with narrowed eyes. The minute Mr Ambrose turned towards him, his features became as neutral as Switzerland, though they remained considerably hairier.

Mr Ambrose didn't speak, but made a few, quick, hard gestures with his hand. Obviously, they must have meant something to Karim, who unslung the bag from over his shoulder and opened it. From its depth, he retrieved... was it a rifle? My eyes widened.

Is he going to shoot at the guards on the wall?

But no. Mr Ambrose was many things, but not a fool. And now that Karim lifted the thing up, I could see more clearly. Contrasted against the moon that rose above the roofs to the north, I could see that, while the object had the same basic shape as a rifle, two slightly curved arms extended from it, one on each side.

And there was something pointy at the end, some kind of arrow with a strange head. What in heaven's name...

Twang!

With a sharp snapping noise, the strange arrow flew upwards and over the wall. Behind it, a sort of tail was flailing in all directions. No – no tail, a rope!

I had to strain my ears to hear the dull thud as the arrow landed beyond the wall. And even so, I only heard it because I knew it was coming. The racket from the other side of the building was still overwhelming.

Mr Ambrose made another one of his cutting, silent gestures. I raised an eyebrow, quizzically.

'That means "move",' he hissed. 'Now *move*.'

Oh, I bet he wished he could use that strange sign language in the office! Then he wouldn't have to talk to me at all, or write, but could just order me about with a twitch of his hand. And what did he mean, move? Move where?

Karim was in motion already. With two steps he was at the rope. Giving it a hearty tug, he tested whether it sat well. Apparently not displeased, he gripped it with both hands.

For the first time, the significance of the rope hit me. Blimey! He was expecting me to climb *up there*?

Bracing his massive legs against the wall, the Mohammedan began to climb, determinedly. Soon, he had vanished into the darkness above me. Mr Ambrose followed, swift and graceful. And I...

Well, I followed, too. Probably more determined than swift or graceful.

After only half a yard or so, my arms began to scream in protest. My palms were on fire, bitten with the hot teeth of the coarse rope from which I hung like a leg of mutton from a meat hook. Clenching my teeth and ignoring the pain, I took one of my hands from the rope and reached upwards. Thank God I was wearing men's clothes! The weight of my usual collection of petticoats would have been enough to drag me to my doom.

Halfway up the rope I decided that, yes, my derrière *was* too fat. I really had to do something about it. Not for the sake of appealing to Mr Ambrose! No, not at all! Simply for the sake of rope climbing. Maybe I should eat less solid chocolate...

Three quarters of the way up, I looked towards the sky, only to see Mr Ambrose's face above me. He made another sign at me, which I immediately understood: *Hurry up! What are you dangling down there for?*

I clenched my teeth again, wishing I had enough breath for a solid, unladylike curse, and reached up once more.

Finally, I felt another hand close around mine and pull me up. It was a hand I knew well. Strong, smooth and hard. Mr Ambrose's hand. His other hand closed around my wrist and heaved. Maybe he groaned a little more than was strictly necessary. My derrière might be a little generous, but I wasn't *that* heavy!

I had just gotten my feet on solid ground once more, when Mr Ambrose grabbed my shoulders, pushing me forward and down. Before I knew what had happened, we were cowering on a stone staircase leading up to the wall, and looking over the edge of the walkway. Immediately, I saw why Mr Ambrose had pushed me. At the other end of the walkway, a soldier in red uniform had just reached one end of his round and was turning towards us. He had to have heard something, for there was a frown on his face when he surveyed the walkway.

Karim, who was kneeling beside us, raised an eyebrow, touching his sabre.

Mr Ambrose shook his head.

The soldier, who had no idea what kind of danger he had just escaped, shrugged and continued, while we slowly started edging down the stairs, away from him.

'Can soldiers of the Presidency army act as soldiers outside of British India?' I hissed. 'That is outside of their jurisdiction, isn't it?'

'Their jurisdiction is wherever Lord Dalgliesh can buy them jurisdiction,' Mr Ambrose replied coolly. 'Now be quiet, and follow me.'

He inched down the stairs, pressed tightly against the wall, his cane, which he had somehow managed to retain while climbing up that infernal wall, clutched tightly in his hand. I had no doubt it was the one with the concealed blade inside. He had come well prepared. For a moment, I wondered what arsenal Karim might have concealed underneath his turban. Probably a large one.

But large enough for an entire garrison of soldiers?

I wrenched my thoughts away from glinting steel and cracking guns. I had more pressing concerns. It was pitch-black here, in the shadow of the wall, and I had to be very careful not to stumble over my own feet and break my neck.

At the bottom of the stairs, we could hear faint voices. Mr Ambrose inched towards them, the grip on his cane tightening even more. Beyond him, I could just make out the outline of a large, wooden shed. The voices seemed to be coming from around its corner. Mr Ambrose leant forward and risked a peek.

Turning to us, he made a quick, jerking movement with his hand.

'It is all right to move,' Karim, who stood next to me, growled into my ear. 'They are distracted.'

He moved past me, behind the shed, and I followed. This must be the shed Mr Ambrose had mentioned. The one behind which we were to change into uniforms.

Opening his bag, Karim threw Mr Ambrose and me one uniform each, and kept another for himself. They quickly slipped into the red coats. The voices on the other side of the shed, meanwhile, moved away, until we were completely alone in the night.

Then, Karim withdrew a rather jaunty-looking blue hat with buttons on it from the bag and put it on his head in place of the turban, glaring at me, daring me to make a comment. Yet I was too busy to comment on his headgear. I had difficulties of my own.

With all the strength at my disposal, I tried once more what I had been trying for the last three minutes: to force the first button on my uniform into its buttonhole.

'There... um... is a slight problem,' I whispered.

'Indeed?' Mr Ambrose asked in a frigid whisper. He was wearing a hat with buttons on it too, and, to judge by the twitching of his little finger, wasn't too pleased about it.

I waved my arms, making the uniform stretch uncomfortably. 'The uniform is rather tight over my other clothes.'

'It may surprise you to hear this, Mr Linton, but *I do not care*. This is not a Paris fashion show.'

'It's not just uncomfortably tight, Sir. It's too tight to wear without popping buttons – at least over my other clothes. I shall have to... um... undress.'

For a moment, I saw a flicker of something in Mr Ambrose's eyes. Nothing hot, not even something warm, but there might just have been the flicker of something tepid at the centre of those dark, icy orbs. Yet he turned so quickly, I couldn't be sure.

'Get on with it, then,' he commanded, his voice as cold as ever.

Karim followed the example of his master and turned, though I had the impression that what he really wanted to do was run and hide behind the next wall.

I was feeling a little queasy, myself. For all my forthright behaviour in other areas of life, I had never been very forthright in the one area of life that usually led a girl to undress in front of men. I had to shiver at the very idea of it. Certainly I shivered at doing it here, in the cold night air, behind this dilapidated shed.

You probably wouldn't despise it quite so much if Mr Ambrose and you were alone, somewhere nice and warm, hm?

Immediately, I kicked that thought out of my mind, where it didn't belong.

Changing your clothes, I told myself. *That's all the reason why you're undressing now. To change your clothes. And he has got his back to you. He is not looking. He wouldn't even want to. And you do not want him to want to, understand?*

Glancing up at the back of the two men, I saw that Mr Ambrose had his arms crossed behind his back, and his little finger was twitching with the tempo of a sewing machine.

'Hurry up, Mr Linton,' he hissed, straightening his perky blue hat. 'If one of the soldiers comes around the shed now...'

'I thought they had gone.'

'They might come back. If they find you like this...'

'What do you think they will do?' I asked in a voice that, for some unfathomable reason, sounded teasing.

'Sound the alarm and come back with heavy artillery,' he growled.

Now that was a blow below the belt! Or not really, because currently I wasn't wearing any belt. In fact, I wasn't wearing much of anything, except a pair of drawers and my corset. It was getting rather chilly, particularly around the shoulders, and I shrugged into the red uniform as quickly as possible. I had expected it to feel awkward, but it didn't. Wearing Uncle Bufford's Sunday best for so long had made me become accustomed to wearing trousers. The military outfit, with its burning colours and padded shoulders, rather gave me a feeling of confidence, though that feeling was slightly offset by the ridiculous hat.

With a deep breath, I fastened the last button.

'All right,' I whispered. 'We can go.'

Mr Ambrose didn't move.

'You are fully clothed?'

'Yes.'

'Karim, turn around and check if sh- *he* is fully clothed.'

'*Sahib*,' Karim protested, not moving an inch. 'I can't...'

'Do it, Karim!'

'Yes, *Sahib*. As you command, *Sahib*.'

One hand over his eyes, with only a minuscule crack open between two fingers that could be closed the moment he detected any sign of indecency or devilry, Karim slowly turned towards me. I rolled my eyes. To tell the truth, I was getting slightly miffed, and had almost forgotten the hundreds of soldiers around us and the mortal danger we were in. I mean, I surely didn't look *that* bad in underwear...

'She is decent,' he announced in a low rumble. Then, thinking again, added, 'As least as decent as she can be.'

'I see. Then let us waste no more time.'

Without turning to glance at me, Mr Ambrose strode to the corner of the shed and peeked out into the courtyard.

'There are no soldiers nearby,' he whispered. 'There are two of them farther down the courtyard, approximately twenty yards away from us. We will go around the back of the shed. When we emerge from behind it on the other side, they will not notice, or think we have come from the other side of the courtyard. From where they are standing, it would be nearly impossible to tell the difference.'

He crossed to the other side of the shed and positioned himself at the corner there.

'Ready?' he asked.

'Yes, Sir,' I said, my heart hammering. By now, the soldiers who surrounded us had more than returned to my consciousness: they had usurped it. Playing dress-up behind the shed was all too well, but now we would step out into the open again, and our disguise would have to hold.

'Yes, *Sahib*.'

'Good. Remember, when you step out, look relaxed and comfortable.'

'You mean like *you* always do?' I asked, sweetly.

'Mr Linton?'

'Yes, Sir?'

'Be quiet!'

'Yes, Sir! Of course, Sir!'

'On the count of three. One... two... three!'

He stepped out into the courtyard, and started marching in the most perfect military step I had ever seen. In his brilliant red uniform he looked the picture of a handsome young soldier. I stared after him, an odd tugging sensation in my gut.

'Come on!' Karim growled from beside me. 'Or do you wish to stand around here gaping for the rest of the night?'

With a hurried shake of the head I started forward.

The moment I stepped out from behind the shed, I could feel them on me: the gazes of the hidden gunmen who were stationed all over the roof. I could feel their eyes boring into me, probing me, as Lord Dalgliesh's eyes had probed me, searching for truth and purpose.

My eyes fixed themselves on Mr Ambrose's back, a few yards in front of me. *Please*, I thought, desperately. *Please don't let them guess the truth about him.*

Would you even see blood on that red coat? Or would there just be a bang, and he would crumple silently to the ground? I didn't know. All I knew was that I didn't wish to find out.

Get a grip, I snapped at myself. *The gunmen aren't watching you. They are watching the outside for intruders, not the inside for their own soldiers, and that's what you are now. It is just your imagination running wild!*

If only I had been better at convincing myself.

Beyond Mr Ambrose, the gigantic double-winged front door loomed. I was just wondering once again how the dickens we were going to get it open, when suddenly, one of the wings swung open with a creak. Two soldiers stepped out. My heart almost stopped. What would we do? What would we say?

Mr Ambrose gave the soldiers a curt nod. He didn't say anything. They gave him a curt nod back. They didn't say anything.

And then we were past them and inside the hallway.

'H-how did that just happen?' I asked, my voice unsteady.

'What?' Mr Ambrose enquired. He wasn't paying attention to me. His eyes were sweeping over the different doors that lead from the hallway in various directions.

'Our getting past them!'

'I nodded, they nodded, we walked past. It's not that complicated.'

'But... why didn't they stop us? Question us?'

'That's why we are wearing a disguise, Mr Linton. So people won't know who we are. Come on. This is the right door.'

And he set off towards a door in the left corner of the room. It opened without resistance, and the three of us entered a narrow corridor, dimly lit by the occasional gas lamp on the wall. Mr Ambrose neither slackened his pace nor altered his brisk gait. I marvelled at how authentic he looked. He could have been a general, or a lord leading his army into battle.

Which maybe he was, in a way.

Shaking my head, I quickened my pace to keep up with him. We passed a door on the left, and Mr Ambrose didn't stop. Again we passed a door, and again he didn't give it a glance. We passed many doors on our march down the narrow corridor, some on the right, some on the left. From behind some came raucous laughter, from behind others came the sounds of swords being sharpened, from behind yet more we heard only silence. Mr Ambrose did not deviate from his straight course once until we reached a bend in the corridor. There, he stopped dead and, without turning, said: 'Around the corner, there is a straight corridor. It should lead directly to the door of Dalgliesh's office. In case we encounter someone, we cannot speak or discuss our route anymore. The closer we get to Dalgliesh's office, the more soldiers we will meet. Karim? Another look at the map, to make sure.'

The Mohammedan fished the map out of his bag, did a quick check and put it back. 'Yes, *Sahib*. You have it correct.'

'I see. Remember. Straight ahead and through the door. Don't speak. Look as though you know what you are doing.'

He started moving again, and we followed. With a few steps we were around the corner – and before us, there was a little room with the corridor splitting off into two different directions.

LION'S DEN

'This,' Mr Ambrose said, gazing coldly at the two doors, 'is inconvenient.'

Karim swore violently.

'What is this?' I demanded, pointing to the bifurcation. 'I thought you said there is only one corridor, and it leads straight on.'

'I also mentioned that the plans were not up-to-date, if you remember, Mr Linton.'

'Spiffing! Absolutely top-hole!' Angrily, I gave the wall a kick. Naturally, it kicked back just as hard, as walls usually do. 'So we're just going to pack our bags and go home?'

'Certainly not,' said Mr Ambrose, who looked as if the whole thing was nothing more than an intellectual problem to be discussed over tea and biscuits. 'There are two corridors. We are three people. Simple arithmetic tells us the solution. We will divide our forces, and whoever discovers Dalgliesh's office or his personal safe will have to acquire the file and make it out of here.'

Karim, who had just been about to follow my example and kick the wall with all his force, stopped. I was rather glad. He might have brought down the house on top of us.

'Of course!' He exclaimed. 'I'm at your service, *Sahib*. Where shall we go? Where shall we send...' His eyes rested for a moment on me, while he searched for the proper pronoun. '...*this individual*?'

I opened my mouth to give him a piece of my mind, but Mr Ambrose was quicker.

'No, Karim. We will not go together. You will go one way. Mr Linton and I shall explore the other corridor.'

Something like hurt showed under the black curls of Karim's beard. I might have been sorry for him if I hadn't been so busy suppressing a gigantic grin.

'You'd rather be accompanied by this creature than by me, *Sahib*?' the Mohammedan demanded.

Mr Ambrose made a terse movement with his head towards the second corridor. 'I'd rather send somebody I can rely on where I cannot go myself, Karim.'

Nice. The grin stopped trying to force its way onto my face. So he couldn't rely on me, could he?

Mollified by Mr Ambrose's words, and probably also by the sour look on my face, Karim bowed.

'I shall do as you command, *Sahib*.'

'If you find the file, leave. If you find nothing, leave. Don't wait for us. We will meet back at Empire House.'

Karim didn't look too happy about that order. But he bowed again.

'As you wish, *Sahib*.'

Without another word, he turned and disappeared down the corridor to the left.

'Come on.' Mr Ambrose motioned down the other corridor and started forward. 'We have wasted enough time.'

I almost ran after him. Not that I would ever have admitted it, but leaving Karim behind sent a tingle of fear up my spine. No matter how many soldiers Lord Dalgliesh had at his command, I couldn't see any of them getting past the huge Mohammedan. Now that he was gone, all Mr Ambrose had for protection was his cane, which just now didn't seem as impressive to me as on the first occasion he had drawn its hidden blade.

Suddenly, Mr Ambrose stopped and held up his hand. That was a sign even I, with my very limited experience in burglary, had no problems understanding. I halted, and waited with baited breath.

When, after a few moments, nothing had happened, I whispered: 'What is it?'

'Voices,' he said in a low, but otherwise normal, tone of voice. 'Be quiet. And if you have to speak, don't whisper. We are soldiers, remember? We are supposed to be here, and if we whisper, it will sound suspicious.'

That actually made sense. 'Yes, Sir.'

'And don't call me "Sir",' he added, still peering down the corridor, his back to me. 'If somebody catches you doing it, we will be under immediate suspicion. We wear uniforms of the same rank.'

A grin spread across my face. 'Do we, now?'

'Mr Linton?'

'Yes, Si- um, I mean, yes, mate?'

'I can *feel* your smile. Dispose of it immediately.'

'Yes, mate!'

'And don't call me mate. Only drunken sailors do that.'

'Yes, Si- ma- um... thingy.'

'Mr Linton?'

'Yes?'

472

'Be silent! I am trying to listen.'

I decided against giving an answer. I had run out of forms of address in any case, and I was just as interested as he to hear what was going on up ahead. Straining my ears, I tried to catch the voices he had mentioned. There was something... Not voices, only indistinct noises. A clang of metal here, a dull thump there, that was it.

Then it came: a low shout, just before the next thump. Again a shout, a bit like a command, but not really, and then another thump.

'What do you suppose it means?' I whispered.

His hand jerked up.

Blast! I had forgotten: no whispering. Quickly, I continued in a more normal tone of voice: 'That doesn't sound like an office, does it?'

He shook his head.

'Well? What is it?'

'I am reluctant to venture a guess with only audible data at my disposal, Mr Linton. But it sounds very much like a dock. Like a ship being loaded.'

'But... we're still a long way away from the docks, aren't we?'

'Yes.'

Without any further explanation, he started forward again.

Yes? That's all you're going to say?

Cursing inwardly, I hurried after him. He still marched along the corridor as if the whole place belonged to him, as if he had a right to be here that nobody could dispute. I did my best to imitate him, but probably didn't quite succeed. Slowly, the noises up ahead grew louder, the voices clearer. It was clear now that things were being loaded. I could hear the recurring thumps of the load as it was let down from high above, and the squeak of what I supposed were pulleys and cranes.

The shouted commands made it certain:

'Two yards to the left!'

'Down! Now!'

'A bit to the right!'

'You've got it! Gently now, gently. This stuff is valuable!'

I could see light up ahead. Suddenly, the corridor opened in front of us into a wide hall. I wanted to duck back, but Mr Ambrose hissed at me out of the corner of his mouth: 'Don't you dare! They have already seen us!'

And he was right. The eyes of several soldiers who were standing on a gallery that lead all around the room were on us. They were out of hearing range, but they could see our every move.

'Oh my God!' I breathed. 'What now?'

'Do as I do,' he hissed. 'Exactly as I do, on the other side. Now!'

And he took a few steps to the right, until he stood at the left end of the corridor, and assumed an erect position, his arms clasped behind his back, his legs clamped together. Having no idea why, I did the same, and felt pretty silly about it.

After a few moments, the soldiers on the gallery seemed to lose interest in us. Their eyes wandered on to more important things, like the crates full of dried cod that were piled on top of one another in a corner of the hall.

I stared at them, fixedly, waiting for the 'Seize them!' or 'Shoot!'. But no such command came.

'What is the matter?' I asked out of the corner of my mouth. 'Why aren't they suspicious? Why aren't they even looking at us anymore?'

'Because we are acting as soldiers are supposed to act,' Mr Ambrose replied. I had no idea how, but he managed to speak without actually moving his lips. 'We are standing guard.'

'Standing guard? Over what?'

'The entrance to this corridor, of course.'

'What would anyone want to guard it for? It's just a corridor!'

'Soldiers aren't trained to think about why they do things, Mr Linton. If they were, nobody would ever get an army together. Now be silent!'

Out of the corner of my eye, I glanced at his face. It was as cool and still as a block of ice. How could he do it? Inside me, fear, excitement and stress were writhing like a wounded snake. He didn't show the least emotion. But then, he never did.

Oh yes, he sometimes does – in your imagination he does a lot of things...

Behind my back, I clenched my hands together. No! I couldn't follow that train of thought, not now, not here of all places. Quickly, I let my eye wander through the hall to find something to distract me.

There was certainly enough to see.

At first, the red coats of the soldiers, flaring up like signs of danger, had distracted me from the rest. But now that they seemed to have lost interest in us entirely, I took in the rest of the giant room.

'Room' probably was not a big enough word. It was a cavern, a man-made cavern, almost as big as the entrance hall of Empire House. I could see that Mr Ambrose and his nemesis had the same penchant for giant proportions. Yet where in Mr Ambrose's hall there had been a monument of cold barrenness, although it was the entrance to his headquarters, this hall in a simple East End outpost of the East India Company was flaming with sumptuous colour.

The walls were dark, red brick, interspersed with wooden beams painted red and white. Up above, the beams arched to support a flat ceiling. Torches hung from the wooden supports, plunging the whole scene into sinister shades of dark gold and orange. In the flickering torchlight, the glinting barrels of the soldiers' guns looked like the torture instruments of Satan's disciples in hell.

Shadows flickered over the ceiling and the gallery that surrounded the room. Shadows also moved with the soldiers who were marching along the gallery, watching the scene below. And shadows were thrown by the gigantic contraptions that filled the centre of the hall.

I hadn't been wrong. There were pulleys, cranes, ropes and even lorries in abundance. They formed a labyrinth through which hundreds of workers scuttled like ants over an anthill, carrying, fetching, shouting. If all things around them left bizarre shadow-paintings on the wall in the flickering torchlight, they themselves painted entire ghastly frescos in black and dark orange. The cranes were the arms of giant black octopi, and the ropes on the pulleys were snakes, waiting to strike and bite.

Under the ghastly play of shadows, on each of the four walls of the hall, hung a gigantic tapestry displaying a coat of arms: two roaring lions on either side of a shield showing a red cross on white ground. Although I had never seen this particular crest before, and the shadowy monsters on the wall made it hard to see, I had no trouble guessing what it was.

We were in Lord Dalgliesh's lair. There was only one thing it could be: the official coat of arms of the Honourable East India Company.

Under the farthest of the tapestries, the one directly opposite me, the entrance to a tunnel gaped like an open maul. Tracks ran down into the tunnel, disappearing out of sight to God only knew where.

One thing was for sure: This was no mere warehouse or office building.

Slowly, I raised my eyes again to the towering golden lions above the entrance to the tunnel. *Come on*, they seemed to say. *Dare approach. Dare enter into our forbidden realm. We will tear you to shreds before you've taken one step.*

Nonsense! Taking a deep breath, I straightened and tried to look unconcerned.

Get a grip, Lilly! Those lions are just pieces of printed cloth. Do you want Mr Ambrose to think you're scared of giant coloured bed sheets on a wall?

No. I did not want that. Particularly after the incident with the wooden dragon.

I glared at the lions, meeting their bold, glittering gaze head-on. My eyes fell on a blue band that wound like a snake under the lions' paws. There were letters on it. Yet even though they were printed in bright gold, in the semi-darkness of the hall they were nearly impossible to make out. Was this English? No, it looked more like a foreign language...

Auspicio... Regis... Et Senatus... Angliae...

What did that mean?

'By the authority of the King and Parliament of England.'

Startled, my eyes flicked to where Mr Ambrose was standing, the perfect model of the British-Indian soldier.

'That's what it means,' he said, again managing to speak in his cool, calm voice without his mouth even twitching. 'The motto under the coat of arms of the East India Company that you were staring at. "By the authority of the King and Parliament of England".'

'How did you know that was what I was looking at?' I hissed.

'Your lips were moving, forming the Latin words. When I say "be silent", Mr Linton, that also means don't move your lips.'

Too preoccupied to argue, I gave a tiny nod and swallowed. My eyes once more took in the soldiers on the gallery, then returned to the roaring lions on the giant tapestries, and to the words they shouted at the world. *Auspicio Regis Et Senatus Angliae...*

No wonder Lord Dalgliesh felt justified in doing whatever he wanted. He had the Queen's Official Seal of Approval.

Beside me, Mr Ambrose tensed. Tensed more than he was already tensed, I mean – which, considering his normal stance, was an impressive feat.

'Out of the way! Quickly!' With those words hissed into my ear, he sprang away and pulled me after him in a decidedly unsoldierly manner. We were behind a heap of crates before I could utter a word of protest. And then I heard *his* voice, and the protest died in my throat.

'...have everything loaded onto the ship immediately, please, Captain. I shall await a full report in half an hour.'

Ice flooded my heart, and I stumbled after Mr Ambrose, not uttering a single word. Just before he pulled me out of sight, and we disappeared behind the heap of wooden crates, I saw it, out of the corner of my eye. I saw the golden mane and hawk's beak. I saw the steely glint of piercing blue eyes.

Lord Dalgliesh was here.

'So it is decided?'

The voice was rough with a hint of cockney, but many other accents mixed into it. Spying over the top of one of the crates, I saw the burly shape of a ship's captain next to the aristocratic figure of Lord Daniel Eugene Dalgliesh.

A hand gripped my collar and pulled me down. Suddenly, a hard body was pressing into me from behind.

'If you intend to spy on them over the top of those crates,' Mr Ambrose hissed into my ear, holding me with a granite grip, 'then I suggest that you remove that blue hat before you do so. It sticks out over the top.'

Oh. I hadn't thought of that. Embarrassed, I snatched the blue hat off my head. He, I noticed, had already removed his. Pity. It really suited him.

'Yes.' That was the voice of Lord Dalgliesh.

'And what decision have you come to, if I may ask, Your Lordship? I don't want to appear presumptuous, it is simply a matter of planning...'

'The file is leaving this building, Captain. It is going out to *Île Marbeau*.'

My head whipped around to look at Mr Ambrose. The file! Had he heard, too? Yes. I could see that he had. His left little finger was twitching.

'If you pardon my asking, Your Lordship...' The captain's voice was hesitant. 'Why did you keep it here at all? Wasn't that a bit... risky?'

I looked over the wall of crates again just in time to see Lord Dalgliesh direct a friendly smile at his captain. It was the same friendly smile that a shark directs at his prey.

'Risky?' He enquired, smoothly. 'Whyever would you think so?'

'Um, well, the means by which you acquired the file were not exactly... you know...'

'No. I do not know. Please, enlighten me.'

The captain met the gaze of the steel-blue eyes just for an instant.

'Nothing,' he said hurriedly. 'I didn't mean nothing, Your Lordship.'

Lord Dalgliesh nodded graciously. 'I'm glad to hear that. I would be very sad to find out that my staff did not think well of me and my methods. You do think well of me, Captain, don't you?'

'Of course, My Lord! I think the world of you, My Lord.'

'How fortunate! Then, I believe, we can continue our working relationship in a manner profitable to us both. Now, where were we...?'

The captain opened his mouth to remind his master, but then thought better of the risk of talking, and shut his mouth again.

'Ah, yes!' Lord Dalgliesh raised a finger. 'You were enquiring why I had not brought the file out of here at once.' He met the captain's eyes. 'Doubtless you were concerned because there are so many thieves and crooks in London, and my rightful property is in danger here, am I correct?'

'Yes, My Lord. Absolutely correct, My Lord.'

'Well, I must admit, it had occurred to me to send the file to a safer location immediately. But, you see, unfortunately, it was in code.'

Puzzlement spread over the captain's face. 'Code? You mean like code of honour and that gentleman stuff?'

'No. I mean a secret language.' Lord Dalgliesh's face was still smiling, but his right hand was speaking a different language. It had clenched into a tight fist, the knuckles white. 'Unfortunately, we have not yet been able to decipher it.'

Out of the corner of my eye, I saw something on Mr Ambrose's face. His non-existent expression didn't change, but I thought I saw a dark gleam of triumph in his eyes.

'And even more unfortunately,' Lord Dalgliesh continued, 'the fact that the documents are encoded makes it difficult for them to be removed from London. The greatest cryptographers of the world work here at government institutes.'

'But... now you're taking the file out of here anyway?' the captain dared to enquire.

'Yes.' Lord Dalgliesh took something out of his pocket and twirled it between his fingers. The object was shiny and yellowish, and looked like some kind of pelt. It took me a moment to recognize the lock of Simmons' golden hair. The hair of a dead man. With a quick, merciless motion, Dalgliesh crushed it between his fingers and let it fall to the floor. 'I have received signs that this course of action would be advisable.'

The captain stared at the remains of the lock in confusion. He didn't know what I knew.

'But... what about these code experts? If, like you said, they live here in London, My Lord...'

'I think they should be encouraged to move. Sea climate is very beneficial for one's health at this time of year. I am sure you can explain this to them, very clearly.'

The captain blanched. 'Your Lordship, surely you are not suggesting...'

He trailed off. Lord Dalgliesh waited, watching him quietly. Finally, he enquired: 'Yes?'

Once more, there was a friendly smile on his face.

The captain swallowed. 'I... My Lord, these are important men. If they should suddenly vanish in a violent manner...'

'Violence? Dear me, who said anything of violence?' Lord Dalgliesh's smile widened a fraction. 'You must have completely misunderstood me, Captain.

You will *encourage* these people to take a *holiday*, nothing more. I am sure they will see the benefit of it when you have explained everything adequately.'

The captain's head slumped down. It was probably pressed down by the weight he knew would come if something went wrong. If something went wrong, everything would be on his head. Lord Dalgliesh's innocent smile made that clear. Lord Dalgliesh would always be innocent.

'Their disappearance will not go unnoticed,' he started a last attempt at convincing his master. 'The press...'

'The press will follow my suggestions and be discrete. I own it, after all.'

'Well... not all of it, My Lord. Some of it belongs to Mr Ambrose.'

The friendly smile froze on Dalgliesh's face. Around them, the workers stopped in mid-stride and turned towards the two. Silence fell over the hall, as more and more pairs of eyes fixed on them. Waves of silence spread out in the pond of the hall from the pebble that had been Mr Ambrose's name.

It seemed to dawn on the captain that he had made a very serious mistake. The last remnants of colour drained from his face.

Dalgliesh took a step toward his subordinate.

'What,' he said very kindly and slowly, in the manner of a patient headmaster talking to a disobedient child, 'did I tell you about mentioning the name of this man in my presence, Captain?'

The captain's mouth opened and closed. No words came out.

'Do I need to remind you again of the consequences if this should occur again, Captain?'

'N-no, My Lord! I remember perfectly, My Lord!'

'Excellent.' Dalgliesh turned again, and continued on his way. At a flick of his hand, the labourers whirled around and started to work again, twice as fast as before. 'Kindly have the file brought aboard and stored in the safe, Captain. Make sure it is in a watertight pouch.'

'As you wish, My Lord.'

The voices receded as the two men walked down the hall. I sank to my knees, so I was completely hidden by the crates, and leaned towards Mr Ambrose, who had assumed the same pose.

'What did he mean "have the file brought aboard"?' I whispered. 'Aboard what?'

'Don't you remember?' he asked, his eyes looking into the distance. 'The entrance to that tunnel down in the hall... It must lead to the docks. That must be how he gets things on ships he doesn't want the government to know about. Intriguing.'

'But not in any way helpful,' I pointed out.

'On the contrary, Mr Linton.' There was a cold gleam in his eyes. 'Think about it. They are going to bring the file aboard the ship. Its current location is probably a separate, heavily guarded room. Even people dressed up as soldiers, as we are, would not be let in without a very good reason. But on the ship, things are different. People of all sorts hurry about, loading the vessel, checking security, carrying messages – it will be the ideal environment for us to retrieve the file. We will wait until it has been put aboard, then we will pretend to be part of the ship's military escort and go through the tunnel. Having acquired the file, we will not return here, but simply leave the ship at the docks, and, discarding our disguise, make our way back to the carriage.'

'What a brilliant plan, Sir. Of course, it all depends on whether this tunnel down in the hall actually leads to the docks, which at present is pure speculation.'

Mr Ambrose gave me a cool look. 'I would rather refer to it as a hypothesis based on circumstantial evidence, Mr Linton.'

'Would you indeed, Sir? And, assuming the tunnel really does lead to the docks, we will, of course, also have to worm our way through countless layers of guards and soldiers, and manage not to get caught and shot in the process.'

'Naturally, Mr Linton.'

The coolness in his gaze intensified. He regarded me like a not particularly interesting bug under a microscope. I knew very well what he was thinking. He was thinking I was afraid.

Well... he was right about that. But *he* didn't need to know that.

'All right.' Taking a deep breath, I stood up again and placed the blue hat on my head. It didn't seem quite so ridiculous to me anymore. It and the rest of the uniform were all that stood between me and a fate I didn't want to imagine. 'Let's go.'

For a single moment, Mr Ambrose looked almost – almost! – taken aback. Then he swiftly rose, too, and re-hatted himself. He was looking at me out of slightly narrowed, immeasurably dark eyes.

'You are really going to come with me?'

'Naturally.' Those eyes... I could drown in them and never even want to breathe again.

'But you just told me how dangerous it is.'

'Well...' I did my best to conjure up a brave smile. It wasn't easy while he was looking at me like this. My knees felt as if they wanted to give way any minute. 'They say fortune favours the brave, don't they?'

'Yes!' Mr Ambrose growled. 'And *they* are stupid. In my experience, fortune favours the powerful and ruthless.'

'Well, we should be all right, then, shouldn't we?' I grinned up at him. 'After all, you've got me on your side.'

He took a step towards me. 'You have a very singular personality, Mr Linton.'

I couldn't hide my smile. 'Singular? You mean special, like Joan of Arc, or Queen Gwendolen[51]?'

'Not exactly.' His hands came up to clasp my shoulders. 'I was thinking more like an *Ifrit*.'

It took me a moment to realize I wasn't offended. Why wasn't I offended? And why the heck was I still smiling? He had just compared me to some kind of demon from hell!

His grip on my arms tightened. The darkness in his eyes flared.

---

[51] A mythological British Queen who fought a brutal war with her husband for the Throne of England. Makes one appreciate modern divorce procedures, doesn't it?

'Mr Linton, I...' For a moment, it looked like he wanted to say more. But I should have known better. This was Mr Rikkard Ambrose. When did he ever want to say more or, for that matter, anything at all?

Instead, he suddenly let go, righted himself and stepped past me. 'We've wasted enough time, Mr Linton. Follow me!' he ordered without turning. 'And be silent. If we encounter resistance, leave the talking to me.'

'And if we encounter resistance that can't be solved by talking, Sir?'

Dumping on the ground the leather bag he had brought with him all the way, he opened it and retrieved an object out of it: a long object made of gleaming wood and silvery metal. I sucked in a breath at the sight of the state-of-the-art rifle. His eyes met mine.

'Leave that to me, too.'

~~**~*~*

Mr Ambrose's snappy salute was so convincing that the guard at the entrance to the tunnel let us through without uttering a single word. He just saluted in return. I, too, attempted a salute and somehow managed one without knocking the blue hat off my head.

We stepped past the guard in silence. Before us loomed the black jaws of the tunnel. I couldn't help it – a final time, I glanced up at the giant figures of the two roaring, golden lions hanging high above us. Their eyes seemed to be trained directly on me, watching my every move, knowing I did not belong here.

'Eyes front, Mr Linton,' Mr Ambrose hissed.

Hurriedly, I did as ordered and hastened my steps. The menacing glint of the golden-maned wardens above me disappeared, and the darkness swallowed me.

Or so I thought.

After a few moments, I could make out a faint glimmer farther down the tunnel. But it was very, very far off.

'Why isn't the tunnel better lit?' I whispered.

'Look around you,' he said in a low voice. 'Do you see any windows or ventilation systems? Both torches and gas lamps produce poisonous fumes that would be hard to get rid of in such an enclosed space. Also, if I'm right about what kinds of illicit activities Lord Dalgliesh is conducting here, the end of the tunnel will have to be completely dark for the purpose of secrecy. We will have to watch our steps very carefully. And from now on, not one more question out of you, understood? Remember, we are supposed to be familiar with this place.'

Thank God I did as he told me and kept my mouth shut. Not two minutes later, a dozen soldiers suddenly appeared out of the darkness right in front of us. Light in the tunnel was so scarce that, even in their bright red uniforms, they were hardly more than shadows. Yet these shadows were armed, and looking none too pleased.

'Are the Ching Chongs[52] still at it?' one growled.

'Ye bet they are!' another answered. 'Damned yellow bastards! Not a night when they can't get to bed like decent folk. And it's the likes of us that has to...'

They went past us, and soon their voices vanished into the distance.

So the Dance of the Dragon was still going on outside, was it? I felt suddenly cold at the thought of what exactly the soldiers had been ordered to do. Why were they marching, as I was sure they were, out into the street to where the Chinese were dancing? I sneaked a sideways glance at Mr Ambrose's profile in the gloom. It was too dark to really see his face. Was he feeling the chill inside, too?

Dumb question. He probably was constantly at a core temperature of – 100 degrees Fahrenheit.

Up ahead, there shimmered a faint light again. Not yellowish light this time, though, but cold, blue light. The light of the moon. As we came closer, I saw that it was falling into the tunnel through tiny cracks in a wooden wall - a wooden wall that ended the tunnel.

I opened my mouth to ask 'What now?' - but Mr Ambrose threw me one of his special looks, and I closed it again. He stepped closer to the wooden wall, which in spite of the few strands of moonlight, was utterly black, and let his hands skim over it. About halfway up the wall his searching hands suddenly stopped. The fingers closed around something, pressed, and pushed.

The door swung open, revealing a view of a narrow stretch of water, and a harbour wall, half covered in algae. Distantly, I could hear the sound of the Dragon Dance, and I was relieved that it sounded as if all the dancers were still alive and perfectly fine.

'How did you know there was a doorknob, Sir?'

'When you have a secret passage that nobody is supposed to be able to find from the outside, it rather makes sense to have the doorknob for the entrance on the inside, don't you think?'

Now that he said it, it sounded rather obvious. But then, how the heck would I know? This was my first secret passage ever, after all! Was it his first? I looked at his face, hard and implacable in the moonlight. Probably not.

Carefully, he leaned out of the open door, his eyes flicking to the left and right without his head moving an inch. In a moment, he was back inside the tunnel, right beside me.

'No guards around,' he said in a low voice.

'Do you think that we've somehow gone the wrong way? That the file isn't here at all?'

'I doubt it. Look.'

Imitating him, I carefully stuck my head out of the door and let my eyes flick to the left, then to the right. There it was! To the right, a narrow catwalk, hardly more than a ridge, led along the harbour wall. It disappeared behind the bulk of a sleek, rather small ship with only two masts. It would have been completely

---

[52] Please, all Chinese readers, excuse the offensive term. People in the 19th century weren't very politically correct.

unremarkable, if not for the dark, even colour of its hull, which was unlike that of any ship I had ever seen.

'You saw it?' he asked, when I ducked back into the tunnel.

'The catwalk? Yes. Cleverly done, that. You probably don't even notice it from up at the docks. And even if you do, what's the significance? But down here, you can sneak from the tunnel to any ship in the dock without anybody seeing.'

He nodded. 'Yes. But it's not the catwalk that worries me. I knew it would be there.'

'Really? But you are worried?'

'Yes.'

'Why?'

'It's that ship. I think it may be...'

From behind us, out of the tunnel, we suddenly heard the sound of approaching feet in lockstep. The sound grew louder.

'Quick!' he hissed, pushing me out of the door and onto the catwalk. 'Onto the ship before they see us and think of asking questions!'

Suddenly, I stood in the moonlight, open and exposed. I prayed to God that there were no guards on that sinister black ship. But even if there were, what was there to see? Just another one of their own soldiers, I hoped. At the moment, however, I didn't feel very soldierly.

Behind me, I heard the door shut with a *click*.

He's out, I thought. *He's behind you, and he's expecting you to move! Go on! Move your generous behind, he's relying on you!*

And somehow, my feet, which just a moment ago seemed to be frozen to the wood of the catwalk with icy fear, started to move. The black silhouette of the ship loomed above me, its masts and ropes throwing a spider's web of shadows across the way in front of me, a web in which I would soon get caught.

I entered the web of shadows, and my heart went cold. Around the curve of the ship's hull appeared the name of the ship, painted in bright crimson that was turned by the moonlight into the colour of dried blood:

NEMESIS

Behind me, I could hear Mr Ambrose suck in a sudden breath. Instinctively, I tried to turn, but hard arms grabbed me from behind.

'Keep going!' Mr Ambrose hissed. 'They may be watching us from the ship, even if we cannot see them. Just keep going.'

'But... you know that ship's name. I know you do. What is the matter? What is so special about it?'

'Keep going, I said! Or do you want us both to lose our heads tonight? Yes, I know the ship. Or at least, I have heard reports of it. If it is the one I think it is, it's the most modern and devastating warship of the world.'

I stared at the slender, black silhouette of the two-master with mingled fear and incredulity. *This?* The most devastating warship of the world? I didn't know much about ships, but most of the Royal Navy ships I had seen entering and leaving the port were much larger than this thing, with a great many more cannons and masts.

He has to be joking.

Then, my eyes fell once more on the threatening, black hull, and I remembered that Mr Ambrose did not ever joke.

'Why?' I asked quietly. 'What makes it so dangerous?'

'It is the first warship made entirely out of steel. Where other ships shatter and crumble under cannon-fire, this thing will simply sail on. It's Lord Dalgliesh's latest contribution to our great British Empire. The flagship of his fleet. Everybody was so pleased when he announced the project. What a great triumph for Britain's naval superiority, *et cetera*. The Queen congratulated him.'

'Does anybody know to what use he is putting his marvellous ship? That he is using it to steal and smuggle?'

'I don't think so. If they did, I think the Queen might have refrained from her congratulation.'

We were almost directly underneath the large, red letters now. The *Nemesis* loomed over me like a spider in the centre of its web, ready to strike.

'Lord Dalgliesh really means business this time,' Mr Ambrose said darkly. 'Nobody would be stupid enough to get in his way while he is on this swimming fortress of steel.'

I shuddered. Mr Ambrose's nemesis travelling on the *Nemesis*... it was fitting, in a poetic sort of way. How unfortunate that I had always detested poetry.

I opened my mouth to ask another question, but quickly, Mr Ambrose grabbed my arm from behind and pressed. Thank God I understood the signal! He had to have heard something, for a moment later, a figure in a dark cloak appeared above us on the deck of the ship. Underneath the dark cloak, I could see a thin strip of bright red. Another soldier of the Presidency Armies.

The soldier made a quick upward motion with his outstretched hand. Mr Ambrose nodded. Non-verbal communication – this was one thing in which he was an expert. A moment later, a ladder was lowered from the ship onto the deck.

Blast! I would have to go up first. My heart hammering wildly, I reached out for the rungs of the ladder.

Do you know the fairy tale about Jack and the beanstalk? You know, the one where this silly chap ends up in a land inhabited by giants by climbing a mile-high beanstalk that leads all the way to the sky? Well, let me tell you, the fellow had it easy! Beanstalks are nothing! The ladder I had to climb to the deck of the *Nemesis* was at least twice as high as the sky. And all the time while I was climbing, and climbing, and still climbing, I knew that something far worse than giants awaited me at the top. Giants were usually really stupid, and not armed with guns.

Finally, I reached the last rung. My hand reached up to grasp the ship's railing – and another hand, large, coarse and hairy, gripped mine. I almost jerked back my arm, and remembered just in time that this was supposed to be the hand of a comrade. Before I could think another thought, the powerful hand pulled upwards and hauled me over the railing, onto the deck of the ship. Immediately, I was pressed down and forced to my knees. An angry red face appeared in front of me. Stinking breath full of garlic and alcohol hit my nose, and I gagged.

'What the hell are you thinking?' the soldier growled, his voice low but seething with rage. 'What are you doing here in that getup?'

I stared up at him, eyes wide.

What the heck is happening? What have you done, Lilly? Have you given yourself away somehow, you silly idiot?

The angry soldier grasped a piece of his black coat that was hanging over his shoulder and waved it in front of my face. 'Completely in red and blue? People will be able to see you from the other side of the harbour!'

Suddenly, I understood. All the other soldiers on the deck, who stood around us in a semi-circle, sinister expressions on their faces, were wearing similar dark cloaks, so as not to be seen by people on the docks. And I didn't have one.

Blast! Of course they were angry! How long would it take for anger to turn into suspicion? How long before they realized who I really was and–

Thud!

Two feet landed on the deck beside me with an impact that resounded through my entire body. I could see the ends of familiar black trousers peeking out under the blue uniform trousers of the Bengal Army. Without looking up, I knew who it was. But I looked up anyway.

Mr Rikkard Ambrose towered over me, glaring down at the man who had his clenched fist just under my nose. I swallowed. He looked a lot more menacing from this angle. His granite aspects increased a thousandfold, he stood there like a true monumental statue, immovable and awe-inspiring.

The soldier beside me seemed to feel the same. Slowly, he drew back his fist.

Mr Ambrose nodded and gave the man a look that made him retreat a yard or two. Crouching down beside me, my employer looked at me. He didn't raise an eyebrow or otherwise disturb the perfect cool smoothness of his face, but somehow I got the impression that his eyes were asking: *are you all right?*

I nodded.

He nodded back at me, and surreptitiously squeezed my shoulder. Warmth spread out from the spot his fingers had touched. Deep inside I knew he had just made the gesture to keep me calm, to prevent me from ruining his plans – but still, this small gesture sent an unfamiliar ache through my heart. An ache that was at once both soothing, and painful.

Mr Ambrose turned his eyes on the red-faced soldier again. And this hardened warrior, used to the glares of dozens of drill sergeants and the hate in the eyes of the enemy, drew back before the cold threat in those arctic eyes.

I couldn't blame him.

Raising his hand, Mr Ambrose made a quick gesture encompassing the two of us, then he pointed below.

The soldier hesitated.

Mr Ambrose's eyes narrowed, and the cold force of his dark eyes intensified.

Hurriedly, the soldier nodded. His thoughts were as obvious as if they had been painted on his blue hat: the sooner these two strange fellows were below deck, the sooner they would be out of his way.

Grasping my arm, Mr Ambrose pulled me across the deck, towards the stern of the ship. There, I could just make out a wooden superstructure in the moonlight, with a small door in it.

'Keep your head down,' Mr Ambrose said in a low voice. 'We wouldn't want to be spotted, now, would we?'

The double meaning in his words was evident – and he was right. I didn't want to be spotted by people on the docks. And I *definitely* didn't want to be spotted by the people on the ship for what I really was.

There was a guard at the door we were approaching. Mr Ambrose made a motion with his head, and he opened the door for us. Without saying 'thank you' or even nodding, Mr Ambrose pushed me past him and down into the darkness. The door closed behind us.

We stood in a narrow passageway, its walls made of dull grey steel. A lamp dangled from a hook in the wall, painting the steel with flickering stains of red and yellow. Turning around, I jabbed at the insignias on Mr Ambrose's uniform.

'Do you have a higher rank than those fellows out there?' I demanded.

'Higher rank, Mr Linton?'

'Yes! They keep doing what you tell them to do. Well, actually it's worse. They keep doing what you want *without* you having to tell them. Are you a lieutenant, or colonel or something?'

Mr Ambrose gave me a look. 'It has nothing to do with rank, Mr Linton. In fact, I am masquerading as a simple soldier. One simply has to act as if one has no doubt that people will do as one wishes. In most cases, that will take them by surprise so much that they forget to refuse. Now come.'

He started down the corridor, and I had already taken the first two steps after him before I realized what I was doing.

One simply has to act as if one has no doubt that people will do as one wishes. In most cases, that will take them by surprise so much that they forget to refuse.

For a moment, I considered refusing, just for the fun of it. But then, I sighed and shook my head. Now wasn't the time.

We continued down the corridor. At more or less regular intervals, we came upon metal doors set into walls that seemed to serve no particular purpose.

'Bulkheads,' Mr Ambrose said when I asked about them. 'Walls separating the ship into smaller compartments. They normally just serve the purpose of giving the vessel more structure and stability. But these look to be watertight. In the event of a cannonball penetrating the outer hull, the door can be closed and the ship can fight on as if practically nothing happened. It's the first time I've seen something like this in a warship.'

His words sent a cold shiver down my spine. I bit my lip to contain my anxiety.

'Where are we heading, exactly?' I asked.

'Nowhere. The ship is not very large. To judge by eye, I would say a length of eighty-four feet, and maybe a draught of six or seven feet. We are going to search it from top to bottom until we find the file. Then we are going to leave.'

'Don't you think that plan might be a little simplistic?'

'No.'

And that was it. I didn't get another word out of him. We marched through dark, dank corridors of steel, now and then opening a door to the left or the right to spy into a tiny steel compartment. They all held crates of different shapes and sizes. Apparently, Mr Ambrose's file wasn't the only thing Lord Dalgliesh was eager to get out of the country.

Finally, we came to a junction where the corridor split into two.

'Should we split up?' I asked, keeping my voice down. I thought I could hear the faint mumbling of voices somewhere, and they had better not hear us.

Mr Ambrose shook his head.

'Smell that?' He pointed down one corridor. 'That way smells of oil and smoke. The engine room will be down there. Lord Dalgliesh would never keep such sensitive papers anywhere near a burning fire. Let's go this way.'

And he started down the other corridor. By now, I had long lost any sense of direction. I only hoped that Mr Ambrose would be able to find the way out again. He certainly seemed confident enough. But then, he always did. Even when, after checking three more storage rooms, we ran smack into a dead end.

Mr Ambrose stopped. He stood there for a moment. His left little finger twitched, once.

'All right. Let's turn around. I think there was another junction not too far back. We can-'

He cut off, as voices came down the corridor.

'...everything been stored down here?'

'Yes, everything, apart from these last few sacks.'

Abruptly, Mr Ambrose leaned down to my ear. 'Stay calm.' His voice was quiet, cool, assured. He must have seen the fear on my face. 'We will just walk past them. Remember, those are soldiers, just like us. We can simply walk past them.'

'And the men didn't open a single crate or sack?' the voice in the distance asked.

'Yes, Lord Dalgliesh,' the other answered.

Beside me, Mr Ambrose stiffened.

'*Just soldiers?*' I hissed, my voice trembling more than I would have liked.

He moved more quickly than I could have believed possible. In a moment, he had flung open the door to my left and pushed me into the dank little room. There was hardly enough space for me there; most of it was taken up by a giant wooden crate, over eight feet high. Slamming his cane between the lid and the walls, he heaved. The lid popped open.

'What-' I began. But before I could finish my sentence or take a closer look at the contents of the crate, I was lifted up by a pair of hard, powerful arms and thrown not very ceremoniously into the wooden container.

The fact that I landed face-first in wood wool muffled the string of unlady-like curses that came from my lips, and probably saved my life. From outside, I could hear shuffling feet.

'Where do you want the sacks, Your Lordship?' I heard a gruff sailor's voice from somewhere outside.

'Over there.'

'Yes, Your Lordship.'

The steps outside approached our little room. A moment later, something heavy landed on top of me, forcing the air out of my lungs, and the lid slammed shut above me. Gasping for breath, and getting only more wood wool, I reached up to shove aside whatever was suffocating me. But it was too hard and heavy to shift. Hell's whiskers, what was it? Was Lord Dalgliesh already in the room, and had his men thrown a sack on top of me, without bothering to look into the crate? My hands reached out, touching, and I felt something bulging under rough cloth. A sack of potatoes, maybe?

My hand reached further up. There, the cloth ended, and my fingers touched something softer. It didn't feel like a potato. It was oval and seemed to have some sort of hole in the middle...

'Mr Linton,' I heard a low voice from right above me, 'kindly take your finger out of my ear!'

Danger! Explosive Cargo!

My finger froze in mid-movement. Outside, I could hear footsteps passing the door of our room. Lord Dalgliesh and his cronies had heard nothing, were not coming to investigate. But right now, I couldn't have cared less what they did or did not do. Turning my head to get my face out of the wood wool, I looked up, but saw only darkness. Mr Ambrose must have pulled the lid of the crate shut over us.

Mr Ambrose, who at present was *lying right on top of me!*

No! Don't think about it! That's not Mr Ambrose on top of you! It can't be! It's a sack of coals, or potatoes, or...

His cool breath tickled my cheek. He moved in a way no sack of potatoes could ever move. A sack of potatoes wasn't as hard as this. A sack of potatoes didn't have muscles that, even through the fabric between us, pressed forcefully into me. A sack of potatoes most certainly couldn't make me shiver all over like this!

It's the cold, I screamed at myself. *You're shivering because it's cold in here! That's all!*

But even though it was freezing inside the crate, I didn't feel cold all of a sudden. I had before, while wandering through the damp, dark passageways of the *Nemesis*. But now, heat was spreading throughout my body. It came from a place deep inside me and climbed upwards, and upwards, until it finally reached my face. Why did my cheeks not light up the crate from inside? They were burning like fire!

Something brushed against my cheek, and my whole body twitched. I could feel him move against me, shifting...

No! Don't think! Don't imagine!

'Mr Linton?' The voice above me was as cool as the winter wind. 'Your finger. My ear. Remove. Now, if you please.'

487

My lips moved aimlessly, in search of something to say. Finally, I struck on an intriguing fact that was worth spelling out.

'You said "if you please",' I whispered, incredulously. 'That's almost as bad as "please" or "thank you". Since when do you have the time to spare for civilities?'

He moved closer. I couldn't see a thing, but I felt it. His face was only inches away from mine now, his mouth at my ear.

'At present,' he breathed, 'I find myself with free time at my disposal. At least until Dalgliesh is far enough away for us to get out of here!'

With my left ear, I could still hear the murmur of voices from the next room – Lord Dalgliesh giving orders to his soldiers. But all my attention was reserved for my right ear – the one that was only separated by a finger's breadth from Mr Ambrose's lips.

'But you are right,' he continued. 'One should never deviate from one's principles. Take your finger out of my ear *at once!*'

My hand jerked away from his ear, touching something soft in the process. A strand of his hair, maybe?

Don't think! Don't think about the fact that he's lying right on top of-
Just don't think!

'Very good,' Mr Ambrose said into my ear, his voice still cold and controlled. Didn't he care that we were... that he was practically... 'Now be still until they have concluded their business and gone. It shouldn't take long. Then we can continue with our mission here.'

He sounded as if he were sitting in his office chair, giving me orders about which file to bring next. But of course he wasn't sitting in his chair. He was lying. Lying on top of...

No! Don't think!

I swallowed. 'Very good, Sir.'

Just as he had said, footsteps soon left the room next door. They came closer.

'Now,' he whispered. 'Not a word until they have gone.'

I held my breath.

And then, the footsteps stopped outside, right in front of the room in which we were hidden.

'What should we do with this sack, My Lord?' I heard one of the soldiers' muffled voices.

'See if there's still space in that room, and put it there.'

'Aye, My Lord.'

That room? They didn't mean... they couldn't mean *this* room, surely?

A moment later, my silent question was answered by the creak of the door as it swung wide open. Hell's whiskers! They were inside, separated from us only by an inch or so of flimsy wood! I pressed my face into Mr Ambrose's chest to keep from screaming. My nerves were stretched to breaking point.

And then, something happened which I would never have believed possible in a million years:

Mr Ambrose put his arms around me.

488

He didn't say anything, didn't try to lie to me, saying that it was going to be all right or that we were sure to get out of this alive. He just put his arms around me and held me, close to his chest, in a way no man ever had dared to do before. I inhaled the clean scent of him – the clean scent of rough, simple soap, with a hint of something musky I couldn't identify. Maybe his own odour – or maybe the smell of too much money. Whatever it was, it was oddly comforting.

How could a smell be comforting? How could it feel so good for a strong, independent girl like me to be held in the arms of a man? This man, whom I hardly knew, and from whom I only wanted nothing more than a pay cheque every month? Why would it make me feel warm and safe to be in his arms?

Memories began to well up inside me, memories long repressed and half-forgotten, of a night at Empire House, and of the same man, doing much the same thing, and a lot more besides. Hard arms around me, hot lips on mine, heat rising inside me...

I tensed in anticipation as I felt his hands move up and cup the side of my face.

'Silence,' he whispered into my ear in a voice so cool and soft it felt like the caress of a snowflake. 'Simply silence. They must not hear a thing.'

You see? I yelled at myself. *He's simply doing this to keep you quiet! Be sensible. Don't dare to imagine there's anything else behind it!*

His hand began gently stroking my face, soft as the first snow of winter falling on rose petals.

Oh God...

Don't think. Don't move. Don't feel. Then, maybe, you can make it through this without contemplating who is just now pressing you to his chest as if you were his heart's desire! Don't think! Don't think!

I forced myself to freeze, to stiffen into an unresponsive block of wood, as dead as the wood wool beneath me. I forced my ears to concentrate not on the breathing right above me, not on the hyperactive thumping of my own heart, but on the voices outside.

And it was as well I did so, considering what came next.

'Hear, Your Lordship?'

'Yes, exactly.'

I heard a dull, metallic thud as something heavy was dropped on the floor outside.

'Very well.' Lord Dalgliesh's voice, muffled by the wall of wood between us, came from somewhere to my left. 'I will go and instruct the captain about our course. You men check that everything is secure and then take up your posts. Understood?'

'Aye, Your Lordship.'

There came several sharp clacks, and I realized the soldiers were snapping their heels together and saluting. Footsteps left the room.

No! Don't go! You're the only thing that keeps me distracted from Mr Am... from the someone whom I can't think about, but who holds me in his arms, so strong, hard, unyielding! Don't go, my dear, deadly enemies! I need you!

The hand on my cheek slowly wandered downwards, over my neck, down my spine, to the small of my back. The man whose name I couldn't think pressed me closer against him. If only it were not totally dark around us! The blackness robbed me of any distractions, made touch the only sense I had and intensified it a thousandfold. I could feel every breath he took, every tiny movement he made against me.

He doesn't mean anything by it! He's only doing this to keep you calm, to keep you from screaming, to keep you from acting as he thinks every silly girl who meddles in men's affairs would act! Keep it together! He doesn't care about you!

I knew it was true, every part of it. Yet the longer he held me, the harder it was to believe.

'It won't be long now.' His voice at my ear was still as steady as stone – so cold and hard it sent another shiver down my back. 'Be still for a little longer... just a little longer...'

How could his voice be so distant while his hands were so gentle? It was a mystery to me – a mystery that tore at my heart.

Suddenly, right when my heart was torn about halfway down the middle, I heard movement from outside. The soldiers still weren't gone. Only Lord Dalgliesh had left.

Think! Distract yourself! What could they be doing? Probably they are checking the room, making sure that nothing has been disturbed, like Dalgliesh said.

'Soon, Mr Linton, soon.' Mr Ambrose's voice was still just as low, just as cold as before. 'Soon they will be gone.'

Suddenly, a voice boomed only a few feet away:

'Ey, look! This crate ain't shut right!'

Above me, Mr Ambrose stiffened. His hand froze at my cheek.

'Well, then what are ye waiting for? 'ere!'

We heard a clinking sound. Only a second later, the crate shuddered under a series of heavy blows – the blows of the hammer that was nailing shut the lid. It took a few moments for the icy realization to flood through me: I was trapped. And, what was far worse, I was trapped with *him* on top of me!

~~*~**~*~*

The moment the soldiers had left, shutting the door behind them, Mr Ambrose's arms unwound from around me.

'They're gone, Mr Linton. You have my official permission to scream hysterically, now.'

'*What?*' I stared up at him incredulously, although I was actually not able to see anything of him except a vague outline in the darkness.

'I don't have the time to listen, though, I'm afraid,' he continued, rising a few inches off me. 'I have to get this lid open.'

At his words, my heart ripped the last few inches and fell apart.

You knew this was going to happen! I yelled at myself. *You knew he was only trying to keep you quiet. So don't you complain now! You had better get cracking on the problem of how to crack open this infernal crate!*

However, Mr Ambrose was already on it. Having lost all interest in me – if he ever had any – he had risen up with his back and was pushing against the lid of the crate. I could see him straining against it in the faint light that fell in through a crack in the crate wall. Yet space was even sparser here than light. He could hardly rise a few inches off me, let alone get any leverage.

I could feel his muscles bunch and loosen, bunch and loosen. Blimey! He didn't look that muscled in his straight-cut black tailcoat, but he had plenty of power tucked away under that simple, smooth black cloth.

My knees screamed under the pressure he was putting on them, but I didn't care. I was too busy trying to ignore the pressure he was putting on certain other parts of my body, parts which were much more private than knees.

'It won't move,' a blizzard-like growl came from above me. 'Brace yourself, Mr Linton. I'll have to get a little more... forceful.'

'You'll shatter my kneecaps if you're any more forceful!' I protested. I shifted hastily, trying to get out from under him, but my elbows hit something hard on either side.

'Don't move!' He commanded. 'There's hardly enough room for us here. If you try to get out from under me, we'll end up in a tangle and will never get out of here.'

I had a mental picture of me, eternally entangled with Mr Ambrose. I swallowed, hard.

'V-very well, Sir. But what will we do?'

'I'll somehow have to get my knees past you, so they won't press down on you when I push. Is there a little space on either side of you farther down? Test with your feet.'

'Yes, there's room there.'

'Well, that solves the problem. Spread your legs for me.'

For a few moments, silence filled the small, black space inside the crate. Utter, complete silence.

'*What*,' I asked very slowly and deliberately, '*did you say?*'

'I said "spread your legs".' He sounded surprised that I hadn't understood, and slightly irked that I hadn't immediately done as he commanded. 'Go on, it's not that difficult. The left leg to the left, the right leg to the right.'

'I know what "spread your legs" means!'

'Well, then there's no problem, is there? Hurry up, Mr Linton, we haven't got all night.'

Now, let me clarify: I didn't know all too much about what went on between men and women behind locked doors. My aunt had never been very specific on the subject of sexual congress, and the one time I had asked her, she nearly bit my head off and told me ladies did not talk about such lowly matters. But I did, at least, know enough to realize that spreading your legs was not something you did for a man, especially if this man was not married to you, not interested in you, and was stuck with you in a crate full of wood wool inside a steel warship on the way to God only knows where!

And he was so close... so terribly close! If he came even closer to me now, pressed to the very centre of my body, I did not know what would happen. I was

491

afraid a lot might happen. I was even more afraid that nothing would happen at all.

'Mr Linton? I am waiting.'

Slowly, tortuously slowly, I slid my legs apart. I could feel his hard thighs pressing against the insides of mine, forcing their way into the opening until they rested solidly there, in my midst.

'That feels better,' Mr Ambrose said contentedly. 'Now we should be able to get going.'

Switch off your imagination, Lilly! Switch off your imagination now!

A moment later, I heard a dull thud as his shoulders collided with the lid of the crate with the force of a rampaging bull. Again and again, he struck out, upward and forward, making the crate rock violently, and needless to say, myself along with it.

There followed a few moments of panting and hammering in the dark. Finally, his attacks ceased, and he collapsed on top of me, breathing hard.

'This is quite vexing, Mr Linton. I cannot get the infernal thing to budge.'

I had trouble finding my voice to answer him. My mind was in a hot, foggy place very far away.

'Err... thing? Thing? What thing, Sir?'

'The lid of course, Mr Linton. Stay focused.'

His hard muscles digging into me... his laboured breathing right above me, only inches away...

'Focused... Focused, of course, Sir!'

'What is the matter with you? You're sweating, and shivering all over. Are you ill?'

His hips bucking into me... his breath hot on my overheated skin...

'N-no, Sir. I simply find it rather hot in here. Don't you, Sir?'

'To be absolutely accurate, I could not care less about the climatic conditions in here, Mr Linton. We have to get that lid open.'

'Why are you in such a hurry?' My voice sounded rather dreamy. I felt rather dreamy all around. The last few minutes had been a.... well, let us call it an 'interesting experience'.

'Don't you see? Mr Linton, if we do not get the crate open, the ship might sail with us on board, and we would be stuck in here together until we reach our destination!'

I gazed up at the dark shape of the man above me. My eyes had grown used to the gloom by now, and I could make out his classical Greek profile, his strong arms and his dark, dark, sea-coloured eyes.

'And that would be bad because...?'

There was a pause.

'Mr Linton?'

'Yes, Sir?'

'I *order* you to focus!'

'Yes, Sir!'

'We must leave this crate before the ship leaves the harbour.'

'Yes, Sir! As you say, Sir!'

It was in this moment that the ship shuddered, and we heard the steam engine start with a deep, menacing rumble. Slowly, very slowly, the ship started moving forward.

~~*~*~*

It was as if Mr Ambrose were a puppet, and somebody had cut his strings. The last tension that had held his panting body upright went out of him, and he collapsed on top of me, a hundred and seventy pounds of solid bone and muscle slamming me back into the wood wool. His heart was hammering like a deranged woodpecker against my chest, and his weight was almost keeping me from breathing.

But he wasn't too heavy. Oh no. The words *too heavy* would have implied I wanted him to get off me. And I didn't want that. How could I? How could I wish him farther away, now that his cheek rested against mine, and his mouth was so close, almost close enough to kiss...

Except that you don't want to kiss him, right? Because you're a suffragette, and he's a chauvinist, and you would never want anything to do with him! You would, for instance, not want to lift your head the few inches that separate you and softly press your lips on his, caressing, comforting...

No. I *definitely* didn't want to do that. I would never even think of it.

Oh well, maybe I would think of it a little.

Unbidden, images attacked me out of the dark. And because of the dark, I had no other images to dispel them. They were images of Mr Ambrose and me in his office, clutched in a passionate embrace. They were images of me practically tackling him and throwing him over backwards. They were images of me wanting. Wanting him. Not just his stern lips, or his granite face, or his deep, dark eyes, but every part of him.

Lies! All lies! That was a dream. An alcoholic fantasy, like Napoleon and the little yellow piggies, nothing more.

Yet the storm of images in my head didn't want to be quieted. It expanded, roaring, and feeding on my anxiety and desperation, until it had finally reached my heart. There, it found fresh strength in the secret recesses of my soul, and turned into a hurricane which swept me along, unable to resist.

My head inched up, my lips moving closer to his.

Mr Ambrose still lay heavily on me, his breathing unsteady. He didn't seem to notice my movement at all. I hesitated. What was I doing? Yes, the images in my memory seemed real enough, but could I really trust them? Mr Ambrose had been cold as an iceberg during the entire time we were shut in here. Even when he held me in his arms, it was not for my sake, it was only to keep me from giving away our presence. Could somebody who was this cold really want me?

And an even better question: supposing he wanted me, did that mean that I should want him? My feminine dignity raised her head and shook it firmly. No. He was the kind of man whom, indeed, I should never even contemplate to want.

493

My mouth was only a hair's breadth away from his now. I could feel the gentle breeze of his breath caressing my lips. It was such an achingly pleasurable feeling.

I didn't dare to move, frozen in indecision.

And then, he spoke. They were just four words, four little words. But they shook the foundation of my world.

'I am so tired.' His head slid to the side, away from mine, to come to rest on my chest. 'I am so tired, Mr Linton.'

He didn't seem to realize, or care, on what delicate part of my body his cheek now rested. At least I hoped for his sake he hadn't realized, because if he had, I'd slap him from here to Honolulu!

But any thoughts of aggression I'd had went out of me as I caught sight of his chiselled face in the half-light. He looked tired. More than tired, in fact – exhausted. There weren't any lines on his perfect face, nothing visible that spoke of exhaustion. There was only the slackness of his normally so stern, hard features.

It was an instinctive decision, born of all the strange, unfamiliar emotions raging in my innermost self. I raised my arms and put them around him. He stiffened for a moment, but then relaxed into me. He did not push me away. What did that mean? Did it mean anything?

My mouth felt bone-dry. I licked my lips and tried desperately to think of something to say.

'What happens now?' I asked softly.

His answer was a long time coming.

'We stay here, shut in this crate, until we reach our destination, Mr Linton.'

You're still calling me 'Mr Linton' while you have your face pressed into my pair of Cupid's kettle drums? You have a problem with reality, Mister!

'I know that, Sir. And then?'

'That depends on the circumstances.'

'Could you elaborate, Sir?'

'I do not feel very communicative at present, Mr Linton.'

'When do you ever, Sir?'

'Adequate point, Mr Linton.'

Somehow, I thought I could feel some life seeping back into him. Was it only my imagination, or was there a bit of dry humour in his voice? I had to keep talking – if only to keep myself from thinking too closely about what part of me his nose was currently pressing into.

'So, what will happen, Sir?'

'Either the crate is opened by a single soldier, or unarmed worker – in which case, we will overpower him and try to make our escape; or it is opened in the presence of Lord Dalgliesh – in which case, we die.'

'Oh.'

'Bravely, of course.'

'Certainly, Sir.'

'At least *I* will. You, of course, have my permission to die cowardly, Mr Linton.' The unspoken words 'You are a girl, after all,' hung in the air. Suddenly, I didn't feel as much like kissing him as I had a moment ago. Withdrawing my arms from around him, I crossed them in front of my chest, shoving him away. My elbow might have grazed his cheek in the process, purely accidentally.

'No, thank you!' I growled. 'I'll go for the brave option, if you don't mind, Sir.'

His words echoed in my head: *in which case, we die... in which case, we die...*

A shiver ran down my spine, half born of fear, half of... wanting?

Not wanting to die, of course. No. I was shivering because I wanted something else entirely – or rather, someone.

If I was going to die anyway, what was the sense in resisting? The silence expanded around the two of us, and in the stillness and the dark I felt him more strongly than ever before. If we were going to die, what was the sense in my keeping my self-esteem? My dignity? Dignity was no good to a corpse. But to spend the last few hours of my life in the arms of another human being, warm and comforting...

Except that he isn't warm. He's cold as ice. He feels nothing for you. And you should not feel anything for him. You can't!

Suddenly, it came. The first wave was almost imperceptible, a gentle swell that hardly moved us, cushioned as we were by the wood wool. But then came another, and another. The rocking intensified. My breath hitched, as I could feel his body press into mine, and draw back. Press down, draw back. Press down, draw back.

'W-what is that?' I asked, my voice sounding strange in my own ears.

'The sea,' he said, cool and resigned. 'We have left the Thames and are now out in the Channel.'

Blast it!

I never liked that darned piece of sea! Why couldn't England be part of the Continent, like every other decent European country? It was simply not fair, the tortures that were inflicted on poor people trying to cross the Channel stacked on top of each other in a small wooden crate!

The motion of the waves grew ever stronger, pressing me against Mr Ambrose with a devilish, regular rhythm. Blood thrummed in my ears, and my breathing became laboured.

'Mr Linton?'

'Y-yes, Sir?'

'Are you sure you do not suffer from fever? Your skin is getting hot again.'

'N-no, Sir. I'm perfectly fine.'

Desperately, I grasped around for something to talk about, something to distract me, so I would not succumb. But there was nothing. Nothing I wanted to say, or do, or know...

Wait a moment. That wasn't strictly true. There *was* something I wanted to know. Something I wanted to know badly enough to even drive thoughts of Mr Ambrose from my mind for a few precious moments.

'Mr Ambrose, Sir?' My voice was unsteady.

He turned his head towards me without bothering to lift it from my chest. I could fell his chin press into my soft flesh.

'Yes, Mr Linton?'

I could feel the breath of his words on my face, smell his scent of rough soap and too much money. What had I been about to ask again? And was it really that important...? I could just surrender and...

No!

'I just wondered, Sir... the centre of the world. What is it? I mean, if we are going to die in any event, you can tell me, right?'

Silence. Silence and darkness. The only other sensation was the feeling of his closeness: omnipresent, omnipotent, omniinconvenient.

Damn him! Why wouldn't he tell me, even now? What could be so important that he wouldn't divulge it even at the brink of my, and his own, destruction?

'Tell me!'

Nothing but silence. I could feel myself yielding, feel my arms snaking around him again, my lips moving closer to his. What did it matter if I betrayed my principles? What would it matter if he pushed me back, laughed at me, mocked me? At least I would get to taste his lips again. Nobody would ever know.

Wrong. You would know. You would regret.

Still, my lips moved ever closer to their destination. I could feel his breath on my tongue now, so close was I.

'Tell me!' I whispered, in a last, desperate attempt to distract myself, though at this point I wasn't sure that even the long-sought mystery of the centre of the world would hold me back. 'Please. Don't people who are condemned to death usually get a last wish before they die? Well, I have one.

Kiss me.

No!

'Tell me. Please. Tell me what the file I'm going to die for is about.'

A shudder went through his still form.

'You want to know what the file contains?' Some part of me marvelled how he managed to keep his voice calm and controlled, even at such a moment as this. 'You want to know what the centre of the world is, Mr Linton? Fine! I'll tell you...'

LESSONS IN POWER

'The centre of the world is a canal. A canal in Africa.'

It took a few moments for his words to register. Had he really... had he really just said that? That couldn't have been the truth! He had to have told me a joke just now, right?

Stupid question. This was Mr Ambrose.

He had been serious. Absolutely serious.

My hands flew up to grasp his collar, and not with the intention of kissing him. I started to shake him like a rattle.

'*What*? A *canal*? I have been risking my life for a *bloody irrigation ditch*?'

His hands shot up to grasp mine, and ripped them off his collar. There was the sound of tearing cloth.

'That uniform cost one pound and ten shillings, Mr Linton! And the tailcoat underneath was almost new!'

'It was ten years old, you blasted miser! Ten years old is not almost new!'

I tried to kick out at him, but he captured my well-aimed knee between his legs. Next I tried to butt heads, but he ducked to the side.

'That is a matter of opinion, Mr Linton. I shall deduct the cost for repairing the collar from your wages.'

'You're never going to pay me any wages, you son of a bachelor, because we'll never get out of this alive! And for what? A bleeding, stinking irrigation ditch!'

'Mind your language, Mr Linton! You have been warned that you will have to address me respectfully.'

'You can take your respectful address and stuff it respectfully up your...'

'Mr Linton!'

With all my might, I shoved against him, and somehow managed to haul him to the side, slamming his back against the wall of the crate. Wood wool flew around us like snow in a blizzard. Only conditions were not cold here. Oh no. They were just about to get hot.

'Mr Linton!'

'My name is Lilly! Do you hear me? Lilly!'

'Mr Linton, I forbid you...'

I tried to bite him. To my credit, I must say that I only missed by inches. My teeth sank into the cloth of his precious, nearly-new-10-year-old tailcoat and probably left a good set of teeth marks. Hopefully, they would be expensive to remove, or better yet, permanent!

'Mr Linton! Be rational.'

'*Rational*? Don't you dare tell me to be rational! It's you who is crazy; crazy enough to risk your life and mine on this damned adventure! And for what? For a bloody irrigation ditch!'

My hands were still firmly caught in his grasp. I tried to bite again, but this time caught only air between my teeth. We rolled around in the little, dark space we had, bits of wood flying all around us, and I flatter myself that I got a few good kicks in now and again. But I didn't manage to free my hands, which was a pity. You need hands for strangling someone.

'You... you... I'm going to kill! Do you hear me! I'm going to–'

Suddenly, he pushed against me with unbelievable force, and I realized that he had been holding back up to that moment. In a flash, he was on top of me again and pressing my arms down at my sides. His legs snaked around me, trapping mine, and preventing me from delivering any more kicks. He had me. I could not hope to escape from his stone-hard prison.

'Firstly,' he said, his voice as cold as a winter solstice night, 'Nobody *made* you risk your life. In fact, I seem to remember locking you up to prevent that exact possibility.'

I hesitated. Admittedly, he had a point there. A small, but nonetheless existent, point.

'Secondly, you *asked* for the contents of the file. It is most ill-bred behaviour to try and bite my fingers off for a truthful answer. And thirdly, if you ever call the masterpiece of diplomacy and engineering which has been stolen from me an irrigation ditch again, I will deduct half your wages for stupidity.'

Colour rose to my cheeks. Thank God it was too dark for him to see.

'So what exactly is this canal, if not an iri...' I remembered his threat just in time, and amended, '...if not what I said before?'

There was one more moment of silence. I waited. I could feel it in the air: he was finally going to talk.

Yet when he started, it wasn't at all how I thought he would.

'Four years ago, a British officer and explorer called Francis Rawdon Chesney submitted a report to Parliament. Nobody paid much attention to it at the time – the country was too busy with the death of King George and the general election. But I heard of the report and tried to get hold of it. Something which, interestingly enough, proved to be more difficult than usual with official Parliament papers. Somebody had taken very good care to suppress this particular paper, which made me only more eager to lay my hands on it.'

He made a pause. By now he had my full attention. I waited with rapt attention for him to resume.

'Finally, I managed to obtain a partial copy of the report by bribing an MP. It was a costly investment, but one that proved worth the expense. I knew that the moment I got to see the report. It detailed calculations of Mr Chesney as to the comparative sea level of the Red Sea and the Mediterranean. You see, up until this point, the sea levels of the two oceans had been believed to differ significantly. According to Mr Chesney's new calculations, however, this was not the case.'

I still couldn't see where he was going with this. Of what earthly importance could sea levels be, no pun intended? Yet I sensed that there was more to come, and so, for once, kept my mouth shut.

'I sent a man out there to check the calculations,' he continued. 'They were one hundred per cent correct. The Red Sea and the Mediterranean were on one level. Yet the fools in the government hadn't seen the significance of this. And I suppose,' he added coolly, 'neither do you?'

I bit my lip. Indeed, I didn't see how it could be of the slightest significance. What could it matter? The Red Sea and the Mediterranean were separated by land, so what could possibly...?

Land.

Land that could be bridged by a canal.

It all clicked into place. Clearing my throat, I said tentatively: 'It was of significance because a canal could be built to link the two, without the different sea levels causing a natural catastrophe?'

He was quiet for a moment.

'Mr Linton?'

'Yes, Sir?'

'Your intelligence is greater than that of an average British Member of Parliament.'

'Err... Thank you, Sir.'

'Don't get too excited, though. Nowadays, this doesn't mean much.'

'Oh.' I hesitated. 'And why is it so important to build a canal from the Red Sea to the Mediterranean?'

He sighed coolly. 'Only *slightly* greater than an MP's intelligence, I see. Well, Mr Linton, why do you think?'

'I have no idea, Sir.'

'What, Mr Linton, is the most potent instrument of power in our world today?'

'Um... guns?'

I could almost feel him close his eyes in exasperation.

'A typical answer, and a very dangerous misconception. The most potent instrument of power in our world today, Mr Linton, is trade. It was trade that built the British Empire, trade that lost it its American Colonies. It was trade that destroyed the might of the Incas, Turks and Chinese and made Europe, and above all Britain, the master of the world.'

'Um... I think guns played some part in that, too.'

'Yes, yes. They played a part.' He waved my comment away as if it were of no more importance than an annoying fly. 'But if not for trade, Europe would never have become inventive and rich enough to develop the gun and put it to its full use. If not for trade, great ships would not have been built, the world would not have been circumvented, the Americas not discovered, the farthest corners of the world not reached and then subjugated. Trade is what keeps Europe's power alive today, and it is what has enabled me to build my very own empire. And now imagine, in such a world, dominated by trade, what you could do if you were able to open a new trade route, a trade route to the richest lands of the East which would be only half as long as the existing ones.'

As he spoke, I saw the map of the world from my father's old atlas appear in front of my inner eye, and I could see red lines flowing across it, marking the most important trade routes of the British Empire. I had never thought about why exactly these trade routes were shown on every map, but now, listening to Mr Ambrose's almost passionate words, I realized: they *were* the Empire. Without them, it would not exist.

And I also realized something else: All of the trade routes to the East ran around the Cape of Good Hope, circumventing the entire continent of Africa before they reached their destination. They did *not* go through the Mediterranean and from there to the Red Sea, because on this far shorter journey, there was a piece of land in the way.

Of course! Lilly, you blockhead, how could you not have seen this sooner!

'Suez,' I whispered. 'You are planning to build a canal at Suez!'

Again, he didn't say anything for a moment.

Then: 'It seems that not just your intelligence is slightly above that of an average MP. Your knowledge of geography, too. Adequate thinking, Mr Linton.'

Would it kill him to say 'good' instead of 'adequate' for once? Yes, it probably would. He'd choke on it.

'How much trade goes around the Cape of Good Hope every year?' I enquired cautiously.

He made a low, derisive noise.

'All the trade with China, India, Indochina, Australia, New Zealand... practically half the world's trade. Certainly the most profitable half. And if everything had gone according to plan, all this was to be channelled through one thin lane of water.' Underneath the coolness, his voice almost became passionate as he spoke. 'All this was going to flow through one centre of the world. All this I was to hold in the palm of my hand. Can you imagine, Mr Linton? Can you?'

I shook my head. I had to work hard to resist the urge to shiver.

'N-no. I cannot.'

'That is because you have never seen a fleet of clippers or East Indiamen set sail for the Far East, or the Americas. If you had, if you had witnessed the majesty of the great white sails coming down, catching the wind, and carrying the ships off to every corner of the world, you would. Ships are my arrows, the sea my bow, the world my target.'

There definitely was passion in his voice now. It was a cold passion, a passion for things, not for people, but it was passion.

'Do you see the power of trade, Mr Linton? The power of the ship? It makes our world what it is today. And I was going to possess the knot where all these strands of power came together. The knot that connected East to West, and made me master of all.'

His last words seemed to echo with significance in our little, dark space.

'East and West...' I murmured. 'That's it. That's why Dalgliesh took the file from you!'

'Yes.' There was resignation in Mr Ambrose's voice, and if I was not very mistaken, grudging admiration. 'If I had been able to go through with my plans for that canal, I would have had him by the throat. His company may have the monopoly for trade in India, it might even rule India as if it were its own empire, it might even have its own army, but its ships still need to pass from East to West. If they cannot do this at competitive speed and cost, the company, like any other business, would collapse within a few years. If I had built that canal, all ships passing through it would have been able deliver goods twice as fast and at half the price of any competitor. *I* could have decided who would get past and who wouldn't. *I* could have demanded *any* price I wanted.'

'And you would have made Dalgliesh pay a lot?'

'No.' The word was a block of frozen stone. 'I would have cut off my right hand before one of the cursed ships of that man ever passed into my canal!'

He still held my wrists firmly in his grasp as he spoke. Thus it was that I could feel his little finger twitch.

'What did you say?' I demanded.

'You heard me.'

'Yes, but... You would have denied him entry? Even though you could have asked any price you wanted?'

500

'Yes.'

'Even though denying him entry would mean driving him into ruin?'

'Yes.'

'Surely that is a little harsh.'

'No.'

'Oh.'

His little twitched again.

'This is business, Mr Linton. Business is about ruining your competitors, burying them so deeply that they never get up again. And I would have buried him. Oh yes, I would.'

By now, his finger was tapping a staccato on my wrist. Somehow, I didn't think Lord Dalgliesh was only simple business competition to Mr Ambrose. Yet I didn't probe further into the matter. Instead, I gently slipped my hand out of his grip and took his fingers in mine. The twitching of his little finger ceased.

He gave a sigh.

'What is the use?' he muttered darkly. 'What sense is there in "would"s and "might have"s? I have played the game, and lost. There will be no centre of the world, no canal at Suez, no new routes for world trade under my direction. There is no chance of getting the file back now. We can only hope, if we are lucky, to escape from this with our lives.' He took a deep breath. 'Now listen. There is a remote chance that not too many men will be present when they open the crate. I will engage them, and it will be your job to-'

'No.'

I think my abrupt interruption caught him off guard. He said nothing for a moment, then demanded: 'No? What do you mean, *no*?'

'I mean no, there still is a chance to get the file back. Think, Sir. Nobody knows we are here. If we could somehow manage to get out of this crate unseen...'

'Which is extremely unlikely.'

'If we could manage it, we could get to the file...'

'How, without being discovered?'

'We still have our disguises. They got us into one of Dalgliesh's buildings – why not another?'

'There still remains the little matter of getting out of there alive.'

I smirked in the dark. 'Since when have I become the one suggesting dangerous schemes and you the pessimist to reject them? Are you frightened of a little adventure?'

'Mr Linton?'

'Yes?'

'If I had enough room to move my arm properly, I would take you by the scruff of the neck and...'

'Yes, Sir?'

Silence.

'Nothing, Mr Linton.'

'Just as you say, Sir.'

Another spell of silence. When he spoke again, his voice was a curious, cold mix of tones I couldn't decipher.

'You are seriously suggesting that on reaching our destination, I get out of this crate unseen, manage to sneak into Lord Dalgliesh's secret hideout, steal the file, and then manage to flee, and that all on my own?'

'No. Not on your own, Sir. After all, I am here.'

'That makes me feel so much better.'

~~**~*~*

The sudden silence was as loud as thunder in our ears. The deep thumping noise that had been our constant companion for the last few hours had suddenly ceased. The vibrations of the ship had stilled. The sudden change woke me from the half-sleep into which I had fallen after hours and hours of waiting in the dark.

'The engine has been stopped,' I whispered drowsily. 'We... we must have arrived.'

'What a brilliant deduction, Mr Linton.'

Instead of making a snappish reply to his sarcastic remark, I asked. 'Do you think we are in the harbour of this place Dalgliesh mentioned? This "Ill Marbow"?'

'Île Marbeau, Mr Linton,' he corrected.

'That's what I said, Sir.'

'No, Mr Linton. You pronounced it like grotesque, half-English gibberish. But I am quite certain the name is French. "Île" is French for "island".'

'Oh.'

'Yes, Mr Linton. An island. Do you see now how getting away with the file might be a bit difficult?'

'Well... we could steal a ship.'

'And man it ourselves?' The cold, disparaging tone of his voice told me that this was not in the realm of possibility. And I believed him. Unlike me, he had been on many ships, most of which he probably owned himself. He knew what he was talking about.

Île Marbeau... The strange-sounding name reverberated in my head and made my breathing quicken. With my mind's eye, I saw a desolate, dark rock rising out of the sea towards a night sky black and grey with storm clouds. On the very top rose the ruins of an old castle, in which the infamous Lord Dalgliesh ruled like the king he saw himself to be.

I cleared my throat.

'We are really and truly outside England now?'

'Yes, Mr Linton.'

'Really? Truly outside England?'

'I believe I have already told you so. Yes, we are. Why?'

I didn't know what to say. All my life I had dreamed of adventure, of leaving England to journey to faraway lands and see the marvels of the world. None of my dreams had included being stuck in a wooden crate with somebody like Mr

Rikkard Ambrose. Still, I found myself glad that he was here. With a queasy feeling in my stomach, I thought back to the fight in the alley, to my fear of being shot down by sharpshooters at number 97. Adventures were neither as easy nor as glorious as I had imagined, and it was good to have somebody I trusted with me.

Wait just a minute! Trust? Are you nuts?

But I did trust him. When had that happened? When I had first met him, I didn't trust him as far as I could throw him. In fact, I was deeply suspicious of his dark business dealings and chauvinistic ways. Some part of me still was. But another part of me wanted him to put his arms around me again.

Suddenly, I heard a dull thump from outside. It was repeated, and repeated again, and again, getting louder as it drew nearer.

'What is that?' I asked.

'Marching feet on the metal floor,' Mr Ambrose breathed. 'They're coming to unload the ship.'

Unload the ship? But... bloody hell! I was cargo now! So that included me! I stiffened.

'Don't move, Mr Linton!' His voice was cold, but his breath was hot at my ear. 'Don't breathe. Don't even think about making a sound. No matter how much they jostle us about, we must remain absolutely still. If they hear us, we are dead.' He leant even closer to my ear and hissed: 'Understood?'

A shiver ran down my spine.

'Y-yes, Sir.'

The door to our room opened, and I heard several people enter. They bent to pick up something, and left the room again. None of them came near our crate. I let out a breath I hadn't realized I was holding. Soon after, another group came, and then another, each time carrying off some of the smaller crates and sacks I had briefly seen lying about in the room. They seemed to want to make room for the big removal – in other words, us. I only hoped the big removal wouldn't include a removal from the realm of the living.

Finally, the footsteps returned.

'All right,' a gruff voice called out. 'Ye and Tom grab 'old on that side, me, Jim and Ezra on this one.'

'Sure. On the count of three, mates! One, two, three... 'ere we go!'

Suddenly, the world swayed. We were lifted into the air.

'Bloody 'ell! That thing ain't no sack of feathers! What did they put in there? A block of granite?'

Granite? I wasn't *that* heavy, was I? My behind wasn't that fat! It was only generous, at most. Although... there was also Mr Ambrose to consider, and he could be classified as block of granite in my book.

'Keep your darn mouth shut!' came the growled reply. 'Don't ye know what 'appens to those as asks too many questions?'

The other man fell instantly silent. From this alone, I knew what happened to curious people in Lord Dalgliesh's employ. Or at least I could imagine.

Groaning and moaning, but not uttering another word, the four men carried us out of the room, down the corridor and... and I knew not where. I heard the sound of waves, saw faint strips of light fall in through gaps in the wooden wall, and once fancied I heard the distant chatter of many voices. Where was I? There was no indication of where we were among the sounds, or where we were headed. Not until the scream, that is.

It was faint, so faint that I might have almost imagined it. Almost. If we had been in another place, I might have taken it for a cry of joy, or the sound of an annoyed child. But I knew better. Where we were going, there were no children, and there certainly was no joy.

But what was it then?

I had already opened my mouth to ask, when I remembered Mr Ambrose's warning.

Silence. Absolute silence.

I clamped my mouth shut again and tried to ignore the gnawing feeling of panic in my stomach.

Silent. You must keep silent.

And I did. Somehow, though, Mr Ambrose managed to be twice as silent as I was. He seemed to radiate negative noise. It was a trick I decided I had to learn, if I survived this.

In the distance, I heard another faint cry. I couldn't suppress the image of a dark dungeon creeping up on me. But both times, the cries had sounded like children. What kind of monster was this Lord Dalgliesh?

What few noises there were soon receded into the distance. We were venturing away from the coast, towards the centre of the island, of that much I was sure. But other than that, I knew nothing of where we were heading. There was only the rocking of the crate and the steady marching sound of the soldiers to indicate that we were moving at all.

Finally, the soldiers slowed down.

'Halt!'

At the command, the soldiers stopped. I heard the jingling of keys and a creaking noise that was probably a door. It didn't sound nearly creaky and sinister enough to satisfy my idea of the rusty hinges of a dungeon door, so maybe there was still hope.

'All right, fellows. Put it down 'ere.'

The soldiers were only too happy to comply. The crate smashed to the ground, and Mr Ambrose nearly squashed me beneath him, pressing all the air out of my lungs.

'Mpf!'

'Gently! Gently! The dickens knows what's in there. 'e will 'ave our 'eads on a platter if anything gets broke!'

There was no need to mention who 'he' was. I understood it as well as the soldiers did. They mumbled hurried apologies, and their footsteps moved away. Not long after, we heard a door lock click shut, and then there was only silence.

They hadn't opened the crate.

'What now?' I demanded in a whisper. 'Are we just supposed to wait here until they come back for us?'

'By no means.' Mr Ambrose's tone was back to cool efficiency. The hint of defeat that had been there earlier was nowhere to be found. He grabbed hold of something lying beside me, and I saw a thin object sliding past my face. His cane?

'What are you doing?'

'If I am not mistaken, the soldiers' rough handling of the crate has loosened one of the boards. I may just be able to slide the blade of my sword into the crack and use it as a lever. Don't move an inch. The blade is sharp.'

I froze as above me I heard the slither of steel on steel. There was a creak and, for a moment, a small beam of light fell in through a crack in the wood. Then, the light was blocked by the figure of Mr Ambrose. He raised himself up as far as he could, sliding his sword into the crack he had discovered. Then, I felt his muscles bunch. There was a crunching sound, and suddenly light flooded into the crate – not the weak, blueish light of the moon, but bright, golden sunlight.

'It is morning!' I exclaimed.

'Of course, Mr Linton. We have been at sea for...' He pulled his watch out of his pocket and let it snap open. The coat of arms on the lid flashed in the bright morning light. '... exactly seven hours, thirty-eight minutes and four seconds. Dalgliesh must have taken a roundabout route to avoid being spotted.'

'Seven hours!' I clapped my hands to my face. 'Blast! That means that by now, my aunt must have noticed I am gone! What am I going to tell her?'

Mr Ambrose gave me a look. Oh, how I had missed that icy, spine-chilling gaze! 'That, I would say, is the least of our worries, Mr Linton.'

'Then you don't know my aunt.'

Instead of replying, he sheathed his sword again, and shoved the cane through the hole that he had created in the wall of the crate. With a sharp pull, he twisted the cane, and another board flew away, clattering to the ground. He repeated the procedure again, and again. Then he nodded, satisfied.

'The hole should now be broad enough for an average person to climb through. I will go first. Wait here.'

And before I could utter a single word of complaint, he was already out of my sight, sliding out of the crate like some sleek, dark spectre. I listened intently, praying that there was no guard posted outside. Not a single sound came from outside the crate. I waited. One minute went by. Two minutes.

What the heck is he doing out there?

Three minutes.

He can't take this long, can he?

Four minutes.

Something has to have gone wrong! What if there is more than one guard out there? What if Mr Ambrose...

Five minutes.

What are you waiting for? Go and look for him! Maybe something has happened. Maybe-

'All clear.' Suddenly, his perfect granite face appeared above me, and I breathed a sigh of relief.

'Where were you?' I hissed.

'Checking.'

'Checking for what?'

'Soldiers, Mr Linton. There are none present, either in here, or out there.'

'How do you know?'

'I climbed to one of the windows and looked out. All I saw was the sea, over the tops of trees, and a path leading downhill.'

'Not even one guard?'

'I do not like to repeat myself, Mr Linton. No. There were no soldiers.'

'But that's strange, don't you think so?'

'Exceedingly. Which is why I would suggest we leave this place before things change from strange to normal. Come!'

He disappeared from my view, and I gathered that now it was my turn. Slowly, I sat up. Every muscle in my body ached from lying down this long, and with so much weight on top of me. I tried very hard not to think about who that hard, muscled weight had belonged to, and gripped the edges of the hole in the lid above me to pull myself farther up.

With a groan at my protesting muscles, I stuck my head through the opening. Looking around me, I saw a large, bare room, with lots of crates piled in every corner and sacks lying on the floor. Light filtered in through a few unglazed but barred windows high up on the wall. Dust motes danced in the light, and somewhere I heard the little footsteps of a mouse, or some other small animal, hurrying across the stone floor.

'What is this place?' I whispered.

'I do not know, Mr Linton. But at a guess, I would say, a warehouse.'

'It looks like nobody ever comes here.'

'Let us hope so, or they will find you still half in the crate when they do come. Now get a move on!'

'Yes, Sir. Immediately, Sir.'

Pushing my arms through the hole, I hoisted myself further up and, bit by bit, emerged into the outside world. This went fine until my waist had slid outside. Suddenly, I encountered resistance. Gripping the boards to either side of me, I pushed harder.

I didn't move an inch.

Again, I pushed harder. Nothing.

'What are you waiting for, Mr Linton?' Mr Ambrose was standing a little way away from the crate, his gaze fixed on the door of the warehouse, prepared at any time for an enemy to come through it. 'We have to go.'

One final time I pushed – to no avail. 'I can't,' I growled. 'I... don't seem to fit through the hole.'

Certain generously-endowed parts of me, anyway.

'The hole should be big enough for an average person, Mr Linton.'

'Well, then maybe I'm a *special* person,' I hissed. 'At least that's what my little sister always says. Will you get rid of another board, already?'

'Manners, Mr Linton!'

'Will you get rid of another board, *Sir*, before somebody comes along and shoots us?'

In two seconds he was on the crate, his cane in hand. Placing it under the nearest board, he pushed down. There was a crack, as if from a pistol shot, and the board flew away. I popped out of the crate like a cork out of a bottle. Hurriedly, I slid down until I stood firm with both feet on the ground, and started to dust off my rumpled uniform.

'Thanks,' I grumbled, my face two shades darker than normal.

He, of course, didn't even deign to notice my flushed cheeks. He was already at the door, sliding it slowly open, and peeking out through the crack.

'There is nobody in the vicinity. Come.' And he slipped outside. Mumbling a very unladylike word, I followed him, and stepped out into a world of wonder.

I didn't know exactly what I had expected the island stronghold of the evil Lord Dalgliesh to look like, but *this* was certainly not it. We stood in a courtyard surrounded by a charming, low stone wall. Moss and other foliage grew out of the cracks in the stone, and it was just the right height to comfortably sit down and have a picnic – an idea to which the rest of the surroundings would have lent themselves beautifully. The courtyard was surrounded by charming, little knobby trees, from which drifted a delicious smell of pines and the sounds of a busy wood. The sound of frolicking squirrels and twittering nightingales mingled with the distant rush of the sea. Bees flew between beautiful flowers which peeked out from between the foremost trees' roots, and a robin fluttered across the courtyard to disappear in the forest on the other side.

'What the heck?' I looked from left to right. 'Did we get sent to the wrong address? Eden, instead of Evil Fortress?'

Mr Ambrose opened his mouth. But I never found out what he was going to say, because all of a sudden, we heard footsteps from around the corner of the warehouse. I hesitated for a moment – and then it was already too late to flee. A man came around the corner, and stopped in his tracks as he spotted us.

Blast!

ÎLE MARBEAU

I wanted to step back, run away, anything, but Mr Ambrose's hand closed around my arm like a vice, holding me in place.

'Don't move!' His voice was barely audible. 'We're wearing our uniforms. He might take us for one of theirs!'

Slowly, the man started forward again. His eyes travelled from me to Mr Ambrose, and back again. Finally, he bowed.

Bowed? To *us*?

'*Bonjour, Messieurs,*' he proclaimed. '*Puis-je vous offrir un verre de limonade glacée?*'

I swallowed convulsively.

'What is he saying?' I whispered. 'Is he telling us that we are going to get shot?'

'No. He is asking whether we want a glass of iced lemonade.'

'What?' I stared at the man, nonplussed. Only now did I notice that he was wearing a white waiter's jacket. 'What does he mean?'

'He means to offer us a drink,' Mr Ambrose told me coolly, as if he had expected all along to be greeted in Lord Dalgliesh's secret abode of evil by waiters wielding glasses of lemonade. He turned to the man in the white jacket. *'Non, merci. Je suis assez frais comme ça.'*

This, whatever it meant, didn't seem to deter the fellow. He smiled a broad smile under his pointy moustache and gave another bow. *'Une tasse de café, peut-être? Ou un repas léger? Messieurs, vous avez l'air un peu pâle.'*

'Non. Mais pourriez-vous nous indiquer le bâtiment principal? Il semblerait que nous avons perdu notre chemin.'

The waiter beamed and bowed once more. *'Bien sûr, Monsieur. Suivez-moi, s'il vous plaît.'*

And he marched off.

'What did you say to him?' I demanded.

'I asked him to direct us to the main building.' Mr Ambrose set off after the waiter with long, determined strides that didn't give a hint of his having been cooped up in a wooden crate for most of the night. I hobbled after him, cursing my burning and itching muscles.

'The main building to what?'

'I have no idea, Mr Linton. I've never been here, remember?'

'But that means this fellow could be leading us right into Lord Dalgliesh's headquarters!'

'I doubt that will happen. Not unless Lord Dalgliesh has started using French waiters to guard his perimeter, which I consider a remote possibility.'

We followed the mysterious waiter along a path thickly lined with ferns, trees and other flora, down a gently sloping hill. The trees were of a rugged beauty – maltreated so severely by the ceaseless wind blowing in from the sea that they were almost bent double, but still stubbornly standing. They were grouped so closely that we could not see anything on either side of the path for some time. Yet suddenly, the flora retreated, and I looked on a sight such as I had never seen before. A horror beyond all the horrors I could have imagined seeing in this stronghold of evil. A terrified gasp escaped my mouth.

'That... can't be!' I whispered.

Mr Ambrose looked on the spectacle for a moment, then nodded gravely. 'Yes. Here, in foreign countries, such practices are not considered... reproachable.'

'But... they are doing it together! Everyone, in plain sight of each other!'

'Yes. As I said, you are in England no longer, Mr Linton.'

Wide-eyed, I gazed down onto the beach in front of us, where multitudes of people were laughing, running about, and swimming in the water. People of *both sexes*! Very well I remembered the bathing places in England where, when women wanted to bathe, they did it in the confines of a bathing machine – a marvellous contraption in the form of a horse-drawn carriage without a bottom, which was pulled into the sea and protected you from all prying eyes. Here, in the country of baguettes and revolutions, women seemed to have no inhibitions about letting the men see them in their swimwear. Moreover, unlike in England, this swimwear did not consist of several heavy, knee-length gowns and a giant hat, under which the woman could hardly be detected. Not only were the feet, calves and knees – yes, *knees!* – of every female on the beach clearly visible, so was pretty much everything else up to an area which, in England, ladies wouldn't even have thought of, much less dared to mention!

I stared at the women for a good two minutes. Then, suddenly, a point of more immediate importance than French standards of morality occurred to me.

'Why,' I asked Mr Ambrose, 'does Lord Dalgliesh have a crowd of bathers on the island that is supposed to be his secret hideout?'

'That is a very good question, Mr Linton.'

'And?'

'And I do not have the answer. Come on. Our guide is getting impatient.'

Indeed, the waiter was already several steps ahead and gesturing for us to keep up. He seemed to find nothing strange about the sight down at the beach, which made my cheeks glow with heat. Frenchmen! Unbelievable...

I sneaked a quick glimpse at Mr Ambrose. He didn't seem to find it unusual, either. Had he been at many such places? Had he seen a lot of female knees?

Quickly, I clamped down on the thought. We were here on a secret mission. Mr Ambrose's bathing habits were none of my concern, and neither were any female knees he might have studied.

By now, the waiter had vanished around a corner. We followed him, and found him pointing up to a building rising up above us.

'*Voilà le bâtiment principal, Monsieur!*'

It wasn't the ruin of a castle.

I admit, my adventurous imagination might have run away with me a bit, imagining Lord Dalgliesh's secret headquarters, but still, I hadn't expected anything like this. The building was large, and painted in a brilliant white. Two rows of wooden supports, one stacked above the other, supported a raised veranda and balcony, and a pair of majestic white steps led up to the first floor. Rows of large windows glinted in the sun and, above the main entrance, words were painted in a cheerful blue:

Hôtel de la Mer azur

'The Hotel of the Azure Sea,' Mr Ambrose translated.

'Thank you so much, Mr Ambrose, Sir. My French extends that far.' I looked from the hotel to the crowd of happily gossiping people sitting on the veranda. 'Do you think it is possible Lord Dalgliesh's ship has landed on the wrong island?'

Silence.

When he hadn't answered after a few more moments, I looked sideways at him. His eyes were glittering.

'I don't think so,' he murmured, and the glint in his dark eyes grew. 'I don't think so at all. Oh, that man. He is a genius.'

A group of children ran by, laughing and screaming. They were not screams of pain. One of the little pests pointed at me and yelled: *'Eh, regardez ce gars! N'a-t-il pas un chapeau totalement ridicule?'*

And they burst into laughter.

'What did he say?' I hissed at Mr Ambrose.

'He complimented you on your manly appearance, Mr Linton.'

'Really?'

'Yes. Focus, Mr Linton. The infant is of no importance.'

Putting a finger in each corner of its mouth, the 'infant' started pulling faces at me and dancing around me, chanting *'Chapeau gaga, Chapeau gaga!'* French brats had a bloody strange way of showing their admiration. His little fiendish accomplices were cheering him on. I tried to chase them away, but I might as well have tried to chase away a swarm of hungry mosquitos.

'This is insane!' I growled.

'On the contrary, Mr Linton.' Mr Ambrose wasn't paying the slightest attention to my fierce battle against the little fiends, but was instead studying the hotel and the beach with dark intensity. 'This is brilliant. Dalgliesh's style, executed to perfection. Blinding people with glamour – so perfect, and so him!'

Bending down, my little tormentor picked up an acorn and chucked it at my hat. I ducked just in time to prevent it being knocked off.

'Glamour? To be honest, I can't see what is glamorous here, Sir. You just wait, you little snot monster, till I get my hands on you!'

'I beg your pardon, Mr Linton?'

'Sorry, Sir. Wasn't talking to you, Sir.'

'Focus, Mr Linton. Focus.'

'Yes, Sir. Of course, Sir. Come here, you bloody little blaggard!'

'Mr Linton!'

'Sorry, Sir. So sorry. What was that you said about Glamorgan?'

Mr Ambrose made an impatient gesture at our surroundings. 'Glamour, Mr Linton, Glamour. This hotel, the tourists, the pretty beaches – all is a disguise for the real purpose of this island – to serve as a centre for some, if not all, of Lord Dalgliesh's less-than-legal operations. That purpose is also the reason for the headquarters being on the French side of the Channel, i.e. outside British jurisdiction.'

He let his eyes wander over the scene before him, the glitter within them reminiscent of freshly fallen snow.

'It is perfect. The perfect place. I must see whether I can persuade Dalgliesh to part with it somehow.'

I was so stunned I nearly didn't manage to duck the next acorn that came flying at me. Had I heard right? Surely he did not mean that he, too, engaged in illegal operations for which he would need a place like this?

I took a look at his cool, granite profile, at the glitter in his dark eyes, and suddenly, I wasn't so sure anymore.

Dear God... What manner of man did you get mixed up with, Lilly? And worse, you didn't just get mixed up with him! You let him kiss–

But no! That had all been pure imagination.

An acorn hit me in the forehead, jerking me painfully from my thoughts.

'Why, you darn little rug-rat...'

'Excuse me, Mr Linton?'

'Didn't mean you, Sir! Sorry, Sir!'

'Focus, Mr Linton. Focus.'

'Yes, Sir. But let me respectfully point out that it is hard to focus while being pelted with missiles, Sir.'

'It is simply a matter of concentration. Now listen closely, Mr Linton. We need to discuss our next move and coordinate our plans.'

'Fine by me,' I said, ducking the next acorn and making a grab for the brat's sleeve. He danced away, cackling like the devil.

'We need to split up. We need to gather as much information about this place as possible, and we can do that more quickly if we do it separately. I will go to the beach and ask questions there. You will go to the hotel, where the staff is likely to speak English. Our aim is to find out where exactly on this island Lord Dalgliesh's headquarters is located. He will have to have privacy for his operations. Try to determine – unobtrusively, mind you – whether there is some place both locals and tourists avoid, or some place that is out of bounds for any reason. Such a spot would be the ideal centre for Dalgliesh's operations. Understood?'

'Yes, Sir. Only, Sir...' I ducked another acorn. 'It will be rather difficult to make unobtrusive enquiries with this little beast on my tail.'

'Is that all?'

Mr Ambrose turned his attention towards the brat a few feet away from him. Only now did I realize that the little snot-monster had so far only chosen me as a target for his missiles, not aiming a single one at His Mightiness, Ambrose the Icy. I didn't have long to ponder the reason for this. Mr Ambrose advanced on the child until he was standing right in front of it. Slowly, he bent down, until his face was on one level with the child. The little brat's fist, already holding the next acorn, slowly sank down until it hung loosely at his side. He made a mistake and met Mr Ambrose's dark gaze. The fist opened, and the acorn fell to the ground.

'*Toi.*' Mr Ambrose said, his voice calm and cold as the Antarctic. '*Va-t'en. Maintenant.*'

The brat gave a little rat-like squeak and whirled around, scampering off as fast as its feet would carry him. I stared after him in disbelief.

'So,' Mr Ambrose announced. 'That's taken care of.'

'What in heaven's name did you say to that little beast?' I demanded.

Straightening, Mr Ambrose shook his head. 'I never disclose my secrets, Mr Linton.'

With that, he left me standing and turned away, off to gather information among the laughing crowds of people on the beach. Thank the Lord he was wearing the uniform, and not his black tailcoat. In his usual attire he would have stuck out like a crow in a flock of popinjays, but in his fake uniform, he fit in quite well with all the officers walking around the hotel in uniforms of different nationalities. In fact, he looked the handsomest of them all.

Quickly, I shook my head, ridding myself of that strange thought. What was it doing in my mind? I had a task to accomplish!

Free of the acorn-throwing fiend, I started up the path to the hotel. But I hadn't gone half a dozen steps when, around the corner of the hotel, I glimpsed another veranda. On this one, several small tables stood, looking very decorative, with white lace tablecloths and vases of yellow iris in the middle. At the end of the veranda hung a sign which, in large blue letters, said: *Café.*

At the tables, people were drinking tea and eating. Delicious smells wafted over, carried by the morning breeze. I hesitated. My eyes wandered between the café, and the entrance to the hotel. I had a duty to perform in there. But then... I also had a pretty pressing duty to my stomach. It gave a big rumble, reminding me of just how long it was since it had been properly filled.

Bad Lilly! Bad! You have work to do!

Yes. My stomach could wait a little longer. I was no ravenous animal. I was a rational, strong, independent lady, and I could resist...

Suddenly, among all the other smells wafting over from the café, I caught one that I hadn't detected before. A smell I would have recognised anywhere in the world: the delicious, mind-boggling odour of chocolate. My feet started moving, and before I realized it, I was across the veranda, inside the café, and in front of a counter with so many delicacies displayed on it that I hardly knew what to choose first.

Bugger! Well, who needs to be a strong woman on an empty stomach, anyway?

Behind the counter stood a broad man with a brilliant smile and a moustache that was so magnificently pointy you could have impaled somebody on it.

'*Um... excuse moi,*' I tried to unearth my few words of French. '*Je vourais... Je...*'

'Oh, do not bother yourself, *Monsieur,*' the man said, his smile lighting up even more brightly. 'Me, I of course speak the language of the Englishmen. We have many Englishmen here, so it good for business, eh? And no worry about English money, either. Now, *Monsieur...*' He pointed to the counter. 'What would you like?'

~~**~*~*

Five minutes later, I sat at one of the little tables, chewing contentedly and sipping a cup of tea. The birds were singing, children were playing – at a safe distance –, the sky was blue, and for the first time in days I felt really content and relaxed. I was about half-finished with my meal, when the calm was disturbed by a cool voice at my ear.

'I thought,' he said, every syllable studded with shards of ice, 'I told you to gather significant information.'

'I have,' I said, pointing to the crescent-shaped object in my hand, half of which I had already devoured. 'For example, I found out that the French are fantastic bakers. They have invented this thing called a "chocolate croissant", which is a kind of crescent shaped bun with chocolate mousse inside, and it tastes simply divine. Do you want to try?'

512

'It appears,' he said, his tone climbing a few more steps down on the thermometer, 'that you and I have very different ideas of what constitutes significant information, Mr Linton.'

'Probably, Sir.'

'Unfortunately, I myself have not been able to ascertain anything useful about the island. People seemed not very inclined to engage in a conversation with me.'

'In spite of your manner being so warm and friendly? Fancy that.'

'Mr Linton?'

'Yes, Sir?'

'Be silent!'

'As you wish, Sir.' I took another bite of my croissant. 'Hm... Something useful like... maybe the fact that there is a ferry service down at the harbour on the other side of the island? Would you consider that useful?'

His eyes darkened. 'How do you know that?'

I took another bite of my croissant and licked a bit of chocolate mousse off my thumb. Then, I jerked it over my shoulder at the smiling man with the pointy moustache, who was just now selling a piece of cake to a young lady in blue.

'My friend over there mentioned it. It's amazing what people tell you once you've bought a cup of tea and a chocolate croissant – for which you will have to pay, by the way. Did you know, for instance, that there is an abandoned salt mine up in the mountains? None of the locals or tourists dare to go there, because it's supposed to be haunted. They know it's haunted, because now and again, they see strange lights up there at night, and because the few people who did go up there, never came back.'

'Indeed, Mr Linton?'

I licked another bit of chocolate mousse off my finger. Somehow, I managed to suppress a grin. 'Yes, indeed, Sir.'

Raising his hand, Mr Ambrose stroked his chiselled chin thoughtfully. His gaze wandered to the mountains rising in the centre of the island. 'Well, in that case, I think we'll have a look at this mine. I would like to meet a few of these ghosts.'

'Can I have another chocolate croissant, first?'

'Mr Linton!'

'Coming, Sir! I'm coming!'

MINE AND YOURS

It only took me one look over the bush to be certain we were in the right place. Quickly, I ducked down again and whispered: 'That's it! Lord Dalgliesh is here!'

'How do you know?' Mr Ambrose enquired, not looking at me, but staring through a gap in the foliage at the man standing at the entrance to the abandoned mine. 'That's not Dalgliesh! I don't see him anywhere.'

'Yes, but the guard at the entrance...!'

'He's wearing a French uniform. He's not one of Dalgliesh's men.'

'Oh yes, he is! That's just it! I recognized him the moment I saw him. He was one of the men on the ship, one of those who were on deck when I climbed aboard.'

Immediately, Mr Ambrose's eyes turned sharper, more focused. They seemed to drill into the man who was standing at the entrance to the old mine, right in front of a worm-eaten old sign that said: *Danger! Ne pas entrer!*

'Hm. Well, if I can forge a uniform, then so can Dalgliesh. He might not even need to. Maybe he is actually in league with the French. They cannot like the idea of a canal at Suez under the control of an Englishman any more than he does.'

I stared at him, incredulously.

'You... you actually think he'd consider treason?'

'It wouldn't be the first time.'

There was a moment of silence while I tried to digest that piece of information.

'All right,' his voice finally cut through the silence, cold and controlled. 'There are two possibilities. Either this guard is genuine, in which case he will turn us back with a few polite *"Pardon, Messieurs"*...'

'I told you he isn't genuine!'

'...or you are right and he is in Dalgliesh's pay, in which case he should take us for soldiers of the Presidency Armies and let us pass.' He shot me a dark look. 'But in that case, there is no return. Once we're out in the open, we have to keep going, down into the mine. Do you understand, Mr Linton?'

I hesitated – then nodded. 'Yes, Sir.'

'I assume it would be of no avail trying to convince you to stay behind?'

I raised an eyebrow. 'After I've come this far, you want me to stay here and miss all the fun? Are you mad?'

'You have a strange definition of "fun", Mr Linton.'

'And you don't have one at all.'

'Mr Linton?'

'Yes, Sir?'

'Be quiet.'

'Yes, Sir!'

Methodically, he took his watch out of his pocket and fiddled around with the dials. I wanted to ask what he was doing, but that would have been rather incompatible with staying quiet. Finally, he seemed to be content, and put his watch away.

'Mr Linton?'

'Yes, Sir?'

'Are you ready?'

'Yes, Sir, I am, Sir.'

'Then follow me.'

Slowly, he rose to his full height. Stepping out from behind the bush, he advanced on the guard in French uniform, his stride perfectly confident, as if nothing in the world could turn him back. I followed close at his heels. The guard turned his head, and spotted us.

Bugger! Please don't shoot us, don't shoot us, don't shoot us...!

He didn't make a move. Was he just too startled to react? For one moment, I questioned my own memory. Was he really one of Dalgliesh's men? His French uniform looked perfect to the last button. He could have come from a parade on the Champs-Élysées. But if he was Dalgliesh's man, and saw through our disguise....

He reached into his pocket. Oh God! What was he going for? His gun?

He pulled out a pipe and lit it. We were only ten yards away now. His eyes followed us closely. Seven yards. Six. Five.

Please don't get suspicious! Please don't! Please!

He took the pipe out of his mouth. Three yards. Two. One.

We were past. He hadn't stopped us, hadn't acted as if we were there at all. The tunnel swallowed us, and we continued on, down into the darkness. I had been right. This was Lord Dalgliesh's lair.

~~**~*~*

I don't know how long we wandered down the gloomy tunnel. In the half-light, interrupted only by the occasional burst of brightness from an opening in the ceiling, time seemed to stand still. Or at least, to me it did. To Mr Ambrose, as the quiet ticking of his pocket watch reminded me, time was always running, and he had to catch up.

At some point, rusty rails began appearing on the ground beside us, and we saw one or two mine carts lying keeled over on the ground. Spiderwebs hung from the rusted iron and from the low, vaulted ceiling over our heads. Ahead, a point of light appeared.

'What is that?' I asked.

'That,' came Mr Ambrose's reply, his voice as dark and cold as the tunnel around us, 'is where Lord Dalgliesh is.'

His pace quickened. I almost had to run to keep up with him. The light in front of us grew larger and brighter, until the tunnel finally opened up spat us out. My mouth dropped open. And this time not because of seeing women display their knees on the beach.

We were standing at the edge of a huge natural cave. The ceiling high above our heads was a monster's jaw, armed with stalactites as tusks and teeth. Torches hung from iron brackets on the walls, their smoke disappearing through a dark hole in the ceiling. With the view thus not obscured by smoke, as it usually would have been in any mine, I could clearly see the figures that stood and marched all around the giant cavern: soldiers.

No French uniforms here. These were all soldiers of the Presidency Armies, proudly proclaiming their allegiance in colours of blood-red and blue. They rolled crates around on mine carts, patrolled along the walls, or carried messages. All was a buzz of activity. And over the heads of the busy little underground kingdom hung the sign of their king: the two golden lions.

'He's not very concerned about concealing who is behind this, is he?' I asked, staring up at the huge banner.

'He doesn't have to be, Mr Linton.' Mr Ambrose wasn't looking at the lions. His eyes were already wandering over the crowds of soldiers, as if he could wrest the file from them by the pure force of his gaze.

'There!' Breath hissed through his teeth, and he made a sharp motion with his head, not daring to attract attention by lifting his hand to point. 'There, do you see him?'

I looked, and I saw. Lord Dalgliesh was stepping out of a wooden building that had been erected on a higher level of the cave, only accessible via a single staircase, built on wooden supports along the stone walls.

'There,' Mr Ambrose whispered. His eyes were not following Lord Dalgliesh, but were fixed on the wooden hut. 'That is where he keeps the file. It's the ideal place. High up, easy to guard, difficult to reach.'

Like an arrow shot from a string, he started towards the stairs. I had a hard time keeping up with him as he wove through the maze of stalagmites and soldiers. We reached the bottom of the staircase in no time at all.

'What if we meet Lord Dalgliesh on our way up?' I hissed into his ear.

With his usual loquacious eloquence, Mr Ambrose made a jerking movement with his hand over his jugular.

'Thank you so much for your reassurance, Sir!'

'You're welcome, Mr Linton.'

Truth be told, I had expected nothing less, but still, the thought made sweat appear on my forehead. Slowly, we began to ascend. We were about halfway up when my worst nightmare happened. I heard footsteps from above us. Mr Ambrose's steps didn't falter. He continued upwards as if nothing had happened.

A man appeared in front of us, in the uniform of a colonel. He stopped dead as he saw us.

What now? Is he going to offer us iced lemonade?

'Hey! You two! What the blazes are you doing here?'

Apparently not.

'Private Williamson and Private Jones, Sir. Change of guard, Sir,' Mr Ambrose said, deadpan, and snapped to attention. Thank the Lord I had enough presence of mind to emulate him.

'Really?' The colonel frowned and took a watch out of his pocket. 'I didn't think it was time yet... No, it *isn't* time yet! You are early. What is going on here?' His eyes narrowed suspiciously, and I had to work hard to resist wiping the sweat of my forehead.

'Really? Early?' Mr Ambrose's voice rang with honest surprise. 'Are you sure, Colonel...?'

'Colonel Townsend.'

'Are you sure that we're early, Colonel Townsend, Sir?' Taking his own watch out of his pocket, Mr Ambrose let it snap open. 'Sorry, Sir, but according to my watch we're exactly on time. Look.'

The officer stepped up beside Mr Ambrose and looked over his shoulder.

'Struth! You are absolutely right, soldier. It's just time for the guard to change. How the time flies.'

'And my watch is very reliable, Sir.'

'Looks like it.' Colonel Townsend glanced at the silver pocket watch with admiring eyes. 'Mine is such a modern piece of trash. Yours looks like a much nicer piece. A family heirloom?'

A muscle in Mr Ambrose's jaw twitched. Suddenly, he didn't look nearly as much like the obedient soldier of a second ago. 'Yes! Why?'

The officer seemed taken aback by such abrupt tones from an underling. 'I just asked because the crest on the lid looks a little familiar.'

With an obvious effort, Mr Ambrose forced a polite mask on his face. 'My... father gave it to me, Sir'

His father? I stared at him out of the corner of my eye. Mr Ambrose had a father? Did that mean he had actually been conceived in connubial congress, not hewn out of the rock of some mountain, as I had always suspected? Could it be true? Or just another lie to put the officer off?

'I see.' The colonel shrugged. 'Well, you may continue, men. I'll have to go and reset my watch...'

And he went off, mumbling about unreliable modern mechanics.

We continued up the stairs. I did my best to try and appear calm, ignoring the fact that my heart was pounding and my head was buzzing with a thousand questions.

'How did you know when they changed the guard here?' I demanded in a low voice, as soon as he was out of earshot.

And do you really have a father? Well, do you? And if so, how did your poor mother ever survive giving birth to a living rock?

'I didn't, Mr Linton. I knew from Warren's report when the guard changed at number 97 East India Dock Road, and, based on the hypothesis that all the Presidency Army soldiers were likely to operate on the same schedule, I set my watch to local time before we went into the mine.'

I had to admit, he had brains, even if they were frozen. But that answer wasn't enough. I itched to ask him just one more question.

Was the watch really your father's? Why is there a crest on the lid? Does it really belong to a noble family, and if so, what the heck are you doing with it? You're no nobleman, right?

All right, maybe that was more than just one question. To be honest, I had a mountain of questions about him, his somewhat scary plans for the domination of all the trade in the world, and his past, and his future. But none of these things were actually any of my business, and with us sneaking into the villain's lair, this was certainly not the right time and place for curiosity. So I swallowed my questions and followed him up the stairs, until we reached a large landing at the top, hewn out of the rock floor of the raised plateau.

We had hardly set foot on the stone when, from up ahead, we heard voices. Among the echoing noises of the busy cave, they were too indistinct for me to recognize – but not for Mr Ambrose.

'Get down!'

Grabbing my arm, he shoved me behind one of the wooden buildings that stood right beside the landing. Stumbling, I fell to my knees, and remained like that, cowering on the cold stone, while the voices drew nearer. Mr Ambrose appeared beside me, his whole body tensed like a panther about to spring.

We waited, in silence. I didn't dare move a single muscle.

'...the men made any progress so far?' A familiar smooth, magnanimous voice came from the other side of the building. It sounded so charming, so relaxed. Even now, knowing what I knew, I could hardly believe this was Lord Dalgliesh, chief shareholder of the Honourable East India Company and close friend to the Crown, discussing criminal enterprises.

'No, My Lord. The code of the documents in question seems to be well developed.'

'I see. Please be so kind as to see to it that they are *properly motivated*, will you? I wish them to understand how important this project is to me and to the Company.'

'Um, yes, My Lord. I shall think of a suitable motivation.'

'Excellent. I'm sure I can rely on you.'

'Yes, My Lord. Certainly, My Lord.'

'And what about the diplomatic treaties that were not encoded? The secret agreements with Muhammad Ali Pasha? Were they genuine?'

'Oh yes, My Lord. Every word.'

'I see. Do we have an East Indiaman scheduled to go to Egypt?'

'Yes, My Lord.'

'How fortunate. Please send one of my agents on board and instruct him to courteously discourage His Highness the Khedive from any such further action. Tell him it would be unwise. He would not want to lose my good will, now, would he?'

The words were so soft, so friendly – not angry at all. And yet, I caught a glimpse of the other man, who walked beside Lord Dalgliesh as they passed by the building behind which we were hiding. At the words 'lose my good will', he flinched as if hit by a whip.

'Certainly not, My Lord,' he said hurriedly. 'The Khedive will surely take that into consideration.'

Lord Dalgliesh smiled.

'Yes. I'm sure he will.'

They began to descend the stairs, their voices fading into the distance. I continued to cower on the stone floor, my heart still hammering like an insane woodpecker. After a while, I tried to get up, but found I couldn't get my legs to move.

'Who is this Khedive-person?' I asked, my voice slightly unsteady.

Mr Ambrose had risen beside me. His legs didn't seem to have been filled with pudding.

'The ruler of Egypt,' he responded curtly.

'Lord Dalgliesh can tell the *King of Egypt* what to do?'

Mr Ambrose lowered his eyes until he met mine.

'Lord Dalgliesh can tell the Queen of the British Empire what to do. Ali Pasha hardly presents a challenge to him. And neither, apparently, do I.' His left little finger twitched, once. 'It cost me a fortune to negotiate these secret treaties! It will cost me another to renegotiate, now that Dalgliesh knows. This is... quite inconvenient.'

'Inconvenient? Dear me. Such strong words, Sir.'

'Mr Linton?'

'Yes, Sir?'

'Shut and get up.'

'Yes, Sir.'

Unsteadily, I got to my feet. 'What now?' I wanted to know.

Holding up a finger, Mr Ambrose took two quick steps to the corner of the building and spied across the corner.

'There is only one other building up here,' he said, his voice hardly audible. I leaned closer. 'Two guards, one on either side of the door.'

'How will we get past them?'

'I will trick them the same way I tricked the officer on the stairs.'

'And what if they don't fall for it?'

He didn't answer. And he didn't really need to. I already knew.

'Ready, Mr Linton?'

I took a deep breath, squared my shoulders and tried to appear as male and soldierly as I possibly could.

'Yes, Sir.'

'Three, two, one...now!'

We emerged from behind the building in what I hoped looked like lockstep, and not like a pair of gallivanting giraffes. The guards' eyes immediately focused on us, and their hands closed more tightly around their rifles. Oh-oh. That was no good sign.

'Afternoon, fellows.' Mr Ambrose nodded to the men. He didn't stop in his move towards them, obviously expecting them to step aside. 'Ye can go and have a nice lie-down, now. Me and my mate, we're taking over.'

The two men didn't move an inch.

'It ain't time for the changing of the guard yet,' Soldierly Exhibit A said. He was a broad-shouldered man with curly, blond hair and long ears. I had never trusted people with long ears. Spaniels had long ears, and so had the Prime Minister.

'It ain't?' Again, Mr Ambrose took the watch out of his pocket and opened it. 'Aye, it is. Look.'

Soldierly Exhibit A took a brief look at Mr Ambrose's watch, then slid his hand into his pocket and took out his own.

'Your watch is going wrong,' he stated after a short examination. 'I swear, it ain't time yet! It's still more than half an hour.'

Mr Ambrose sighed. 'My watch ain't never wrong. Yours must be. Look, if ye don't believe me, go ask Colonel Townsend.'

The soldier's long ears twitched at the name. 'Colonel Townsend? He knows ye're here?'

'He's the one that sent us up here, pal. You can have it out with him, if ye want, but you ain't gonna stop me and my mate from staying. This is our shift, and we're gonna do as we was told.'

The long-eared guard bit down on his lower lip. The name of the officer had apparently eradicated his suspicions and simultaneously sown doubts in his mind about the reliability of his watch. You could almost hear the words – *after all, the modern trash today ain't very reliable, things ain't what they used to be...*

'All right,' he growled. 'But if I find out ye've been pulling one over on me, pal, I'll get back at you, don't ye doubt it.'

Mr Ambrose gave a little snort of derision. 'Why d'ye think I'd wanna do that, eh? Do I look like I enjoy pushing my legs in my liver? I'd rather sit down and have a drink than stand around all day for no good reason.'

'There's a reason, all right,' the guard growled. 'Whatever's in that place,' he pointed to the hut he had been guarding, 'is pretty important.'

'Aye, aye, be off with you.' Mr Ambrose waved them away. 'Don't ye fear. We ain't gonna let anybody nick My Lord's stuff.'

'Ye'd better not.'

With that, the long-eared guard waved to his silent companion, and the two disappeared down the stairs.

I opened my mouth to speak, but immediately Mr Ambrose held up a warning hand. I shut my mouth again. With a jerk of his head, he indicated for me to follow him, and took up his position to the right of the door. I placed myself to the left and stood straight, arms hanging loosely down my sides, just as he did. In this position we remained – one minute, two minutes, three. I was beginning to wonder what we were waiting for, when I heard it, or rather its absence: footsteps. They were gone. We had been waiting until the guards were out of hearing distance.

As soon as there was silence, Mr Ambrose sprang into action. Fishing two small pieces of metal out of his pockets, he bent down in front of the door of the wooden hut and began fumbling at the keyhole.

'Where in God's name do you have the keys for this place from?' I hissed.

'I don't,' was his calm reply. 'These are no keys. They are lock picks.'

'*Lock picks?* What does a respectable gentleman want with lock picks?'

'Nothing, probably.' He threw me a cool glance. His fingers didn't stop. They moved in an intricate dance, producing clicking noises from the lock. 'But then, I never claimed to be respectable.'

He turned his eyes towards the lock again.

'Listen closely now, Mr Linton. We have exactly twenty-six minutes and thirty-one seconds until the next shift of guards arrives – less even, if those two who just left should happen to meet Colonel Townsend and discuss with him our appearance here. I will need approximately another three minutes to open this lock, and there might be other, more complicated locks between us and the file inside the hut, so we will have to move fast. As soon as the file is in our possession, we will move to the tunnel at the end of the cave...'

'What tunnel, Sir?'

'Didn't you see the tunnel at the other side of the cave as we came in?'

'No, Sir.'

'Well, I did. As I passed it, I felt a breeze come up the tunnel. It smelled of sea air. There's a direct connection to the coast through that tunnel. Judging from the general direction of the passage, it should come out somewhere near the harbour you told me about. If we go by that route, we might be able to make our escape before the soldiers realize they've been hoodwinked.'

'And we might end up at a dead end and be trapped.'

'We might. But better a risk in life than certain death, Mr Linton.'

I couldn't argue with that.

'What should I do?' I ask him. 'Can I help?'

'Yes.'

'How?'

'Be quiet.'

I bit back a sharp reply. This time, his terseness might actually be more than simply annoyance at my presence and general feminine existence. I had no idea if one needed quiet to pick a lock; it might very well be.

'And you can keep an eye on the stairs,' he added in a voice that wasn't quite as granite-hard as usual – rather more akin to slate, or sandstone. 'Tell me immediately when somebody approaches, understood?'

For some reason, a smile appeared on my face. 'Yes, Sir.'

I had been staring at the empty stairs for a few minutes when from behind me, I heard a click.

'Done! Let's go, Mr Linton.'

When I turned my head, I saw that the door was indeed standing open a crack.

'What now?' I whispered. 'Should I stand guard outside while you go in and get the file?'

'No,' he said. 'I don't want you to stay out here alone.'

He gave no more explanation, but silently beckoned me to follow him inside. I did so, feeling confused. What was that supposed to mean? That had sounded almost as if he wanted to keep me at his side because he cared more about my safety than about securing his precious secret file, the key to all his greatest dreams of wealth and power. But that couldn't be the case, surely.

Compared to the distant, echoing hum of voices and clatter of cargo out in the cave, it was almost eerily quiet inside the hut. It was only a small, one-room building, made of wood, but still I felt as though I had entered a church, or a throne-room, or another place of majesty. And at the other end of the little room, only a few yards away from Mr Ambrose and me, stood the throne, the Holy Grail of this palace: a small, black safe, with a lock on its door that looked considerably more complicated than the one on the door outside.

Mr Ambrose took two quick steps towards the safe and bent forward to examine the lock. His eyes narrowed the faction of an inch.

'Mr Linton?'

'Yes?'

'We might have a slight problem.'

'Indeed, Sir?'

'Yes. I calculate I will need about twenty minutes to open this lock.'
'And how many minutes do we still have left until the guards appear, Sir?'
'Twenty.'
'Oh. That might be a problem Sir.'
'Yes, indeed.'

Without another word, he shoved his lock picks into the lock and started fiddling. The sound of metal clinking and scraping was nerve-wracking, and after only a short time, I was hardly able to stay still. I started to walk up and down the hut, trying not to think of what would happen if the real guards walked in on us now. They probably wouldn't look kindly on two of their supposed colleagues trying to crack Lord Dalgliesh's safe.

'Mr Linton?' came a terse voice from floor level, in the direction of the safe.
'Yes, Sir?'
'Stop walking about. You are distracting me.'

I forced myself to stop, and instead leaned against the wall and started to nervously flex my fingers. I wouldn't have thought anything could distract Mr Ambrose. But then, the prospect of being shot would probably even faze a stone statue such as he.

'Mr Linton?'
'Yes, Sir?'
'Stop flexing your fingers. I can hear your knuckles cracking from over here.'
'Yes, Sir. Of course, Sir.'

I clenched my hands into fists and folded my arms in front of my chest, just in case. I even tried to breathe more evenly so as not to disturb him. *Please let him be quick*, I prayed. *Please!*

Click.

'Done!' he exclaimed. Was that a tiny hint of excitement I heard in his voice? Whatever it was, it was gone immediately. He gripped the handle of the safe, and I launched myself forward, eagerly gazing over his shoulder. After weeks of searching, weeks of wondering what the bloody hell we were after, I was finally going to see the mysterious file. What would it look like? I imagined a black steel case, with the letters 'top secret' printed in dark red on the top, and a padlock on the side. Or maybe...

The door of the safe swung open. Inside lay a thin, beige envelope, about the size of a standard letter.

'Yes!' Mr Ambrose reached inside, grasped the envelope and flipped it open. Quickly, he skimmed through the contents. I saw dozens of sheets, covered with column upon column of numbers, and a few pieces of paper covered in a squiggly, foreign script I could not decipher.

'That's it?' I demanded.

'Yes. Everything is here!' He didn't notice the dire disappointment in my voice. Or if he did, he chose to completely ignore it. His dark eyes were glittering with an inner frost, as if he had just been given an award by the International Miser Society.

With silent reverence, he held up the envelope for a moment, as if it indeed were the Holy Grail to him. Maybe it was. Then he slipped it into his pocket, and from his other one withdrew a similar-looking envelope, which he placed inside the safe before closing and locking it.

What was that about? Why not just take the envelope? Why leave one behind? Was it an apology letter? *Sir, I am deeply regretful to have had to disturb your criminal operation, but it was necessary to retrieve an item which you stole from me. My sincerest apologies, Rikkard Ambrose.*

I glanced at Mr Ambrose's chiselled face and shook my head. No. He wouldn't write anything remotely like an apology, or write or say anything at all for that matter. He would just stay silent, in the knowledge that he had given his opponent a solid figurative kick in the bollocks. So what was the envelope for?

I burned to ask, but this was neither the time nor place. We had to–

'We have to get out of here,' Mr Ambrose cut short the very same words in my mind. He sprang to his feet and strode over to the door. Carefully, he peeked outside. 'The guards are still nowhere in sight. If we hurry, we can reach the tunnel before they arrive and the alarm is raised.'

He was already about to open the door when, suddenly, an idea struck me and I grabbed his arm.

'But why leave at all?' I demanded.

Turning, he threw me a look that could have frozen lava. 'Would you prefer to stay and ask for hospitality? I imagine Lord Dalgliesh would be delighted to receive you for tea and biscuits. Especially when you will have such interesting topics of conversation as where the most precious document on this entire island has disappeared to.'

'I meant,' I said, trying to be patient, 'why should we run now, before the guards arrive? We could shut the door of the hut and stand outside like real guards until the next shift arrives. They will think we are the real guards, the ones they're supposed to be relieving, and we'll saunter off without anybody ever being the wiser.'

It may have been only a trick of the torchlight, but I thought I saw Mr Ambrose's mouth drop open slightly. He was quiet for one or two moments. Then he said:

'This... actually sounds as if it were a reasonably feasible plan.'

'Blimey! Don't be all over with me with your compliments!'

'Don't worry. I won't.'

'So we're going to do it?'

He hesitated. I could see the struggle in his eyes – the same struggle as on the day I had asked for a dress and a bag of onions. He hated to adopt any plan of mine, probably because it meant admitting I actually was of some use. But he was nothing if not practical, and – I could see the thought enter his mind as clearly as if it were painted on his forehead – at least *this* plan wouldn't be expensive.

'All right,' he conceded. 'We will.' And he stepped outside to take up his position beside the door.

˷˷**˷*˷*

523

To my own great surprise, my plan actually worked perfectly. The two guards showed up only two minutes after we had left the hut, greeted us in a quite friendly manner and sent us off downstairs. I followed Mr Ambrose down at a steady pace, although what I actually wanted to do was run.

Stay calm, I told myself. *There is no need to run. Nobody knows the file is missing. You can walk out of here slowly and nobody will ever know. Everything is going great.*

Yes, everything was going great – until, as we passed under a shadowy arch of stone, I saw, a few dozen yards away, the two guards we had relieved of their duty half an hour ago. They were engaged in an energetic discussion with Colonel Townsend.

'I? Send them up there?' the colonel was saying. 'No, why in God's name should I do something like that. I thought they were the regular shift that...'

Mr Ambrose had seen them, too. He stiffened.

'Seems like not attracting attention is no longer an option,' he stated icily. 'Move. Now!'

Grasping my hand, he tugged me away from the colonel, towards the entrance of the tunnel he had pointed out earlier. He didn't have to tug hard. I hurried after him, trying my best to keep up with his long strides. He was right. We had to get out of here right now, or we were as good as dead. Quickly, we neared the entrance to the tunnel. There was a soldier standing beside it. A guard?

'Do you think he'll try and stop us from entering the tunnel?' I asked out of the corner of my mouth, nodding towards the soldier.

'It is interesting how you always seem to assume that I know everything about this place, when, in fact, I haven't been aware of its existence any longer than you have, Mr Linton. I have no idea.'

'Well, what if he does?'

No answer.

'Sir?'

Silence. So I just continued on, trying to ignore the rising feeling of panic in my stomach. The guard definitely looked alert and suspicious enough to justify my fears. He had a narrow rat's face, with a long, twitching nose. I had never trusted people with long noses.

'Sir?' My voice was a harsh whisper. 'Mr Ambrose, Sir, what will we do if he doesn't let us pass? Sir?'

More silence. I looked up at his face and saw that, although it was cool and serene as ever, his eyes were totally focused on the guard, burning with cold ice. Maybe, just maybe, he didn't know what to do yet, either.

We were only ten yards or so away from the tunnel entrance now. I tried to look as innocent as possible.

If you think about it, we are innocent, right? After all, we're just stealing back something that had been previously purloined.

One hundred per cent correct. My ears, though, didn't seem to agree: they were red hot with guilt. Never before had I been so thankful for my tanned skin, which would at least hide the blush on my cheeks.

Five yards.

524

Four.

The guard didn't move.

Three yards.

Without warning, the guard stepped sideways, blocking our way. My hands clenched into fists, and it took a conscious effort to relax them, and to look the man straight into his little rat's eyes.

'Hey, you there! You know nobody is allowed in the tunnel without permission from the colonel.'

'But we 'ave permission,' Mr Ambrose said, his voice absolutely credible, almost affronted at being questioned like this. 'We're to stand guard at the other end. New safety measures.'

'Oh? Let's see your permission slip, then.'

'Certainly.'

Reaching into his pocket, Mr Ambrose withdrew a slip of paper. What was this? Had he somehow managed to magically forge Colonel Townsend's signature? I was beginning to think that nothing about him would ever surprise me again.

I was wrong.

'Here.' He held out the paper to the guard, who leant his rifle against the wall and took it.

'Hey, wait just a minute! This isn't–'

Mr Ambrose's fist moved so fast I didn't even see it coming. Neither did the guard. He flew backward and crashed against the stone wall beside the tunnel, sliding to the ground, unconscious.

'Run,' Mr Ambrose said. He didn't yell. He didn't shout. He just said it.

'Y-you knocked him unconscious!'

'Yes, Mr Linton. Now move.' And then he was running, pulling me after him. I stumbled, still staring at the prone figure at the floor. Out of the corner of my eye, I caught a glimpse of the shocked faces of hundreds of soldiers all over the cave, staring down at us, and then I was inside the tunnel, being dragged along the rails towards the foremost of the mining carts.

'Get in!' he commanded.

I looked from him to the cart and back again. 'Into that? But why–'

'Get in, I said!' His tone was so deadly cold that my legs moved without consulting my mind on the matter. With a painful thud, I landed on my knees inside the iron cart. I had hardly had time to grab the wall to steady myself, when I felt it: the cart started to move.

Bloody hell! What...?

I raised my head and stared at Mr Ambrose, who was grinding his teeth, both of his hands clasped around the back wall of the cart, pushing it forward. My head snapped around to look in the other direction, where the rails led down a steep decline, then it whirled back to face Mr Ambrose. Suddenly, I realized what he was planning to do.

'Are you crazy?' I yelled over the creak of the metal wheels.

'Not that I'm aware off, Mr Linton.' How he managed to sound cool and distant while his muscles bunched with the effort of pushing the cart forward was a mystery to me – but not one I cared to solve right now. I had more pressing matters on my mind. Such as...

'Are there even any brakes on this thing?'

'Not that I'm aware of, Mr Linton.'

'Well, are you aware of what'll happen if we run into a dead end?'

'Have you ever tried making meat-and-bone pancakes, Mr Linton?'

'Stop this at once!' I started to rise. 'I'm getting out of this thing right now. I won't–'

There was an ear-splitting *boom* that echoed all around the cave. Something ripped my ridiculous blue hat from my head, and it smashed against the wall. I had just enough time to see the large hole in the middle before it rolled out of my field of vision. My incredulous eyes flicked from the place where my muti-lated hat had lain, to the entrance of the tunnel where, in a patch of torchlight, I saw a soldier standing, his rifle raised. Others were appearing around him, shouting and yelling curses. Not bothering to consult my mind again, my legs dropped me to the floor.

'Um... all right. Maybe I'll stay in here after all.'

'How gracious of you, Mr Linton.'

The cart was gathering speed now; we were almost at the slope that would carry us away. Mr Ambrose shoved harder and harder, scarcely breathing heav-ily at the effort. I would never have thought that there was this much raw power in that cold, hard body of his. He looked focused and determined, as if he had been pushing mine carts all his life.

'Hold on, Mr Linton,' he hissed. He gave a last shove, and then jumped into the cart behind me. The force of his jump carried us forward another few feet, just far enough to reach the edge of the slope. We started to gather more and more speed. Wind rushed against my hair and tugged at my brown locks, mak-ing them fly all around me. Behind us, I could hear more shouts, and then there came another shot.

The car reverberated with a sound like a bell, and a scream tore from my throat. They had hit the car!

'Keep your head down!' Mr Ambrose hissed.

'Thank you for the valuable advice, Sir,' I growled. 'I'd never have thought of that!'

Another shot, and another. Stone dust rained down on us as it hit the ceiling above. The light around us dwindled fast as we gathered speed. The torches of the cave were only a distant glimmer by now, while the dark before us was a gaping maul waiting for a scrumptious meal of Ambrosia and Lilly. Somewhere out of the half-light behind us, I could hear the creak of more metal wheels, and knew what it meant.

They're following us!

Then, all thoughts disappeared as we shot around a corner and down, down, away from all light, down into the darkness.

The Tortoise and the other Tortoise and no Hare

Our race into the darkness ended rather abruptly when, after a few dozen yards, the rails levelled out, and our cart rolled to a halt.

Having expected a thrilling race through the dark tunnels of the mine, this was something of an anti-climax. It was also quite worrying, considering a bunch of bloodthirsty soldiers, armed with rifles, sabres and God only knew what else, were not far behind.

'Now what are we going to do?' I demanded. 'Get out and push?'

'Not quite,' he said drily, and in so calm a voice it made me want to strangle him. 'Climb over there. Quick.'

Jumping over the front wall of the cart, he landed on something solid – wood, not the stone of the tunnel floor, I could tell from the sound his shoes made. He gestured for me to follow. Looking over the edge of the cart's metal wall, I saw that it didn't actually end at what I had taken to be the front wall. There was a flat, wooden extension, a kind of platform, attached to the front, and in the middle of the platform there was a construction that looked like a strange sort of metal see-saw.

The only difference from a see-saw was, it didn't have seats at the ends. Instead, it had wooden handles, one of which Mr Ambrose was already holding.

'Well, what are you waiting for?' he asked. 'Grab hold, and let's get going!'

'Get going with what?' I demanded, though I already had an inkling.

'Grab the other handle and start moving it up and down,' he ordered. 'This isn't just a mining cart. It's a draisine.'

'A what?'

'A draisine. You move it by it by moving the handles up and down.'

'You mean you want to try and escape the murderous hordes that are chasing us by pumping up and down?'

'Essentially, yes.'

'You must be joking!'

He considered this. 'No,' he stated. 'In fact, I'm quite at liberty to be serious. Which I am in general, and in particular at the moment.'

'You don't say.'

'Yes, I do. Now get moving, Mr Linton.'

I opened my mouth to argue – then, I heard the screech of another mining cart, not far behind us. However much I might have *liked* to argue – there was no time. Quickly, I grabbed the other end of the see-saw and, immediately, Mr Ambrose began to move up and down at a prodigious rate. The cart – or draisine, rather – shuddered, and then began to move forward at a leisurely pace. I felt as if we were sitting in an old ladies' carriage, with a tame old horse in front, so the venerable grandmother wouldn't get jostled.

'Can't this thing go any faster?' I panted.

'Of course it can,' was Mr Ambrose's reply. 'If *you* move faster.'

And he picked up the pace. It was all I could do to try and follow his movements and not dangle off at the end like a sack of potatoes. I doubt I contributed much to our forward thrust. Nevertheless, sweat soon began running down my forehead.

'Don't shove the lever upwards like that,' Mr Ambrose commanded. 'It comes up automatically on your side when I push down. We have to move in turns. First you push down, then I, then you again.'

From then on, we alternated in the movement, and I had to bear half of the burden. As we moved along at an agonizing pace, we could hear the soldiers slowly coming closer behind us. They didn't seem to have nearly as much trouble as we with getting their draisine moving.

Well, they probably don't eat as much solid chocolate as you do, said a nasty little voice in my head. *And, oh yes, all that soldiering they do, that running around and marching with heavy packs on their shoulders all day long, that probably doesn't hurt either...*

Gritting my teeth, I swore to myself to take more regular walks in the park. Maybe if I had done that, maybe if my behind wasn't so... generous, I wouldn't feel as if my lungs were bursting now.

'You're not up for this,' Mr Ambrose stated in a calm tone, not interrupting his rapid movement for a second. 'You are already exhausted.'

'I'm fine!'

'You do too little exercise, Mr Linton. Your figure...'

'There's nothing whatsoever wrong with my figure!' I snapped. 'I said I'm fine. I do plenty of exercise!'

'Such as?'

'Um... walks in the park?'

'How long? How fast?'

I felt my ears heat. About ten minutes long, slowly back and forth between the bench and the duck pond. But he didn't need to know that. 'Do you want me to talk or to move, Sir?'

He narrowed his eyes a little more, but didn't say anything else. He just kept moving, and so did I, hoping fervently that the red colour of my face came from my exertion, and not from his remarks about my personal appearance. What in heaven's name had he been going to say about my figure?

Probably that you're fat, the tiny voice in my mind whispered. I told it to shut up and help me move. Somehow, I would manage! I would get through this alive! And then I would start exercising until I was strong enough to handle a draisine, and to strangle Mr Rikkard Ambrose!

I had just reached that resolution when we came to the foot of the hill.

It started slowly, so slowly I hardly noticed at first. The cart tilted slightly, and my arms, which had already been screaming before, were now howling in agony. At first I thought it was just the exhaustion, but the rise became steeper and steeper, until I finally realized: we were going up a hill.

'Bloody... hell! This has to be... the slowest chase in the... history of the world!'

'Shut up and push, Mr Linton!'

On the plus side: the hill turned out to only a small one. On the minus side: after it came another, and another, and another. God! Wasn't this ever going to stop? My fingers were raw from the rough wood of the handle, and all thoughts of what Mr Ambrose thought of my figure had left me. I couldn't think of anything, anymore. There was just the next push, the next turn of the wheel.

Finally, I collapsed onto the wooden platform. My arms felt like burning splints of tinder, my clothes were drenched in sweat, and my last piece of strength was gone. I couldn't move an inch.

'Get up,' Mr Ambrose's voice commanded from somewhere above me. 'You can't keep the cart moving if you're lying on the floor, Mr Linton.'

'Geez... you don't... say!'

'Yes, I *do* say. Get up!'

'I... I can't.' The voice that came out of my throat didn't sound like my own. It was the croak of some half-starved crow. 'I... can't. I'm sorry.'

Unsurprisingly, he wasn't very moved by my apology.

'I order you to get up, Mr Linton!'

'Oh, go stick it where the sun doesn't shine!'

There was a pause. Then:

'I knew it.' The ice in his voice sent a chill down my back. 'I knew this would happen sooner or later. You're nothing but a weak, feminine girl! A man in your place wouldn't–'

He broke off. But he didn't need to finish the sentence. I could imagine its ending all too well. Suddenly, energy surged through me. Not strength, no, but something even better: anger!

'A man would what?' I snapped, raising my eyes from the floor to glare at him. He just shook his head.

'Forget it, Mr Linton. It doesn't matter anymore.' Letting go of the see-saw, he stepped back, his expression stoic. He wasn't even looking at me! He was gazing off into the distance, his mouth set in a resigned line. He was giving up! Giving up *because I was a girl*!

'It bloody well does!'

With a gut-wrenching effort, I scrambled to my feet and grabbed hold of the wooden handle. 'Where's your stomach? Get hold of that handle and start moving! We're not beaten yet! Not by a long shot!'

He observed me for a moment through slightly narrowed eyes, as I stood there, legs shaking, hands clasped around the handle.

'But you're too weak to do this. You said so yourself.'

'I? I never said anything of the sort! Let's get going!'

Something twitched at the corner of his mouth. I blinked. Had I seen right? Could that have been the shadow of a smile? But no! Why would he smile? What was there to smile about, here and now?

'All right... If you're sure you can handle it...'

I had to be mistaken! Rikkard Ambrose never smiled.

'Yes, I'm bloody sure! What are you waiting for?'

Another moment of silence passed. Then he gave a curt nod and abruptly took hold of the other end of the see-saw once more.

'Well, if you insist, Mr Linton.'

He shoved down so hard it nearly lifted me off my feet. I gathered all my strength and pushed, and let loose, and pushed, and let loose. From then on, I kept up, although the pace he set nearly killed me. I wouldn't give up again for anything, not after what he had said! Ha! Weak, feminine girl indeed...!

We were already halfway up the hill when it occurred to me that he might have said that on purpose, just to get me off the floor and moving again. But no... He didn't know me that well, did he?

Yes, he does, that little annoying voice whispered in my ear.

I told it to shut up and help my aching arms.

I pushed and pulled and pushed. But although I gave it my best effort, we still were only moving as fast as an old lady's carriage drawn by a horse with two lame legs. I estimated our stunning speed at about one mile per hour. Fortunately, the soldiers behind us seemed to have troubles, too. To judge by the voices I heard echoing behind me in the tunnel, there appeared to be more than two of them on the draisine, and the added weight was making it difficult for them to get up the latest hillside.

But that didn't make my burning arms feel any better.

'Mr... Ambrose?' I gasped.

'Yes, Mr Linton?'

'Next time... you pick a cart to flee on, Sir... pick one that is steam-engine driven!'

'Mr Linton?'

'Yes... Sir?'

'Be quiet and move faster!'

'Yes... Sir!'

From behind us came the boom of a shot. I nearly dropped the handle and threw myself to the floor.

'Don't!' Mr Ambrose commanded. 'They can't hit us! The metal container shields us from any gunfire!'

'As long as... they're behind us.'

'Yes.'

'What happens... when they realize that they... could probably catch up... by jumping off and... running after us?'

'Mr Linton?'

'Yes... Sir?'

'One of the advantages of being silent is not giving your enemies any ideas while they might be in hearing distance. Now be quiet!'

'Yes, Sir!'

~~**~*~*

It was about five minutes later, and we were just struggling up another slope, when we heard the sound of heavy footsteps behind us.

Mr Ambrose shot me a dark look. He didn't say anything, but he didn't need to. His look said it all: *faster!*

Another shot whistled over my head. And another, and another! The last one came so close that I could feel the air move as it whizzed past. Then came the sound of panting, and I knew they were catching up. Quickly, I risked a glance over my shoulder.

There they were! Halfway up the hill, only a few dozen yards behind us. The red and gold of their uniforms shimmered menacingly in the light of the torches they carried, the steel of their rifles adding another deadly colour to the mix of blood-red and gold. They were three in number, and were dashing forward at a dead run. One of them in particular, a slim-built fellow who looked as if he were used to running from Bristol to Bath and back again every morning before breakfast, seemed intent on sinking his claws into us. He was catching up fast.

'We'll never get away from them,' I panted. 'They'll get us!'

'No, they won't,' was Mr Ambrose's cool reply. 'Not if we make it to the top of the hill in time.'

'How...?'

'Be quiet and move! Faster!' And he started shoving down the handle twice as fast as before. Now, even *his* breathing sounded a little laboured. A single drop of sweat appeared on his chiselled forehead and ran down the side, disappearing into his collar.

Ha! So he is human after all, not some inanimate statue into which the God of Mammon has breathed life by accident!

Unfortunately, I wasn't a living statue either. My tortured, aching muscles made my humanity all too clear to me. Gripping the handle more tightly so my slippery hands wouldn't lose their grip on it, I tried to keep up with his insane tempo.

Think of Joan of Arc, I told myself. *She threw an entire invasion of men out of her country! And you are going to be defeated by a stinking mining cart? What are you? A baby?*

Well, at the moment I definitely felt like lying down and crying.

Blinking the sweat out of my eyes, I stared past Mr Ambrose and, in the dim light of the torches that our pursuers carried, could make out a dark black outline rising above us. The top of the hill? I couldn't tell. It seemed miles away yet, but in the gloom, distances were impossible to gauge. Behind us, the sound of panting breath was growing louder.

'Stop!' The shouted command from behind me came so suddenly, and sounded so near, it nearly made my heart jump out of my chest. 'Stop or we'll shoot!'

How very kind of you to warn us... Of course, you have already shot at us, so it's not much of a warning, but still, very thoughtful.

'Don't stop,' hissed Mr Ambrose.

'Of course not! What do you take me for? An idiot?'

Silence. Very meaningful silence.

'Well, thanks so much!' I growled.

'I did not say anything, Mr Linton.'

'You didn't have to, Sir! You were thinking loud and clear.'

'Just keep moving, Mr Lin–'

The crack of a shot cut off his words brutally. It was so loud, so terribly near now that my ears stung from the impact of the sound. Mr Ambrose's eyes burned into mine, and again I could read the same message in them: *Faster! Faster!*

And I did move faster. Up and down and up and down – the repetitive movement sent shocks of pain up my tired arms and down my back. I kept going, but didn't know how long it would be before I collapsed again. Even my thoughts of Joan of Arc didn't comfort me anymore. Surely, beating an army of men had to be easier than this? There probably was some way to just hoodwink the stupid fools into falling on their own swords. But a mine cart... a mine cart was devious, and unrelenting. Up, down, up, down–

And then, we were suddenly rolling forward easily, and I nearly fell forward as the cart began to gather speed, without any help from me, and plunged downwards.

Yes!

'We've done it! Let go, Mr Linton! Let go!'

I couldn't. My hands were glued to the handle, my eyes half-closed with exhaustion. Another pair of hands gripped mine and slowly pried them loose. 'Let go! We have to lie down! Now!'

Lie down? But why?

The answer to my question came a second later, when two shots echoed through the tunnel. Something heavy collided with me, throwing me to the floor and landing on top of me. Something – no, *somebody* familiar. Mr Ambrose.

'They're shooting,' he told me in his cool, precise tone. 'They have a better angle now, from above. Stay absolutely still.'

Oh no, I plan on running a marathon! After all, I feel so rested right now.

I didn't say anything, though. I couldn't have moved a muscle if I had wanted to, not even my lips. And I didn't want to, really. To lie on the rough wood, his arms wrapped tightly around me, felt very comfortable for some reason.

But why is he lying on top of you?

Good question. It was almost as if he were shielding me from the gunfire. But that couldn't be. That was something only the heroes in penny dreadfuls did if they happened to be in love with the heroine...

The next shot sounded farther away. The one after that could hardly be heard. We were gathering speed now – I could feel it from the wind rushing past us, tickling my face. We were really getting away! Really and truly!

'Why...' My voice sounded like a crow with a cold. I cleared my throat and tried again. 'Why aren't they following us?'

'Oh, they will, eventually' Mr Ambrose said in a dry tone. 'But they jumped off their cart halfway up the last hill, in order to run after us. It will have rolled downhill by now. They'll have to push it up all the way before they can follow us. That will take time. We have a good head start.'

There was a last, faint echo of a gunshot, but even I, with my limited knowledge of firearms, knew it didn't have a hope of hitting us anymore. We were much too far away by now, the darkness gathering around us. The distant red flicker of torches subsided into grey gloom, and then the grey turned to black, and the last noises of our pursuers faded. All noise faded, except for the song of wheels on the rails, the whistling of the wind in my hair, and Mr Ambrose's breathing. We were alone. We should get up and try to find a light, try to find out where we were, maybe. We should definitely get out of this embarrassing position, Mr Ambrose lying on top of me, his arms pressing me to the floor. Yes, that was definitely something we should do.

But then, why didn't he get up?

Why don't you get up yourself, Lilly? You still have two arms and two legs, don't you?

I checked, just to make sure. Yes, all the necessary limbs were still attached, and hurting like hell. He might be lying on top of me, but I could have pushed him away, or tried to slide out from under him, or said something to him. Yet I did not. I simply lay there, his body pressing against mine in a way that made me ache to pull him even closer and put my arms around him. I could feel his breath on my cheek. He was so close. Almost close enough to ki-

'We should get up,' he said. His voice sounded strange, rough even. It still was his usual cool tone, and yet, it wasn't.

'Yes,' I agreed.

Neither of us moved.

'Well?' he said. 'What are you waiting for, Mr Linton?'

'Um... excuse me, Sir, but what are *you* waiting for? You are the one lying on top.'

On top of *me* – the second time in a row! But I didn't dare say these words aloud. They made heat rush to my face just thinking them. Was it just coincidence that we always seemed to end up like this?

'Well? I asked. 'What are you waiting for, just wasting time lying here? Knowledge is power is time is money, isn't it?'

He was silent for a moment.

'You remembered, Mr Linton.'

'Of course, Sir.' Before I knew what happened, my hand had reached out and touched his face. Bloody traitorous limb! 'You're a very memorable man.'

Another moment of silence.

A long one.

A really, really long one.

Then his weight was suddenly lifted off me, and his arms were gone. I gasped with surprise.

'You're right of course,' I heard his voice from high above. 'We have to get moving. I must have received a blow on the head when falling to the floor and been temporarily stunned. That is the only explanation for such unforgivable inactivity. Now... let's see...'

I could feel him climb past me, back into the metal container of the cart, and had to fight hard to suppress a sense of stinging disappointment. But why? Having a man so close had been highly improper, and against my every principal and yet...

And yet, now that he was gone I wished him back. Bloody hell!

'Mr Linton! Look what I've found!' His shout roused me from my dangerously unfeminist thoughts.

'I can't look,' I pointed out, turning towards where his voice had come from. 'It's dark.'

'Actually, I was aware of that, Mr Linton.' Suddenly, a light flared up, making me raise my hand instinctively to shield my eyes.

'How...?' I demanded, grasping for the edge of the cart for balance. The bright yellow shine forced its way through my fingers and, after the long time spent in utter blackness, almost made me dizzy.

'There is a wooden case with spare equipment attached to the back of the cart,' I heard the voice of Mr Ambrose from beyond the golden glow. 'A safety lamp, knife, flint, food, water – you can say what you like about Lord Dalgliesh...'

'Really? Well, then I'd like to point out that he is a pretentious, lying, blood-thirsty ball of slime!'

'That was not meant as a prompt, Mr Linton.'

'Oh. Sorry, Sir.'

'As I was saying, say what you like about Lord Dalgliesh, but he does take all possible safety precautions. And this time, they work to our advantage.'

Slowly, I lowered my hands from my eyes and let my eyes get used to the brightness. Slowly, I looked around, and for the first time since starting on this mad, muscle-tearing ride, actually paid attention to my surroundings.

The orange glow of the safety lamp fell on rugged stone walls rushing past at a prodigious speed. They rose up about three meters, forming a vaulted ceiling above our heads. Both in front of and behind us, the tunnel disappeared into seemingly endless darkness, not giving away any of its secrets about where it would lead. For the moment, I couldn't bring myself to care very much, as long as it brought us away from hostile men with guns. What I did care about was the ice-cold wind in my face, making my sweat-drenched clothes feel as if they would freeze any second.

My teeth began to chatter.

All right, maybe I cared a little bit.

'Come.' Suddenly, Mr Ambrose was beside me, nodding towards the rear of the cart. 'Get into the container. It will shield you from the wind.'

He was right. The metal was cold to sit on, but it was a relief to have the biting wind out of my face. And there was an old sack in the metal container. The material was rough, but warm, and we huddled together, pulling it around us.

'Where do you suppose the tunnel leads?' I asked, after a while.

'As I said before, I smelled sea-air from down there. I still catch a whiff of it now and again. Also, the tunnel is going down, and we started at the centre on the island, inside a mountain. This all would support my theory that the tunnel leads to the coast.'

As the last words left his mouth, the scene around us suddenly changed. Where before there had only been the stone walls of the tunnel rushing past, there now gaped a black opening. For just a moment I glimpsed another tunnel, and another set of rails splitting off from the ones we were riding on and heading down the other way. It was gone as quickly as it had come.

I hesitated for a moment.

'And how do you know that *that* wasn't the way which leads to the coast?' I asked, my voice unusually timid.

'I don't.' His voice wasn't timid at all. It was as cool and composed as a cucumber on ice. 'But since this car does not have brakes and is going too fast for us to change direction, it is of little consequence. Cheese?'

'Excuse me, Sir?'

'I asked you whether you want some cheese.' He held out a piece of something yellowish towards me. 'Or bread. There are some emergency rations in the container in which I found the lamp.'

Again, I hesitated. We were supposed to be in a desperate rush to escape our enemies. That hardly seemed the right time to be eating cheese. But then, I had worked harder today than ever before in my life, and a chocolate croissant wasn't much to go on.

'Some bread, please, Sir.'

'Here.'

He handed me a neatly cut-off piece, and took another for himself. We sat in the semi-darkness and ate in silence. The bread was dark and coarse, but I didn't really mind. It was hearty and gave me new energy.

Only after a while did I notice that Mr Ambrose was watching me. In the shadowy half-light, the planes of his perfect, stony face stood out more sharply than ever. The look in his dark eyes as he watched me nibbling on a piece of cheese made my skin tingle.

'What is it?' I asked.

'What is what, Mr Linton?'

'Why are you looking at me like that? And don't you dare deny it, because you are looking at me, and not like you normally look at me.'

'Indeed?' He cocked his head. 'How do I normally look at you?'

'Like you want to strangle me and ship my body to Antarctica. And don't try to distract me! I want to know why you were staring at me!'

Silence.

'Why were you staring at me? Please, Sir?'

'Well...' His cool voice was hesitant, his eyes calculating. 'You don't seem to mind the bread much. Most ladie– most people like you would have turned their nose up at brown bread.'

My lips twitched. 'Most ladies? Was that what you were going to say?'

Silence.

I shrugged. 'Most ladies would have turned up their nose at being shot at, too.'

'I imagine so, Mr Linton.'

Was the scant light playing tricks on me? Yes, that had to be it! How else could it be that I thought one corner of Mr Ambrose's mouth turned up into a quarter-smile, for just a second?

'I'm used to tough food, Sir. I live with my uncle, and the only thing he ever puts on the table are potatoes, bread and cheese.'

'Sounds like a sensible man, your uncle.'

'He's one of the greatest misers in the world. You'd like him.'

Again I saw that trick of the light, that play of the safety lamp's illumination on Mr Ambrose's face that made it almost seem as if he were smiling. Quickly, I looked away.

'You know,' I said, 'this is not at all how I imagined a mine cart chase.'

'How did you imagine it, Mr Linton?'

'I don't know. More exciting. Less... cheesy.' Ponderously, I took another bite. The cheese really tasted quite good, once you got used to it. Those French really had a culinary talent.

'Well, I think I can promise you some excitement soon enough,' Mr Ambrose told me, drily. 'Once we reach the end of the tunnel, we have to manage to get on a ship before they catch up with us. If we don't get to one in time...'

His voice trailed off. But I didn't need him to finish the sentence. I knew.

We lapsed into silence for a while. I was busy with eating, and Mr Ambrose, who only took an occasional bite now and then, seemed to be very busy staring at the tunnel floor, as if the stone whizzing by told a fascinating story.

'I was right,' he said, suddenly. 'This tunnel leads to the sea. We are not that far away from the exit anymore.'

Startled, I looked up.

'How do you know?'

'Do you see this? And this?' He pointed at the floor, and I barely managed to catch a blurry glimpse of a small stone before we rushed past.

'What about it? Looked just like a pebble to me.'

The cool look he gave me made me shut my mouth.

'This "pebble" was quartzite – not the same type of stone as the mountain around us. Such pebbles are only found on beaches. They must have been accidentally carried up by soldiers who passed this way from further down, because up at the mountain there was not a single quartzite anywhere in sight.'

He sounded as if he had spent his life burrowing through all kinds of different rock and knew all of them by name. I wanted to open my mouth to argue, but then I remembered the ease with which he had pushed the mining cart, his familiarity with the functioning of a draisine, and I shut my mouth again. Somehow, I was suddenly certain he knew what he was talking about. If you looked at his chiselled granite face, you simply had to believe that he knew all there was to know about stone.

'But will we get to the exit fast enough?' I asked. 'Before Dalgliesh's men catch up with us?'

'As I said, Mr Linton, we have a good head start.'

'But don't you think they'll catch up with us quickly once they've pushed their cart to the top and roll downhill, after us?' I asked. 'After all, they're three, and we're only two. Their added weight should make them move a lot faster.'

'Yes, they are three, and we are only two, that is true,' agreed Mr Ambrose. 'But still, the difference in weight might not be as great as you might ima–'

He eyed me, and then suddenly lapsed into silence. A very lengthy silence, and, for him, a very healthy one. Had he continued his sentence, I would not have been responsible for my actions. I gave him my most fiery glare.

536

'There *will* be a difference in weight,' I huffed, and pushed him away, sliding out from under the sack. 'A *very great* difference in weight. Just you wait and see, they will catch up with us fast!'

~~**~*~*

Ten minutes. Twenty minutes.
I glared morosely at the tunnel walls, doing my best to avoid looking at him.
'Do you hear anything?' I asked.
'No.'
'I could have sworn I heard voices behind us!'
'I didn't hear anything, Mr Linton.'
Silence.
'They should have caught up with us long ago. How long has it been since we left them behind?'
'Exactly twenty-five minutes and thirty-seven seconds, Mr Linton.'
'It can't be that long already!'
'But it is, Mr Linton.'
Silence. Calm silence from him, grumpy silence from me.
Suddenly, my ears pricked up.
'Do you hear that?' I demanded.
'Mr Linton, I told you, they are not–'
'Not from behind! From there!' Anxiously, I clambered to my feet and pointed into the darkness ahead of us – only that it was not complete darkness anymore. There was a tiny point of light moving towards us, getting bigger as it approached. But not white light. Not the light of day.

Suddenly, Mr Ambrose appeared beside me. His eyes were as dark as the bottom of the ocean, his mouth pressed into a grim line. Well, it was *always* pressed into a grim line, but now it was a *very, very* grim line.

'What do you think it could be?' I asked.

The moment the words were out of my mouth, I suddenly heard the noise I had been both dreading and hoping for: the faint squeak of a mine cart's wheels! But it wasn't coming from behind. It was approaching from ahead of us, from where the light was.

'Prepare yourself,' Mr Ambrose commanded, reaching into his jacket and drawing out something hard and shiny. I only caught a glimpse of the metal barrel of a gun before it disappeared again, hidden behind his left hand, where it was easily accessible. 'We will have company, soon.'

SHOTS IN THE DARK

'You have a firearm?' I demanded, my breath catching. He regarded me with supreme disdain. 'Sir,' I hurriedly tagged on.

'Of course I have a firearm, Mr Linton. Do you think I would go into a situation such as this without being prepared?'

'But why didn't you use it on the soldiers before?'

'Because they had long-range weapons and could have shot me long before I could have returned the favour. You don't bring a rifle on an infiltration. It is cumbersome and slow to load. This,' he patted the weapon hidden behind his hand, 'is a Colt Paterson improved model prototype with loading lever, 36 calibre. If our friend there,' he nodded towards the approaching light, 'gets close enough, he will be swiftly and terminally perforated.'

'Meaning, Sir?'

'Meaning that I will put a hole in his head, Mr Linton.'

I threw a worried glance at the walls of the tunnel, which were still rushing past in a blur, then directed my gaze at the light that was approaching alarmingly fast.

'I hope we survive long enough to have to worry about fighting him. If we keep going at this pace, we'll probably die when we ram into him. We're moving too fast and, as you said, this thing has got no brakes.'

'I doubt it'll come to a collision. Look.' And he raised the safety lamp high over his head, pointing to something beside the cart I hadn't seen before: a set of tracks, running parallel to our own.

'Why have two sets of rails in a mine?' The confusion in my voice was evident.

'One for sending up the salt, one for sending down empty carts again. It makes sense.'

'Well... I suppose you're right. And you think he's on the other set of tracks?'

'Yes. But...'

'But what, Sir?'

'But be ready to jump, just in case I'm wrong.'

How very comforting.

As we raced closer, I could see that indeed he was not on another set of tracks. But there was no need for me to jump, either. Long before we reached the other mining cart, the tracks flattened out. We began to slow down, rolling along the track at a leisurely pace. Now we could see that the other mining cart hadn't, in fact, been moving towards us – it had only seemed that way because we had been catching up so fast. It was, in fact, moving in the same direction as we, only at a considerably slower pace. A single, rather fat man, whose red uniform and bushy white beard made him look distinctly harmless, was gripping the handle of the draisine. As we came nearer, he raised his hand.

Mr Ambrose raised a hand, too – the one with his gun in it.

I noticed just in time to grab it and push it down again.

'No!' I hissed.

He gave me a don't-interrupt-my-important-business look, which I completely ignored. I clung to his arm tenaciously. 'Why not, Mr Linton?'

'Because he hasn't got a gun in his hand, Sir!'

'He might be going for one, Mr Linton.'

'Then wait until he does, Sir. You can't shoot an unarmed man!'

'That, Mr Linton, is usually the wiser and more effective policy.'

'Ahoy there,' the man called, waving genially in our direction. 'Caught up to me and my little ship on wheels, have you? Well, I ain't the fastest, I got to admit that.'

'See? He didn't want to shoot! He just wanted to wave at us.'

'For now, Mr Linton.'

Suddenly, the old soldier let go of the end of the see-saw with which he had been pushing along his cart and jumped off.

'I'm going to take a little rest and have my supper,' he announced, appearing perfectly content to let the draisine stand where it was. 'Want to join me?'

I looked at Mr Ambrose.

'Don't even think about saying yes, Mr Linton,' he hissed. 'We're being chased by a whole army of soldiers! We don't have time for supper!'

'I wasn't going to say yes, Sir,' I snapped back, miffed. 'I was going to ask how we'll get past him without arousing suspicion! He's blocking the way!'

'I had noticed as much, Mr Linton. Do you still object to my shooting him?'

'Yes!'

Mr Ambrose gnashed his teeth in silence, and didn't answer. It was obvious that of all the dangers that we could encounter on our wild chase for survival, he hadn't factored in a jolly old fellow asking us to stop for supper. Well, neither had I, to be perfectly honest. You just didn't reckon with those kinds of things when you were hunted by a horde of evil villains. Everybody was supposed to be chasing after you in a panic, not cheerfully unpacking sausages and a bottle of ale.

The white-bearded fellow pulled out a second bottle from the sack slung over his back and held it out to us. We were only a few yards away from him now, and our draisine slowly came to a halt.

'Want to try it? It's a damn fine brew, if I do say so myself. The name's Ben, by the way.'

'No!' Mr Ambrose bit out, jumping off the draisine and striding towards the old man.

'I assure you, it is. My mother picked it out. Father was never the creative one, so she picked all our names. Ben for me, and Tom and Elsie for my–'

'I meant,' Mr Ambrose said, enunciating each arctic syllable, '*no thank you*, I do not wish to partake of your alcoholic drink. And neither does my friend. Will you be so kind as to move your mine cart out of the way, so we can continue? We have schedule to keep.'

'Oh, today's youth!' Old Ben sighed and took a large swig of ale. 'Always in a hurry, always in a hurry. You got to take a breath, youngsters, and learn how to relax. All this panicking will kill you before you get old, you know.'

'Actually,' I said, throwing an anxious glance over my shoulder, 'we're trying to *avoid* getting killed before we're old.'

Old Ben didn't seem to hear that. He was busy carving up a sausage, holding one slice out to Mr Ambrose, who looked down at it as if it were a rotten rat's carcass.

'I really must insist, Sir, that you–' he began.

'There they are!'

The shout cut him off abruptly and made us all look back up the hill, from where we had come. There was a yelp from old Ben, who had probably cut his finger instead of the sausage. But I didn't pay attention, nor did Mr Ambrose. We only had eyes for the draisine with all three soldiers on board, racing down-hill at a dangerous tempo.

Dangerous for them, and for us.

Without wasting another word, Mr Ambrose stepped up beside old Ben's draisine and heaved. With a strangled groan, half from his throat, half from the protesting metal and wood, the vehicle keeled over, and everything that had been inside toppled onto the tunnel floor.

'Hey!' Old Ben rose from his sitting position, waving his sausage around threateningly. 'Now, look here young fellow, you can't just...'

I didn't hear any more. Mr Ambrose came running towards me. He jumped onto our draisine and uttered a single, decisive word: 'Move!'

Knowing all too well what he meant, I jumped on, gripped one end of the see-saw, and pushed. We shot forward, past old Ben and his bloody sausage, to-wards... towards what? Freedom? Escape?

'Get them! Get them!'

A shot whistled over my head, and I ducked, my heart hammering faster.

Well, at least we were rushing away from the heavily armed hunting party, that much was sure. The draisine tilted, and off we went down another decline.

'Hands off the see-saw!' Mr Ambrose commanded. 'Get down and stay out of sight!'

He didn't follow his own advice. Instead, he knelt down right behind the mine cart container and laid the barrel of his gun on top of the metal, narrowing his eyes. I was beside him in a flash.

'What are you doing, Sir?' I demanded.

'I thought I told you to stay out of sight, Mr Linton.'

I cupped one hand behind an ear in a mock gesture. 'Excuse me? The wind is so loud I hardly understand what you are saying. You want me to stay by your side?'

'*Out of sight*, Mr Linton. Out – of – sight!'

'By your side it is, then, Sir.'

Another shot whistled over our heads. Mr Ambrose didn't move an inch. Only the barrel of his gun made a minuscule movement, going half an inch up-wards. He didn't look at me.

'You, Mr Linton, are the most irritating personage I have ever encountered in my life. If you must risk getting shot, do it quietly. I am trying to concentrate.'

'What are you doing, Sir?'

'I mentioned quietude just now.'

'I'll be quiet if you tell me what you are doing.'

'I am trying to shoot those inconsiderate gentlemen behind us.'

'But I thought you said they were too far away to be hit with a revolver.'

Suddenly, an ear-splitting explosion jarred my skull. It threw me backwards so hard I smashed painfully into the wood of the draisine's floor. If the other gunshots had been loud, this was beyond loud – because it came from right beside me. A flash of light flared up at the mouth of Mr Ambrose's revolver, and from somewhere up the tunnel I heard a roar, mingled with curses.

Mr Ambrose turned to me, his sea-coloured eyes glinting in the gloom. 'They were before,' he said. 'No longer. They're catching up. *Stay down!*'

For once, I could find no words to reply. I didn't know much about shooting, but I knew enough to guess that this had been one hell of a shot. A much better one than any city financier should be capable of. But then, I had already known that Mr Ambrose was more than that. Much more.

Two gunshots answered him out of the darkness. They slammed into the tunnel wall not far above our heads, and at the same moment, I saw grim satisfaction flashing in Mr Ambrose's eyes.

'Why do you look so content?' I groaned. 'They nearly hit us!'

'Yes.' With a soft click, he rotated the cylinder of his revolver. The next bullet was in place. 'But only twice. The third man wasn't shooting.'

The meaning of his words came to me in a rush – the man had to be gravely wounded – or dead. For a long moment, I wondered if that should bother me. It probably should. I knew that Ella would be weeping or screaming in terror in my place. But all I felt was... excitement.

'Can you teach me to shoot like that?'

Mr Ambrose's hand, resting on the wall of the metal container again, jerked, and his next shot flew wide of the mark.

'*What?*' he hissed.

'Can you teach me to shoot? I'd like to learn.'

A shot hit the metal wall of the draisine, which reverberated like a church bell. Mr Ambrose ducked, as a second shot raced over his head.

'You cannot be serious!' he hissed.

'Of course I am, Sir. Wouldn't it be useful to have some more firepower right now?'

'But you... you are a...'

'Yes?'

'Nothing, Mr Linton.'

My eyes sparked.

'You were about to admit that I am female!'

'Nothing of the kind, Mr Linton.'

'Stop with the Mister already! I am a girl! And girls could use guns just as well as men, if somebody took the trouble to teach them.'

Another shot hit the draisine. And another.

'This is hardly the right time to discuss gender politics, Mr Linton.' Mr Ambrose glared at me with a cold intensity that would have sent a pack of lions running for the hills. I didn't back down an inch.

'Indeed? And why not, Sir?'

'Because,' he said in a deliberate voice, 'we are about to reach the end of the tunnel. And when we do, we need to run.'

My head whirled around – and light stung my eyes.

He was right! I had been so focused on him and the men who were after us that I hadn't noticed how the tunnel around us had become steadily brighter and brighter. It took my eyes a few seconds to adjust. When they had, I could make out a patch of bright blue. Sky? No, it glittered. The sea! The Mediterranean. Dear God, the tunnel didn't open onto the sea, did it? I had a brief flash of Mr Ambrose and me plunging three hundred feet to our deaths, to provide a meal for the lobsters of the island, eager to take revenge on humans for the massacre the cooks of France had committed among their people. Not a jolly thought. Especially since I hadn't eaten a single lobster in my life.

Suddenly, though, there was brown and green mixed in with the blue. I caught the blurred forms of bushes and grass. Grass didn't grow on the Mediterranean. Huzzah!

Behind me, another shot from Mr Ambrose's revolver ripped the air apart. Quickly, I pressed my hands to my ears. My head was beginning to hurt.

'Why don't you take your own advice, Sir, and do that more quietly?'

'I am afraid nobody has yet invented a noiseless gun, Mr Linton.'

'How disappointing!'

He didn't even glance at me, which, under the circumstances, I suppose I could understand. His eyes were firmly trained on our pursuers. 'Back to the matter at hand, Mr Linton. Do you see the exit?'

'Yes.'

'Is it far ahead?'

'No, I don't think so.' I growled. 'These aren't the best circumstances to judge distances, though. I don't have a yardstick, and I've never sat on a draisine racing downhill in a mining tunnel with shooting maniacs right behind me, before.'

'You don't say. What do you see outside?'

'Why don't you look yourself, Sir?'

'There's this small matter of me trying to shoot our pursuers before they shoot us; it is distracting me slightly. Now – *what do you see?*'

I squinted in the direction of the opening again. The light outside was still so bright in comparison with the tunnel's gloom that I could hardly make out anything.

'Some bushes, I think. Grass.'

'Good. As soon as we leave the tunnel, we are going to throw ourselves into those bushes.'

'To disrupt the nests of innocent nightingales, Sir?'

'To cushion our fall, Mr Linton. Cover your face with your arms so your eyes won't be stabbed by a branch. And... be careful.'

I had just opened my mouth for a witty comeback, but closed it again. Had I heard right? Mr Rikkard Ambrose had just wasted valuable time and breath telling me to be careful? Not only that, but he had sounded genuinely concerned. Could it be that he...?

Another gunshot sheared through my half-finished thought. Hurriedly, I turned my gaze from Mr Ambrose to the approaching exit. I had to keep an eye on it. He was guarding our backs, making sure those sons of bachelors didn't get us. I had to do my part.

'We're getting close,' I announced. Sweat had started to bead on my forehead again, although the air in the tunnel was still icy, and I was just sitting, doing nothing, only watching. 'On the count of three we have to jump.'

He gave a grunt, and fired again. I took a deep breath.

'One,' I called.

Two more shots burst from his revolver, and the enemy answered.

'Two.'

He slowly pulled back his revolver and crouched lower, preparing to jump.

'Um... two and a half.'

'*What?* Mr Linton, what is that supposed to mean?'

'I misjudged the distance, all right? Two and three quarters!'

'Your version of a countdown is not very reliable, Mr Linton!'

'Why? I said on the count of three, and on the count of three it'll be. Two and four fifths!'

'*Mr Linton...!*'

'Three!'

I snatched his arm and hurled myself sideways, into free air.

RISING WAVES

Mr Ambrose had suggested that the bushes would cushion our fall. I didn't know what kind of cushion he preferred, but the landing in the bushes gave me a pretty good idea. Basalt, maybe? Sandstone?

By the time I came to a stop at the bottom of the hill on which the bushes were perched, I felt as though I had been squeezed through a meat-grinder. A strangled moan escaped from my throat.

'You should have rolled,' a cool voice commented from above me.

'I did roll! I did nothing but roll and jump and bump! I feel like a flipping football!'

'I mean *actively*. To break your fall.' A firm hand gripped mine and pulled me up so quickly I couldn't even try to protest. In a moment, I was standing beside Mr Ambrose, whose red uniform – curse him! – somehow still looked immaculate. He hadn't even gotten one twig in his smooth, shiny black hair.

For a moment, we stood like this, each close enough to hear the other's heart beating, our hands intertwined. Then he let go and abruptly turned.

'Let's go!'

'There they are!' The gruff voice from the tunnel entrance was much too familiar. 'Get them!'

Behind us, a shot rang out. It was the starting signal for our race. We dove into the brushes, and now I blessed the thick foliage I had cursed a moment ago. Bullets whipped through the forest to my right and left, but none hit Mr Ambrose or me. We were too well hidden among the green leaves. As quickly as possible, we slid between the trees, farther away from the tunnel.

Suddenly, Mr Ambrose stopped.

'Be quiet!'

'Oh really?' I hissed. 'This isn't the right time for your obsession with silence! We've got to run, and I don't care how loudly we do it! We–'

'No. I mean, I heard something. Be quiet and listen, just for a second.'

Grudgingly, I did as he told me. Over the hammering of my own heart I couldn't hear anything, at first. Then, slowly, I began to hear a low chatter, far off on the other side of the undergrowth.

'Voices!' I exclaimed.

Mr Ambrose nodded. 'Yes. Probably the crowd at the harbour. If we can reach it in time, we'll be safe!"

Without another word, he dove between two bushes and disappeared.

Muttering a low curse, I followed. The farther I got, the louder the voices became. I redoubled my effort, almost running headlong, raising my arms to shield my face from the sharp branches that attacked me from all sides. It was with a shocking suddenness that I stumbled out of the trees and into the open, onto a square paved with cobblestones.

The harbour. We had really managed to reach the harbour. In front of me stretched a wide, seaside promenade, with dozens of people strolling up and down, enjoying the view. Some of them glanced towards the forest when I burst out from between the trees, and looked more than a little surprised by the sight of a soldier with leaves and twigs in his bird's nest of hair, but most were too busy watching the ships arrive and leave.

Or, to be more precise – two ships arriving, one ship leaving. The ones that were arriving looked older, but the one that was about to embark was a brand-new steamship. Passengers were just getting on board the shiny, new vessel, all looking like wealthy tourists returning to England after a wonderful holiday. For a moment, my eyes fixed on the cursive word emblazoned on the ship's hull: *Urania*.

Quickly, I threw a sideways glance at Mr Ambrose and saw in his eyes the mirror of my own thought: our only chance. We rushed forward, slipping into the line at the gangway of the luxurious ship, and ignoring the protest of a thick-set French gentleman right behind us.

'Two tickets to England, please,' I gasped, slamming my hands on the counter of the official at the gangway to steady myself.

'I beg your pardon, *Monsieur*?' the man asked, looking at me with his nostrils instead of his eyes. But I worked for Mr Rikkard Ambrose! This little Frenchman's derisive glances were nothing in comparison to the ones I had learned to withstand.

'Tickets. To England. You do sell tickets to England, don't you?'

'*Naturalement, Monsieur* – since this is our vessel's only destination.'

'Well, then, you heard my companion.' Mr Ambrose stepped up beside me and fixed the official with an icy glare. 'Two tickets to England, third class.'

The official didn't back down. If anything, his look became even more disgusted. '*Third class, Monsieur?* I am afraid you have the wrong vessel. This is a ship of a respectable line, offering its services only to the better classes of society. We have no cabins of third class on board.'

Behind the granite mask on Mr Ambrose's face, a momentous struggle seemed to be going on. A muscle in his jaw twitched. His left little finger jerked erratically. Finally, he managed to say: 'Fine! Second class, then! How much does it cost?'

The official seemed to decide that looking at us with his nostrils was too great an honour for us, and he switched to regarding us with his wobbly chin instead.

'There is no second class, either, *Monsieur*. Please remove yourself. You are holding up the line.'

I saw Mr Ambrose's little finger twitch again, violently.

'Two tickets, first class, to England,' I said, before he could do anything he would later regret.

His head whipped around to stare at me. 'What are you doing?' he demanded, his tone low and hard.

'Saving our skins from your miserly ways,' I shot back amiably. 'I hope you have enough money on you.'

He opened his mouth to reply, but was cut short by the official.

'First class? As you could pay half the sum required! I have no time for your silly jokes, *Messieurs*. Remove yourselves immediately, or I will be forced to call security.'

Slowly, Mr Ambrose turned back towards the man. When the Frenchman caught sight of his eyes, he flinched back.

Mr Ambrose reached into his jacket and drew out a wallet. Opening it with deliberation, he pulled out two one hundred pound notes and slammed them down on the counter.

'You can give me my change when we arrive in England,' he said, his voice cold enough to freeze sunlight in mid-air. 'I wish to be shown to my cabin. Now.'

'W-why, certainly, *Monsieur*. At once, *Monsieur*.'

Staring incredulously at the banknotes, the official waved one of his underlings over. 'Quick! Pierre! Take these two gentlemen to the best cabins on the ship. Now!'

'But *Monsieur*, the best cabins on the ship are occupied by...'

'Do it!'

As we were led off by the bewildered young man, who kept sneaking glances back at his superior, Mr Ambrose leant over to me and whispered:

'The money for the tickets shall be deducted from your wages, Mr Linton.'

And for some reason, this didn't make me want to snarl back at him. It made me smile.

~~**~*~*

'Get them! Get the–'

The soldiers fell silent the moment they stumbled out of the undergrowth onto the seaside promenade, and several hundred people turned to stare at them. They seemed to realize several things at once: firstly, their prey was nowhere to be seen, secondly, they were wearing British Indian Army uniforms

545

on French territory, and thirdly, the crowd did not seem to appreciate the guns they were waving around.

'Ehem.' One of the soldiers, probably the commanding officer, cleared his throat. 'S-sorry if me and my friends gave you alarm. We... just had a bit too much to drink. Got a bit above ourselves, that's all.'

Weak though the explanation was, it was generally accepted, and as the soldiers lowered their guns, the crowd slowly returned to their business. The men – there were only two; Mr Ambrose had indeed hit the third one, apparently – huddled together and began whispering.

Up on the deck of the *Urania*, Mr Ambrose and I crouched behind the ship's railing, peering through the gaps down into the harbour.

'What do you think they will do now, Sir?' I asked.

'They are alone and do not know what to do. They will not risk attracting the attention of the crowd in order to find us. They have no authority here. Were Dalgliesh present, it might be different, but with things being as they are, we have a chance – if the ship leaves before they get reinforcements or, worse, support from the French authorities.'

'Do you really think the French are in on this?'

Mr Ambrose's face was grim. Even more so than usual.

'I'm convinced of it. Dalgliesh is no fool. He wouldn't set up his base in an environment he cannot control. Our only chance is to get away before the authorities can be notified.'

As he spoke, one of the soldiers darted off and up towards the centre of the island like a bullet shot from a gun. The other one began moving among the crowd, stopping people, asking questions. We remained where we were, watching, our anxiety rising with every minute. Or at least *my* anxiety was rising with every minute. I wasn't sure about that of Mr Ambrose, or about whether he had any at all. His face still looked like the bust of some stoic philosopher, only without the long beard and the toga.

The soldier down on the promenade moved closer and closer to the *Urania*. Not long and he would figure out that it was the only ship due for departure, the only way his prey could get off this island. But at the same time, the line in front of the *Urania* was dwindling. People were hurrying to get aboard. The sun was setting, and they seemed eager to get to their warm cabins before the cold of the night set in.

Beside me, I could hear Mr Ambrose let air hiss through his teeth, and turned my head to see what was wrong. He was staring at a point far above the crowd, where a road led up towards the centre of the island.

'What is it, Sir?'

'There might be slight difficulties for our departure. There, Mr Linton. Look!'

He pointed to the very top of the road, where several riders in blue uniforms, accompanying a rider in red uniform, were racing down towards the harbour. Slight difficulties indeed.

'Don't tell me those are the French, Sir.'

'Those *are* the French, Mr Linton.'

I grimaced. 'Thank you so much, Sir.'

By now, the soldiers were halfway down the road. I saw the foremost rider waving, trying to catch the attention of somebody on the ship, but the crowd was getting in the way. He shouted, but his words were drowned in the babble of the people admiring the sea view. Never had I been this grateful for the thriving French tourism industry.

'What will they do if they catch us?' My mouth felt dry. For some reason, my hand snaked along the railing, towards that of Mr Ambrose.

'The French? Or Dalgliesh?'

'I don't know. Which is worse?'

'Both.'

'Oh.'

My fingers found his. He twitched, and I was about to draw back, but then his fingers closed around mine like a vice, and held them tightly in place. I was so surprised that I almost didn't hear the shout from directly beneath us.

'*Larguez les amarres!*'

'W-what does that mean?' I whispered. '"Seize the spies'?'

'No.' Mr Ambrose's voice was just as cold as ever, but underneath the ice, there was triumph, waiting to break through. 'It means "Cast off"!'

Before I could even process what that meant, I felt a shudder underneath us and saw the gangway retract. Helpless, the faint cries of the French officers rose over the babble of the crowd as the ship detached itself from the jetty and lurched forward, its steam engine roaring to life like some giant, ancient beast. But unlike the *Nemesis*, this was a friendly beast. It had come to take us to safety.

With a dizzying mix of relief and disbelief, I watched as the harbour moved away from us, slowly at first, then faster and faster, as the ship gathered speed and moved away from the island into the channel. The French and British Indian soldiers shouted in vain, their voices drowned out by the engine that carried us farther and farther away from the danger.

Mr Ambrose's hand didn't loosen its grip on mine.

'We made it!' I whispered. 'We actually made it!'

He turned towards me. There was something in his dark gaze – not cold, this time. Something else. Something indefinable. He opened his mouth. But before he could speak, we heard a gentle cough from behind us.

Letting go of his hand as if it were a block of ice, I whipped my head around and stared up into the concerned face of a member of the ship's wait staff, looking down at the two of us crouching on the floor with concern.

'Um... we do have seats on this ship, *Messieurs*. It is not necessary to sit on the floor. Would you like me to show you?'

˷˷**˷*˷*

The helpful young member of the wait staff guided us to our cabins. I didn't know what Mr Ambrose did after disappearing into his. Stand in a corner and calmly calculate how much money he was going to make out of his new canal, maybe? I, for my part, slumped onto the thing that vaguely resembled a bed nailed to the wall. Bunk, dunk, shwunk – I couldn't care less what it was called or what it was for. It was relatively soft. That was all I needed to know.

The knock that woke me from my sleep was tentative but resolute. I blinked and yawned. How long had I been out? I didn't really care. My clothes had dried, so it had to have been some time.

Again, there came a knock from the door. Drowsily, I lifted my head. This didn't look like my room at my uncle's house. What was this? Oh yes, the ship! It all came back to me then: The island, the mine, the race, getting on the ship...

What was its name again? *Urania*. Yes. Had we really managed to escape, or had it all been just a dream? Was I still dreaming?

A third knock came from the door. I could tell from the sound alone that it wasn't Mr Ambrose on the other side.

'Yes?'

'*Monsieur?* Diner is ready in the dining hall.'

That decided it. I had managed to have some pretty strange dreams in my lifetime, but never could I dream up a French waiter calling me 'Monsieur'. Crazy things like that were reserved for reality – my reality with Mr Rikkard Ambrose.

Groaning, I pushed myself up from the bunk bed and stumbled towards the door. 'I'm coming,' I called. 'I'm coming.'

'Very well, *Monsieur*. You are, um, well? You seemed a little pale, earlier.'

Well, what do I say? Getting shot at does that to me.

'No, no. Everything is fine. Thank you.'

'Excellent. I shall return to the dining hall. Your companion is awaiting you there.'

Not long after, I stepped out onto the deck of the ship and closed my eyes for a moment as I breathed in the fresh sea air. It was cool, harsh and salty – not the best combination for a city girl like me, under normal circumstances. But just now, I revelled in it, revelled in the fact that it was no longer the dank, dusty air of the mine I had to breathe in, revelled in the fact that I could still breathe because I was alive.

Opening my eyes again, I looked around. I stood on the upper of two decks aboard the *Urania*. The wooden structures supporting the deck, as well as the walls of the cabins, were painted in a cheerful golden-yellow and only served to re-emphasize the point: I was out of the dark. I was safe. We both were safe.

Stepping towards the railing, I took another deep breath and looked back the way we had come. Past the roiling clouds of smoke from the engine that propelled us forward, past the churning waters behind it, I could see, in the distance, the faint shape of a mountain on the horizon, rising out of the distant waves. *Île Marbeau*. It looked like nothing more than a molehill from here. And regardless of how angry the mole that lived there might be right now, regardless of how much he might resemble a lion in his fury, we were out of his reach. I smiled.

Leaving the sea view behind me, I turned and went in search of Mr Ambrose. I hoped for his sake he hadn't eaten without me and already left, or there would be hell to pay!

It didn't take me long to find my way through the luxurious, wood-panelled corridors of the ship. They were not like the corridors of the Nemesis. Light shone in through curtained windows, gold and silver glittered in every corner, and everywhere there were helpful people willing to show you the way, instead of evil people willing to show you the way to your grave. One old lady, Lady Timberlake, even entangled me in a conversation about how small and underfed the young men in military service, like my good self, looked nowadays, when I asked her for the way. She discovered I had the cabin right next to hers, and it took me some time to pry myself away from her. She was sorry to see the young soldier (i.e. me) go; he reminded her so much of her grandson, the brave darling...

I hoped fervently this was due to the excellence of my disguise and not to the freakish anatomy of her grandson.

When I finally entered the dining hall, a grand room with plush leather chairs arranged around small, intricately carved tables, and crystal chandeliers dangling from the ceiling, the first thing I saw was Mr Ambrose, sitting at one of the tables and arguing with one of the waiters over the price of a glass of water.

'...two shillings for one glass?' Mr Ambrose was saying, trying to nail the poor waiter to the wall with his cold glare. The other guests were watching him with apprehensive looks on their faces. 'What do you put in that water, man? Gold dust? This is not acceptable!'

'But *Monsieur*,' the waiter protested. 'This is special mineral water with many beneficial properties for your health, directly from the wells at...'

'Well, as it happens, I do not feel sick in the slightest. Is it within your ability to procure some non-healing, but reasonably priced water?'

'*Monsieur*! This is a vessel of the very first class. We pride ourselves on the excellence of everything we serve, and it would be a disgrace if we–'

'Can you or can't you?'

A pained expression crossed the waiter's face.

'I might be able to, um... obtain some low-quality fluid out of the provisions for the ship's personnel, if *Monsieur* wishes it.'

'Yes, *Monsieur* wishes it.'

'*Alors*, I shall do my best. Before I leave, what does *Monsieur* wish to eat?'

Mister Ambrose eyed the bread basket placed in the middle of the table.

'Does this cost anything?'

'The bread basket? No, of course not, *Monsieur*! That is just an appetizer. Which of our delicacies does *Monsieur* wish to taste?'

'The one that doesn't cost anything.' With one hand, Mister Ambrose pulled the bread basket towards him, with the other, he waved the waiter away. 'This will be quite sufficient. That will be all.'

The waiter was near tears.

'*Monsieur* cannot be serious! Water and bread? Water and bread? This is a first-class vessel, not a prison bark!'

'More's the pity. On a prison bark, I wouldn't have had to pay for the voyage.'

'*Monsieur*! I beg you to reconsider. Please, here, I have a menu, will you not look and see if there is something that will please your palate? We have the best–'

He was interrupted by a hand snatching the menu from his grasp. *My* hand.

Casually, I flicked through the pages with golden corners and embossed, italic writing. Something caught my eye.

'I would like... *Foie Gras avec Sauce Espagnole*, then a glass of Champagne...'

'The sparkling variety or pale red?'

'Sparkling, definitely sparkling. And as for dessert... well, we shall see. I look forward to tasting your delicacies.'

The waiter bowed so deeply that his head almost smashed into the table.

'*Thank you, Monsieur*. Thank you so much!'

Shooting a last, lofty glance at Mr Ambrose, he glided away. I, meanwhile, sank down into the chair opposite my employer and gave him a bright smile.

He did not return it.

'The price for that extravagant meal shall be deducted from your wages,' he warned.

'If you keep this up, Sir, there won't be anything left of my wages when you've deducted all you wish.'

'That would be very convenient indeed, Mr Linton.'

'Oh, don't be so grumpy,' I admonished. 'You got what you wanted, didn't you? We have the file back. We should celebrate!'

'I am celebrating. I ordered a glass of water, didn't I?'

'Dear me, you're right. Your extravagant exuberance is overwhelming, Sir.'

He, oh great surprise, didn't reply. The waiter arrived with our drinks, and I raised my glass of champagne towards Mr Ambrose.

'A toast,' I declared.

He regarded me with those cool, dark eyes of his.

'Similar to jokes, Mr Linton, toasts are a waste of time and breath. They also present the added hazard of spilling a drink one has paid for.'

'Well, I like to waste a little breath and time now and again!'

'I noticed.'

'A toast,' I repeated, and to my utter astonishment, Mr Ambrose hesitantly raised his glass towards mine. 'To a successful operation. May you make so much money out of your canal that you choke on it!'

We clinked glasses. I didn't spill anything of my costly drink.

'A pleasing prospect, Mr Linton. However, quite unlikely. I have never had problems digesting monetary gain.'

I hid a smirk behind my champagne glass. 'I can readily believe that, Sir.'

He watched me drinking, his eyes narrowing infinitesimally. 'Should you be drinking, Mr Linton? Remember what happened last time.'

My smirk widened into a grin.

'Yes, that was fun.'

His eyes narrowed another fraction of an inch.

'There was a gunfight. You were hallucinating. We nearly died.'

'As I said, fun.'

'I think we must agree to disagree on that, Mr Linton,' he said coolly.

We lapsed into silence again. I wet my lips and opened my mouth – then closed it again. There was something I really wanted to ask. I didn't, though. I was afraid of what the answer might be.

'*Messieurs! Voilà*, your meal has arrived!' The waiter swooped down on us like an eagle on a rabbit, only instead of grabbing us for his next meal, he brought us one. A steaming plate was set down in front of me, with a glistening, brown piece of something on it that looked incredibly soft and succulent. It also looked like nothing I had ever seen before, let alone eaten.

Bowing and smiling at me, the waiter departed. He completely ignored Mr Ambrose. I looked down at my plate, and tentatively picked up the thing on it with a fork. It wobbled.

'You have no idea what *foie gras* is, do you?' Mr Ambrose asked.

'Of course I do!' I sent him an indignant look. How dare he adopt this superior tone with me? I was a member of the gentry, after all. He was nothing but a paltry financier. Why should he just assume he knew more about French cuisine than I did? Granted, he might be right, but it was still a pretty darn cheeky supposition.

'Indeed?' The way he said that word alone made me want to stuff a fork down his throat. 'Well, what is it, then?'

'Um... it's...' I stared at the brown lump, trying to make deductions from the form and size. 'Fish?' I suggested, hopefully.

'Not quite. Actually, it's goose liver.'

'Oh.'

Suddenly, I was acutely aware of how the ship pitched and rolled in the power of the waves, and I wasn't quite so keen on tasting the French delicacy as a moment before. Raising my eyes, I saw Mr Ambrose watching me, his face perfectly expressionless, but his dark eyes slightly smug.

Ha! I'll show him!

Quick as a flash I cut off a piece of the poor goose's innards and stuffed it into my mouth before I could think better of it. Carefully, I bit down. It tasted surprisingly good. Not squishy at all, but soft and buttery.

'Hmmm...' Swallowing, I cut off another piece. 'Quite nice. Yes, really quite nice.' I tried the sauce that came with it, and the grin returned to my face. 'Those Froggies really know what they're doing in the kitchen.'

Cutting off another piece, I offered it to Mr Ambrose. 'Do you want to try?'

Demonstratively, he took a piece of baguette from the bread basket and took a bite.

'Oh well, suit yourself.'

We ate in silence for a while. I really enjoyed the meal. When you live off potatoes most of the time, tasting *foie gras* is something special simply for the scarcity value. Add to that the exquisite taste, and... well, it was just about heaven. I treasured every bite, knowing I wouldn't taste something like this again for a long, long while. Even with my own wages, I would hardly be able to afford this on a regular basis. Especially if...

There it was again. That question. That question I didn't want to ask.

I did it anyway.

'Am I really that bad?'

My voice was quiet, hesitant. Mr Ambrose looked up from his plate, where he was cutting his baguette into geometrically similar pieces. 'What?'

'You intimated that after you had deducted money from my wages for all the things I had done wrong, there wouldn't be anything left. Am I really that bad at my job, Sir?'

For once, there was no teasing, no scorn, no antagonism in my voice. That seemed to throw him off. He stared at me as if really seeing me for the first time. His dark eyes turned even darker.

'No,' he said, finally. 'You are not. In fact...' His jaw worked for a moment. 'In fact, one might say your services have been moderately satisfactory, thus far.'

'Satisfactory?' Had I heard right? Had he just uttered praise? Praise, moreover, which in Mr Ambrose's limited complimentary vocabulary equalled heavenly trumpets announcing a triumphal procession in honour of my utter perfection?

'Relatively speaking, of course, Mr Linton. You are still no match for a real man, of course.'

For some reason, this didn't make me want to bash his brains in. Instead, my lips twitched. 'Of course.'

'But for a member of the unmasculine persuasion, you showed considerable lack of fear, down in the mine.'

'Courage, you mean, Sir?' I inquired sweetly.

'Courage would be too strong a word. I would be more inclined to attribute your actions to an impetuous nature and a tendency to rash behaviour. However, whatever the reasons might be, you exhibited a considerable lack of fear and weakness.'

'You mean I was resilient, Sir? Strong, even?'

'Those words are not the ones I would have chosen. It is more likely–'

'–that my actions originated from some irrational part of my inferior mind, which simply didn't grasp the danger, than from any real strength of character?'

'Exactly.'

'Why, thank you, Sir.'

'You're welcome, Mr Linton.'

Why was there a smile on my face? His compliments were badly disguised insults! He still was just as abominable a chauvinist as on the first day I met him. I should be shouting at him, demanding recognition of my work and my loyalty. I definitely should not be moving my right hand across the table towards where his left rested on the tablecloth.

And why was his hand suddenly starting to move, too, sliding over the table until his fingers touched mine? His fingertips brushed the back of my hand, and a little gasp escaped me. Suddenly, my mind felt very irrational indeed.

'Will you pay me my wages?' I asked softly. 'Will you let me stay on?'

He seemed to weigh my words for an eternity.

'I shouldn't pay you a penny,' he said, finally. 'I should get rid of you as quickly as I can.'

It was I who remained silent now, for once. It hadn't escaped my notice that he had told me what he thought he *should* do, not what he *would* do. So I waited in silence.

Without knowing why, I squeezed his hand. For some reason, it felt good to hold his hand, as if I were a ship in a storm, and he the line holding me in my safe harbour. Ridiculous, but there it was. The feeling wouldn't go away.

'Why?' I asked, still in this soft tone of voice that was so totally unlike me. How had I managed to suddenly come up with it, without practising? Why was I even using it? 'Why would you want to get rid of me? I was helpful, wasn't I? We got your secret file back. Soon, you'll be the unchallenged master of world trade. That's what you wanted, isn't it?'

His fingers grasped mine more tightly.

'But the danger...'

'Well, there was a danger of not getting the file back. But it's passed. So why worry?'

His eyes flashed with sharp shards of ice.

'I was not talking about the file, Mr Linton!' His fingers closed even more tightly around mine. It was as if they were squeezing my heart. I suddenly found I couldn't speak.

'What were you talking about, Sir?'

His dark eyes bored into mine, answering my question without words.

'You remember how I told you to be careful?' he asked, his gaze keeping mine prisoner. I nodded.

'Down in the mine you were not careful. You never are!'

I swallowed, dislodging the lump in my throat that had kept me from speaking, and attempted a smile.

'It would take all the fun out of life.'

His hand clenched around mine, almost breaking my fingers. Why the heck did feel good anyway?

'You could have died!'

'So... that's why you want to get rid of me?'

'I want to dismiss you from your job all right.' He leaned forward, his chiselled face not betraying a hint of what he thought or felt. His eyes, though... His eyes were another matter. 'That's not the same as getting rid of you.'

Another one of those lumps had appeared in my throat. I swallowed, hard, but it was a stubborn lump that didn't like attempts to dislodge it. 'What other reason could I have for staying around, Sir?'

'What if it's not up to you, Mr Linton? What if I don't want to let you go?'

I felt the floor under my feet sway in a way that had nothing whatsoever to do with swell.

'W-what do you mean?' I asked.

He opened his mouth to speak.

'Excuse me, *Messieurs*?'

Our hands jumped apart as if hit with a horsewhip. We stared up at the waiter, who had walked up to our table without either of us noticing. He bowed and flourished a second set of menus. 'Would you like dessert, now, *Messieurs*?'

~~**~*~*

We ate our dessert in silence. That is, *I* ate my dessert in silence, while Mr Ambrose chewed another piece of baguette in silence, following the waiter through the room with a venomous, icy glare.

I was glad for his lack of loquaciousness, for once. I had enough to think about – most of all about Mr Ambrose's words. He had said he should get rid of me. And yet... and yet... he hadn't looked at me as if he wished to get rid of me. Quite the contrary, in fact.

'What if it's not up to you, Mr Linton? What if I don't want to let you go?'

I shivered. What if he didn't plan to sack me? What if he was planning on doing something even worse? Exposing my disguise, maybe? But no. That would also expose himself. But what then? I could not for the life of me decipher his dark, intense looks or sparse words.

My dessert was soon gone. There was plenty of baguette in the bread basket still, but Mr Ambrose didn't seem in the mood to continue eating, even if it was for free. That fact alone was very worrying. He simply sat there in brooding silence, a brooding silence that was about three times as brooding as his usual brooding silences. Again, I couldn't suppress a shiver. I thought I had managed to prove myself to him, at least to some extent. To prove that I could be a valuable and reliable asset in spite or even because of my femininity. But the way he was staring at the table, avoiding my eyes... He looked like he had all those times when he had contemplated getting rid of me. What was wrong?

'Is... is everything all right, Sir?' I asked.

He nodded.

'You did get all of it? The file, I mean? Is there something missing?'

'What?' He looked up, seeming to need a moment to realize what I had asked. 'No, no. The file is complete. Mr Linton?'

'Yes?'

'Are you hurt at all? I didn't get a chance to ask before. I should have made sure, after we got away from the soldiers. Are you all right?'

Why did he want to know? Was he worried I had gotten blood on the fake uniform he had paid for?

'No, Sir. I'm perfectly all right.'

'Hm.'

He lowered his eyes, and started glaring at the table again. It was a wonder that the piece of furniture hadn't fled from him yet.

Soon after, the waiter appeared with our bill, which didn't exactly improve Mr Ambrose's mood. He paid, but not without giving me a look twice as icy as that he had directed at the poor table. I really hoped my wages would be high enough to cover this bill, otherwise I would be in big trouble.

The waiter bowed and left. For a moment I considered asking Mr Ambrose what was the matter. I hesitated briefly, looking at his chiselled granite face. I hesitated for an instant too long. Pushing back his chair, he rose.

'I'm tired, Mr Linton. I'm going back to my cabin. You should, too. When we arrive in England, we still have a long coach journey ahead of us.' His dark eyes met mine, holding them for a moment. 'And we'll have a lot to discuss.'

Before I could say anything, he was gone. I shrugged. It wasn't as if this was the last chance we would ever get to talk. I'd have to get to the bottom of what was the matter with him sooner or later. But it could just as well be later as sooner.

Besides, I had to admit, a few more hours of rest would probably do me good. My muscles still ached from pushing the draisine up those hills, and all I wanted to do was lie down and relax.

When I stepped out onto the deck, Mr Ambrose was nowhere to be seen. Strange. Why was he in such a hurry to disappear? Was he avoiding me? But why would he do that?

The question kept nagging at me, even when I had entered my cabin and lain down. No matter how much I tossed from side to side, or how many blankets I pulled over myself, I couldn't find sleep. The sun started to sink and disappeared behind the horizon, and still my eyes hadn't closed. Mr Ambrose's strange behaviour continued to gnaw at me. Besides, the roar of the steam engine was doing its best to keep me awake. It felt like trying to go to sleep with a raging rhinoceros next door.

In the end, help came from unexpected quarter: the sea. As time passed, its motion became more turbulent, its rush became louder, until it tuned out the drone of the steam engine. The repetitive up and down of the waves, instead of making me sick, turned out to be comforting, like the movement of the cradle, lulling a child into sleep.

Don't worry so much about Mr Ambrose... Whatever his problem is, he'll calm down... Everything will be all right...

With that comforting thought, I drifted off into sleep.

I awoke, startled into consciousness by the ring of a bell. A bell? But why would I hear a bell? There was no church in the vicinity, was there? No, of course there wasn't. I was on a ship! The *Urania*. Did ships have bells? And when did they ring? Surely not for a wedding?

It was then that I noticed that the motion of the waves had once again changed. Before, it had been like a mother, rocking a child to sleep. Now, it rather resembled a mother bent on infanticide! Over the roar of the sea I could hear thunder rumble in the distance. And were those running feet outside my cabin? Yes, they were! And they were coming closer.

With an almighty crash, my door burst inward, slamming against the wall – and there, framed in the doorway stood Mr Rikkard Ambrose, his silhouette only visible for a moment as lightning arced across the sky. Then he disappeared into darkness, and I only heard his voice, cold and controlled:

'Get up! A storm is coming!'

MAN AND WOMAN

For a moment, I was frozen. Which was ironic, in a way. I had always thought of Mr Ambrose as cold and immobile, but now I was the one who couldn't move. He marched over to me and grabbed me by the arm.

'Get up, I said, Mr Linton! Now!'

Half running, half dragged by Mr Ambrose, I stumbled out of the cabin and onto the deck. The deck? No. This didn't look like the deck I remembered. This looked more like pandemonium. All I saw, before a wall of water hit me in the face, was a strange still life in black and white, with men, women and children arranged around the ship like living corpses, waiting to die again, their faces thrown into stark contrast by the flash of a lightning bolt.

Then, the wave was on me, and the light was gone. My lungs filled with salt-water, and I was thrown back against the outer cabin wall. Only the hand that still clasped mine held me upright. The hand of Mr Ambrose.

'Steady. It's all right. I've got you.'

Spluttering and coughing, I emptied a mouthful of saltwater onto the deck, and a goodly piece of half-digested goose liver, too. I hardly noticed the stench over the strange and unfamiliar scents wafting over the *Urania*. Dark scents. Cold scents. Scents of the deep sea rising.

'Please, ladies and gentlemen! Please, there is no need for concern! Calm down, please!' An officer was striding towards us, down from the bridge, his hands raised in an attempt to calm the frightened crowd. Even if he had ten arms, I doubt it would have worked. 'We are doing everything we can to get the situation under control. Please, ladies and gentle-'

'And how,' Mr Ambrose cut him off, cold steel in his voice, 'do you plan to get a storm under control? Are you St Peter? Can you close the sluice gates of heaven and stop lightning from striking us down?'

The officer opened his mouth, but no sound came out. His frightened eyes flickered from Mr Ambrose, to the rest of the terrified crowd gathered on the deck, to the roiling sea around us.

'How many lifeboats are on this miserable wreck?' Mr Ambrose's voice was still deadly cold.

'Please, Sir, you have to stay calm. The captain-'

'The captain obviously isn't worthy of scrubbing the deck of a ship, because it was he who got us into this situation in the first place. Now - *how many lifeboats are on this vessel?*'

The officer hung his head. 'Not enough for everybody.' His voice was mere whisper. It didn't matter. Everybody heard him. And a moment later, he could have yelled himself hoarse, and nobody would have understood a word. The crowd exploded into panic, everyone demanding that they would get on a life-boat first, screeching insults, pressing to see the captain. As if that would help.

Mr Ambrose didn't yell. The moment he heard the officer's words he squeezed my hand even tighter, and began to drag me along the slippery deck, away from my cabin. I didn't protest, or try to stop him. I felt numb. Somewhere, deep inside, the realization had already settled: I was going to die tonight. I had fulfilled my dream, gotten my own job, lived through all those adventures and dangers, and now I would die tonight, on this measly little boat, far, far away from home.

At least Mr Ambrose was with me. That made me feel a little better, though also sad, for some reason.

Why?

Yes, *that* was the reason: I didn't want him to die. The realization came as a surprise to me. Most of the time during our short acquaintance, I had felt like strangling him myself. But now that the sea was about to choke him for me, I didn't want it to happen. And yet, I was glad that I wasn't alone. Strange. Very strange.

'Please! Ladies and Gentlemen!' I heard the officer call from somewhere behind me. 'The situation is not as dire as it seems. The sea is just a little rough, I assure you. Please stay where you are! We have the situation under complete control. The captain...'

'Where are you going?' I yelled to be heard over the howl of the wind. 'He says we should stay where we are!'

'He also says they have the situation under control!' His voice had never sounded like this before. Even when he had been furious, it had always been a cold fury – cold, precise and calculated. This wasn't calculated. It was out of control. It was almost as if he were showing emotion. I, on the other hand, couldn't feel anything, not even fear. I was beyond that now. I could hear our fate in his voice, and if you already knew you were doomed, what was the point of being afraid?

I grasped his hand more tightly.

'Where are we going?' I asked, more because I wanted to go inside, away from the cold, than because I really wanted to know his destination. If I was going to die, I wanted to damn well spend my last few minutes in a warm, comfy cabin, and I wanted him with me!

But he turned his head from left to right, not giving the cabins a second glance. His eyes were wild, as if desperately searching for something.

'I don't know!' he growled. 'There must be something! Some way to... You can't... you can't just...'

Another voice, amplified by a speaking trumpet rose over the raging storm and drowned out his stuttered exclamations.

'Attention! Attention, please, ladies and gentlemen. This is the captain speaking. This vessel is nearing a storm that we might not be able to circumvent. Please remain calm. Everything is being done to ensure your safety. Everybody proceed to the lifeboats, please, and prepare to embark, in case of an emergency. Women and children first. This is an order!'

Mr Ambrose's head snapped around to the origin of the voice as if he were Tantalus starving in the underworld and it had just offered him a slice of apple pie. I thought he would start running in that direction, but no: he started to drag me off again, heading away from the voice, not toward it. Soon, we were back at my cabin. Mr Ambrose ripped the door open and pushed me inside. Stepping in, he slammed the door shut behind him. Suddenly, the howl of the storm and sound of the thunder were muted. It felt like another world – a warmer, safer one. If not for the bucking of the ship beneath us, I might have believed we were far, far away from danger. I might have believed we were not going to die.

I was glad Mr Ambrose had brought me in here. This was what I had wanted. To not be out there, in the cold and wet, at the end of my life. I smiled at him in silent thanks, but he glared back at me as if I had offended him somehow.

'Well?' he demanded. 'What are you waiting for? Strip!'

I blinked. This wasn't what I had been expecting.

'S-strip, Sir? Strip what?'

'Your clothes off, of course!'

'M-my clothes?'

'Yes, your clothes! Get out of those ridiculous army trousers and into a skirt! Right now, Mr Linton!'

This didn't do anything to detract from my confusion.

'*You* want me to put on a skirt, Sir?'

'Are you deaf? Yes. A skirt, a dress, a hat and all the rest of it. All those things that make a girl actually look like one, and not some cheap imitation of a man!'

Slowly, anger started rising up inside me. I had wanted to spend my last few minutes of life in peace and quiet, and here he was, insulting me, trying to get me to do the very thing he had forbidden me from doing for weeks now. And for what? Because I wasn't worthy to die in a man's shoes and trousers?

'Well,' I snapped, 'you'll have to do without the entertainment of a charade, I'm afraid. I'm not playing dress-up for you! Lord, we're about to die! What is going on in that sick head of yours?'

'I told you to strip, Mr Linton! Strip and put on women's clothes! This is an order!'

'Do not call me Mister! And I do not care if it's an order or an anchovy! I'm about to drown and don't have to do another word you say.'

He advanced towards me. His eyes were beyond wild now. They were dark pits of death, as dark as the sea that was about to swallow us up.

'Put on girl's clothes. Now!'

I stepped forward, too, facing him directly.

'No! I will not. I would not, even if I had them – which I don't.'

'*What?*'

'Use your head, if it hasn't turned to a block of stone yet! Where should I get girl's clothes from? I didn't take anything onto the ship with me. I only have the clothes on my back, nothing more!'

'But...' He looked around, frantic ice in his eyes. 'You must have something! A dress, or a night shirt, or... anything!'

My hand hit him in the face with enough force to make him stumble back three steps.

'You bastard!' I shouted. 'We're about to die! Do you understand? Die! I don't care about what clothes I wear. I care about...'

I stopped.

What did I care about? I couldn't really find the words for it. But as I gazed up into his deep, dark eyes, I thought I found at least one of those things in there.

'You must have,' he muttered, as if he hadn't even registered the fact that I had slapped him. 'You must have some girl's clothes.'

'No.' For some reason, my voice was suddenly soft, hardly loud enough to be heard over the roar of the storm in the background. 'Why do you care? They're clothes, Sir, just clothes.' Almost involuntarily, my hand reached up to clasp his trembling fingers. 'It's what's underneath that matters.'

'Not right now,' he murmured, his voice more controlled again, but just as ferocious as before. 'Don't you see, Mr Linton? The captain said "women and children first". *Women*.'

It took a moment for the penny to drop. I had gotten so used to my disguise, to pretending that I was a man, that I hadn't even thought of the meaning of those words. *Women first*. I *was* a woman. I could get a place on one of the life-boats.

I can survive this.

My eyes, which had reached out into the far distance, snapped back to Mr Ambrose.

But he can't.

He seemed to read the thought on my face.

'Mr Linton,' he said, his voice colder than I had ever heard it, 'you will be on one of those lifeboats. No discussion. This is an order.'

'You can order as much as you want,' I whispered. 'I don't have any girl's clothes. Nobody will believe I'm a woman.'

'They will! I will *make* them believe!'

'Why do you care anyway?' My voice suddenly sounded hoarse. Was I catching a cold? Well, on the bright side, it wouldn't really matter, because I would be dead soon. 'Why do you care if I survive? If I drown, at least you'd be rid of me at last!'

He took a step closer. His dark eyes, burning with cold fire, didn't leave mine for a second. 'Maybe I don't want to be rid of you.'

I had to swallow. It was hard. 'And maybe I don't want to leave you behind.'

He went rigid, as if suddenly paralysed by some hellish poison – or a heavenly one.

'Mr Linton, I...'

Suddenly, the ship, hit by another wave, gave a violent lurch, and I was hurled forward, towards Mr Ambrose. His arms came up reflexively to catch me and, just as reflexively, his lips parted. There I hung, limply, in his arms. The force of the wave was spent. I was no longer being forced forward, and yet I was, by another wave, a wave of unknown emotions welling up inside me, keeping me moving, until his face and mine were just inches apart.

I stared into his fathomless, sea-coloured eyes and saw in them volumes of unspoken words. For just the briefest of moments I thought I felt a gentle caress of his lips on mine – then, another wave hit, and I was thrown back, away from him.

Crying out, I reached for something, anything to hold me upright and grabbed a coat hook on the wall. With my other hand I reached up to brush my lips. *God almighty...!*

Mr Ambrose, too, had grabbed a coat hook to hold onto. He let go of it now, and fixed his eyes on me. The shock of the second wave seemed to have shaken him out of his momentary paralysis.

He grabbed my hand.

'What are you doing?' I demanded, my voice breathy.

His hand tightened around mine. 'I'm going to see to it that you survive this night!'

'I said I didn't want to leave you!'

The fire in his eyes sparked in a way that was both infinitely hot and infinitely cold. 'Is that so? Well, you are just going to have to, Mr Linton.'

'You can't make me!'

'There you're wrong.'

Before I could say or do anything, strong arms took hold of me and I lost my footing. It took a moment to realize: Mr Ambrose had swept me off my feet! I was so stunned, I didn't even contemplate my natural response, which would be bash his head in with a parasol.

But since I didn't have a parasol, that wasn't really an option, anyway, was it?

Crash!

Dazed, I watched him kick open the door and march forward. He was moving as if I weighed no more than a feather, and in a heartbeat we were outside again. If anything, the chaos had increased. The waves were twice as high as before – high enough to easily reach over the railing and roll over the ship's wooden deck as if it were already part of the ocean. The passengers were all crammed together in one corner beside two flimsy-looking boats, secured to the deck by ropes. Each and every one tried to jostle forward, to get into one of those fragile promises of safety.

Nobody paid attention to what we were doing – and that was a good thing. With me slung unceremoniously over his back, Mr Ambrose marched right up to the door of the cabin next to mine and drew back his foot. It came forward again in a lightning-fast movement and connected with the door with a thunderous crash that nobody noticed over the roar of the wind and the sea.

'Mr Ambrose!' I protested. 'That's Lady Timberlake's cabin!'

'Exactly,' he said, and drew his foot back again. 'That's why I'm kicking the door down.'

Once more, his foot shot forward.

Crack!

The door burst inward, splinters of wood from around the lock flying everywhere. Not waiting for me to protest again, Mr Ambrose marched inside and slammed the door behind us. For a moment, we were in darkness. Unlike my

560

cabin, where I had left a lamp burning, Lady Timberlake's cabin was not illuminated, and even though there was a window, no light came out of the dark storm outside. The clouds had long blocked out the moon and the stars. They were gathering to cast the world into shadow, to use it as the dark anvil for the bright hammer of lightning.

Suddenly, Mr Ambrose slid me off his back and more or less shoved me away. Panicking, I tried to grab him, but caught only empty air.

'Mr Ambrose?' I turned my head left and right, but could see only black. I didn't want to be alone! Not in this dreadful chaos of death that was coming down on us. 'Mr Ambrose? Where are you, Sir?'

Silence.

'Where are you, darn it?'

Without warning, a light flickered to life in the corner of the room, and I had to shield my eyes from the bright invasion. Mr Ambrose stood there, holding a safety lamp, next to a large trunk that stood open beside Lady Timberlake's bunk bed. As I watched, he bent down and pulled out something enormous, pink and frilly, which glittered in the lamplight. He held it out to me.

'Put this on!' There was no doubt in his voice, no room for hesitation or argument. It was a command. And I didn't care.

I crossed my arms in front of my chest.

'Never!' I didn't want to leave his side. I couldn't. Besides, I, unlike poor old Lady Timberlake, actually had some dress sense.

He took a step forward, the dangerous glint in his eyes intensified a thousandfold by the light of the lamp he held up. The flickering flame shone on his face and gave it a whole new appearance, the sharp angles thrown into clearer contrast, the hardness now more clearly visible than ever before.

'You are going to change into female attire this minute, Mr Linton, or I swear, by all the banknotes of the Bank of England, I will rip your clothes of and stuff you into a skirt myself! Do you understand?'

At any other time, the thought of him ripping my clothes off might have unleashed a torrent of forbidden images and dreams. Not now, though. Now, there was a real torrent coming for us. From somewhere not far away, I heard wood splintering, and the ship shuddered. It wouldn't be long now.

'*Do you understand*, Mr Linton?' he repeated, enunciating each word, his teeth clenched. I couldn't escape his penetrating glare. And somehow, I found, I couldn't deny him.

'Y-yes, Sir.'

'Adequate.' He nodded, turning on his heels and marching towards the door.

'I'll be waiting outside,' he said over his shoulder. 'Don't take too long. Your dressing room is sinking.'

˷˷**˷*˷*

I stepped out onto the deck. Mr Ambrose already awaited me.

'You took your time,' he observed.

'It was difficult to get the dress on,' I said, my voice as lifeless as the rest of me. 'The buttons are at the back.'

There were so many things I should have said. Yet that was all I could think of. *The buttons are at the back.*

The ship swayed, and I grabbed the doorframe to steady myself. Mr Ambrose didn't move an inch, somehow seeming able to sway contrary to the ship's motion, so he was always standing ramrod straight. He held out his arm to me.

'Shall we?'

I stared down at it. Having dressed up as a man for so long, I had almost forgotten how a gentleman was supposed to behave to a lady, and that he was the former, while I was the latter. To have this resurface now that we were in danger of sinking into bottomless depths forever was the cruellest of mockeries. With shaking hands, I clutched his arm, and we proceeded down the ship, towards the clamouring crowd beside the lifeboats.

Again, I heard the ship's alarm bell ringing high above me. It suddenly, painfully, reminded me of church bells announcing a wedding.

Ha! As if this was anything like a wedding. At a wedding, everything was white. Tonight, everything was in black. At a wedding, two people were joined for life. Tonight, two people would be divided in death. At a wedding, two people loved each other. He only hated me, didn't he? He had said it often enough.

I glanced sideways at Mr Ambrose and saw that he, too, was watching me, his dark eyes burning with cold fire. I remembered his lips skimming over mine, and suddenly it struck me that in this last respect, maybe tonight wasn't so unlike a wedding after all. My jaw began to quiver, and I could feel moisture at the corner of my eyes, threatening to spill over.

'Don't, Mr Linton.' The voice was Mr Ambrose's – but it was neither as hard nor as cold as usual. It sounded almost gentle. 'It's wet enough as it is.'

I nodded hurriedly and clenched my teeth. I wouldn't cry! I would be strong.

We arrived at the sodden altar of our deadly wedding. The wedding guests didn't seem too pleased to see us. Particularly, when Mr Ambrose started pushing through the crowd.

'You there!' one of the men shouted. 'Stand back and wait your turn, like any of us!'

Mr Ambrose shot the man a glare that could have frozen lava and held up our joined hands. 'I'm not seeking a place for myself, but for this lady here.'

'What the hell is that supposed to mean?' The man growled, not even bothering to look at me. 'There are already heaps of women in the boats. All that were on the ship!'

'Apparently not.' Mr Ambrose's voice remained calm and cool, but I when I glanced at the little finger of his left hand, I knew the truth behind the mask. The finger was twitching in *prestissimo*. 'As you can see, there is still this young lady left, and...'

'What, that strumpet?' the man growled, glancing in disgust at my less than orderly attire. 'Not a chance she's getting into the boat with us. It's time that honest men got a pla-'

Mr Ambrose's fist moved faster than a lightning bolt. The man was thrown backwards, driving people right and left, and slammed into the ship's railing.

'Just to clarify,' Mr Ambrose said, still as cool as an iceberg. 'I'll be staying behind to make sure she gets on board safely.'

'No!'

The word was out of my mouth before I knew why or how. The crowd's eyes snapped to me. Then, from me, they went to Mr Ambrose, and back to me again. Something appeared in their eyes then, some understanding I couldn't quite reach, and they backed away. Mr Ambrose led me through their midst, though now I had started to struggle. I was finally starting to realize all of what he meant to do.

'No!' I protested. 'You can't stay behind! You can't! I won't let you!'

He said nothing, just picked me up and deposited me in the lifeboat as if I weighed nothing at all. I tried to scramble out again, but the hands of other women grabbed me, holding me back. I could feel wetness stream down my face. Were those tears, or was it rain? The storm roared louder and louder.

'Look after her, will you?' Mr Ambrose asked Lady Timberlake, who was cowering in the boat, right beside me.

The old lady nodded.

'I will, young Sir! I promise. Such a lovely girl. She looks just like I when I was younger. Why, even her dress looks like one of mine! It's almost like fate. I promise, nothing will happen to her.'

'No,' I mumbled, helplessly, not looking at her once. 'No! Don't do this!'

I tried to reach for Mr Ambrose, but he retreated far away. Other people started to climb into the boat after me. Were they were men or women? I did not know. They could have been elephants, for all I cared. All that mattered was: he wasn't one of them. He didn't even try to get a place on the boat. He just stood there, staring at me as if his gaze, connected to mine, was his lifeline. I stared back, knowing that all too soon, that line would no longer hold. In such a moment, another man might have spouted goodbyes, confessions – he said not a word.

From somewhere far away and unimportant, I heard a shouted command. The boat rose into the air and slowly began to be lowered over the side of the ship. I held Mr Ambrose's gaze until the very last moment. When he vanished behind the side of the ship, I buried my face in my hands and slumped to the boat's floor.

This couldn't be happening! We were supposed to have won! To have brought back the prize in triumph! This was impossible!

With a violent jerk, the boat touched down on the roiling sea. Someone shouted commands – a man's voice. So there were men aboard. But *he* wasn't. He wasn't.

Over the yowling of the wind I heard the splash as oars dipped into the water. The little boat was carried away, dancing like an empty nutshell on the surface of the water. I felt just as empty. There were arms around me, and the voice of an old woman was muttering soothing nothings into my ear, but I didn't feel able to respond, or even to hear. Some part of me wanted to fight her off, but my arms felt so weak, so terribly weak. This could not be happening!

Glancing up through the wild veil of my hair, I saw the ship, far above and away, atop a giant wave, just as much at the mercy of the ocean as we were in our tiny vessel. For just a moment, I thought I saw a lone figure standing at the prow. Then my head slumped down, the rest of my energy used up. Tonight had simply been too much to be real. It had to be a dream.

But you know it isn't, came a voice from the back of my mind. *Just as his kiss was no dream, either.*

I cringed, shuddering with pain. From above, I heard a crash, a giant roar, and thought *That was the ship, splitting apart.* I wanted to look, wanted to look so much, but could not. I didn't have the strength.

All I could do was listen. My ears strained to hear some noise, some sign that would tell me that the ship was still afloat, that he was still alive – but no such sound ever came. There was nothing but the crashing of the storm waves against the bow of the boat. And then, even that was gone, and there was only silence.

THE END

SPECIAL ADDITIONAL MATERIAL

A CHAPTER FROM

MR AMBROSE'S PERSPECTIVE

None of your Business

Can't you read? This is *none of your business*! I am not going to tell you what you want – and most certainly not for free! Close this book and leave. Now!

…

Did you not hear me? That was an order!

…

Why are you still here? Did I not give explicit instructions for you to leave? Let me put it another way: you are dismissed. Scram! Scat! Get thee gone! I know what it is you want, but I am not going to do it! I am not going to tell you my story.

Why?

You dare ask *why*?

You have some nerve! Do you know who I am? No, you obviously don't. If you did, you wouldn't still be here, pestering me. Well, if you will not stop making a nuisance of yourself, you useless layabout, I'll tell you why. Here are the reasons why I will not share my story, in order of significance:

10. It's mine. I don't share what's mine.

9. I'm too busy.

8. Very busy indeed.

7. You are no more than a bug to me – easily squashed.

6. I don't waste my time on bugs.

5. I don't waste my time on anyone. Knowledge is power is time is money.

4. This story contains secrets of immeasurable value. Secrets must stay secret. That's the point of a secret.

3. This story is mine. Do you hear? Mine! I don't share. Not ever.

2. And it's about *her*.

1. Remember what I said about never sharing?

…

You still haven't left, have you?

You still want my story?

Well, I have to say I admire your persistence. If it is persistence, that is. More likely, you're just too thick-headed to comprehend my warning.

Very well…

On your own head be it.

~~**~*~*

'Ah! Just breathe in that breeze! Feel that air filling your lungs! A hundred of Neptune's sea-horses couldn't get me and my ship away from here again! Old Blighty, England, home – there she is! Isn't it a wonderful sight, Sir?'

Silence.

'And the weather – perfect for a coming home! Perfect for anything really! Smell that air, will you? I tell you, there's no air anywhere in the world like good, clean English air! Don't you think so, Sir?'

Silence.

'Ah, I know what you'll say! You'll say I'm being sentimental!'

Silence.

'But it ain't that, Sir. I swear, it ain't that. This old sailor's been all around the world, from the Cape of Good Hope – which didn't inspire me with much hope, let me tell you – to the rocky cliffs of Norway and back again, and let me tell you, there's no place like Old Blighty!'

Silence.

'The green hills, the fields, the decent ale – and the people! The people are always friendlier at home, don't you think? I always say the French are stuck up, the Germans stiff, but Englishmen – you won't find a single Englishman who isn't kind, polite and warm.'

Stone-cold silence.

'No wonder, considering. Who wouldn't be cheerful on such a wonderful day! Ah, just breathe in the breeze, Sir, breathe in the breeze! Isn't that wonderful weather, Sir?'

Icy eyes turned on the captain of the ship. My icy eyes.

'Which part, Captain? The fog, the cold wind, or the drizzle?'

The captain, apparently immune to all forms of sarcasm, smiled brightly. 'All of it! Isn't it wonderful to be back in England? Admit it, you don't get weather like this anywhere else.'

I shook my head to rid myself of the worst of the incessant wetness, and pulled my hat deeper into my face. 'Indeed you do not.'

'Aren't you happy to be back home, Mr Ambrose?'

I threw the captain another look.

'England is many things – but certainly not my home. I don't have or need one.'

'Ah, come on, Sir!' A huge hand slammed into my back, and I had to suppress the instinctive reaction of grabbing it, twisting it and forcing its owner to his knees with a gun put to the side of his head. Old habits die hard. 'Everybody has a home! After all the time you've been away in the colonies, I'm sure your family is going to give you a big, warm welcome back! Your mum and your old man will be tickled pink to see you!'

'Captain?'

'Yes, Mr Ambrose, Sir?'

'We're very close to the shore now.'

'Yes, I know, Sir.'

'But do you also know what that *means*, Captain?'

'I'm afraid not, Sir.'

I gave the man a very meaningful look. 'It means that I don't need you anymore to reach my destination. Shut up or I will throw you over the side.'

'Um... Yes, Mr Ambrose, Sir. Of course, Mr Ambrose, Sir.'

After that, the captain didn't seem to feel quite so jovial anymore. He made himself scarce. I didn't even glance at his retreating back. Instead, I continued to stare at the distant cliffs of Dover, rising in front of us out of the mist.

Home...

A foreign concept to me. After years in the colonies, what was there about this place that could be home to me?

How about the Bank of England?

Not a bad thought, actually. I would have to see what could be done about buying it.

'*Sahib?*'

Still, I didn't turn. There was no need. I knew that voice coming from behind me.

'Yes, Karim?'

'The captain says we will approach the coast in about half an hour. He asks if you wish to land in London, or a place called Dover.'

'London, Karim. I paid for the whole trip across the Atlantic, and I don't plan to get off this ship before I reach my destination only to have to hire a coach to go the rest of the way.'

'Yes, *Sahib.*'

There were a few seconds of silence. And this time, they didn't just come from me.

'*Sahib?*'

'Yes, Karim?'

'Do you think he's waiting for us? Dalgliesh, I mean. Does he have a surprise waiting for us?'

I glanced at my bodyguard. Behind the bristly barrier of his beard, his black eyes were narrowed, staring suspiciously at the shore.

'Do you expect him to?'

'Yes, *Sahib.*'

'Then he won't have a surprise waiting for us, Karim.' Reaching into the pocket of my tailcoat, I pulled out my revolver and whirled the drum. All six chambers were loaded. '*Something you expect is never a surprise.*'

Even through the beard, I could see one corner of Karim's mouth twitch. One of his massive hands curled around the hilt of his sabre. 'Wise words, *Sahib.*'

I said nothing. Instead, I looked again towards the distant cliffs.

'I shall go and check on the goods, *Sahib.*'

'Do that.'

'And... *Sahib?*'

'Yes?'

'Are you sure you wish to go to London? Do you not want to sail somewhat farther North? Maybe to your fam–'

I felt a muscle in my cheek twitch.

'Go check on the cargo, Karim," I cut him off.

'Are you sure? We could–'

'Go!'

'Yes, *Sahib.* As you wish, *Sahib.*'

~~**~*~*

There was a welcoming committee present when we arrived in the harbour. However, the committee did not consist of smiling family members. What a big surprise. The lights of cameras started flashing the moment I stepped onto the gangway.

'Mr Ambrose! Mr Ambrose, why did you suddenly decide to come back to London after all those years?'

'No comment!'

'Mr Ambrose! A statement, please, Mr Ambrose!'

'No comment!'

'What do you say to the rumours that you ruined Harlow & Sons to take over their company?'

'Yes.'

The reporters were so startled at my reply that they actually stopped badgering me with questions for a moment. The one right in front of me nearly dropped his pen and notepad. 'W-what do you mean, *yes?*'

I took a step towards him, off the gangway and onto the embankment. 'I should have thought that was obvious. I say yes to the rumours. I ruined their company to take it over. And if you don't get out of my way I'll do the same to your paper.'

'Are you threatening me? I'm a member of the free press, and—'

'—in my way.' Taking the reporter by the scruff of the neck, I lifted him off the ground and, with a splash, dropped him into the harbour basin right beside me. He resurfaced a second later, spewing dirty seawater. I looked at the remaining reporters gathered all around me like a pack of hungry jackals, and cocked my head. 'Do any of you gentlemen still have questions for me?'

They scattered.

'The press here appears to be easier dealt with than in America,' Karim commented, thoughtfully.

I nodded.

'What about them?' asked my bodyguard, pointing to a crowd of gapemouthed gawkers who had gathered around the dock to stare at the splashing reporter, at the huge Mohammedan with the sabre and the turban on his head, and most of all – at me. Now that the reporters were gone, the gawkers were the only thing in our way. 'Should I remove them, *Sahib?*'

I shook my head.

Stepping forward, I focused my gaze on the foremost of the spectators: a spindly little half-bald man with enormous ears. I lifted my hand, with three fingers outstretched.

One finger retracted.

Three...

Another finger followed.

Two...

I met the spindly man's eyes. My last extended finger twitched.

The man moved faster than the fastest race horse. He stepped back so quickly that he stepped on the toes of the fat fishwife behind him. Instead of reacting in the usual manner of a fishwife and hitting him over the head with a haddock, she caught sight of me and stepped back just as hurriedly. As did the man behind her, and the one behind him, too. A corridor through the crowd began to open.

Any other man might have smiled, maybe even felt triumph. I didn't. A lion doesn't feel triumph when his prey steps aside.

At least I didn't think he did. I had never actually asked one.

Stepping forward, I brushed past the people, easily parting what was left of the crowd in front of me. All around, I could hear whispers:

'...Ambrose! Rikkard Ambrose...'

'...richer that Croesus, they say! Richer than Midas!'

'Back from the colonies...'

'...should have stayed there! Who does he think he is?'

'Psht! If he hears you–'

'I heard,' I said.

From one moment to the next, a blanket silence fell over the crowd. Without looking, I pointed my cane over my shoulder, directly at the man who had spoken.

'You have one week to get out of the city. By then, I will have squashed the company you work for and your job along with it.'

I reached the exit of the harbour without any further interruption, Karim close behind me.

'I see you are in a good mood, today, *Sahib*,' he said in what was, for Karim, almost a jovial voice. 'You gave him a week.'

Nod.

'That was very generous of you.'

Shrug.

'Shall I order a cab for you, *Sahib*?'

Headshake.

'Are we going to walk?'

Nod.

'The address?'

I handed him a piece of paper on which I had noted the address.

'This is where your new offices are?'

Nod.

'Very well, then, *Sahib*. We shall walk.'

Nod.

I so enjoyed these lively conversations with my bodyguard. They really brightened my day.

Ten minutes later, the massive supports of a two-columned portico rose up out of the morning mist in front of us. The door under the portico stood wide open, and some strangely deluded fool had unrolled a red carpet all the way into the street. His idiot friends, meanwhile, had been busy decorating the outside of the building with garlands. *Coloured* garlands!

Very slowly, I turned my head towards my bodyguard and gave him a long, long look. 'Karim?'

The Mohammedan shook his head. 'This is not my doing, *Sahib*.'

'I see.'

Taking a deep breath, I stepped through the door – and was almost blasted off my feet by the fanfare of the brass band arrayed at the opposite end of the hall. Quickly, my eyes took in the scene:

The brass band, the cheering people arrayed along both sides of the wastefully expensive-looking red carpet, the committee of what was probably senior staff awaiting me by the reception desk, headed by a sallow-faced man in a grey waistcoat. Behind them, the walls and ceiling were bedecked with banners and garlands.

I didn't know any of these people. This was the first time I had set foot on British soil for over a decade. I'd had this office established in my absence. Not a single one of the staff members had I met in my entire life, and they had hung up garlands and banners for me?

I had to admit, they were accomplished bootlickers. But they had made a mistake, or even two. The first was that they, I was sure, had not paid for this welcome out of their own purses. And the second...

Well, the second was that one of the banners, the largest, right behind sallow-face, read 'Welcome Home, Mr. Ambrose'.

Welcome home?

Home?

'Silence!'

My voice cut through the brass music like a guillotine through the neck of a luckless French aristocrat. The musicians lowered their instruments. The cheering people stopped cheering and clapping, their hands frozen in mid-air. They watched cautiously as I marched to the welcoming committee in front of the reception desk.

'Why are you not working?'

Sallow-face seemed a bit taken aback by my curt demand. 'S-sir?'

'It's a simple enough question.' Reaching into my waistcoat pocket, I pulled out my silver watch and let it snap open, not even glancing at the coat of arms on the lid. The times when that had made me flinch were long past. 'It is eleven thirty-one a.m., and not a single one of you is doing the job he is supposed to. Do you think I pay you for lazing about?'

'N-no, Sir.'

'And what is this litter cluttering my entrance hall?' Raising my cane, I pointed at the banners, the garlands and the members of the marching band. 'Sell everything you can find a buyer for, and throw the rest in the Thames!'

'Yes, Sir. Of course, Sir.'

'Excuse me?' The conductor of the marching band stepped forward, red in the face. He apparently wasn't used to being treated like this.

Well, he's in for a novel experience.

'Who the bloody hell do you think you are?'

'Rikkard Ambrose,' I told him. 'That's much too easy a question. I can think of a better one. What are you doing here? You are not members of my staff!'

'No, Sir, but–'

'Out! This building is only for authorized personnel.'

'But, Sir, our fee–'

'Out, I said! I didn't hire you. You won't see a penny from me, unless it's one you find at the bottom of the River Thames!'

To judge by the speed with which they ran from the hall, they believed me.

I was standing at the door, glaring after the marching band, when Sallow-face came sidling up to me.

'I have prepared some refreshments for you after your long journey, Mr Ambrose. Is there anything you would like particularly?'

'Yes. For you to stop licking my boots.'

'W-what?'

'They're quite clean enough at the moment. But don't worry.' Whirling, I marched towards a door that looked as if it led upstairs. I had to find myself an office in this place. 'If I ever need a shoeshine boy, I'll remember your talents.'

'Um... yes, Sir. Of course, Sir.'

'Which of these goggling buffoons is my secretary?'

'That would be Mr Simmons, Sir.'

'Send this Simmons upstairs with a progress report and an annual balance. It's time someone took this place in hand!'

~~**~*~*

Plink.

I heard the noise of the little metal capsule landing on the desk on the other side of the wall and nodded, with something that almost approached contentment. The decision to install the pneumatic tubes had been an excellent one. If I'd had to communicate with my secretary in the ordinary way, I would have had to get up, open the door, holler his name and march back to my desk again before continuing to work. Right now, I had saved at least ten precious seconds. Over the last few days, I had been able to save at least three hundred and seventy-one seconds. If I managed to do that every hour of every workday, I would save at least forty-three thousand eight hundred and fifty-five seconds this year.

Or maybe not.

Because my secretary, it seemed, didn't share my work ethic today. He wasn't answering my call. Shoving another message into the tube, I pulled the lever.

Plink.

Nothing.

Plink.

Still nothing.

Plink! Plonk! Plink!

I was just about to shove the next message into the tube when I realized this was turning into a senseless waste of perfectly good paper. Cupping my hands around my mouth, I called: 'Simmons!'

No reply.

Where was the blasted fool? Kicking my chair back, I rose and marched over to the connecting door between our two offices and pushed it open.

Two minutes later I was back in my own office, lifting the mouthpiece that connected it with downstairs.

'Karim? Get up here! Simmons has vanished!'

Karim marched into my office after only a few moments. Without asking, he continued to Simmons' office, and I heard rustling and clanking. I waited. The man was good at his job. There was no sense in interfering while he did it.

'Nothing, *Sahib*.' His bushy eyebrows drawn together in a frown, Karim reappeared at the door. 'No clue to where he's gone.'

'Search the building.'

'Yes, *Sahib*.'

'And if the idiot has accidentally locked himself in the archives again, demonstrate to him what I think of time wasters.'

'With pleasure, *Sahib*.'

When Karim returned half an hour later, his frown had deepened. 'I could not find a sign of him anywhere, *Sahib*. He's gone.'

'You mean permanently gone?'

'Apparently.' Karim hesitated. 'When I searched his room just now, I didn't just not find any clue to his whereabouts – I found nothing at all. No personal possessions, no loose cash, nothing. He cleaned his desk out completely. It seems Mr Simmons decided to leave your employ.'

'Leave? Why now? He's worked here for three years.'

'Maybe your charming personality overwhelmed him, *Sahib*.'

'Karim?'

'Yes, *Sahib*?'

'Was that sarcasm?'

'No, *Sahib*. Of course not, *Sahib*. I would never take the liberty, *Sahib*.'

'Good.'

There was a pause in the conversation. Something unusual for me since, under normal circumstances, I would not condone such a frivolous waste of time. But the behaviour of my secretary had thrown me off course for a minute. The bloody cheek of the man! He didn't even have the decency to let himself be sacked for his ineptitude!

'*Sahib*?'

'Yes?'

'Should I put an advertisement about an open post for a secretary in the papers?'

Those words jarred me out of my paralysis. 'Have you lost your mind, Karim? Do you know how much an advertisement in the *Manchester Guardian* costs these days? Let alone in *The Times*?'

'No, *Sahib*.'

'Well, I do! There has to be some other way to find the right man for the job. In the meantime, I'll do the work myself.'

₊₊**₊*₊*

There are a few things you tend to forget about secretaries. One is that you pay them to do the work you don't want to do yourself. So, when your secretary is suddenly gone, he leaves you with a big pile of idiotic correspondence and an intense wish to shoot him for the deserter he is.

Icily, I stared at the pile of letters on my table. When I did this with people, they usually turned and ran. The letters, unfortunately, seemed to feel no such inclination. They just lay there leering at me. Most of them seemed to be from charities, or from mothers who wanted nothing so much as to invite me to a ball, shackle me to a wall and feed me tea and biscuits until I agreed to marry their daughter out of desperation.

'Have you changed your mind yet about the advertisement, *Sahib*?' asked Karim from behind me.

Without a word, I grabbed all the letters in pastel-coloured envelopes and dropped them in the bin.

'It is conceivable that prospective business partners might send correspondence in pastel-coloured envelopes,' Karim pointed out.

'Not ones with whom *I* wish to do business.'

'Yes, *Sahib*. Of course, *Sahib*.'

'Have you heard anything new from the estate agents we've been contacting?'

'No, *Sahib*.'

'Pressure them, Karim. I need a place in the country for my negotiations.' I looked around my perfectly designed office – bare, grey stone walls, bare stone floor tiles and a single wooden chair in front of the desk. 'For some reason, people I invite up here do not seem comfortable discussing business.'

'I can't imagine why, *Sahib*.'

I was just about to tear open the first of the letters that remained on my desk, when there came a knock from the door.

'Enter!'

A message boy stuck his head in the door. 'Guv? I 'ear you was wanting a place in the country?'

'What's it to you?'

'Mr Elseworth sent me. Mr Elseworth of Elseworth and Brown, estate agents. He's got a place for you, if you was interested.'

'I was, or more grammatically correct, I am.' Throwing aside the letter, I rose from behind the desk. 'Come, Karim. Let's meet this Mr Elseworth.'

'He's downstairs,' the boy piped up. 'Your man said you was looking for a place real quick, so 'e didn't want to lose any time, Guv.'

'A man after my own heart. Lead on.'

Downstairs at the entrance, Mr Elseworth was waiting. The good feeling created by his promptness was not supported by his appearance. The man was fat, with small, piggish eyes that made him look like a nasty, greedy bastard. But I knew better than to judge by appearance. After all, by popular opinion I was the most handsome man in London, and I was a nasty, greedy bastard myself.

'Ah, Mr Ambrose!' Spreading his arms, Mr Elseworth sent me an ingratiating smile. 'How very kind of you to spare some minutes of your valuable time for me! I truly think I have an offer that will interest you greatly. Shall we go up to your office and–'

'No.'

'But I really–'

'I have a business appointment in...' I let my watch snap open. '...exactly fifteen minutes and twenty-seven seconds. No time to waste.'

'But–'

'We can talk on the way. Move.'

I brushed past a slightly dazed Mr Elseworth, not even slowing my steps. A few moments later, he was beside me, huffing and puffing in an attempt to keep up the pace.

'Don't you... think we should... get a cab?'

'No.'

'Oh.'

'We'll walk. You have an offer to make? Make it.'

We started down the street, Karim and a group of his men surrounding us, while Mr Elseworth extolled the virtues of Wilding Park, the country estate he was desirous of selling. Apparently, it had not only ten *huff puff puff* bedrooms, but also *gasp* modern *huff gasp* bathing facilities *gasp*. Amazing.

By the time we reached the street that was my destination, I was already getting tired of Mr Elseworth. One country place was as good as another, and I was not prepared to waste any more time on this matter.

'... tell you, it is in perfect condition,' Elseworth was blabbing. 'The best of all the houses I have.'

'Indeed? Interesting that you are willing to part with such a treasure.'

'It is out of the goodness of my heart, Sir, out of the goodness of my heart! Wilding Park is a treasure, and I hate to part with it, but I know that with you it will be in good hands.'

Not far away I spotted the bank where I had my first business of the day to conduct. Dismissively, I waved Elseworth away. 'Bah. I have no time for this. Karim, pay the man and let's be done with it.' Pointing a finger at the fat estate agent, I fixed him with my eyes. 'However, you should remember: If you haven't told the truth, I shall be very... displeased.'

My words had the desired effect. If Elseworth had sold me a pup, he knew what was coming for him.

'Karim?' I snapped my fingers. 'The money.'

Karim stepped forward – but then hesitated. I was just about to turn and demand what he was waiting for, when I heard someone clear their throat.

'Excuse me, Sir?' The voice was high, clear, and a nuisance. I had already wasted enough time today. Whoever this was and whatever they wanted from me, they were going to be disappointed. Through the mist, I saw only the out-line of a smallish figure stepping towards me before Karim intercepted the bothersome stranger, grabbing him by the arm.

'On your way, you lout!' he growled. 'On your way, I said! The *Sahib* has no time for beggars!'

'I don't want any money from him,' the stranger retorted, almost sounding offended. I was just about to start towards the bank again, when I heard his next words: 'In fact, I want to help him save some!'

I stopped in my tracks.

Maybe this strange fellow wasn't that big of a nuisance, after all.

'Save money? Karim – let him go, now!' I turned my eyes on the stranger, for the first time bothering to look at him properly. He was a rather odd-looking young man with a rather fat behind, although his true figure was hard to divine under the baggy trousers and too-large tailcoat he was wearing. His chubby cheeks were tanned from long hours in the sun, and an overlarge top hat set on a mop of chestnut brown hair that looked as if it wasn't on first name basis with Mr Comb. All in all, a rather unusual appearance for a financial advisor.

'You!' I gave him my best intimidating glare, which has been known to send bloodhounds off howling. He didn't move back an inch. Impressive. 'What do you speak of? How exactly can you help me save money?'

The young man's Adam's apple bobbed, nervously. He tried to step towards – yes, actually *towards* – me, but Karim stopped him. The boy really had guts.

'I couldn't help overhearing part of your conversation with...'

'Mr Elseworth.'

'...with Mr Elseworth. Am I right in thinking that you intend to purchase Wilding Park, Sir?'

I gave a curt nod. 'You are.'

'If you don't mind my saying so, Sir, I would advise against it.'

'Why?' I studied the youngster intently. There was no sign of deceit in his eyes. Trepidation, certainly, but not deceit. What was his game? Did he even have one?

'My... my grandmother lives in the vicinity of Wilding Park, Sir. I visit her now and again and have caught glimpses of the house. It is not pretty.'

I waved that away. 'I am not concerned with whether it is pretty or not. Is it sound?'

'That it is, Sir, that it is,' Elseworth threw in. From the look he directed at the young man, our young friend had made an enemy today. 'Don't listen to this foolish youth!'

'It is not sound,' the fellow snapped.

Ah, so he has some fire under that big topper of his, has he?

'And you know that how?' I wanted to know.

'Half the roof tiles are missing and I have seen unhealthy-looking stains on the walls,' the young man started rattling off. 'Once, in passing, I heard the steward complain about the wilderness in the grounds and an infestation of rats. The road up to the house, from what I could see from my coach as I drove by, also looked in bad disrepair.'

'And you remember all that just from passing?'

I looked at him again, and this time from an entirely different angle. He was young, true – there was not a shadow of beard on his chin – but not *too* young. His behind was rather larger than usual, but still I didn't get the feeling that he sat on it all that often. There was a fire in his brown eyes, a desire to prove himself that burned in all people who had long moved out of Lazytown.

'Yes?' It sounded more like a question than like an answer. But it was answer enough for me.

I gave a curt nod. 'I see. Exactly what I have been looking for.'

The young man blinked. 'But I just told you the house is dilapidated and...'

I cut him off with a jerk of my hand. 'Not the house, young man. You.'

'*Me?*'

'Yes, you.' Glancing over my shoulder, I waved towards Mr Elseworth. Or should I say the late Mr Elseworth? In the world of business, he was as good as dead. 'Karim, get rid of that individual. Our business relationship is terminated. I have no further use for him.'

'Yes, *Sahib*.'

'Now to you.' Ignoring the protesting shrieks of the pig that was being carted off to slaughter, I focused all of my considerable attention on the young man in front of me. 'I know a good man when I see one, and I need a bright young man with a good memory and quick mind as my secretary. The last one I had has just left my employment for some unfathomable reason. I think you would be exactly the man for the job.'

The young man's eyes bugged, and he coughed. Overwhelmed by my generosity, probably.

'Err... the *man* for the job? Sorry, but I don't quite think that I'm the one you want, Sir.'

What the heck? Why was he being difficult?

'Can you read and write?'

'Yes, but...'

'Do you have employment?'

'No, Sir, but...'

Bloody hell, what was this? He should be kissing my feet! I didn't have time for this.

'Well then, it's settled.' My gaze drilled into him, making clear that by 'settled', I meant 'very, absolutely, finally settled'. 'Be at my office, nine sharp Monday morning.'

Taking a step towards the youngster, I held out my card to him. Having those cards printed had been abominably expensive, but having to waste my time reciting my address would cost me even more time and money.

'Here.'

As I stepped forward and the last remnants of mist between me and the young man disappeared, his jaw suddenly sagged and a glazed look came into his eyes, as if he were seeing a unicorn with an extra horn sticking out of its behind. Why was he staring at me like that? Impatiently, I waved the card.

'Hello, young man? Are you listening to me?'

'Err... yes. Yes, I am.' The young man shook himself. 'You just surprised me, Sir. I must admit, that it's not every day I get an offer like that.'

'See that that you're not "surprised" too often when you are in my employ. I have no use for baffled fools standing around gawking for no good reason.'

Still, the youngster hadn't taken the card I was holding out to him. What was the matter? Was he mentally retarded?

'My card!' I said, waving the thing impatiently. He finally took it, and studied it as if it were a particularly peculiar bug. Maybe I'd better rethink hiring him... But no. I needed a secretary, and fast. If I had to deal with one more charity request for helpless little orphans, I was going to shoot someone. Probably the orphans.

Bah! What was I waiting for? I had wasted enough time on this little worm!

'Don't be late.' I sent him another significant look. 'I don't tolerate tardiness.' With that, I turned and marched away down the street. If he showed up, good. If not, he wouldn't have been tough enough for the job, anyway. Soon, the young man disappeared in the mist somewhere behind me.

'Where to now, *Sahib*?' Karim asked from beside me, keeping pace.

Wordlessly, I nodded at the bank down the street.

'Very well, *Sahib*.'

There were quite a few customers in Bradley & Bullard's Bank, waiting at tables, writing documents, busily chatting. At least they chatted until Karim, his sabre, his turban and his beard stepped into the main hall. All voices died, and all eyes were drawn to the huge Mohammedan. Then I followed him inside, and Karim was forgotten. There are things with which even a sabre and a turban cannot compete.

Ignoring the line of people in front of the counter, I marched up to the closest bank clerk and fixed him with my gaze.

'You there! How much does this bank cost?'

'Um... we offer very affordable bank accounts, and our fees for stock management are also–'

I cut him off with an impatient gesture. 'That's not what I asked! How much does *this bank cost*?'

The man blinked at me, the confusion in his eyes slowly changing to disdain. His eyes wandered over my simple black tailcoat, my lack of silk, satin and gold embroidery, and I knew he was busy judging by appearance. Bad mistake.

The bank clerk's eyes narrowed. 'I'm afraid I don't have the pleasure of understanding you, Sir.'

'Rest assured, understanding me is no pleasure.'

'I can readily believe it, Sir.' He sniffed, derisively. 'Will you please remove yourself? You are holding up the line.'

Reaching into my pocket, I took out one of my business cards and slammed it onto the counter. The bank clerk's eyes focused on my name and widened in shock.

If I hadn't lost the ability years ago, I might have smiled. Sometimes, a business card says more than a thousand words.

The man's frightened eyes rose from my name to meet my gaze.

'Get me the manager,' I ordered.

When we left the bank five minutes later, Karim was carrying the documents detailing the sale in a suitcase that the manager had, in his generosity, gifted to me. People tend to be generous like that when they are scared of losing their jobs.

'Is our business here concluded to your satisfaction, *Sahib*?'

Taking a deep breath of filthy London air, I glanced back at the bank.

'Well... It's not the bank of England, but it'll do for a week or so.'

'Quite so, *Sahib*.'

'Where to next...?' I hesitated on the sidewalk, thinking. Bloody hell, I really needed a secretary to keep track of my appointments, and fast! Hopefully, that youngster would live up to my expectations. He seemed like a bright young man. Where to now... where to–

'Chauvinists!' a shout rudely interrupted my thoughts. Or, to be exact, it was more of a shriek. 'Oppressors of womanhood!'

I turned, just in time to see... *What the hell?*

Farther down the street, a figure was being dragged down the front steps of a polling station by two police officers. A figure I knew. I stared. Was it really....? Yes. My future secretary.

No. Oh no, this would not do. Not at all. If the police had caught that foolish youth breaking the law, they would just have to forget about it, until I had found someone cheaper and more law-abiding.

'Officer!' In three long strides I was in front of them. I was damn well going to get to the bottom of this! 'Officer, what are you doing with this young man, may I ask?'

The sergeant turned and, when he caught sight of me, paled. Unlike the bank clerk, he clearly knew with whom he was dealing. If his facial expression wasn't enough proof, his hurried salute definitely was.

'Good morning, Mr Ambrose, Sir!' he mumbled, trying his best to keep hold of my prospective secretary, who was wriggling like a rattlesnake in an attempt to get free. 'Um... Sir, if I may ask, what young man are you speaking of?'

My eyes slid from the policeman to the young man in his clutches and back again. Was he daft? Who else would I be talking about?

'That one, of course. Are you blind? What are you doing with him?'

'Not *him*, Sir.' Reaching up, the sergeant gripped the young man's top hat and pulled. It was like that silly trick magicians did when they pulled a rabbit out of the hat – only in this case, I would have actually preferred it if a curious bunny poked its nose out of the hat. Instead, masses of wild chestnut hair tumbled out. I felt a cold hand clench hard around my vital organs. '*Her*. That's a girl, Mr Ambrose, Sir.'

Impossible.

Silence.

I stared.

More silence. And for the first time in my life, it wasn't because I didn't want to say something. It was because I did absolutely not know what to say. Or to yell. Or to bellow.

No. No, this is impossible.

'Something wrong, Sir?' the sergeant inquired dutifully. He got no answer from me. I didn't have one. After a long moment of waiting, he cleared his throat. 'Well, if you'd excuse us, Sir, we have to take this one away to where she belongs. Maybe a night in the cells will teach her not to do what's only for men.'

'Aye,' one of the constables chuckled. 'Women voting? Who ever heard of something like that? Next thing we know they'll want decent jobs!'

Jobs.

Women.

Jobs for women.

A job for a woman.

No. No. No. No. No. No!

I only distantly heard the laughter of the policemen. Most of my attention was focused on the seething volcano of ice-cold rage that was rising inside me. Taking a deep breath, I met the girl's eyes. She met my gaze head-on, not looking away, not even blinking. Other people had died at my hand for the kind of defiance I saw in her eyes right then.

A woman.

A job for a woman.

But she wouldn't really...!

Paralyzed, I watched the policemen drag her away. Just before they pulled her around the corner, she turned her head back towards me and, grinning in a way that made me want to strangle someone, shouted:

'Looking forward to seeing you at work on Monday, Sir!'

She wouldn't! Would she?

THE BEGINNING...

ABOUT THE AUTHOR

Robert Thier is a German historian and writer of historical fiction. His particular mix of history, romance, and adventure, always with a good deal of humour thrown in, has gained him a diverse readership ranging from teenagers to retired grandmothers. For the way he manages to make history come alive, as if he himself lived as a medieval knight, his fans all over the world have given him the nickname "Sir Rob."

For Robert, becoming a writer followed naturally from his interest in history. "In Germany," he says, "we use the same word for story and history. And I've always loved the one as much as the other. Becoming a storyteller, a writer, is what I've always wanted."

Besides writing and researching in dusty old archives, on the lookout for a mystery to put into his next story, Robert enjoys classical music and long walks in the country. The helmet you see in the picture he does not wear because he is a cycling enthusiast, but to protect his literary skull in which a bone has been missing from birth. Robert lives in the south of Germany in a small village between the three Emperor Mountains.

OTHER BOOKS BY ROBERT THIER

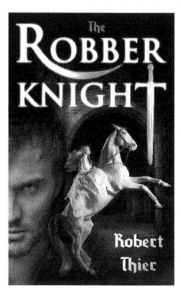

The Robber Knight

When you are fighting for the freedom of your people, falling in love with your enemy is not a great idea.

Sir Reuben, the dreaded robber knight, has long been Ayla's deadliest enemy. She swore he would hang for his crimes. Now they are both trapped in her castle as the army of a far greater enemy approaches, and they have only one chance: stand together, or fall. Welcome to "The Robber Knight"—a tale full of action, adventure, and romance.

Special Edition with secret chapters revealed and insights into Sir Reuben's mysterious past.

ISBN-10:   1499251645
ISBN-13:   978-1499251647

Upcoming Titles

At present (2016) *The Robber Knight* and *Storm and Silence* are Robert Thiers's only books published in English. However, book two of the Robber Knight Saga, *The Robber Knight's Love*, is being edited for publication, and the sequel of *Storm and Silence* is also in the works. Keep updated about the books' progress on the internet.

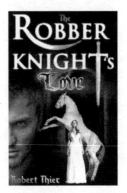

Website: www.robthier.com
Facebook profile: www.facebook.com/robert.thier.161
Facebook page: http://de-de.facebook.com/RobThierHelmHead
Twitter: http://twitter.com/thesirrob
Tumblr Blog: http://robthier.tumblr.com
Goodreads: www.goodreads.com/author/show/6123144.Robert_Thier

34928436R00365

Made in the USA
San Bernardino, CA
10 June 2016